Royal Secrets

Royal Secrets Box Set Cover Design by: Pretty in Ink Creations

Royal Secrets Typography by: Pretty in Ink Creations

Map Designs by: J.L. Wilson/Something Wicked Creations

Title Typography by: Killerbookcovers

SECRETS AMONG THE TIDES

This series contains content, themes, situations, and tropes that may not be suitable for all readers.

Some of the triggering concepts include:

-Abelism against disabled main character.

-Classism

-Violence

-Attempted murder

-War in a fantasy setting

-Poison

-Choking

This book also features themes, situations, and tropes such as:

-Virgin FMC

-A slow burn romance

-Bisexual mermen and MM relationships

-Cliffhanger ending (the series is complete, don't worry!)

-Group sex scenes

-Angry sex scene

-There is a scene where the FMC has sex with one of the MC's in a case of mistaken identity. This could be considered dubious consent. Please proceed with caution.

Pronunciation Guide

THALASSAR: TAL-UH-SAHR

Kappur: Kay-purr

Draconi: Dray-cone-e

Iol: Yo-l

Ventlaer: Vent-lair

Gvulis: Vool-liss

Brague: Bra-aag

Eramaea: Era-may-uh

Malabella: Mahl-ah-beh-yaw

Oriana: Or-ee-ah-nuh
Fraema: Fray-muh
Ytgar: Eet-gahrr
Valmundur: Val-mone-doorrr (heavy R roll)
Odalaea: O-dah-lay-uh

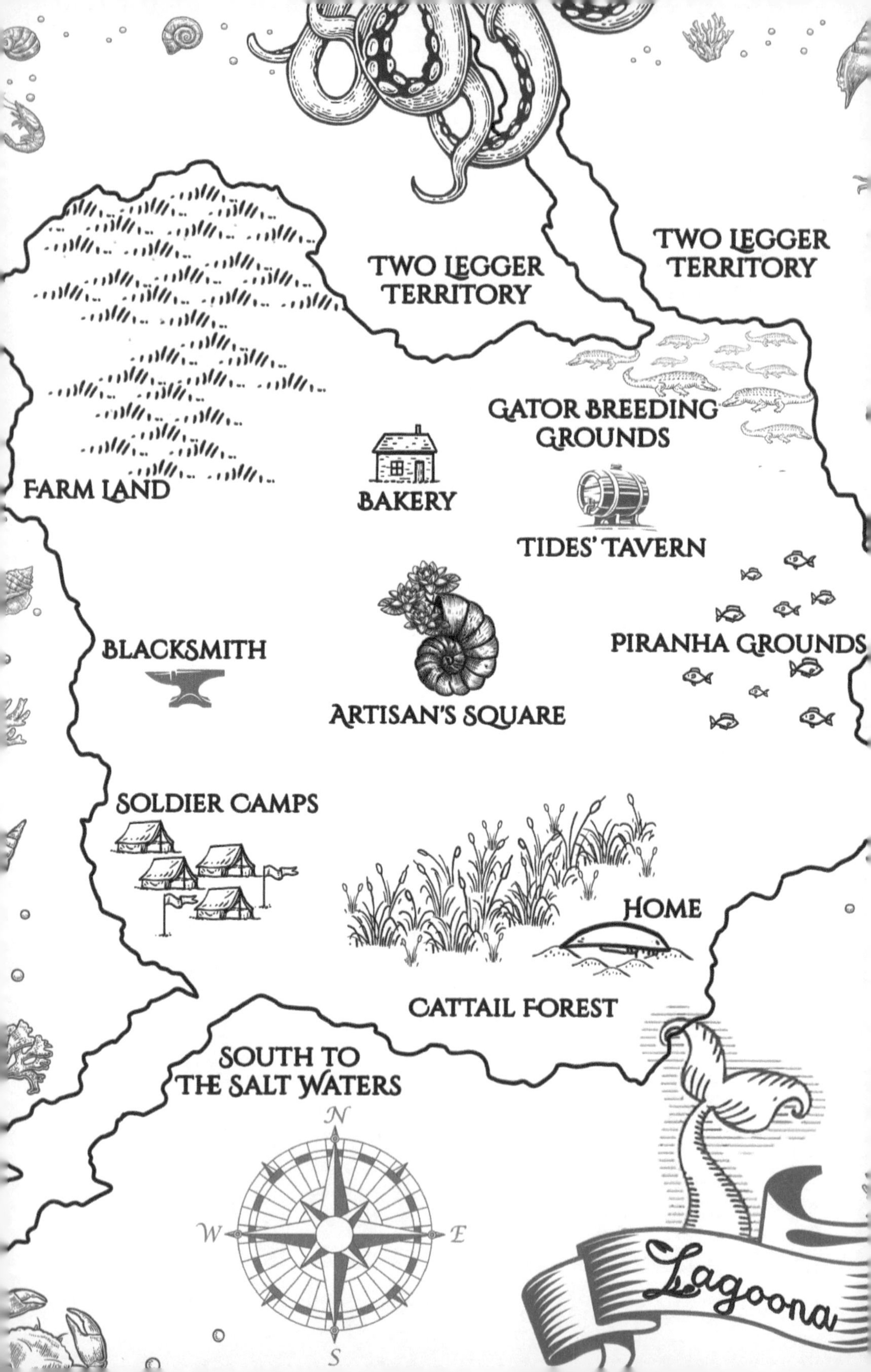
TWO LEGGER TERRITORY
TWO LEGGER TERRITORY
GATOR BREEDING GROUNDS
FARM LAND
BAKERY
TIDES' TAVERN
BLACKSMITH
PIRANHA GROUNDS
ARTISAN'S SQUARE
SOLDIER CAMPS
HOME
CATTAIL FOREST
SOUTH TO THE SALT WATERS
N
W
E
S
Lagoona

IOL
TWO
LEGGER
ERRITORY
TWO LEGGER
TERRITORY
DRACONI
TWO
LEGGER
TERRITORY
THALASSAR
KAPPUR
GVULIS
VENTLAIR
BRAGUE
N
W
E
Kingdoms

DEEP IN THE FRESHWATERS of Lagoona, in a backwater pond of the mer Kingdom of Thalassar, the current stirred. The waters today were in a torrent, a sure sign that a storm up top and had only just begun. It was a cold and dark day, like the skies reflected the somber mood of the ocean, rivers, and ponds below.

Thick forests of cattails beat a relentless, violent, back-and-forth rhythm against the walls outside of Tides' Tavern, and I was sure that by the end of the night, the place would need repairs. Made of two-legger materials that had fallen into our waters, the structure of the tavern was already weak and shabby. Square with rotting, wooden walls, algae and moss covered nearly every surface inch. The ceiling was a sheet of metal, tied down in place with rope from a fisherman's net. There was a second floor where Josiah—the tavern's owner—lived and it was just as ill-kept as the bottom floor.

Not that anyone seemed to mind the drear of the place. It was still one of the best in Lagoona because food and drink were both affordable and tasty. The customers didn't seem to mind that gators swarmed through the backyard. They knew that they were safe as long as they didn't venture further north into the breeding grounds.

I wished I would have been smart enough to realize that sooner, but I couldn't blame Josiah for where he'd decided to settle. Perhaps it was because he was from up north. From the swamplands, deep in the bayou that bordered our own little town. He'd wanted to keep his past close and so he had. Hence, the gators.

Despite the day, the tavern was full, though voices were kept as low as a funeral dirge as opposed to the usual loud chatter that tended to fill the place. I could only blame one thing for the quiet, and that was the Selection that would take place tomorrow.

I didn't want to think too hard on it because I knew it would fill me with emotions that beat in tandem with the currents. Rage. Disgust. Fear. But not thinking about it, not talking about it, not *accepting* the feelings inside my chest seemed like I was somehow laying down and letting the royals of Thalassar slit my throat. They had soldiers by the thousands, but still they went from village to village, selecting able-bodied mer to fight in their war against the enemy kingdom of Kappur.

Any one of the mer currently in the tavern could be chosen tomorrow to go and fight off an enemy we scarcely knew about. What we did know was speculation, whispers that reached us from the palace. That, and the deaths of our loved ones. That knowledge made me smile wider at them, if only to brighten their moods before the truth came crashing down on their shoulders.

"Another bowl?" I asked one of the customers, a merman with webbed hands and feet like a frog.

His face had been etched in grave lines. At my words, he startled, looking up at me and at the warm smile on my face. His amphibious features softened as he pushed the bowl and cup towards me. "Fish eye stew," he said quietly. "And a bit o' ale."

Picking up the bowl—a large two-legger plastic hat—and the cup, I turned and swam behind the counter. Josiah was shining cups with a strip of kelp as I passed him, going to the kitchen in the back. Enormous pots sat on small mountains of sand on the ground. They were like small volcanoes, containing hot blue lava on the inside that bubbled out heat to keep the food warm. I went to one of the pots and ladled up a spoonful of thick stew and then poured fermented ale into his cup before taking it back to him.

"Enjoy your meal, sir." I smiled.

He returned the gesture before grabbing the bowl and dunking the contents into his wide mouth.

I was already moving towards the next table, stopping to take the order of the merman there. "How are you doin' today, Christof?"

The distracted merman almost startled out of his chair at my inquiry. I'd never known the seamstress' son to be jumpy, but he was staring at me with wide eyes and a panicked expression that made me want to offer comfort.

"Oh." He chuckled nervously. "I—" He broke off. "A little nervous? I don't know. Just want a meal before—"

He didn't need to finish his sentence. I already knew what he meant.

Before Selection.

"I'll bring you some stew."

Once the plate was in front of him, he devoured it with loud slurping noises, earlier troubles all but forgotten.

If there was one thing mer came to Tides' Tavern for, it was the food. Josiah teased that they only came to see me because I was so "exotic". I thought he was full of sand. Although, my features *were* rather extraordinary for a pond mer. My hair reached down to my waist and bordered between dark purple and blue. Not quite one but not the other, either. My tail shone in the same shade as my hair, while my skin was the color of a pearl, that strange, shining combination of pink and white. I always knew I looked different from the mer here with their webbed hands and feet, snake tails, or dull green scales.

I stood out, but by no stretch of the imagination was I *beautiful*. I had a plain face, with a slightly upturned nose and wide eyes. My frame was thin and tall, and even if my coloring was pretty, I knew what the truth of my clothes hid. Scars ran down the side of my tail and trailed up to my hip and waist. I swam with a limp, due to the aquamarine fin on the side of my tail being shredded. When I first started working with Josiah, I'd been attacked by a gator. My own stupidity had almost cost me my life, and my body had never been the same since. The scars made navigating the deep pond slightly difficult.

Still, Josiah liked to tease me. So I'd self-consciously taken to wearing my hair up in a hat to hide it. My tail was harder to hide, but at least the long, dull tunics I wore covered most of it.

I leaned against the counter on my forearms, my tail curling leisurely under me as I smiled at my boss. He didn't return the gesture. He shined the cups with great fervor, his knuckles going white with the effort. He wasn't even looking in my general direction. His eyes were glued to the ivory clam shell that rested on a high shelf behind the counter. The center of the shell held a floating bubble, which glowed a bright yellow and depicted moving images.

It was the fanciest thing in Tides' Tavern.

Despite the poverty in Lagoona, all mer were required by the king and queen to have a telly shell. The royals liked to project images all over the kingdom of their grandeur, if only so that we would be informed of the events at the capitol.

Josiah complained that the royals wasted valuable resources, like the mages and their magic, only to fabricate outlandish stories that they wanted the mer to see.

Mages were rare magic-wielders. The seven sea kingdoms were filled with their own special magic and a science that differed from what existed on two-legger territory. It was a mixture of both. Magic and science blending together to create the world we lived in. It allowed things like soup to stay within the confines of its bowl instead of drifting through the water. Our own foods were denser than two-legger liquids, so it wasn't too complicated to comprehend the differences.

Josiah thought differently. "They're trying to manipulate us!" he said angrily, gesturing with the strip of kelp towards the image of the King and Queen of Thalassar greeting the foreign Prince of Draconi.

The images had no color to them, but they were high-quality, and I felt my attention snag on the foreign prince. His features were rather striking, his expression severe as he bowed stiffly to the king and queen.

"They're trying to distract us with announcements of the royal wedding so that we can take our eyes off the war. It's their way, you see. They dangle shiny things in front of us so we don't realize that they're sharpening the knives intended for our backs."

I rolled my eyes but didn't dare interrupt. Josiah was all about conspiracy theories. He spoke of nothing else and since he had an audience, I knew he was just getting started. I wondered if he was hoping to start a riot, to raise arms against the King and Queen of Thalassar. A part of me relished in the idea of a revolution. I'd seen first-hand how we suffered during the Selection. It had been going on for years now. And none who were chosen ever came back. Those who tried deserting suffered the consequences of their actions.

"They send out the poorest of us to fight a battle they started while they lounge about in their fancy castle surrounded by experienced soldiers, planning the princess' wedding! I'd like to see the king go out and die beside the best of us."

I hissed from between my teeth and glanced warily over my shoulder. "Quiet, Josiah," I warned. "You know they double security 'round these parts before the Selection. If a guard hears you, you could be executed."

Josiah snorted. "Let them come!" he shouted. "Not even royal guards are strong enough to get past the gators!"

I sighed, knowing he wouldn't let up any time soon. He'd scream and shout for an hour more and the customers would scream and shout with him, as they always did. But in the end, nothing would change. We were nothing; we had no power and little resources. We'd never start a revolution or raise arms against the capitol city. To speak of it was to welcome death. To not speak of it meant cowardice. Living under these circumstances was a double-edged sword.

I turned my attention back to the telly, frowning. The images moved around, waving, elongating, and stretching with the movement of the bubble. In them, the Prince of Draconi sat next to the Princess of Thalassar at a state dinner. The prince's face was grave, and even I could tell he had no desire to be there. His fiancée, however, smiled widely, relishing in the attention.

I rolled my eyes at their images, knowing Josiah was right. How could they sit there all day, eating from diamond-encrusted silverware while their kingdom suffered greatly from the effects of their war? It wasn't just Lagoona who suffered, but the swamplands and most other backwater towns who sent their young mer off to war. The war had led them to poverty and near starvation, it had instilled fear and had made life nearly unbearable. Out of fear of being Selected, some mer would rather try and swim away. Those who were caught were executed in Artisan's Square to remind the rest of us what should happen if we tried neglecting our duties. A law, cruel and barbaric, passed down by the royal family.

A sudden, violent part of me had the urge to reach through that bubble and strangle the princess on her pretty little throne. I'd seen enough images of her to know she seemed as daft as a tadpole. I turned my gaze abruptly away from the image of her and the prince trailing about through the palace gardens.

"Spoiled is what they are," Josiah continued.

I reached out to place my hand over his own. He stopped polishing the cup to look at me. "You've been cleaning that same cup for thirty minutes," I pointed out. "How 'bout I take over?"

His ruddy features softened as he offered me a warm smile, revealing his sharp teeth. Josiah was slightly robust, with gray hair that was cropped short. His skin was covered with the gray and green ridges of an alligator's scales, and his tail was long and thick, with stumpy fat legs at the end. His eyes were yellow with slit pupils that would have been frightening had I not known the merman my entire life.

"You're a blessing straight from the gods, Maisie." He released his hold on both kelp and cup to reach out and cradle my cheek for a split second before pulling away. "I don't know what I did to deserve you, but I'll pray to them that you aren't Selected tomorrow."

His words were a reminder that I wasn't completely safe and that I never would be until this war was over. Tomorrow was the Selection. Up until now, I'd avoided such a fate. The tides could turn at any moment. No one—save for business owners, mothers, mer younger than sixteen, and the elderly—were exempt from it. I was nineteen and could be chosen at any moment.

The war had been going on for as long as I could remember; the Selection had begun when I'd been thirteen. The royals had probably been tired of sending their own into battle in a war that was happening leagues away, where the borders of Thalassar and Kappur met.

Despite the fear gnawing at the center of my stomach, I smiled at my boss. "You'll not be rid of me so easily. I plan on inheriting the place once you die." I winked, and he laughed.

"You're meant for bigger things than running Tides' Tavern for the rest of your life, Mais."

"Yeah, yeah." I waved him off before pulling more cups towards me to continue shining. As I did my job, my gaze frequently found the telly, looking at repeat images of the princess and her prince, Josiah's words playing over and over again in my mind.

I wanted to desperately believe what he was saying, that somehow *I* was meant for a life bigger than this one. That I was destined to help the mer here in a way that extended to more than a smile to ease their fears. But that was utterly ridiculous. I wasn't a princess. I was no one but an orphaned mer from the backwaters of Lagoona.

And never, in the history of anything, had a backwater mer made a worthwhile change in the world.

Artisan's Square was located in the centermost part of the small pond of Lagoona. It was one of the prettiest sights because it boasted the market. Every Finsday, artisans from all over the ocean came to set up their stands and sell their wares. Everything from foreign foods to garments and jewelry. Despite the poverty of Lagoona, the market still burst with merchants.

I couldn't afford half the things displayed there. Not many could except the lords and ladies of Lagoona, whose rich homes bordered the Square. Though it was ways away from my own home, I still liked to visit after work to see what it was they had to offer.

"Pearls! Get yer pearls here!"

"How 'bout a lovely necklace for the merfriend? The diamonds are *real*."

"Beautiful rubies, straight from Her Majesty, the queen's crown. Half off!"

I inhaled the scent of the market. During the day, when the sunlight from up top pierced through to illuminate the waters below, the yellow glow of it would hit the jewels just right, casting an underwater rainbow against the pond floor. Colors of magenta, red, cerulean blue, and gold would dance with the movement of the water. It was always an enrapturing sight.

The stands all seemed to blend together to the point where it was hard to tell where one ended and another began. They were made up of all materials ranging from deep sea coral shelves, as well as wood and metal. They used the finest looking sea silk as mantels, the bright colors obviously more expensive than anything I'd ever own.

Lined up on one half of the square, the other half was occupied by a very large dais that was used for public announcements and executions. In the middle of the Square sat a gargantuan nautilus shell, its opening of the chamber spilling out bright pink water lilies. As far as sights went around here, it was all we had besides the cattail forest and the alligator breeding grounds.

I navigated my way through the crowd at a leisurely pace, bumping past locals as well as soldiers keeping watch. The day was almost over, nighttime soon approaching, and already some vendors were packing up to leave. My eyes darted everywhere at once, taking in what sights and colors from the outside world I could. Coral, shells, sea glass and jewelry; some vendors even sold two-legger objects thrown into the sea.

I paused before a weapons' table, my gaze holding on a winking, black blade.

"Like what you see, little mer?" the vendor asked. He was a surly merman with spikes trailing from his forehead down to his spine. His body was a pale gray, mottled with brown spots. He held the blade up before him for my examination, balancing it on his palm. It was the length of my forearm with a sharp tip but curved edge. It was polished black, immaculate. The hilt was studded with a single sapphire jewel. "Polished obsidian," the merman continued. "A rare blade, made by Thalassar's finest." He handed it to me, placing it in my reluctant fingertips. "Go on," he urged. "Give it a swing."

Tightening my grip on it, I took a stroke back, observing the blade as if it would move itself. I'd never held a weapon before, certainly nothing this expensive or of this caliber. I could practically feel how the blade oozed coins and knew immediately it was priceless.

"Go on."

I took a deep breath and swung the blade in an arc over my head. I had no idea what I was doing and felt entirely too ridiculous, like a child playing at soldier.

The blade differed from a kitchen knife, its purpose clear in the weight as I made a series of jabs. This blade was meant to defend, to protect. It was a blade made for battle. For killing.

I froze, holding the weapon away from me, breathing heavily, my shredded fin pulsing from the exertion.

"Very light, as you can see."

"It is very pretty," I observed.

The merman made a noise of impatience. "If you're looking for 'pretty' I suggest you go get yourself a necklace. This weapon here is meant to be dangerous, to kill. It is *not* a decoration."

He said it as though beauty and danger could not go hand in hand. As if you could not be one without the other. I saw the beauty in this danger, and just because it was meant to draw blood, did that in turn make it *ugly?* The act itself was ugly. The weapon, however, was not.

"I meant no insult," I said cautiously.

"It is not I who you've insulted, but the blade's maker."

I twirled the weapon, captivated by the movements as I asked, "Who's the maker?"

"That weapon was made by none other than the infamous Black Blade."

I stopped, looking at him with bright curiosity. "The Black Blade?"

The merman leaned his forearms against his algae covered wooden tabletop, pushing aside a range of dull silver blades as he did. His eyes were wide with brittle excitement that he didn't want to contain. "The Black

Blade," he repeated in darker tones. "The most wanted outlaw in the entire Kingdom of Thalassar. You mean to tell me you've never heard of him?"

I lowered the weapon to my side, feeling its weight suddenly very heavy. "No, never."

His smile was mischievous. "There's a reason for all the extra security during the Selection and it's because of the Black Blade. He was chosen once too, if rumors are to be believed. But before he could be taken, he escaped, taking down some royal soldiers along the way. The first ever escapee in history."

"Nuh-uh." But even as I said the words with disbelief, I leaned closer to him, captivated by his tale.

"No one knows how he did it, only that he did. They couldn't find him afterwards. They say he moves as quietly as a shadow, as quick as a current. That whenever Selection comes around, he is there to help those chosen escape their fate. He's a thief of the night, a whisper between the waves, and he's made a mockery of the royals on more than one occasion. No one who has seen him has lived to tell the tale. A hero to many, and a criminal to the crown."

His words blanketed over me, filling me with something I'd long forgotten. Hope. The sensation lasted but a moment before I snorted. "Who just so happens to make weapons during his free time? Sounds too good to be true."

An escapee? Certainly we would have heard about it by now. Even as separated from the rest of Thalassar as we were, we would have heard the whispers. No, he couldn't possibly exist, whoever he was, because once you were selected, there was no escaping it. You belonged to them, to the *crown*, and you would go off to war to fight and die for them. Whether you wanted to or not.

"Don't doubt the existence of the merman of shadows. You'll never know when you might need him to save your tail."

I was about to mumble that his story was nothing but bullshark when the blaring of a horn had me turning abruptly.

All chatter ceased as one by one, every mer in the square turned to the dais. I felt my heart tumble inside my chest at the sight that greeted me there.

Several guards were floating atop the structure. They wore the colors of the royals they served; dark blue uniforms with black and gold trimming. One of the guards held a conch shell in his hands, the source of the noise. Another held up a very large, thick flagpole. The flag of Thalassar—a blue background with a golden and black hippocampus stitched on the front—was attached to it, flapping against the current.

There were two other guards, and between them they held a merman, a commoner from Lagoona. His head was hung low, so I had no way to tell who he was. Blood rose from his body in smoky tendrils before disappearing. His clothes were the simple rags of a workman.

When he lifted his head to look up at the crowd, shock rippled through us all.

It was the seamstress' son, Christof.

"On this Finsday of the forty-fifth year of the Malabella-Oriana reign, I condemn this mer, Christof Ket, to death for the crime of attempted desertion a day before Selection." The guard holding the conch's voice rang out loud and clear through the square. "Let this remind the rest of you that cowardice is rewarded only with death, and all deserters who are captured will *die* at the end of a blade."

As he said those words, the guard carrying the flagpole suddenly flicked the bottom of it, and out came the sharp, long point of a blade.

After a gesture from the guard who spoke, the two holding the merman came forward, hauling Christof before the center stage. My heart beat wildly, uncontrollably as they brought Christof to a kneeling position. There was panic in his eyes and his shoulders shook with sobs.

To be so young, for he was my age, and to face such a fate… He'd tried deserting before the possibility of being called on to go out and fight. And he'd pay the price for his actions.

"In the name of the queen and king and the entire royal family of Thalassar, I condemn you to die."

My stomach churned and bile rose high to my throat as I watched the guard lift the blade over Christof's head.

I wanted to look away. I *should* have, but I couldn't, even if I wanted to. I let the fear that pervaded through the water paralyze me. It consumed with vicious talons, making my breath come out in shallow spurts. I was playing into the royals' hands. This was what they wanted to instill in us all. This cloying sensation of being trapped with no escape at all.

Then the blade came swinging down.

And there was nothing but silence.

Silence and blood.

"By the order of the royals, so it is done," the guard said in a soft but firm voice. "Long may they reign."

"Long may they reign!" Only the guards echoed those words, banging their fists against their chests, clattering their leather armor, before they promptly left, leaving Christof's body to sink to the stage.

I tried to blink back the image of his head rolling, of the blood that burst through the water to darken our pond. But the memory was there. I'd witnessed so much death at my young age already that this should have been easy to bear, but it never was. Friends, acquaintances, strangers… Their faces were etched so deeply into my mind that they followed me into unconsciousness every night when I closed my eyes to sleep.

A touch at my arm brought me back to reality. I whirled around to face the vendor of weapons. He was looking at me, his yellow eyes soft, with both sorrow and caution.

It was then that I realized I was gripping the hilt of the blade so tightly that my fingers began to hurt, and I held it in a position poised to strike.

Taking in a deep, shuddering breath, I loosened my hold on it and held it out in front of me, balancing it on my palm as he had. He merely observed it with an expression in his eyes I couldn't quite read.

"Looks like your infamous Black Blade is nothing but myth." And one too good to be true, at that. No one would ever come to free us from this tyranny. No outlaw. No royal. No guard.

We were on our own.

And always would be.

The merman's gaze flicked from the blade to my face. Something in him seemed to soften and I knew he understood every emotion running through me right now.

"Keep it," he said. I blinked and he leaned forward, closing my fingers around the hilt before pulling away.

I stared at him with disbelief. "I can't take this. I've no money."

He clicked his tongue in annoyance. "I'm not asking you for money. I'm *telling* you to take the blade." He bent beneath his table and emerged a second later with a black scabbard and a leather waist strap that were as finely made as the blade. He handed those to me as well.

"But, why?"

He sighed. "Because maybe the Black Blade cannot come here to save you or your mer, but that weapon is a piece of him and maybe it will give you the strength you need to save yourself. Now get. I'm about to close shop."

I weighed his abrupt words the way I'd weighed the weapon in the palm of my hand. There was a possibility I could be selected tomorrow. If I was, would I face what was to come or would I run? There would be no outlaw to help me, and the merman was right. I knew firsthand we could rely on no one but ourselves if we wanted to be saved.

I stuck the blade into the scabbard. "Thank you," I whispered before turning around and swimming away, out of Artisan's Square. Noticing that all had gone quiet now, as the weight of death settled deep into our bones.

Like most homes in Lagoona, mine was made from discarded two-legger material. But unlike most homes, mine was entirely secluded, deep in the cattail forest. It had been my grandmother's, and when she'd died, it became mine.

A small and shabby place, the house was made from an overturned blue boat that was chipped and furry with algae. A long, wide board had been pried loose, leaving a gaping hole in the front that served as a doorway. I swam through it now and into the confined space. The inside had been carved out, the mud hollowed to give the illusion of space.

There was a small kitchenette with a table and a few supplies I used to make my meals with. To the right was my sleeping area. I had no bed, or rather I couldn't afford it, so I'd taken cattails, kelp, and tadpoles and woven them together to form a hammock.

After placing the blade carefully on the table, I made my way to the hammock. It was made of fraying thread, the color dulled over time. Two ends spread out and were hammered into the wooden walls. When I climbed into it, my tail hanging off the end, it groaned like it wanted to break.

The boards holding it up creaked as I settled in comfortably, resting my hands on the flat of my stomach. Looking at the wall, I sighed. My telly hung there, albeit it was incredibly smaller than Josiah's. The shell was chipped around the edges, but it still projected images just the same.

I looked at them now, at the Queen and King of Thalassar sitting upon their coral thrones, and felt hatred stir within me anew.

Years ago, the king had been married to the *true* Queen of Thalassar. She'd been good and kind and just, but she'd died so many years ago when the princess was only five. She'd soon been replaced by another. By her *cousin.* This new queen was rather cruel, as she'd been the one to start the war with Kappur and had plummeted the kingdom in darkness.

I closed my eyes against their forced images and turned away, wrapping my arms against myself. The cold still seeped through my bones, spreading throughout my entire body until it was numb. And pretty soon, I felt nothing at all.

Maisie

I DRESSED QUICKLY THE next morning, pulling off my black tunic, switching it for a brown one so that I blended in with the crowd. It was old, so it fit me tight around the chest and waist, but at least it covered half of my tail. Sweeping my long hair above my head, I hid the tresses beneath a hat. When I finished, my gaze wandered over to the blade on the table. My hand itched to reach for it and belt it to my waist, but I shook that feeling off.

The guards would double—or triple—today. If one of them saw me with it, they wouldn't hesitate to take me down. They were the "kill first, ask later" type of mer. So I left it where it was and swam out towards town.

Artisan's Square was packed with royal soldiers. Some were setting up watching posts while others swam lazily about, laughing and joking as though they hadn't a care in the world. As though they hadn't come to destroy lives.

The waters were a blur of royal colors. Everywhere I turned, there was a soldier and no doubt there were many more of them posted all over the outskirts of our town, waiting for escapees. I wondered if they relished in it, in the ones that tried to flee, because it was all just a game to them and they knew that there was no chance of escaping.

An image of a faceless, shadowy merman swam into my mind. The Black Blade. If the story was true, then he'd escaped their clutches. There had been someone out there who the soldiers hadn't been able to catch.

And that filled me with satisfaction.

To be honest, it was hard to believe in a merman of the shadows, and yet I clutched onto that image like a lifeline. Maybe that's why heroes were created. Because people like me needed something to believe in.

Bodies pushed up against mine as I tried swimming past the crowd. I'd swam directly to the Square even though it was more of a trek to come here instead of swimming directly to the Tavern. I'd just wanted to get a feel of the atmosphere this year, of the soldiers and the brand of cruelty they brought with them.

Selection did not require to be gathered together, at least not until nighttime. I wasn't sure how they chose us, just that they looked through the list of population names the lords and ladies of Lagoona provided for them.

Funny how the wealthy were never chosen.

So, today would be a normal work day until tonight. Tonight, everything would change.

There were no stands up today. No sign of the merman who had gifted me with the blade, no sign of anyone but nervous mer swimming to work and an endless sea of soldiers.

Shaking off my nervousness, I started to turn directions, to go to the Tavern. It would do no good to make myself anxious over this. Best to just get to work and bust my tail until I temporarily forgot.

But as I turned, I was caught off guard as a wall of solidity rammed against me. I staggered a stroke back, trying to right myself but, *blast my torn fin*, I lost my balance and fell to the mud.

The crowd didn't slow as I sprawled to the ground. They swam past me, hitting me in the face with strong tail fins.

Briefly blinded, I cried out, throwing my hands up to protect my face. When the pain eased and the impact lessened, I looked up to find a royal soldier staring down at me indifferently. His eyes were barely on me, flickering behind me with an expression that said he'd rather be elsewhere.

"Forgive me," he said stiffly. "I didn't see—" He suddenly froze, his hand outstretched, palm up as if he meant to help me up. His bright eyes grew wide as he took me in, as if seeing me for the first time.

My face flamed under his scrutiny and, ignoring his hand and trying to preserve the scraps of my dignity, I got up on my own. As I did, I felt the tresses of my hair float against my cheeks. Great. I looked to the ground to find my hat trampled in the mud. With a groan, I bent and picked it up, shaking the clumps of mud out of it.

When I looked up, the soldier was still staring with a gaping mouth, making me feel entirely too self-conscious. He was a tall merman with a wide, muscular frame. His uniform was the same blue with black and gold trimming the other soldiers wore except his, I noticed, had starfish embroidered on his breast. His skin was golden-kissed, hair blond, the color of sunlight, and cropped short. His aquamarine colored eyes matched the bright color of his tail; a tail that fanned out beneath the long, flowing tunic he wore beneath his jacket.

All in all, a handsome sort of face that was ruined due to the uniform he wore and what he represented.

I said nothing as I started to swim past him. I was brought up short by the tight grip of his hand on my forearm. He whipped me back in front of him, so close I had to place my hands against his chest, both to keep me steady and to keep space between us. My heart pounded as I looked up at him.

"Look, mister," I began angrily, hoping my voice wouldn't shake. "You knocked *me* over, so if it's an apology you're wantin' sorry to disapp—"

"Odele?" he interrupted breathlessly.

I felt my heart stutter at the way he asked. At the intimacy with which he whispered that name.

"Looks like you're confusin' me with someone else." I pushed him away and, to my surprise, he didn't tug me back. Good. He dropped his hands to his sides, tightening them into fists.

He blinked a couple of times, like coming out of a trance and then stiffened completely. "Forgive me." He looked around cautiously. To see if someone had witnessed his odd behavior, or to see if anyone witnessed him speaking to me? My fins flared defensively at the thought. "Might I speak with you in a more private area?"

My breath caught as I stared at this merman, at this stranger, at this *soldier.* What was wrong with him? The audacity! Anger boiled hot in me, like the workings of an erupting volcano. These soldiers had some nerve. They came to murder us, destroy our lives, and now he was asking me for a private meeting?

"I don't know what kind of a mer you take me for, mister," I gritted out from between clenched teeth. "But I'm not some concubine at your beck and call. Now, if you'll excuse me…"

I started to swim past him, slamming my hat back onto my head as I did. But he was beside me again, his hand reaching out to grab my arm. I suddenly wished I had brought the blade.

"You won't take no for an answer, will you? Back off!"

"Wait!" When he made a move to grab me, I slapped his hand away and darted off into the crowd. Pushing my way through bodies, I swam, putting all the power that I could into my tail. When I found an opening, I sped through it, praying he wouldn't follow behind me.

I zipped through town until I put Artisan's Square behind me and didn't slow until I was sure he hadn't followed. Still, just to be safe, I took different routes, cutting through the farmer's market and taking the back way behind the pastry shop. When Tides' Tavern finally came into view, I didn't breathe until I was safely inside, door closed behind me.

I leaned against it, chest rising and falling with every rapid breath I took.

Josiah floated behind the counter, took one look at me and whistled. "You alright, Mais? You look like you've been chased by a wild pack of piranhas."

I forced my heart to calm it's thundering and turned my gaze to my boss. Though his tone had been lighthearted, his face was etched in worried lines. I knew that if I told him the truth, soldier or no, he'd feel obligated to defend my honor.

I plastered a smile on my face. "All's good, Jo." I moved away from the door and went to join him behind the counter. "The square is packed today," I commented as I took my apron from a fisherman's hook on the wall and put it on. Pulling the hat from my head, I observed it closely. A hole had been torn through it from the trampling it had received. Well, it was ruined, I decided and tossed it into a disposal bin.

"Crawlin' with soldiers," he spat.

Since I could see his temper start to rise, I pierced him with a hard look. "Now, Jo, don't go startin' stuff with them. Especially not today."

Jo snorted and continued to wipe down the already clean counter. I knew he was just keeping his hands busy because of the stress of the day. I wanted to remind him that he had nothing to fear. Business owners were exempt, more often than not, from Selection. Their workers, however, were not. And under the circumstances, I felt calmer than what he was displaying.

Reaching into the pocket of my apron, I pulled out a spare strip of kelp I tended to carry around with me and began tying my hair back, away from my face. When I finished, I looked to the front door of the tavern as it opened and a small group of soldiers poured in. They stopped at the entryway, looked around with scrutinizing gazes, their eyes roaming to the muddy floors, to the furry green walls, and to us behind the counter.

I felt Jo stiffen beside me, and I knew what he was probably thinking. His anger was practically a palpable thing, and I knew it would take very little for him to erupt.

"Great morning, 'gents." I swam around the counter and gifted them with my widest—and fakest—smile. "A table for three?" I held my hands behind my back so they wouldn't see them tightening into fists.

Their eyes roamed over me, gazing a bit too long at my hair for my liking. I cursed the soldier who had knocked me over, ruining my hat in the process. My face heated with self-consciousness and I cleared my throat before saying, "Our special today is river snakes stuffed with leeches, served over salad."

They all blinked, absorbing the words.

"Leeches?" one of them asked.

I nodded, smiling. "We also have fish-eye stew if you prefer."

"I'll take a snake," another said. The two guards turned to stare incredulously at their companion. He shrugged. "What? I like trying new things!"

"If you'll follow me to a table?" I turned and led them to the table furthest away from the counter. After they were seated and I'd taken the rest of their orders, I went back over to Jo.

He was scowling. "You're too kind, Maisie."

Shrugging, I began pulling out bowls and cups. "They're paying customers."

"They're little more than royal dogfish," he hissed quietly.

"Yes, I know. But they're dogfish with pockets full of coins, and it's just your luck that I convinced them to order a whole jar of moonshine."

Josiah's eyes widened. "That's our strongest and most expensive drink."

"I know."

The drink had them dizzy within moments. And after half an hour, they were a mess. We had more customers arrive, all seated as far away from the soldiers as they could get. The soldiers had gotten loud and obnoxious and it made everyone cautious. All I could focus on was the money that would soon fill the tavern.

When they'd drank the last of the moonshine, I swam over to them, my smile already in place. "Anything else y'all require?" I asked sweetly, though inside I was seething at the sight of them.

"Ay! She's back!"

"And as pretty as a pearl." Their words slurred together, making my skin crawl.

Ignoring them now, I leaned over to clear the dishes when a strong arm went around my waist. I let out a yelp as I was hauled into the soldier's lap.

"You don't look like most mer out here." His breath fanned against my cheek, warm and overpowering. I struggled in his lap, only to be pulled tighter against his body.

"Let go of me!" I demanded, using my elbow as a weapon against him. It did little but ruffle his uniform, and the more I struggled against him, the tighter he held me, and the more pain flared in my fins. And it seemed that no amount of fighting would get him to ease his grip.

Panic clawed at my chest, the desperation to get away lost behind the blind haze of that sensation. Soon, all I could hear was the thunderous beating of my own heart. All I could feel was the warmth of his breath on the back of my neck, the pain as his arm dug into my stomach.

And then I heard Josiah's voice, loud enough to break through the panic and bring me back. "Release her or I'll have your brains blown all over this table."

The soldiers froze, though the one holding me didn't let go, nor did he loosen his vice grip. Then slowly, he turned with me in his lap, and I saw Josiah pointing a spear gun in our direction.

If I expected the soldiers to tremble in fear, I was wrong. In unison, they laughed and the one holding me pressed his face into my shoulder as he wheezed.

I think I would have preferred death by gator than to suffer in his grasp any longer.

Finally, he sat up straighter. "You think I'm afraid of your little weapon, freshwater freak?"

"If you aren't then you're dumber than you look, soldier. Now, let her go."

I could tell the soldier was offended because he stiffened. "Now look—"

He didn't get the rest out because at that moment the front door of the tavern burst open and a voice—rumbling and familiar—sounded.

"What is going on here?"

The soldiers turned their gazes to the door and, upon seeing who it was, quickly got up from their seats. I was pushed forward, colliding into Jo. He righted me with one arm, but kept the other tight on his weapon.

I whirled around to see the mermen come at attention, their bodies straight and their gazes wide on the wall. I recognized the merman that swam before them and felt the claws of panic dig in deeper.

Aquamarine eyes found my own. Gone was the shock and tenderness he'd looked at me with earlier. In its place was hard anger but all his anger was directed at the other soldiers.

"Captain Saber—"

"Did I give you permission to speak?" The merman who had knocked me down—the *captain*—was suddenly looming over the one who had held me. His eyes were flickering like two-legger fire. When the soldier clamped his mouth shut, the captain backed away and glared down the line at them all. "This is how you spend your time during Selection? Harassing the locals?"

"Captain, we—"

"I still do not recall allowing you to speak, cadet."

Dangerous. That was what the captain looked like in that moment, his body poised like a blade waiting to strike and kill. The soldier trembled and bit down tightly on his bottom lip.

"You're a disgrace to the royals you represent. All of you." The captain's glare didn't ease, his eyes piercing. "Now pay what you owe and leave, back to your posts. Your punishment *will* come later." When no one moved, he snarled, "Well?"

The soldiers practically scrambled over each other to dump coins onto the table before turning and bowing low in mine and Josiah's direction. "We apologize for our behavior," they said. When we didn't reply, they straightened and took their leave, tripping from the tavern like guppies. Only the captain stayed.

He turned to us. Josiah kept his weapon raised and pointed, but the captain didn't so much as blink. Instead, he looked at me. I felt my breath catch in the back of my throat.

"I don't care if you're a captain. Get out of my tavern."

The captain didn't flinch, or even look in Josiah's direction. My face flamed under his scrutiny. "Gladly," the captain replied. "But first I would like a word with *her*." He nodded at me.

I went cold down to the marrow in my bones and had to fight away the urge to reach for Josiah's arm in support. Instead, I tilted my head high and glared at him.

"Absolutely not," Josiah replied, his hands tightening on his weapon.

"Please," he whispered, and I could have sworn that was desperation in his voice. "It's urgent that I speak with you. In private."

I didn't know why I did it, why his words convinced me. I didn't lower my guard, but I did place the palm of my hand on Jo's spear gun to lower it.

"It's okay, Jo," I whispered. "I'll speak with him."

I led him out the back after assuring Josiah that I'd be fine on my own. Even as I muttered the words, I slipped a kitchen knife into the belt of my tunic. Just in case. I also didn't say a word to him until I led him deeper towards the back, near the gators. If he tried anything, I knew I'd be safe. I knew these grounds and he didn't. If things got rough, I could swim away, leaving him to a fate of teeth and blood. It was cruel, and my stomach clenched unpleasantly at the thought of leaving him to a fate I'd suffered myself.

But fear made even the bravest of us act irrationally.

When we were far enough away to not be overheard, I whirled around to face him, hands on my hips. "What do you want to speak to me about?"

His posture was stiff, his hands frozen behind his back. He was staring at me, eyes roaming up and down over my every inch.

My fins flared defensively. "So?" I prompted. "What do you *want?"*

His eyebrows furrowed. He looked as though he were at war with himself, grinding his teeth, jaw straining with the effort. Finally, he spoke, "I have traveled all over the kingdom and never in all that time did I think I'd come across someone like you."

"Someone like me?" What was that supposed to mean?

"Ma'am, what I am about to tell you… it is of the utmost importance that you keep it to yourself. The entire kingdom could be in danger if you do not."

How dramatic. I pushed away the eye roll that threatened to emerge and raised an eyebrow. “What are you talking about, mister?”

He lowered his lashes, took a deep breath and then said slowly, cautiously. “I’ve traveled all across the kingdom of Thalassar and never before have I met a mer like you. Because *you*, ma’am, are a perfect likeness of Princess Odele Malabella of Thalassar.”

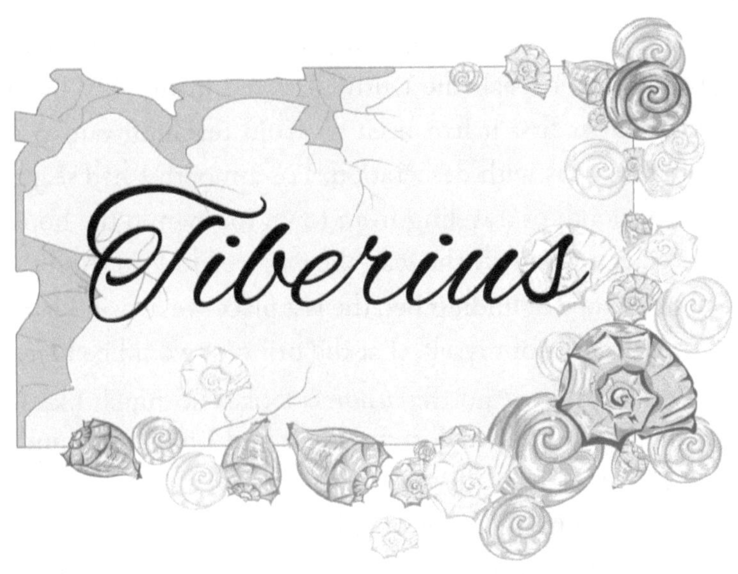

Tiberius

SHE WAS THE PERFECT picture of incredulity. Black eyes, like smooth marbles of obsidian, stared back at me. Eyes that were so familiar, they tugged at my heart, almost as if meaning to rip it straight from my chest with the intensity. And yet, *she* was so different from the princess I'd confused her with hours earlier.

The similarities were striking, but whoever truly knew the princess would notice this mer's posture, the subtle tilt of her chin, the set of her brow, the roughness of her palms. This mer, with her torn fins fanning at her sides beneath a dress that was too tight and too short, was no royal.

But she was enough like Odele that even I, with all the attention I placed in detail, had been taken aback.

She glared at me now. The princess had never glared. At least not like that. "You're insane!" Her hands were placed on her lean hips, her voice coming out in that twangy, Lagoona accent.

I couldn't stop myself from comparing every miniscule detail and judge.

"I can assure you, I speak the truth," I stated firmly. My hands were behind my back. At first it had been to avoid reaching out to her and taking her in my arms with desperation. For a month I had searched for the princess. A month of traveling from town to town in the hopes that I would find her. But wherever she was, she was well hidden. And this place had been my last hope of finding her, the last place we'd visit. I had hoped, with every raging fiber of myself, that the princess would be here.

Instead, I'd found *her*. And this *waitress* looked so much like Princess Odele that my heart thundered in my chest and I had to remind myself she was *not* who she looked like.

Her next words reminded me of this. "Right." She let out the most unladylike snort. "So you grabbed me because I look like the princess." Her words dripped with an icy coating of disbelief. "You're full of sand, mister. The princess is at the palace with her betrothed. I saw it on the telly. You're wasting my time." She started to swim back to the tavern. But I couldn't let her leave, not with the future of the kingdom hanging on by a thread. And she may just be the answer we'd been searching for all this time. A temporary solution. If I could only convince her.

"Please listen," I commanded. "Let me explain."

Her obsidian eyes flicked over me and she sighed, placing her hands on her hips again in a gesture that obviously meant impatience. "Five minutes," she said. "That's all you get before I go back."

I took in a slow breath. This... this would be the hard part. Swearing her to secrecy, convincing her of my maddening plan.

"Four minutes!" she snapped.

I pierced her with a hard look and dug deep inside to muster up the patience for this conversation. "You see what the king and queen want you to see. Princess Odele and Prince Kai? Those images had been recorded months ago and are being projected to make the events seem recent. They do it all the time."

She looked taken aback by that revelation but quickly re-masked her features. She was much easier to read than the princess, that I noticed.

"So?" She tilted her chin up in defiance. "So what if she's missing? Even *if* I look like her—which I don't—what business is it of mine?"

"What I'm about to tell you is one of the biggest secrets in all of Thalassar. I need your word you will stay silent. You can tell *no one*."

"I can make no promises."

I narrowed my eyes at her and took a stroke forward, just as she took one back. Yes, that was fear in her stance. I stopped, jerking my hands behind my back once again. It would do no good to frighten her into submission, though I wasn't opposed to the idea if necessary.

"Your word," I threatened darkly. "No one can know."

She sighed with obvious exasperation. "Fine. I give you my word."

And I believed her. It was the expression on her face. Everything about her seemed so openly honest.

"The princess has been missing for months."

She didn't even blink, as if the news hardly surprised her. "So what, she swam away?"

"I don't know," I confessed. No one did. "It remains a mystery. She was in the palace surrounded by guards one moment and gone the next. But she *is* gone, and we don't know where."

She bit at her bottom lip, pensive before looking at me with curiosity. "Do you think she's gone from the palace because she does not wish to be there?"

I had asked myself the same question for days. She wanted for nothing, she'd had it all and now she was gone. It couldn't be a kidnapping. The culprits would have sent word by now, demanding a ransom.

Another possibility was that it had been Kappur and they were biding their time, waiting for the perfect moment to announce it. After all, Thalassar would never think to attack Kappur if they had the princess.

"I do not know," I confessed again. "But she is gone and her absence is being noticed by the courtiers. The queen and king have lied and told them that the princess is ill and is to be confined to her rooms. That lie cannot go on forever."

The waitress nodded. Finally, she was catching up with the conversation. "Yes, I can see how that would be problematic."

I nodded. "Yes. But if she has gone, *if* she has swum away, then our enemies will see it as Thalassar's weakness. They may attack while we are weak, while we are frantically searching for her return. The kingdom cannot afford such a loss."

She nodded in understanding, though there was a crease between her brows. I wasn't exactly sure what she was thinking in that moment. A part of me itched to ask, but a larger part of me did not care what she thought or felt. Because all I needed was for her to agree to my plan.

"So you agree that saving lives is important? That we need to stop this bloodshed?"

"Of course."

"Then you agree to come with me to the palace?"

She started to nod then froze. "What?" she stammered and placed her palm against her chest, as if she meant to steady the beating there. "Why would I go to the palace?"

I fought to keep my patience in place. "You are a perfect likeness to the princess," I explained slowly. "You are the temporary solution to the problem until we find her again."

"W-what are you saying?"

"I'm saying that I need you to come with me to the capitol. I need you to disguise yourself as the princess."

He was crazy. He had to be. Or there must have been something wrong with his eyes, because there was no way that I, an orphaned backwater mer, could look like royalty. Crazier yet, he wanted me to disguise myself as her, parade around the palace in silks and jewels to avoid an attack on the royals?

I took a deep breath. "No," I stated firmly.

He blinked, as if he hadn't quite heard me correctly. His brows pulled together, forming a crease of displeasure between them. "No?"

"No. I won't do it. Now if you'll excuse me, I have to get back to my shift." I tried swimming away, leaving this whole crazy mess behind me and get back to my reality. But as I tried to get away he was there, pulling me by the arm, whirling me to face him once more. His grip was tight and his gaze was angry.

"You *must* do it." He gritted his teeth, eyes blazing furiously. "Lives are at stake. The balance of this very kingdom—"

I pushed down the panic before it could rise again and slowly let my fingers drift towards my belt, reaching for the knife there. "*Royal* lives," I spat as my hand tightened around the hilt. "Mer who do not care about me or anyone else in Lagoona." I brought the blade up quickly, but the captain was faster, or he'd seen it coming. I felt pain explode through my arm and I yelped, dropping the knife and taking a stroke back. "Ow!" I pierced him with an accusatory glare.

He didn't even flinch. "You must do right by your kingdom and the crown," he lectured in irritating tones.

I glared at him. "Why should I? The crown hasn't done me any favors besides kill off my friends. You say you want to save lives, Captain? Then start by ending the war. I don't care about some stuck-up princess who shunned her duties."

I knew I'd said the wrong thing the moment his entire posture stiffened and his hands fisted at his sides. I saw the workings of his jaw, the veins at his temples strain against his skin. "Never speak ill of Princess Odele again, waitress. It may be the last thing you ever do."

A chill shivered down the length of my spine, all the way to my torn tailfin. But still, I stood my ground. I'd not let this soldier intimidate me. "The crown hasn't done me any favors," I repeated unkindly, rubbing the pain in my arm.

"If you do this for them, if you replace the princess for however long they need, until we can *find* her, the crown will be in your debt."

Pausing, I looked at him with wide eyes. The crown in my debt? That sounded like an insane notion. That a freshwater mer, a *nobody* from

Lagoona, could be of use to the royal family and that they could give her something in return. It was insanity and yet, I gave pause, imagining myself in the palace. Imagining myself in the softest of silks, in the richest of jewels, swimming through palace gardens, wearing a crown and sitting on a coral throne. The fantasy played so vividly in my mind in that moment, an image that I could surely reach out and touch… if I dared.

No.

I shook the image off. I couldn't parade around in another's skin while the mer of Lagoona suffered in poverty and fear. I would not sit on riches and pose for paintings and take turns around the garden with the prince instead of actually getting involved and making a difference…

I paused, breath catching. But… If I did this, if I pretended to *be* her, could I? Could I be involved? Could I make a difference in the kingdom somehow?

"The Selection—"

"You will be exempt from it," he interrupted. "However, as we cannot tell anyone the true reason for you leaving, we will have to lie and say you've been selected."

I gulped, pressing my hands to my chest. I felt my heart there, pressing back and forth against my palm. Taking a deep breath, I lowered my hands and looked at him, looked at his uniform, at the colors of the kingdom. Of *my* kingdom. When I saw those colors, all I saw was cruelty and death, the arc of a blade, heads drifting. The blood of friends, family.

"Do I have a choice?" I whispered, tearing my focus from the memories to look at him.

"You do," his answer was too slow. I wondered if he just wanted to give me the illusion of freedom. "You will come back." His voice was softer now. As if he meant to comfort. "You'll see your friends again."

Little did he know I had no friends left.

The crown had taken them all.

"I—" I gulped, cleared my throat. "I don't know." This was too much, too soon. "I need time. I need to think…"

The captain nodded his understanding. I wondered if he truly did. "I will give you until tonight. Until Selection. Meet me in Artisan's Square by the nautilus shell before names are called." I registered his words, nodding absently. I could feel his gaze on me, hard and unyielding. "Your kingdom needs you. Please think about it."

"Yes, um… I have to get back."

"Of course."

I started to swim forward, stopped and looked at him. "What's your name?" I asked. It was strange. I'd never thought of any of them as anything other than soldiers. Murderers.

He gave me a formal bow, and I knew I shouldn't have, but the gesture did make me feel like a royal. "Captain Tiberius Saber," he whispered, bright eyes flashing. "At your service."

"I'm Maisie. Maisie Fauna, Captain."

I got back to work slowly, offering Jo a small reassuring smile. Still, I found myself lost in my own thoughts, thoughts of what he'd said, about the princess. My eyes wandered to the telly on the shelf. Her image floated in the bubble there and I found my gaze locked on her, looking for any sign that what he'd said was true. *Did* we look alike?

The princess was always in such long dresses that appeared to be made of the richest materials like silk, tulle, and gossamer. Her hair always appeared to be coiled beneath extravagant crowns, the shade of it was dark, as were her scales. Her eyes, like my own, appeared to be black.

I'd never looked too closely at her, but now I analyzed her every detail. The angle of her chin, the curve of her cheekbones. Everything.

I tore my gaze away from the telly and focused on wiping down the counter. I scrubbed the rag vigorously across it, mind racing.

I didn't stop until I felt a hand jerking me back to reality. I turned sharply over to Josiah. "You okay, Mais?" he asked, concern in his eyes.

I realized my knuckles were white, my grip tight on the strip of kelp. I released it slowly and laughed nervously. "Yeah. Sorry, Jo." *My mind is elsewhere.*

His eyes roamed over me. "What did that soldier say to you?"

I knew he only meant well, but I couldn't possibly tell him the truth. "He just wanted to apologize for his comrades' behavior," I lied.

"Huh," he mumbled, as if he couldn't quite believe it. Probably because it hadn't been true. What apology took ten minutes? I bet he knew I was lying through my teeth.

"Jo." I sighed and turned fully to him. Josiah had been my boss for so long, but even more than that, he'd been a mentor, a parent. And a part of me longed to tell him the truth, for his guidance. I wanted him to tell me what I needed to do, what I *should* do. "If you had a chance to make a change, would you?"

My question had so obviously caught him off guard. I hoped—prayed—he wouldn't suspect a thing. I'd given my word, after all. But I needed guidance. What could I do? Even if I accepted, would there be a chance I could change anything?

"Of course I would. In the beat of a heart." His eyes softened as he looked upon me. "Is this about the Selection? Are you nervous?"

"Yes." It wasn't a lie. I was nervous just not about the Selection. I was nervous about something that seemed all the more dangerous than fighting in a war somehow. "I just—" I broke off, running a hand through my hair. I found myself looking at the purple strands and thinking of the princess. I quickly dropped them to place my hands on the countertop. "I just wonder if someone like me could ever make a change."

He raised his eyebrows and I wondered if he was amused. "Someone like you?"

I nodded once. "Someone like me. Someone poor. Someone from Lagoona. Someone—" I cut off again, gesturing wildly at my body, at my torn, crippled fin. "Me."

"I think anyone can make a difference," he said with certainty. "It doesn't matter if it's a fish, or a frog, a soldier, a king, or *you*. If we set our minds to it, if we *really* want it, we can make a difference."

"But how can someone like *me* ever change anything?"

Jo sighed. "I think you need to stop asking yourself *'how?'* and start asking yourself *'should I?'* The how's can be so easy and you know it. The hardest question out there is asking yourself if you *should* do it."

"But how do I answer those questions, Jo?"

"By looking *around* you, child." His voice rose, passionate and eager. "By looking inside you and looking around you. You will see what it is that is wrong, what it is that *needs* to be fixed, and you'll do it. *Be* the change you wish to see."

He gave me one last look before he went back to the kitchens, leaving me alone in my thoughts. I understood what he meant. I looked around every day, saw what was wrong with the Lagoona, saw the injustice and the poverty.

There was already a fiery rage inside me.

Everything was wrong here. Everything needed to be changed. Obviously, the royals weren't doing anything to help us, to fix what was wrong. If anything, they made an even bigger mess. The princess had done nothing. They *chose* to live that way. And now I had an opportunity to really fix things, to really make that difference. Would the royals listen to me? Maybe, maybe not. But if I wore the mask of Princess Odele, the merpeople would listen to me. And that could be enough. Enough to give hope.

Enough for change.

My gaze went to the telly once more, to the images of royalty floating there and in that moment, I knew what it was I had to do.

Night fell in the waters of Lagoona as the mer gathered about outside. The population was small and diminishing, but with all the extra soldiers around, everywhere seemed to be packed. I couldn't turn without running into nervous and stiff bodies. Mothers held onto their grown children and husbands tightly. This was all too familiar to me; the heartbreak, the cries. It chipped away the pieces of my heart each time, leaving a hole in its wake. A hole that would *never* again be filled.

I wrapped my arms around myself as I swam slowly through Artisan's Square. The night was cold, pressing up against me in an icy embrace. I braved it, pushing forward through the crowd. They all gathered near the stage, forming neat rows as they awaited names to be called. Soldiers floated on top of the dais, surrounding it as well. All eyes were alert on the citizens, waiting—hoping—there would be an escapee. That they would get their adrenaline rush for the night.

It was all a game to them.

But it wasn't to me.

I hung back from the crowd. The Selection would soon begin, and I needed to meet with Captain Saber to let him know what I'd decided. The thought of voicing it out loud, of seeing him again instilled fear in me. But I'd thought about it for hours, thought about what Jo had told me. Every day I passed poor children. I'd seen so many executions, had known so many attempted escapees, and things were only getting worse. To change things, to get them the way I wanted them to be, I had to first change myself.

And I was ready. So ready to do something about this life.

When I approached the nautilus, Captain Saber was already there. His hands were stiff behind his back, broad shoulders tight and alert. His aquamarine eyes assessed every single thing, darting left and right as if he expected everyone to rise up in arms at any given moment.

He turned his body when he saw me, but didn't smile. His lips were in a too-tight line. I feared if they were any tighter, they'd snap off his face. I didn't greet him as I approached and he didn't greet me. We just looked at each other briefly before he asked, his voice strained, "Well?"

I took a deep breath, calmed my shaking hands by tightening them into fists at my sides. "I'll do it," I said. His face changed into a look of obvious relief before he masked it again. "I'll do what you asked."

Tiberius

Relief crashed through me, but I suppressed it quickly. She'd agreed with my plan. I'd had doubts she would, but floating before me, she looked so determined, so *ready* to face what was coming. I admired that for a moment before cleansing myself of emotion and nodding, as if that had been the answer I'd expected of her all along.

"You've chosen to do the right thing," I whispered. Then I looked around, to the stage. It was time and they were all waiting on me. The other generals had all gotten together with what few lords and ladies this small pond of Lagoona had, and chosen names based on a complicated, randomized system of numbers and letters. "Tomorrow, I will come for you at your home." I did not know *where* she lived exactly, but I could easily find out. I just couldn't bear to look at her any longer, to remain in her presence. I did look one last time to see if she'd heard me. She had and was nodding slowly. I let loose a breath and, without a goodbye, left.

It was slightly unnerving, being in front of her, looking at the shade of her hair, at the shape of her eyes and not seeing Princess Odele in her place. But Maisie was *not* Odele, and I feared those words would soon become my mantra, my daily reminder. It would be what I told myself any time my heart started beating frantically at the sight of her.

Once I got to know her, I knew my body's reaction to her appearance would change. My palms would no longer sweat and I'd no longer look at her lips, longing for something forbidden, for something I could never have.

Shaking off those thoughts, I weaved around the labyrinthine crowd until I was near the stage. I swam to where the generals and lesser ranked soldiers were waiting for me. As soon as I was on the dais, a soldier handed me a kelp list with the names written on them. I glanced at them all. Maisie's name wasn't on here, but when I announced them, I'd be naming her regardless.

I knew how the Selection hurt some of the mer, knew there was a slim chance that they'd see their families and loved ones again. But that was the price to pay when there was a war. It was for everyone's own good, for the safety of the entire kingdom. They were no more or less important than the mer in the capitol or at any other town.

This had to be done.

I looked out into the crowd. They were all silent, holding their breaths it seemed like it, waiting to see who would next be chosen. I did a sweep of the crowd, my gaze catching on the flowing movement of purple-blue hair. Maisie had woven her way into the crowd. She was at the very back, next to the merman I recognized as her boss.

My eyes stayed on her, on this mermaid who was so different from the rest in Lagoona. No one else had her hair, her coloring. Where did she come from? Why was she here? And, more importantly, why did she look like the princess?

Taking a deep breath, I opened my mouth and called out the names.

FIFTEEN NAMES TOTAL, INCLUDING mine. When Captain Saber opened his mouth to call those who were selected, I'd held my breath the entire time. And when he got to my name, I felt my heart drop like a boat's anchor to the pit of my stomach.

I tried not to gasp aloud, but the sound seemed to tear out of me. I knew, logically, I had not been selected to fight in a war. I'd been selected for something else entirely. I'd be safe inside the palace, I'd be able to make a difference. But all of the logical thoughts flew away when I heard my name. For a brief moment, I was deep in the horror of the selected. For a moment, it had been real.

Josiah grabbed my arm and I wasn't sure if he'd meant to steady me or himself from the shock of it. I kept myself upright with his help, tried not to crumble to the ground like so many had already done upon hearing the names. I wouldn't do that. I'd be strong.

"Mais," Jo whispered. I barely heard him. There was a rushing in my ears that hadn't been there before. A painful cacophony of sound accompanying the panic in my chest. I took a deep breath, trying to get my emotions under control as I turned to look at my boss, at my mentor. I did not misread the heartbreak in his eyes. "I'm so sorry, Mais."

This part was hard. The pretending, the lying. He believed I was going off to fight, to throw myself amidst blood and sword with the rest of them when, in reality, I'd be wearing the mask of a royal, trying to stop it all from continuing.

A sob rose in my chest. I tried to push it down, but it slipped through, cracking my words. "It's okay, Jo," I nearly gasped. "It'll be okay."

And then I was in his arms, feeling the scales of his skin against the smoothness of my own. I held him tightly, as tight as I could in the hopes that it would prevent me from crying out, from somehow blurting out the truth. Instead, I held him in our final goodbye. And even though everything else was a lie, my love for him and the heartbreak I felt were very, very real.

Pushing aside groups of cattails, I made my way through the forest and towards my home. The home I would soon leave behind. Tomorrow morning this place would be empty, the place where my grandmother had raised me. The place where she had died.

One day, I would come back here, after I made things right in Thalassar. In the meantime, I'd asked Jo to look after the place for me, to not let it get overrun with weeds and critters. I knew he'd do it for me. I saw the raw emotion in his eyes. He didn't want me to go, hadn't been expecting it. I could have asked anything of him at that moment and he wouldn't have questioned a thing.

But all I wanted was this place well kept. "In case I come back," I'd whispered.

I saw his eyes shutter. I knew he didn't believe I'd ever be coming back. No one who left ever did.

I pushed aside the doorway and swam through, into the confines of my little space. I had nothing of value to take with me. The telly would stay, obviously, and the blade… I swam over and grabbed it, running my fingers lightly across the smooth hilt. It was the nicest thing I owned and I didn't plan on leaving it behind.

I wondered if the captain would approve of me—the soon-to-be fake princess—carrying a blade around. Probably not, but I wouldn't give this weapon up. Not to him or anyone else. I'd only had it for less than a day, yet I felt so strongly about it. If it had been fashioned by the Black Blade, by a merman who had made history by defying the kingdom, then I'd keep it.

Because, like the Black Blade, I planned on making history too.

I took my time packing the next morning. I had few belongings, so it didn't take long to stuff three tunics and a few hats into a carry-on bag. I wore a black tunic, long enough to cover my tail and loose enough to move around comfortably in. I'd need it, for I had no idea what was to come. After stuffing my hair into a hat, I went to the table where my sheathed blade sat. I debated on tying it around my waist but decided against it, instead stuffing it out of sight with the rest of my belongings.

As far as possessions went, that was all I owned. It was a good thing because it meant less to carry. And besides, if I was going to parade around as the princess, her things would become mine. At least temporarily.

The morning after Selection ranged between being harder and being easier. This morning we would find out if anyone had tried escaping, if the guards had caught anyone sneaking about to run away from their duties. And those selected would leave.

I wouldn't say goodbye to anyone. I'd already said my goodbyes to Jo the night before. Doing it twice would have hurt more. No, this way seemed easier. I looked around at the inside of my home, breathed in the smell of water lilies one last time before I had to go. I would miss this place. The feeling lodged itself so deeply into me that I almost faltered, but I straightened, pushing back the tears.

I had to do this. If no one else was going to change anything, then I had to do it.

An abrupt knock tore me out of my thoughts.

It was time.

With my head high, I swam out to meet Captain Saber. He was by the entryway, his body as stiff as ever. I nodded in acknowledgment. "Captain," I mumbled.

His eyes roamed over my face; more specifically, my head. I wondered if he was trying to see through the material of the hat, to get a glimpse at my hair. When he finally tore his gaze away, he seemed a bit more relaxed.

"Good morning, Maisie," he said. I noticed there was something in his hand, and when I looked at it, he was stretching his arm out to offer it to me. "Put this on." I took it from him and I swore my hands burned from touching the material. From touching the uniform jacket he handed to me.

I scrutinized it. "Why?"

"The moment we leave these waters, we will be passing through more civilized towns with a lot more merfolk. If they see royal guards and if they see you or your hair, they may mistake you for the princess."

I stared quizzically at him. "But isn't that the point?"

"Yes, but not yet and not here. Especially not dressed like that." His chin jerked at my outfit and I felt myself prickle at the judgement. He hadn't said it unkindly, not exactly, but it still made my face flame. "Just put it on. We are going to move out soon and I don't want to wait on you or draw attention to you, either."

I blinked at his words, at the way he seemed to spit them out with irritation. Weird how he could go from one somber mood to annoyed in a split second. It made me wonder if the trip was going to be entirely dreadful.

Sighing, I dropped my pack and shoved my arms through the sleeves of the jacket. Once it was on, I secured it with the black pearl buttons all the way up to my neck and looked down at myself with heated cheeks and distaste. It felt like a betrayal to wear this. To wear the colors of the kingdom that was destroying Lagoona. But for the good of everyone, I had to suck it up.

"There," I held my arms out at my sides. "Do I look like the princess now?" My words were meant to be sarcastic, but they came out in a breathy whisper.

Captain Saber looked me up and down, gaze lingering at the bottom part of the tunic that covered most of my tail and then back up at my face. "Not at all."

"Good."

Before he could drill me about hurrying up, I turned to the overturned boat one last time. Emotion swelled in my chest, threatening to suffocate me, but I ignored it, pushed it down. I reached forward and placed my palm against the decaying wood and kept it there. Maybe I could draw its energy to take with me on my journey, if I held it long enough. But I didn't need its energy. Not when the memory of it was there in my heart.

And I'd come back. Once everything was set to rights, once they found the princess, I'd come back to my home.

Hoisting my bag onto my shoulder, I turned to face Captain Saber. He was looking at me with the oddest expression, but I ignored it and forced a tight smile to my lips. "I'm ready."

THE CAMP WAS NEARLY packed up completely and for that I was glad. I counted down the minutes until we could get out of this town and go back to the palace. It was urgent I speak with the queen and king. It was urgent they meet Maisie and decide what was going to happen.

She swam beside me, her body tense as she took in the sight of the soldiers' camp. Not much of a camp now that mostly everything had been taken down. Still, her eyes were wide and I wondered if that was with fear or delight.

I tried pushing away the image of her that surfaced. The image of her placing her palm against her little blue home, head bowed almost as if praying. When she'd turned around, there had been something in her eyes. Some raw sort of emotion that was hard to describe. I'd never seen anyone look the way she had. With so much emotion that it was unnerving.

I caught sight of the other mer selected. There'd been fifteen total. They were all packed together, huddling and trembling with fear. There'd been no escapees this time around. Good.

Maisie's eyes went to them and stayed. I knew she would have to go to them, to feign as though she would be learning the basics of how to wield weapons. But I could not let her out of my sight. Not when she had such an important role to play for the kingdom.

"Stay with me," I whispered softly to her. We had to draw as little attention as possible. It would be easier now that she was covered from head to tailfin. No sign of purple hair or scales. It was for the best. It wouldn't do for the soldiers to ask questions later, to ask what had happened to the bright-colored mer who had been selected for the war. I'd have to help fake her death later on. It wouldn't be hard to do in the chaos of war. I could even forge military documents with her name on the training list. No one would remember her anyway. Not with everything else going on.

I supposed that was one of the benefits when you worked directly under the Queen and King of Thalassar.

She shot me a skeptical look. "Shouldn't I be with the other selects?" she asked, equally quiet. "To make it more believable?"

"No."

"But—"

"I said no."

She grumbled something barely audible beneath her breath. I caught the words "tadpole" and "grumpy guppy". Sighing, I continued forward, letting her trail after me. I could already tell this journey was going to be a long and frustrating one with her. She wouldn't go easily or quietly for that matter. But soon that would all change. Once she went before the queen and king, once they decided what to do with her, she would learn the ways of the courts she would temporarily be a part of.

We wove our way through the hustle of camp, determination in my stride. We would ride hippocampi; some would pull carts with our tents and supplies behind us until we stopped for the night a town over. It would be days before we actually reached the palace.

I saw my own hippocampus being tended to by a cadet. He was being brushed down with an ivory comb, his large head hanging low with relaxation as it was passed through his strands of long, yellow hair. His ears were plastered behind his head, his long, serpentine tail curling and uncurling. The beast was massive, blue and yellow. His ears perked up when he saw me approach.

"Cadet." I nodded my head and the cadet returned the gesture before taking a stroke back, giving me room to swim over to my beast and palm his thickly corded neck. "Ready to journey home?" I asked him in a soft voice. He threw his head back and whinnied.

A small gasp had me tearing my gaze to look over at Maisie. She was holding her arms to her chest, staring with wide eyes at the large beast before her. It was only natural she seemed surprised. Lagoona was hardly a diverse place; their preferred method of transportation was on fin. When everything was in swimming distance of each other, there was no need for a majestic creature like a hippocampus. She'd probably never seen one up close before, even if the capitol bred them.

"You're excused, cadet." The cadet bowed his head before swimming off to get to other duties. My eyes never once left Masie's. I watched her closely, watched the wonder in the depths of her black eyes. "This is Geronimo," I introduced, giving him a pat on his neck. "He will be our ride on the journey home."

She startled, looking at me, a choked sound escaping her lips. "You can't be serious, Captain." She looked from me to Geronimo. "I'm not riding *that.*"

Geronimo, displeased with being called *that,* stirred uneasily. I calmed him by rubbing my hand against his scaled skin. "Geronimo," I clarified, eyes narrowing, "is quite safe, I assure you."

She shook her head so vigorously, I worried that the hat would fall from her head, but it held steady. "I think not. I'll just ride in the back of a cart." Her head jerked in the direction of said carts, big scallop shells attached to thick rope.

"Don't be ridiculous," I lectured. "Everyone is required to ride a hippocampus."

Her eyes assessed Geronimo again, from his large head to his front paws and the long, thick tail that ended in a set of jagged looking spikes. I could practically hear her gulp. "I'm sorry, Captain." She took an unsteady stroke back. "I—I don't think I can—"

"Don't worry yourself unnecessarily." I grabbed Geronimo by the reins, tugging slightly at them. "New selects ride with officers and cadets until we get back to the palace. There they will learn sword fighting, war, and how to mount a hippocampus. When training is finished, the queen and king give new soldiers hippocampi of their own."

Meaning to ease her nerves, I pulled Geronimo forward. He pawed at the water and started to follow, but Maisie let out a small shriek and darted backwards, only to trip and fall into the muddy ground. I halted Geronimo, ordered him to stay with a gesture of the hand, and then reached down to help Maisie up.

Her face was flushed and I was glaring at her. Annoyance flowed through me. "You'd best get over this fear of yours before it can even fully develop." I tried pushing the harshness away, but it slipped into my words, making her flinch and pull her hand from mine quickly. "The real princess is a skilled rider."

Her glare was mutinous, but it affected me none. "I'm *not* the princess."

"I know." She didn't need to remind me. It was apparent in her lack of good sense and education. "You needn't say so."

Maisie huffed loudly and opened her mouth to say something but caught herself. Good. I did not want to argue in front of my soldiers. It was time to leave. Ignoring her, I turned back to Geronimo and took his reins. At my signal, the whole camp would begin marching out of this town. And I was beyond ready to go.

"Time to move out!" I called to the camp. Affirmatives responded all around and they began mounting their hippocampi. I looked down to Maisie, who was glaring at me from her position. I loomed over her, gripping tightly at the reins as if that could help control the anger and annoyance I felt inside because of her cowardice. "It is time to go," I said firmly, reaching my hand down for her to take. She stared at it a long distrustful moment. "Nothing bad is going to happen to you, Maisie," I promised. "You will be safe with me."

My words burned past my lips, though my chest felt hollow as I said them. I hadn't been able to protect Princess Odele, what made me think I could protect Maisie? What made me think that I could even begin to keep her safe? Those words were my haunting, my greatest sin. But I vowed I would keep her alive and well, if it cost me my life. Because if she went missing because of me, I didn't think I'd ever be able to live with myself again.

"Please," I whispered, quieter.

Maisie visibly swallowed, nodded, and took my hand.

The beast thrashed tail and head, darting through the water at an easy pace that felt too fast, the height too high. I gripped the reins and didn't let go, my knuckles white, and my stomach churning unpleasantly for what felt like hours. I'd closed my eyes tight against the cold waters that slapped at my face, the current a fast sting against my skin.

Captain Saber's arms were like a firm cage, locking me in, preventing me from falling. The hard press of his chest was tight on my backside, muscles bunched and tense. After a while, I focused on that instead of the speed, focused on him instead of the beast beneath us. The captain was holding me tight, making me realize that he would indeed protect me as he'd said.

Hours later, we were out of Lagoona. I knew I'd seen the last of my home when the scenery began changing, when gone were mer with webbed features, long, thick whiskers, and sharp teeth. The waters seemed to change as well, becoming thicker, denser. I knew soon we'd reach the saltier waters of the ocean. Soon we'd be in Eramaea, the capitol of the kingdom of Thalassar, and then the palace. Soon, I'd meet the king and queen.

It was hours later that we stopped in a kelp forest of a neighboring town to make camp. I was glad for it. My tail and backside were saddle sore from sitting for hours, my hands going numb from gripping the reins too tightly.

Captain Saber brought his large blue beast to a halt. The hippocampus pawed the water before settling down. The captain hopped off first with incredible ease. I looked at the drop below. Easy to just hop off, stretch my tail, and swim. But I was cramped up and my fins didn't make swimming easy.

But when the captain made no move to help me down, I decided to do it myself. I was independent, I could do this. I'd lived my entire life without him there to guide me through it and I could do this without his help, too. Setting my palms against Geronimo's side, I leaned against my tail and hopped down. I fell lightly through the water, fanning my fins out at my side. My left fin didn't catch water, so I nearly tripped but righted myself quickly.

My face flamed when I looked up to find Captain Saber scrutinizing me. I fought hard not to snap at him, though everything in me wanted to. I didn't want to draw attention to myself. He was right and it wouldn't be wise. I'd hated the attention back home, hated the stares I got at Tides' Tavern because of my appearance. I didn't know how I'd handle it if I were dressed as the princess. All eyes would be on me. I dreaded that part the most.

But for the greater good of Lagoona, for my mer and the lost souls of Thalassar, I'd do it.

I watched as Captain Saber started forward and began barking out orders to set up camp. It was amazing how quickly everyone moved when he spoke, how they watched him with rapt attention. He was powerful, influential. That much was evident.

Soldiers started hopping off of their hippocampi, going to the carts and began pulling out supplies. Once everyone was hustling, even the new selects, he turned to me and gestured with a jerk of his head that I follow him.

He led me to a cart, a very large scallop shell that was clamped closed. He propped it open, revealing the contents inside. It was the material of a tent, thick seal skin with bamboo poles and braided rope.

"Selects usually sleep in a supervised area together," he explained quietly, firmly. "Yours is a special case. I do not want you staying with them, but I do not want them asking questions either." He pulled out the hefty tent, barely grunting as he lifted it.

"I think, to avoid rousing suspicion, I should sleep with the other selects." The idea of drawing attention–even worse, the idea of sleeping *near him*—was nerve wracking. I didn't need him scrutinizing my snores along with everything else he already scrutinized.

He shot me a look as he turned with the tent in his arms. I quickly grabbed the pile of bamboo sticks into my own and followed him. They were slightly heavy, but nothing I couldn't handle.

"I don't think that's a good idea."

I rolled my eyes, hoping he'd see it in his peripheral vision. "The idea is to not draw attention to me, right? If I sleep in my own private tent, or even with you, don't you think everyone will raise their eyebrows in our direction? Don't you think they'll try to figure out *why*? Try to figure out who I am and what I am to you?"

He was quiet so long I thought he wouldn't reply at all, but then he finally nodded. "You're right." He came to a clearing and dropped the tent into the muddy ground, causing silt to fly up in a small cloud.

"Just treat me like you would any other select," I added, placing the bamboo down with much more gentleness. "When we get to Eramaea, things can change. For now, no attention."

I straightened, watched him tighten his jaw. I wondered why he was so at war with himself, why he looked so…torn. I watched as he let loose a slow breath and then bent to begin putting up the tent. "Fine," he conceded. "But I'll supervise you and the other selects. You'll ride with me until we get to the palace and don't, for the love of the gods, slip up."

I snorted and began helping him pitch the tent.

Night fell quickly and I, with the rest of the selects, sat around the comforting blue glow of lava. The blue liquid was contained tightly inside of a hard glass ball. Attached to the ball was a small metal tube with a handle that was used to safely release the lava in small quantities. A small volcano had been formed in the earth, lava released in the centermost part of it. The heat of it caused warm bubbles to emerge to the top, and we all sat in a circle around it, relishing in its warmth.

It was comforting, sitting with mer who knew what this change felt like, who were living what I was. We'd all been chosen for something bigger than ourselves. There was a possibility that they would die. But there was also the possibility that I could save them.

I sat between two mer, one from Lagoona and another from an equally small backwater pond in Thalassar. The merman from Lagoona had worked for the blacksmith, a young mer of only seventeen. The other mer was a bit older than me and quick to smile, despite the circumstances. He was quite handsome, with short dark hair and skin covered with a series of prickly spikes. There was webbing between his hands and feet. He sported a jacket identical to mine, but unlike me, he wore his with glowing pride.

"Why do you seem so okay with all of this?" I asked skeptically, nursing my cup of warm, frothy tea.

"It's not about being okay with this." He gestured at the entirety of the quieting camp. "It's about accepting what's been thrown your way and making the most of it."

The mer from Lagoona snorted. "I'd like to see you make the most of it when you're face down in the sand with a spear gun in your back, friends and family dying around you." He took a sip of his own tea then splashed the rest of it into the lava angrily. "War is not glorious. It's not *fun,* and it most certainly isn't a *game*."

That sobered the other merman up quickly. "Of course it's not a game. It flipping sucks. Do you think I *want* to go to war with Kappur? A war we don't even know how or why it even started in the first place?" His voice had started to rise with contempt. It was the same tone that Josiah had always used when he spoke of his theories and of the royals.

There were so many theories about what started the war, each one crazier than the last. Some said it was because Kappur wanted Thalassarin waters, others said it was because Thalassar had stolen something valuable from Kappur, and the craziest story of them all claimed it was because of a love gone wrong.

Personally, I didn't care how it started.

I just wanted it over.

I struggled to keep up with the conversation. Their voices rose, arguing the different reasons of war, arguing over what to expect, arguing over whether or not the Selection was justified.

When silence descended, I looked up to see what had prompted it only to find Captain Saber looming over us, a glare mutinous in his bright eyes. I gulped, fingers tightening around my cup. His gaze swept over them, halting on my terse form. The smile that had been on my lips died, the warmth in my belly churning into something unpleasant.

"I suggest you all *stop talking* about the kingdom that keeps you fed and alive and get some sleep." He seemed to grind the words out through his teeth. "Tomorrow is going to be a long day."

"Yes, Captain," they said in unison as they got up and began clearing away the space. They dispersed and I started to do the same, but when I tried swimming away, the captain caught my arm, holding me in place.

"You call that being discreet?" he hissed through his teeth.

"I don't know what you mean," I replied calmly, tearing my arm from his grasp.

I could feel his anger emanating from his body like a pulsing beat of a current. I tried hard not to quake under it, instead straightening and looking at him with the calmest expression I could muster. "Insulting the kingdom with your friends is the surest way to draw attention to yourself."

I frowned, eyebrows drawing together. "I didn't say a *thing* about your precious Thalassar. Besides…" I darted a quick look around. "You're drawing more attention to us with this conversation." His entire body stiffened so hard it looked like he would snap. He glanced around the camp before turning his attention back to me. I probably shouldn't provoke him, but it was impossible to resist doing so. I smirked. "Good night, Captain."

He didn't try to stop me as I swam away, following the other selects towards our guarded tent. I gave my cup to a passing soldier before reaching the tent flaps. I gripped them tightly into my fists and paused a moment. I looked over my shoulder to find Captain Saber still floating where I'd left him, looking after me with ice in his eyes. The look sent a shiver of awareness down my spine and all the way to my tail fin. Taking a deep breath, I turned back around and went inside.

Our temporary quarters were spacious, with enough room for all of us to stretch out and leave space between us. We each had a rolled-up mat that had been provided by the soldiers as well as a very thin blanket. The tent would keep out most of the night's cold, but I didn't doubt I would toss and turn most of the night.

I reached for my mat and unrolled it on the muddy ground, then laid on it and pulled the blanket over my body. No one spoke, and I doubted they would. Not when solitude pressed through every crevice of our bodies, our hearts. Not after being berated by the captain. I was sure there were things on their minds, like their families and everyone they'd left behind.

My thoughts wandered to Josiah and Tides' Tavern. I would miss the smell of the backyard in the mornings, the soft growls of gators. I would miss the smell of richly cooked food and moonshine, miss the sound of Josiah's booming voice as he screamed out theories at the telly.

I would miss that little blue boat that I'd called home for the past nineteen years. Where I'd been raised by my grandmother and where I'd learned of her death. Home. It seemed so far away now, and I wondered how long it would take before Lagoona was nothing but a distant memory to me. I vowed that I would never let that happen. I would never forget where I came from, nor the merpeople who needed me.

I was doing this for them, after all. I couldn't lose sight of that.

So I pushed away those thoughts and closed my eyes to fall asleep.

The cold beating of water against the tent awoke me. So did the harsh sound of rapid breathing. My eyes flew open to be greeted by darkness. I blinked a few times, listening intently to the moans and groans around me. For a brief second, I'd forgotten where I was. But when my body pressed deeper into the cold mat, I remembered.

My limbs ached from the temperatures, the lack of warmth. My torn fin throbbed, as it tended to do when the weather was cold and unforgiving. I sat up, the thin blanket pooling around my waist, and stretched my arms over my head. My wrists popped with the movement, bringing me temporary relief.

I cast my gaze around the darkness, at the shadowed bodies of the other selects lying around me. Some of them slept soundly, others shivered, though most of them tossed and turned, groaning as if they were plagued by nightmares. I almost wondered what they dreamt of. If they created a bloody battle in their minds with dozens of Kappurin soldiers tearing them to pieces.

I used to dream of such carnage. Of rotting corpses with the faces of friends and family floating in their deaths. Tonight, I dreamt the same nightmare I always did, watching the swing of an axe come down. Only this time, the scene changed, and the faces of friends became my own reflection.

Sleeping was beyond me now.

I got up and went to the entrance of the tent, tossing the flaps aside. Guards floated at attention outside. The second I swam out, their weapons were at the ready, their gazes dark and tense. I froze, hands going up in total submission.

"I just need to relieve myself," I lied breathlessly. Their spears pointed at my faces made me nervous.

"No one is allowed to leave the tent after dark."

Captain Saber hadn't told me that. He hadn't told me much of anything. All he seemed to do was scrutinize me instead of actually taking the time to go over camp rules as they would with any other select. I supposed I had to remind myself that I wasn't *like* any other select. I was supposed to be the princess. But of course, these mer didn't know that.

"I promise I won't be long. I really need to go." *I really need to go and get away from the haunted sounds. I can't stand the torture.* I needed a breath of freshwater, needed to calm the beating of my heart. I knew if I said this to them, they'd take no pity on me. Not these soldiers with their cruel faces and weapons poised to kill. I wondered if they were hoping for me to fight back, to argue. If only so they could stick me through the heart.

"At ease." Captain Saber was suddenly there, between the two soldiers. At the sight of their commander, they relaxed their grips and postures, however slightly, and saluted.

"Captain Saber," one of them began, "this mer—"

"I will deal with her," he interrupted. His piercing eyes swept over my frame, landing on my face with just enough intensity to make my cheeks heat. I didn't doubt there'd be a tongue-lashing after this. "Come, Select. I'll escort you." He turned abruptly and began to swim away. I followed behind at a much slower pace, already dreading the upcoming conversation.

He led me away from the cluster of tents, hippocampi, and soldiers, into a small forest of grass that flowed and slapped against the icy movement of the current. He stopped, forcing me still behind him. When he turned to face me, I almost expected familiar severity to flash in his eyes, but his expression was surprisingly gentle. That scared me so much more.

"I think this provides enough cover for you. Unfortunately, there aren't better accommodations for you, nor will there be throughout the journey until we reach the palace." When I did nothing but blink at him, his eyebrows furrowed. "You wanted to relieve yourself did you not? I can turn around..."

Laughter bubbled out of my chest that I released on a soft sigh. "I lied," I murmured, bringing my fingers up to my lips. "I just needed to get a breath of freshwater. I was suffocating in there."

He frowned and I waited for it. For the demands, for the chastising, but he surprised me again by nodding as if he understood what was plaguing me. Then, he cast a cautious glance around before turning back to me. "I can give you a few minutes only. But you must promise me you won't swim off."

"I promise."

He gave me one tight nod. I wondered why he believed me so easily. "I'll be over there." He gestured little ways away. "When you're ready I'll come for you." And then he turned and swam away to where he'd indicated.

I watched him go before I ventured over to a patch of grass and sat in it. It was scratchy and cold, the texture of it against my skin and tail reminding me so much of my own cattail forest back in Lagoona. Sighing, I tucked my tail under me and wrapped my arms around myself.

My thoughts wandered to my home, to all that I'd left behind and all I planned to gain. Even if I told myself why I was doing this, who I was doing this for, it didn't hurt any less. There was still this pressure in my chest that threatened to suffocate me. I was giving up my life for the freedom of my merpeople, to help end a war. I had no idea what my life would be like from now on. I had no idea *how* I'd even go about with stopping this war that had plagued us for years. But I knew I had to try.

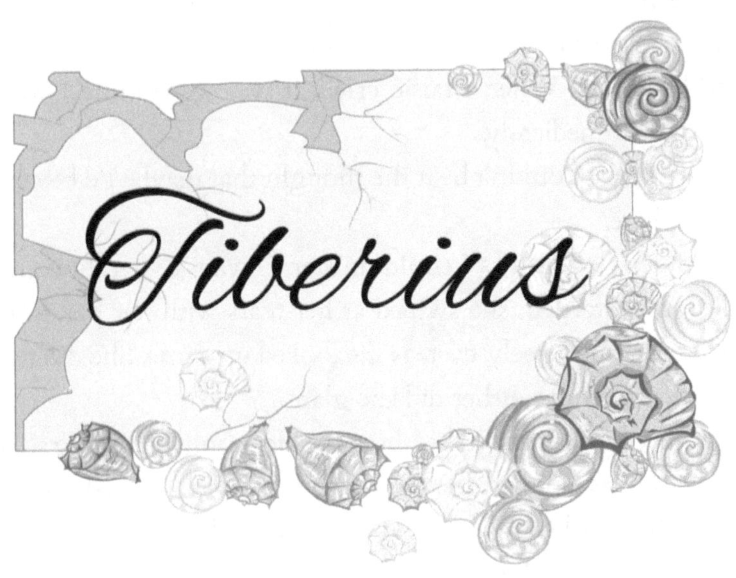

Tiberius

I WATCHED FROM THE shadows. The freshwaters were nothing like the salty expanse of the sea. Here, there was brightness. Being closer to the surface of two-legger territory meant more natural light. The beams of moonlight pierced passed the surface of the water and moved along with the fluctuation of the waves below. The light was blue in its hue, illuminating Maisie and the tears she wept.

Small bubbles rose from her eyes, swirling around her. I knew that two-leggers cried tears of the salt of the ocean, but the mer cried tears of air. Something inside me clenched at the sight of those bubbles rising through the water.

Once again, I was struck by how much she looked like the princess. Except, the princess had *never* cried. When she did, something about her tears seemed artificial, as if she were producing them in order to manipulate those around her. Even I, for as much as I cared about her, had noted her flaws. When Maisie cried, it was so genuine I wanted to put a stop to it immediately.

I didn't like tears. Couldn't bear the thought that maybe I'd been the one to put them there.

With as much slowness as I could muster, I swam to her, hovering over her small frame. Startled, she swiped at her tears with her hands, but the tiny bubbles swarmed freely, even as she looked up at me. She did not force a smile on her face but neither did she glare.

I didn't know what to say to her, how to offer comfort. Doing so seemed beyond my abilities and besides, she knew what she'd signed up for when she came with me. She was wasting her tears and my time. I didn't have all night to watch over her while she moped. I straightened my posture and hardened my resolve.

"You've had enough time," I said tersely. "It's time to get back to the tent before anyone starts asking questions."

Her gaze sharpened and she clenched her jaw, almost as if she was biting back the words she desperately wanted to slice out at me. *Good*, I thought. It would be better for her to learn now how to hold her tongue, that way when we got to the castle, I would not have to lecture her constantly on court etiquette. I could already imagine the scandal she might be capable of causing before the queen and king, not to mention the courtiers. If she placed a fin out of line, it was quite possible she'd lose her head.

Tensions were high in Eramaea, especially at the palace. With the war plaguing and the disappearance of the princess, nothing seemed safe, and no one could be trusted. The minute we arrived, I'd have to be on high alert, watching her every move.

To protect her from others and her own defiance.

Maisie floated up, her movements slightly jerky. I'd noticed before that she swam with a limp, though she tried furiously to hide it. I didn't ask her what had caused it, even if I itched to. Her life before this was none of my business, and I didn't care. But the limp made her clumsy and I despaired, as it was just another thing on my list of things to teach her. The princess always swam with grace and her head held high. Maisie would have to as well.

But not tonight. Tonight, I would not criticize her. The tears flowing from her eyes prevented me from doing it. I'd wait until tomorrow. As we rode on Geronimo, I would go over the rules and etiquette so that by the time we made it to the capitol, she would know exactly what she was doing.

She smoothed out the front of her jacket then stopped herself, closing her palms into fists mid-action and then dropping them to her sides. She still wore the dark hat, hair hidden under it. At least she'd done something right. I watched her every movement closely, my own body tense. From the jerk of her wrists to the tilt of her chin.

"How kind of you," she said slowly, and there was enough ice in her voice to slice at me. "Thank you for giving me all of thirty seconds to take a breath."

My hands fisted at my sides and my jaw clenched. Irritation surged through me, hot and quick. Insubordinate. Sarcastic. What else would she surprise me with? "Be thankful you got any time at all. It's more than what other selects receive."

She scoffed and jerked forward, back towards the tent. She moved too quickly, though, and her fins weren't strong enough to stop her from falling forward. Everything in me reacted on instinct. I rushed forward, wrapping my forearm around her stomach and pulling her up before she could hit the silt.

I blinked and realized that I had her pressed tightly against my chest, so tightly that I was sure she could feel the way my heart pounded against her backside. Her hair had fallen from the confines of the hat, fanning against the back of her neck. I took in the bright tendrils and felt something rush through my body at the sight.

"Let go of me." She was breathless and shivering in my arms.

The illusion shattered at the sound of her voice, at the careful anger placed there. *Fool!* How many times did I have to remind myself that *she wasn't the princess* before my body understood? Slowly, I released my hold on her and took a stroke back.

Maisie loosed an audible breath and straightened, tucking her hair back into her hat. She didn't turn around, didn't give me eye contact as she whispered, "Good night, Captain." When she started forward, I watched her go and disappear back behind the tent flaps. For a moment, the moonlight shone down on the lodgings and I was gifted with the moving image of her silhouette. I watched as she climbed onto her mat, pulled a blanket over herself, and turned. When I blinked, the image was gone.

And with it, the incessant pounding of my treacherous heart.

THE NEXT MORNING, AFTER a quick breakfast of a cold and tasteless marsh salad, we packed up camp and headed out. I barely looked at Captain Saber all morning, though I felt his heavy gaze following me. I'd gotten very little sleep the night before, plagued by heated thoughts and the memory of his arm wrapped around my waist. My ears had filled with the musical rhythm of his heart against my backside, pounding as if he'd been afraid of what would happen to me. And that sound, that erratic beating, was the only way he knew how to show it.

Maybe a part of me wanted to believe that he did care, but I knew when the hair had fallen from my hat and the illusion was broken that he'd been imagining the princess. The thought shouldn't have stung—not when I'd *come* here to be her—but it did. I pushed those emotions away. It's not like it mattered, anyway. I needed to stop feeling and start *thinking*, start coming up with a plan that would help save the kingdom from a war.

So when Captain Saber pulled me up on Geronimo and we marched off, I finally found my voice. "Is there anything I should expect from the royal life?" My hands were tight on Geronimo's reins, and my voice quivered from the fear of the altitude.

"There is a lot to be expected of you, if you disguise yourself as the princess." He'd dropped his voice to a very low whisper, his breath tickling my ear.

"Like what?" I whispered back.

"You will need to learn proper royal etiquette. This includes how to address other royals, fine dining, proper speech, how to swim, and lessons on politics. You'll need to study and memorize everyone in the royal family so that you can address them as Princess Odele would. You will need to learn every single aspect of her life to truly become her."

"That's—" I broke off on a gulp. "That's a lot to learn, don't ya think?"

"Don't *you* think," he replied stiffly.

I twisted to raise an eyebrow at him. His face was the perfect picture of annoyance. "What?"

"It's 'That's a lot to learn, don't *you* think?' If you are going to pretend to *be* royalty, I suggest you start acting like it. Speak in complete and proper sentences and drop the accent."

My face flamed with embarrassment, so I twisted back around, gaze ahead. He had a point, but it still irked. "Don't worry yourself," I said, dropping my accent to mimic his own. The words were properly elegant and lilting. "I think I can manage to speak eloquently."

His whole body tensed, and his next command was harsh. "Don't do that."

"Do what?"

"Don't talk like that."

"I thought you wanted me to be more proper?" I fought back an eye roll. The merman was insufferable.

"Yes, but not here. Certainly not now." His body moved side to side, and I couldn't see him, but I imagined him looking around to see if anyone had heard me.

"Why not? Isn't it better I get the practice in as we go along?" I still hadn't dropped that strange Eramaean accent. I wondered if I used it enough, would I forget my own?

"You proved you can speak with at least a small amount of elegance. Do not draw attention to yourself by overdoing it."

Tadpole!

"Fine," I dropped the accent, replacing it with my own once more. "Then what should I practice?"

"Once we stop, we can work on your swimming."

It was my turn to tense, so hard my body might have snapped. So it hadn't mattered how hard I'd tried to hide it; he had noticed my limp. My knuckles went white against the reins. I slowly released them, feeling pain in my fingers. The last thing I wanted to do was to be taught how to swim like some guppy.

"No," I replied.

"No?"

"No. Teach me somethin' else."

I could feel him glaring daggers at the back of my neck. "I'm afraid you have no choice in the matter."

"Please..." I hated that I had to beg, that I had to be reduced to this. I did not want the embarrassment of him watching me, of the freezing bite in his words as he judged my every move when I failed. Because I *would* fail. I'd been trying to swim like a normal mer my entire life until I realized I would *never* be normal. I would never swim in a straight line; my fins would *never* be the same. While I was at peace with that, it didn't mean I wanted to suffer that humiliation.

"It's best you get the notion of embarrassment out of your head now, Maisie," he said, not unkindly but roughly. "If you think I am a harsh judge, know that every royal mer in Eramaea will be a thousand times harder. I judge you because I want to see you succeed. I want you to *convince* them."

There was a truth to his words that eased a bit of the turmoil in my chest, gifting me with a fraction of confidence. He was absolutely right. I had no idea what the royal life was like, had no idea what was in store for me. If I wanted this to work, then I had to be convincing. And the only way to do that was to *practice* so I wouldn't fall on my face once I got there.

"Fine," I conceded. "But I think we should multitask. Teach me to swim like royalty and quiz me on etiquette while we do it." Determination filled me. There was so little time before we made it to Eramaea and once we arrived, I would be prepared.

To convince them all that I really was Princess Odele.

"Head up!" Captain Saber commanded.

I lengthened my neck, chin turned up, eyes straight ahead. My back was curved, my tail graceful beneath me. Well, it would have been graceful if it weren't for my torn fin. It was a hard thing to do, to try and keep my balance with fins fanning out at my sides, especially when one of those fins was shredded.

We were away from the camp, away from prying eyes. My hair was undone, flowing down the length of my back. On my head, the captain had placed a thin stone slab. He'd commanded me to swim without it falling. So far, it hadn't worked out.

"Arms lightly at your sides or clasped together in front of you," Captain Saber instructed. I did as I was told and started forward. "You look too stiff. The movements should be more natural." I fought back a groan and focused on what I was doing. My fin was hurting. It usually did when I put too much strain on it. It throbbed as I flapped it to keep me balanced. "You're tilting to the side," he commented.

I supposed the good thing about this was that the dresses were not only long enough to hide my tail and my deformity, but also loose enough that they could move around as freely as I willed them.

"Why must royalty swim so precisely?" I grumbled, unable to stop myself.

The captain didn't grace my comment with a reply. Instead, he began quizzing me on the brief information he'd given me before our swimming lesson. Since it was all basic history, I answered them with ease.

What are the names of the King and Queen of Thalassar?

King Xristo Oriana de Malabella and Queen Circe Malabella.

How many children do they have?

None.

Who was Princess Odele's mother?

The late Queen Odette Malabella.

Who was the supreme ruler of Thalassar and why?

Queen Circe. In Thalassar, the queens have more rule than kings because they are direct descendants of the Malabella line. Only the daughter of a daughter can rule on the throne.

It was all quite simple.

But soon he started quizzing me on distant relatives of Princess Odele, relatives I'd never even heard of before. Cousins, second cousins, aunts and uncles on Princess Odele's mother, father, and stepmother's side. Pretty soon, it all became a muddled mess in my mind. Names blurred together, one after another until I couldn't remember a thing.

When my tail started to cramp up, I finally sat down to take a break beside the captain. I longed to lift my skirt up and run a hand across my battered fin, to ease the pain, but I'd never shown my scars to anyone, and I wouldn't start now. Especially not to the Captain of the Royal Guard. Not when he was eyeing my tail like it was something to be ashamed of...

"What happened to you?" he asked, his voice sharp and prying. His eyes never strayed from my tail. I almost wondered if he stared at it long enough, would he be able to see through it?

My lips pressed tightly together before I opened my mouth to answer. "That's not your business, Captain."

He stiffened, and I knew that our time of amiability was over. He got up, adjusted the lapels of his jacket, and tossed my hat to me. I dropped the stone slab and caught it in my fingers. "We should be getting back."

Well, so much for a break, I thought as I began stuffing my hair into the hat and securing it on my head. When I finished, I followed him out of the thick forest of grass.

After moving on from this town, we'd be making it to the salt waters and then to Eramaea. I couldn't deny either the excitement or nerves that tingled through my body. Soon, I'd be in the capitol city of Thalassar, in audience with the queen and king, disguising myself as the heir to the throne, stopping a war, and saving the mer.

We fell into an easy routine within the next few days of our journey. While we rode Geronimo, Captain Saber would school me on the history of Thalassar, the royal family, and Princess Odele's busy schedule. There was a lot to learn, and I held onto every scrap of information like I would hold onto change at Tides' Tavern. The princess, despite the shallowness I believed she possessed, was skilled in a number of things. Riding, sewing, fencing, dancing, and music, among other things. And I was expected to learn every single one of her abilities. For now, though, we stuck with the easier aspects.

At nights, after everyone went to bed, Captain Saber would discreetly escort me into a more private area, and we would practice swimming like a royal for a few hours as well as proper speech in the Eramaean accent. The lessons were exhausting, to say the least, but I was determined to push through.

I was so occupied in my lessons that I barely noticed when we'd left the sweet waters behind us and arrived at saltier places. My body wasn't used to the excess salt, and I worried my skin would break out in hives. It seemed harder to breathe the salt in, the gills on my neck flared briefly when we'd arrived before settling. I could tell many of the other selects were also having trouble. The water here felt heavier, harder to swim through. The soldiers and their mounts had more experience. I felt Geronimo speed faster through the water.

I held on to the reins, shutting my eyes against the viciousness of the current's sting. Captain Saber's arms were around me, caging me in so I wouldn't fall. I should have felt safe, instead I felt nothing but dread. My stomach roiled with nausea until the captain finally pulled Geronimo to a halt. When I was sure the beast wouldn't make a move forward, I lifted my head and looked around at the vast expanse of the ocean.

"Have you ever traveled outside of Lagoona?" the captain asked me, lips close to my ear.

I shook my head, eyes still glued to the sights before me. I'd never seen anything like it. Never seen a space so open or so… blue. The waters of Lagoona were nothing like this. My home was muddy, bathed in colors of pinks and greens and yellow sunlight. It seemed there was barely any sunlight here. Fish darted in and out of coral reefs of red and pink. Though there weren't any merpeople in sight.

"Wait until we make it to Eramaea," the captain said, almost as if he'd read my mind. "The closer we get, the more populated it will become."

With that, he started forward and we made our journey through the ocean. By the end of the day, when the waters darkened, we set up camp and sat quietly around the warmth of glowing blue lava. My eyes wandered over everything, from every flickering fish to the bioluminescent specks that floated in particles around us.

The captain had set up more guards than he had when we'd been in fresher waters, and I wondered if it was to protect us from the dangerous creatures of the ocean like sharks, or if it was to prevent the selects from swimming away. The closer we got, the more reality seemed to crash over us. I could tell from the way their eyes widened as they stared into the bubbles of the lava, or by the way their hands tightened around their cups. We were getting closer to our doom.

"Can you believe tomorrow we'll be in Eramaea?" one of the selects asked. His webbed fingers were tight on his cup, I believed it would shatter under the force of his nervousness.

"It's so surreal," I replied quietly. To think, tomorrow I would be in the palace, and my new life would begin. My gaze flickered around at the rest of the selects. The blue lava casting soft hues across their skin and scales, my heart clenched at the fear in their eyes. My life would begin, but theirs might just end on a bloody battlefield unless I could stop it.

"Would you all laugh at me if I told you I was scared?" the mer went on.

No one replied.

Because they were all terrified as well.

I awoke in the middle of the night to the sound of a scuffle, to shouts. We selects nearly jumped up at the sound, looking around the tent warily. I noticed that one of the mats was empty. The shouting of the guards echoed louder towards us.

Nervously, I got up and swam to the entrance of the tent, ignoring the protesting sounds of the other selects. I pushed the flaps aside and peeked outside, suppressing a gasp. The merman who had confessed his fear hours earlier was pinned to the ground by the end of a guard's spear. He struggled against their hold, his cries muffled in the sand. One of the guards kicked out at his face with his tail fin, silencing him immediately. I watched with dread in my heart, the bioluminescent light illuminating Captain Saber as he calmly swam up to the scene.

"We caught him trying to escape, Captain," a guard said.

The captain looked down at him. There was disgust in his eyes, so shocking that I almost staggered a few strokes back, but I stayed still, watching in silence. I should have gone back inside. I couldn't. Like I had to witness this, what I knew was going to happen. Like I needed it to remind myself what I was doing here, and who I was doing this for.

Or maybe I was watching because I wanted to see if the captain was as bad as the rest of them. As the ones who had killed my friends, my neighbors. Maybe I just wanted to hate him.

The captain bent down low, observing the struggling merman. The merman lifted his head. From here, I could see the tears swarming from his eyes, and the captain batted them away with a furious gesture of his hand. "Please, Captain," the merman begged. "I'm not a soldier. I can't fight in a war!"

Compassion almost seemed to flash through Captain Saber's eyes, but he masked it just as quickly, expression going hard, angry. Every bit the fierce commander he was. "You know the penalty for fleeing." He straightened and looked at the guards, giving them an almost imperceptible nod.

I felt fear thrum my heart into an erratic rhythm as I watched the guard pull back his spear and then brought it crashing down to the merman's head.

I jerked back, letting the opening fall back into place. A sob was stuck in my chest, but my breathing was harsh, chest heaving. Nausea roiled in me, worse than when I'd been riding Geronimo. I knew what the punishment was for fleeing Selection. We all did. I'd seen the consequences so many times that I should have been used to it by now. But this was somehow worse than any Selection I'd witnessed. It was worse because of all the time I'd spent with Captain Saber. In the time we'd been together, it was like I'd somehow forgotten what he was and who he worked for. He was carrying out orders from a corrupt monarch, and I'd fallen prey to his scheme. I'd started to trust him, as much as I could trust a soldier. But the truth of *who* he was lay beyond this tent, at the end of a sharp point of a blade.

Captain Saber was a soldier. And I was a fool for forgetting.

Tiberius

I KNEW SOMETHING WAS wrong that morning when we left camp behind. In a few hours, we'd be in Eramaea, and Maisie had not said a word, sardonic or otherwise. I wondered if she was nervous about what was to come, and though a small part of me wanted to comfort her, I could not. Above all things, I had to be honest regarding what was expected of her. She did not have the luxury of choking on her nerves. The kingdom was at stake.

I leaned forward to guide Geronimo by the reins, and when my chest brushed against her back, she stiffened and leaned away from me. My jaw clenched at that minuscule action, but I tried to push it aside. She hated soldiers. Why would I be the exception?

We spent what felt like hours in silence, with nothing but the slapping of Geronimo's hooves and tail pushing against the current. Finally, I opened my mouth to speak, "We should continue our lessons before we reach the palace."

Already, we were arriving at more populated towns on the outskirts of the capitol. Mer swam about, some of them bowing to us as we thundered past. It was a sign of respect for the royal guard that kept them alive and protected. I was used to the bowing, to the mer thanking me as if I was something close to royalty. I wasn't. Far from it. But I accepted their praise with grace. They needed to believe in the crown. And I would ensure that they did.

"You'll need to know how to greet the queen and king at the palace."

Maisie kept leaning closer into Geronimo's mane the more I spoke. Her shoulders shook and her body flinched. My brows pulled together with confusion. Was she going to be sick?

My hand came to rest lightly on her shoulder, but she suddenly jerked away and twisted around to glare at me with obsidian eyes. "Don't touch me," she hissed through her teeth.

I dropped my hand back to where it had been, calculating the hard anger in her gaze. I matched it with a look of my own, lips thinning into a tight line. A thousand retorts came into my mind, though only one word came out of my mouth. "What?"

"I said get your murderous hands off of me, *Captain.*"

"Ah." I frowned, staring at the back of her neck. A few loose strands of purple-blue hair had slipped from her hat to curl in floating tendrils. My fingers itched to move them aside, but I kept them in place. "I take it you saw what happened last night, then."

Her silence was confirmation enough. I sighed. Of course she would see it that way. Of course she would think me cruel. I'd been doing my job as Captain of the Royal Guard and all she could think of calling me was a murderer.

I knew that there were mer who saw me, saw *us*, that way. Coming from her, I felt a little insulted.

"You know those who try to flee are penalized by law. What would you have me do?"

Her back was ever tight, shoulders bunched nearly to her ears. She didn't turn around to face me to reply. "Show some leniency?"

"Why? He was abandoning his kingdom. The law is the law."

"The law is only made to benefit the royals. It does nothing but jeopardize *us*. But, of course, *you* can't see that."

I bristled, hands tightening along the reins. "The law was made to protect the merpeople of Thalassar."

She snorted unkindly, mockingly. "Right. Keep telling yourself that, Captain."

She was quiet a long moment after. I should have let it go, but something ran down my spine, my mind swimming continuous laps. I couldn't just leave it alone. How dare she presume to understand the complexities of war? This little hobbling chit had never even left her backwater pond before, and yet she insulted *me*? "We aren't monsters, Maisie. We are just following the law."

Maisie sighed and turned around then. I wasn't prepared for the intense look in her eyes as she glared at me. "Following a law made by tyrant royals. A law that is meant to protect *them*. Keep *them* safe while the mer at the bottom suffer and are killed in a war that no one knows who started or why it has been going on for years. If it was a law meant to protect the mer, then the royal guard and soldiers would be out there fighting. Not farmers and weavers. And if your law was meant to protect us, then you wouldn't be killing us in the dead of night to honor your queen and king."

Lies. All lies. What we did, we did for the good of the entire kingdom. Soldiers were out there fighting just as much as the farmers, as those selected. They were all shedding blood together for the same cause. She just didn't see it yet. Maybe life at the palace would open her eyes to the truth.

"What we do, we do for Thalassar. We all have our part to play," was all I said before staring ahead, promptly ignoring her.

Of course, she had to get her last words in. She sighed and turned back to face the front. "I don't want to argue with you, Captain. You seem like you could be a good merman. But kingdoms fall when good mermen do nothing."

I knew what the hidden message behind her words was. A message she'd never dare say aloud, not if she wanted to keep her head. Thalassar could not fall. It was a kingdom of old, good and just. The mer just didn't understand it yet. They didn't understand what the royals did this for. They couldn't see past their own ponds, if you asked them to look further into the future. And I hoped Maisie meant no harm by the words she'd said. Because if the mer planned to rise up against Thalassar, then I was afraid that she was very much correct.

They would fall.

We didn't speak to each other at all the rest of the journey. I had nothing else that needed saying and he brooded from behind me. Besides, the closer we made it into Eramaea, the tenser he became. As if he dreaded the upcoming moments as much as I did.

And despite my hesitancy, despite the rage that boiled deep in me because of the royals and the rich, I could not help but admire the capitol city of Thalassar once we arrived. I was sure the water left my lungs entirely as I gazed at the entrance to the city.

A sprawling, vast expanse, the city was bustling with color and light. I'd never seen anything like it. Flurry with activity, crowds of beautiful, exotic mer swam through opened archways carved from red and white coral. Buildings, restaurants, and houses in all colors and textures seemed to be pushed together closely. Nothing like the wide spaces and forests of Lagoona. Out here, things glowed with bioluminescent lights. And the rays of sun that ever so slightly pierced past the surface of the water above, shone down onto cerulean-diamond castles to cast a rainbow hue over the seafloor.

The royal palace was an incredible structure, towering over everything else. It appeared to be structured from rose quartz and aquamarine, the colors spiraling through the water in spires and peaks. The light hit it at an angle that lit up Eramaea in hues that could only be described as a sunset.

The exclamation of awe that escaped my lips was involuntary. I didn't care. The place was incredible.

We swam deeper into the city and my eyes tried following every little thing at once, darting around furiously to take everything in as quickly as possible. There were mer of all shapes and sizes. Mer with the lower bodies of sting rays, eels, and jellyfish. Most of them had long, iridescent tails in bright, flashy colors. It was with a start, I realized that in appearance I fit in more with *these* mer than I ever had in Lagoona.

I pushed that thought to the side as we made our way through the sandy roads. Young mer swam about, hawking their wares, from food to jewelry to conch news shells. And the strangest thing happened as we passed… The mer stopped to observe and bow.

It happened all throughout the trek towards the palace. Mer would stop and call out joyously to the royal soldiers, throw flowers at their fins and scream out in thanks. Captain Saber was relatively still and quiet behind me, though every time someone called out to him, he acknowledged them with a nod.

I hated feeling like I was being stared at. I hated the thanks they called out to me and the other selects. What were they thanking us for? For being forced from our homes to come here, to train and fight in a war? For dying? My rage boiled hotly at their ignorance, at their lack of knowledge and compassion.

It was obvious from the streets and homes of Eramaea that the mer here lived lavishly, meanwhile those in Lagoona were starving. They had to work their fins off to scrape up the next meal and lived in fear of the Selection. I was willing to bet none of these mer had ever been selected or even knew anyone who had been.

By the time we made it to the palace, I was trembling with anger. I barely noticed when we'd parted from the other selects to travel to a stable. Hippocampi were behind stalls, their hooves pounding against the doors of their confinements. I trembled as Captain Saber hopped from Geronimo's back.

I didn't wait for him to offer his hand to me. Instead, I positioned myself and hopped down. My fins fanned out at my sides, cramping from all the time I'd spent on top of the beast. I took a moment to stretch my limbs as Captain Saber handed the reins over to a groomsmer and gave him instructions. When he finished, he turned to me, looked me up and down.

I glared at him.

"It's time," he said.

My insides became leaden and as heavy as an anchor inside me. It was time.

Time to meet the queen and king of Thalassar.

"Your Majesties, it is an honor to be in your presence once again." Captain Saber's voice was booming, his bow elegant as he swept low towards the polished quartz floor.

The inside of the palace was as lavish as the outside of it. Paintings, decorative swords, and so many valuable objects adorned the halls. Objects that could have kept Lagoona fed and well for years. Swarms of guards were posted at nearly every door, and I was floating next to one at the very back of the throne room.

Captain Saber had insisted upon meeting with the queen and king first. He'd left me there, without having briefed me on anything, as he swam out to greet his rulers. I watched from my spot, nervously twisting the hem of the black jacket in my fingers, feeling entirely too exposed.

I wore no hat. Captain Saber had pulled it from my head and straightened my floating tendrils of hair with adept, elegant fingers before we swam through the entrance. They were going to look at me in all my limping glory. Would they see their daughter the way Captain Saber had seen the princess? Or would they debunk his idea, claiming him a mad merman and lock the both of us up for knowing too much?

So many scenarios passed through my mind, each crazier than the last. In that moment, I longed for the comfort of my bag at my back. The comfort of the blade I'd hidden there. In my nerves, I'd forgotten to ask for it. Not that it would have helped; no one was allowed into the throne room with weapons. That much had been made perfectly clear.

Besides, the captain promised he'd give me my bag later. If I was to parade around as the princess, I probably wouldn't need it, but I still wanted the comfort.

I strained my ears to listen to Captain Saber's conversation, and I cringed at the words of King Oriana.

"Have you found my daughter, Captain?"

From here, I could see the tightness bunched in his shoulders. "I have not, Your Majesty."

The king tightened his hand against the arm of his golden throne. Golden, with a long arched back carved to look like an ivory scallop shell. The queen's throne was even grander somehow. A crown of carved coral and sea glass adorned both their heads, seeming to loom high above them.

"I recall," the king began tightly, "that I told you not to come back unless you found her."

"Yes, Your Majesty."

"Then why are you here?" the king shouted, losing any sort of composure he may have possessed.

Even I flinched, but Captain Saber kept his poise. His hands were fisted tightly behind his back, closing tighter and tighter with each word that was spoken. "We traveled throughout the entire kingdom of Thalassar, Your Majesty, and there was no trace of her anywhere. Although my hope remains that she is out there somewhere, I soon discovered a temporary solution to our problem."

I gulped. Me. I was a temporary solution. And the queen and king didn't even know it yet. That tadpole of a captain had led me to believe they would be okay with this. With me.

"What if we cannot find the princess for many more months?" Captain Saber asked, his voice firm. "What if the kingdom starts to question her absence? And Prince Kai will notice. He is living here at the palace, and we cannot keep avoiding him and—"

"Get to the point, Captain," the king interrupted with a note of impatience.

"My point is, Your Majesty, that we need to trick the merpeople, the *prince*. And I know just the way to do so." He turned then, eyes locking onto mine.

This was it. This was the moment I made myself known. Taking in a deep breath of salt water, I swam forward slowly into the illumination of their throne room.

Don't limp. Don't limp. Don't limp.

I kept my head held high, my hands clasped together near my stomach, just as Captain Saber had taught me. I resisted the urge to look at him as I swam towards the throne, and towards the queen and king. I moved slowly, deliberately. My nerves wouldn't let me go faster. I was too afraid of falling onto the shining floor and breaking my nose.

When I arrived at the fin of their thrones, I dipped into a curtsy, my head bowed low.

At the sight of me, King Oriana gasped. But I did not look up.

"Your Majesties, I present to you, Maisie Fauna of Lagoona."

I rose then and looked up at the Queen and King of Thalassar.

The king was floating above his throne as he gazed down on me. There was only one way to interpret the expression on his face. Shock.

"Odele..." He reached a hand towards me, but then seemed to realize himself and slumped back onto his throne. "No, you cannot be..."

So Captain Saber hadn't been full of sand. I actually did look like the princess.

"Yes, the resemblance *is* rather striking," the queen, who had remained silent the entirety of the exchange, suddenly spoke up. My gaze went to her.

They were both beautiful. The images on the telly had done them little justice. The king was a very tall merman, his tail long and green and powerful. His hair was black and ran down to his waist, clipped back with golden jeweled pieces and bands. He wore an elegantly cut red jacket with golden trimming at the lapels and a long, richly made cloak at his shoulders. His black beard was long and jeweled, dark eyes regarding me sadly.

The queen was rather remarkable. Her hair as golden as sunlight to be, her eyes the brightest blue. She wore a special crafted dress in magenta, and glittering diamonds adorned her neck and ears. Her tail was the purple-blue coloring of the Malabella lineage and curled leisurely at the fin of her throne.

"Where did the captain say you were from, dear?" the queen asked with icy politeness.

I drew in a breath before I answered. "I am from Lagoona, Your Majesty."

Her long fingers came up to stroke her chin. "Strange, that a mer that looks like you could come from a backwater pond such as that. Tell me, do you have family?"

I shook my head slowly. "No, Your Majesty. My family is dead."

"And how did they die?" the king asked gruffly. He was looking at me like I was either an amazement or an oddity. Either way, it unnerved me. His eyes were too intense, too focused.

"My grandmother died a few years ago. She ventured out to northern lands to exchange handwoven baskets for currency but was caught up in the current of a sink hole." It still hurt to remember it. To remember when the village soldiers and merchants had brought me the news. They'd gone out as a group for trade, but not all of them had made it back alive. She'd left me an orphan that day. And I never even got to say goodbye. "I never knew my parents. I was told they died after I was born."

The queen stroked a long fingernail down the arm of her throne. "Interesting," she mused.

Maybe to her. To me, it was heartbreaking.

"Captain Saber, what do you mean to accomplish by bringing this peasant forth, again?" The queen turned to the captain, glaring mutinously. How easily she'd brushed me off. Typical royalty. I tried not to frown.

Captain Saber took a stroke forward, so I was gifted with the image of his strong back. "Your Majesties, surely you can see it? The resemblance is uncanny. When I first laid eyes on Miss Fauna, I had thought for sure it had been Princess Odele. Of course, to our disappointment, she is not. But I had the beginnings of an idea. To avoid the questioning of the mer and of the Draconian Prince, why not have Maisie disguise herself as the princess?"

The queen's eyes widened just before she scoffed. "Have this peasant disguise herself as my beloved stepdaughter? I think not."

I felt my face heat unpleasantly. I was all too aware of how I looked. Aware that my dress had a hole at the hem, that it was too tight at my chest. I knew I wasn't the prettiest mer or the most well-mannered. But if

I looked like the princess as they all believed I did, then I would certainly try my hardest to be her. To save this kingdom and the merpeople from downfall.

"And why would we allow such a thing to happen?" the king asked slowly, stroking his beard in thought.

"How long will we be able to hide the fact that Princess Odele is gone? We cannot claim illness forever, Your Majesties. Not with Prince Kai asking questions and demanding to see her. What will happen if this gets out? The balance of the kingdom lies in this charade. If she can pretend to be the princess, then we will have bought some time to find Princess Odele's whereabouts."

The queen and king looked from the captain to me. And their gazes were scrutinizing, intimidating, and I tried not to falter.

"It's ridiculous!" the queen exclaimed finally, looking back to Captain Saber. Her fins unfurled at the base of her throne, slapping at the water angrily. "The very notion is demeaning. A servant disguised as the princess? I can see the kingdom in ruins now."

"Forgive me, Your Majesties, but what other choice do we have?"

The queen seethed, and I was so sure she would command someone to swoop in and cut off the captain's head then and there. "How about you do your job and find my stepdaughter, Captain, since you are the one who lost her in the first place?"

Captain Saber's whole body tensed even more so than it had been. I wondered what thoughts were going through his head at that moment. If he was plagued by guilt and anger. He'd conveniently left out the part where he'd been the one to lose her. Perhaps that was why he was so desperate for this plan of his to work.

"She can be taught, Your Majesty. She can be taught to move, talk, and act like the princess. No one will know the difference."

"How can you be so sure?" the king cut in. He was looking at me. At my hair, at my eyes. I kept my hands clasped near my stomach to avoid fidgeting.

"We cannot be sure of the future, Your Majesty. We can only take measures to prevent scandal and invasion from Kappur."

Both royals stilled at this, turning to look at one another. They silently communicated using nothing but their eyes. Then finally, the queen turned. She did not look happy as her gaze found mine. She looked murderous.

"Fine," she conceded hatefully. "Let us try this plan Captain Saber suggests. You will keep our secret, girl, and you will be Princess Odele's doppelgänger for a brief amount of time. Take heed that you do not ruin this or slip up. For if you do…" She smiled, her fingers curling around the arms of her throne. It chilled me to the bone. "…you will long for something as sweet as death."

The guards at the throne room entrance escorted me quickly and quietly to Princess Odele's room. Captain Saber stayed behind, as the queen wanted to have a word with him.

"Escort her to the princess' rooms while I speak to the captain," she'd sneered.

I was all too eager to swim out and avoid being part of *that* conversation. The queen looked like a piece of work. She and the king both, actually. I could only imagine what the princess had been like. If the rumors that spread through the market back in Lagoona had even a vestige of truth within them, then I knew. She was vain, rude, and hateful. And I was going to have to pretend to be her, for however long it took them to actually *find* her. It could be months or even a year. Maybe more.

I tried not to let that dark thought loom over me. However long I had, I'd make the most of it and change as much as I could. I was sure of it.

I was so lost in my thoughts, that we arrived at the princess' rooms within moments. I hadn't gotten a chance to take in my surroundings, but I could feel the opulence of the palace threatening to close in on me. The guards opened the double doors for me and I swam inside.

"Captain Saber will fetch you later," a guard said. "Stay."

He spoke to me as if I was a dogfish. Grumbling, I pointedly avoided his gaze and his command and turned about the room. A soft click echoed, and I knew they'd closed the doors. With them gone, I could freely let out the gasp that was trapped in my throat.

Princess Odele's bedroom was bigger than Tides' Tavern and my dinky little house combined. A glorious expanse of a room, I swam through it, awestruck at the lavishness of it.

Her bed was a massive ivory scallop shell with a cushiony middle and bright, fat anemones lining the outside of it. She had a line of white and red coral shelves with expensive decorations, from dolls to glass and diamond figurines aligned along it. The walls were polished rose quartz, with images etched on the surface like a tiny maze of sculptures. Her closet was enormous, practically a room of its own, piled with hundreds of dresses, jackets, and accessories in materials of silk, velvet, gossamer, pearls, and diamonds.

A plush anemone carpet was in the middle of the room, their fat fleshy fingers grabbed at me as I swam past it and towards the double glass doors by her bed. I reached for the pearly handles and tried at them, but the doors were locked. I wondered if that was for security purposes or for another reason entirely. Sighing, my face met the blue and green panes of sea glass, eyes catching sight of the exotic plants on the other side of the balcony. They swayed along with the flow of the current, a gentle, hypnotic lapping.

My palms pushed away from the glass as I continued exploring what would be my new home. Princess Odele's washroom was a porcelain wonder. With a long claw-footed shipwrecked tub, shells filled with different colored sands, and her very own lava seam to help heat the bath, it seemed like a place I could get lost in. She had two tellies; one in her washroom and another in her bedroom. They were huge things, the floating bubble in the middle depicting images of Eramaean beauty.

I certainly wasn't in Lagoona anymore.

A part of me wished I was.

The spacious room felt like *too much*, too soon. The walls would carry out my echoes and bring them back to me in incredible loneliness. Had that been why the princess had left? Had she been lonely surrounded by all these clothes and things? Maybe she'd been trying to fill some void with this stuff and it just didn't measure up.

I swam over to her shelf along one of the walls and ran my fingers across its smooth edges. Trinkets were aligned on this one. Not expensive, sapphire structures and dolls, but these were simpler… mundane. My fingers ran over them. A seashell the size of my thumbnail, a piece of driftwood the size of my forearm, a shark and alligator tooth. My fingers stopped to finger the alligator tooth before roaming across the rest of her things. A two-legger fishhook, a leather-bound book—the pages already dissolved beneath the water—a vial full of purple and pink sea glass, and a very old and chipped conch shell.

I wondered if she'd collected these things as a child. They were certainly poorer in comparison to everything else, not as eye-catching as the blue dolphin figurine, nor the glittering diamond necklace on display.

I tore my hand quickly from the shelf. It felt like a violation, to wander through her room and touch her stuff. Even if this was to be my life for the next few weeks, it felt wrong somehow. To go about wearing discarded clothing, to treat her stuff as my own.

I was gripped with the sudden longing to hold my own bag in my hands. To cradle that obsidian blade in my arms and dream up an image of the Black Blade as I did so.

Feeling suddenly overwhelmed, I swam quickly to the bedroom doors and wrenched them open to swim out into the hall. The guards weren't there, probably deeming me unworthy of being protected. Good. It gave me a chance to escape. I swam without knowing where I was going, as if my problems were snapping at my tail fin but I wasn't fast enough.

I didn't stop until I turned through various hallways and then ran, *smack*, into a body.

I jerked back, fanning my fins out at my sides, only to trip and fall hard onto the polished floor. My face flushed as I looked up and found myself staring into the dark eyes of the most beautiful merman I'd ever seen.

He blinked at me, almost as if he was surprised to see me. He probably was. After all, how many peasant mermaids wandered around the palace like maniacs and ran into royalty? From the surprise on his face, I would say the answer was none.

Brown eyes flicked over my body with cold calculation. Long hair was pulled away from a porcelain smooth face. It flowed in black tendrils down to his waist. The merman was clad in a bright red kimono that swept over his beautiful tail. It was white with bright orange and black spots, resembling that of a koi fish.

There were two mermen fanning his sides, and guards wearing dragon-scale armor behind *them*. Due to the similar tails and features, I assumed they were from the same kingdom. Though, these mermen wore opposing kimonos in black and white. And they were staring at me with barely concealed distaste.

My face heating, I got up quickly and swept into the lowest, most dignified bow I could muster. Because floating before me, was Kai Li.

The Crown Prince of Draconi.

"Princess." I blinked once, twice, just to be sure my eyes were not deceiving me. Unfortunately for me, they weren't, and I was really in front of the Princess of Thalassar. She was the last mer in this palace I'd wanted to see—or had even expected to, for that matter.

For weeks, I'd been informed that the princess was bedridden with sickness. One so great she could not make an appearance to any of the regular royal activities we were meant to attend. Together. As an engaged royal couple.

While her mysterious ailment had given me reprieve from her overbearing presence, it had caused quite a fuss between my father's advisors. The two mer bristled behind me, and I knew they were judging the princess even while they wore stoic masks.

I was surprised by her appearance as much as they were.

She was wearing the rags of a commoner, a black military jacket over it. Her hair was unkempt and slightly tangled behind her back. But what surprised me the most was the respectable bow she was presenting me with.

"Your Majesty, sorry, I didn't see ya," she whispered breathlessly. Her gaze was still lowered and something about her voice, the way she pronounced and spoke the words seemed… off.

"Excuse me?" I asked, tilting my head to the side. As if that little action could make me register the words any clearer.

She cleared her throat and straightened to look me in the eyes. "What I mean to say is," she began, so quickly in her Thalassarin accent that I forgot she'd even sounded odd in the first place. "Forgive me for running into you in such a way. I was in a hurry and didn't see you as I rounded the corner, Your Majesty."

Your Majesty? I looked her over. She was acting so strange. Usually, she greeted me with the term 'Lizard Prince.' The words were more insult than endearment, and when she'd said them to me the first time we met, I knew she was just as unhappy about our engagement as I.

"Princess, I was told you were ill. That you required constant bed rest for an indefinite amount of time…"

My advisors fanned out at my sides. I could feel their hands hovering near my sides, ready to pull me away from Princess Odele if she so much as coughed. Ever protective, the royal advisors. And ever irritating. I fought back the glare I longed to shoot them and instead stared at her.

Her black eyes swept over my advisors before settling back on me. They were wide, and something about them seemed… different. Fearful, even. She was usually always the perfect picture of indignation. Always sneering, always finding fault within me.

"I *was* sick, Your Majesty," she whispered, almost a little shyly. "But I can assure you, I am well now."

"I am glad to hear it." I was sure she could sense the lie the moment it left my lips. It had been peaceful without her, I had to admit. But we were to be married, and I was shunning my duties and honor. I knew my advisors were taking note on the exchange, eager to report back every detail to my father. Like the princess, he was always looking for new things to chastise me about. However, his was a crueler hand.

Forcing a smile to my face, I reached forward and took her hand. She tensed as I it brought it up and bowed over it. Strange, how they felt so rough and worn. They had been soft before; I could have sworn it. Still, I brought her knuckles up to my lips and pressed a kiss to them.

"Forgive me, Princess, for not greeting you properly." I dropped her hand gently, felt my lips burn where I'd touched them to her skin. "I was merely surprised at finally seeing you up and about, is all."

Her face was flaming as she brought her hand—the one I'd kissed—up to her chest and tightened it into a fist. I noticed her every flicker of movement, the fearful way she floated before me. It made me eye her closely. She appeared to be nervous, though I couldn't quite possibly fathom *why*. Last time I'd seen her, she'd looked down through her nose at me. She'd been rude and quite bratty.

"Forgive me if I startled you, Your Majesty."

I narrowed my eyes, wondering if this was some type of joke. If she was mocking me. My lips twisted into a smile. "You may call me Kai. We *are* to be married, after all." The last time I'd said those words to her, she'd gagged and called me a disgusting reptile.

"I—uh—" She took a stroke back and tripped over empty water. Her palm slapped against a painting on the wall to right herself. As soon as her skin touched it, she gasped, jerking her hand away and turned to look at it with a visage of guilt. Like she'd committed a crime.

Odd, indeed.

"Are you sure you're well, Princess Odele?"

"I think so…" she replied distractedly. I followed to where her gaze lay. Paintings in golden gilded frames of her ancestors. Faces of relatives distant and close, dead and alive. I knew them all by name. I'd been forced to learn everything about my betrothed and her family history before I came to this dreadful kingdom. And she'd taken me on a tour through the halls the day of my arrival, her demeanor rather pompous as her fingers flicked in the direction of her family.

"No need to tell you their names," she'd said. "They're all dead."

"Princess…"

Her hands went up to the painting, fingers tracing the edges of the face there. I wondered if this was some sort of test, somehow. She was always testing me, always questioning me. I pushed down my irritation and swam up close to her side. She tensed briefly before relaxing her posture. Yes, there was something changed about her. She even smelt different, too.

"The late Queen Odette," I said, in *case* this was a test. So she'd know I really did show an interest in uniting our kingdoms. "Your mother." As if she didn't already know. That could be why she'd paused, why she fingered the portrait so tenderly. Because that was her mother. A mother she had inherited every feature from.

She dropped her hand and turned abruptly to me. The tentative smile she gifted me was staggering, and something inside me clenched. She never smiled at me unless it was for telly recordings. I looked around cautiously. Maybe there was a recording somewhere and she was trying to catch me unaware.

There was an uncomfortable tightness in my throat when our gazes clashed again. "Now that you are up, I suspect we will be seeing more of each other?" I almost dreaded her answer.

"I—uh—I mean—"

"Princess!" Princess Odele jumped in the water and turned to face the Captain of her Royal Guard. He swam quickly over towards us, his posture tense. I watched him carefully as he loomed over the princess, wearing a tight, angry expression on his face. "What are you doing out of your rooms?" he asked quietly, though there was no mistaking the rage boasting his words.

I raised my brows at him. Since when had it become appropriate for a guard to question a royal? "Captain Saber," I said in way of greeting. "What a surprise." It wasn't, and we both knew it. He was always trailing after Princess Odele, always in her shadow, and when the two of us were together, always glaring at my hands. Like I'd shift them into claws at any moment and slit her throat, just to remind everyone why I was called the Dragon Prince of Draconi. But with the princess ill, I'd been spared those glares and rejoiced in the news that he'd been sent away to find selects for his kingdom.

The captain turned, bringing his fist to his chest and gifting me with a half-bow that could have been considered mocking. "Prince Kai," he greeted. "Forgive me, Your Majesty."

"I hadn't expected to see you back so soon, Captain." Unlike when I'd first met him, the captain was disheveled. His uniform jacket wasn't straightened, and his short hair was floating all over the place. I knew my advisors were scrutinizing everything, and I fought to keep that judgmental expression off my own face. I was not like them and refused to be.

"It was a speedy Selection," he replied.

Beside him, the princess stiffened, her eyes glaring daggers at the captain.

Interesting.

I catalogued every interaction and knew the advisors were doing the same.

The quiet afterwards was disconcerting. Never before had things with the princess been so awkward. It was always sharp words spitting from her tongue. Now, she just stared at the floor. I wondered if something had happened to her, wondered what had made her change so suddenly.

"I suppose I will see you around the palace more often, Princess?"

She snapped her attention up to me, a blush brightening her face. The captain tensed, and he was the one who answered coolly. "Of course you will be, Your Majesty. Although I fear the princess must take her leave now. Her schedule is filled, and there is much to do to ready for your anniversary dinner."

My hand closed into a tight fist at the reminder. I had almost hoped she would be unwell enough to miss that.

The princess made a squeaking noise that startled my gaze over to her. Her face seemed to get redder by the second. "Anniversary dinner?" she echoed.

The captain glared at her. "Yes, Princess. I know you've been sick for months, but surely you remember you are *betrothed* to Prince Kai?"

She squeaked again and looked at me with a complete unreadable expression on her face. It was an amusing sort of look that involuntarily had me smiling at her. "It's alright, Princess," I reassured her. Maybe it was the look on her face that prompted me to joke darkly, "I don't bite."

If she had spikes down her back, surely they would have bristled. Her fins fanned out as her brows pulled together and her eyes narrowed on a glare. "Maybe I *do.* Did you ever think of that, *Prince*?"

I found myself chuckling at this sudden humor and defensiveness. Maybe I was just on edge because I hadn't seen her in so long. Whatever the case, I took a stroke forward and reached for her stiff, unyielding fingers. I brought them up to my mouth and whispered against her knuckles, "Every day, Princess," before pressing a kiss to them and easing away from her.

I got the satisfaction of watching her face brighten once again before I turned and left with my advisors and guards.

There was definitely something *very* different about Princess Odele Malabella Oriana of Thalassar.

And I liked it.

Even if I couldn't quite place what it was.

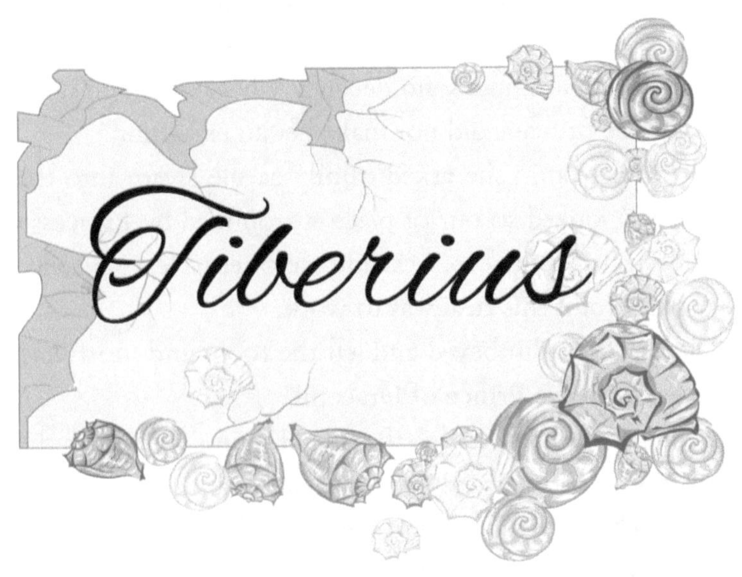

Tiberius

"What were you thinking?" I demanded as I closed the doors to the princess' quarters.

I always prided myself on my impeccable self-control. I'd been trained to confront any situation with a stoic mask. To bottle up any and all feelings, lest they flow like rapid currents for all to feel. For so long, emotions raged within me like a storm. I felt so deeply, so keenly, all the time. Until I learned to not feel at all. Because feelings interfered with duty.

I didn't want to think that my carelessness in regard to the princess had led to her disappearance. I'd always been an unmovable force between her and anything that would harm her. I'd kept my mask in place. I'd done what I was supposed to do.

With Maisie, it was different.

She stripped away all my good sense with a single look. My anger rose higher by the second because of this mer. *Disobedient. Sarcastic. Rude.* She acted like she was raised in a stable. Which, in her case, was probably true. Small town mer had absolutely no decency whatsoever, and just because she looked like the princess did not make her an exception.

"What do you mean?" she asked calmly as she swam into the center of the room. She looked so out of place surrounded by Princess Odele's things. But even if I wanted to, I couldn't ask her to leave or relocate her to a new room. Not if this ruse was to work.

I glared at her. "You disobeyed and left the room and nearly blew your cover out there with the Prince of Draconi!"

"Really?" She cocked her head to the side. "I thought it went rather well." As she said this, her fingers flexed at her sides, and she slowly brought them up to her chest, pressing them there as if she wanted to wipe off the memory of the imprint of his lips against her skin.

I glowered, unsure why that simple action made my fins want to flare. "That went the opposite of well. Did you somehow forget that the princess and him are engaged to be married? Because it certainly appeared that way."

She let out an exasperated sigh and went over to the bed to sit at the edge of it. The bright anemones reached out for her with caressing, fat tentacles. I glared at those, too. She lifted and lowered her tail almost absently, leaning her hands against the soft cushioning of the bed.

"What did the queen and king say?" she asked quietly, effectively changing the subject.

I pinched the bridge of my nose and sighed. That conversation had not gone well at all. As soon as she'd left, the queen had floated up to her regal height and screamed her rage in my direction with all the force of a maelstrom. Words had soon blurred together in a chorus of 'beggar,' 'peasant,' 'demeaning,' and my personal favorite, 'this is all your fault.'

Did she think I didn't know that?

The king had sat at his throne, stroking his black beard and twirling the enormous ruby ring round and round on his finger until he finally silenced his wife.

"You will teach her the ways of royalty. You're right. The mer are growing suspicious. So groom her and prepare her for the anniversary dinner and let this doppelgänger be presented to the courts."

"If she slips up in any way, I will have both of your heads!" the queen added. "And you will keep actively looking for our daughter or so help me…"

"Captain?"

I broke out of my reverie to look at her. Smiling and words of reassurance were beyond me. "The queen will have both of our heads if we slip up in any way, Maisie," I explained coldly.

Her whole body tensed, but the realization seemed to settle quickly over her shoulders. Her teeth snagged at her bottom lip, chewing it furiously before she nodded. "I understand," she murmured.

"Do you really?" She'd agreed, but I still couldn't seem to rein in that tight feeling in my chest. The anger that made me want to lash out at her. As if it was her fault the princess was gone. Like she was a substitute for the real thing. I didn't care, though. "This is serious, Maisie. You cannot go wandering around the palace halls without an escort. A princess must always be protected and accompanied. Even if you aren't really her."

"So I have to have you follow me around everywhere I go?" Her voice rose, holding a trace of anger within it.

"Yes. Though if a murderer like me makes you so uncomfortable, we can always assign my most trusted guards to be near you at all times."

"Gee, will they spoon feed me, wash me, and brush my hair like a little tadpole, too?" she muttered just before she threw her hands up. "Fine. If this is what royalty must go through, then I'll do it."

I nodded once. Good. It was better she comply with minimal complaint. It was in everyone's best interest. "Now," I began, pacing across the floor with powerful strokes of my tail and my hands behind my back. "We must first fit you for dresses and perhaps alter hers. Though you look like her, you are much skinnier and her clothes would not fit you."

"Yeah, hunger has a funny way of doing that to a mer…"

I ignored her comment and went on. "Since the princess has been deemed sick, they'll only assume you lost weight because of it. We have that in our favor, at least. We will begin lessons right away."

"More lessons?" she groaned.

"Speech, swimming, riding, and you still must learn the princess' schedule and who she takes tea with, who are her closest friends, and who she confides in."

"Right." She got up and there was a new light around her as she widened her smile. Determined. Ready. It was almost breathtaking. I staved off that feeling and replaced it with one of annoyance. "Let's get started, then."

Maisie

The next few days were pure torture. I kept telling myself I had to get through it, remind myself *who* I was doing this for. I whispered their names over and over as I suffered through facial massages, aggressive baths, hair trimmings, and clothes fittings.

Josiah.

Christof.

The seamstress.

The blacksmith's son.

The Black Blade.

Lagoona.

Maids swam in and out. No one had been told who I really was, yet every time they came in, I held my breath. Waiting for someone to claim me an imposter. It never happened, though. They all curtsied and bowed reverently, almost fearfully whenever they came into the room.

The way they acted around me gave me a little insight onto how well-liked Princess Odele was with the staff. The way they watched me warily, as if I'd snap and order their heads chopped off at any given moment, told me all I needed to know.

At one point, a maid had been trembling so badly as she served me afternoon tea, the cup had fallen from its saucer, spilling the frothy foam through the water. She'd frozen, staring at me slack-jawed before bursting into airy tears and apologizing.

"Forgive me, Princess Odele. I did not mean to—"

"It is quite alright," I reassured her, using my perfectly practiced Eramaean accent.

The whole staff present froze at my declaration and stared at me as if I'd suddenly grown gator legs and danced on them.

I tilted my head to the side, feeling a flush rise up my neck and cheeks. "Accidents happen, it's alright."

It had been the wrong thing to say.

Captain Saber had barked at everyone to get out. He then spent the better part of the hour berating me.

Lessons dragged on longer after that mistake, in which Captain Saber treated me like I was an incompetent fool, though I knew he'd never admit to his faults. He was a very impatient teacher and seemed to enjoy insulting me anytime I answered a question incorrectly.

Insults like 'foolish', 'childish', and 'irresponsible' became the norm for me. I was sure he was used to me calling him a tadpole under my breath. Under any other circumstances, I would have probably felt guilty about the way I spoke to him, but he deserved it. He was being a total piranha and was asking for it.

Josiah.

Christof.

The seamstress.

The blacksmith's son.

The Black Blade.

Lagoona.

I thought those names many times the more my princess training progressed. I mainly thought of the faceless Black Blade and tried not to mourn the loss of my weapon. Throwing myself into my studies helped to take my mind off the fact that Captain Saber hadn't given me my stuff back.

"You will receive your belongings once the princess is found and you leave the palace," he'd said. I'd argued profusely, but he interrupted me. "A princess does not need weapons. Especially not those made by a criminal to the crown."

And that was that.

I'd cried over the blade that first night and had thrown myself into my studies with great fervor the next morning. Maybe a part of me had hoped that if he saw how hard I was working, he'd be lenient and give it back.

That was not the case.

Weeks had already past, and I was about as close to getting my blade back as I was to changing the fate of the kingdom. Which meant I wasn't really close at all.

Lessons were usually confined to Princess Odele's—*my*—room. The captain didn't want to risk anyone else seeing me. Not yet. Not until I was ready. I felt ready, but he didn't believe I was. So for now, I suffered through my confinement, studying the long names and faces of royalty that were close to Odele. I studied who her friends were, what her schedule was, how to take tea and how to swim and speak with elegance.

More often than not, I laid awake at night, listening to the current slap at the sea glass windowpanes. Small bioluminescent jellies floated on the canopy above my head, illuminating the room in a soft blue glow in the darkness. I looked around her room, at the richness in décor, at the quartz wall covered in a thick painted seaweed tapestry. The painting was in pinks, golds, and blues. The city of Eramaea.

I wondered how Odele could go through this life without a care in the world. How she could spend her days riding hippocampi, taking tea with her royal friends, or dressing in such finery while there were mer out there who were suffering under her parents' rule?

Why hadn't she done anything to stop the tyranny? Instead, she'd swam away from her problems—whatever those were. I couldn't help the angry thoughts that sliced through my mind. Thoughts of a selfish princess who obviously cared about nothing and no one but herself. She hadn't done a thing to change Thalassar. In all her life, she'd done nothing to help.

And I vowed I would never be as weak and as spoiled as her.

THE NEXT MORNING, THE captain deemed me competent enough to swim the hallways of the palace. He'd checked with his trusted guards and considered the halls would be empty enough in the early morning. Royalty slept in late, so I could have a bitter taste of freedom without the risk of embarrassing anyone with my stupidity.

How generous.

I was wearing a beautiful pink silk dress with long, shimmering sleeves that were threaded through with the thinnest strings of gold. The waist was belted with a thicker golden rope, the ends of the dress billowing out around my tail. My hair had been adorned with the most subtle of gold clips, as I'd refused the extravagant headpieces the princess apparently liked to dress in. I sparkled with each careful stroke I took.

These past few days, my fins had been hurting more than usual. Perhaps it was the constant use, the trying methods Captain Saber used to get me to swim without the limp. So far, nothing had really worked. My limp was still prominent as ever, and it wouldn't be something that could just go away after a lesson or two.

So together, we swam the halls of the palace, passing row upon row of royal portraits painted with colored squid ink. He kept a respectable distance behind me, as was usual for a guard. I almost wished I could swim ahead, if only so I could have a moment alone.

"You are swimming too fast," the captain judged from behind me in a soft voice that would make it difficult for others to overhear. "Slow your pace and keep your head up."

I rolled my eyes and, just to mess with him, flipped my fins behind me and put a small burst of speed. I heard his audible sigh and gave a small smile of satisfaction. He would probably grill me over a pot of boiling lava later, but out in public, he seemed to mostly keep his commentary in check. It made me love the freedom from the confines of that room.

"Oooodeeeelleeee!"

The shriek was unexpected. I startled as a sudden heavy body pushed against me and wrapped me in the most crushing hug I'd ever experienced. The mer who was hugging me was also shrieking in my ear, causing a dreadful ringing in it. I struggled beneath her heavy weight and was glad when she finally pulled away.

Her hands were clasped tightly to my upper arms, and her smile was wide, toothy, and white. Her skin had a slight pink tone to it and her tail was more blue than purple. Bright eyes regarded me with happiness, and I smiled tentatively back.

"I've missed you so much!" she said, though it sounded more like a scream. Her voice was booming and loud, and I tried not to flinch. The rotund mer was wearing a dress in an alarming shade of yellow and an enormous tube hat with dozens of dangling jewels that twinkled together as she bobbed before me.

My eyes darted to the side where Captain Saber rigidly floated, his own eyes screaming in panic. He obviously hadn't expected this turn of events. He probably expected me to mess this up entirely. I told him I was ready and I would prove it.

I smiled an incredibly wide smile, the kind I imagined Princess Odele would give. "Jessinda!" I greeted happily, kissing either side of her cheek. "It's so great to see you!"

"I *knoooow*! We all thought you'd *died*. They told us you were ill."

I gave the most flippant, shallow look I could muster. "I *waaas*," I exaggerated. I had no idea if the princess spoke like that, but Jessinda did, so I would, too. "It was terrible, to be confined to my room with nothing but the telly to keep me company." I pouted, jutting my bottom lip out. From the corner of my eye, I saw Captain Saber's surprise slash across his features.

Yeah, suck a blow fish. I'd *told* him I was ready.

"Tragic, O, tragic." She took a stroke back and looked me up and down. "Although…" She paused, her eyes narrowing over me. I held my breath. "Something about you seems different…"

The captain shuffled closer to us. I wondered if he'd panic and pull me away from her and shut me off in that room again. My heart was pounding frantically in my chest at this exchange, but I tried as hard as I could to keep the façade going. I flicked my hair over my shoulder and struck a pose, hand on my hip. "You think so?"

She laughed loudly and nodded. "You lost weight, didn't you?"

"You noticed!"

"The tides will love it." That was Eramaean slang. It was a term used to describe the popular mer, or the crowds. "I have to go now, but we *have* to get together for tea and catch up on all the latest gossip spinning through the tides."

After nodding vigorously and promising I'd meet her for tea, she swam away. It wasn't until she was well out of range of sight and hearing did I turn to Captain Saber with the biggest eat-squid grin I possessed. "You were saying, Captain?" He rolled his eyes. "C'mon!" I gestured wildly and so not princess-like that he frowned. "Tell me that wasn't epic?"

"It wasn't."

"Whatever. I did a good job and you know it." Without waiting for his reply, I started forward again, swimming with much more lightness in my fin and a heavy weight off my shoulders. If I was able to fool Princess Odele's *cousin,* then I was positive I could fool everyone else, too.

The captain caught up with me. Instead of trailing behind, he swam up to my side. "Fine," he sighed. "You did well for your first time. Is that what you want to hear?"

"I should have brought a recording conch with me," I said playfully. "Because I doubt I'll ever hear that again."

"Do not let one success get to your head. There is still a long way to go."

I snorted. "I'm ready to take on the royal court. I'm ready for tea, and I'm ready for that stupid anniversary dinner—" I stopped short as we rounded the corner and bit down hard on my lip.

Like a reoccurring nightmare, he was there. Finely dressed, and beautiful in a silk black and white kimono, long hair swept low behind his head and dark, penetrating gaze. At the sight of him, the hand he'd pressed his lips to tingled, and I cursed myself to the abyss and back for my loud mouth.

Because before me, once again, was Prince Kai.

Stupid anniversary dinner...

My lip twitched into a mocking smile. "Princess." I bowed low and when I straightened, had the satisfaction of seeing a flush brighten her skin. My eyes lingered over her modest pink dress and golden clips keeping her long purple tresses back.

Her teeth were biting down hard on her lower lip, and I couldn't help but stare at her mouth. She released her lip and stuck her tongue out to trail over them. There was something different about the shape of her lips, the arch of her throat… I'd never given either thing a thought before, but now something about her seemed shy and almost tantalizing.

However, her words had been more than enough proof that there was no change in her. She was still the same spoiled little princess she always has been. That thought alone pulled my gaze away from her mouth and to her eyes.

I smiled dutifully, pretending as though I hadn't heard a word as I looked from her to the captain, who was leaning a bit too close to her instead of waiting at a respectable distance like he should have been. When he saw where my gaze lingered, he took a few strokes back and stiffened, his hand going to the hilt of the weapon at his waist. As if I'd be capable of hurting my betrothed. No. Even if I felt nothing for her, I would never harm her. Not when I—my *kingdom*—relied on this engagement.

"How are you today?" I asked.

She let out a breath. "I'm fine, Your Majesty."

"I am glad to hear it."

An awkward moment of silence stretched out before us. One of my advisors coughed, breaking the tension. I turned to them, to their sour faces. For a moment, I'd almost forgotten they were there. My father had insisted they come with me to Thalassar to begin grooming me on the foreign politics of this kingdom and on the princess. As if I needed their help to understand her. As if I needed them trailing behind my every move. As if I needed them to tell me how to woo a mer.

"You are dismissed," I told them firmly in Dracon. Their eyes widened, but they stayed where they were. They never wanted to obey me. I cleared my throat. "You may take your leave… *now*." They looked at me reluctantly, looked at the princess, and I knew what they were thinking. They didn't think it safe for me to be alone with her before we were wed. It was scandalous, to go around without a chaperone. What century did they think we were in? I had no interest whatsoever in her, and her guard was there, besides.

Not that Captain Saber could ever defeat me in a battle. I'd probably seen more death and killed more mer than he could have ever dreamed of meeting. In Draconi, we became warriors when we first chose our dragons. We became adults when we drew first blood in battle.

I was known for bloodshed and malice.

I did not need them to guard me.

They turned around and swam away slowly. Only when they were gone did I turn back to Princess Odele. "Princess, will you take a swim with me about the palace?" I offered her my arm out of politeness, almost expecting a clever or irritable retort. If she didn't take my arm, there was nothing I had to lose. Taking a turn around the palace with her gave me the perfect excuse to get away from my advisors.

If she declined, it gave me the perfect excuse to get away from *her*.

In this moment, she just seemed the lesser of two evils.

"That would be lovely." She smiled widely at me, surprising me entirely as she placed her arm in mine. She'd never touched me willingly before unless news conches were present, recording our every move for the kingdom. Even then, her touch had always been cold, callous.

Her palm was warm.

We began our swim. It was slow and awkward those first few moments, but then the silence stretched into something far more comfortable as I peeked sideways at her. There was a tentative smile on her lips as she looked around at the high arched ceilings and windows of the castle. Her facial expressions made it seem as though she were seeing the place for the first time. As if she hadn't grown up here.

Almost as if… as if she were an outsider looking in.

I was so enthralled in her expressions as she looked around, so lost in the trance of her eyes that I didn't notice or register the words that came out of her moving mouth.

"Excuse me?" I blinked.

She turned to me then. "I apologize for what you heard. I—I don't know what came over me—"

"I assure you, it's alright."

"It's not, though. It was cruel of me to say that."

I blinked at the mer who would be my wife, and inexplicable anger swelled up inside me. I'd never lost my temper around her. I never raised my voice or responded to any of her grievous comments because I knew it would give her satisfaction. But this pretending?

I could no longer hold back my words. "Really, Odele, there's no need to pretend. I know our engagement was one of convenience and no love exists between us. I'm not a fool. I know you dislike me. Do not insult me by feigning otherwise."

Her relaxed posture tensed in an instant. Slowly, she pulled her hand from my arm and brought it back to her side. Something in her face fell, completely broke in that instant. And for a moment, the look in her black eyes broke me too, despite my words.

I came to a halt, grabbing her arm to stop her. She gave a tiny gasp. The captain started forward, so I dropped my hand, took a stroke back. I wanted to groan, shout. Instead, I ran a hand through my hair with frustration.

"Princess, forgive me. I haven't seen you in months. In all that time, whenever I inquired about you with the queen and king, they told me you were not well enough yet. Now, you are here and..." I trailed off, looking over her lithe form.

"And now I'm different?" she asked with a sad smile on her lips. I nodded and she sighed.

I found myself once again enthralled in her every detail. My emotions contrasting with my head because this situation was so different from what it had been since I'd arrived. She was different. Not just in the way she moved and the way she spoke, but in the way she dressed and carried herself. She was not weighed down with heavy layers of makeup and jewels. She was no longer rounded in figure but thin, muscular. Her nose was a little sharper than usual, the tip of it tilting up ever so slightly. Her eyes were a darker shade of black, hair a darker shade of purple.

"Maybe the illness has changed me a bit," she said quietly but firmly. From the corner of my eye, I saw the captain shoot her a warning glance. "Maybe I want a chance now to make things right."

I wasn't sure if I believed her or if she was just playing me for a fool. But gods, I wanted to believe her every word. Perhaps I was a fool to hope for affection. But I wanted an amicable marriage. So I found myself smiling at her and offering her my arm once again. "Then shall we continue our swim, Princess?"

"We shall, Prince."

And she put her hand in my arm, and I felt in that moment something shift between us.

Maisie

I FELT THE WARMTH on my arm and the tingles running up my skin throughout the night. I felt them the next day when I got up and the maids readied me for the anniversary dinner that would take place late in the afternoon.

The prince's touch had provoked an unrest over my body. In a way that I'd never felt from anyone before. Even now, when I'd lathered every inch of my skin with sand in the tub, I could still feel the heat of his mouth. It lingered, a phantom against my skin.

The whisper of his soft voice echoed through my mind. His beautiful face like a painting in my memories. One I wanted to trace the strokes of with my fingertips. I wanted to study the artistry of his panes. The sharp curve of his cheekbones tapering down to a pointed chin, the deep brown eyes that held secrets and mischief.

"How different is Thalassar from Draconi?" I'd asked. The question had caused a low growl of disapproval to emanate from Captain Saber as he trailed behind us. He obviously went ignored.

The question seemed to startle the prince. He blinked at me slowly, taking me in. It felt like he was seeing me for the first time. I supposed, in a way, he kind of was. He'd seen Princess Odele plenty, but he hadn't seen *my* version of Princess Odele.

"It is… very different."

I'd heard stories of all the seven sea kingdoms. They were whispered by merchants who went to Lagoona to trade. Draconi had been just another kingdom they whispered about. A kingdom of dragons and malicious rulers. They boasted a mighty army who rode atop dragons like hippocampi. No warrior was fiercer than the Emperor of Draconi.

And none more powerful than the Dragon Prince at her side.

It seemed weird to think of him in battle. She supposed those long fingers were made for more than gentle touches against her arm. They were made for wielding swords. For taking lives. It seemed so at odds with those gentle eyes and soft words.

"I hear you… have a dragon…"

His hand tensed over my wrist before his grip eased a fraction. He smoothed the action out with his fingers. "I do."

I heard the longing in his voice, and it made my heart ache.

"Why didn't you bring her?"

He cleared his throat. "My father thought she would frighten you Thalassarins. I left her behind as a show of good faith."

Right.

"What is she like?"

I wasn't sure who the question startled more. Captain Saber, who scoffed, or Prince Kai, who sucked in a breath.

There was a moment of contemplative silence in which I wondered if the prince was deciding whether he should answer me or not. He finally did, and it was in a tone that told me how much his dragon meant to him.

"She is wonderful. I have no adequate words to describe her. In Draconi, we have a tradition where, when we come of age, we must choose our dragon by swimming through their breeding waters."

"Isn't that… dangerous?"

He chuckled. "Yes. But how else are we to prove we are worthy of such amazing creatures? My dragon chose me in my coming-of-age ceremony." His eyes got a distant look. "I do miss her."

We spent the next few minutes talking about his dragon. His eyes lit up as he spoke, holding me enraptured in every word. I was almost sad when we arrived at the princess' rooms.

It wasn't just because of his beautiful face or kind, soft voice. I tried to tell myself that I wanted to get to know him, to be kind to him, because I wanted him and the princess to get along.

A happy couple was a happy kingdom.

Right.

I reminded myself not to get attached to anyone in this kingdom. I was here for one thing and one thing only. To fix it for the good of the mer. My life and Lagoona's future were at stake. I couldn't afford to be distracted by pretty, dark eyes. Or warm lips that had hovered a bit too long over my knuckles when we'd said our goodbyes the night before.

My face flushed at the memory. At the way his eyes had glowed with newfound mischief as he looked up at me through dark lashes. The captain had been off to the side, glaring daggers my way the entire time. When the prince had left, I hurried into the room and closed the doors before the captain could utter a word.

I didn't need them. I knew what I was doing. Didn't I? No. I pushed doubt away. I had to stick with the plan. I wouldn't make it if I couldn't fake it, and I *had* to fake being the princess. That meant inheriting her entire attitude. But what was she like, really? From what I'd gathered studying telly casts about her and from studying the personalities of those around her, she seemed to be no different than other royals.

She probably didn't hold doors open for mer. She didn't dress herself or care about the staff. Prince Kai obviously had no affection for her. Maybe she was just as bad as my mind had conjured up. But could I really dive into that personality and come out with my soul still intact?

I was starting to think I had no other choice.

An anniversary dinner at the royal court was more than what I imagined. It was lavish. Overwhelming. I didn't know why I'd expected it to be a small affair with only close family and friends. I was so wrong.

Diplomats from all around had shown up. Princes and princesses, dukes and duchesses, lords and ladies. There were distant cousins so far removed that they were no longer even on the royal coral branch. Friends and their families, guests of all shapes and sizes, dipped in finery. And reporters recording every single moment on their enormous conches.

I swallowed the sudden lump in my throat and clasped my hands together to keep them from trembling. It looked like everyone in the kingdom was here. Everyone they deemed important enough to attend, anyway. My fins quaked and I fought to keep them steady under this heavy weight of reality.

I was terrified.

The captain was behind me, keeping a close eye on every flickering movement near and far. He was decked out in a dark blue military jacket with red coral trimming on the lapels. The color really offset the bright blue of his eyes. He wore a military hat, in black as well, and a scabbard at his waist with a long, needle-thin blade. The sight of it only made me miss mine, so I tried not to look too long in that direction.

I was floating next to the queen and king. They were both very beautiful. The queen made it a point to ignore me unless a conch recorder was pointed our way. She was in an extravagant dress made in a deep shade of purple that matched her tail. Her crown was silver and studded with blue sapphires that were so dark they looked violet. Heavy jewelry adorned her long neck and thin wrists.

The king didn't speak a word to me, but he did look at me from over his wife's crown, eyes narrowing. He was wearing royal blue robes with thin silver threading and a tall silver crown. Silver clips were threaded through his hair and his beard. The massive expanse of his shoulders was intimidating.

I had dressed, not in colors as bright as theirs, but in a more modest attire. A dress in beige-pink embroidered with silver flowers. The dress had a heart shaped neckline and sleeves that reached to my elbows. It hugged me tight enough against my upper body but was loose and in gossamer layers down at the waist.

The crown on my head weighed heavily, even though it was thin and wiry, glittering with colorful gems. It felt like a mockery. I was just an imposter masked in jewels and finery to look like the princess. But I wasn't her.

The soft touch of fingers tugging at the back layers of my dress brought me away from that panic. I glanced back, but the fingers were gone. Captain Saber's bright eyes held mine a brief moment before he resumed his duties of monitoring the royal dining hall.

That small touch of faith gave me the confidence to hold my head high and smile. In my mind I repeated the names that got me through it.

Josiah.

Christof.

Lagoona.

The Black Blade.

Repeating it in my mind reminded me who I was floating next to. The tyrants who were destroying my mer and the poor. I had to pretend to love them, and I had to make a change. There were diplomats, leaders, and other important mer at this anniversary dinner, if I could get involved in conversation, I could make something happen, like a wave crashing against the shore.

Our arrival was announced, and the blaring of horns silenced the entire hall. I held my breath as the conch recorders found us and halted there. They'd record our every move, and I had to be flawless. I smiled as we descended the stairs in slow, even strokes. I concentrated hard on not tripping, willing my fins to go on despite the strain I had them under. It was a difficult task, to hide my limp, and I nearly sighed with relief when we reached the bottom of the steps.

The mer bowed to us as we passed, and I noticed the females look at me before whispering behind their sea fans. I tried not to let that trip me up. They were probably just surprised that I—rather, the princess—was up and about after being hidden away for so long.

We made it to our seats at the end of the table, the queen taking the seat at the very head while the king took the place to her right and I the one on her left. More arrivals were announced, among them Prince Kai and his advisors. He looked rather dashing in his long black robes. When he took the seat next to mine, I noticed up close the silver and red embroidered dragon at his back.

He smiled softly at me and, once everyone had been announced and taken their respected places, dinner was served. The conversation around me picked up. I tried grasping bits and pieces of it, pulling the words to me and tucking them into my pockets for examination.

My eyes and ears were everywhere at once, staring at the diplomat from Iol across from me, and the Prince of Ventlair next to *him.*

"Are you well, Princess?" Prince Kai's voice cut through my examination around the room. My gaze jerked over to him. He was staring at me, though I couldn't be sure what was in his dark gaze. "You haven't touched your food."

I looked down at the plate before me. Food sat in the finest China I'd ever seen. It was a light and frothy green soup that looked more like sea foam, the surface sprinkled with little brown unrecognizable specks. Though Captain Saber had given me lessons on dining etiquette, he'd never given me *this.*

Ugh.

"I'm fine." I smiled at him and picked up my spoon. When I tasted the soup, I wanted to cringe. This is what they ate at palace parties? It had somehow tasted worse than the food I'd been given during my lessons. Or maybe I was just sick of the awful taste and texture. Either way, I wasn't sure I could down this whole thing.

When I looked over to Prince Kai, he seemed to be playing with his soup as well.

I smirked. At least I wasn't the only one who thought it was atrocious. "What's your favorite food, Your Majesty?" I asked him.

The prince appeared surprised by my question. I wondered if that novelty would ever wear off whenever I opened my mouth. Had Princess Odele never bothered to ask him, to get to know him? Or had she already asked him that and I'd blown it? I waited nervously for his reply.

"There is this food in Draconi called Nii-chin. It is a ball of seaweed stuffed with cooked shrimp and Wasagri peppers. The commoners eat it, and my sister snuck out one day and brought a whole bundle back. I'd never tasted anything so delicious." His smile was sweet as he recalled this pleasant memory.

I smiled right with him. "How many sisters do you have?" I asked impulsively and regretted it immediately. Odele would have probably already known that. I should already know that. All of Captain Saber's lessons blended together and I found myself forgetting every single one for a brief flash.

Luckily, he didn't startle or freeze at my question. His smile grew wider. "I have about ninety-eight sisters."

I choked. "Ninety-eight?" My eyes widened to an impossible fraction.

"Half-sisters, really," he explained. "My father, as I'm sure you're aware, has many concubines."

Concubines. Right. His father was the emperor, and from what I'd studied, he was allowed to do what he wanted and rule as he wished. All of his children, even if they weren't born of the empress, were considered royalty. How different the two cultures seemed.

"I am his only son," he went on, his voice getting tighter. "And when he deemed it time for me to marry, he arranged it with the richest, most desperate available bride he could find." He winced and looked at me. "Sorry," he muttered apologetically.

I smiled a little sadly at him. Thalassar was desperate for troops and Draconi was rich in warriors. It was rumored that even their princesses rode out to war. I could see why the alliance would be beneficial to Thalassar. But why would *his* kingdom need the alliance?

I didn't ask.

"What's *your* favorite food?" he asked after a moment.

The smells of Tides' Tavern stews suddenly assaulted my memories and my stomach growled. I pushed away my embarrassment with a laugh. "Stuffed pond slugs and leeches." Just thinking about my favorite meal was making me crave it. I looked distastefully down at my bowl.

"That sounds like an odd sort of food…"

I laughed at his hesitancy. "It sounds gross, but I promise it's very *riptide*."

"Prince Kai, if I may interrupt…" We looked up from our conversation to find Iol's foreign diplomat looking at us. There was a smile on his face, but it didn't seem genuine. It reminded me a lot of a barracuda. With his icy eyes and pale, blond hair, there was something strangely sinister about him. "How are things in your kingdom? What with the raids and impoverished streets…" He picked up his goblet and took a sip, watching Prince Kai closely over the rim of it.

Prince Kai tensed, his hand wrapping around the base of his own goblet as if to keep himself steady. The tension was palpable as I stared between the two. And suddenly I remembered. Raids. Poverty. My heart sank.

That's why Kai desperately needed this alliance. His kingdom was being nearly overrun with two-leggers. The vile creatures were hunting through his waters, leaving parts of his kingdom—villages and the like—in an impoverished state.

Their alliance was meant to fortify the kingdoms. It was meant to be a show of force. Would Kappur really attack Thalassar if they had the aid of thousands of warriors and dragons? And it was said that Thalassar had the best mages that could protect them from two-legger invasions.

Only mages could weave spells and manipulate matter to the benefit of the kingdoms. Not every kingdom had one, and it left them vulnerable to attacks.

It was why we'd remained so safe from them for years, even being so close to them in Lagoona.

And if I was guessing correctly, the kingdom of Iol despised Draconi.

"We are doing all we can to fortify our kingdom against the two-legger raids," Kai replied smoothly.

The diplomat put his goblet down and chuckled cruelly. "I'm sure the emperor is fortifying your kingdom… straight from the sheets of his concubines' beds."

There was enough venom and judgment packed into his voice that Prince Kai stiffened. I looked at his hand and was sure he'd crush the goblet beneath his tight grip.

It seemed the whole table had gone silent as they watched the exchange. Even the queen and king had paused mid-sentence to see what retort Prince Kai would come up with. My mind raced in circles as I tried keeping up with names, faces, stations and politics. I vaguely remembered that Iol didn't approve of Draconi's violent way of ruling.

I picked up my own goblet and brought it to my lips. "Tell me, Mister Shallows, how is your Prime Minister faring?" He turned his startled gaze to me. I bet he hadn't counted on me to speak.

"Faring, Princess?"

I nodded, took a slow sip, swallowed, and smiled. "It cannot be easy, having to tax the mer grievous amounts of coin to feed them while keeping it for himself before he's run out of office. Such a shame, to let his poor subjects *starve* in the streets without medical aid or governmental assistance…" He sputtered and I held my goblet up in a mockery of a toast before taking another sip then setting it down.

I had no idea if what I'd said was true. Iol was the kingdom we knew less about. We knew they had a monarchy but were ruled by the Prime Minister. We did not, however, know what this monarchy looked like or who they were, really. Captain Saber had told me Mister Shallows was here to change that. To start to build relationships between Thalassar and the secretive, northern kingdom. Regardless of what we didn't know, Josiah had been filled with enough government conspiracies from all around to last me a lifetime. Anything to get his attention off Prince Kai.

The shocked gasps that rang around at my words were followed by tense laughter coming from diplomat Shallows himself. "My, what an imagination you have, Your Majesty."

I smiled mockingly at him and didn't lose the expression even when the queen leaned in to hiss in my ear. "What are you doing?"

I turned to her, smile still in place. "Blending in, *mother*."

The queen had the power to kill me where I sat. I shouldn't provoke her. But right now, I was safe. Right now, I was the princess and there were reporters crammed in every corner of the room, keeping a watchful eye on us all.

She leaned away from me, but I didn't miss the slashing anger in her eyes. And the king, he merely looked at me while stroking his beard. As if he knew a secret that I didn't. It was unnerving.

Soft fingers against the back of my hand had me turning to Prince Kai. "Thank you," he whispered low.

"My pleasure." I picked up my spoon and began eating what was before me, listening intently as the conversations picked up once again. Trying to grasp any words regarding the war or Kappur that I could jump on and join in.

I'd almost given up on the royals entirely. Their conversations were filled with nothing but shallow babble. Most of them seemed as dumb as guppies and as clumsy as tadpoles. The conversations left much to be desired, and I wondered if the princess hadn't swum away from home just so she'd never have to deal with another minute of this torture.

"Come Wavesday, the new selects should be ready to head over to enemy lines for battle."

My attention snapped up to the queen. She was deeply engaged in conversation with the king and diplomat Shallows. I leaned closer to listen.

"And how are the selects looking this month around?" Shallows asked.

"Stronger than the last. No one has tried escaping yet, so we can thank the tides for that," the king replied.

Shallows snorted as he reached for his goblet. "Ungrateful mer. You'd think they'd be proud to service the royals that keep them fed and alive."

My nails scraped against the polished table, anger bubbling up my throat.

"You know how the freshwater mer are." The queen flicked off his concerns with the wave of her fingers. "They cannot think past the ponds they see. Think everything revolves around them."

I couldn't hold my words back any longer. "That's not true!" I nearly shouted. When every head turned to look at me, I cleared my throat and repeated in a much softer but no less firm tone, "I am sure that's not true. The freshwater mer are not born and bred for battle, after all."

The queen glared at me, and I was sure she'd kill me with her eyes if she could.

"No one is born and bred for battle, Your Majesty," Shallows said dismissively. "It is something that is taught. Only cowards swim away from their duties."

I tried to keep my voice civil, but my teeth were grinding in my rage. "It is not the job of farmers to wield weapons of war while royal soldiers remain safe at the palace." They all looked at me as though I'd sprouted a bulbous squid head. Still, I pushed on. "It could be the reason why Thalassar is suffering under this war."

They sent selects out to do their fighting so they wouldn't have to pay soldiers, so that their coffers wouldn't suffer. Why pay widows of war when they were sending out widows to fight in the first place? Another lesson learned from Josiah.

"The soldiers remain at the palace in case of the event of an invasion. Who else to protect the kingdom's rulers? It is thanks to them that Eramaea remains safe." Shallows had his chin resting on intertwined fingers and was watching me intently, almost as if he couldn't quite believe that the princess was involving herself in the first place.

Had she really been that daft?

"The wine is going to her head, I'm afraid," the queen said, and then she leaned closer to me. "If you want to keep your head intact, I suggest you keep your mouth clamped shut."

I wanted to argue, to convince them to look for peace instead, but I turned away and let them resume their conversation without me. Had I really thought it would be so easy? That I could convince royalty who had thrived off lesser mer's hard work to change their ways over one dinner?

I felt his fingertips trail against the bare skin on my arm. I turned to look at Prince Kai, and he offered me a sad smile. "Are you okay?"

Yes. The word was stuck in my throat. But the truth was, I wasn't okay. They didn't seem inclined to listen to me at all. I was the princess, but I was a foolish one at that. How could I get them to listen to someone who had never cared for politics in the first place?

A waiter showed up and placed a pitcher of wine before us. Prince Kai reached for it immediately, topping off his own goblet and then mine. "When they see you as a child, they will brush you aside until you are useful to them." He picked up his goblet and gestured that I do the same. I reached for it and held it up. "We are smarter than they think and know more than what they'd like to admit."

I smirked; he was right. "They fear the knowledge we hold."

He nodded once and then clinked his glass to mine. "When we become better rulers than they ever were, they will see."

I brought the cup to my lips eagerly and downed most of the drink in one go. It wasn't princess-like or even merlady-like, but I did not care. I set the goblet down and turned to smile at Prince Kai, only to have my world spin wildly around me.

A sudden, blinding pain clenched my gut within seconds. I groaned, reaching for my stomach.

"Princess?" Prince Kai was looking at me with concern, but his face blurred across my vision. A vicious wave of nausea roiled over me, and I tried to get up, but only managed to knock over dishes.

"Princess!"

Shouting around me became distant in my ears as my tail gave in under me and I went crashing to the polished floor. My whole body trembled, and I felt arms pressing up against me.

There was the whisper of "Poison…" just before I gave in to the darkness.

I WATCHED HER FALL to the floor. Before I could register what was happening, before I could even rush to help her, Captain Saber was there, pulling her into his arms.

I watched, heart thundering a wild beat in my chest as he looked her over. For a moment, everything froze. I knew of nothing except the stillness of her body and how fragile her thin frame looked as the captain cradled her in his arms.

"Poison!" His eyes flared with rage, with pain of a loss, and the thunderous need for violence.

Before I knew it, the goblet I held was being slapped out of my hand by an advisor. I felt numb as I looked over to him, to the panic in his eyes. I knew what he was thinking. I was the emperor's only heir. If I were to die, our kingdom would be doomed.

But I didn't care about that. I didn't care about anything but Princess Odele being held tight in Captain Saber's arms. Blood began to dribble from the corner of her mouth and float in tendrils above her body. She wasn't moving. *Why wasn't she moving?* And more importantly, who had poisoned her?

"Escort Prince Kai to his rooms and keep him there!" The captain began barking out commands to the soldiers rushing through the sudden chaos of the situation. And then he was swimming away, clutching the princess tightly to his chest, his hand cradled at the back of her head to keep her in place.

I was suddenly grabbed, pushed among the sudden frenzy of the crowd as I was ushered toward the stairway. I followed on a numb fin, and I couldn't help but look back to where we'd been sitting and laughing mere moments ago. To where she'd been hurriedly taken from the room.

Poison. Poison. Poison. The words mocked me, enraged me. But above all, they worried me.

Something in me started crumbling. Just when we had begun to get along. Just when I was beginning to crave her nearness, to want to be around her, the world had been cruel enough to try and take her from me.

Something deep inside my chest, my soul, that had slumbered for so long *snapped.* I could hear it. The beast inside rumbling, awakening. Phantom claws raked through my insides, threatening to emerge. Threatening destruction. Retribution.

Vengeance.

I turned to my advisor and said to him in our mother tongue, *"Find who did this."* His eyes widened at the menace in my usually calm voice. At the flash in my eyes as the Dragon Prince was awakened once more. He bowed his head in acquiescence. *"When you find the mer, bring them to me. Alive."*

I KNEW ONLY DARKNESS and pain. Nothing else existed. Nothing else could slip within the edges of the two. My body raged with fever one moment before trembling against an icy cold the next. I drowned in nightmares that were so vivid, I couldn't help but scream as though they were real.

Shadows flickered and slithered against the scales of my flesh, threatening to drag me under, to hold me down.

And to never let me resurface.

Agony pulled me awake. I rolled over in the darkness, knowing nothing about where or even who I was. All I knew was the pain that held me in a tight fist and had me heaving. My stomach roiled painfully, and I clutched at it, but there was no easing whatever was inside.

The light brush of something against my face had me swatting against the darkness in fear. My head was too muddled to think clearly. But I breathed in and out. In. Out. Until finally, my brain cleared for a mere moment, just enough for me to remember who I was. *Maisie Fauna*. And where I was. *The palace.*

I sat up, gently easing my tail from the side of the bed. A mistake, because pain shot straight through my skull, nearly blinding me. I heaved a breath and fell forward, hitting the wall beside the bed. My limbs ached and screamed in protest as I tried getting up, fingernails clawing against the wall. They came in touch with something soft. I struggled to remember what it was. Oh, right. A tapestry. I hauled myself up, shoulder sliding up against the wall.

I tugged…

And the tapestry came falling down.

I groaned in pain. Poison. Someone had poisoned me. Why? Did it matter? My hands slid up the wall to keep myself upright. I put pressure on my palm and heard the sliding of stone against stone. And suddenly, the wall that was keeping me upright was gone and I was falling through empty space.

I reeled back before I could hit the floor, causing a pain I'd never known to electrify me all the way down to my tailfin. Wiping a hand across my vision to clear it, I looked up at where the wall had been and stared into a hallway of sorts. Inside, nothing but blackness greeted me.

This can't be real.

I pushed through it, my fins screaming at every movement. The darkness was too thick to see anything through, anyway. I pressed my hands against the outer edges of the doorway, pushing my fingers against stone. A piece of it caved in and then the wall seemed to materialize once again.

My stomach heaved as I bent down, fingers fumbling for the tapestry on the floor. When I finally gripped it, I tried for what felt like an eternity to hang it back up where it had been. That miniscule task had worn me out, had my body on the edge of collapsing.

Trembling, I took a stroke, then two, but it was all I managed before I let the darkness drag me under once more.

Small rays of light beams shone down against my eyes. I blinked several times, though my lids felt heavy with the weight of sleep. I managed to open them and glance around at my surroundings. My body was shaking from the cold, and I soon saw why. I was sprawled on the floor by the bed and still wearing the dress I'd worn to the anniversary dinner.

I lifted myself up on shaking arms and looked around the room. Small rays of phytoplankton pierced past the sea glass to cast a rainbow of illuminative colors against the floors and walls.

My whole body ached and my mind raced, struggling to remember events from the day before. There had been the anniversary dinner. Arguing with diplomats about the selects. And then… I'd toasted with Prince Kai. After that there was nothing but darkness.

Poison.

I'd been poisoned.

But the question was, were they trying to poison *me* or the princess? Not me. No one here knew who I was aside from Captain Saber, the queen, king, a few guards. No. I couldn't have been the target. That much was clear even through my poison-addled mind. So, an even bigger question still, was who wanted Princess Odele dead?

I swam jerkily over to the bed and sat on the edge. Every muscle in me ached. The pain reminding me of the gator attack that had destroyed my fin. Except this was much, much worse. I hunched over my tail and breathed in and out as an attempt to control it.

When I looked up again, my gaze fell on the wall beside the bed. The tapestry that had hung there was crooked, hanging on by a single hook. I narrowed my eyes at it when the memories suddenly came back to me in an instant.

Last night, the panel on the wall, the doorway…

Had it been real? Or had it been a dream?

I got up slowly and swam over. My shaking fingers moved the tapestry aside to reveal the wall behind. Polished quartz, like the rest of the palace. Maybe it *had* been a dream. I was about to turn away when something caught my eye.

I pressed my face closer to the wall, squinting my eyes to see the thin outline against it, like a crack in the stone. Taking a breath, I pressed my hand against it and there was the familiar sound of stone scraping against stone as that small piece of quartz was pushed inwards.

A dull scraping sound filled the room, and I jolted back as the wall suddenly parted to reveal the dark entrance of a doorway. My heart thundered wildly, my breath hitching as it struggled to catch up with my racing mind. It hadn't been a dream. I hadn't imagined it in a delirious fever.

The princess had a secret passage in her bedroom.

Fear tried to slide doubt into my mind, but my curiosity got the best of me, and I swam slowly into the entrance. But it was dark, too dark to see anything in front of me. I made it five swim strokes in when the sudden touch of something slimy against my fin had me shuddering and racing back to the entrance.

Something was in there, something more mysterious than the creature that had slithered over me. It could be the answer to the mystery of her disappearance. How had she disappeared straight under the noses of guards and palace courtiers? Could this be a passage that had led her out? And if so, did no one else know about it?

I'd have to explore it, to find answers at the end of it.

A knocking at the door pulled me out of those thoughts. Quickly, I pressed the panel again and the wall slid back into place, then I straightened the tapestry until it looked as though it hadn't been bothered in the first place and swam as quickly as I could manage into the bed.

The doors opened a second later, and mer I didn't recognize shuffled in wearing white medical robes. Following behind them was Captain Saber. His eyes locked on mine, and I swore I saw relief slash through his blue depths.

The medics rushed to my bedside and bowed respectfully. "Your Majesty, it is such a relief to see you awake."

I managed to give them a weak smile, though my own gaze remained on the captain. He was at the fin of the bed, his posture rigid straight, hand on the hilt of his sword. Maybe he meant to cut the medics down, if they even touched me wrong. Funny, it almost seemed like he truly cared.

"Yeah." I sat up again the cushiony mound at my back. Speaking hurt my throat, made it burn. "What a crazy night."

The medics looked to each other. "Your Majesty… you've been unconscious for seven days."

My breath froze as soon as it climbed up my throat. "Seven days?" I choked out.

They nodded. "The poison left you unconscious. You are lucky to be alive."

"Right." I fought back the panic. Seven days. I'd been knocked out for seven days because someone had poisoned me.

I kept my gaze focused straight ahead if only to avoid looking at the tapestry by the side of the bed.

The medics got to work, checking my temperature and looking me over. "Are you in pain?" the medic asked.

I turned to look at him. He was an old merman with kind eyes and gentle, firm fingers. "My body hurts," I confessed.

He nodded. "That's normal. The poison is flushing from your system. Sea wasp poison is quite deadly, indeed."

Which meant that the culprit had meant to kill, not maim. I shuddered at the idea. When I'd agreed to being the princess, I hadn't known the dangers it would entail. After all, why would anyone want to kill someone so daft and selfish? Unless… unless she hadn't been as daft as she seemed.

"Where is she?"

I looked up with a startled expression to the entrance of the room. Prince Kai was pushing past the captain's trusted soldiers to get through. My heart fell to the pit of my stomach.

"Let him through," the captain ordered tightly, though his eyes never once left the prince as his mermen moved aside and let him into the room.

Prince Kai didn't seem to notice the distrust circulating through the room. He swam right over to the bed, nearly pushing the medic away as he perched himself on the edge and reached for my hands. I felt my face flush as he lowered his head and pressed kisses to the backs of my knuckles.

When he looked up, his dark eyes were distraught. "Princess…" The word came out strangled. "Thank the Great Dragon…" He lowered his lids as if praying before searching my face, looking for any sign of the sickness.

I was suddenly self-conscious, all too aware of the heavy, leaden texture of my tongue, the parched lips, and my more than likely pale parlor. I was still in the dress from the dinner, for tides' sakes. I probably smelled.

He didn't seem to care as he pulled me gently into his arms, pressing his hand against the back of my head to hold me in place briefly before leaning me back against the bed. "Prince Kai…" My head spun quickly, and my breath came out in small pants.

His hand came to rest against my cheek, pushing away a stray lock of hair with the pad of his thumb. "They refused me entry for days. They refused to give me any news of you." I reached for his hand, the movement subconscious. The tips of my fingers grazed against his knuckles, feeling the split, scabbing skin there. My brows furrowed but he pulled his hands away, hiding them within the long sleeves of his kimono. Almost as if he didn't want me to see.

"Her Majesty's condition was critical," Captain Saber said from his position at the end of the bed. He was glaring at the prince, his posture rigid, distrustful. "She was not well enough to receive visitors."

Prince Kai slashed the captain with a glare that startled me. His otherwise gentle demeanor was gone. "I am her betrothed," he ground out tightly. "I have a right to see her. To inquire about her well-being. To worry."

The captain's lip twitched. "Yes. Though I have to wonder, and forgive me, *Prince,* but were you actually worried for the princess' well-being or for your own position should she die?"

Prince Kai's face went red at the declaration, and I couldn't help the pain that squeezed at my heart. I wasn't the princess. I knew that if and when she was found, I would leave and never see the Prince of Draconi again. But the cold cruelty in the captain's voice, the flushing of the prince's face was all the confirmation I needed.

He cared about himself. About his kingdom. The expression in his eyes suddenly made much more sense. The relief hadn't been for me at all.

"Princess…"

I wasn't the princess. But already I was falling into the illusion that I was. That Prince Kai somehow belonged to me. Otherwise, why did the truth hurt so much?

I clasped my hands in my lap, and before the prince could open his mouth to argue, I spoke, "Please leave." My voice was as cold as the captain's words and as quiet as a whisper. When I looked up, Prince Kai's face was shocked; hurt, even.

"You cannot think that's true…" He reached for me and froze when I cringed back. The stiff posture was back in an instant. Gone was the caring expression and in its place a mask of indifference that he seemed to have perfected so well. "As you wish, Your Majesty." He gave me a stiff bow. When he rose, those dark eyes of his flashed like a bolt of lightning. It somehow filled me with both fear and anticipation. Like I was prey and he was predator. But then it was gone.

And so was he.

"If you could all please leave. Everyone but Captain Saber."

The medics gathered their supplies, bowed awkwardly and left, closing the doors behind them. Even with them gone, his posture, his expression didn't change. I looked up at him through my purple lashes. Everything in me ached. Somehow, the emotional hurt worse than the physical.

"Did you find the culprit?" I asked.

The captain stiffened and then slowly shook his head. "We are actively looking. Even the prince has been—" He broke off with an irate shake of his head. "It does not matter. We have not found them."

The prince has been what? I didn't ask that, but I thought back to Prince Kai's bruised knuckles and couldn't help but wonder… But that was ridiculous. I swallowed and met the captain's gaze. "I want my blade back."

"No."

I glared. "Captain, someone is trying to murder me—the princess, you know what I mean—and I do not want to go around without protection." The blade would offer some sort of comfort, even if I didn't know how to wield it. But he didn't need to know that last bit.

"You have protection," he said tightly.

I snorted. "Sorry, but how well has that worked out? I don't want to be rude, but you and your soldiers couldn't keep the real princess safe, and you certainly couldn't stop me from getting poisoned. I need *more*."

"Then we will double the soldiers—"

"No," I interrupted. "What happens when one of your soldiers turns out to be the culprit? I cannot rely on guards at every second. I need my blade."

"A princess cannot swim around—"

"I am not the princess!" I shouted then, hands fisting the blankets. Sensing my distress, the anemones flowed over to me and caressed my arms in the slight sting of their embrace. I pushed them aside, calmed my breathing. "I am not the princess," I repeated. "And I will never be the princess. No amount of pretending will turn me into her. I am not a helpless royal, and I want my weapon to defend myself should I ever need it."

The captain was quiet a long moment after that. From where I sat, I could make out the slow workings of his square jaw as he contemplated my words. The side of his mouth twitched, and he sighed. "I will think it over."

I scowled at him. What else had to happen to me for him to agree to give me my blade back? Did I have to get attacked on Eramaea's streets for him to finally see reason?

"Get some rest." That was his goodbye as he turned and swam from the room.

The dragon reared its head from within, banging against the cage of my mind. My bruised knuckles throbbed at my sides, and I tried to hide the evidence of my more violent side from beneath the long sleeves of my clothes.

It was common knowledge throughout the seven sea kingdoms that I went by the name of Dragon Prince. Not just because I came from the kingdom of dragons, but because of what lived in my blood. A monster. A beast that transformed me into something dangerous.

Something deadly.

If anyone dared to ask, I would have confessed that the dragon was a separate entity, but the truth was we were one and the same.

So when I was dismissed from Princess Odele's rooms, I forced myself to leave because I swore if I didn't, that feral side of me would show and I did not want her to see that part of me. So when her fingers grazed along my bloody knuckles, evidence of what I'd done in an attempt to locate the scum who tried to harm her, I had to hide them.

I didn't know why I even cared. Perhaps Captain Saber was correct and I feared more for the fate of my own kingdom and not the princess, but in my heart I knew it wasn't true. The princess was changed. Different. And something in me felt a pull towards what I saw in her.

I cared.

And though she'd tossed me from her room due to doubts, I would not stop caring.

Maybe our relationship had started off on bad terms, but I would not let it continue to be that way.

I swore, on the rage of the dragon that lived inside me, that I would prove to her that I cared. And if the scars on my knuckles weren't enough for her then I would decimate the entire kingdom of Thalassar until it was.

I DRANK THE TONICS the medics had left me, albeit reluctantly. When the pain had become too much, I'd downed them in one go and prayed I wouldn't fall into more feverish dreams of poison. The pain receded, but my lids closed involuntarily, and I fell into a dreamless sleep.

When I finally awoke some hours later, I sat up in bed. There was a dull ache where the terrible pain had once been, and I was grateful it was finally subsiding. Because I couldn't sit for one moment longer in this bed. Not when I had a mission to accomplish.

I didn't need to peek out the doors to the bedroom to know that Captain Saber had probably posted guards there. If I was going to go through that mysterious passageway, I didn't want them finding out. Who was to say one of the guards hadn't been the culprit? I could trust no one until I found out more information.

So I went over to the telly and opened the top shell like a compact. The bubble that emerged immediately began dancing and playing images. Royal tellies were obviously way more advanced than what we had at Lagoona. The sound inside the bubble was loud. Perfect.

After that, I went to the vanity table and, as quietly as I could, pulled the chair over to the doors and propped it just under the handle. If they wanted to get in, I'd be alerted to it. Then I searched through the princess' things, not caring what I knocked over or broke in the process. I'd taken poison that was meant for her; if she couldn't forgive me, then that was her own problem.

Finally, I found a large tube of red squid ink and a palm-sized lava globe. I swam quickly over to the wall, pulled the tapestry to the side, and pressed my palm against the panel. When the walls opened, I took a deep breath and swam inside, letting the tapestry fall back behind me.

It was dark, but the small lava globe gave off enough illumination so I could navigate my way around the space. I made sure to mark red squid ink along the walls as I swam through. If I squinted through the darkness, I could barely make out the barnacles crusted on the ceiling.

This passage wasn't made of quartz like the rest of the palace. It was stone and element, rocks that were chipped away over the years, seaweed growing and critters of the darkness hiding through. I swallowed my nerves as I pushed on.

The hall was small and confined, and so far I'd not come across any bends or forks. I felt like I'd been swimming for too long when I finally came to a dead end. I frowned, turning in a slow circle with the lava globe in my hand. I was sure I hadn't passed any other ways. This couldn't be the end of it.

I shone the light on the floor and smiled when I saw the small hole of a tunnel. It was big enough for a mer my size to fit through. I crouched low on the murky, muddy ground and shoved my hand through the hole cautiously. Empty space greeted me on the other side.

I pressed myself low against the ground and pushed my tail, sliding through the tunnel. Silt clouded my eyes and I coughed it away as I slid further and further through the tunnel. Gripping the lava globe tightly in my fist, arm outstretched, I crept low on the ground. I breached it and fell through the open water of a small cove.

Gripping the lava globe tightly in my hand, I spun around. Phytoplankton illuminated the walls and the drop down below. The cavernous space was covered with all sorts of surprising things. I swam down to get a better look.

It was like a shipwreck had exploded down here.

Two-legger objects were scattered everywhere in piles. Tables with missing limbs covered in furry green algae and barnacles, chairs without their cushions, a rusted porcelain bathtub, and a large, full-length mirror with a golden gilded frame that was already rusting away in the water. A chest full of gold coins, rubies, and jewels spilled over on a slab of stone, and then there were conches. Hundreds of conches littered the floor and tabletops of the cavern.

I swam down and rummaged through the things, my fingers passing over two-legger and mer objects alike. It was a mess of paraphernalia that I didn't know what to make of. Was this some kind of secret room that the princess locked herself away in? To be surrounded by junk?

I swam over to the table to look through the objects on top of it. There was a mer device there that I recognized. It was a thin, circular disk made of a material that looked like coral and stone. In the center of it was a placeholder and on it sat a small ivory conch. I'd heard of these objects before. They were very old devices used to project conch recordings. I bent low, wondering how it worked, but when my hand touched the conch in the center, something seemed to activate.

The conch began spinning in slow circles around the disk. From the top chamber of the shell, bubbles began rising to form a single, large floating one.

I held back my surprised gasp as I looked at the image of the princess.

Her image was only a bit blurry. Since the contraption was old, the images projected were strange, faded. But it was clear enough who she was. Her hair was fabulously long, and she wore an extravagantly jeweled crown on her head. She was smiling in my direction, though I knew logically she had been smiling at whoever had recorded her in the moment.

"Is this thing on?" she asked, her voice wispy and melodic. "Hello? Testing, testing. I think it's on. Hi! It's me. The most *fabulous* princess who ever lived in the sea. Odele Malabella Oriana." She flicked her hair back, and I rolled my eyes. She really did seem overly flippant. "Anyway, this is the *fabulous* documentation of *my* life. Follow me as I journey from princess to *queen*."

I reached forward and stopped the recording, prying the conch from the center placeholder. Then, I looked around at all the discarded conch shells on the floor. The princess had documented her life and she'd hidden everything in this cave. Her schedule. Her thoughts. Her *life* was all down here.

I grabbed a conch at random and put it in the center of the disk and started it. It twirled, bubbles rose, and her image appeared once again. This time, it was alarming. Her hair wasn't decked out in jewels, she wasn't smiling. In fact, she looked frightened. Her breathing was heavy, and she sniffled on occasion. Had she been crying? I looked closely at the image.

"It's me," she whispered and took in an airy breath. "Princess Odele Malabella Oriana. And if you're watching this, I want you to know that they're after me—"

The recording suddenly stopped, her image in the bubble bursting and falling around the disk. No! I looked down. What had happened? The disk suddenly gave a jerk and the conch shrieked to a halt. I moved it, trying to start it up again. All it did was make an infuriating scraping noise.

With a groan, I pried the conch off and set it down gently, picking up the disk to examine it. I had no idea what I was looking for, but I had no doubt that it was broken.

Cursing it to the abyss, I dropped it back on the table and bit the inside of my cheek to avoid screaming.

They're after me…

This information changed *everything*. Maybe her disappearance hadn't been because she was a spoiled brat, after all. Maybe she had disappeared because of another reason entirely. But for what reason? Had she known something, seen something she shouldn't have?

The answers were here in this cavern.

But first, I needed to get this disk fixed.

I made it back into the room, secret wall closing behind me, just in time to hear a knock on the bedroom doors. Making sure the tapestry was well adjusted, I hurried to move the chair and then dashed into the bed just as the doors opened and Captain Saber swam through.

His eyes narrowed on me with suspicion immediately. "What's wrong?"

I blew out a breath and tried to appear as casual as possible. "Nothing."

He looked at me a moment longer, and I knew he didn't believe me.

"I—I'm sore."

His expression softened then. Softer than I'd ever seen it. He closed the door behind him and approached the bed. His fingers drifted towards his back, and when they reappeared, they were wielding the black blade. My heart soared at the sight of it. The obsidian hilt, the sharp tip… It was all intact. I longed to lurch for it and pull it from his prying fingers. I didn't need to.

He laid it gently on my lap.

THE JOY THAT LIT up her eyes was unique, beautiful even. The shine in her round depths matched that of the blade she now held in her palms. I did not understand her attachment to that weapon, nor did I want to. Not if it meant treason, given its maker.

"If you are going to *carry* the blade, then I will teach you to *wield* the blade." She blinked at me, surprised I'd even offered. I could see her thoughts racing with all the questions she wanted to ask, so I answered them before she had the chance. "The princess is a skilled fencer. Sooner or later, you will need to learn. I will teach you how."

She closed her gaping mouth and nodded. Gently, she placed the blade next to her on the cushioning of the bed and patted the spot next to her. I didn't move to take a seat. Though she was not the princess, it still wouldn't be proper. I did not want her to get too comfortable with me the way she had seemed to be doing with the prince.

It was best she got any illusions of friendship out of her mind now.

We were nothing to each other.

"I came to speak with you about a few things."

She sighed and leaned back. "What?" The accent we'd worked so hard to instill was gone now; in its place, her harsh pronunciation of words. Her small act of rebellion to grate on my nerves.

"Methods will be taken to ensure that what happened at the anniversary dinner doesn't happen again. That means there will be more soldiers monitoring every hall, taste testers at every meal, and the blacksmith will be here in a few hours to install steel bars on your windows."

She jolted at that and then pierced me with an angry glare. Since I'd expected this, I wasn't fazed. "Bars?" she asked incredulously. "Really? It's not like I could open the window anyway."

"It is for your protection—"

"I'm not your prisoner!"

I sighed. Why was she prone to such tantrums? She was more like Princess Odele than she'd probably want to admit. "I assure you, it's for your safety. To keep intruders out."

"Or to keep me in." She brought her tail up and rested her chin against it, turning her gaze from me to the telly.

"Let's talk about the anniversary dinner to celebrate Princess Odele's and Prince Kai's marriage," the mer on the telly said. I narrowed my eyes at her as if she could see my discontentment. "The tides are bursting with excitement at the latest fashions to be found at the palace. I want to talk about Prince Kai's outfit. It was very traditional and elegant, and he's so beautiful that it *worked*. I love how he wants to remind everyone in Thalassar *where* he's from by honoring the colors and symbols of his own kingdom. And that embroidered dragon on his back?" She shuddered. "He doesn't want anyone forgetting that he's the Dragon Prince of Draconi, known for his skills in the battle waters. And hopefully in other places, too."

I fought back my eye roll and looked over at Maisie when I heard her breath hitch. I wondered if she agreed. If she thought Prince Kai was beautiful, too. She must've, considering the way her face flushed when he was near or the way she flexed her fingers ever so slightly after he pressed his lips to them.

"Now let's talk about Princess Odele's dress. The princess usually follows the tides, keeps up with the latest fashions and outdoes herself each time. But she seemed to dress down for her anniversary dinner. A beige dress with silver threading? How very boring!"

When she took in another sharp breath, I looked at her. She seemed to hug her tail tighter to herself. And I noticed she was still wearing the dress they were talking about.

"I wonder if her newly found modesty was in protest to the engagement. Or maybe she just didn't want to outshine the prince with her own extravagance. We all know she was in bedrest for a few months because of an illness. Well, honey, we could tell. Bags under the eyes? Loss of weight? Come on! Haven't you ever heard of cosmetics?"

I swam over to the telly and slammed the shell closed, cutting off anything else that mer had to say. When I turned back to Maisie, a small bubble tear rose from the corner of her eye.

"She's a bottom feeder," I said unkindly. "She insults everyone. It doesn't matter."

Maisie sniffled. "Yeah." She offered me a sad smile. "It doesn't matter. Hey, Captain, I'm tired. Is it okay if I rest the remainder of the day?"

"Of course."

Without even waiting for me to leave, she pulled the blankets up to her chin and turned away. I didn't miss the shaking of her shoulders or hear the muffled sniffles she tried to hide from beneath the covers.

My hand tightened into a fist to avoid reaching out for her and comforting her. She had to harden her heart or else she'd never survive among these tides. Everything in me screamed to reach out for her, but I ignored the part of my mind that demanded it and turned, leaving her alone.

After the mermen came to install the bars—an event which I shamelessly hid in the bathing room the entire time—I swam out and finally got into a change of clothes. I picked something easy to move in, something dark and not so fashionable, snickering as I slid it over my body.

The merlady on the telly could kiss my fin.

I chose a black dress that I found hidden deep in the recesses of the princess' closet. It was unlike any other attire she had, which made it the perfect fit for *me*; black with long sleeves and a short train that was easy to flap my fins in. I tucked my hair beneath a dark hat and attached my beloved blade to my waist before shoving the chair in front of the doorway and getting the lava globe.

If the princess *had* escaped from under everyone's noses, then she'd most likely done it from the inside of this room. Specifically, from the inside of that cove. That meant there was probably another hidden doorway down there that led somewhere else. And I intended to find it.

After securing everything in place, I went to the panel, pressed my palm against it, and swam all the way to the cove. I scoured the muddy floors until I found a messenger bag that I wrapped around my shoulder and shoved the disk into, as well as a handful of golden coins and rubies. Once I found the doorway, I would find someone who could repair the disk. I needed it fixed so I could watch that recording, find out *who* had been chasing her, and discover who ended up poisoning *me.*

After securing everything tightly against me, I began looking for a possible exit. I pressed my palms against the cold stone walls and began feeling for a panel like the one in the bedroom. I scoured nearly every inch of that cove, swimming up the ceiling and along the walls. There had to be a way out. There *had to be.*

The more time passed, the more frustrated I became. The princess couldn't have gotten out if there hadn't been a doorway. Was it hidden like the entrance to the cove was? Or was it simpler? I pressed my hands along the edges of a dark wall, and to my luck, I heard the now familiar sound of stones scraping together. I held my breath as bricks parted to form a small doorway. I swam through it and turned around in time to see it close by its own volition.

I hoped there was a way back in, or else Captain Saber would have my head.

Loosing a breath, I turned to observe my surroundings. I was in a dark alleyway of some sort in a place I didn't recognize. Granted, I hadn't been given the royal tour of Eramaea, so that wasn't surprising. Beyond where I floated, noises and activity could be heard. I looked up and saw the pink spires of the castle behind me. Okay, so I was close to the castle, but why did everything look like I was in a poor part of the city?

I dropped my lava globe inside my bag to avoid drawing attention and swam forward a few strokes. I didn't make it far before I suddenly found myself with company. Three mermen swam into the mouth of the alleyway. I froze and watched as the three hauled a fourth merman and shoved him painfully against the stone wall.

Their voices were too low to hear, but then one of them shouted a curse and shoved his fist straight into the fourth merman's gut. The merman grunted in pain and slid down the length of the wall, his dark tail curling under him. The others didn't waste time and began attacking him, kicking at him with their tail fins, throwing fists and curses in his direction.

I floated in petrified silence until one of the mermen pulled out a two-legger switchblade.

My tail was moving before I could command it to stop, hand reaching for the blade at my waist and pulling it out. I charged at them with a fierce cry, placing myself in a protective stance over the injured merman. The three mer looked at me with eyebrows raised. Here in the mouth of the alley, the light from algae was bright enough to see their faces.

They had the features of sharks and eels. Sharp rows of teeth sneered at me and lidless black eyes that looked like they could devour my soul glared. I fought back my shudder and held the blade tightly in my hands.

"I reckon y'all should get goin' now," I said breathlessly. My body ached in places where the poison still lingered. I refused to let it back me down, though. This merman was in trouble. He needed my help.

"And who are you to be givin' us orders, bottom feeder?" One of the mermen puffed his chest out and looked at me with indignation. I refused to acknowledge his question.

"Leave him alone," I spat.

The three of them looked to each other before turning and smiling at me. Their smiles chilled my bones.

I barely blinked as the one with the blade lunged forward. I dodged, blocking the blade with my own. Too late I realized he'd been the distraction because the mer to my left grabbed my wrist in his tight grip. The one to my right slapped my other wrist, sending the weapon clanking to the ground. I thrashed my tail out, hitting a solid body. I smiled with satisfaction when one of my captors gave a grunt.

Fighting back only seemed to make them angrier. Suddenly, they had me pressed against their bodies, a forearm at my throat and blocking my gills from taking in water to my lungs.

"Seems like you need to be taught some manners, bottom feeder." I thrashed, but he only held me tighter. My gaze flicked down to the merman they'd hurt. He was slowly getting up, his hand sliding up along the stone wall.

"Don't you know it's not polite to harm a lady?" he asked. His voice was deep, smooth, and dangerous. It was the kind of voice where nightmares were born. The kind that lived in shadows and held secrets. The kind that was a weapon itself. The kind I imagined whispered in mermaids' ears promises of pleasure and adventure. He looked up, and I swore I caught a glimpse of evil in his black eyes. The merman holding me loosened his grip, the surprise in his gasp evident. Before he could say anything, however, the black-eyed merman was attacking.

I barely had time to cry out as he lunged towards us, the blade I'd discarded tight in his fist. When had he picked it up? The tip of the blade came crashing towards us, piercing the flesh of the merman behind me. He howled his pain and dropped me. I fell through the water, fanning my fins and twisting just in time to see the battle that ensued.

The merman crumpled to the muddy ground, holding at his bleeding wound. The other two advanced, but they were no competition. With a few kicks of his tail and twirls through the water, the others fell, injured as well.

The mysterious merman pointed the tip of the blade at them in threat. "You know now who I am?" he asked. It chilled me to my very core. The mermen stared at the tip of his blade and released shocked gasps before nodding vigorously. "Leave now, scum, before I change my mind and run you through."

The three mermen didn't need any more persuading. They got up and swam away as fast as they could. And they didn't look back.

My heart beat so loudly I was sure the black-eyed merman could hear it. He turned to me, illuminated by phytoplankton in the dark. His hair was black and curly, the strands spinning down the back of his neck. His skin was a dark, coppery color, his tail black with jagged, pointy fins. He wore a black jacket with the spiked teeth of barracudas coming out from the shoulders. His nose was straight and pointed, lips full. A single silver cross dangled from his ear, and with the blade in his hand he looked frightening.

He tossed his hair aside with a single jerk of his head. Commanding. Powerful. Dangerous. I held my breath as he swam towards me. But I didn't back down. Would a merman I really just tried to save, a merman who had *saved me*, really harm me?

"Foolish little fish," he muttered.

I blinked. "Excuse you?"

"Those mermen would have chewed you up and spit you out like this morning's breakfast." He lifted the blade up and pushed it through a sheath at his waist.

"Give me my blade back." My hand snapped out in command. I didn't just get it back from Captain Saber to have it be taken all over again by some tadpole.

His thick dark eyebrow raised. "You might want to look again, little fish." He nodded at the ground. Cautiously, I took my eyes off him and found *my* black blade on the ground where I'd dropped it. I quickly picked it up, weighing it in the palm of my hand as I looked at the one sheathed at his waist.

"Where did you get that?" I asked, sudden curiosity nagging at the back of my mind.

"I made it." Those dark eyes danced with mirth, his lips tightening into a line that made me think he was trying not to laugh at me.

"Don't lie to me," I snapped. I was sick of everyone lying and treating me like I was incompetent and stupid just because I was from Lagoona. It was insulting at the palace, and it was definitely insulting coming from this stranger. "That weapon was made by the Black Blade."

His eyebrows rose, his lips twitched into a smile of mischief. "I know."

"B-but—"

He made a noise of annoyance, and quicker than I could blink, he was suddenly grabbing me and pushing me against the stone wall. The rough edges of rock and barnacles dug painfully into my back. I gasped, lifted my weapon, but his hand clamped against my wrist, pressing it tightly against the wall.

"Enough talk, little fish. You owe me for saving your life just now."

I gasped, my breathing heavy but quick. "*You're* the Black Blade?" That was all I managed to choke out. All I could think to say. It was the only thing my whirling mind could grasp onto. *This* merman was the outlaw? The one who had escaped the tight clutch of Selection? He was the one who freed mer from their fates?

The image I had conjured up of him suddenly fell apart, and I didn't know if I should weep, laugh, or rejoice. I didn't want to believe that he was telling the truth. I swore I'd never be so gullible again. Not after what happened the last time I'd believed a lying merman. My fin flared in response to the thought, and I shoved it away. He couldn't be the Black Blade, but… I'd seen him move with my own eyes. Quick, sharp, and silent. A shadow in the night. He'd been all but a blur slashing through the water.

"You've heard of me, then?" He was warm against my skin. Close. He was *too* close to me. I trembled in fear. "Then you'll know what I am capable of." His free hand, the one not holding me down, suddenly came up to my face, fingers sliding down my cheek. "And you know I will not leave without payment for my services."

The slimy barracuda! And here I'd pictured him to be heroic.

"I have money in my bag," I gasped.

He shook his head. "A pretty mer like you? No. I don't want your money."

I swallowed the rising tightness in my throat. Somehow, I managed to push the question out through my fear. "Then what do you want?"

He smiled and hummed a dark sound that slid down my neck and to my fins. "A kiss," he whispered.

My heart thumped a rapid beat in my chest as the two simple words registered. I became suddenly all too aware of his dominating presence looming over me, pressed against me. Of his flashing white teeth. The curves of his dark lashes. The hungry gleam in his eyes.

"A kiss?" I whispered back, disbelief heavily coating the echoed words.

His fingers toyed with the skin at my cheek before gripping my chin in a tight grip. He inspected me in a way that made me feel all too vulnerable. And still, my heart was beating faster and faster the longer he stared.

"One," he said. "One kiss for your savior."

I didn't want to yield. But there was something all too hypnotizing about his expression. About the way he looked at me. I promised myself I'd never let another merman pull me in like this, and yet I couldn't help myself as I leaned towards this beautiful stranger.

One kiss.

One kiss couldn't hurt, right?

"Okay," I found myself whispering. My breathing grew heavy, languid, and so unlike myself. I tried not to think about that. "One," I agreed. "Just one."

He smiled triumphantly, and that was all the warning I got before he bent down and crashed his lips to mine.

Elias

THE LITTLE GASPING NOISE of surprise she made against my mouth only spurred me on. What I'd intended to be just a press of lips against lips suddenly became something more as the blade of my making fell from her hand and fell to the ground below. My tongue speared past her lips and into her mouth and that action alone had her melting into my embrace.

The skin beneath my fingertips was soft, and I trailed them over her cheek, down to her throat, her collarbone, tracing a pathway of caresses that made her shiver. Finger stopping against her collarbone, I began trailing circles around her flesh.

And then she bit me.

I jerked away from her, pressing a hand to my lips in surprise. She was breathing heavily; the fast rise and fall of her chest was all I noticed at first. Then I looked into her eyes. Eyes that were as black as my blades.

"D-don't do that again..." she stuttered, hand coming up to wipe at her mouth, as if she meant to get rid of the taste of me from her tongue.

Good luck, I wanted to tell her.

One kiss was all it took for her taste to be imprinted into my soul forever.

I smiled. "That your first kiss, little fish?" She was nowhere near being a little fish. This mer was on the taller side, with a strong purple tail and muscular arms and back. I noticed how she inclined slightly to the right, as if she favored that side more.

A single glance and I saw every detail about her.

Her hair was purple, like her tail. Her eyelashes had been a dead giveaway. Her fingertips looked calloused, though the skin on her face had been soft. She was young, I'd guess nineteen, only three years younger than myself. And there was something absolutely *fierce* about her.

"You tadpole! You never said *that* was the type of kiss you wanted!" She bent down to grab her blade and hold it up, pointing it at my chest. Her gaze stopped there, and I wondered if she could see the pounding of my heart or if she was picturing how she would skewer it with the very blade I fabricated.

I could have laughed in her face.

She didn't know who she was dealing with.

Or maybe she did and just didn't care. She did know my alias, after all. It seemed my reputation preceded me. I looked at the blade that was a smaller, twin version of my own. I recalled the day I'd made them, weeks after I'd escaped Selection. Mine had been the first, studded at the base with black gems I'd stolen. I remembered looking at it and feeling a sudden crippling sensation of loneliness. So I'd made its twin. Its pair. Its mate.

One that was studded at the base with sapphires, a glimpse of color against the darkness. It should have made me happy, but I'd sold it soon after.

And now here it was again, being wielded by an angry, impulsive, *beautiful* mer.

If that wasn't a sign from the tides that she was meant to be mine, I didn't know what was.

"Put that down before you hurt yourself." I smirked because I already knew the action irritated her. "And tell me, what is your name?" She didn't put it down and she didn't offer me her name, either. Stubborn little fish. "Since I saved your life, I'd think you'd have the decency to at least give me some answers."

She growled low. "I was trying to save *your* life, you guppy!" I liked her already. Anyone who was brave enough to scream at me, knowing who I was, deserved my respect. "And if you could beat them all easily, why did you let yourself get pushed around like that in the first place?"

"All part of the game, little fish." I held my hands out at my sides in mockery. It was amusing, to watch her reactions. I wanted to know how deep I could sink my hooks into her skin. How far she would let me go.

"You're supposed to be the Black Blade?" She finally sheathed her weapon, probably deeming me not to be a threat anymore, and crossed her arms against her chest. My eyes followed her every movement with burning curiosity. "You're the one who freed mer from the Selection. The very first escapee in Thalassarin history?"

Ah, a title to be proud of. An outlaw to the crown. A criminal who sold blades like rare candy and who kept secrets more valuable than money. I was proud of who I was, and if I was not mistaken, there was a hint of awe hidden beneath the blatant disgust.

"The one and only."

Her dark eyes shone beneath the bioluminescent lighting of the alleyway. Yes, that was praise there. She just didn't want to admit it.

"I expected more."

I chuckled but didn't take offense. "Did you expect a phantom? Sorry to shatter your illusion, but even us legends are mere mermen."

"So, *Black Blade,* do you have a real name?" She leaned her back against the wall casually.

"Do *you*?" I countered.

"Maisie," she replied slowly, if a little cautiously. Good. What a foolish thing, to throw your name to strangers.

But for her, I would be honest. "Elias Blackfin, at your service." If I had a hat, I would have taken it off to bow. Though the gesture itself would come off mocking.

"Elias..." she repeated quietly. I liked the way my name sounded coming from her lips. I liked it a lot. "Well...." She straightened, adjusting the strap of the bag over her shoulder. "Thank you for your assistance. I really do appreciate it." She gave a little wave and started to swim away.

That wouldn't do at all.

I blocked her exit, placing my body too close in front of hers. She startled back, shooting me a glare. "You can't leave. Not when you still owe me."

If she could have killed me with her eyes, she would have. "You took your payment."

I liked the way her voice quivered at those words. It almost made me want to take her mouth again, but I vowed that the next time we kissed—and I'd make *sure* there was a next time—she'd tremble and beg me for it. And not wipe her mouth in disgust.

"You think that's enough to satisfy the Black Blade?"

She scoffed. "First, don't refer to yourself in third mer. It's weird. And second, as I told you before, I have coin." Flipping the flap to her messenger bag, she opened it to reveal the contents inside. I caught sight of a flash of gold and rubies, but what held my attention was the disk.

Without asking for permission, I reached inside and pulled it out despite her cry of protest. When she made a lunge for it, I held it out of her reach.

"Give it back!"

She obviously cared for this thing a great deal. It was more valuable to her than any gold pieces she had in that bag. I looked it over. It was one of those old conch projectors. Why would this be more valuable than anything else?

"Are you done gawking?" she snapped.

I smirked, holding the disk tightly in my fingers. "Where could you possibly be going with this?"

"I'm going to have it fixed, if you *must* know." She huffed angrily as she lunged, snatching the disk from my fingers and shoving it back into her bag.

"I'll fix it for you," I offered with a mischievous smile.

She snorted. "No, thank you."

My smile only widened. This little fish obviously didn't know that I never backed down from a challenge. She was no exception. "Do you even know where to go to get it fixed?" I inquired. "Or were you planning on swimming around the streets of Eramaea without a clue?" Her face flushed and I knew I'd been right.

"I'm sure I'll manage well enough alone." She tried to swim past me but found herself blocked again.

"You'll be fresh bait for thieves and criminals out there, little fish."

She looked down at her outfit, then back up to me. "I blend in."

I snorted. "You think they won't notice that the thread on those clothes is made from expensive sea silk, or that your purse clatters when you swim? You think they won't notice the color of your lashes and your tail?" My irritation rose higher the quicker my words were spoken. I reached forward and yanked the hat from her head, watching her purple hair slowly float down past her shoulders. "Did you really think I wouldn't know who you were, *Princess?*"

I noticed everything. I'd known from the moment she'd appeared in that alleyway, the moment I'd set eyes on her.

She appeared too startled to move or even speak. Her eyes were widened with shock that she didn't bother to try and hide behind glares or sharp words. I'd expected more than her silence…

Then, "You really are as incredible as the stories say."

I hadn't expected *that.* I smiled and tossed the hat back to her. She caught it in her fingers. "I'll take it to get fixed for you," I offered again. "I know a mer. He owes me a favor."

The look of awe vanished immediately and was replaced with the narrowing of eyes and distrust. "Why would you help me?" she demanded.

I shrugged. "Who wouldn't want to have the Princess of Thalassar in their debt?"

She scoffed. "Despicable tadpole."

"Lesson one, nothing in this world is free." I held out my hand, smiling and expectant. "So?"

She thought for a long moment, so long and with an unreadable expression that I thought there was a possibility she would be stubborn and turn me away. But what had happened moments ago in this alleyway had been proof enough that she was not ready for the streets of Eramaea. Her royal sensibilities and upbringing would be a dead giveaway.

Strange, how she didn't act like any royal I'd ever met. And I'd met my fair share of royalty, after all. I was the Black Blade. Escapee. Seller and vendor of secrets. Leader of the uprising. Hero to Thalassar. King of the slums of Eramaea.

Finally, she dug through her bag and pulled the disk out. I took it from her and tucked it under my arm. "Fine. But I'll need it back as soon as possible."

"As soon as possible, little fish. Though I have to wonder, you have servants at your beck and call. Why not get one of your palace maids to do it?" Her stiffening was answer enough. She was so easily readable, the little thing. I waved her off with my fingers. "Scurry away back to where you came from," I said. "The hour grows late, and you'll soon be missed."

Her black eyes narrowed, and she pointed an accusing finger at me. "You promise you'll get it back to me as soon as possible?"

"Oh, little fish…" I took a stroke closer, but she didn't scuttle back. She straightened, looking up into my eyes. I bent down, feeling the challenge pulse and hum through my every nerve. Our lips were but a kiss length apart. I whispered near the edge of her mouth, "I *always* keep my promises."

Maisie

THE NEXT AFTERNOON, I dressed with great care in a light blue dress with a long train that gave into soft puffs of white. It looked like a wave crashing to shore. Though I imagined it to be what a two-legger sky would look like. The dress was comfortable and easy to move around in, as my limbs were still a bit sore from the poison.

I'd wanted to stay in bed, ignore the duties that awaited me—the princess—beyond the palace, but Captain Saber had insisted I make an appearance. Besides, that morning, there had been a tentative knock on the bedroom doors. When I opened them, Prince Kai had been on the other side, his hands clasped tensely behind his back, the soldiers in charge of my protection glaring at him, though what he'd done to garner those looks, I hadn't known.

I hadn't invited him in.

The pain of his last visit still stung. It shouldn't have. We weren't anything, despite what he thought had shifted between us. I wasn't the real princess, and we would never marry. Once my business here finished, I'd never see him again.

But the prince had kind eyes and a gentle touch. Something about him drew me in like sea bugs to jellyfish stingers. No matter how badly I wanted to ignore it. I knew he was only in the engagement with the princess because of his own benefit, to help his kingdom. Royal marriages weren't based on love or even affection.

And because I wasn't the princess, I couldn't let myself believe that he felt anything for me. Because I wasn't the princess, I had to release my hurt. After all, wasn't I parading around as her for the exact same reason he'd come to Thalassar? To better conditions, to help the mer?

"I was wondering if you'd like to have a turn around the gardens with me," Prince Kai said, forming the sentence as a command rather than a question. While his posture had screamed of confidence, his eyes were beseeching and uncertain.

I wondered what Princess Odele would have done in that situation. Would she have turned him away? Would she have told him she needed to check her schedule? I pushed those thoughts aside and found myself nodding. A turn around the gardens couldn't hurt. It may even help my aching limbs since my fin had been hurting me since I'd ingested the poison. As if the contents in it had made my limp prominently worse.

Prince Kai nodded once, agreeing to meet me later, and turned to swim away.

When I finished dressing, I looked at myself in the mirror. Purple tresses were pulled away from my face and held together by a blue jewel. Few wisps curled loose over my temples, and as I stared at myself, I had to force away the cutting words from the mermaid on the telly.

Plain.

Perhaps I was.

Turning away from my reflection, I went out the door to find Captain Saber waiting for me with a gaggle of soldiers on the other side. He bowed low when he saw me. "Princess Odele, we are here to escort you and the prince around the gardens."

I tried not to glare at the mer who had been keeping watch. I would have liked to swim alone without the eerie sense of them following me. But after being poisoned, I couldn't be too careful. I would hate to die before I'd even had a chance to rule and change things.

"Do we really need so many soldiers?" I asked, looking them all over. There were about ten of them. A tad too many, in my opinion.

"It's for your safety, Your Majesty."

I sighed but nodded. Then I followed Captain Saber down hallways and stairs until we made it out to the royal gardens. There, Prince Kai was waiting for me, and he was accompanied by his royal advisors as well as a set of Draconian guards of his own.

He was wearing his traditional kimono in a royal blue that really offset the dark color of his hair and eyes. When I swam over to him, he smiled softly and took my hand, bending over it to press a kiss to my knuckles. Like always, his lips against my skin made my whole body tingle. Except this time, the heat of his lips reminded me of someone else's.

Dark eyes flashed in my mind, the hot press of the Black Blade's body. His lips and tongue. How he'd made my fins curl beneath me and when he'd pulled away, all I wanted was more.

I snatched my hand away without meaning to. A quiet look of hurt flashed through Prince Kai's eyes as he straightened, and I tried to push aside my guilt.

"Your Majesty," he greeted. "You look lovely."

The advisors and guards floated around us, not bothering to turn away or give us privacy. "Thank you," was all I managed to say. How could I say more or even think about complimenting him with so many eyes and ears on us?

"Shall we?" He offered me his arm and I placed my hand on it, only to be guided through the gardens.

It was a beautiful splash of colors. Coral and exotic plants burst in bloom all around. Magenta, cerulean blue, and yellow flowers swayed with the gentle breeze of the current. Fishes darted in and out of anemones, colors in splotches of purple and pink sea roses blotted blue bouquets.

"It's beautiful," I whispered quietly as we passed a small forest of water lilies. The sight of them reminded me so much of home, I was nearly crippled.

"It's my favorite place in the whole palace," the prince admitted quietly. "Because it reminds me of home."

I turned with a surprised look to him. Then I looked over my shoulder. The soldiers and advisors were following behind us at a steady pace. There was enough space between us that they wouldn't openly eavesdrop on our conversation, but close enough still that they could hear what we said if we spoke loudly.

I rolled my eyes and the prince stiffened.

"Sorry. I wasn't rolling my eyes at *you.*"

"Okay."

"I wasn't!" Then, to change the drift of the conversation, I said, "It's my favorite part of the palace, as well." Not that I'd seen all of the palace yet. But this was too beautiful to hate. It gave me an overwhelming sense of nostalgia that made me smile despite it.

"Lilies are my favorite." The prince stopped and broke away from me. He bent over the bright pink water lilies and picked one. When he turned back, it was with his arm outstretched shyly. "I wanted to apologize," he said as I took the water lily, face heating brightly as I did. "I did not mean to offend you or hurt you the other day. Your captain implied that I only cared about your well-being because my kingdom needs you. While that may be true, I've found in the past few days that you aren't entirely what I thought you were at first. Something… something seems different about you. You have something in you that I didn't see before."

I was at a loss for words, not knowing how to reply or what I could say that wouldn't ruin this moment. My eyes darted quickly over to the soldiers behind us. They had stopped at a respectable distance, the majority of them looking around the waters for any possible threat. Captain Saber was looking at me with narrowed eyes. For a brief second, I wondered if he was chastising me with his gaze, if he didn't approve.

My fingers tightened against the water lily, and I brought it to my nose to sniff. I was here to make a change in any way possible. Why not start with Prince Kai? Just because I pretended to be her didn't mean that I had to be as mean, flippant, and daft, right?

I was here to make a positive change.

"I felt it was time for a change," I said slowly, lowering the lily from my face. "And I was hoping that maybe we could start over. Get to know each other?"

I was sure Captain Saber was shooting daggers in my direction, but I avoided his gaze. It would do no good to dwell on what the princess would or would not do in this situation. I didn't have it in me to be rude or indifferent to Prince Kai. Not when my heart beat faster when he was near. Not when my fins curled and my stomach twisted into knots. Not when my fingers tingled at the touch of his lips.

"I'd like that, Princess." He smiled down at me.

"Please, call me M—" I cut off, sucked in a sharp breath, and then breathlessly added, "Call me Odele."

He took the lily from my hands and tucked it behind my ear. "Then call me Kai."

IT WAS HARD FOR me to believe that anyone could change within such a short amount of time. Princess Odele had proven me wrong.

She was far different from the mermaid I had first met all those months ago. Gone was the selfish demeanor, gone was the judgement, looking down on servants, looking down at *me*. It was like a different mer swam next to me.

She spoke softly, almost hesitantly, and when she laughed, she laughed freely, genuinely. And I couldn't help but smile along to her words, with her happiness. There was so much I hadn't known about my betrothed. If we could have gone back in time, and she would have been this way from the start, I was sure that by now, I'd have loved her.

"You did *not*!" She squealed with laughter.

I chuckled. "In my defense, I was a child."

"Sixteen is hardly a child. I can't believe you snuck a box of puffer fish into the royal hall during a state dinner." She began shaking her head, the smile lighting up her eyes and face.

"My elder sister, Ting, convinced me to do it." Rather, she had manipulated me into doing that. But she didn't need to know how conniving and insane my sisters could be just yet.

"I would have liked to see your advisors faces!" She snorted and had to stop as she bent over laughing. When she laughed, there was a slight snort that she gave through her nose. Something about her changed entirely. It took my breath away.

"They were furious," I admitted. "But not as furious as the emperor. I still have the scars from the lashing he gave me." The remembrance stung. One day, she'd see the slight silver marks crisscrossing my arms. Would she cringe away from them? Or would she press her lips against the ridges of them? The thought froze my insides. For the first time since meeting her it made me *desire* her.

"That seems rather cruel," she pointed out quietly. Purple lashes fanned across the sharp jut of her cheekbones as she looked up at me, a plaintive curiosity in her gaze. And beneath that, *pity*.

I brushed it off with a strained smile. "It's normal in royal life." I was sure she was familiar with lashings. How else would they learn everything they needed to know if not through that particular method of discipline? Or so I'd been told. I thought it rather cruel and heartless myself. I'd vowed that our children would not be educated that way…

When had I gone from despising her to thinking about our future children?

"I think royal life should change."

I blinked at her words. "Change in what way, Odele?" It felt odd, saying her name without the respective 'princess' in front of it. It was pleasant, though.

"There's a lot that needs to be changed, don't you think?" She gestured around the gardens with her hands. "I mean, royalty doesn't really think of anyone but themselves, don't they?"

"I'm sure that's not true—" She shot me a look that had my lips clamping shut.

"Look around you, Kai. We have such lavish lives while there are mer beyond these walls dying of hunger and being murdered for trying to swim away from a war they want no part in. How is that fair?"

"In Draconi, it is considered an honor to fight alongside the emperor and soldiers."

She sighed. Though I didn't miss the passion burning deep in the depths of her dark eyes. "But your royals fight *by* your mer. They defend them in battle."

They did. All royals, advisors, and mer of my kingdom were skilled in combat. When there were disputes or wars, even my sisters followed our father out into battle, with no fear in our hearts and with ferocity saturating our weapons. The mer in Thalassar were obviously much more delicate in their upbringing. My mer would never swim away from a fight, not when it could bring honor to their family for generations to come. And my emperor and the princesses would never think of sitting with their arms crossed in the palace while soldiers risked their lives. They were always at the front lines.

"There is no greater honor than to die beside our emperor."

Odele bit her bottom lip, and my eyes followed the movement longingly before she released it and shook her head back and forth, as if she were clearing the thoughts there. "But that's what they *choose* to do. The mer of Thalassar are forced into battle."

I looked at her, assessed her, and then slowly said, "If you are in disagreement with the laws, why not help change them? You're the princess. You have more power than your father; surely you have the queen's ear."

Her face flushed as she tensed. "I'm tryin'," she whispered. Something about the way she said it was strange, different. Her accent… She blinked and her head snapped up, face flushing. "Of course," she said, her Eramaean, lilting accent back in place. "If I had more royalty backing me when I go before the queen to make my case…"

I smiled, accent now forgotten, and nodded. "Of course I'll help in any way I can. Though we find honor in fighting, it does not mean that it is something we like to do."

She bumped her shoulder against mine. The move was starling, warming. "I'm glad to hear it."

She seemed to move closer to me then, her shoulder brushing mine. The skin of our bare fingers grazed and impulsively I reached for her hand. My heart beat rapidly as I threaded my fingers through hers, almost afraid that she would snatch her hand away again as she had earlier. But when she gave my hand a squeeze back and held tightly, I loosed a sigh of relief.

"I want to show you my favorite part of the gardens." I smiled tentatively as I pulled her forward, and we swam through the labyrinthine gardens. The soldiers followed, matching our pace. But I didn't care about their presence. I didn't care that they'd later talk about the fact that we held hands and it might seem inappropriate for us since we were not yet wed. All I cared about was her. So I pulled her forward until we made it into a small clearing of the garden.

There was a patch of neatly cut sea grass, and in the center, a large wooden and stone statue of a mermaid. The statue looked like it had fallen from a pirate ship and had sunken deep into the garden in an upright position. The base was cemented deeply into the sand, seaweed and sea vines climbing up the base of it, looking like small green fissures in the structure. Tube worms were in bright blooms around the carvings of her scales.

Surely, Odele had seen this a million times already. This was her palace, her kingdom, after all. But there was something special about being here with her for the first time. When I looked down at her face, her fingers were pressed tightly against her lips and her eyes were widened with awe. I watched with fascination as a small tear bubble emerged from the corner of her eye.

Never before had she looked so beautiful.

It was then that I realized that, after this short swim through the gardens, I was falling in love with my betrothed.

That was my last thought before the spear zipped through the water, heading straight for Princess Odele.

It happened so fast. I wish I could've seen it coming sooner. I wish I hadn't failed at my duties. One minute I was watching them so closely it was all I seemed to be focused on. The two of them, their intertwined hands, and searing jealousy soaring through my chest.

I didn't know why the sentiment filled me. So I reminded myself that it was because of who she looked like and how much princess had meant to me. And seeing their hands clasped tightly together, seeing them laugh and joke, and then seeing her eyes fill with tears wrenched the envy straight out of me.

I was so focused on them, on the feelings in my chest, that for a brief moment, I forgot my duties. For a fraction of a second, I nearly missed the spear spiraling through the water, heading straight for her.

I gave a shout, my body already moving on instinct. I gave a kick of my powerful tail and rushed forward to knock Maisie into the silt, just as the spear hit the ground a second later, right in the spot where she'd been floating. My body hovered over hers, arms caging her head in at their sides. The silt clouded around us and she coughed. When it cleared, our lips were but inches apart.

"Are you okay?" I whispered. I was sure she could feel the thundering of my heart through her own chest. "Are you hurt?"

"I'm fine," she whispered. Her eyes looked dazed, as if she wasn't quite sure what was happening.

"Stay down," I ordered as I shot up in the water, turning to give a precarious look around. Already, my guards were dispersing, fanning out at all sides. Prince Kai's guards were corralling the prince, his advisors, and Maisie into a protective circle, while others swam towards the direction the spear had come from.

I tightened my hands into fists and unsheathed my sword. Every bone in my body told me to stay with Maisie and the prince. To protect them. But the bigger part of me told me to catch the sea scum that was trying to kill her. I turned to my soldiers and ordered them to protect them with their lives. Knowing they would, I looked to Prince Kai and brown eyes met my own.

"Protect her." It was a plea, a menacing command. Probably not the appropriate way to speak to royalty. But if anything happened to Maisie, I'd kill anyone that played any part in it. Including the prince.

He glared at me, as if to say he didn't need to be told, because he was the Dragon Prince of Draconi. That was all confirmation I needed before I shot off towards the direction the spear had come from. I was a fast and sure swimmer, and within moments, I'd caught up with my guards and had surpassed them. I put in a burst of speed through the garden and that's when I saw the merman.

Dressed in black with a spear gun at his side, he was zipping through the shrubbery in an attempt to escape. Rage boiled hotly inside of me. He had tried to kill her. And once I got my hands on him, he'd wish he were dead.

I zigzagged through the maze. He didn't see me coming and I tackled him to the silt from behind. He twisted and we struggled. There was a scuff of fists and pain as he hit me against my vulnerable spots. I grunted but kept him pinned, using my own fists to punch and maim. The spear gun dug into my side, and I gasped as I felt the sharp tip of a spear slice my uniform.

He was a strong fighter, but I was a soldier, my rage making me stronger. I smashed my forehead into his and he grunted, going limp beneath me. It took but a moment for me to haul him up by the throat of his collar. It was then that my soldiers caught up to us. They advanced quickly, pulling the spear from his hands and then bringing his wrists to his back and holding them there.

I tried to keep my cool, but my head was fuming, my thoughts swirling. He'd tried to kill Masie. He'd tried *shooting* at her.

I shook him by the collar. "Do you know who you were trying to murder?" Though how could he not? The princess was too recognizable. Her entire lineage was.

The merman, a small, greasy bastard, laughed. "The Princess of Thalassar."

I could have killed him right then. But I needed information, and there were rules and laws in place. I was not the Dragon Prince. I would not beat prisoners to death until they gave me answers. Yes, I knew what he'd done. How despicable and dishonorably he'd acted within Thalassarin waters.

It was just another reason to hate him.

"Why? Why were you trying to kill the princess?"

The merman scoffed. "I don't ask questions," he spat. "My boss tells me to kill, and I do it."

Sea scum. I wanted to bash the hilt of my sword into his nose but refrained from those primal urges. "Who sent you? Who hired you to kill the princess?"

He laughed. "I don't have to tell you a thing."

I gritted my teeth together. "If you don't, I'll make you suffer. I'll rip your scales off one by one until you're in tears, begging for mercy. You think I won't?" I slid the tip of my sword down his flesh, and he trembled. A lie, one that savored bitterly against my tongue, but he didn't need to know that. "Tell me who sent you."

Bubbles swarmed from his eyes. When he opened his mouth, I waited eagerly for his answers, but he let out a gasp and all that spilled forth was blood. It was then that I noticed the arrow piercing his chest.

Cursing, I yanked it out and tossed it. "No, no, no. Don't die on me now." My soldiers crowded around me, their weapons drawn, eyes scanning every inch of the water to protect. "Who sent you? Tell me who sent you!"

But the blood was bursting from his mouth, clouding in front of us. His eyes and body twitched.

"Captain, the arrow was poisoned," one of my soldiers said as he examined the tip of the arrow, bringing it to his nose to sniff.

The merman convulsed and made terrible gasping noises.

He was dead within moments.

I let out a curse and dropped his body to the silt. "No sign of the sniper, Captain," one of my soldiers said. I growled out my rage, the sound rumbling deep in my chest. He'd been hired to kill Maisie and then someone had killed him. No loose ends. No witnesses.

It seemed as though my job had gotten a lot more complicated.

Maisie

My heart still raced miles in my chest. I tried controlling it, tried calming that nervous sensation that ran down through my veins and bones, but it just wouldn't leave. Someone had tried shooting me, had tried to kill me. Now I knew it was urgent I get the disk back and watch every conch down in that cove.

But first, I was before the queen and king. And they were both fuming, directing their anger straight at Captain Saber. I sat in the background, my hands clasped in my lap, my mind racing miles a minute.

"...no use to us if you cannot keep her safe!"

"What will they say if the double dies and the princess is found?"

"Find the culprits or your life is forfeit!"

It was the king who swam up to me moments later and took my surprised hands in his own. "Are you well?" he asked, genuinely concerned. "Were you harmed?"

The queen scoffed before I could answer. "Of course she wasn't harmed, Xristo. She's alive and well as you can see."

I held back my glare. I knew the queen ran things in Thalassar, but I hated her. I hated that the Selection was alive because of her. My merpeople had died because of her. And she cared about no one but herself and her image.

King Xristo dropped my hands and then swam back to his throne while his wife glared at him. After he sat back down and fixed his gaze on me, she began screaming at the captain all over again. I ignored most of what she said, my mind too focused on other things.

Someone was trying to kill the princess. *They're after me.* Had that been why she'd disappeared? Because someone had been chasing her? Who? And why? What did she know, and why did they want her dead because of it? I had to get to the bottom of this and stop whatever was happening. Because if someone killed me, thinking I was the princess, then I'd never be able to change a thing in Thalassar.

After the queen and king dismissed me and stayed with Captain Saber to talk, I was escorted to the princess' rooms, where I barricaded the door and swam quickly down to the cove. I needed to go into that alleyway, find the Black Blade and get that disk back. I needed to watch every single conch and learn more about the princess.

I was positive a confession would be in one of them. There had to be answers there.

And I wouldn't rest until I got them.

Stone scraped harshly as the opening was formed. I swam cautiously out, holding the black blade tightly in my hand. When I swam out, the secret passageway closed behind me, the noise seemed loud in the quiet and dark alley. I looked around, my eyes alert to every threat. Almost as if I expected a murderer to come spiraling through the water to try and kill me again.

But there was no one.

No sign of suspicious mer, and certainly no sign of the Black Blade. He hadn't really told me *how* he would get the disk back to me. Only that he would do so in a timely manner. I wondered stupidly if he'd duped me, if he'd taken the disk just because he could. The Black Blade—*Elias*—obviously wasn't what he seemed, what I'd thought he'd be.

I imagined someone serious, a shadow of the night, a faceless mer with mysterious magic, an older mer with a heroic streak, someone who would ask for nothing in return. He was none of these things. He was young, a few years older than my nineteen, and though his features were dark and mysterious, he smiled like he was a demon. And he obviously only helped mer so they'd remain in his debt. That didn't sound heroic at all to me.

He was just a barracuda. An infuriatingly handsome barracuda who liked to steal kisses from mer he knew nothing about. Yes, he'd known I was supposed to be the princess—even if I really wasn't—because of my coloring. He was observant, I'd give him that. But obviously not *that* observant.

I swam to the mouth of the alley and peeked my head around the corners. He wasn't there. Just the hustle and bustle of Eramaea night activity. Would I risk swimming out to look for him? No. I had no idea where I'd be going or even where he'd be.

I swam back into the alleyway and started to make my way towards the secret passage when a bag that was hung on a hook on the wall caught my eye. I swam over to it slowly. The bag was identical to the one I'd worn last time I'd come here. But the one I had was hanging safely within the confines of the cove. I pulled it off the hook and opened it. Inside was the disk and a note written on kelp parchment.

I pulled them both out.

You owe me, little fish. The words were scrawled with dark squid ink, under it a drawing of twin black swords crossing each other, the signature obvious if the nickname had not been. The Black Blade.

Smiling, I placed both things back into the bag and went over to the secret entry again. I pushed the panel and it opened. I swam back into the cove. I was eager to watch every single conch. Eager to finally uncover the secrets that Princess Odele had tried to hide.

The secrets she was being hunted for.

"…they're after me…"

I held my breath as I watched Princess Odele's image in the bubble. She was crying, breathing heavily. Her hair was down, floating above her shoulders with each brusque jerk of her head. She sniffled, brought the back of her hand up to her nose and wiped at it. The other hand was out of the image, presumably holding the conch that had recorded this image in the first place.

"They're out to get me, I know it," she whispered between sobs. "They want to ruin my life!" Her head jerked to the side, and there was the noise of a door knocking. "They're here," she whispered quietly.

I leaned forward, my heart thundering as I watched her swim and place the conch down. If I looked closely, I could make out the outline of her bedroom.

"They're coming for me," she sobbed. "This conch will be the evidence."

There was a loud clang as her bedroom doors were thrown open. I flinched when she did, watching with dread as someone else appeared in the image, within the range of recording of the conch.

The queen.

My hands flew to my lips, stifling the gasp that ripped through me. No. It couldn't be! Had the queen killed the princess? I scooted forward on the chair I sat in, holding my hands against my tail to steady myself as I watched the scene unfold before me.

"What do *you* want?" Princess Odele spat.

The queen placed her hands on her ample hips. "Look at you. Have you no shame? The hour is late and you still have not dressed!"

Princess Odele sobbed. "I don't want to! You can't ruin my life this way!"

The queen rolled her eyes. "Again with this complaining? Go ahead, get it out of your system. Keep crying about how we are ending your life and out to get you and blah, blah, blah."

"It's true!" Princess Odele shrieked.

"Yes. Poor princess, she's being forced into an engagement with the Dragon Prince Kai. It must be so difficult to be you."

I blinked at her words. What? *That's* what was going on in this conch? The princess had cried, had made me believe that someone was coming after her because of some secret knowledge she possessed, but in reality, she'd been crying because she didn't want to meet her betrothed?

I slapped a hand against my forehead and groaned. I'd worried at my nails for the longest time because of her idiocy. The blasted guppy of a princess! How infuriating! I had the sudden urge to rip the conch from the disk and chuck it across the room.

There *had* to be a secret around here somewhere. There had to be something that the princess had hidden away to explain her disappearance. She couldn't have just vanished into thin bubbles. I bent to the floor and began sorting through conches. I noticed the sides had small numbers etched into them. The order that she'd recorded them in, perhaps?

It took me close to an hour to sort them all by number. If every conch here was as ridiculous as the one I just watched had been, I feared for my sanity. But I needed to watch them. I needed to get an insight on the princess' life, who she spoke of, her secrets, who appeared beside her in images.

So once they were finally sorted, I picked up conch number one and placed it carefully onto the disk and sat back to watch the Princess of Thalassar's life unfold.

My head was pounding. I'd gotten through twenty conches and there was nothing. *Nothing.* There was just a buoyant attitude regarding every situation. She detailed who had kissed who, which royal she thought was riptide, cute, or a total shipwreck. In some videos, all she did was stare at the conch and make kissing, puffer fish faces.

And I was supposed to believe that *she* held knowledge that was getting her hunted? Maybe someone just wanted her dead because of how *stupid* she was. That wouldn't surprise me. Rubbing at my temple with one hand, I reached the other out to take the conch from the disk and set it gently on the table.

This princess would literally be the death of me. In more ways than one.

Feeling drained, I swam up the cove and through the small opening until I made it back to the bedroom. I didn't bother changing out of my clothes as I climbed into the bed, swatting away the anemones that sucked at my scales as I passed. As soon as my head hit the soft cushioning, I fell into a deep sleep.

That night I dreamt. The dream was so vivid, I could have sworn it was real. I tossed and turned on my bed, peeking my eyes open to find a mer in the room with me. My body ached from the strain it'd been put under the past few days, my fin flaring with cramps that never seemed to disappear. I was too exhausted to scream, to call out for help.

Instead I watched this mer in the darkness, a darkness that was only illuminated by the slight buzzing of the jellies that hung in the canopy above my head. The mer was small, at around my size, which made me think it was a mermaid. Her shoulders were cloaked, a hood covering her head. She was by the coral shelves on the other side of the room, near the small collection of shells, glass and other knick knacks. The mer was fiddling with objects there quietly. When she finished and turned, she froze mid-stroke when she noted my heavy-lidded gaze on her.

And it was like looking into a mirror.

I'd watched so many conches with the princess, that I was starting to hallucinate her, too. Sighing, I turned on the bed, pulled the covers up to my chin and fell back to sleep.

I had to keep to my schedule the next morning. Apparently, nearly getting murdered wasn't cause enough to stop my duties. And those duties? Taking tea with my cousins. I'd almost expected it to be sitting in on meetings with foreign ministers, but no. Teatime was something very important that I could not afford to miss.

I dressed in a dress of sea foam green to meet with Jessinda, Silviya, and Scarlet. Since watching the conches of the princess, I knew intimate details about these mer that not even Captain Saber had been able to provide. And I was dreading every second. I'd much rather take a turn about the gardens with Prince Kai again, rather than hang out with flippant guppy royals.

Granted, Prince Kai *was* a royal, but something about him was different from the rest. He was kind and honest. A warrior. And I admired him. I wished the princess' stupid schedule would allow for more time with the prince, but it was limited to seeing him twice a week on Moonsday and Starsday, as propriety allowed. Royal rules were ridiculous.

I was escorted there by Captain Saber and his guards. He hadn't said a word to me since the day before, when he'd saved me from the spear that very well could have killed me. I hadn't even had time to properly thank him for risking his own life to protect mine. I'd known he went after the culprit and had caught him. The merman had been killed before he could give any useful information.

I promised to make time among the stupid busy schedule of the princess to get him alone and thank him for what he'd done. Even if it had just been duty and not because he liked me enough to save me, I was grateful. And he needed to know that. He needed to know that I wasn't just some ungrateful freshwater mer playing too hard at being a royal. That I wasn't like *her.*

When I arrived to teatime, the three mer were already there waiting for me. They got up and gave low, proper curtsies before taking their seats in front of fine, shipwrecked China. I sat among them, feeling like the oddity of the group as they began falling into easy chatter, serving a light frothy tea. I reached for a little pastry in the center of the table when Jessinda finally spoke to me.

"Is it true you were attacked again, Odele?"

I paused with the pastry halfway to my mouth before I set it down again. "It is true," I replied.

They gave little gasps of astonishment. They sounded so fake, I tried not to roll my eyes.

"How ever did you survive?" Scarlet, a rotund mer with bright red hair, asked.

"Well, it was only thanks to Captain Saber and his soldiers that Prince Kai and I survived."

"Prince Kai was there, too?" Jessinda inquired with a quirk of her brows. She picked up her teacup, took a sip and set it back down. "Strange that he's been there for both of your attacks so far, isn't it?"

I didn't like what she was implying. My eyes narrowed. "Not at all. He *is* my betrothed."

"Well, yes, but did he even try and protect you as Captain Saber did?" Jessinda intertwined her fingers and rested her chin on them.

"Well, no, but—"

"Strange, that he wouldn't jump in front of that spear to save his betrothed." Her voice was as low and sharp as a barracuda. It was how I knew she was up to something, trying to manipulate me somehow. "He does come from a kingdom of warriors, after all. You'd think he would have battled alongside the good captain and his soldiers to save your life."

I ground my teeth together. Just because he was a warrior didn't mean he had to fight. Besides, everything happened so fast. Right after Captain Saber had gotten off me, we'd been corralled into a tight protective circle. And it was during that time that Prince Kai had gripped my hand tightly in his, had pulled me close by the waist with a grip that told me he never wanted to let me go.

"You know they don't care for each other, Jessinda," chastised Silviya, a mer with long silver hair and scales. "Is it really a surprise that he didn't want to save her? You know they hate each other."

"Hold on…" I waved my hands out in front of me. "I don't hate Prince Kai. And he doesn't hate me."

The three mer shared a look before looking at me with… pity? "You confessed to us when he came here that you had no interest in a pathetic little lizard prince. Did you change your mind?"

My mind was actually racing. Had the princess really said that to these mer? To reduce Prince Kai's title of the Dragon Prince to something as little and as demeaning as a lizard? She really *was* a guppy. How could she not see kindness when it was staring her in the face?

"If I did call him that, it was in the past," I said stiffly as I reached for my teacup and brought it to my lips. "You will do well to remember, though, that Prince Kai is my betrothed and you will address him with the respect a prince is owed."

They were shocked into silence because none of them spoke for a long while after that. I took the time to dig into my tea and pastries. They were surprisingly good. So unlike the tasteless food they'd given us at the anniversary dinner. These were much, much better.

Chatter eventually picked back up, though no one really directed any words at me. As if sensing my earlier hostility, they moved on to simpler subjects that had nothing to do with the royals, the war, or anything of importance. All they could do was talk about who had the latest dresses and who was kissing who in secret.

I fought not to bring my elbow up to the table and rest it there. Bad table manners.

A servant eventually came to switch out the now empty pastry plate for a new one. Smiling, I reached for the empty plate and handed it to the merservant, who looked at me incredulously as she took it in her fingers.

"Thank you," I said as she sat the new one down.

"No need to thank a simple servant, O," Jessinda cut in cruelly. She was watching me with cold eyes and glaring at the servant. "She probably can't even read."

The servant's face flushed a bright shade of red, and my own heated right alongside hers. I'd worked at Tides' Tavern for years as a waitress, cleaning up after mer and feeding them, and never once had the freshwater mer treated me like these royalty treated their own.

"Whether or not she can read is irrelevant," I ground out tightly, scraping my nails across the top of the table. "Saying 'please' and 'thank you' is common courtesy and politeness. Something none of you seem to comprehend."

Jessinda's eyes widened, as did Scarlet's and Silviya's. "What is your problem today, Odele?" Jessinda asked angrily. I knew this was going to be a shipwreck of epic proportions. The ice in her voice told me so.

"I don't have a problem."

"Something is so different about you. Thanking a servant? How beneath you." She flicked her long hair behind her shoulder.

"I'm just doing what any decent mer should do. You don't have to treat servants or anyone who isn't a royal badly just to prove that you can, you know."

They all blinked at me, and then Jessinda laughed. "Oh, please, Odele. Do not come at us with this righteousness like you're some type of angelfish. You treat everyone badly, more so than any of us at this table ever could. Stop pretending like you're better just because you said 'thank you' once."

My hands curled into fists. "I don't treat anyone badly."

She scoffed. "Oh, please. A few months ago, you had the stable merboy whipped because he put the wrong saddle on your hippocampus. You are such a hypocrite."

I shot up, scraping the chair against the polished quartz floor. My breathing had grown ragged and heavy. I wasn't a monster. The princess may have been one, but I *wasn't,* and I hated the looks in their eyes. They were looking at me as if I was her. As if I was the princess.

"Well at least I didn't kiss Scarlet's merfriend behind her back," I called out, and I regretted the words as soon as they were out of my mouth. I'd watched so many conches, had memorized nearly every word and secret the princess had spoken, that I couldn't help but blurt the words in the same cruel voice she'd used. If only to take the attention off me. If only to get them to stop looking at me like I was a monster.

But by doing this, I became the one mer I swore I never wanted to be like.

I became the princess.

Scarlet's eyes had widened as she turned to glare accusingly at Jessinda. Jessinda's face was as bright as coral, and I had to take a stroke back. "I'm sorry," I gasped quietly. But they weren't paying attention to me. The three girls were yelling at each other.

I didn't want to stay and watch this aftermath turn ugly. I dashed away, going as fast as my limping fin would allow me. It wasn't until I was in front of the princess' bedroom doors that I was whipped around and staring into the angry gaze of Captain Saber.

He opened the door himself and practically shoved me in, closing it behind him. "What in the tides was that?" he demanded angrily. I didn't blame him. I'd messed up. I'd ruined the image of the princess that I was supposed to maintain. But I didn't want to maintain an image. I didn't even want to *be* her.

"It's not my fault," I whispered weakly.

"Do you *want* to blow your cover? Do you *want* the whole palace to find out you're not the princess? You have one job, Maisie, and that is to *be* her. And you can't even do that."

I exploded. It was too much; the pressure, the poison, the almost getting killed, those mer without a speck of remorse or empathy in their bodies… I couldn't handle it.

"I'm not the princess!" I shouted. "I could *never* be the princess! And why would I want to be someone so spoiled and bratty?" My breathing was heavy as I went over to the coral shelves and lifted a glass statue. Impulsively, I threw it across the room and watched it shatter. "Why would I want to be a mermaid who does nothing with her time but drink tea with daft cousins or doesn't give a flip about anyone else in Thalassar but herself? No, I'm not the princess, Captain Saber. And I'm glad of it. Because I'd never want to be someone so weak, annoying and *worthless*—ah!"

Captain Saber was suddenly in front of me, his hands gripping tightly at my upper arms. The rage on his face was plain to see in the flaring of his nostrils, in the blazing of his eyes. He shook me and my head rattled.

"Shut your mouth, bottom feeder!" he snapped. His face was so close to my own that I could feel the heat of his anger coming off him in waves. "Don't you *ever* speak of Odele that way again or so help me—" He cut off abruptly and shoved me away.

I watched him as he seemed to try and physically compose himself, to rid himself of that explosive anger he'd displayed only a moment ago. He ran a hand through his hair, tried to steady his breathing. But his face was flushed and so were the tips of his ears.

I was too shocked to do anything but lower myself to the fin of the bed and press my hands into my lap. I stared at him as he paced from one end of the room to another, as if he wasn't quite sure what to do with himself.

Odele. He'd called her Odele. When he spoke to me of her, he was always so careful to use her title and speak of her respectfully. And when he did, it was with praise.

I blinked, the realization finally dawning on me. The understanding of why he'd gotten so angry. I remembered so vividly the way he'd whispered Odele's name at Lagoona, when he'd mistaken me for her. The expression of hope on his face…

"Captain, do you… Are you *in love* with Princess Odele?"

ARE YOU IN LOVE with Princess Odele?

And here came this mer from the freshwaters, a mer I hadn't known for that long, and she was wrenching out the secrets I would have killed to hide. Saying the words I'd been ashamed of feeling so easily, bringing them straight out of my heart and into the light.

I pointed a finger at her, fear melting into anger, anger rising to lash out at her. "Shut your mouth," I ordered, and I cursed my trembling voice, betraying me entirely. I'd never given myself time to accept those feelings coursing through me. I never wanted them there in the first place.

I could not love Odele. Because she was royalty, a princess, and I was the soldier that had failed her when she most needed me. I did not deserve her.

"You do," Maisie whispered, her eyes wide with awe as if she'd just discovered some fortuitous secret.

I supposed she had. And she was pulling it slowly out of me to leave me crippled, bleeding. It was easier to push feelings away rather than bring them forth, and she didn't seem to care what she was doing to me.

"I told you to be quiet." I had the sudden urge to zip forward and shake her again until she obeyed. Until she did what she was told. Until she started acting like the princess would. Until she *became* the princess.

And that was the core of the problem. I was so desperate for the princess to be back that I was forcing Maisie to try and change her every aspect, if only to become Odele. But Maisie would never be Odele.

"Why?" she snapped with irritation. "It's the truth. You love her. It all makes sense now…"

"Don't try to analyze this, Maisie," I warned. It would only end in heartbreak.

She acted as though she hadn't heard me. "If you love her, why didn't you ever tell her?"

A frustrated growl tore straight out of me. Finally, I'd lost all composure I'd built up within myself. Everything I'd worked so hard for came tumbling down because of her. "Would it have made a difference?" I shouted. "She's a princess and is to be married to Prince Kai." It was the closest I'd ever come to admitting what I felt for Odele.

"Why?" Maisie demanded. "Why do you love her?" She looked me over as if she couldn't quite fathom what I was thinking or if I was out of my mind. Maybe I was. But she'd brought it up, she'd pulled this straight out of me.

"She is not what she seems." Only I saw her day and night. Only I saw the heavy burdens she carried on her shoulders. There was the weight of an entire kingdom there, the weight of a marriage she didn't want or desire.

The weight of trying to be perfect. Only I noticed the shadows beneath her eyes and heard the cries that were carried to me by the current at night while I guarded her doors.

"She's exactly what she seems." Maisie got up and swam to me, her eyes begging to hear me out. She placed her hand on my shoulder and kept it there. "How can you love someone who doesn't care about her kingdom? Who can only belittle others?"

Angrily, I tore away from her, letting her hand fall back to her side. "Don't you dare try to tell me who I can and can't love or what she's like. You may be wearing her clothes, sleeping in her bed, and swimming beside her prince, but do not make the mistake of thinking you know who she is."

She chewed on her bottom lip. "Maybe I never spoke with her, but she never lifted a finger to help those in need. You cannot convince me she was good. Those who are good do not hide behind their closed doors to be that way. If she were really good, she would have shown it."

My temper rose again, exploded into something I could no longer control. "You know *nothing* of her!" I reached forward, grabbed her again and shook her. I shouldn't have. I should have treated her delicately. I should know to never harm a mer like I was harming Maisie. I stopped shaking her. She was pulled close to me, our chests touching and rising and falling together. One in anger, the other in fear. Her face was only inches from mine, our breaths mingling together hotly.

"Let go of me, *Captain*," she ordered.

My eyes darted involuntarily down to her mouth. She looked so much like Odele that it hurt, that it made me realize what I was doing was *wrong*. And for the first time since her disappearance, my heart broke. I'd locked my feelings so deeply inside that I hadn't had time to actually process what had happened.

And Maisie had ruined it all.

Slowly, I released my hold on her, bringing my fists to my sides. But she didn't move. She didn't take a stroke back. She stayed in place, her breath fanning across my lips.

I swallowed the sudden tightness in my throat and took a stroke back. "Don't let it happen again, Maisie," I told her, turning away. I couldn't look into her eyes again. Not without seeing Odele. "Try *harder.*" And before she could reply, I swam away and out the doors of her bedroom. Only to run into Prince Kai.

I NARROWED MY EYES at the captain, looked over his shoulder and saw Princess Odele in the middle of her room. Tears were falling from her eyes to swarm in tiny bubbles above her. Her expression was so broken, so angry. The captain pulled the doors closed behind him before I could look in any further.

A fierce wave of protectiveness crashed through my chest. "Why is the princess crying?" I hissed. I'd heard shouting earlier, though I couldn't make out the words behind the raised voices. I could make out *his* voice clear enough.

I'd been coming to see how she was doing. I knew it was far from proper, as we were courting and it was her custom to only see me twice in a week. But to the abyss with those traditions. I wanted to see her. I wanted to see how she was, if she was still shaken up from everything that had happened. I was about to knock when I'd heard the raised voices.

I shouldn't have tried to eavesdrop, but I had been worried. I had waited to hear crashing, fighting, so I could barge into the room and put an immediate end to it.

Now Captain Saber was in front of me, his anger almost palpable. And I'd never wanted to drive my fist into his face more than I did now.

"What did you do to her?" I advanced, my hands tightened into fists. If he'd done anything to her, I'd pummel him to the floor.

The captain's eyes narrowed, and he took a stroke forward. Our chests bumped together. Tension, dangerous and palpable, flowed between us. It had never boiled this hot, like a lava seam, threatening to consume us entirely.

"The *princess*," he spat, "is fine. She is distraught over being forced to have extra guards follow her. I assured her it was for her safety."

I despised the captain with every fiber of my being. I hadn't thought much of him before. All he ever did was glare at me and trail behind Odele like he owned her. But then that day in the gardens, when he'd pushed me aside to cover Odele's body with his own, I noticed something between them.

Something akin to passion.

And I hated him for it.

"The princess is *my* betrothed," I reminded him. He blinked before he started to swim away at a tight, slow pace. I swam after him, keeping up at his side. "It doesn't seem proper that you spend so much time in her room. Even if you are her protector, there will be talk—"

The captain turned so abruptly I startled to a stop, eyes widening as he looked at me with unconcealed fury. "Do not worry yourself unnecessarily,

Your Majesty," He packed as much sarcasm as he could into the title. "I would never jeopardize her reputation."

I nodded stiffly. "Good," I replied. "I would hate to see her suffer because of your mistakes."

The captain usually didn't reply to clever retorts. Today was different. His rage just kept rising. He snorted. "Do not pretend to care for her suffering. You never did before."

"Things change." *She changed.*

The captain shook his head. "Am I supposed to believe you suddenly love her?" I didn't reply. But the answer must have been plain on my face because a moment later, the captain was pulling me forward by the collar of my kimono so that we were close. "You do not love *Odele.*"

I let loose a breath. I could easily break his fingers and leave him writhing in agony. I was not called the Dragon Prince as a term of endearment, and he would do well not to test me. I just pried his fingers from my clothes, and he seemed to realize what he'd done. His eyes widened and he took a stroke back.

"How do you know how I feel?" I asked quietly. Who was he to dictate what was inside another's heart?

He grumbled low in frustration and turned around. I didn't bother to ask where he was going.

I didn't care.

Maisie

I COULDN'T STAND IT. I couldn't stand the way the tears flowed from my eyes or the way my heart pounded like a painful gong inside my chest. I wanted to stop feeling, to tear it out of there and tuck it away. I didn't want to care what the captain thought of me, didn't want to dwell on what I may have ruined.

Mostly, I didn't want to feel like a failure.

I barricaded the door and swam away from all the troubles, trying to leave them behind as I swam into the cove and out into the alley. It was broad daylight, unlike the other times I'd visited, and the reflection of pink towers shone down to illuminate the shadows. The alleyway was empty. But why had I expected it not to be? Was I starting to be so entitled that I just expected the Black Blade to be here, waiting for me? I was even starting to act as selfish as the princess.

Shaking my head to clear my foggy brain, I swam forward and into the bustling streets of the city. Bodies pushed past me, not one apologizing. And my eyes tried to go everywhere at once. The colors of the water seemed to blend together in bright blues, pinks, purples, and oranges. I tried to contain my awe as I watched a school of manta rays swim above my head, darkening the waters into shadow for a brief second.

Mer rich and poor swam about. The richer mer were sitting on top of ivory clamshell carriages, being pulled by strong hippocampi with long serpentine tails. Stalls and stores could be seen all around, mer with bright colored tails and impressive dresses swam around.

I'd hidden my hair beneath a hooded cloak of periwinkle. I looked rich, royal, and I knew it. But I hadn't wanted to take the time to change. I'd needed to get out of the palace as quickly as possible. I wanted to see the only other person in this city who could quite possibly even remotely understand me. The Black Blade. But where would I even begin to look for him?

I swam deeper into the city, past the rich housing and stores, past diamonds and gold and into poorer parts. Though not as lavish as the places closer to the palace, these stores were still rich in colors. The mer looked a bit more unsavory, their stalls a bit shabbier. I'd swam out without my blade for protection, too distraught to even think of bringing it. I regretted it now as I looked at the mer here but shook off those thoughts. How pretentious did that sound? These were the type of mer I was used to back in Lagoona. It was like I'd already forgotten where I'd come from.

Trying to be as inconspicuous as possible, I swam up to the store of an elder merman. He was selling hippocampus riding gear. I waved to him in greeting. "Excuse me, sir." He perked up at the sight of a possible customer and smiled. "I was wonderin' if you could help me with somethin'." Out here, I didn't bother hiding my accent. Out here, I wasn't the princess but any other mer.

"Anything, dearest."

I looked around, leaned down and whispered, "Do you know where I can find the merman they call the Black Blade?"

The merman's shoulders tensed, his smile dying quickly. He looked me up and down, took in the richness of the dress and cloak, the diamonds I'd worn at my throat. He took in my every detail before sniffing. "Can't say that I know what you're talking about. Now get, I'm about to close shop." I blinked at that sudden abruptness and hurriedly swam out as he waved me away and then closed the doors to his store, turning the sign from 'Open' to 'Closed'.

How odd, his behavior. I went to the next store. The owner was an older mermaid with brightly colored hair threaded through with white. There, it was much of the same thing. She was all smiles until I mentioned the Black Blade, and then she was ushering me out and closing the doors behind me.

And it happened in every store I visited.

What was going on here?

Unease bent through me, and my fin throbbed as I swam further through the city. Some mer, as if sensing what I wanted, slammed their doors before I could make it inside to talk to them. What were they so afraid of? The Black Blade? Or me?

I was about to turn back around and go back to the castle. I'd been a fool to think I could find him, to think that I could ever have someone in my corner, confide in anyone. I was on my own, and I didn't even think I had the right to be sad, to want to vent out my frustrations. I'd signed up for this, after all.

I turned slowly when the sudden hands tightening on my upper arms startled me into opening my mouth to scream. A hand clamped over my mouth before that could happen, and before I knew it, I was being dragged between two buildings, hidden from the eyes of the public.

I thrashed my tail, trying to fight off my attacker. My hood fell down with my movements, and more panic surged through me. If my attacker hadn't known who I was, they would now. A sob rose in my throat as I was brought crashing onto a hard body.

"When you go searching for an outlaw," a voice began in my ear, "you do not ask for them by their name, little fish."

The hands that held me loosened their grip and I whipped around to stare into familiar dark, dangerous eyes. Elias Blackfin, the Black Blade, was leaning against the wall behind him, but his hands were hovering over my upper arms. His lip twitched into a smile that was mocking. And even if I wanted to punch the look from his face, I couldn't help the relief and joy that surged through me at the sight of him.

"I knew you'd come looking for me eventually."

His voice was so cocky, so sure, and everything that had happened these last few days came over me in one overwhelming shove. I couldn't help the sob that rose in my chest or tore out of my throat. I couldn't help the tears that flowed freely from my eyes. I couldn't help any of it.

I threw myself into the Black Blade's arms.

And I wept.

SHE WAS GLARING ONE moment and distraught the next, tears spilling from her eyes as she threw herself into my arms. Her hug was crushing, and I was all too eager to keep her in place. She buried her face into the dark shirt of my tunic, and I held her there with one hand, the other skirting around her waist. Sobs racked her body and something inside of me clenched.

"There, there, little fish." I pressed a soft kiss of comfort on top of her head. "Who has wronged you?" I'd kill whoever had hurt her without blinking twice. I did not like to see a mermaid cry. It crippled me.

She sniffled and pulled away, but her fingers were still fisted at my shirt. "I'm sorry," she whispered. "I didn't come here to weep all over you."

I almost told her it was alright, that she could weep all she wanted. I liked her there, pressed up against my chest, showing a vulnerability she'd tried to hide the night we first met. Before I could say anything in response, she was pulling away and wiping away at her tears, ever strong and fierce as she looked up at me.

"I've been looking for you," she said.

I smiled. "I know, little fish. I was told. Take more caution around this part of Eramaea. Though the mer know I am here, they don't use my name. It would bring soldiers straight to their shop doors. Now—" I broke off and looked around. "Let's go somewhere more private so we can talk, yeah?"

She complied and didn't protest when I slipped my fingers into hers, pulling her deeper into the alley and through an opened door. I closed it behind us and led her into the comforts of a small home. She stopped by the door and looked around at the place.

"Is this yours?" she asked. Her eyes glued to the décor. It was rather bare, a small couch, a table, and a clutter of trash and various human paraphernalia.

"This is the back room used for storage," I replied, guiding her to the couch and sitting her there. "It's not mine, but the owner lets me use it on occasion." I perched myself on the edge of the table across from her. "Now, tell the Black Blade all of your troubles."

She glared at me. "Don't mock me," she snapped.

"I would never do such a thing." I smiled. Anger was better than sadness, and if I could rile enough emotion out of her, she'd forget she was ever sad in the first place.

"You're a liar, Elias."

I *really* liked the way she said my name. I liked it a lot. My eyes roamed over her slowly, from the aquamarine color on her tail fin to the purple-blue of the exposed part of her tail. A sea foam green dress floated loosely over her body, and at her shoulders she wore a purple cloak. The outfit did not do her beauty justice.

"Perhaps. But you must like something about me, since you came calling. Want another kiss?" I raised my eyebrows, smirked, knowing it would infuriate her. When her face flushed angrily, I knew it had worked.

"Ugh, why did I come to see such a barracuda like you?" Her words were angry, but there was no bite to them. And then she answered her own question. "Because I needed a break. I needed to get away from *them.*"

I crossed my arms over my chest. "Them?" I echoed.

She nodded and sighed, tossing her head back on the couch. "The *royals.* I was suffocating in there. I wanted to get away from the pressure. I wanted something... normal..."

She looked so sad sitting there. I sighed and looked around. There was a lot I had to do. Blades needed making to be sold, and there were some locals I'd promised I'd help out by moving furniture and tending to their animals. But... I looked at her lip stuck between her teeth. The locals could wait.

"You fancy swimming around town with me, little fish?" I asked, hopping off the table. I didn't wait for her reply as I began digging through the clutter around the floor. I picked up a long strip of black cloth from the corner of the house and went to the other side to rummage through an old chest.

"I'll probably draw attention to you," she said. "The Princess of Thalassar out in Eramaean streets with the kingdom's most notorious criminal. I can hear it on the broadcasts now."

I found what I was looking for and turned back to her, handing her the folded fabric. "Ditch the dress and cloak," I ordered. "And put this on."

She took the folded fabric from my hands and let it unfold to reveal a long, black dress. Her eyebrows rose. "Yours?" she asked sarcastically.

"Wouldn't *you* like to know?"

She chuckled as she floated up and untied the strings of her cloak at her throat. I watched the workings of her long, slender fingers move, jerking the strings and dropping the cloak from her body to float to the floor. My throat tightened.

"Do you mind?" she asked, eyes narrowing.

I laughed and crossed my arms against my chest. "Not at all, little fish." She glowered and I laughed again before slowly turning around to give her enough privacy to change.

I heard the swishing of fabric, felt the stirring in the water as she moved. I had that sudden urge to turn and look at her, to steal a glimpse at the curves of her waist, the shape of her scales, her perky breasts…

"Finished," she announced.

I couldn't turn fast enough. The dress fit her a bit tightly, pressing up against her chest. It ran down tight across her tail, though the sides were slit to allow free movement in the fins, it was obviously designed for a thinner mermaid. She still looked stunning, the material pressing against every dip of her body.

"Come here," I demanded quietly, my voice heavy. She swam forward until we were nearly touching. "Turn around." She did as she was told and my fingers got to work, sweeping her hair behind her head and tying the black strip of cloth onto her head like a swashbuckling pirate. I ended up braiding her purple strands in with the remaining strips of black cloth and tying the end. When I finished, she turned back around. "There," I said. "Now you're just a simple mermaid named Maisie taking a swim around Eramaean streets with a simple merman named Elias."

I loved everything about Thalassar, though the royalty of Eramaea were the exception. There was something about Eramaea that was rather beautiful. It could have been the colors, swathes of pinks, golds, and blues that cast a sunset-like hue over the entire city. Maybe it was the food sold in stalls along the streets. Maybe it was the variety of mer that swam about with all sorts of tails in all shapes, sizes, colors, and styles.

Today, I loved Eramaea because of her.

Her eyes widened as she took everything in for what seemed like the first time. It had me observing every little thing about her. There was always so much to learn, so much to see, new details to pick up. Like the fact that she swam with a slight limp that she seemed to be desperately trying to hide. Or the fact that her eyes shone almost blue when the golden rays of the palace shone down on her. Or the way she spoke in a small pond accent with much more ease than when she spoke in the Eramaean one.

We swam side by side, though I didn't reach for her hand again, and she didn't reach for mine. I didn't mind. It was enough to swim beside her and enjoy her reactions to the city. When we passed a stall that sold river frogs stuffed with water leeches, I noticed her nose twitch in that direction.

"Do you want one?" I asked, stopping her.

She looked so excited at the prospect of real food. They probably starved her with nonsense that they passed off as meals in that palace. I ordered two frogs skewered on kabobs and handed one off to her. She dug in without hesitation, smacking her lips as she swam.

I ate mine much more slowly, and when we finished, we went to discard the kabob sticks into a fishing net used for trash.

On and on our adventure went. She'd stop at stalls and look over the things there. Before I could offer to buy anything, she'd move on to the next. The only things she truly held an interest in were foods. Foods, I noticed, that were authentic from the small pond of Lagoona.

She was devouring snail stew from a to-go bowl like she was starving.

When she finished, she used the back of her hand to wipe her mouth. "So…" She set her bowl onto her lap. We had stopped near the public park. There were coral benches and reefs with hundreds of fish swimming all around. I lifted my finger up to stroke a passing clown fish. "Why are you here?" she asked.

I leaned back on the bench. "Because I wanted to wipe the sadness from your eyes."

She flushed but shook her head. "No, no, no. I mean why are you here in Eramaea?" She looked around cautiously, afraid someone might overhear, then she leaned closer to me. "You're an outlaw," she whispered.

My eyes glittered in amusement. "You don't have to whisper, little fish. I know I'm a criminal."

She rolled her eyes. "So if you're wanted by everyone here, why stay? Why not leave Thalassar and live somewhere without having to look over your shoulder at every turn?"

I batted away a shrimp that came over to buzz around our faces. When it was gone, I smiled. "Misdirection," I explained. At her confused look, I elaborated. "That's what everyone expects me to do, little fish. I'm the most wanted mer in the capitol. I've fled Selection and have helped other mer flee Selection and find sanctuary. Where? At the one place they'd never think to look."

Her eyes widened and she smiled. "Right under their noses."

"Exactly. They wouldn't expect the Black Blade to be hiding a few strokes away from their palace. They never look. And all those mer you saw today? They were all Selected at one point. After a few weeks in hiding, they change their appearance, change their names, and they can live comfortably in the only kingdom they've ever known." Home. I had no home. Not anymore. Mine was brutally stripped from me by tyrant royals who did not like the idea of a free merman.

"Why do you do it?" she asked.

No one had ever asked me that before. The smile on my face died. Everyone always thanked me for what I did for them. They treated me like a hero, like the savior of the broken. I'd never wanted to be that. I never wanted titles that weighed heavily on my shoulders, and I hadn't been born with them. They'd been bestowed upon me because of what I could do and what I'd done.

"Because I love Thalassar." My reply was simple enough. I didn't think I needed to explain my love of it to her. I didn't need to elaborate and tell her I loved the mer, I loved the currents, the schools of fishes. Her eyes were bright with understanding. Royals would never understand the love I had for the ocean we resided in. But she held the in-depth understanding of someone who had been Selected would.

Her hand found mine, and instead of looking down at it, I was captivated by her eyes. By her smile. "Thank you," she whispered.

And she didn't need to explain to me what she meant.

I already knew.

Tiberius

I WATCHED FROM ACROSS the park. She had not yet seen me, and I probably would have missed her if I hadn't heard her laughter or seen a quick flash of purple. So I stuck to the crowd, followed at a steady pace. My eyes had not failed me. There she was. Maisie. Wearing drab clothing, out of the palace and with a merman.

I tried to simmer the rage down, but it would not stay. My eyes narrowed as I took the merman in. His tail was long and black, his fins looking as sharp as razors. Everything about his demeanor told me that he was a criminal from the fishhook sticking from the lobe of his ear to the way his hair floated wildly over his coppery cheeks.

And then I saw the rings adorning his fingers. Lavish things of sapphires and rubies. One in particular caught my eye. A black, obsidian ring perched on his left hand. The hand Maisie currently held. There was so much confidence in the gesture, so much trust. I gritted my teeth together and loosed a slow, steady breath.

I'd come to the city to clear my head, to get Odele and Maisie out of my mind and regain my composure. And now here she was, swimming through the city streets with none other than the Black Blade. The outlaw the crown had been looking for.

I didn't need to get close enough to listen to their conversation to know who he was.

Everyone knew the stories of the Black Blade. Of a legend of cloak and shadow, and of the rare obsidian blades and accessories he possessed.

And Maisie… Did she know she was in the presence of a criminal? She had to. She had to know who he was. She had his blade, for tides' sake, and she worshipped it like she would a god for reasons I simply could not fathom.

She should have been at the palace, in her rooms. How had she gotten out without the guards noticing? I'd ordered them at her door and to follow her every move. Had she somehow slipped past them? If so, how?

But more importantly, what was she doing with a wanted criminal of Thalassar and why was she smiling at him as if she were in love?

Maisie

When night started to fall, Elias—he was *Elias* now, a name that seemed far more intimate than just calling him 'the Black Blade'—escorted me to the mouth of the alley where we'd first met. He didn't ask questions about how I got in and out of the palace unseen, though I suspected he already knew.

Our goodbye was bittersweet, and he didn't wait to watch me go in through the secret passage before he was turning and swimming away. I watched him disappear into the throng of mer before I left, swimming into the cove. My heart was filled with a glee that hadn't been there since Selection. Glee that hadn't been there for such a long time.

I felt giddy, felt hope surge straight through me entirely. Elias had given that to me with his words and actions. He believed in the tyranny of the royals just as much as I did because he'd seen it. Even though he thought I was the princess, he'd been kind. I wondered if he could believe I could make a change as much as I wanted to believe that myself.

His belief in me made me think that perhaps this hadn't all been for nothing. That I was suffering through dress fittings, teatime, and everything else for a reason. And that reason was because the change *would* come.

I spun aimlessly through the water, twirling in circles with my arms out at my sides. I laughed happily, fanning my fins out at my sides only to have them cramp up and send me hurtling to the ground.

I didn't have enough time to right myself as I crashed to the floor onto a pile of conch shells. Pain pierced my skin, and I heard the painful sound of a crack as a conch broke beneath me. Cursing, I sat up and moved aside.

"Abyss take me," I muttered as I bent to dust away the cracked broken bits of a conch. I'd broken three. Three conch shells that held recordings of the princess. Recordings I'd hoped had been nothing, but now I'd never know.

I picked up a cracked conch shell and was about to toss it in frustration but stopped when I noticed something sticking out of the cracks. I brought it closer to my face to examine it. Something was buried deep into this conch. Sticking my fingers in, I grabbed whatever it was and pulled it out. It was a folded piece of kelp. I unfolded it to its true size. It was long and rectangular, with pretty handwriting sprawled across the front of it in squid ink.

Why had it been hidden in there?

My eyes scanned over the page, reading the words.

"On this Starsday of the one hundred and ninth rule of the Malabella lineage, it is hereby decreed that Princess Odessa Malabella Sanitorum of the mer

kingdom of Thalassar, on the day of her twentieth birthday wed Prince Xristo Oriana of the kingdom of Brague, uniting both kingdoms in a contract that can be broken only in death. In the same note that it is hereby decreed that Princess Odette Malabella Sanitorum of the kingdom of Thalassar shall wed Prince Dorian Knoll Gennivus of the mer kingdom of Kappur that same day."

I tore my eyes from the page to steady my breathing. This… What I held in my hands was a *marriage contract.* A marriage contract between Princess Odele's mother, Odette, and the Prince of Kappur. The prince who was now an unwed king.

Odele's mother had been *engaged* to King Dorian. The royal signatures of the old king and queen as well as advisors and witnesses were on this scroll. So why hadn't Odette married Dorian? I looked over the names again. It said here that Odessa had been engaged to Xristo. Odessa was the late Queen Odette's twin sister. She'd died before any marriages had taken place. There weren't many details regarding her death, none that I'd heard anyway.

But even if she'd died, why had Odette married Xristo instead of Dorian like she was supposed to? If this document was correct, even despite her death, Odette should have married Dorian, thus sealing ties between Thalassar and Kappur.

Had this been what the princess had kept secret? Had this been why someone was trying to murder her? Could she possibly know the story behind this?

Kappur and Thalassar had been in a contract to join forces. A legal contract that bound them and had been broken. The question was, who had been the one to break it? This could very well be the reason why the two kingdoms were at war in the first place. A broken marriage contract was serious enough for the royals to go to war over.

I read it over three more times, memorizing every word and name on that scrap of kelp before I folded it up and tucked it into conch shell number twenty-three. I'd keep it there until I found more out. Until I knew what exactly I was going to do with it and the information on it.

"There's a lot of secrets in these royal tides," I said to myself. And I meant to uncover them all.

Small specks of light flickered through the water. They clung to my skin, the brightness a contrast to my shadows. The bioluminescent algae likely illuminated the smile that curved my mouth. Nothing could diminish my happiness right now. The thought was a flicker in my mind as I swiped the specks away, smearing them against my body until I glowed.

Damn.

A joke rose up in my throat at my own expense, but I pushed it back with a chuckle. My dark fins pushed against the breeze of the current, and I emerged from the alleyway and out into the bustling streets of Eramaea.

I hadn't lied when I told her that I hid at the capitol to avoid detection. It was not because I was afraid of the soldiers. Fear had left me long ago in those moments when I'd been selected. When they'd called my name, the frightened young mer within me died. When I'd been thrown into a cage with others, I'd been born anew.

I'd worked from the shadows ever since. I wanted to help those who couldn't help themselves. It was why I stayed on the poorer side of Eramaea. It was why those mer protected me and my reputation with a ferocity.

When their own monarchy betrayed them time and time again, it was no wonder they turned to criminals for protection. The royals liked to call me a villain. What they didn't know was that villains were just heroes in disguise. Everyone thought themselves righteous and good here because of the blood they were born with.

I was scum, and I knew I was scum. No amount of jewels on my fingers or in my pockets could change the circumstances of my birth. Of where I came from. Yet I knew I was better than half the mer at the palace on principle alone.

They flipped their fins at the mer on the ground while I helped them swim up to heights they never thought possible.

I pushed through clusters of bodies, letting the crowd swallow me up when I felt the first tingle clawing down my spine. I wasn't foolish enough to look over my shoulder and give anything away. Only a fool let their stalkers know that they knew they were being followed.

I was no fool.

I weaved through the crowds, disappearing into shadows, clinging to them like a sticky phantom. When I was sure I was out of sight, I paused, waiting. I was a patient mer, and though I couldn't make out who it was who was following me, I knew the moment they were gone. The feeling of being watched abated and the adrenaline that had started to build eased.

This time, when I swam, I made sure to stick to the shadows. When I made it to the poorer side of the city, I was about to creep through the backs of houses and sneak into one when I felt that sensation once again.

A stirring in the water, a sensation down my spine.

This time, I started to turn and confront the problem, but I was too late.

Pain splintered through the back of my head. I was knocked forward, my fins flapping to try and right myself. I twisted, landing hard on my back in the silt. My blade was in my hand before I could blink, clashing against the sword of the royal guard looming over me.

A feral grin twisted my lips. The adrenaline was back, pumping through my blood, rushing like a fast-moving current. I rolled in the silt, pushing myself up and meeting the soldier. I studied his features in between parries. Slash, dodge, push. We fought with vigor, and I was confident I would win.

And that confidence was my downfall.

A moment later, I was surrounded. Soldiers burst from all sides and within moments, took me down. I grunted as the water was knocked from me, and I would have laughed if I'd been able to do so. The sound was stolen from me as fists and fins punched and kicked my face. The blade was wrenched from my grasp, my rings pulled from my fingertips. It didn't matter how much I fought back; it was useless.

At least for the moment.

I was not one to believe in hopelessness. There was always a way to freedom.

Always.

And when the soldiers hauled me up between them, I chuckled as a soldier appeared in my blurred vision. I recognized him all too soon and couldn't help the laughter that bubbled out of me.

"Quite far away from the princess, aren't you?"

Captain Saber sneered at me as if I were the scum on his fins. Because how else would this well-groomed palace guard see me?

"Shut your mouth, criminal," he snapped. His fists tightened and I knew he wanted to hit me, but he was too uptight for that. He would not strike me. Not abuse his power.

Pathetic dog fish.

"I don't think I will."

"Well, you do not have a choice. Not where you're going." He bent low so we were close. I wondered what he would do if I pressed my lips to his. How shocked he would be by the action. "Your days of hiding are over, Black Blade."

I didn't see the next blow coming.

Then there was nothing but darkness.

THE NEXT MORNING I was escorted to the queen and king at the guards' request. They wanted to see me, and so I'd go to them even if I didn't want to. I wore a long silk dress in purple so that it matched my tail. Today, I didn't really care what I wore. I just wanted to get this over with, whatever it was they wanted me for.

I arrived at their sides. They were wearing fancy dress, their crowns sparkling on top of their heads. When I arrived, the queen looked me over with disdain and ushered me forward quickly.

"Suffering tides, you are slower than a sea turtle. Bend down." I did as she bid and tried not to wince as she set a small silver crown on my head. When I straightened, her gaze seemed to scrutinize nearly everything about me. "We have much to do today," she said. "So please no more repeats of what had happened at the anniversary dinner."

I just nodded to avoid arguing, though I made no specific promises to her. It seemed there was a royal event going on of some sort, because a moment later, Prince Kai arrived with his guards and advisors. He gave me a shy nod that I returned before we were ushered out of the palace and towards awaiting shelled carriages tethered to massive hippocampi.

The queen and king rode together in one while Prince Kai and I took the other one. We sat in the soft cushioning and then the beast was off, following behind the queen and king's carriage.

"Do you know what this is about?" I asked him.

Prince Kai shook his head. Interesting.

"Princess, are you well?" he asked me suddenly.

I turned away from the pretty sights of Eramaea to smile at him. "I'm fine, thanks."

He looked doubtful. "Yesterday I was outside your room. I heard you and Captain Saber shouting."

My face went bright red, but I turned from him before he could make note of it. "It was nothing," I said, waving his concerns off. I didn't want to think about Captain Saber today. Not when I'd had a good night. Not when he was nowhere in sight.

Prince Kai must have noticed I didn't want to talk about that business any further, because he kept his silence. It was a few minutes later that we made it to wherever it was we'd needed to be. It was an enormous coliseum, a building shaped with circular walls like an amphitheater. Had we come to see a play? I let a guard help me down and escort Kai and I to the entrance.

We were led up a flight of stairs where four thrones awaited us. Behind one of them floated Captain Saber, his posture stiff and rigid. He cast one glance at me, the expression hard in his eyes, before he turned away. Good. I didn't want to look at him either.

We took our seats, me beside Kai and King Xristo beside Queen Circe. I leaned forward in my chair to look down. It wasn't as big on the inside as it was on the outside. We were close to the stage below, and seats around the place were filled with mer. Not a single seat was left unoccupied.

"Why are we here?" I whispered to Kai.

He shrugged. "I do not know. I was hoping you could tell me."

I guess Princess Odele would have known. Captain Saber and I never went over this bit in our training, unfortunately. I fought not to turn and glare at him for that. I wondered if he deliberately had wanted me to fail at this.

I almost turned around and glared, but before I could there was the loud blaring of a horn. I leaned over the edge of the balcony eagerly, placing my hands on the railing. Would there be an orchestra? I'd always wanted to see live music.

A hush descended upon the crowd as an old merman swam onto the stage below. He was wearing black robes, his long white hair braided behind his back. Was he the orchestra master? I tried to lean closer but felt the tug at the end of my dress. When I turned, Kai was looking at me with concern, like he was worried I'd fall over the edge. I rolled my eyes at him playfully.

Turning my attention back to the merman, I watched as he cleared his throat. "The Minister of Justice comes forth to present the charges to Her Majesty, Queen Circe Malabella and King Xristo Oriana de Malabella."

The queen at my side replied in a booming voice that carried through the water. "Proceed with the charges, Minister."

Charges? What was she talking about? A sudden feeling of unease crept through me. Still, I kept my hands tight on the balcony and watched with rapt attention.

"On this day on the one hundredth and nineteenth year of the Malabella reign, I, the Minister of Justice, hereby condemn this mer for the crimes of fleeing Selection as well as aiding other criminals to the crown of fleeing Selection."

My heart sank to the pit of my stomach. My fingers trembled on the balcony. A sudden intense feeling of nausea washed over me, but I pushed it away and tried to focus.

"And what is the punishment for these crimes?" the queen asked.

The minister rolled his kelp parchment up again. His answer was clear and sent frozen icicles straight through my veins. "The punishment is death."

The queen nodded. "Bring forth the prisoner."

I wanted to close my eyes when they brought the merman out onto the stage. This scene was so familiar to me. I'd seen it a day before Selection in Lagoona. I'd seen soldiers bring Christof down and behead him. And I would witness it here in Eramaea, from the comfort of my throne with the heavy weight of a crown bearing me down.

This merman, unlike Christof, did not fight his captors. He swam with dignity despite being covered in the gray cloth of a prisoner and with a sack over his head. My breath caught in my throat, a sob froze waiting to be unleashed. More mermen swam out onto stage. One with a large swinging axe. The other to place a block before the condemned.

"By royal permission do I decree that this merman known as Elias Blackfin, alias the Black Blade, be condemned to die."

The gasp tore through my throat as the hood was pulled away to reveal the merman underneath. His black hair was ruffled, the silver cross at his ear gone. The side of his face was bruised as if he'd been beaten. When he looked up in our direction, his eyes found mine…

And he smiled.

WHISPERS
BENEATH THE
DEEP

"I SENTENCE YOU TO die . . ."

My fingers felt numb from how tightly I held to the railing, watching from my place on the balcony high above the arena at the coral-made stage below. The crown that had been placed on my head by the queen an hour before this moment, though wiry and adorned with very few jewels, suddenly felt too heavy. Its weight threatened to drag me down into an abyss of despair as the sack was pulled from the criminal's head to reveal the identity of the merman underneath.

Elias Blackfin.

The infamous Black Blade.

If they hadn't said his name, I still would have recognized him, even from this height. Even with his dark skin mottled and swollen with bruises, even without the obsidian rings adorning his fingers, even as he now wore the gray rags of a criminal, his presence was dominating, commanding.

From across the space that separated us, Elias looked up, dark eyes finding my own amidst the crush of mer filling the stadium, and he smiled.

My next breath stuck to the back of my throat.

There was a reason he had looked up at me and no one else, a menacing danger in the curve of his too-sensual lips. A danger that I could read all too well.

You owe me, Princess.

A sudden cheer trembled the waters of the arena. I tore my gaze from his to look at the merpeople of the kingdom of Thalassar, jumping from their seats and cheering at the prospect of death. The words they shouted spun through the violent riptide of waves in my mind, threatening to overwhelm me.

"Finally!"

"Kill the Black Blade!"

"Off with his head!"

My gut clenched. Nausea roiled over me, and I tasted bile rising in the back of my throat. This scene was familiar to me. The victim, officials, their swinging ax. I'd witnessed it a thousand times before. But this… the cheering, the jeers, it was all new. Back home in Lagoona, deaths were mourned, fueling our hatred for the capital city, Eremaea, and the royals of Thalassar who resided here, where they relished in the death of a mer.

Because we meant nothing to them.

The weight of jewelry and silks adorning my body suddenly pressed too hotly, like the finery itself was speaking to me in vicious whispers, begging my frigid body to move. To do *something.* My fingers dug into the rail, and I felt my painted nails crack. I ignored the stinging pain. I doubled over, and the dainty little crown toppled and spun down to the waters below.

A gentle hand pressed against my lower back.

"Are you alright, Princess?"

I half turned to look at the merman who spoke. Brown eyes met my own, and I could see the severity in those depths. Prince Kai kept his hand placed lightly on my back, and I wished his warm touch could help anchor me. Instead, it just gave me a harrowing sense of dread.

"This is barbaric," I ground out from between tightly clenched teeth. I wondered if Prince Kai thought these actions to be just as vicious as I did but shook the notion off. He was a royal himself. Surely this was not a new occurrence to him. Even the kingdom of Draconi held their own executions, and I knew they were more brutal than to just suffer at the swing of an ax. I'd heard in whisperings that criminals in Draconi suffered death by dragon.

I jerked away from him, pressing my body tighter against the rail, as far away from him as the confines of the balcony space would allow. He looked at me, a brief expression of hurt passing over his elegant features, before he set his gaze back to the scene below, expression hardening.

Behind him, Captain Saber was studying me with apprehensive, aquamarine eyes. Looking at him made me equally ill, so I turned back down in time to see the guard haul Elias forward violently and bend him over to expose the back of his neck. The cheers became a deafening roar now, vibrating the waters. The tendrils of Elias' dark hair floated up, like tiny wisps of a shadowy curtain parting to reveal his face. Broken, bruised, his eyes still held mine from down there.

The executioner swung the ax in a few test tries that had me seeing blood. I was familiar with the swing of a merman who didn't care who he killed. I'd seen that carelessness before. Like they did this for sport, or worse still, like they just wanted to get this nuisance over with before they could go back home to their lives, unencumbered by the scum of Thalassar.

He lifted the ax high over his head now, strong, muscular arms cording and bunching up with the strain.

And those dark eyes were still on me. They weren't begging, pleading, but *demanding*. A sharp, dark reminder of what I owed him for all he had done for me since we'd met. He wanted to be saved, and only I had the power to save him.

That wasn't technically true. Princess Odele Malabella Oriana of Thalassar, future ruling queen, could save him, and though I wasn't her, nobody knew that except for a few seated near me. The queen, king, and Captain Saber. They knew I wore her mask, and that I was just a figure for the mer to look at. I held no real power. I was nothing. Nobody.

But the *mer* didn't know that.

It was high time I tried to make a change.

Fingers shaking, I straightened to my full height and shouted over the roar of the crowds. "Stop!" My voice did not quiver. I was fueled with the implacable desire to protect. To stop this madness. I always used to sit back and watch the inevitable death of those around me. Not this time. This time I would try to do something about it.

The mer did not hear me. Those in my company did. "What are you doing?" the queen hissed from beside me. "Sit down, foolish child." I did not spare her, decked out in jeweled finery, a glance.

"Princess…" Captain Saber's voice was stern, a command that I chose to ignore.

Straightening my shoulders, I pushed myself off the balcony railing, feeling Prince Kai's adept fingers tug lightly at my dress, trying to hold me back. I flicked my tail, ignoring the pain of my shredded fin on the left side of my body, and swam down from the royal enclosure.

As the mer saw me descend, they began to hush, sitting back in place, some bowing as I passed. I ignored them. Hateful creatures. All I was focused on was Elias, bent over, beaten and tied, ready to face a death he did not deserve.

I swam to the edge of the stage and stopped. I didn't know what my facial expression looked like at that moment. All I knew was that the executioner took one frightened look at me and dropped the ax to bow low on the coral-made stage.

"This has to stop," I whispered angrily, then turned to the crowd. They were all staring at me with confusion and irritation. I glared at every single one of them, and finally, up to the balcony where the queen and king sat. Prince Kai was floating where I'd been only moments before, his hands gripping tightly at the ledge. Captain Saber kicked off from the balcony and started towards me. "This must stop!" I called out to the audience. I had too much practice using that Eramaean accent; it rang out confidently, firmly. They shifted in their seats. "This merman does not deserve death. Stop the violence. No more!"

"Majesty." The executioner spoke reluctantly like I was no more than a petulant child. Odele may have been one, but I was not. "This merman has committed many crimes against the kingdom. The law clearly states—"

"The law is wrong!" I interrupted. Shocked gasps rang out through the arena. I turned back to them, eyes beseeching them to listen. "The kingdom of Thalassar has been ruled too long by tyrant laws. Children, mothers, and fathers are sent out to fight in the war with Kappur. Those who fear the striking of blades, those who *flee* are punished with death. What message is this?" I turned, gesturing at Elias with a wave of my hand.

"Violence is all this kingdom is now. Violence and death. Surely there was a time when this kingdom shone with the same radiance as its castle, when praise was given to the queen and king. Now, the mer whisper of their hatred for the royals." I banged my fist against my chest, and the aggressive sound reverberated along the rippling of water. "They hate us, and it is their very right. Because we steal them. We take them from their homes and we murder them without a second thought."

Captain Saber was getting closer now, his face tight with disapproval. I turned and went over to Elias. The guard behind him froze with uncertainty, watching as I swept low and grabbed Elias by the elbow. Slowly, I helped him up so that his face and bruises were visible to all.

"No more!" I shouted. "The violence stops now. And it stops with me."

"Princess, he is a dangerous criminal," the guard stuttered.

I glared. "Unbind him!"

"Princess… the law…"

"I said *unbind him*."

The guard started forward reluctantly. I didn't miss the way he shot glances up the arena where the queen and king were seated, as if he were hoping her command could supersede my own. But in her rage, she kept silent. He'd be a fool to disobey the rulings of a princess. And I *was* his princess as far as he knew. He bent and took a knife from a holster at his side, and in a couple of sawing motions, Elias was free of his restraints.

I smiled just as Captain Saber reached the edge of the stage, a sword held tightly in his hand, as if it had been there all along. "Princess, get away from that sea scum, now."

I glared at him, too. "No more violence, Captain."

"He's dangerous."

"He is not!"

I felt Elias's chest brush against my back and my body heated. I felt his hand snake up to rest on my shoulder, giving me a tiny squeeze of gratitude. I didn't turn to look up at him, but I saw Captain Saber's eyes narrow on the hand of the criminal behind me.

"Unhand the princess and face your sentence."

I glowered. The captain was disregarding every word I had said publicly.

"Oh, little fish…" I felt Elias's warm lips against the lobe of my ear and my face flushed. With just the proximity of his mouth, I felt my mind drift back to a few weeks ago. When those lips that whispered darkly in my ears now had pressed against my own. When his tongue had invaded my senses and made my fins curl. When, for the first time in my life, I felt *desire.* Involuntarily, my eyes went up to the balcony, where I saw Prince Kai's murderous gaze even from here. Suddenly he was swimming towards me as well, with his Draconian guards and his advisors. "You should have listened to your captain…"

Before I could gift him with a questioning glance, I felt his forearm snake around my shoulders and go around my neck, pressing my body tighter against him. I startled and Elias squeezed, closing off my gills and water supply.

I choked, clawing at his hand. "Elias…" I gasped.

He held me tightly and backed away from the captain and the guards. "Come closer," he threatened, loud enough for the entire arena to hear, "and I will kill the princess."

What are you doing, Elias?

I wanted to scream the words, but they constricted in my throat. I couldn't breathe in the water that my body so desperately craved. I didn't want to believe that Elias would hurt me. How could I, after all we'd shared? A favor, a shoulder to cry on, an understanding… A kiss.

But I should have known. I should have known things would end this way. He was a criminal, after all, and he'd made that little fact known since the first moment I'd met him.

In this one swift action, of placing a forearm against my throat, everything I thought I'd grown to feel for him shattered, like the fragility of an old conch breaking under a rough touch. Hatred rose, surging through me like the hot current of a lava seam.

"Drop your weapon, Captain!" Elias commanded, his voice menacing, dangerous. For a moment, I was transported back into the mouth of that alleyway to the first moment I'd seen him. He'd transformed right before my eyes. Funny, how he could look helpless and weak one moment, and completely change into a deadly shadow. Into what he was truly meant to be.

The Black Blade.

Captain Saber pointed the tip of his sword in our direction. His stance was battle-ready. I hadn't seen him in action, didn't know the extent of his force, but the two of them facing one another? They'd be formidable.

"Let the princess go!" the captain commanded.

I raked my nails down Elias' exposed skin. Water… I needed to breathe. He only jerked me tighter against the hard panes of his chest and pressed his cheek against my own. His skin was warm, but when I tried to jerk away, his grip on me tightened.

"Put down the sword first." As he said the words, his arm slid around my waist to pull me closer, if that were even possible. He already felt close enough, and things were starting to blur around my vision. Darkness wasn't too far behind.

The indecision on Captain Saber's face was all but obvious. His eyes darted up to my own, then to Elias, assessing, and I wondered what he saw. With great reluctance, he finally dropped his sword to the stage where it fell with a clang.

And then I could finally breathe.

I sucked in water, gills and lungs burning with the action. I could feel the heavy imprint of his violence against my skin. Now, his arms were wrapped around my waist, keeping me as a shield between him and the wrath of both Captain Saber and Prince Kai, who swam up at the captain's side.

I couldn't keep the heat from rising up my neck and cheeks at the sight of Prince Kai. How was it that he could look both elegant and dangerous? The finery draped over his body only accentuated the murderous gleam in his eyes. It was a look I'd never seen before.

"Looks like the cavalry has arrived!" Elias laughed harshly in my ear, tugging me back. "What an honor it is to float in your presence, Prince Kai Li." He mockingly bowed, chest pressing into my back, forcing me to mimic the gesture as well. My hair fell over my cheeks in thick tendrils, and when they parted, I glimpsed Kai's expression.

It was nothing short of murderous.

"Release her," Kai demanded. The cadence of his voice was different, almost guttural in a way that sent shivers down my back.

Elias edged us backwards again. What was he doing? Surely he must know that this couldn't end well, that there was no way for him to escape? We were surrounded by guards and citizens. He couldn't use me as a shield forever.

"Or what, Dragon Prince?" he mocked. "Will you spit ice? Will you eat me with sharpened teeth?" He chuckled with feigned amusement.

Kai's hand twitched at his sides.

"Please feel free," Elias continued. "But know this: if you do…" He bent us down then, and it was then that I realized what his intent was. He picked up the ax that had been meant to end his life. He held the heavy weapon in one arm, bringing it up to the base of my throat. "I will kill your precious princess."

And before anyone could reply, Elias brought his arm back and then forward, releasing the ax in one violent, strong throw, aiming straight at Captain Saber and Prince Kai.

I screamed, but he didn't let me see the aftermath of the blow. He whirled me around and hauled me away after creating the perfect distraction to escape.

Using me as bait.

I SAW THE AX twirling through the water in our direction. We were pressed so close together, and the weapon traveled at near impossible speed, that the sharp curve of the executioner's blade could very well have ended us both. Adrenaline coursed through my bloodstream as I watched the weapon hurtle towards us, threatening death.

But then Prince Kai was shoving me aside. I grunted, not registering his movements. He was a blur of black and blue silk, like the strong push of a current in the water. A moment later, he stilled, and in his hands he held the handle of the ax that should have ended us both.

Annoyance I couldn't avoid surged through me.

"Don't do that again!" I snapped. *I* was the guard. Not him. Despite his reputation as the Dragon Prince, I was meant to throw myself into the path of danger to protect him. Not the other way around.

He glared at me with changed eyes, the dark brown having vanished to make room for something absolutely feral. Slit pupils and a bright blue iris, focused like a beast hunting for prey. No longer was he Prince Kai Li of Draconi, but he became the Dragon Prince right before my eyes. The one that was so terribly revered. And like the rumors whispered, his eyes glowed with fearsome might. His nostrils flared, catching scent of the enemy he meant to catch and destroy.

Without a word, he dropped the ax and whirled around, speeding forward in the water to chase after that criminal and Maisie.

Cursing myself for wasting a moment to gawk at the abnormal prince, I bent down to scoop up my sword and darted after them as well. I should have never let her swim down from that balcony. I'd made a vow to protect Maisie like I'd failed to protect Princess Odele, and I couldn't break my promise now.

I put in a burst of speed, coming up beside Prince Kai. He may have had a special set of skills that set him apart from other royals of his station, but I was made for this. Meant to protect and defend.

The amphitheater was shaped in a circle, with different levels for seating arrangements. I caught sight of a purple and black tail ahead, heading for one of the many exits around the stadium. If they made it out, it'd be harder to catch them. Harder, but not impossible.

And I meant to catch him and send him straight to the gallows. Whether Maisie, that fool of a mer, wanted the Black Blade dead or not. I'd see to it myself. Because he'd threatened her life, and he'd taken her.

And now, the only thing between her and death was me.

WHEN I FIRST ARRIVED in the kingdom of Thalassar to formally announce my engagement to Princess Odele before the courts, I had vowed I would never show my true self to these mer. My reputation as the brutal Dragon Prince followed me all the way from Draconi. I heard them whisper about me and the lives I'd taken, about my other form, though they hadn't seen it.

"They never will," I'd said as I left the home I knew for these warmer waters, for these strange mer with their strange traditions.

Today, I had broken the leash I had on the dark violence inside of me.

And the Dragon Prince had been unleashed.

The sight of that criminal holding Odele to his chest, his filthy hands roaming all over her, sparked a rage in me that I hadn't even known I could feel on her behalf. I'd already killed for her. I'd beaten servants and guards in interrogations in the days following her poisoning. But I'd never been unhinged. *Unleashed.*

I wanted to protect her, and I would drop my facade if it meant getting her back. No matter what my advisors said. No matter what they reported back to the emperor.

For Odele, I would face my father's wrath tenfold.

For her, I would lose myself entirely to the savage part of me, if only it meant that I could hold her within the safety of my arms and rip apart the criminal who dared touch what was mine.

Maisie

WE BURST OUT OF the arena and onto the Eramaean streets. I struggled the whole way, but Elias' grip on my upper arm was strong enough to leave an imprint against my skin. He pulled me by his side forcefully and into the fray of bodies swimming through the streets.

I was hauled through traffic, passing by a speeding hippocampus pulling an ivory shell cart behind it. It nearly trampled us, rearing back at the last second, giving us just enough time to dodge it.

My heart was racing harder than it ever had before. I tried dragging my tail behind me, but my torn fin cramped unpleasantly, nearly crippling me into the silt. Elias, though, was having none of it, yanking me up whenever I fell down.

"Keep up!" he spat over his shoulder.

The anger in him was new. I hadn't known the Black Blade long, but I didn't associate what he was doing with who I thought he was. Maybe I was just a fool. Maybe I'd only seen what I'd wanted to see. Or maybe that had been his true self but when threatened, he would risk everything to get himself out of that situation.

Even me.

"Let me go!" I responded, clawing at his hand. I felt betrayed. Betrayed by the one mer in this whole city who I thought understood me more than anyone else. A sob threatened to rise in my chest, but I pushed it down. Tears would do no good now.

We swam hard, my chest heaving and every limb and muscle in my body aching. The pain in my fin was nearly unbearable. It throbbed incessantly, each pang a sharp warning that I should stop and rest.

We made it to the market. Like Lagoona, the stands and stalls were made up of all types of materials. From coral tables and kelp woven mantels to two-legger objects like sheets of metal or rotting wood. Vendors hawked their wares to the mer passing by, offering everything from fresh eel meat to an array of water fruits and greens.

I was pulled between the long aisle of stands, voices shouting all around me, blending together in one cacophony of confusion. But above the rising voices of the mer citizens there was one I recognized over all others.

"Halt!"

The voice was so commanding that Elias obeyed, but not without pulling me to his chest as he whipped around to face him.

Prince Kai.

The Draconian royal floated before us, his posture menacing, coiled tight and ready to spring forward. He looked so different, his features somehow changed. His face seemed elongated, teeth sharper, eyes *blue* instead of brown. Like the blood of dragons pulsed through him. Like all the whispers claimed him to be.

My heart pounded against my chest, and I was sure Elias could feel it on his hand as his palm pulled me closer. Meanwhile, Kai took in every movement, narrowing his eyes at the intimacy with which Elias held his palm against my chest.

"Release her, criminal," Kai growled. His voice was a darkened threat, rasping like rocks were scraping along the back of his throat. "Now."

I could feel Elias smirk against my hair, as if that were the kind of thing one could physically *feel*.

"I think not."

I squirmed against him, which only served to have him tighten his grip around me, palm splaying wider on my chest, palm hovering over my breast. I gasped and tried to lurch forward, but he pulled me back.

Kai's eyes darkened further as he drank in the movement. Activity around us seemed to fall away from me and there was nothing but this moment. Nothing but Elias and Kai, with me between the two. But our little party soon grew, because Captain Saber swam just behind him, along with a group of Eramean and Draconian guards and Kai's stiff advisors.

My face heated at the sight of them and at the intimate way Elias was holding me. We were pressed so close together and I knew we probably looked like lovers.

Captain Saber dared to nudge Kai aside and point his sword. "Enough talking!"

"Captain Saber…" My breath hitched when he looked at me. The rage and fear there was frightening enough to have me shaking against Elias. The look in those aquamarine eyes screamed murder. I knew if he got ahold of Elias, the Black Blade would not make it out alive. Between the prince and the captain, there would be little else left of the mer but whispers and his blades.

Yes, I felt betrayed, but I did not want Elias to die. Death wasn't something I'd wish on anyone. Not even my worst enemy.

Just as the thought swam through my mind, Captain Saber lurched forward, sword poised to strike at an angle. I wanted to close my eyes but was pulled back before I could. Elias twirled our bodies away from the tip of the blade, and in one quick movement, he grabbed the edge of a vendor's table and flipped it.

Hundreds of water apples went flying through the water. The vendor screeched at Elias, but he ignored him, taking advantage of the distraction to pull me away, leaving behind a chaotic mess.

I chanced a glance over my shoulder. Kai made a move to lunge after us, but his advisors and guards reached him, pulling him back and away from the threat of Elias. He bucked and thrashed against their grip, holding an arm out as if he could reach me with the sheer force of his will.

I turned away from the sight before I could burst into tears. Not because I was afraid of what would happen to me, but because I wasn't who Kai thought I was. I wasn't the princess he was desperately trying to save, but a mermaid who just looked a lot like her.

We wove through crowds of vendors and buyers, Elias shoving them aside to get through. Some of them called out in a feeble attempt at protest. Others elbowed and shoved back. Limbs, hard and angry, slammed against my skin and temples. The pain tripped me up, but I found myself being hauled up again by Elias before I could truly fall.

We were close to exiting the market now. Beyond the fray of stalls and the stench of raw meat, there were coral reefs, houses, stores, hippocampi pulling carts, and an array of fish and merpeople.

Once we made it into the throes of traffic, I didn't doubt Elias would camouflage the both of us.

His strokes became more urgent, his movements more commanding. He jerked my arm hard enough that my muscles cried out.

And then someone slammed into him from behind, knocking him face first into the silt. The force of the collision was enough to knock his grasp from my body and send me flying to the ground.

When the silt cloud around me settled and my eyes ceased to ache from the grains, I watched as Captain Saber turned Elias over and pummeled his fist into the side of his face. The sound chilled me to my core. The unbridled violence behind it. Too similar to the memories of how the guards treated deserters back in Lagoona, I cringed, hands flying to my mouth.

Elias defended himself, fists flying up. They were a blur of blows and grunts, facing each other off in a terrifying rage. I could only stare numbly as they battled. This seemed to be more than just the captain catching a criminal to the crown. This was personal, and I knew the captain wouldn't stop until he had Elias' blood.

They rolled through the silt, crashing into a stall, sending the heavy contents tumbling down from their table. Two-legger kitchenware rained around them.

When the fray cleared, it was to reveal Elias beneath Captain Saber. He thrashed against the larger mer's heavy weight, but the captain was pure muscle and rage, pinning him down with his tail and arms. The captain's hand went to his waist, unsheathing the sword there.

"No!" I cried aloud.

The captain ignored me and sneered down at Elias right before plunging the blade through the Black Blade's flesh.

THE PAIN OF BEING stabbed was near blinding, causing me to cry out. Once. One shout of weakness was all I was willing to give. I wouldn't allow this royal soldier a chance to hear me scream a second time. My hands fell to my sides, palm coming into contact with something hard. I grabbed it, whatever it was, raising it overhead and smashing it into the side of the captain's face with all the strength I could muster.

It was my turn then to relish in the loud sound of his surprised cry. Once the sound pierced out of him, I couldn't stop. I smacked him over and over with my makeshift weapon, my only thoughts of escape. I would rather fight until my death before I gave in to a soldier or the royals.

He went slack above me, and I used that to my advantage, throwing him off my body with a powerful push of my tail. I shot up, body protesting in pain. Every instinct in me told me to flee now before it was too late.

I started to leave. There were plenty of mer around these parts of Eramaea who owed me favors. I could find refuge with them, disguise myself, lay low until they forgot about me like they always did. But her voice stopped me mid-stroke.

"Are you alright?" She was eyeing my wound with wide, surprised eyes, and I couldn't help but smile. Even after what I'd done to her, even after witnessing my brutality for herself, she still found it within her to care for my well-being. She was either very foolish or very kind. Or both.

Her attention drifted down towards her guard. Her posture was tense, and I knew there was a touch of fear inside of her at what I'd done to the captain. At how easily I dove into violence. How easily I could betray her trust.

A part of me wanted to comfort her, but now was not the time for that. Just like it wasn't the time for the flare of jealousy that rose up as she bent to check his pulse. Would she do that if she knew that he was the reason I'd been captured in the first place? That he'd been the one to order the guards to strip me, steal from me, beat me?

"All is well, little fish." A lie, but it tasted so sweet when her attention pulled back in my direction, her eyebrows tugging together.

I *was* hurt. My body ached. I should turn, leave. But instead, I reached for her once more, and it was like the missing piece of me finally settled into place.

"I need you," I whispered, and even as the words left my mouth, I wasn't sure what I meant by them. Even so, she didn't resist this time as I pulled her out of the market, leaving behind the noise, the chaos, and her unconscious guard.

The wound at my abdomen pulled each time I moved. The sharp stabs of pain and the smoking trail of blood was a painful reminder that I should find some place to rest.

But not yet. Not until we were safely hidden from the watchful eyes of Eramaea.

We'd stopped our quick pace. It'd look suspicious, so we kept steady strokes with our heads down. I held tightly to her arm. I told myself it was to keep her in place so she wouldn't swim away, but it was more to keep myself from flopping to the silt into unconsciousness.

Tugging her along gave me purpose. Though she kept her head down, I was aware she was drawing attention to the both of us, and I wasn't entirely inconspicuous, wearing the rags of a common criminal and leaving a trail of blood in my wake.

We passed an old merman selling cloaks from a basket. With quick, adept fingers, I snagged one, pulling it around my shoulders and tying it together at the front of my neck with the string. Then, I pulled her close. She was stiff against me, and a sudden swell of irritation passed through me. I didn't want her to fear me any more than I wanted to die. Some things were just necessary evils. Like knocking a royal guard unconscious, like throwing an ax at the crown prince of Draconi. Like betraying her.

I pressed my lips to her cheek and she jolted, but I kept them there, letting them graze across the warmth of her skin until I reached her ear. "Easy, little fish," I whispered. "I'm not going to hurt you."

A shiver went through her that I felt vibrate on my own body. A small smile of satisfaction touched my lips. Before I could even make a clever comment regarding the state of her obvious desire, she turned to press her own lips against my bruised skin. I fought back a wince.

"In your state," she said slowly, "it doesn't look like you could hurt *anyone*."

Proving her point, she wrapped her hand around my waist, where she dug her fingers tightly into my wound. White lights danced behind my eyelids. I grunted, doubling over to take in sharp breaths.

"You…" I couldn't even get what I wanted to say out, because she was jamming her fingers into my side again. "Alright, alright, swim down, little fish. Don't kill me yet."

She chuckled without much mirth and helped me to straighten again. By the time we were away from the busiest part of the capital, she was practically dragging me through the streets. Even through my haze of pain, I could tell that the castle guards and officers had all been alerted to the abduction of the princess. They frantically swam around looking for her.

Nowhere would be safe.

Nowhere except…

"Take me to the castle," I ordered her, my voice coming out as more of a guttural growl.

Thankfully, she didn't argue. She must have known how much pain I was in because she steered me in the direction of the palace of Thalassar. The grandeur greeted us even from leagues away. Tall peaks and towers the color of rose quartz and gold winked and beckoned.

"To the alleyway," I rasped.

She gave a tight nod, knowing what I meant. It was the alleyway where we'd first met, what seemed so many nights ago. The night she'd thought she was saving my life. The night she met her hero. Now, I was the sea scum who had used her as bait to swim from my fate. Just like I always found myself swimming away from that which did not suit me. War. Soldiers. Death.

And now she realized just how much of a barracuda I truly was. I'd made her believe I cared for her, and then I'd been quick to use her as a shield.

I didn't expect her to understand, though. She owed me. A life for a life, and once she got me to safety, her debt would be paid in full.

At the mouth of the alley, we waited to venture in until the streets cleared. I was grateful we were close, so close, because I didn't think I could take much more swimming. Once we reached the dead end of an algae-covered stone wall, she stopped and turned to me, letting me go and putting a stroke of distance between us.

"We're here," she commented quietly.

Narrowing my eyes but lifting my lips up into a sarcastic smirk, I made a noise of disapproval deep in my throat. "Now, now, little fish, you know where I want you to take me."

I wanted inside her secret hideout. Her lair. Somewhere on the side of this stone wall where she was able to sneak in and out of the suffocating confines of the palace.

Her eyes became a cold mask, and because of that small action, I knew that there was a secret doorway here. I'd not be fooled otherwise. Not when she was tensing up, readying herself to deny it with her very last breath. The space was obviously sacred to her. A secret.

I didn't care.

"I don't know what you mean."

"You and I both know there's a door to your hideaway here. I want you to take me there. Now."

Her head shook back and forth, the silky strands of purple hair flying around her face. "There's nothing like that here."

Because I was running out of niceties, I took a single stroke forward until our bodies were pressed up against each other, so close I could feel the rise and fall of her chest against my own. The press of her turgid nipples against these rags stirred my own cravings, but I tamped whatever desire I felt for her deep, deep down.

"So the night we met, you just happened to be hanging around the dead end of an alleyway?" My voice was menacing enough to send thieves and thugs swimming for their lives. Her heart beat frantically. I felt it. But she still met my own gaze with a level stare of her own.

"That's exactly what happened, *Elias.*"

Stubborn little fish.

My hand went up to wrap around her throat. She gasped, but I didn't squeeze. I kept my palm there, feeling the pulse at her skin. My fingers traced along the lines of her gills, my thumb going in circles along the sharp edge of her collarbone.

"You will take me there now, little fish," I drawled. She shuddered. "Because if you don't..." I let the sentence trail off, and let my fingers trail down the length of her skin, touching the edge of her delicate neckline, just where the cloth met the swells of her breasts.

Her breath hitched, and like I knew she would, she moved a little to the side, out of my grasp. I dropped my hand, staring at her intensely.

"Fine," she conceded. Then, she turned to the furry green wall of stone. Her palms met the dirty surface, moving them around briefly before the sudden, startling sound of stone scraping against stone filled the darkness.

I cast a cautious glance towards the mouth of the alley. No one came. I looked back to see the stone part to form a doorway. Darkness greeted us beyond.

"Come on," she urged. She swam halfway into the threshold and held her hand out for me to take. I smiled and placed my hand in hers, letting her lead the way.

"Not here, Dragon Prince." The words from my advisors were spoken in Dracon, whispered harshly in my ear, cutting through my haze of rage.

I thrashed against them, a roar building in my chest. They shouldn't have been stronger than me. They were older, and yet that did not matter when you were Draconian. In our kingdom, everyone was a warrior. Everyone knew how to fight. And they, along with my guards, were doing all in their power to hold me back from reaching Odele. My princess.

Mine.

The dragon in me reared its vicious head, demanding vengeance against the Black Blade. It demanded death against all those who blocked the pathway between me and her.

"The Emperor will have your head!" Ichiro hissed in my ear. "If you become the dragon, you will frighten the Thalassarins."

It was only the mention of the Emperor of Draconi that tore me from my rage and made me think clearly. To my father, our image was everything. Our self-control was something to be commended. If he knew, and I had no doubt that he likely would within moments, he would be furious.

I winced at the thought as phantom pain splintered through my spine. The whispered memory of his beatings and disapproval ached something fierce. And all it took was a single moment of distraction, a split second of compliance, for my advisors and guards to pull me away from the market despite my protests.

"Her guards will bring her back," Ichiro assured, though he sounded dubious. "And when they do, let us hope it is with her reputation intact."

I wanted to snarl at him but swallowed the sound. My princess was in danger and he was worrying about her reputation? To the Great Dragon with her reputation. I cared about *her*. Her safety, her life. I wanted to go after her, but they were already pulling me away. We were swallowed whole by the chaos and I was shoved into a carriage that immediately made its way towards the palace.

I choked back the anger that was threatening to burst. But it lived inside me, a creature waiting for havoc and destruction. I was denied a chance to save Odele, and if my princess wasn't brought back to me safely, I didn't care who they were or what they meant to the emperor…

I would become the Dragon Prince and *end them.*

HIS FINGERS THREADED THROUGH the spaces between mine. The movement was so natural, I could have almost forgiven and forgotten what he'd done to me earlier. The ease with which he had pressed the blade of the ax to my throat, or had cut off my waterway, or had beat Captain Saber with two-legger kitchenware.

Almost.

The doorway to the cove closed behind us, and we pushed our way inside the darkness. We swam in blind strokes. I was familiar enough with the inside that I knew when to curve at the drop. The phytoplankton stuck to the walls at the top of the cove weren't enough to illuminate the way, but just enough to catch the smallest outline of silhouettes.

When the drop came, I tugged at his hand, indicating that he should swim down with me. We were closer to the ground now; to the explosion of two-legger things strewn about. I'd discovered this hideout weeks ago through a secret passageway behind a tapestry of Eramaea in Princess Odele's chambers. It was a wide expanse of space, the cavern's walls covered in furry green algae, barnacles, and tiny specks of phytoplankton. The floors were another matter, however, looking like a shipwreck had exploded throughout the place, leaving behind a bunch of two-legger paraphernalia. Not to mention the hundreds of conches carpeting the ground.

I led Elias over to where I knew the two-legger couch was and sat him down. He went without a fight, grunting as he lowered himself onto the cushions. Then, I turned in the darkness, remembering the layout of the room. Perhaps Princess Odele had hidden a lava globe for illumination here somewhere that I hadn't yet come across.

Blindly waving my hands in front of me, I began moving across the space in search of something that could be used for light. I bumped the left side of my fin onto the sharp edges of what felt like a table. A gasp of pain tore out of my throat. Pangs were sent spiraling down the entirety of my tail.

Ever since Captain Saber had escorted me from my pond home of Lagoona and brought me to the capital, my tail had hurt so much more than I was accustomed to. It had been shredded by a gator back home, and I'd swam with a limp for years. Since coming here, I'd been forced to speak and swim just so, having to move straight-backed and with an elegance I'd never before possessed. Not to mention, the strain of having to swim fast through the market earlier was trying my fins and limbs.

I took a breath, willing the pain to relax. When it did for a brief moment, I started forward again, grateful when I finally made it to the massive treasure chest on the floor. I kneeled down at the tail, feeling for the latch in the front of the chest keeping it closed. Opening it, I dug my hands through the contents, pushing aside two-legger golden coins, rubies, and diamonds to feel for something rounder, smoother.

I moved aside a pile of coins, and a blue light greeted me. Giving a silent cheer of triumph, I dug the round glass lava globe from the inside of the chest and pulled it out, holding it to my body. I swam up and turned. The light on the inside of it illuminated at a distance of three strokes in front of me. The lava was still strong. A soft blue light fell across the space, showing Elias's face contorted in pain.

I swam towards him and sat next to him on the couch, placing the lava globe between our bodies, giving the illusion of distance. Despite what had happened between us, despite him threatening my life, I couldn't bear to see him suffering.

"Let's see the wound, then."

He drew in a ragged breath as he first tugged off the black cloak he'd stolen and then unbuttoned the gray prison rags he wore. His fingers trembled as he went down the line of old, rusty buttons. I didn't dare offer him help, scared that I'd find my fingers trembling as much as his were. When he finished, the scraps of cloth parted to reveal the panes of his chest. I found myself watching in fascination as he slipped one arm out of the shirtsleeve, then the other. The material bunched down at his waist, just where his black tail began.

My face flushed and I hoped he didn't notice in the dimness of the cavern.

"That sea slug got me good."

I broke out of my musings to look down at the wound on his abdomen. It was an ugly, bleeding scrap of flesh. I hissed through my teeth.

"It needs to be cleaned and sewed shut."

Elias gave a tight nod. "So do it."

The haughty, arrogant way with which he commanded me grated on my nerves. I glared at him, crossing my arms over my chest. His eyes flickered to the movement before looking up at my face again, wearing a frown that was contagious.

"Why should I?" I demanded. "You were so willing to threaten my death in order to escape. Now you want me to help you? No. Absolutely not."

Dark brows pulled tightly together, pupils narrowing into thin, angry slits. He seemed to push away any pain he felt in that instant, mustering up a new, darker emotion. Something dangerous that made me shiver involuntarily. And I wasn't entirely sure if it was from fear or... something else.

"You *will*, little fish," he purred, leaning forward. The pretend space I'd placed between us really had been just an illusion, because he closed it within seconds until his lips were a breath from mine. "Or I will tell everyone that you are not the real Princess of Thalassar."

If the room hadn't been shrouded so dark, he would have seen the sudden paleness of my face, the tightening of my features, and the way my lips thinned into a near invisible line. My brain raced laps inside my mind, each thought more anxious than the last.

He knows.

He knows. He knows. He knows. He knows. He knows.

One of the most carefully kept secrets of this kingdom lay in the hands of the Black Blade, enemy to the crown. He knew I was an imposter princess. That I was just pretending to be Odele until the missing mermaid could be found. My next words were crucial, this situation fragile, dangling on the balance of my ability to lie and swindle the most notorious criminal in the whole kingdom.

"I don't know what you're talking about." My voice quivered, and because it did, he smirked.

"You're not a very convincing liar, little fish."

He leaned forward, despite the pain it so obviously caused him, and rested an elbow on his lap. The other hand went low until his palm came into contact with the dress I wore. I startled but remained surprisingly still as he slid the dress up the length of my scales. My face heated as his fingers suddenly stopped at the side of my tail where my shredded fins were. No one had ever come this close to me, and I was too nervous to do much but stare.

"You think I didn't notice this?" His fingers were gentle, passing over the jaggedly thin edges of what used to be perfect, aquamarine fins at my sides. "You swim with a limp, Maisie."

At the use of my name, my *real* name, I flinched.

He smirked. "The moment we met, you introduced yourself as 'Maisie' easily enough. And you speak with a Lagoona accent with so much ease, it's like you're from there, as opposed to when you try to keep that Eramaean accent in place…"

I was breathing heavily now, so unsure what to do, how to rebuff his every claim. There seemed to be no way to do so, no denying what I'd so desperately tried to hide. Elias had seen through me since the very beginning.

"Not to mention on our little outing yesterday." He leaned back on the couch again, the gesture appearing slightly nonchalant. "You ordered almost every food native to Lagoona. Your sympathy for peasants, and your sympathy for me facing a beheading… You risked a lot for a criminal and I know the real princess would rather starve than sully herself like that."

He *knew*, and there was no going back from this now. I could deny it until I was as purple as my hair and tail, but he would see right through any lie I'd try to whip up. There was nothing to do now but proceed cautiously.

"You're very observant," I commented, dropping my practiced Eramaean accent completely, replacing it with my native one. The one of Lagoona.

"In my line of work, I have to be."

"Right. Thieving."

"And deserting, and spying, and blade-making."

The arrogant piece of kelp. I huffed indignantly and got up from the couch. "Fine," I conceded. "I'll heal your wound. But I don't have anything to sew it up with." I'd have to go through the little tunnel on the opposite side of the cove, the one that led to the princess' chambers. "Wait right here." I turned and swam up, feeling my way up for the little tunnel. I didn't take the lava globe with me because I'd bring another one on the trip back. To sew up his wounds, I was going to need all the illumination I could get.

Squeezing myself into the little tunnel, I crawl-swam through the silt and debris until I made it out into the dark stone hallway that led to the rooms. I was lucky there were no twists and turns here, or I'd be completely lost in darkness. Swimming forward and trying not to imagine what creatures slithered along the walls, I finally made it to the end of the hall and pressed my hands against the stone. The doorway opened, and I pushed aside the tapestry to swim into the room.

It was brighter in here, swathed in hues of gold, magenta, lilac, and blue. The ivory shell bed looked so inviting after the trying day I'd had. I longed to throw myself into it, letting the soft kiss of the anemones against my scales lull me to sleep. But Elias was waiting.

I swam around the room looking for sewing notions. The princess didn't seem to have anything useful in her rooms. There was nothing but figurines, toys, and pampered princess things, like jewelry and makeup strewn about.

Making my way to the bathing room, I searched through the stuff there until I finally found a little shell container. The inside held sharp needles and sea thread. I also grabbed a hidden bottle of fermented sea wine that the princess kept hidden there as well. I knew she kept it because I'd watched dozens of conches on her miserable, royal life.

I shoved the contents into a simple messenger bag I found lying in the princess' closet and grabbed a lava globe on my way out. The stone doorway closed behind me. I went down the hall, then wriggled my way through the tunnel, coming out on the other side with silt buried in my hair.

I shook myself off and coughed before I realized that the silence in the cove was eerie. Cautiously, I looked around. The lava globe I'd left with Elias was no longer where it had been. In fact, it wasn't anywhere in sight. And there wasn't any sound of Elias gasping in pain, either.

Unfortunately. Okay, maybe I didn't want to see him die, but I was petty enough right then to want him to suffer, at least a little.

Holding the lava globe in my palm, I started to turn and gasped when I felt the sudden cold, sharp edge of something press to my throat. I froze.

"Are you alone?" Elias' voice whispered in the dark.

I started to nod but stopped when my skin dug into what felt like a blade. "Yes," I answered.

There was a pause as he waited for a minute, and then another. When it was obvious I'd come alone, the blade pulled away from my throat, and Elias swam out into the illumination of the globe I held in my hand. He gripped at his wound with one hand, and in the other he held a silver-studded blade.

I eyed it suspiciously.

"Found it in that treasure chest of yours." He started for the couch and I followed.

"That's the second time you've held a weapon to my throat today."

Once we made it back to the couch, he tossed the blade across the cavern and shrugged, looking at me unapologetically. "One can never be too careful when it comes to survival."

"One can never be too careful when choosing their friends, either."

Elias just pierced me with a look that I chose to ignore as I made my way to the couch and sat down on it. He followed much more slowly, this time sitting as close to me as he possibly could. I tried to ignore the proximity, but I couldn't help how my heart sped up.

"I never claimed to be your friend, little fish." He moved his hands aside so I could examine the wound. "We just owed each other favors."

My face heated with the beginning of humiliation. I always saw goodness where there was none. Imagined friendship where it didn't exist. I should have known by now that mer were liars. The proof of that lay in the scars on my side.

There was so much I wanted to say to him, so many replies that came to mind. None of them would have been productive to the situation at hand. Instead, I bit my tongue and bent over to look at his skin. I'd been a fool to think we were friends. To think that the Black Blade, a merman I once admired, turned out to be sea scum instead. The idea of him was better than the bundle of flesh and blood I had in front of me.

I pulled out the bottle of fermented sea wine and uncapped it, dipping it over to pour the contents onto his wound. The dark color of wine floated gently down onto his flesh, looking like swirls of squid ink vanishing through the water. He winced when it touched him, and let out a hiss and a curse.

I took out a needle, threading it, and bent over to pinch his separated pieces of flesh. He jumped, as if my hands tickled rather than hurt him. I didn't look up, though. I paid attention to my task, sticking the needle through his skin and I began to sew.

We sat like that in the silence for a moment. I worked methodically to make sure I did it right. When I pressed my fingers to the flesh above the wound and pulled the string back, Elias took in a sharp breath.

Finally, he asked in a quiet voice that I felt deep in my bones, "Where did you learn to do this?"

I didn't look up from my task. "I've had my fair share of scrapes and bruises." Working at Tides' Tavern near gator breeding grounds resulted in quite a few accidents all around. Plus, through a delirium of pain, I watched the seamstress sew up my own side after my attack. But he didn't need to know that. We weren't friends. "And I've had to mend and tailor a lot of my own clothing when money was tight." I almost regretted the words as soon as they came out of my mouth but shook it off. He already knew the truth about me. Saying this was nothing. Besides, sometimes it felt nice to pull that mask off, even if it was with this criminal who was blackmailing me.

I felt the light touch of his fingers against the floating tresses of my hair. I tensed, and then he pushed them back, dropping his hand.

"You're amazing, little fish. You know that, right?"

My face heated despite myself. "I'm nothing special," I dismissed.

"It takes a special person to disguise themselves as a stuck-up princess for weeks. Though, I still don't quite understand *why* you're doing it."

I bit my lip. Released it. "Don't worry about it."

It was like he didn't even hear me. "The real princess is either truly sick or gone, that much is quite clear. But what's in it for *you*?"

I bit my tongue and kept sewing. He was baiting me. I knew it. And I wouldn't fall prey to him. I wouldn't spill my secrets, giving him more information to blackmail me with. Did he think I was *completely* daft?

"Did they offer you jewels? Money? Or do you like pretending to be royalty? Maybe you just want an excuse to kiss a pretty prince—*ssssttt*." He winced when I stuck the needle hard into his skin. I didn't like what he was implying. That I was just as shallow as the princess. That'd I'd jump at the chance to be someone else, to live in finery, to be the center of attention.

The truth was, I hated it.

"Sorry," I whispered, my throat tight with an emotion akin to anger. "I slipped."

I was sure he glared at me, but I didn't reply. I resumed my task with faster fingers. The quicker I got through this, the sooner he could leave. I would go back to pretending to be Princess Odele and suffer the consequences of my actions today.

When I finished sewing his wound, I sat back and placed the needle and thread into the little shell. I set it aside and stuffed the now-corked bottle of sea wine into the silt.

"Well," I began. "I suppose you'll be on your way now..."

Elias chuckled unkindly, and I knew that there was no chance he'd be leaving now. "I think not," he said. "The whole kingdom is looking for me. And if you haven't noticed, I'm vulnerable." He gestured at his wound. "No, I think I'll stay here for a while."

Just like that, the one sacred space I had, the one place where I could irrevocably be myself and hide away from the watchful eye of courtiers was snatched from me. "Y-you can't!" I protested.

He raised a dark, slender eyebrow. "I think I can. You forget I have vital information that could determine your future. What do you think the kingdom will do to an imposter princess? Do you think they'll be lenient with you? Perhaps they'll do to you what is done to selects."

His words had me seeing blood. The swing of an ax. A head rolling. Not Christof's this time, not one of my friend's from Lagoona, but mine.

"I thought so."

I glared at him and his luxuriating way of lying there on the couch. "You're such a tadpole!" I cursed him.

He smirked. "I never claimed otherwise."

I scoffed and got up from my seat. It was time I left here. Being in his presence just made my fins stand on edge. I started to turn away but felt his hand suddenly tighten on my upper arm.

I tensed.

"Wait..." he said quietly.

Turning, I narrowed my eyes at him only to find him wearing a startling expression. He was looking at me with softer eyes, and I wondered if that was a tinge of regret there or maybe it was something deeper. As quickly as it appeared, it was gone, replaced with a reticent curve of his lips. Perhaps I'd just mistaken the look for something it wasn't. For what I wished I could have seen.

"You have to know, little fish, I never would have hurt you."

I wanted to close my eyes against those words because they were exactly what I needed to hear to forgive him. But words, I'd learned, meant nothing in the grand scheme of things. Actions always spoke louder, and so far, his had given me insight as to who he really was. Even if a part of me wanted to grab that version of an apology and keep it close. Even if I wanted to smile like I had just the day before.

"You certainly fooled me."

His eyes went to my throat, to where he'd cut off my waterway. I was sure, even in the dimly lit cove, he could make out the shadowing of a bruise there. He tugged lightly at my hand, but with enough command that I found myself falling into his lap. His arm went around my waist to hold me there, to keep me from protesting.

I didn't.

Maybe I was weak. Maybe I always had been. Or maybe it was just him. Elias' energy was something else entirely. He was hypnotizing and I wanted to be closer to him, despite what he'd done or would do.

I sat there, breath hitching up in my throat as I watched every single thing about him soften. His whole demeanor changed. Fingers came up to brush along my throat. I swallowed, a lump rising up my throat that I was sure he could feel with his fingertips.

"I am sorry," he whispered.

I tried not to shiver and failed. "I don't believe you." My voice was hoarse with some unknown emotion that clenched tightly in my gut.

He leaned forward, so close that our noses almost touched. Then he bent to my neck and pressed his lips against my bruised skin. The feel of his warmth at the base of my throat had my pulse quickening to an impossible speed. I was sure he felt it. Felt the way my heart was racing against his mouth. He kissed me there, and I remained entirely too still under his care. He kissed his way lower, lips touching my collarbone, and then lower still, to the top swells of my breasts.

He stopped, pulled away when I was sure I would melt like molten lava.

Elias looked me in the eyes with lowered lids. A soft smile touched his mouth, and my face and body heated in response. I wasn't sure why my gut was tightening, why my belly coiled in his presence.

"I would never truly hurt you, Maisie." He said the words like they were a promise he meant to keep forever between the two of us.

My breath hitched. "If that were true," I began, "then you wouldn't really tell anyone my secret."

His fingers grazed down the length of my arm. "I had to ensure you would help me and that was the only way I knew how."

"By abducting me. By tricking me. By hurting me."

His own breath hitched at that. "You were safe with me, little fish. I had to pretend. That's all. You have to know…"

"Know what?" I was breathless and the words came out in a panting whisper.

His touch glided against my collarbones, up my neck. His eyes seemed bright in the darkness as he drank me in. "You have to know that you are my second blade. My match. My other half."

I closed my eyes against the words, feeling them carve a pathway down to my soul. I should have replied with something similar. But I didn't. I opened my eyes and said, "Then there's nothing stopping me from telling the guards where you are and turning you in."

He smiled, but it wasn't the arrogant smile I was so accustomed to seeing on him. It was derisive but beautiful just the same. "You won't," he said. It was a dare. A challenge.

I bit my bottom lip, and his eyes followed the movement. Slowly, I released it and sighed, shaking my head. "You're right, I won't."

And he'd seen right through me. Because it didn't matter what had happened. Deep down, the Black Blade was still my hero. And Elias Blackfin was still my friend, no matter the lie he whispered when he said we weren't. I knew the truth.

He'd been ready to face certain death, and I'd made myself an easy target. He had done what he always did: survived, using whatever means he could. It stung my pride, made a strange vulnerability bury itself in my chest, but I understood. We were one and the same, after all.

I was suddenly aware of our position. Of me on his lap, tail curling beside his. His arm around my waist, fingers hovering over my bare skin. We were pressed together intimately, and for some reason, in this moment, my mind flashed to Prince Kai and to Captain Saber.

Prince Kai was not mine. I had to remind myself of that. He belonged to Princess Odele. Once she was found, they would marry, have children, and rule a kingdom. And Captain Saber? I wasn't sure why I thought of him. All I knew was that he belonged to the princess as much as the prince did. He was in love with her and would be happy to be rid of me.

I was just Maisie. And maybe Elias and I could actually be together, but for some reason even he suddenly seemed far away. He was the Black Blade. He was doing something for Thalassar, for its merpeople, while I was failing from the inside.

"I have to go," I whispered abruptly.

Elias did not look surprised. He just gave me a single nod and pushed lightly at my waist. I flushed and slid off of him, taking a few strokes back. Maybe distance would clear my head. Maybe distance would make the burning feel of his lips against my skin vanish entirely.

Or maybe it wouldn't.

"Goodbye, Elias," I said before whirling around and swimming away from him. At the top of the cove, my hands pressed against stone. The doorway opened and I swam out, practically gasping once it closed behind me. When it did, I pressed my back against the wall and tried to calm my erratic breathing. My heart was incessantly pounding in my chest.

I swallowed and started forward. If I stopped now, it'd only give me time to think about Elias and the confusing feelings coursing through my body. That was something I didn't need. Not now.

So I swam to the mouth of the alley and down the street. There were guards all around and merpeople screaming. My blood went cold at the sight of it. Were they looking for me?

I stopped a passing guard, and when he saw me, his eyes widened.

“Excuse me,” I began, accent falling into place. “I am Princess Odele, and I’d be grateful if you escorted me to the palace.”

I knew true fear as I was led to the palace. Guards swarmed behind me, holding their spears and swords, alert for any threat. As if the Black Blade would somehow materialize from within the walls to try and take me again.

I swam through the halls just like a princess should, hands clasped at my stomach demurely, back straight, looking ahead as if everything and everyone were beneath me. Elias had been able to see through me, and I could not let anyone else do so. Even though my fins were screaming in protest, begging for rest, for a moment of reprieve, I would not let them see me falter.

We finally made it to the throne room, where I had no doubt the queen and king were already atop their lavish thrones, waiting to rip through me for what I’d done. The guards opened the doors, and I swam through.

My heart was still pounding in my chest. It was painful. I looked up as the door behind me closed. The queen and king were on their thrones. The queen’s hands perched on the golden armrest of her throne, nails digging into them. It was perhaps the only way she’d let her anger show, for her face was the image of regal beauty and indifference. Her long neck was held delicately high, as if the crown on her head weighed nothing at all.

The king was another matter. His head was lowered, forehead resting in his hand. There were creased lines of worry around the corners of his eyes, and I tried not to let that startle me or wonder on it at all.

At the fin of the thrones were Captain Saber and Prince Kai.

The sight of *them* almost made me falter.

I looked to Captain Saber first. The side of his face, where Elias had smashed kitchenware onto him, was red and swollen, still bleeding. His expression was tight, angry. He remained stiff and scowling even as he took me in. I turned to Prince Kai. There was a contrast between the two. Where the captain's hair was fair and short, Prince Kai's was black and flowed down to his waist, dark against his royal blue kimono that looked like it was made of the softest sea silk the kingdom had to offer.

At the sight of me, Prince Kai's expression of visceral anger faded to relief. He darted forward through the water, and before I could even blink, I found myself enveloped in his strong embrace. His arms wrapped around my body, and he held me close, pressing my face into his chest.

I inhaled the scent of him briefly, of water lilies and something darker, before he pulled away, hands cupping my cheeks. I was too surprised to do anything but stare at him, at the soft curves of his features. High cheekbones, warm brown eyes and lips.

I was so worried," he practically gasped. And then he leaned down and kissed me.

If only everyone else would fall away. If only I had the time to hold her and memorize her very essence, her scent… her taste. But my kiss was chaste, a quick press of lips against lips. There was no time to explore, and even if I wanted to, Odele seemed too stunned to do much but float there.

Behind us, the Queen of Thalassar cleared her throat in annoyance.

I broke away from Odele in time to see her eyes flutter, her cheeks heat. But I took even longer letting go, relishing in the feel of her soft skin against my palms, in the way she seemed to lean into me. Her breath had hitched, and I could just make out the pulse at her throat jumping.

I didn't care that I was breaking the bounds of propriety or that her family was watching such an intimate display. Just the sight of her, well and obviously unharmed, had been enough for me to break free of the bindings of etiquette.

Had it not been for my advisors, I'd have made it to her in time. Unlike Captain Saber, I would have caught the criminal and hauled him from the market by his fins and killed him myself. Alas, my advisors were as strong and as skilled as I, and they'd shoved the Dragon Prince back into his confines before all of Eramaea could witness it.

My fingers trailed down her cheek to her neck, where I rested them, running my thumb across the pulse at her throat. Her pink skin was tinged with the beginning of a bruise. A feral growl rose to my throat, but I shoved it back.

"You are well?" I asked. My own heart beat a wild rhythm in my chest, mimicking the sounds of the battle drums of Draconi. I was nervous. Nervous and glad she was in front of me, that I could touch her. I wanted nothing more than to desperately pull her away from this blasted throne room and take her to my rooms and…

"That will be quite enough of that!" The queen's harsh voice broke me from my wandering, improper thoughts. My cheeks heated as I let go and turned to face the queen and king. I didn't dare take a stroke away from her this time.

The queen was glaring at her stepdaughter unkindly, and I didn't miss the way she made an attempt at smoothing her features over, placing on a mask of feigned worry.

"Dearest daughter," she began tightly. Her voice was as sweet as candy and confections. I didn't particularly like how false it was. "It warms my heart to see you in one piece."

Odele tensed next to me but swept into the most proper low bows. Odd. She'd never bowed before her stepmother before. Even if she was queen.

Odele had made it known time and time again that the queen's rule would not last and her own rule would surpass that of her stepmother's once she came of age.

"Thank you, Majesty."

"Although, I am quite curious as to how you managed to escape Thalassar's most notorious criminal in the first place." Her voice was laced with nothing but suspicion.

I hadn't wondered about that question myself. I'd just been glad she had survived at all. When that blackheart had placed an ax to her throat, I'd seen red.

"It may be hard to believe, *mother*, but he let me go."

The queen stroked her pointed chin in thought as she gazed down at Odele. Her bright eyes were narrowed on my betrothed in an expression I didn't like at all.

Finally, she dropped her hand back on the armrest of her throne, flicking her fingers absently. "Perhaps," she purred, "he would not have had you in the first place had you not been so foolish to challenge the law."

Odele snapped her head up, and it was her turn to glare. She didn't even bother trying to mask it. Royalty usually did. "I won't apologize for swimming up for what's right."

The queen's gaze flickered with annoyance. "Right?" she huffed. "Who are *you* to say what is right for the kingdom of Thalassar?" She pushed herself up from the throne in one angry stroke, as if she meant to loom over and intimidate the rest of us from her position.

Odele looked far from intimidated. "I am just trying to *help.* The merpeople of Thalassar are *suffering.* Surely you must know that? Do you really think that violence and death is the way to rule?"

Never before had I seen the queen move as fast as she did in that moment. She sped through the water until she was face to face with her stepdaughter, nose to nose, and the tension between them was all too palpable.

"How *dare* you speak to me that way? Insolent little wench!" She reached her hand up high and brought it down in a swing.

I grabbed her before I could blink. Catching her wrist in my hand, squeezing tightly. I felt the dragon in me stir into the wakening of unbridled violence. "Don't..." I warned in a voice that was as deadly as the heat of lava on bare skin. "...harm her."

The queen was staring at me with the most shocked expression ever. Her eyes, bright and wide, held only disbelief. She couldn't quite fathom my sudden change, my sudden willingness to stand up for her stepdaughter. I'd been so meek before, so quiet and proper and polite in this dreadful kingdom. I'd have never dared to lift a hand to them before even if I was more than capable.

Things were different now.

Everything was different.

"Drop the queen's hand. Now." Captain Saber was suddenly at my side, and I didn't need to look over to him to know that he was pointing the tip of his precious sword at me. I could have disarmed him easily. Instead, I dropped the queen's hand, placing my own, clasped, behind my back.

The queen took a jerky stroke away from me. She was staring at me as if she couldn't quite believe who I was. Like, instead of having a prince before her that she could easily manipulate into doing her bidding, she found an untamed beast in his stead.

"Forgive me." I calmed the heat that had built up inside of me, took the slightest of bows, if only to conceal my expression of rage. I should never lose myself in front of these merpeople. Ever. And yet Odele had awoken that part in me more than once.

I straightened and turned to look at Captain Saber. There was a calm among my features that could be akin to the stillness of waters before a storm. I wondered if the good captain realized just what a mistake he had committed. If so, he didn't show it. He looked at me, sword still pointed in my direction.

"I was told weapons weren't allowed in the throne room." The sarcasm that left my lips really couldn't be helped.

The captain sneered. "I am a trusted guard, and I have sworn on my life that I would protect the Malabella lineage until I draw in my last dying breath. That includes the princess *and* the queen. No matter who or what I face."

I did nothing but raise a brow. Nonchalance, I knew, went a long way. In some cases, it also served to annoy those who thought themselves better than me. And though he was merely a captain and I a prince, I knew he thought me no worse than a bit of stray kelp stuck to a hippocampus' hoof.

"If that were true, then you would have stopped at nothing to save my betrothed from danger earlier, yet you let a common criminal get the best of you." I'd hit my mark. His face reddened with humiliation.

"That criminal was—"

I turned away before he could get the rest out. A dismissal. Not a method I was practiced in, but effective. Usually, I was averse to the lesser treatment of others. Not now, though.

I looked to the queen. "With your permission, Majesty, I would like to set one of my own guards and my advisor to watch over the princess." I gave a side look at the captain and then back again. "Security in your kingdom is quite lacking."

Odele huffed from her place. "I don't need a guard!"

"She already has guards," the captain ground out tightly.

I flicked my fingers in his direction. Another dismissal. "They seem to be doing a poor job of things so far. She has been poisoned, shot at, and abducted by a criminal among hundreds of Thalassarins. My guards' and advisor's skills are equal to my own. They would not let harm come to her."

The queen pinched the bridge of her nose with her thumb and forefinger. "I will allow it."

Captain Saber took a stroke forward, mouth opening as if he meant to argue, but he reeled back last minute, holding his fists tightly at his back. Remembering his place.

I smirked.

The queen cleared her throat. "If you please, Prince Kai. We'd like to speak to our daughter. Alone."

I did not trust her to not raise a hand to Odele again. Still, she was the ruler, and I'd already challenged her once. To do so a second time could very well wage a war between our two nations, marriage contract or not. So I settled with piercing her with a look that was menacing, a warning. Then, I turned to Odele. She looked unhappy about my current suggestion but let me take her hand in mine.

"Until we meet again, Princess." I pressed a kiss to her knuckles, wishing with everything inside me that it could be her lips instead.

His kiss was quick, yet it still managed to warm me all over, despite how unhappy I was at his suggestion. I didn't need another guard, especially not Prince Kai's. If I had mer swarming all around me while I tried to go about my fake life as the princess, I didn't think I'd survive the end of the week.

It was difficult enough trying to uncover the secrets of the royal tides, I didn't need the added difficulty of being followed around everywhere. That would mean I'd have to be constantly alert. Constantly worry about someone discovering my secret. Not to mention there was a greater chance of Elias being discovered if I wasn't left alone.

Prince Kai straightened and turned, swimming out with an elegance that only he seemed able to muster. Once he was gone, and the double doors to the throne room closed behind him, the queen turned to me with a hateful glare over her beautiful features.

"You may have enchanted the Dragon Prince, peasant, but we know who you really are."

Her words speared through me, even if they were true. I was beneath them. But the way she said it made me feel entirely too small. Like a mere speck riding the current.

"If he knew who you really were, do you think he'd be so quick to come to your aid?" When I didn't reply, she smirked, and the cruelty that lived in that single gesture was unparalleled. "I thought not."

She turned haughtily away from me and swam back up to her throne, sitting on it with her back straighter than ever, and her neck held too high. She sniffed once, looking down on me. I wondered if she was waiting for me to bow. Rebelliously, I did not. For a fleeting moment, I imagined the real Princess Odele would have cheered me on for this bit of defiance.

"Now that he is gone, we can speak freely. You are swimming in thin tides here, little mer. When Captain Saber brought you here, it was my understanding that you'd be nothing more than an image for the merpeople of Thalassar to look at. Not an ambassador for peace and unity." She scraped her nails against the golden armrest of her throne. "You have tested my patience at *every* single turn, and I am fed up."

A lump caught in my throat. Would she send me away? Back to Lagoona? My hand went to my neck as another thought occurred. Would she have my head on a spike along with deserters and criminals to the crown? Fear coiled tightly in my belly, making me suddenly nauseous. I'd seen so many of my friends and neighbors die at the end of a royal blade, it was only a matter of time before it happened to me as well.

Tears burned behind my eyelids, but I pushed them away. I would not give her the satisfaction of seeing me cry.

"Your meddling ways have become quite tiresome, and the fact that you practically aided in that criminal's escape means you cannot be trusted with this task. You are a foolish, incompetent, *crippled*—"

"That's enough!"

Her rant was interjected by the king's sudden angry shout. He pushed himself up from his throne and looked to the queen with a furious expression. The queen seemed to recoil from his gaze, though I wondered why when she was the supreme ruler of Thalassar. If anyone should have feared, it should have been him. And then I wondered if there was any love between them at all. His wife had died, only to be replaced by this mermaid a few months later. He hadn't had a proper mourning period because the kingdom could not have anyone on the throne unless they were of the Malabella lineage. Odele had been too young to take over the kingdom herself at the time; she was *still* too young. It wouldn't officially be hers until she turned eighteen and wed Prince Kai.

"How *dare* you speak to me that way?!" The queen regained her wits quickly enough, dropping the shocked hand from her throat to tighten in her lap.

The king rolled his eyes at her theatrics. "Be quiet. I am sick of hearing the ugliness you spout from that impetuous mouth of yours." He turned away from her, as curt a dismissal as Kai had given Captain Saber minutes earlier. The king swam down from his throne and came before me. There was compassion now in his gaze as he took my hands in his. He pressed a kiss to the back of my knuckles, and I had to force myself not to tear them away. He was treating me as if I were true royalty, and I wasn't sure how I felt about that.

"Are you really fine?" he asked.

Numbly, I nodded.

He let out a sigh of obvious relief, let go of my hands, and turned to his wife. "The most important thing to us is that you are here, alive and *safe.*" He put emphasis on the word as he glared at the queen, daring her to contradict him. I felt like I'd been dropped in the middle of a feud and was watching a battle war out between the two royals. But the queen said nothing, so he continued, "The details of the consequences of your behavior can be discussed at a later time. Right now, I suggest Captain Saber escorts you to your chambers, you soak in sand scrubs, and change into something more comfortable while we deal with the gossipmongers."

"Your Majesty…"

He smiled at me. "Not all royals are complete barbarians." That brought out a smirk in me. I dared not let my heart melt in my chest, but a part of me couldn't help it. I'd never had a father, and the king was very fatherly in his countenance. "Your actions were impudent, but I am sure after your trying time today, you realize this and regret it. Please, Maisie, do not let it happen again."

That last part was said so sternly, I could only nod in agreement, to which he smiled and shooed me away with a wave of his hands. I started to turn, Captain Saber swimming up beside me as we started for the door. I didn't look back, but I heard the queen practically screech at the king.

"You are a soft-hearted fool! Babying her the same way you babied Odele!"

"You would do well to hold your tongue—"

The rest of the king's reply was cut off by the door opening, and the captain ushered me out of it quickly. It closed behind us, and I regretfully didn't hear the rest of their rising shouts.

I'd vowed not to let myself become overwhelmed by this sensation, but for the life of me, I couldn't very well help it. The king had kissed my hands. He'd looked at me with worry. He'd said my name. And a strange sort of happiness bubbled up in my chest, despite everything that had happened that day.

Because I let myself believe that the king loved me, the way a father loved a daughter.

And for a moment, I let myself believe that he was mine.

Tiberius

IN ALL MY YEARS of living, I'd never known anyone to be more foolish than Maisie Fauna.

The moment we exited the throne room, I grabbed her by the upper arm and pulled her along the hallways of the palace. The more we swam, the more I seethed with a quiet rage. So lost in my anger, I didn't even stop to think about the consequences that pulling her around would bring. It was improper to haul around the princess through the palace, as if she were nothing more than a common servant.

But Maisie wasn't Princess Odele. She *was* practically a common servant.

A part of me must have forgotten that the moment I'd seen the Black Blade's arm snake around her throat and threaten her precious life.

I'd been blinded by rage and desperate to get her back.

And I'd been bested because of it.

It was only after I'd woken from the unconsciousness that the Black Blade had put me under that I felt something in my gut that I knew I'd deny until my very last breath. Had it been worry that I felt? Yes. Worry about what the mer of Thalassar would say about the princess because of Maisie. There'd also been rage. I'd wanted to throttle her for what she'd done. For putting herself and the princess' image in jeopardy to save a criminal that had not hesitated to harm her.

We made it to the door of her chambers. I opened it and shoved her inside, closing it behind me.

"Captain, you're hurting me."

Her voice broke through my haze of anger. I hadn't realized how hard I was holding onto her upper arm. I eased my grip, pulling my hand away and stretching my fingers at my sides. I breathed in and out, but the calmness would not come.

I glared at Maisie. "Do you have any idea what you have caused?"

Maisie avoided looking at me. Instead, she swam over to the ivory bed and plopped herself down on the soft cushioning in the middle, anemones hugging her curves.

"I don't know, Captain, but I'm sure you're about to tell me."

"This isn't a *joke,* Maisie!" I shouted.

She sat up in the bed quickly, her hair floating above her like the tendrils of the tail of a snake. She pulled it back in a frustrated gesture. "I know it's not." Her eyes narrowed. "You want me to admit I made a mistake? Alright, I did. The queen has made it abundantly clear. What do *you* want from me?"

What *did* I want from her? Even I could not answer that question myself, as I did not entirely know the answer.

"I want you to realize how your every action affects Princess Odele."

She scoffed, rolled her eyes. "Right. Because every royal here thinks about how their actions affect the poorer mer, right? How it affects Lagoona?"

"Again with this argument?" I crossed my arms against my chest, if only to give myself something to do. Something that didn't involve punching my fist through the wall. "Why must you insist on having it? Why do you even care so much?"

Her face flamed with evident rage. She shot up from the bed, pushing her hair back, and she paced back and forth at the fin of it. "Have you ever seen your friends die, captain? One by one, every month like clockwork? To be chosen and to never come back? Gods forbid they even show the slightest bit of fear and weakness, lest they meet the end of a blade. You wouldn't understand."

My eyes narrowed in a carefully placed glare. "I understand perfectly," I said darkly. "Do not think for a moment you are the only one to lose someone, Maisie. I have watched my friends, soldiers, go out and fight for the kingdom they loved. To keep it *safe.* And one by one I watched my friends *die* because of Kappur. Don't think *for a moment* that you're the only one in Thalassar who has lost someone you care about. My friends bravely went out to battle, sacrificed their lives for the luxuries you are now getting. So forgive me if I don't feel a single ounce of empathy for cowardly deserters who cannot find it in them to help or shed blood the way the rest of us are doing!"

Her expression softened, and gods take me, I hated that look. Her anger I could take, her disdain as well. Maybe I even wanted it, *craved* it. I wanted her to shout and be furious with me. I could not take sympathy.

Her voice was low when she replied, "No one deserves to be killed for feeling fear, though."

My lip pulled back in a sneer. She did not warrant it, but I wanted to lash out every time she spoke. Her own ignorance was astounding. A part of me wanted to say it was not her fault she was raised in a small pond that knew nothing of the workings of royal life. Another part despised her for everything she said. "We cannot afford to feel fear. Not in times of war. You'll do well to remember that next time you decide to flounce around in the light of day with a known criminal on the streets of Eramaea."

She sucked in a breath. Observed me. My face and posture were rigid, angry. The realization of my words sunk in for her, and she dropped her mouth open, closed it again.

"It was you…" she whispered.

I did not acknowledge what she said, just stared at her with my expression unchanging. But something like dread started to rise in me. I tried to shove it away.

"You followed me?" she demanded to know.

She wouldn't even try to deny it. Princess Odele would have denied it until she was blue in the face. But Maisie was not Odele. The princess never would have allied herself with common criminals. "I did not," I replied smoothly. "I saw you with him."

Her fists clenched, and I eyed the movement, wondering if she would try and take a swing at me. I would welcome the action. I would let her pummel me to the ground. It still would not change a thing.

"You were the one who turned him in." It wasn't a question, but I nodded just the same. "You tadpole!" she shouted. "How could you?"

"He was a wanted criminal, Maisie, and you are supposed to pretend to be the princess. I am not sure how you got out of these rooms undetected, but I vowed I would keep you safe. That is something I cannot do if you are panting after a criminal like a dogfish."

My words were cruel, I knew it the moment I said them. But I hadn't expected that look on her face. The hurt. The way her expression crumpled as if I'd struck her.

There was a long moment of seething silence. Had my point gotten across? I'd hoped so.

But then she spoke, "Is it truly me you care about, Captain? Or yourself?" Before I could inquire as to what she meant by that, she took a stroke forward. "See, I don't think you care about me at all. I could die right now, and I'm sure you wouldn't even bat an eye." She took another stroke. "The one mer you truly care about is yourself." Another stroke until we were almost touching. "You are upset with yourself because you couldn't keep Princess Odele safe, so you want to blame *me* for it. That's why you hate me so much. You failed your duty to her. You are a failure as a guard and you think you can lock me up, put bars on these windows, have a trail of your sentinels follow me, put my friend at the gallows…" Another stroke forward and our chests bumped together. "But no matter what you do to keep me here, it won't change the fact that *your* impudence is what may have killed your precious princess in the first place."

I grabbed her arms and shook her once, twice, and held her at arm's length. Fury shot through my every crevice, electrified my every nerve. I wanted to shake her, to scream that it was not true. But every word had pierced my heart, leaving me open and vulnerable, naked before her.

It wasn't true. It *wasn't.*

My breathing had grown heavy. Hers mirrored my own. She did not look into my eyes with fear at my outburst. Her gaze was challenging. And I would fold.

"Get out," she demanded. "I don't want to see you ever again."

For a moment, as she said those words, my mind betrayed me. For a moment, I didn't see Maisie in front of me but Princess Odele, and something inside me broke because of it.

I released her arms and took a stroke back, putting distance between us. My back bumped against the door.

"I do not want you as my guard."

I closed my eyes, willing those words to go away. Maybe when I opened them, things would be different, and she would change her mind. When

I did, she was still glaring, but her expression was laced with something else. Disappointment.

"Get out."

My heart cracked in two, but I did not give Maisie a chance to tell me a third time.

I turned and fled from the room.

Maisie

The doors slammed closed behind the captain's tail. I could only stare at it numbly before it all gave way to a boiling anger inside my chest. Ever since I'd met the captain, my life had been a riptide wave of chaos. He had tried giving me the illusion of free will when we met, but I realized now that he wouldn't have let me stay behind. He would have done *anything* for Princess Odele, even if it meant sacrificing me in her stead. The only reason he'd chased after me in the arena was because the merpeople believed me to be her. Because he wanted to protect her reputation.

Ever since I'd gotten to the palace, he'd been controlling and judging everything I did. I understood why, but he was harsher than most, harsher sometimes than even the queen. They never ceased to remind me who I was and where I came from. That I'd never measure up to the inerrant princess I pretended to be.

And for the first time since I'd come here, I'd found a friend in Elias. We were alike, he and I. Two poor mer, trying to survive under the tyranny of Thalassar. Two outcasts. Two selected. In a way, I had been selected too.

Then Captain Saber had tried to take away the one friend I had in the whole of Eramaea. Like he wanted me to be miserable. And maybe the princess had been miserable, too. Maybe he'd been as controlling and as protective with her as he was with me. Maybe her parents were just as cruel. Maybe that had given her the courage to flee. Someone out there was already trying to kill her, so what was leaving everything behind and starting a new life in the grand scheme of things?

I still had so many secrets to discover.

But first, a nap.

I swam over to the mirror by the rose quartz wall and looked at myself, wincing. I looked like I'd been dragged through the streets of Eramaea. My dress was torn at the hem and covered with speckles of mud and silt. My hair had tangles through it, and it floated in disarray above my head. There were shadows under my wide, red eyes.

Well, silt.

I stripped the clothes off and tossed them by the door. I wasn't the princess, but I knew that if she came back, she wouldn't want to set sights on that outfit again. I certainly didn't want to. I'd lost the crown in that arena of death and wore no other jewelry, so when I was naked, I swam into the bathing room.

The claw-footed shipwrecked tub looked so inviting. Back at home, I hadn't had the luxury of one. Back in Lagoona, most of the mer lacked tubs. To bathe, we dumped sand in buckets and scooped out handfuls to scrub our skin and scales with. It was a nice change, to finally experience this lavish life. But at what cost?

I went over to the sea fan shelves and pulled off a couple of jars of pink sand from the shores of two-legger territory. Turning, I uncapped one and bent over to dump the contents into the tub. The grains fell to the bottom. I put down the jars on the floor and knew that the servants would later refill them. There was a lava seam in the room, located just below the tub, and a lever to release small quantities of heat to warm the contents inside. I pulled it and waited. Once it heated, I adjusted the lever again and then swam into it.

Sinking myself into the sand, I let out a pleasurable sigh, my tail burying beneath the grains. The color was light and warm against my dirty scales. It felt good, not having to scrub off grime and slime from my tail with Lagoona sand.

Out of every horrible thing the palace had to offer, I had to admit that this was the least horrible of them all.

I picked up a handful and started scrubbing my arms slowly, scraping it against my skin in circles, smoothing it out and making it shine. I scrubbed everything, making my way down to my chest, where I paused, remembering the feel of Elias' lips there, just on my collarbone, and lower still.

I looked down at myself. I hadn't had much of an education in Lagoona. The school there only served to teach the young ones how to read, write, and do math. Afterwards, the mer were expected to work. Those who were lucky enough to leave Lagoona had probably enrolled in a school somewhere else in Thalassar, if they hadn't had the misfortune of being selected later on.

Needless to say, I wasn't very well educated in things like the anatomy of the mer. I mean, *I knew*. I worked at Tides' Tavern, and there we got all manner of creatures, male and female alike, and I'd heard talk. I knew what made us different, how everything worked, and how babies were made. I knew mer kissed and touched, the same way Elias had touched me. I just never knew it could feel so… pleasurable.

I trailed my fingers lightly over my skin, over the swells of my breasts. Where mermaids were soft and supple, mermen were all hard panes and muscled skin. I let my fingers roam lower, over the dip of my stomach. It wasn't so thin anymore. Not like it'd been before I'd come to Eramaea. The palace had given me curves in places I never thought I'd see. My hips flared at my sides and the skin that had clung to my frame was fuller. I was muscled from the constant swimming and exercise I'd done. My touch veered lower where my skin met my tail, touching what my dresses hid. My skin dipped below my waist in the figure of a V where it met the lining of purple-blue scales.

I touched that V, fingering the line where the scales met. I knew that this was how the mer mated. There was a small slit that ran down the center of the V that opened to accommodate a merman's member. I slid a finger up the line then, pushing against the slit of myself. A tingling sensation ricocheted through my body and that slit opened, allowing me to push a single finger inside.

My face heated as I explored myself. I'd done so before, back in Lagoona when I felt curious, but it had never felt like this. I'd never felt like I was filled with such urgency, and I'd certainly never imagined someone else while I was doing it. But I did. I could all but feel the Black Blade's kiss on my skin, the shape and imprint of his lips against my body as my own fingers moved to the slow rhythm of that memory. I was reaching for something that I couldn't quite grasp. I had no idea what it was or why it was so unreachable…

I dropped my hand into the sand with a groan and grabbed a fistful of it and resumed scrubbing at my body, trying to push away the feelings and sensations Elias had awoken in me. The very thought of it frustrated me. I wasn't here to feel these things. I was here to stop a war, discover what had happened to the princess, and go home where I belonged.

Scrubbing vigorously until my skin shone, I finally finished and swam out of the tub. I reached over to a claw-shaped hook on the wall and pulled off a pink robe, slipping the garment on. When I made my way out to the room, I lifted the ivory shell of the telly in passing. A bubble rose from it, depicting clear recorded images of happenings in Thalassar.

As it started to play, sound resonating through the room, I swam into the closet and grabbed a comfortable—miraculously, as the princess only seemed to own extravagant, uncomfortable garments—dress. I slipped it on, the silk pooling around my sand-sensitive skin and swam back into the room to plunk myself down on the bed.

Anemones reached for me, caressing my skin and scales. I was about to plop back onto the cushioning of the bed and fall into a long sleep when the voices and words on the telly caught my attention.

I stared at it. On the telly was a mermaid and merman, two mer I recognized. They were news reporters, and they reported all major events on Thalassar broadcasts.

"...have informed us that the princess is in the palace, and that she is alive and well," the mermaid said.

"That's quite a relief! I think it's safe to say that we were all worried about the princess facing this dire situation." The merman smiled at his co-host, like they were having a normal conversation, pretending that the conch recorder wasn't in front of them. Like they weren't being watched by thousands of Thalassarins.

"I think this whole situation deserves a conversation, don't you? What is your opinion on what the princess did at the execution? Do you think she was in the right to stop it?"

I leaned closer to the edge of the bed, holding my breath to wait for his reply.

"It was certainly a surprise. Up until now, we've only ever seen the princess take part in lavish state balls and parties. We've never actually seen her take an interest in political affairs before. I have to say, and this is my opinion, mind you, that it was refreshing to see how our future leader cared so much about the merpeople, even if it *was* just a criminal. Let's have another look at the footage, shall we?"

He turned his body and suddenly, him and his co-host disappeared, the image of them on the telly replaced by another one. This one from a high angle inside that death arena, images depicting me before the mer, pounding a fist against my chest.

"Stop the violence! No more!" I'd cried out.

I wasn't sure how or what to feel about seeing myself on a telly screen like that. All I knew was that, in the moment I had gone to save Elias from death, I had looked fierce like I never had before.

The screen switched back to the mer hosting the news. "A very brave thing for her to do!" the merman complimented, an enormous smile on his face.

"Or very foolish," the mermaid added. I glared at her. "She put herself in harm's way to save a criminal. That rouses another question; do you think she should be punished for what she did? Though she is the princess, she acted above royal law—a law set by *her* ancestors—and aided in a wanted criminal's escape."

The merman laughed off the mermaid's reply as if it meant nothing. "She's going to be queen once she marries Prince Kai and comes of age. She can change laws on her whim if she so wishes. As for punishment… Well, according to interviews we've conducted since the incident, polls state that the middle and lower class mer are enamored with her suddenly, all because of what she did. If she is punished, there are sure to be riots. Let's have a look at more footage we've gathered…"

The telly changed again, this time showing the image of hundreds of mer gathered near the palace of Eramaea, screeching and screaming. Some of them held up signs that were hard to make out. The screen cut to another image of a merman interviewing a mermaid.

"Can you tell us why everyone has gathered here today?" he asked.

The mermaid was middle-aged, wearing a simple commoner's dress similar to those I wore in Lagoona. She smiled into the conch. "We are gathered here to celebrate Princess Odele for her valiancy in saving the Black Blade from death!"

"You do realize that the Black Blade is a criminal, right?"

The mermaid frowned. "To some of the upper class he might be. To others he is a savior, a symbol of hope. Sometimes he's the only hope mer like us have."

The interviewer looked genuinely confused. "Mer like you?"

She nodded vigorously. "Poor mer selected or living in fear of being selected to fight against Kappur. He's given more to our community than those in the palace have."

They cut to another merman. "I always thought that the princess was just another stuck-up royal and that she didn't care about any of us. Today proved differently. For her to sacrifice herself to save the Black Blade? I never thought I'd live to see the day when a royal fought for a poor mer's life."

"The Black Blade threatened the princess. How can you all admire a criminal willing to harm the princess you now admire?" the interview asked, perplexed.

The merman shrugged. "I don't think he would have harmed her. That's not the Black Blade's way. He doesn't kill or hurt anyone. He's like a miracle sent to us from the gods. He has more of a heart than the queen and king, that's for sure. Besides, she's safe in the palace. He didn't touch her."

The scene cut off and went back to the hosts of the news. They began talking, but I didn't hear them. My mind was reeling so much that I almost forgot I was still holding my breath. I let it loose slowly and then dropped back onto the bed cushioning.

What I'd thought would end disastrously had actually ended in something else entirely. The mer of Thalassar were happy. They were rejoicing. They loved the princess…

No.

For once since I'd come here, it wasn't the princess they loved.

It was me.

PAIN DRAGGED ME IN and out of unconsciousness for hours, until it was the cold of the cove that finally pulled me from the darkness. My teeth clattered together, the sound echoing across the cavernous stone walls.

Darkness enveloped me, the only source of illumination was a dusting of phytoplankton floating around. I reached a hand up to grab the particles but they dispersed while I cringed in pain.

Never, in all my years as an outlaw had I been caught until the night before last. Since Maisie had swam into my life, I'd been captured, beaten, and nearly killed. Now, I was the most wanted merman in the whole kingdom. Not that I hadn't been before, but this was different. Before, I'd just escaped Selection. This time, I'd abducted their princess. I tried to make myself despise Maisie for what had happened, but in truth it was my fault.

I'd grown careless. The moment I'd dropped her off in the alleyway, I'd turned and had been filled with nothing but thoughts of what it'd be like to have her body flush against mine. I'd neared the poorer half of Eramaea when they'd grabbed me. Seven royal guards pummeled me with fists and the blunt ends of swords. When the beating stopped and I'd opened my eyes, I'd seen him.

Captain Tiberius Saber.

They'd parted to let him swim through, and he'd tried so hard to look the formidable opponent as he bent to glare at me from my position in the silt.

He'd smiled at me in a gesture that was neither fortuitous or boastful. He smiled at me with manic possessiveness. A look that said much more than words ever could. Moments later, I was hauled up, bound, gagged and blindfolded, taken away to what could only be the dungeons.

I'd been stripped, beaten by prison guards, given dirty rags that reeked of mud and a rotting corpse, and awaited my fate.

I guess the greatest joy I'd gotten out of this entire situation was bashing the captain's face in with two-legger kitchenware. I hoped he'd bruised, both his body and his ego. That and the way Maisie's body felt against my chest. The way she'd defied all rules to protect me. The worry in her gaze.

That mer was invading my every waking thought. I tried pushing her out. After all, she hadn't given any indication that she dreamt of me with the same fevered passions I'd dreamt of her.

But even so, I knew that there was a reason we had met. Like the gods themselves were pulling our futures together, threading our fates. There must have been a reason she wielded the other half of my blade, and the reason was only one I could fathom.

Maisie was meant to be mine.

I sat up in the dark with a groan. This place, though I couldn't see well in the dark—I'd shoved the lava globes away so I could sleep—was too spacious, it was nearly suffocating. I got up and wrapped the rags and cloak around myself, swimming blindly through the cove. My tail bumped into hard objects as I passed. I tried to remember the layout of the place, swam up and forward, until my hands came into contact with a wall. It was furry and covered in barnacles. I pushed down on the stone, feeling my way across the surface, the imperfections digging into my palms. I pushed against the stone and it gave way, screeching together loudly, the wall parted to form a doorway.

Smiling, I swam into the alleyway, the doorway closing behind me.

Night had fallen in Eramaea. For hours, I'd succumbed to the pain and darkness. It didn't matter because this, I could deal with. I could become one with the shadows and do what I needed to do before anyone was the wiser.

I was the Black Blade, after all.

I pulled the hood of the cloak over my head, tying the drawstrings together at my neck. I started forward to the mouth of the alleyway, looking around. The streets were relatively empty, save for the occasional mer strolling about.

There were a few guards patrolling, but I was careful to let them pass before I slipped out into the shadows of the streets. I stuck near the underside of buildings, letting the cover of darkness camouflage me.

I swam cautiously through back streets, making my way by memory instead of sight. There were no lights to illuminate the way here. Not that I'd need it.

I made my way out of the busier parts of the city into the poorer parts of Eramaea. I paused, straining my ears, and feeling for even the slightest of stirrings in the water. I would not be foolish enough to swim blindly there and get caught a second time.

And there were ways to sneak in undetected, secret ways, and I knew each and every one of them.

I swam slowly, taking my time to circle around the area, swimming in between homes. I made my way to one specific house, looking around before trying the back door. It swung open with ease and I darted in, closing the door behind me.

The house was as dark as the waters outside, but like the outside, I knew every nook and cranny of this place.

I swam to the corner of the room where I knew a chest was located. I dug through the contents until my hand came in contact with something cold and sharp. I wrapped my hand around the hilt of my black blade and pulled it out. Though the weapon was dark, the obsidian shone in the room.

The blade was the length of my forearm, bigger than the one Maisie wielded, though no less deadly. They were mates to one another. Hers, studded with a single sapphire gem, while the hilt of mine glittered with the hint of black diamonds. I dug into the chest again, pulling out the black leather scabbard and belt. After securing the blade in its place, I pulled out a long, black tunic.

After stripping, I changed into clean clothes, strapped the belt around my waist, the sheathed blade bumping against my hip and tail with comforting familiarity.

Just then, a door opened to the room I was in. Defense came easily. I whipped the blade from the scabbard and held it out before me. A bright blue light shone from the inside of a lava globe, a globe held in the hands of an old and bent merman.

My weapon lowered, and I sheathed it back into its rightful place. The old merman's face was set in a wrinkled frown, cast into the soft shadowing of blue and white light. His expression changed as he saw me, eyebrows rising, mouth dropping open.

"Elias?" he asked incredulously.

"Mr. James, sorry if I disturbed you."

"Not t'all, son." He gestured that I follow. I did so without reluctance, following him out of his back storage room and further into the small house, to the kitchen and dining area. He placed the lava globe in the center of his table—a slab of stone with piled rocks holding it up—and pulled out a chair, seating himself.

I kicked out a chair with my fins and sat myself in it.

"Heard you had an exciting day, son." His face was clearly amused, though with a slight undertone of worry.

"Yeah?" I pressed my elbow into the table, resting my chin on my palm. "What have you heard?"

Mr. James rolled his eyes at me. "You have ears, son. Don't act like you don't know what the mer are saying about you and the princess just so I can stroke that big ego of yers."

"And what are the mer saying about the princess?" I asked, genuinely curious. I hadn't heard what they'd said, though I could imagine.

The old merman's thin shoulder lifted before his palms met the surface of the rough stone table. "There are a lot of rumors going around that you hurt her."

I leaned forward, eyebrows raising. "Really?" I asked.

His eyes narrowed. "Load of bullshark, if you ask me. You wouldn't hurt a mermaid, let alone a princess. But the things that are floating around about *her*, that stuff I can believe."

"What exactly are they saying about her?"

"So many things. The loudest of the rumors is that she's a changeling."

My skin tingled at the sound of that. *Changeling*. I schooled my features into a mask of nothing but sarcasm, so as to not give anything away. In a way, a changeling was what Maisie was. Someone put into Princess Odele's place. Impersonating her. Living her lavish life.

But if there was one thing I was absolutely certain of, it was that Maisie was nothing like Princess Odele.

"Indeed?"

Mr. James gauged my reactions, to see how much I cared. Whatever he was trying to read on my face, he would find nothing. I would show nothing.

"It's all so strange…" Mr. James continued. "How quickly someone can change…"

Strange, indeed. I smiled and got up from my chair. Mr. James followed the movement with his eyes. "Thank you for keeping her safe for me." I patted the side of my sheathed blade. "And for hiding the rest of my belongings."

Mr. James got up himself. A sign of respect towards me. I didn't bother telling him not to. It wasn't as though he'd listen. The mer revered me despite my protests. They treated me like a hero. I was, but a real hero did not want recognition and neither did I. I just wanted change. "No problem t'all son. It's the least I could do after all that you've done for us."

I frowned at that. There was always endless heaps of gratitude among these mer. As if I was doing it so they'd owe me. I didn't want that, either.

"I've done nothing, sir," I denied.

Mr. James snorted. "You've done plenty and you know it. And should you need anything else, the mer here are loyal and would gladly help."

I knew that, but I was being hunted right now. I wouldn't put the mer in danger. I'd already been here too long. No. The safest place for me and everyone else right now was hiding in Maisie's cove.

I started to turn. Stopped. "There is *something* you could do for me." I dug into the pocket of my tunic.

"Anything."

So quick to agree… I thought with wry amusement. I flicked a cold coin at him, which he caught before it could spiral through the water.

"Take that to old mer Seth Spiketail. Tell him thanks for the cloak."

Mr. James started to smile, but I turned before I could see the full extent of his admiration. It wasn't something I deserved. I professed myself a hero in their story and even in my own. Yes, I'd helped them evade Selection and start a new life. I kept them hidden and gave them money…

But I was still a criminal to the crown, after all.

Waking up hours later hadn't seemed to settle my exhaustion at all. My fins still ached terribly. I hiked the dress up, fingers reaching for my shredded fins. Massaging them lightly brought temporary relief, but soon my fingers started cramping up. Maybe I just needed to swim at a leisurely pace. Get up, stretch my limbs.

I did just that. My body felt tingly all over, like my every nerve had fallen asleep. I swam around the vast space of the room, hoping that the aches would ease. It only made them worse.

I was nearly tempted to call for a maid, to bring me a salve or something. The only thing stopping me from doing that was that if I told anyone, it wouldn't be long before royal medics were rushed into the chambers to look all of me over and they realized the princess had scars that didn't belong.

No.

Instead, I went over to the door, making sure it was secure, then went to the tapestry on the wall.

I needed to check on Elias, to see how he was faring. Hopefully his wound hadn't gotten infected, I thought as I swam through the passageway and crawled through the muddy hole. I made it to the other side, dusting myself off. The light of two lava globes beckoned me down to the couch.

Elias lay there, his eyes closed. I froze beside him and took a moment to observe him in his stillness. The shadows of the blue glow that the lava globe cast over his features was soft, making his features look even darker. Black lashes, long and thick, fell across the top of his cheekbones. His nose was straight, pointed, and his mouth was wide, lips full.

That mouth had pressed against my lips, tongue invading the most private aspects of me. He'd shamelessly tasted my flesh, and not for the first time, I wondered why he'd done such a thing. Had it really been a claim to the payment I owed him, or was his reason something else? Sinister? Dark? Selfish? Or had he simply wanted me in all my limping glory? I doubted it.

"Do you like what you see, little fish?" His voice startled me in the dark. Black eyes suddenly fluttered open to stare at me with an amusement that matched the smirk of his lips.

"Are you feeling better?" My voice was a raspy whisper that could have been contributed to the pain, but I knew that wasn't it. I just hoped he couldn't read the treachery in my voice. I hoped he couldn't hear how much I wanted him, even when I shouldn't.

He sat up straighter, dropping his tail from the couch so I could sit next to him. I did, keeping a modicum of space between the two of us.

"As *better* as I can be."

My eyes went down to where his wound was and I narrowed my eyes. The prison rags and cloak he'd been wearing were gone, and in their place, a black tunic, belted at the waist with black seal leather, a scabbard, and his obsidian sword hanging from it.

My cheeks heated as I glared at him. "You went out!" I accused.

He grinned. "As lovely as that prison attire was, I couldn't stand another moment of the stench."

"What if you'd been caught?" I near-shouted.

He raised a dark brow, sarcasm lacing his every gesture. "Worried about me, little fish?"

Yes. Curse him to the abyss and back.

"That was reckless!"

"I've been known to do a reckless thing or two…"

Fuming, I shot up from my seat. "Stop joking!" I tried to take a stroke back, but my fin—*blasted flipping fin*—gave in. I cried out, nearly falling onto a pile of conches. But Elias moved like a shadow, pulling me up against his chest before I could fall.

I sprawled onto him as he fell back onto the couch. His hands were warm around my waist, holding me steadily in place. The lava globes illuminated the worry on his face, and likely my own shame. My breathing grew labored, coming out in quick pants. My hands were splayed across his chest and for the briefest of seconds, I tightened my fingers against the neckline of his tunic.

I let go and begged for him to do the same. "Let me go, please."

He looked reluctant to do so. I almost wished he wouldn't. But I was so confused. My body was drowning in heat, a heat I didn't know if I completely understood, and his touch only made it worse. It made me desire him like I'd never desired anything in my life before.

He slid a hand down the side of my dress. When he reached the hem, he slowly hiked it up. I sucked in a sharp breath. I didn't move as I felt the warmth of his palm begin to slip up the length of my tail, sliding along my scales. When he fingered my fins, I moaned, dropping my forehead to his chest. I wasn't entirely sure if the sound had been in pain or pleasure.

Then he moved his hand against my fins, massaging them with gentle fingers. His touch eased the cramping, the pain.

"Does it hurt a lot?" he asked in my ear. There was a sensual curl to his words that had me pulling away to look into his eyes.

I never spoke to anyone about my injury. Not even Josiah, my old boss from back home, knew to what extent it shamed me. With Elias, the line of boundaries was blurred. It was something that had been washed away in the current. He wanted to extract my secrets, and so he would, whether I told him willingly or he had to pull them from the whispers of waves in the deep. He'd get them. One way or another.

"If I exhaust it," I replied slowly.

He nodded as if he understood but did not stop rubbing it, one hand steadying me by the waist.

It felt so deliciously good that I could hardly bring myself to tell him to stop.

I'd never let anyone touch my tail before, let alone my fins. With Elias, everything was different. Like he was the only one who could ever understand. And I wanted him to.

"I was fourteen," I whispered. Never before had I spoken these words aloud. They were my greatest shame. Back home, everyone knew what had happened and they pitied me for it. I was a fool. And perhaps I was only giving him more information he could possibly use against me. But it wasn't until this moment that I realized, I desperately needed to share this with someone. "I'd just started working at Tides' Tavern."

He listened to me, his fingers not stopping once.

"At the time, there were other waiters there. Before..." He didn't prompt me to continue, because he knew what I meant. Before Selection had taken them away and left me there alone. "They were my friends. We were all young. And stupid." I said that last part lightly but could find no humor in it. "There was one merboy, a waiter a few years older than me. He smiled at me all day, would find reasons to swim by me, let our hands touch…" My face heated. "At the time, I thought it was all terribly romantic. And then he asked me to meet him after my shift in the back." I took in a shuddering breath, willing myself to continue. "I thought I'd be safe. There are nets separating Jo's land from the gators, but…" I shook my head back and forth. "I waited for hours. He never showed. By the time I realized he wouldn't, it was too late. A gator had gotten me. The rest was just darkness and pain."

Elias, who'd been ever quiet, suddenly stilled. The hand on my waist tightened while the one on my fins touched me softly, tenderly.

"I guess I swam to Jo's house in my delirium. I woke up there, being tended to by Lagoona's doctor. After I healed, my merfriends told me that he—the one who invited me there—had been laughing about it in Artisan's Square. About how he'd tricked me into waiting for him. He'd never meant to show."

It was my biggest shame. I'd been young and impressionable. I'd believed that a few seemingly accidental touches as I passed a bowl of frog-eyed stew and a couple of smiles had meant something. And because of that, I'd been changed irrevocably. I didn't care about the ugliness of my fins. Not anymore. What hurt was the pitying looks. Being *different* because of one stupid mistake, and being reminded of it every time I swam.

Elias let out a slow breath. "What was his name?" he asked, strangely calm.

"Does it matter?" I didn't like thinking about him.

"It does. I need to know who I am going to kill. I have a few mer who owe me favors, who sell in traveling markets. I would love nothing more than to run him through myself, but I'm indisposed at the moment."

I believed his every word, and they humbled me, that the Black Blade would think about killing someone for me, however morbid the gesture. However averse I was to violence.

"It doesn't matter, Elias. Because weeks later he was selected."

It was the first time I'd been glad to see someone leave. And that still shamed me to this day. Possibly more than my own injuries.

"Good." Elias nodded. "Then I hope he's rotting ten strokes under the silt."

His hand had stopped moving on me, and I realized that the pain had vanished completely. And I was all too aware of how close we were, so close, the rasp of his breath fanned across my mouth.

There was this maddening urge I had to kiss him. Instead, I pulled away, getting off of him and taking a seat on the spot next to him.

Even as I sat down, he pulled my tail into his lap, and resumed massaging his fingers against my fins.

"You really are special, little fish."

Not this again. I rolled my eyes. "Right."

"No, really. You should hear what the mer are saying about you around Eramaea."

I'd seen what the mer on the telly had said, but I dared not hope.

"They're calling you a changeling. And they're completely enamored with you for saving *me*. I'd say that makes you special. They love *you*. Not the princess."

I knew it was true, they loved me, but it still didn't make me special by any means.

"You earned their love, Maisie."

"Yeah, but do I deserve it?"

One merman. I'd saved *one*. So far I wasn't any closer to stopping a war or discovering why the princess had vanished.

"I guess that depends on *why* you're here. What do you have to gain from this?"

This wasn't the first time he'd asked me this question, and I wasn't sure I should answer. Sharing aspects of my life, my biggest shame was one thing but sharing *this*...

What was it? Was it really any different? I needed someone to confide in. And Elias' goals were practically the same as mine. To stop the war with Kappur.

And maybe... maybe he could be the one to help me accomplish that.

I decided to take the dive.

"The princess has been missing for months..." I said slowly. But of course, he knew this part already. "And I think she left because someone was trying to murder her."

It took an hour to recount everything to him. From the moment Captain Saber disrupted my quiet little life, to nearly being murdered twice, to the passageway, to the conches and to the marriage contract.

I retrieved it from its hiding place, stuffed safely inside one of the many conch shells. He read it in silence by the light of the lava globe, and I anxiously watched his expression. It was rather serious, and he gave nothing away. When he finished reading, he looked up at me.

"Do you realize what you've found, Maisie?"

Yes. Evidence. Evidence of why there was a war with Kappur.

"We could finally find out *why* there's a war. And stop it."

He nodded and looked down at the kelp parchment held in his hands.

"We need to find out why this contract didn't go through. To do that, we need to find those witnesses and ask them what they know."

I swam over to him, looking down at the marriage contract as well. There were four names signed on the witnesses' lines.

"Lysandra Mako. Percival Pike. Nigel Gillson. Jesse Fenson. Well, I don't know any of these mer…" However, the name Percival rang familiar.

Elias shook his head. "Me neither. But they must be royals or royal associates. Witnesses from each kingdom." He folded the contract up and handed it to me. "You need to find out who they are, little fish. Ask them if they know anything."

I nodded gravely. I wasn't sure where to begin. "I'll need to keep a low profile from now on. The queen was quite angry with me for what I did." I placed the contract back into its respected conch, and set it on the cave floor near the chest.

"No more saving criminals?" he joked.

I shot him a look. "No. Definitely not."

"That's certainly too bad." He came forward and tilted my face up by tapping my chin. "I liked the way you felt against me."

My face heated, and I was glad for the dimness of the cavern and that he couldn't see me. Because I knew my coloring would betray me entirely.

"We should probably watch some of these conches…" I whispered. If it wasn't the color of my face the thing that gave me away, then it would certainly be the low rasp of my voice. I turned away from him and went over to the recorder, trying to remember what conch I was on. Flustered, I bent and picked one up, looking at the number before placing it on the device and starting it up. When I turned, Elias was on the couch, beckoning me to sit next to him.

I did, as far as I could be on his other side. He rolled his eyes and tugged on my dress, causing me to fall onto him.

"Come closer. I'm not a shark, and I won't eat you, little fish."

That was the problem. Maybe I *wanted* him to eat me. I wanted him to devour me, and that feeling scared me, yet still I settled in at his side, resting my head on the crook, just where his neck met his shoulder. He wrapped his arm around my waist and held me, and I prayed he couldn't hear my heart pound, as a recording of the princess began.

Elias

THE PRINCESS OF THALASSAR was perhaps one of the most daft, spoiled, irritating mer I'd ever known. Or at least, her recordings portrayed her to be that way. After a while, I started nodding off. Maisie had long fallen asleep, resting her head on my shoulder.

I marveled at the ease and trust she was placing in me. Hours ago, I held an ax to her throat. I certainly did not deserve this, but abyss take me if I lied and said I did not want it with every bone in my body. Not just this… but more. I wanted more of her. Her body, curling beneath mine, tails twining together, bodies opening up as I thrust inside her, wringing pleasure from her body, pulling cries of ecstasy from her mouth.

Maisie stretched delicately, tilting her face up, nearly touching her mouth to mine. I groaned at the proximity. If she kept at this, I'd not survive the night or keep the promise I'd made about not touching her again.

I shook her slightly. "Maisie…"

She jerked up, and our heads cracked together.

I flinched slightly. The brief touch was more painful than I'd like to admit because of my bruising.

Captain Saber's lackeys had given me the beating of a lifetime. He'd locked me up in a dark, dirty cell and had turned away just as they pummeled into me as if they meant to end my life. There had been evil in the captain's eyes, just moments before; evil and a jealousy I could not fathom.

It wasn't until I'd pressed the ax to Maisie's throat that I realized why he'd gone through all the trouble. Who he had done it for.

"Sorry." Maisie stretched her arms over her head. My pain forgotten, I was captivated by the movement, by the way the delicate curves of her body pressed against the material of her dress. She dropped her arms, and looked around the cavern, rubbing her eyes. She was too cute, with the traces of sleepiness fogging across her vision. "What time is it?" She yawned.

I smirked and couldn't help but tease her. "Let me just get out my diamond-encrusted timepiece…"

That woke her up quickly. She glared and scoffed out something that sounded like "tadpole."

"You fell asleep and left me to watch these horrid conches by myself," I accused with only the slightest bit of chagrin in my tone.

She made a slight mocking noise deep in the back of her throat. "Poor you," she teased. "Now you know how I've felt the past few days." She peeled herself off of the couch, swimming slowly over to the conch recorder. Her stiff body tilted her sideways. She tried to straighten her posture, but there was a strain in her muscles that made her movements jerky, perhaps the only indication that she was in pain.

I tried not to tighten my fists at her discomfort. I did not want her to see it and think I pitied her. On the contrary, she was strong. Stronger to have survived that vicious ordeal. What sliced through my body was rage. I wanted to murder the bastard that had taken advantage of her innocence. I wanted him to meet his death at the end of my blade.

She pried the conch from the recorder and bent down to pick up another one. She placed it on top, started it up, and swam back to the couch. It was almost instinct to wrap an arm around her shoulders, and pull her towards me. Her presence had a way of calming the shadows that stirred inside me. Things between us had changed. A door to secrets and intimacy had opened, spilling a closeness I doubted either of us had ever shared with anyone else before. She tucked her head into the crook of my neck, and it was like the last piece of a perfect life slipped into place.

The bubble rose up to show the familiar images of the princess in all her finery. Jewels adorned her neck and ears by the dozens, glittering diamonds and sapphires that covered up the entire length of neck, making her skin look bejeweled. An ornate headpiece rested on her head, jangling bells and objects dangling from shining thread to twinkle around her face. She was ostentatious to the point of it being blinding.

At the same time, Maisie and I groaned.

"Me again!" she exclaimed flippantly. I rolled my eyes. It was really rather incomprehensible how no one could tell that Maisie was not the princess. Odele spoke with venom and mischief curling her tongue. "And accompanying me today is none other than the Lizard Prince—oops—I mean, the *Dragon Prince*, Kai Li of Draconi. Say hi to the conch!" The image turned to reveal Prince Kai.

The Dragon Prince was surrounded by his kinsman, mer who shared similar features; dark eyes, bright tails, and long, dark hair. His personal guards, advisors, and courtiers. They all looked upon Odele with disdain.

Prince Kai frowned in her direction, displeasure evident on his too-beautiful face that he obviously tried to mask. She used the conch to close in on his face, a close up of those intense brown eyes.

"Princess," he greeted, his voice a wisp of mystery and disdain.

"Hey, Lizard Prince," Odele said venomously. "How is Thalassar treating you?"

His eyes narrowed into thin slits. "Splendidly."

"I am so glad you're finding Eramaea to your liking."

Beside me, Maisie snorted, and I looked down at her. She was looking at the bubble, and the image of Prince Kai there. Her eyes were wide, and even in the dimness of the cavern, I could make out the flush on her rounded cheeks. Even if I hadn't been able to see it, the heat of her skin against mine would have been a dead giveaway.

I lifted the end of my tail up to the couch and nudged hers with it. She shot a glance up to me and I smirked, a small twist of my mouth. "I see that gleam in your eyes," I teased. "Are you in *love* with Prince Kai?"

She sputtered out a stream of nonsense that I construed as a mixture of truth and embarrassment. "Of course not!"

A chuckle pushed past my lips. "Oh, I think you are." It was obvious from the way she stared at him, as if she had the moon in her eyes.

She blew out an exasperated breath. "He's a *prince,*" she said.

Ah, so no more denial? And her excuse was rather pathetic. My eyebrows pulled together in a frown, though the smile still touched my lips. "And I'm an outlaw."

"So?"

"So…" I drawled. "If you can kiss an outlaw despite your scruples, you can kiss a prince."

"First of all, you kissed me."

I waved her words off with a simple flick of my fingers. "Semantics…"

"And secondly, I can't kiss a prince. Don't be ridiculous."

Something inside of me flared to life. Like a volcano erupting. "But you can kiss *me,* little fish, is that it? Why? Because I'm on your same wavelength? Because he's a royal and we are not?" I could not keep the venom from my voice. Maisie scooted away from me, taking away warmth and leaving the cold of ice between us. I turned to glare at her. I shouldn't have taken offense at the words, but I did. I knew she hadn't meant it, but she made me feel unworthy. Worse than that, she made herself sound unworthy when it was the royals who should have been bowing down to *her*. She had the power to command kingdoms and win hearts, she just didn't realize it yet. And that infuriated me. "You won't kiss Prince Kai because you think you're not good enough for him." An accusation. One that had her looking away from me before turning back, tilting her chin up in the slightest gesture of defiance.

"I'm not the princess," she reminded me. "It's not my place to… *seduce*… a merman who isn't mine."

"And yet he looks at you like you're the only star in the sky. Like you're his favorite treasure among the hoard. Like he wants to make you his Dragon Queen." I reached out and grabbed her wrist, she pulled, and I pulled back. "Like, if given the chance, he would devour you, drown you in the ice of his passions like the Dragon Prince that he is." She pulled, and this time, I let her hand smack back to her chest. Then, I leaned back against the cushions and smiled. "I've seen the way he looks at you, little fish. He wanted to tear my head from my shoulders for taking what he thought was his."

She was quiet for so long. And finally, she whispered, "That's because he thinks I'm the princess."

I made a disgusted noise in the back of my throat, flicking her words off as what they were. Foolish.

"I've no doubt in my mind, little fish, that Prince Kai Li of Draconi knows exactly who you are." And I didn't mean her name, her station. I meant something else entirely. A veritable kindness that lived and shone through the cracks of her smile and the orbs of her dark eyes. She opened her mouth to protest, but I cut her off. "He may not realize it yet, but I'm sure he is questioning why he's suddenly fallen head over fin in love with a mer he hated weeks ago."

I settled back onto the couch and watched the image of the princess in the moving bubble. I could practically hear Maisie mulling my words over, the thoughts in her mind spinning through an abyss.

"Sometimes I fear your attention to detail," she practically cursed me.

Laughter rattled out of me, tugging at my wounds and making me wince. I doubled over, holding my side. When the pain eased, I sat back up, tossing my arm over the back of the couch.

"All in a day's work, little fish. It's my job to know things about Thalassar's finest..." I looked her over, smirked. "And it's most beautiful."

She rolled her eyes, snorted then looked at me mischievously. "So you think Prince Kai is beautiful?"

"Yes."

She blinked when I answered with no hesitation. Her mouth dropped open, then closed again. Clearly, I'd caught her off guard.

"I—you—what?"

I winked. "Not the answer you were expecting, little fish?"

"Well, no, not really. You really think he's beautiful?"

I shrugged. "Is it so rare for a merman to appreciate the beauty of another merman? I'm comfortable enough in my sexuality to admit it."

"Wow..." she breathed, falling back to the couch. "That's... surprising..."

Considering the past few days we'd had, I could name some things that were more surprising than finding out I appreciated the finer aspects of a beautiful mer.

"I enjoy mermaids and mermen in equal measure," I said coolly, wondering what her reaction would be. If she would be disgusted or... No. That was a blush rising to her cheeks. I wondered if she was suddenly picturing as vividly as I was. Of the prince and I devouring one another's mouths, tearing at one another's clothes. And an even better fantasy, with Maisie between the both of us, writhing and gasping against the heat of our bodies as we brought her pleasure in tandem. I could feel myself hardening just thinking about it and adjusted my posture so she wouldn't notice.

But she wasn't looking at me at all. Her gaze was fixated on the recorder, but the brightness of her flush was telling. I leaned closer to her, the rub of our bodies hinting at the desire I felt. My own hardness pressed against the cloth of my tunic and onto her. She felt it through the material of our clothes and her breath hitched.

"Can you imagine such a thing?" I whispered, my words fanning across her skin.

"Imagine what?" Her voice was but a whisper.

"Three bodies." My fingers trailed up the length of her arm. A slow seduction. A promise. "Three mouths." My thumb swiped against her lower lip. "You, me, and Prince Kai, twisting together between the sheets…" I pulled away, letting the promise dangle between us. And Maisie? She could find no words to question me or point out the fact that Prince Kai despised me. I smiled and for the next few moments relished in the heat of her body and her silence. I knew what she was thinking, dreaming, *wishing.*

I thought it, too.

I dreamt it, too.

I wished it, too.

More than she could ever know.

Off and on I fell asleep in the Black Blade's arms, the voice of the real Princess of Thalassar lulling me to sleep with the incessant details of her boring life. Eventually, I had to leave his side, letting secrets and whispers, plots of discovery waiting until the next night.

I ventured up to my room, just as lights outside my windows began to expand in swaths of magenta, orange, and periwinkle. Phytoplankton illuminated whatever shadows the surface light could not reach, covering the ocean in a dusting of golden and blue particles.

I stopped and stared beyond the bars of my pretty prison, and even that black steel refused to put a damper on my mood. Eramaea was so beautiful, my heart ached.

Sighing, I took a stroke away from the windows and slowly peeled the dress from my body. It slid down in a tuft of gossamer and silk past my tail and onto the quartz floors. I turned and froze for a moment, transfixed on the vision of myself in the mirror.

My hair was tousled, the tips floating over my bare shoulders. There was a smattering of scales raining down my shoulders and lower back. I tried to see myself as what Elias claimed me to be. Was the mer before the mirror really beautiful? Could she be, or rather, could *I* be?

My skin held the slightest tint of pink, like it had been coated over with the dustings of a pearl. And my hair and tail… Thin aqua fins ranged halfway below my hip and nearly down to the tip of my tail on either side of my body. They fanned out at my sides, in a way I imagined a bird took off for flight, and when the light caught them, you could make out the darker tracings of veins running through. The left side was shredded, and there was the small silvery sheen of scar tissue spiderwebbing on my tail.

If it weren't for this scar, I could almost trick myself into believing that I was actually part of the Malabella lineage. I shook that thought off as soon as it formed. No. I was nothing. No one. Just because my hair held the undertone of blue in it, though it was on the darker side of purple, it didn't make me royalty.

I was letting the silk gowns get to my head.

With a sharp shake of it, I turned from the mirror and waded into the bathing room. First, a scrub. I could never get enough of those.

I took my time soaking in the sands before getting out and choosing an outfit for the day. The princess had very little assortment of simple clothes, and I'd exhausted them all already. I grabbed a dress in the pretty color of purple, one that matched my tail, but glittered with diamond jewels.

I slipped it on. The dress had thin straps that crisscrossed at my upper back. There was a heart shaped neckline, and the oval cut behind the dress left my back bare. The skirts were puffy, the whole thing rather superfluous, and so like Princess Odele that I had a maddening urge to rip the dress from my body. I didn't. I had to make up for my mistake the day before. Which meant I had to don her face. For real this time. If I wanted to make a change, discover secrets, and stop a war, I had to be her. In every way.

So I picked out jewelry and extravagant headpieces. Diamonds glittered at my ears, a necklace of purple stones, as big as a sea robin's eggs, was heavy at the base of my throat.

I grabbed a pack of cosmetics and slid a bright dusting of ground mother-of-pearl across my eyelids, brightening my cheeks and lips with pink until they sparkled.

When I finished, a knock sounded at the bedroom door. I answered it slowly, imagining that Odele would take her time before answering, all haughty arrogance.

I moved the chair propped up against it and opened it. Palace guards floated on the other side, among them, I noticed, was also one of Prince Kai's own guards. They bowed low before straightening. "Princess," they greeted in unison. "The queen requests an audience with you immediately."

Of course she did.

"We are to escort you to her, at the behest of Captain Saber."

Just the mention of him made my gut clench angrily. The tadpole. He'd followed Elias and I. He'd turned him in. Because of him, Elias had nearly died.

"I never want to see you again."

I'd meant it, and he had obviously heeded the venom in my words if he'd sent his guards in his stead.

I tilted my chin up, the same way I'd seen Odele do it hundreds of times in those conch recordings. "Fine. Take me to her."

I swam with dignity, my limp hurting a great deal less than it had yesterday. Still, if I had been in pain, I wouldn't have let my weakness show. Especially not in front of the queen.

I was guided into the throne room, where the queen awaited, and much to my inner turmoil, the king did not. There was another merman in her presence, though. He was decked out in royal finery, robes in bright colors with silver thread and clips holding the material together at the throat. He was old and a little sleazy-looking. Wrinkles sagged his face, ever slightly. His nose was long and crooked, eyes a tad too small beneath drooping eyelids. Wisps of white hair were plastered onto his scalp as if by magic.

I didn't like the way he spoke in hushed tones with the queen. And I certainly didn't like the way they lapsed into silence the moment they saw me.

The guards left me to swim in alone, closing the doors after me. I swam up to the fin of her throne and bowed low, a respectful mask already settled into place.

"You called for me, Your Majesty?" I asked politely. The queen looked me over, eyes narrowing over my every inch. Finally, that sharp gaze settled on my face.

"Dearest daughter," she began tightly.

My eyes flicked over to the merman at her side. He didn't know who I really was. Good.

"I have been giving it a fair bit of thought. Since your sickness has passed, I believe it best to continue on with your lessons once more."

Lessons. I tried to remember the captain's words. He'd explained to me in detail what exactly the princess' duties entailed. Fencing. Riding. Lessons in politics. Tea time. He had started to oversee my princess training. I hoped that would no longer be the case.

"With Captain Saber being busy with… more pressing matters, we have doubled your security. Prince Kai has sent over one of his own guards, as I'm sure you're aware."

More pressing matters. I read between those lines. The more pressing matters obviously meant he was out there looking for the princess he so obviously loved. The sooner he found her, the sooner he could get rid of me.

"And so, you will continue your lessons with Percival as though they never ceased." She nodded to the merman at her side.

Percival. I racked my mind for a hint of recognition. Why was his name so familiar? Then it clicked. Like the whiplash of a strong current, it all came rushing back to me. Percival Pike. The name of one of the witnesses on the marriage contract I'd found. And, if I was remembering Captain Saber's teachings correctly, he was the queen's royal advisor.

And I was meant to study with him.

"These lessons will keep you occupied and less focused on the other activities you think are worth your time."

What she really meant was more focused on becoming the princess and less focused on the things that truly mattered. Like the fate of criminals and selects.

I nodded my acquiescence. "Of course, stepmother." The words burned out my throat.

She waited a couple of heartbeats, as if I would object, and then she turned to her advisor. "Off to the schoolroom, both of you." A curt dismissal. "I have matters to which I must attend."

Percival and I bowed to the queen respectfully; or at least, as respectfully as I could manage. It came out rather stiff and angry, but I bore through it. Surprised at how something as simple as a bow could seem as condemning as if I let the ax drop on my own neck.

I straightened but didn't look at her again. I turned and exited the throne room, leaving Percival to follow me. It's what I imagined Odele would do. Wait for no one. Act as if I owned the world because, well, Odele *did* own it. At least, she owned Thalassar. Daft as she may be, she was still a princess, the future ruler. She waited for no one.

I didn't slow when I heard and felt Percival approach behind me. He swam to my side, matching my pace, with my ever faithful guards trying to make themselves invisible behind us. There was something sleazy about this merman that made me uncomfortable. I put discreet space between us.

"I cannot express how glad I am to see you alive and well."

Alive and well. What a strange way to word it. My eyes narrowed, but I assumed the most flippant expression. Like I had not a care in the world. I was wary of him, the same way prey are wary of sharks. The same way one should be wary in rock fish-infested waters.

"How kind of you to be so attentive towards my well-being, Percival."

"Yes, well, you are the future of Thalassar, and as your mother says, you must be up to par in your studies. They've been put off for too long."

"My stepmother," I corrected haughtily.

He stiffened, causing me to smile. I'd sounded just like Odele then. How she never ceased to remind those around her that Queen Circe was *not* her birth mother. So many conch recordings. Her personality was embedded deep into my brain.

"Of course, Your Majesty." He sniffed once. "Well, then, shall we venture to the library?"

"It's not like I have a choice, do I?"

I could feel the glare emanating from his body but gave no acknowledgment of knowing I'd upset him.

We swam to the royal library in silence. I hadn't yet been to the royal library; in fact, there hadn't even been a tour of the palace. So when we finally arrived, I tried not to let my awe show when I beheld it.

White columns marked the open doored entrance to the place, and it seemed palatial in its own right. Blooms of brightness burst, like lanterns, stars, and fire had melded together to illuminate the vast expanse of space. The colored glass windows on the far side of the library ranged like the shelves did, from floor to ceiling. Each shelf was filled with conch shell recordings and scrolls of kelp parchments.

In Lagoona, we'd never had libraries this grand. In fact, we hadn't had a library at all. We'd had a house of public records, but it was nothing like this.

There were tables made of quartz and coral, chairs all around them, rows and rows of shelves, and a desk behind which sat a very old and bent merman with skin that glowed like the light of a lantern. Off to the side, there was a room that was closed off from the rest of the library, encased in walls and darker windows. A sign on the door informed me: 'Royal records. Royal access only.'

Percival swam up to the desk with the glowing merman. Without a polite word, he pulled a large, leather-bound book open and began flipping the delicate kelp pages. I watched curiously as he took the quill—the elongated and sharp tooth of some creature—and dipped it into an opened vial of squid ink, signing on a page. Turning, he handed the quill to me.

I shouldn't have been nervous as I went up to the book and looked at the scrawling letters. It was a sign in, sign out ledger.

"Princess Odele, how nice it is to see you well again!" the old, glowing man exclaimed. His voice reminded me of the whistle of the current blowing between cattail stalks. It was the pleasant sound of home.

I smiled widely as I bent gracefully over the book and started to sign Odele's name as neat as I possibly could. "It's good to be back."

"We missed you around here. I was hopelessly lost without my little helper."

I froze mid-letter. The Princess of Thalassar helped the librarian? That wasn't something she ever mentioned in any of her conches. I had to admit, it caught me off guard, and I couldn't very well imagine her inside this place, joyously stocking shelves or among the conches. That seemed like servant's work, something she would deem beneath her.

I finished signing her name and set the quill aside. I wasn't sure how to respond to him, so I just gifted him with a smile that he returned a second too late, for he'd been observing my hands. Before I could contemplate his stare, Percival impatiently waved me away from the front desk and to a table in the center of the library. I sat and watched as he went to gather conches and parchment in his arms. He worked quickly, long fingers pulling things from shelves efficiently. His long robes flowed behind his tail, like a dark wave or a sinister shadow following his every move.

He came over and gently laid the contents down onto the table before taking a seat across from me. "Let's begin where we left off, shall we?" He opened a roll of parchment and tapped his fingers against the looping scrawl of handwriting written there. A beat of silence. "Well?" he asked expectantly.

Internally, I panicked. My lessons had started from the beginning. Eating. Drinking. Swimming. What did I know about the lessons of the princess? Foreign languages, history of the Malabella lineage, things that an outsider couldn't possibly know.

And that was what I should know. The queen had known that. So had this been some sort of test on her end? To humiliate me? As if to say, 'imposter,'

Imposter. Imposter. Imposter.

But Percival didn't know that.

I scoffed and pushed the parchment away. "Ugh." I made a noise of disgust deep in my throat. "How *boooring.*" I looked down at my nails. Flippant. Rude. Wearing her mind was too easy. And I was good at it.

"Princess." Percival sounded exasperated. "We *must* study."

"I am sure we must, Percy. But I really don't feel like it." I slowly got up from my seat, palms pressed tightly against the surface of the table. "There are many other things I'd rather be doing." I made a move to turn away.

"If you could at least *listen* to the lessons?" A vehement demand.

Nothing bad could come from just listening. As long as I pretended. I let out a suffering sigh and plopped myself indignantly back into the seat. "If you *must.* But make it quick. I have things to do today."

As it turned out, there were things I'd wanted to do that day—visit Elias—that Percival didn't allow. I barely got time to breathe. Lessons were shoved down my throat. At first I feigned disinterest, but after a while, though I still refused to write and answer questions, I paid rapt attention.

There was so much to learn. About politics, foreign trade, strategic battle planning… It was all insider information. Things to be tucked away in my mind for future use. Whatever use I'd find for them.

After lessons, we went in for a light lunch that I fought hard not to devour, despite its bland taste. When we finished there were more lessons, listening to conches, and to my immense fear, hippocampus riding.

I tried not to tremble as I was brought before the massive beast. It was gargantuan, and it wasn't so much the height I feared, but rather falling and then being trampled by it.

I recalled the first time I rode one of the beasts, the gut-clenching fear, and the way Captain Saber had felt behind me. The protective way his arms caged me on the animal. The heat of his body against my back…

No. I had to stop thinking about Captain Saber. A feat that proved difficult without his presence. I expected to see him around every corner or trailing the shadows behind me. I'd been the one to chase him away. I never expected to feel his absence like a phantom, or to feel an ache for the slightest bit of teasing and banter.

Pushing thoughts of him away, I swallowed my fears and nervously approached the beast, trying to appear confident, though I was sure my features were pulled tightly into a grimace. I gripped the reins and hauled myself up, hugging my tail to the side of its body. I rode slowly with the instructor at my side, an instructor that didn't give me much instruction, and the guards at my back, flanking almost all around me like a wall of bodies.

The guards were supposed to make me feel safe. I felt anything but. The excess number of mer were just a reminder of everything I still had to figure out; marriage contracts, why a war had been started, and what Percival knew about it.

I was having a hard time figuring out how to approach the subject. It wasn't until later that I got my opportunity.

After surviving the hippocampus ride, we went back to our studies. I was listening to a recording on marriage contracts and found my opening.

"Why must marriage contracts be so tedious?" I pushed the shell away.

Percival glared. He did a lot of that, I noticed. "You and I both know that marriage contracts are a matter of state, Princess. Very important."

"Yet it all seems so… *cold.* Like pawning off a hippocampus. I am a princess. Not an animal."

Not for the first time that day, he sighed with exasperation, making me think that perhaps the princess was prone to those sorts of conversations with him.

"Marriage is a promise between two nations. Contracts are meant to assure each country that the other won't look elsewhere should a better prospect arise." He looked at me as if to say, 'You already know this.'

I ignored it and went on, "I'm sure there have been many broken marriage contracts throughout history."

He glared suspiciously. "Of course there have been." His tone grew a darker edge. "And they've all ended in the same conclusion: war."

My bones chilled. War. A broken marriage contract could lead to war after all. His words confirmed just what Elias and I already knew. Now to confirm my other suspicions…

"And if the contract between Draconi and Thalassar were to be broken?"

He let out a gasp, his face raging red. Bushy eyebrows pulled together. "Don't even speak such things aloud!"

I leaned back in my chair, eyes widening in surprise at his outburst. I tried pushing away his words with a flippant expression and a wave of my hand. He didn't let me finish half the gesture before he was bearing down on me again, reaching for my hand and crushing it in his grip.

"Kingdoms have gone to war for less than the mere mention of such treason. Thalassar has fallen victim already to the hardships of war, and you will not let it happen again. You *will* marry Prince Kai Li. Do you understand?"

I let out the shakiest of breaths but nodded. Only then did he release my hand.

Yes, I wanted to whisper. *I understand.*

"So did he tell you that's why Thalassar and Kappur are at war?"

Elias paced a short distance from one side of the cove to the next. He claimed he needed to stretch his muscles to help his wound. I wondered if it was really because he was anxious at the information I was bringing him.

"Not directly. But I've no doubt he meant to imply it."

You will not let it happen again.

Was it too farfetched to think that that's what he'd meant? It had felt like a warning.

I held the marriage contract in my hands, fingers tracing the edges of Percival's neat scripture.

"He obviously knows something." Elias finally stopped pacing and turned to look at me. His black eyes were intense, shadows cast against his cheeks and beneath his eyes, making him look even more formidable.

"Obviously. I mean, his signature is on the contract, and the old barnacle has been advisor to the Malabella lineage for decades. He knows why we're at war."

"Getting him to talk will be difficult." Elias stretched and cracked his knuckles.

My eyes narrowed. "Don't," I warned.

His eyebrows lifted, and the side of his mouth twitched. "I wasn't planning on hurting him, little fish. I was actually going to suggest you use your feminine wiles to seduce the old mer."

My face heated and I felt the words like a jab. "Don't tease." I glanced down at the contract to avoid looking at him. But there was the soft rustling of clothes, and a moment later, his warm hands covered the tops of my own. I set the contract in my lap, eyes finding his.

"Don't doubt your abilities to seduce, little fish. You've ensnared the Dragon Prince easily enough."

I snorted. "It's one thing to seduce a pretty prince and another entirely to seduce a barnacled, saggy merman."

"And what about the merman of the night?"

My breath stuck shy at the entrance of my lungs. There was no mistaking that tone, the sudden darkening of his voice that curled the hairs on the back of my neck and had goosebumps rising over my skin. He was good at that. Too good. At changing the rhythm of a conversation that would otherwise be lighthearted, into one that made my heart pound.

This was unfamiliar territory with a merman who had become familiar; a comfort. Things between us had never gotten further than that kiss in the alleyway, than the light tracings of a touch, than heated words that promised passion like I'd ever known. But something inside me wanted *more*. My body burned with the demand for it. Only fear kept me from taking that first stroke. And I knew he'd only go as far as I wanted him to go. He'd only go as far as what I allowed.

"What are you so afraid of?" he whispered, darkly, like he could read my every thought. Curiosity and a challenge all packed into the tenebrous lilt of his voice.

You.

The word hung unbidden between us. Then there was the way my heart pounded, and how he could surely hear it, each thump daring to make that first move.

Ba-dump. Ba-dump. Ba-dump.

"Elias." My voice was hoarse as it shattered the quiet. I dared to place the palms of my hands on his arms. His skin was hot and warmed the chill in my bones.

"Maisie..."

As if we hadn't seemed intimate enough, he had to go and say my name. Like it was the only name he knew, and the only one he wanted to know.

I closed my eyes against the sensation. As if it hurt. And it did. Just not the way I'd expected.

What are you so afraid of?

The pain in my fins reminded me. I'd been foolish once. You'd think I'd have learned my lesson by now. But with Elias, I wanted to be foolish all over again, only this time I wondered how different the outcome would be. Would I be hurt again? Would blinding pain splinter through every nerve, every bone, and leave me a mangled, crippled mess? Or would I find something different on the other side? Would I find light and stars and wishes? Pleasure, happiness, a future? Something worthwhile?

My eyes opened, and I finally found the voice to answer. "*Nothing.*" And then, I kissed him.

I'd always imagined what it would be like to plunge my hands into two-legger fire. With Elias, I got my answer. It was all-consuming, from head to fin, my body heated, blazing. Like I was glowing hot from the molten core of lava, and I was pulling the Black Blade down with me.

Our mouths opened for each other's secrets and we took, pushing and pulling until somehow, his body had slanted over mine, and I felt the comfort of his heavy weight.

His lips brought me to depths I never knew existed until now. His tongue traced over the seam of my lips, and I found myself gasping, only to take him in deeper.

My hands fumbled in their nerves. The only way to steady them was by bunching my fingers into the material at his shoulders.

Elias pulled away just long enough to murmur against my cheek. His dark curling voice was a whisper beneath the depths of the secrets that joined us. And then he was kissing me again.

Our bodies didn't know the meaning of the word space. How could they when we fit so perfectly together? His hands gripped my shoulders with the same urgency I gripped him, and then his fingers moved, slipping to the sides to press down on the sharp ridges of my collarbone. Then further still, to the straps of the dress. He paused, broke away and looked in my eyes, wordlessly asking: 'Is this okay?'

I nodded, and his fingers nearly tore the material. He pushed it aside and hooked his fingers into the bodice of the dress and pulled. I gasped as it was torn from me, the material sliding down the length of my body. And Elias pulled me in with a hunger in the shadowing of his gaze that was both frightening and thrilling.

I was finally bare before him. The whole of me on display. From the dusting of purple blue scales across my abdomen and shoulders, to the torn fin flapping nervously at my side, and finally to the rest of me. Naked. Breasts suddenly heavy with desire and the urge to feel his touch. I felt I just might burst if he stared at me much longer.

His hands went to my shoulders, and with half-lidded eyes, I watched as he traced the shadows contouring my body, down to my collarbone, lower to my breasts.

A place that I let him explore without reservation.

He cupped them in his hands, and I never knew how one little gesture could send desire pulsing through every nerve in my body. I didn't need to look down to know that I was opening up to him, preparing for our joining.

I felt it. Felt the need pulsing there, begging to be touched. I held my breath as Elias bent down and to my surprise, pressed his tongue where his hand had been. Right on my nipple.

I groaned, arching into his touch, fingers clinging to him as if I'd be lost otherwise. Maybe I would be. He switched his ministrations from one side to another, and my head whirled faster and faster the more insistent he got.

Finally—*finally*—he slid back up my body and took my mouth in a kiss that left me gasping for water.

It was overwhelming, to have so little between us and feel like we were leagues apart. I clawed at his tunic, slipping the material from his shoulder.

Elias pulled away long enough to chuckle and press the tip of his nose to my own. "Give me but a moment, little fish."

"Hurry." I barely recognized my own voice, but I didn't care. All I wanted was to feel him over me again. But he was pulling away, unfastening the belt around his waist. It slowly floated away from him, along with his scabbard and blade. I swallowed as his hands hiked up his black tunic, past his tail and higher still, discarding it completely. I'd seen his chest before, but I'd never seen him like this, bared before me so intimately.

His muscles looked all the more prominent in the shadows of the cave, cords on his arms bunching and straining. He was holding back from pouncing. As if from fear of hurting himself—for he still wore a strip of gauze around his wound—or the fear of hurting me. No. His gaze spoke differently.

The Black Blade feared nothing and he, above all others, saw a strength in me that I had yet to see.

His hesitation was due to something else entirely. I realized because he was giving me a chance to admire him. Just another bit of the Black Blade for me and me alone. The proof of what would soon come to pass between us in his posture and…

My gaze lowered *there.* His body opened for me, like mine did for him, and if I'd ever been unsure about his desires before, I no longer was. Not with the evidence rising strong against his stomach. Like with mine, the V of his hips had a slit running down the middle, but where mine was flat, his bulged. It opened, and that part of him that made him male, his member, was thick and long.

Nervously, I opened my arms to him. an invitation, and he gladly went into them, body covering mine. His hands were all over me, each light caress of his fingers punctuating all the secrets between us, bringing us together.

Thumb against my hip bone. *I know who you are.*

My hands running down his chest. *I love Thalassar more than anything.*

His fingers through my hair. *Fake Princess.*

A savage kiss between our lips. *Savior of the broken.*

Hand on my breast. *An outlaw but so much more.*

A scared mermaid.

And then he entered me in one swift thrust, pressing me into the cushions of the couch. A gasp tore out of my throat at the sensation. My tail curled around his tightly, pulling each other closer. He moved, and I *felt* him inside me. Hard and heavy, velvety and warm. Lights danced behind my eyelids the faster and harder he moved, and throughout it all, we never ceased touching and never stopped sharing the most intimate of silent secrets.

And when that final sensation came over me, a shuddering that had me crying out and gripping him to avoid spiraling into that abyss, another secret followed.

One we didn't need to say aloud for either of us to understand.

I love you.

I'D HELD ONTO HER as long as she would allow. Which, despite what we'd just shared, had been very little. Her body was warm and flush and left an ache in me when she got up to dress.

Watching her move with limping efficiency made my heart clench with want and something else entirely. Pain? An emotion that cut me as painfully as the quick stab of a sharp blade.

Just look at how quick she wanted to leave.

Soon, I'd be forced to do the same.

Not that I could tell her now when we'd just shared our bodies and hearts. She would think I was abandoning her to pain and sorrow. That I'd tricked her for my own gain like that bastard before me had. But would it be better to leave in the shadows of the darkness? To disappear, leaving nothing but the traces of a shadowed memory in the back of her heart?

I could. It was my nature. To be a trickster. A heartbreaker.

She turned and smiled at me and I returned the gesture. I smiled more around her than I ever had in my entire life. I knew why she brought out the best in me. Even if we hadn't said the words aloud, our bodies had confessed what our mouths couldn't.

"I'll see you later?" she whispered. There was such hope packed into that single question that my heart fractured in my chest because I knew I was going to have to lie to her.

That I was going to break her heart at some point, some time, down the line.

"Yes," I said.

But even if I left, I *knew* that no matter how hard I tried to get rid of it, the one being followed by shadows would be me.

Lessons with Percival were as dull as ever. There were no more tracings left of our conversation about marriage contracts, or talk of treason, or anything else I could take back to Elias in order to continue our investigation. Not that we spent much time investigating. In between conches on the princess' life, we spent time talking or wrapped up in each other's arms. Sharing every aspect of ourselves. Every secret through quiet touches and glances.

We were closer than any two other mer could quite possibly be, and we didn't even really need words at all.

My face flushed, and I felt the sudden whack of a whip on the backs of my hands. Pain broke me from embarrassing reverie. I cried out, yanking my hands to my chest. Red welts began rising on the backs of my knuckles. Unfortunately, I was well-versed in Percival's punishments. My hands wore the bruises and hard skin of his beatings. He'd started hitting me often enough in the past few days that my hands should have been used to the pain by now. They weren't. The first time he'd struck me, I'd been so surprised that tears had welled behind my eyes. The second time as well. By the third time, I'd learn to expect the lashings.

"Pay attention!" He waved the whip around in front of me. The tadpole. "Now, I'll ask you again, when was the treaty of Fraema signed, who signed it, and what did the treaty consist of?"

I racked my brain for the correct answers. So. Much. History.

"It was signed on the… thirtieth? … year of the Malabella rule. It was signed by… Thalassar… Prague and… Iol?"

The whip came crashing down onto the table with such a force it rattled it. Luckily, my hands were pressed tightly to my chest and didn't suffer the brunt of his wrath.

"Wrong!" he snapped. "The treaty was signed by Thalassar, Prague, and Ventlair. What did the treaty consist of?"

My hands trembled, but I did not dare bring them down. Tears prickled behind my eyelids, threatening to swarm out. I pushed them away. I'd not embarrass myself by crying in front of him. It'd be like placing a loaded speargun in his hands just so he could shoot me with it.

Gone was that docile, exasperated merman from that first day. Now, he was a cruel teacher. And this obviously wasn't the first time he'd administered such punishments.

No wonder Odele had fled.

"It allowed for free passage between the nations to supply equal trade and commerce?" I was doubtful of my answer and tried hard not to be.

A princess must be sure of all things, even if she is unsure and incorrect.

Again, he slapped the whip onto the table.

"Hopeless and brainless," he critiqued.

He liked to do that, to toss out insults that made me forget myself. The confidence I feigned while wearing Odele's mask waned as, bit by bit, he tore into my every action. Soon, I'd not be able to take it anymore, and I feared that day's arrival.

Besides, how had the queen's advisor come to be little more than a glorified nanny to Princess Odele? Was it because she was the future ruler and he was passing on his experience?

I could tell him now that if he treated Odele half as bad as he treated me, the moment she ascended the throne, he'd be out on his fins in the streets.

The welts on the backs of my hands stung.

"That is enough study for now. Unfortunately nothing stuck. Hopefully you carry yourself better in the gardens while taking tea with your cousins."

Dear Tides. Not again.

After what had happened between me and Odele's cousins that first round of tea time, I had no desire to repeat such an incident.

I'd single handedly turned Odele's closest confidants against her.

Not that they hadn't deserved it, the wretches. But it had been a harrowing experience. They'd no doubt accept me with disdain.

Percival got up from his seat and gestured to a nearby servant, who began gathering up all the conches and kelp parchments quickly. I smiled at her almost absently before I caught myself.

A princess does not thank the help.

"Hurry along now," Percival urged. "You have a schedule to keep."

The schedule. To the flippin' abyss with the schedule. It was like swimming in shackles. I was told what to do, how to speak and dress, what to eat and even who to see. And to my regret, this schedule did not allow for many breaks or to see Elias or Prince Kai at all.

I probably shouldn't have even been thinking of the Prince of Draconi, considering all the intimacies I shared with Elias, but I couldn't help it. He *was* beautiful. He was a prince. I could hardly help it if my heart fluttered whenever my thoughts went astray to him, especially when I caught sight of his guards trailing after me alongside my own. Besides, Elias hadn't helped with whispered words in between kisses of what he would do to me, to Prince Kai. Sultry fantasies feathered against my skin and made me imagine things I shouldn't.

Prince Kai was kind, a stark contrast from other royals I had met. *And* he had kissed me. It hadn't been anything like the feverish caressing between Elias and I. Kai's had been sweet. A promise of something else.

I couldn't help but want to see him again. I could pretend to be Odele with everyone else, but with him, it was harder. I so desperately wanted to mend whatever rift was between them, even if I had to be myself to do it.

At least, that's what I told myself, denying with every fiber that I was actually getting close to him for myself.

"Hurry along, now." Percival signed off on the ledger.

I followed slowly and did the same, taking the quill and signing Odele's name. At first, I'd worried about the handwriting and how it wouldn't match. Now, I could make the excuse that the signature was different because my hands hurt.

It's not like anyone but the old librarian seemed to notice anyway. Thankfully, he never made comments about my wretched handwriting. Especially not with Percival around. The last thing I needed was him prying into who I really was.

As we exited the library, Percival began speaking in that clipped, dull tone of his that spoke of lectures and chastisement. "You have an hour and a half of tea time. I'll escort you there and the guards will escort you to your rooms, where you'll change into your riding habit. I shall wait for you with your instructor in the stables."

He spoke as though I didn't know my own schedule, the barnacle.

I didn't bother replying.

We passed through the opulent hallways of the palace where rows of Eramaean royalty stared at us and made me uncomfortable. The portraits veered into statues and vases that looked like old relics. It wasn't until we neared the end of the hallway that the sounds from the opened doorway registered.

Clank. Swish. Pant.

Percival swam right past, but I stopped at the entrance and peeked in. My curiosity got the better of me. Usually all we passed were vacant rooms or spaces filled with courtiers that were either desperate to speak with me or desperate to avoid me. These sounds were wholly new and I wanted to investigate.

As I did, the water left my lungs and my gut clenched, flittering with nerves.

Prince Kai was in the room. It was a training room if I ever saw one. Weapons adorned the walls of the place, and the floors had thick leather-like mats in square sections.

The Prince of Draconi was in one of those sections, and I breathed him in. Every detail, every contour, every *breath.* It'd been so long since I'd last seen him, and yet his beauty was still so staggering. He was all high cheekbones, and soft, refined features.

Although, from what I was currently witnessing, the last thing he'd be considered was *soft.*

Prince Kai was engaged in a vicious sparring session with one of his guards. A long katana was gripped tightly in his fingers, the blade clashing against that of his guard.

He became a blur of silken black robes and steel as he danced through the water around the other mer.

Clash. Clank. Swish. Dodge.

It was like watching a dance choreographed in vicious savagery. There was something elegant about the way he moved but dangerous as well. His posture, and the formidable way he attacked, made my heart thump a little louder in my chest. Here he was.

The Dragon Prince.

Steel sparked against steel; it was obvious his opponent was good. Not good enough. Kai made a series of blows with katana and tail, and a moment later, the katana went flying from his guard's hands, all the way to the ground at my fins.

It rattled and settled, and I couldn't stop myself. I bent and picked it up by the hilt. It was a heavier blade than what I was used to, but it felt comforting nonetheless in my hands.

"Princess!" Percival was suddenly at my side—probably having noticed a bit too late that I was no longer following—screeching. His loud voice seemed to draw every eye over to us. Kai's. His advisors. His guards.

My grip tightened on the hilt of the katana.

My eyes—and Kai's—found each other. Where I expected that sudden politeness he was known for, something else glowed in his eyes instead. It was daring, dangerous, and it heated the blood coursing through my every vein. Still high off the adrenaline of this battle, his eyes took me in like a predator hunting for prey. He looked like he had weeks ago, in those moments when I was caught in the Black Blade's grasp. It was feral and untamed, the darker side of him he kept hidden.

Excitement swelled in my chest, causing me to smile. He smiled back and then sauntered forward with purpose in his every stroke.

I braced myself for the impact of his voice.

"You're holding it wrong." His Draconian accent clipped the words out in slow resonance, but there was a romantic lilt to it. I looked down at the foreign sword. He placed a hand over my own, fingers adjusting my grip on the weapon. "Use both hands," he instructed coolly, pulling his own hand away from mine for a brief second. I did as I was told. With the blade pointed down at the floor, I grasped the hilt, one hand encircling at the top, the other at the bottom like he'd instructed.

Once my grip was adjusted, he moved off to the side so I could lift the katana.

Percival sputtered. *"Princess!"* he chastised, suddenly appearing behind me and making me jolt. "You will be late for tea with your cousins. You cannot dally around here and partake in heathen Draconian behavior."

Kai raised an amused, delicate eyebrow in Percival's direction. Behind him, his advisors and guards seemed to ruffle indignantly at his tone. I didn't blame them. If this was supposed to be Odele's betrothed, why was he blatantly insulting him for all to hear?

And he'd chastised *me* on war and treason. Old fool.

I half turned to Percival and commanded, "Cancel it."

His face reddened. "Cancel it? I couldn't possibly—the schedule!"

I shrugged, feeling bold with the blade in my hand and Kai's near-glowing eyes on me. It gave me courage, that stare. "Throw the schedule into a lava seam for all I care." I turned back to Kai.

His smile was breathtaking. "Are you looking to battle, Odele?" he asked with amusement.

I hated when he called me by her name. Just once, I had the impulsive desire to be called by who I really was. To hear him say *my* name in his beautiful accent. For him to know exactly who I was and who I was not. But that's who I was pretending to be, after all. Princess Odele.

"That depends on the opponent."

He smiled wider, obviously pleased with that coquettish answer.

"Clear the floor!" he ordered.

Everyone rushed to obey, moving aside so he could pass. It was rare to see him so commanding. To see him take charge. And I rather enjoyed the layer of niceties stripped away. I had not bowed to him, and he had not kissed my fingers as royal propriety dictated we greet one another.

I swam over to the mat. My guards and Percival filed into the room after me. More to watch what would surely be a spectacle rather than to protect. I had no experience with sword play.

'The princess is a skilled fencer,' Captain Saber had told me those first days on our journey from Lagoona to Eramaea.

I wasn't skilled at anything, and Prince Kai would soon find this out.

But the challenge in his gaze was impossible to ignore. So I took my place opposite of him on the mat.

And waited.

Kai paced back and forth, a prowess in his posture. The katana was held lightly in his hand, almost carelessly. He knew I'd be no match against him. But it'd still be fun to try.

"A powerful blow does not come in the *strength* of your swing..." He held his own katana at the ready. "...but in the *angle* of the swing." He demonstrated by bringing the sword over his head and flying down in a graceful arc, then a few more at opposite angles. The sleeves of his bright training robes slid down his arms, giving me the perfect view of long forearms... and the scars crisscrossing his skin. "Brute force does not win battles, my gem." He twirled through the water in a series of swings until he had closed the space between us, the distance of the blade the only thing that kept us apart. A blade he slashed against the sleeve of my dress, tearing it down to the elbow. "Skill and cunning do."

I stared down at my sleeve with widened eyes then back up at him. He was already retreating back to where he'd been before.

Mischief gleamed in his eyes. A dare glowed there as well. A challenge to come towards him. My eyes narrowed. "I was fond of this dress."

"I wasn't." He smirked. Even that was beautiful and distracting. My tongue felt suddenly heavy and I couldn't swallow. Was this a mistake? Was I in over my head? "I'd much rather see you without it, anyway."

My face flamed, and I cautiously looked around to see if they'd heard. But of course they'd heard. We were locked in a room where sound traveled through water. They gave no indication that they were listening, except for Percival, who was fuming with rage at the very suggestion.

I turned back to Kai and pointed the blade at him. My voice shook when I replied, "Is that a challenge?"

His eyes were alight with adrenaline. Yes, there was something spectacularly different about him. I wouldn't doubt it if he had a hidden personality in there somewhere. The soul of a dragon lingering, ready to break through that carefully construed surface of politeness.

His eyes roamed over the length of my body, and I could almost feel his fingers on me, pulling each garment slowly from my skin. Funny, just how much a single look could convey.

It was like it was just the two of us, and everyone else was falling into an abyss.

"It could be, my gem. In fact…"

I didn't see him coming. He was a blur before my eyes. I felt the snag of the blade on my clothes, the other sleeve ripping at the seams. The flaps of the material floated to my elbows.

"Try and bare me before your merpeople."

A challenge.

"Alright then."

I swung the blade.

SHE SWUNG AT ME.

I'd heard rumors, whisperings that the princess was a skilled fencer. I hadn't seen it, as she'd kept herself all but hidden since I'd arrived in Thalassar. Fighting with a katana was not like fighting with a sword as thin as a needle. But even as she charged at me, there was no trace of her rumored skill. The ability to be grand was there, surely. In her stride, determination, and stubbornness.

She swung the katana with such a force that would have made any normal mer tremble. But I was no ordinary mer.

Just before the blade came swinging down, I whirled so she struck empty water. She cried out, turned again to me, a vicious whirl of pink and purple.

"Skill and cunning, Princess," I teased, then I held my sword up. "Where should I slice next?" The tip of my blade touched her shoulder. She stilled as it slid down the top of her bodice. "Here?"

She sucked in a breath and pushed the tip of my blade away with her own before stroking back.

"Maybe you'd like to be sliced yourself?" she threatened.

There went that wicked mouth of hers. I was so busy staring at it that I didn't predict her next move. She sliced forward, aiming for my chest. I barely had time to jump back before the blade sliced across the front of my *bei zi*. It was a garment I used for training. Long colorful robes that depicted the images of dragons with snarling teeth and vicious claws.

The material tore.

"Huh..." I observed the slit. "Impressive."

Odele smirked, obviously pleased with the compliment. The dragon in me roared, bashing itself against the surface of my consciousness. Ready to claim its mate. The legends surrounding my family were unclear in the line of truth and myth. One thing in the legend was clear enough. As a lineage who bred dragons, it was no surprise when an ancestor consorted with one.

And so every single one of his descendants had the blood of dragons. Inside us, there was a beast buried beneath our surface.

It was my nature to be wicked. To breathe ice. To win battles. To collect treasures. To claim my mate.

Only a slip of the dragon came out now. It was him who fueled me. Adrenaline and carelessness pushed my actions. I supposed... the dragon and I were one and the same, I'd just pushed that nature away so often, that the primitive part of me had become something separate in my mind.

It was slowly unleashing now as we parried. I struck, and she responded. There was no real skill to her, but she was a quick learner. *Slash. Swish.*

The blades of our swords struck, the force vibrating my arm with pleasant familiarity. We twirled and hit, the tip of my blade ripping another seam on her dress. This time at her hip. The material parted to reveal the scales on her waist.

The dragon in me roared a second time.

A taste. A taste. A taste.

Her cheeks heated with a blush, and then she was advancing. I blocked, but she was relentless. Her sword came at me from every possible angle. But the sword wasn't her only weapon. She struck with fists and tail. Her outburst of strength was so surprising, I staggered back and she advanced.

Clang. Clang. Clang.

The sword fell from my hands when she whacked my fingers holding the hilt. It clattered to the floor between us, and unarmed, she still came after me, punching the small of her fist into my chest.

I took it for all of two seconds before I smacked her wrist. The katana clattered to the floor next to mine. She gasped, from surprise or pain, I couldn't be sure, but I pushed her back by the shoulders.

The princess lost her balance and started to fall backwards, but not before she gripped the lapels of my clothing and I fell to the floor with her.

I wrapped my arm around her head to cushion her fall; that didn't stop the breath from whooshing from the both of us.

A sharp silence descended, cut through only with the sound of our mingled breathing. Our chests pressed together, they moved where it was near impossible to discern where one ended and the other began. Her heartbeat was captured by my own.

Then, the princess chuckled. "Now I know," she panted, "why they call you the Dragon Prince."

The world had fallen away around us. There were no advisors to lecture me on propriety. There was no carefulness between us any longer. There was nothing but warmth, and dare I hope it? Love.

I touched the tip of my nose to hers, and you'd have thought it had been a kiss from the way her cheeks warmed.

My tresses of hair fanned out, a few strands having fallen from my tie, and curtained the sides of our faces. There was tenderness in her gaze as she pushed a strand behind my ear.

"Prince Kai?"

"Yes, Princess Odele?"

"We should get up now."

I didn't want to. Everyone else could damn themselves into the abyss for all I cared. All I wanted was *this.*

"Of course, Princess." I got up, pulling her up with me. Floating before each other, I pulled the torn strips of her dress together, my fingers confident near her hips. "Sorry." I smirked. "But I really *don't* like this dress." I pulled my hands away.

She looked at the flaps hopelessly and shrugged. "It's just a dress."

Before, she had yelled at a merservant for knocking food onto her clothes. That had been the princess of the past.

Instinct, and desire, had me grasping for her hand. I brought it to my lips, pressing the softest of kisses against her knuckles. My eyes went down to her skin, at the red welts there.

Noticing my attentions, she pried her fingers away, almost self-consciously.

My blood boiled.

"Princess!" a snake-like voice hissed. An oily looking merman, with long, disdainful features, string-like strands of hair slicked onto his shiny scalp, came over beside Odele.

Knobby fingers wrapped around Odele's upper arm. She winced. The action was slight, and she tried to hide the gesture by schooling her features into a mask of impassiveness.

I turned my glare to him, unleashing my consciousness into my other self. Into that part I desperately tried to push down. My veins filled with ice.

"You…"

His eyes left the princess to look at me. Yes. There'd been just enough cold packed in my voice that he froze.

"Un*hand* the princess," I ordered. "Now."

He sputtered. "I *beg* your pardon, Your Majesty, but *I* am the queen's advisor." He still did not release her. As if he had the *right* to put his filthy hands on her.

"And I am *Prince* Kai Li of Draconi, heir to the throne of Draconi, son of the war general and Emperor Jiang Li. I am the Dragon Prince of my kingdom and that mer is my betrothed, so I will tell you only once more, *unhand her.*"

Only fools disobeyed my orders once.

No one dared do it twice, unless they wished to be corpses, rotting in the silt.

And this mer obviously wanted to be. His hand still rested there.

"Your Majesty," he snapped with a flourish. "As advisor to the queen, it is also my duty to advise the future queen, and this *repulsive* display was inappropriate and *barbaric.*"

My own advisors huffed in breaths of indignation. Though they would have disapproved of the display as well, they'd not tolerate the likes of *him* insulting us in such a way.

I'd long since mastered the art of calm fury. "Then I suppose sparring is as barbaric as flaying the princess?"

I did not want to announce such a thing in front of everyone. I'd wanted to spare the princess this embarrassment. But I was cruel. It was inside me. And it was time he see it unleashed.

I grabbed his collar, hand shoving out in the midst of his sputtering. In the shock of the action, he released Odele and clawed at my hand instead. I brought him close to me, the tips of our noses touching.

"You think I didn't recognize what those welts on her hands were? You think I don't know what you *did*?" I was well versed in royal lashings. And to see the evidence marked so prominently on the skin of *my* princess?

If I still held my katana, I'd run it through his flesh.

"It is necessary to—"

I cut the rest of that filthy sentence off by shoving my thumb into his throat. He gurgled. "The only thing necessary is that you stop talking and listen. Do you understand?"

I eased my grip and he immediately opened his mouth. "You—argh!"

I dug my thumb in deeper, and when his gurgling ceased, he nodded.

"Good." My smile was a blood-curdling, cruel thing, and there was a glare emanating from him somewhere beneath the droop of his saggy eyes. "Because I want you to know that if you ever, *ever* touch my future queen again..." I choked him for emphasis. "I will kill you."

Silence ensued. And only when I thought he'd absorbed my threat completely did I let him go.

He scrambled backwards, gasping for breath like he'd been drowning on air.

I turned to the princess, who was staring at me with such wide eyes. The tame part of me would have apologized for such a display. Right now, I was not tame. Either she'd accept me in all my savage, raving, murderous glory or not at all.

"I believe, my gem, you had a schedule to keep?" I only said it to gauge a reaction. All she did was stare. With disgust? Or was that a gleam of delight in her eyes, a precious obsidian glow that drew me in as all treasures did to dragons?

She opened her mouth to reply, and I ached to hear those next words. But the voice that spoke wasn't her own.

"The princess, in fact, *does* have a schedule to keep."

I turned slowly, but not before noting Odele's sudden pale pallor. The appearance of Captain Tiberius Saber had nearly every single one of Odele's guards scrambling over each other to float in a single line. He ignored them to swim by Odele's side. He gripped her upper arm, much more gently, but her own face could not mask the venomous reaction to his touch.

"Captain Saber." My way of greeting. "Pray, tell, where have you been?"

His posture was stiff. Saber was a big merman, wide and muscular, as opposed to my lither body and thin frame. Yet, I had no doubt that I could crush him if I really wanted to.

Ice was trapped in the depths of his eyes, encasing around his entire body and demeanor. Cold. Emotionless, even when he wore the depths of his heart in his eyes.

"Forgive me for the bluntness, Majesty, but I do not answer to you. Where I was is none of your concern."

I really wanted to stab her guard.

"It becomes my concern when you are absent from doing your duty to my betrothed. Perhaps, had you been present, such violent liberties against her would not have been taken."

"You know what?" The princess huffed out a laugh that was all too fake. "I *do* have a schedule to keep. Since it's too late for tea, I think… I think I'll go change for riding." She discreetly pulled her arm from the captain to rush closer to me. She was such a sight to behold, in a dress that was mere tatters now. Stretching out on her fins, she pressed a kiss to my cheek, where her warm lips lingered. Heat stirred inside me, and I kept very, very still as her lips traveled to the lobe of my ear.

"Thank you, my prince." Another kiss, and then she pulled away. Her absence made me shiver.

"Until next time, my gem."

She smiled at my parting words and swam past Captain Saber, acting as if he wasn't there in the first place.

He didn't follow her immediately. His eyes were like chips of glaciers threatening to crash into me and plummet me to an icy death.

Little did he know that I was forged in ice and jewels. And if anyone was to bring about the ruin of a merman, it would be me, and Captain Saber wouldn't live to see tomorrow.

Tiberius

I'D SLIPPED INSIDE THE training room for but a moment. I hadn't meant for Maisie to see me, not after she'd made it abundantly clear just how little she wanted to do with me.

I'd conceded to her wishes, if only because I thought the space would help quench my own anger. I furiously spent the past few days looking for any sign of Princess Odele and of the Black Blade. I swam to the mouth of that alley, the one where that criminal had dropped her off, near the rear of the palace. I had been searching for a clue as to how she disappeared out of thin water.

All my efforts had been fruitless attempts.

So much investigating left me with little answers, too many questions, and a bout of cold fury.

There'd been nothing to do but monitor Maisie from afar. And that's how I found myself here, watching, raging.

It had been like a perfect dance between the two, yet entirely unplanned. Even I was fascinated by the choreography of the push and pull between them. Of the Dragon Prince challenging Maisie to go faster, push harder. She'd done it, making it a feat I had not been able to accomplish. Gone was the prominent sign of her limp. There'd been a confidence in her that, with a start, had reminded me of Odele.

That resemblance was the only explanation I had for the jealousy searing in my chest.

Every movement, every swipe of the blade against her clothing pushed her further away from me and into another's arms.

But she wasn't Odele.

Even if she was, she didn't belong to me any more than Maisie belonged to Kai. They were wishes that were about as impossible and far away as the stars in a two-legger sky.

I bowed briefly to the Draconian Prince before excusing myself to go after Maisie. I left behind the other guards with a gesture of my hand. Not even Percival followed.

I knew she did not want to see me. I didn't care, because I wanted to see her. Her, or the princess she represented? It didn't matter.

She was swimming slowly, if a little distractedly. I wondered if she even noticed me beside her.

"Are you here to lecture me about how I ruined the princess' image?" she asked quietly, sadly.

I startled at the tone. Something in it seemed… broken, defeated. Her hands were red, blisters marring the backs of her knuckles. She kept rubbing her fingers across them. Seeing that hurt skin made my blood suddenly boil, rage raining high.

I was familiar with the sight of welts and bruises. I'd seen them before, had sustained them myself on behalf of Odele. At the time, I'd wanted to protect her from such a fate, as it was my duty to protect her from *all* harm.

Percival had whacked her once across the backs of her hands. I could still hear the gasp of pain ripped from her throat. Offering my hands in her stead had been easy. Watching her suffer was not.

What I'd done had been selfless. All I'd wanted was to spare her such cruelty. I had, but I still remembered the words she'd said to me right after.

"I didn't ask you to save me. You aren't a hero. You're nothing to me, so stop pretending otherwise."

Her words had cut through me like a knife just before she slammed the door to her room in my face. I'd leaned against it. I should have turned away, but I couldn't bring myself to leave. Especially not when the sounds from inside suddenly drifted towards me. The sound of Odele weeping.

"No," I replied. Contrary to her belief, I did not enjoy lecturing and yelling. And this time, I didn't plan on doing it. "You look like you've suffered enough."

If I expected her to chuckle, she did not. She still ran fingers across her bruised skin in anxious movements. Instinct made me place a hand over hers. All I wanted was to ease that pain. She stopped. A weary sigh pushed past her lips, and she pulled her hands away from mine, putting space between us.

"You know," she began as we turned in the hallway, "the longer I'm here, involved in all of *this*..." She gestured her arms around, at the walls, and ceiling. "The murder attempts, the suffocating lack of privacy, the lessons..." Her fingers fluttered absently, flexing. Finally, she turned to look at me. It was then I realized we had stopped swimming to face each other. "I am starting to understand *why* she swam away."

Those words were a dagger to my heart. To think that she'd left of her own accord, that there had been nothing to make her stay.

Not even me.

An impossible wish. To think she even noticed me. She scarcely did. I was just another servant to her. Just another mer she could yell at and misuse. Still, I loved her. I was starting to think that loving her had been a far greater mistake than losing her.

I almost hated the mer in front of me for making me realize that but couldn't bring myself to feel such a sentiment.

"Then, are you thinking of swimming away too?" I knew my words had come out colder than I'd intended, frigid like the cold freeze floating through water.

Her attention snapped away from me and resumed forward, leaving me to follow.

"I'd hoped you'd understand me better by now, Captain," she chastised, annoyed. "I am not one to just swim away from duties and leave behind the mer who need me. I said I'd help, and I *will*."

Determined as she was, I knew it wasn't to help Thalassar but to shake the royal foundations of the palace and challenge the laws of war.

"Then I hope to see you do your duty to Thalassar and help," I commented as we turned down the hallway to Odele's rooms, "rather than cause more chaos by freeing the criminals of their cells."

She stopped, just in front of Princess Odele's room, and turned sharply to me, her glare in place. "I'll kindly thank you to stop insulting me every time we meet, Captain. If I recall correctly, I gave you an order to stay away."

Her chin was tilted up, her hands clasped delicately at her stomach. Though her clothes were in tatters and wisps of hair floated out of her chignon, in this moment she looked and sounded every bit as regal and demanding as Odele.

"Well? You are *dismissed*, Captain."

She exuded power. Command. Both which were staggering. I blinked, for I could not find the will to do much else. A choked laugh escaped me. "Oh, Maisie." I shook my head back and forth. "You're more like Princess Odele than you know."

Her spine steeled. To her, there could be no greater insult than to be compared to the mermaid she despised the most.

"Goodbye, Captain." She whirled around, opened the door to her temporary lodgings, and slammed it in my face.

I stared at it long after she'd done it, willing my heart to cease its infernal rapid beating. Deny it as she might, there *were* some similarities they shared, similarities that ran deeper than just an outwards appearance. Odele used to slam that door in my face as well.

Odele. Odele. Maisie. Odele. Maisie. Odele.

Maisie.

Maisie.

Maisie. Maisie. *Maisie.*

Was this mermaid from Lagoona pushing the princess from my mind, or were they starting to blur together, becoming one single entity that made my heart pound with affection for the both of them?

No.

It couldn't be true.

Or rather, I didn't *want* it to be true. My head knew which mer was which. And it was time for my heart to learn who it belonged to.

THE TEARS CAME UNBIDDEN, swarming from my eyes in the most annoying little bubbles. I swiped at them, but the harder I tried to push them away, the more came out. A part of me didn't even know why I was crying so suddenly. Captain Saber's words tipped me over that ledge I'd been so carefully balancing on, and into an abyss. Leaden tail weighing me down, I could do nothing but sink.

I lowered myself to the floor in the princess' rooms, back leaning against the door as my heart betrayed me. Suddenly, it was all very overwhelming, crashing over me like a tidal wave. Doubts were but whispers in the deepest parts of my mind, growing louder now. Fast moving images like recordings from a conch bubbling. The marriage contract. Elias. The swing of an ax. Captain Saber. Odele. Prince Kai.

You are like the princess…

Elias. Kai. Tiberius.

"Gah!" I shot up and paced the room desperately trying to remove the thoughts that currently plagued me by the dozen. At the tip of that overwhelming peak were *them*.

Elias.

Kai.

Tiberius.

My body was a treacherous shell of a thing, and instead of being hollow inside, empty, my blood flowed and my heart pounded, my mind pulsed with thoughts of them.

Elias was my honesty. My greatest secret and my greatest truth. We were the same, him and I, or at least, the opposite sides of the same tarnished coin. Poor, longing for a better tomorrow, for a day when the waters of Thalassar no longer ran on currents of blood. We were matching blades set with different stones.

Prince Kai… My heart pounded just thinking of him. Dangerously beautiful. Like capturing the image of an erupting volcano. I'd be damned if I got too close to the heat of the Dragon Prince, but damned if I didn't want to find myself trapped in the steel lock of his jaws. He was an impossibility. Because he had a duty to his kingdom to save them by marrying a princess. I was but an imposter longing for the greatest jewel of all in the dragon's den.

And Tiberius… He was the hatred in the swing of my blade. The danger and the beauty that went hand-in-hand in the making of a weapon. The line separating enemy from friend was unclear. I could not deny that I saw something in him. Maybe it was just an illusion. Maybe I just saw what I wanted to see, but there was a goodness in him, just past a surface that I dared not scratch. Lest I find my heart falling into the betrayal of feeling something other than hatred for a royal soldier.

It wasn't hard to fathom why all of these mermen invaded my thoughts—my heart. It was quite possible that I cared for them all. I mean, the proof was in the beating of my heart and the tears I shed. But it didn't matter what I felt. Not for the Black Blade, not for the Dragon Prince, and certainly not for an infuriating captain. In the end, I would leave them all behind.

I went into the closet after barricading the door with a chair. Stripping down completely, I went for a simple camisole and nightgown. The material slipped over my body, hugging me like a second skin. That was all I donned before I made my way over to the tapestry, went through it, then the tunnel, and into the cove.

Ominous quiet greeted me. A light below beckoned, so I followed the soft glow of lava. But down by the cavern's floor, the couch was empty, and there was no sign of Elias.

I picked up a globe, held the heavy weight of the cold orb in my hand, and turned slowly.

"Elias?" My voice echoed against the walls. That echo was my only reply.

Panic wrestled into the center of my chest. He was gone? How could he be?

A gasp tore from my throat. Had the royal guards found him somehow? I discarded that thought. If soldiers had found him in here, they likely would have awaited my return to arrest me for aiding him if they knew whose rooms this cavern led up to.

No, perhaps he'd foolishly gone out, thinking I would be none the wiser. He *had* left a conch playing on the recorder. I swam closer to the device. A conch sat mouth-down upon it. It twirled and twirled, but no image seemed to flow from it. I placed my hand over it, moving it slightly to fit on the centerpiece. As soon as I did, bubbles rose into a soft recording glow of gold.

I took a stroke back, eyes widening as Elias' image appeared on the recording.

I'd never seen him in a recording before. It was strange to see his lively face a little devoid of color, like a phantom wisp of silver around his edges. He was looking into the conch record, but I felt like he was looking at me.

"Little fish," he breathed, his voice strange and echoing. "Forgive me…" I lowered myself onto the couch, keeping my hands clasped tightly in my lap. "I should have waited for you to get back to say goodbye, but I couldn't." A pause. He ran a hand through his hair, and I swore he almost looked remorseful. "We both have things to do. I'm off to see some of my contacts…" Another pause. He was cautious about giving away too much, in case this conch fell into the wrong hands. "We will see each other again, little fish, but do not come looking for me." His eyes looked up at me, and I swore I could feel his commanding presence in the room with me. "Goodbye."

The bubble burst and fell into a tiny dusting of silver and gold, the device stopped turning, and only the quiet followed.

No tears came, and my heart didn't break. Where sorrow should be, instead there was an unending loneliness, and a lack of surprise.

What had I expected? Elias was not a pet. He couldn't have stayed here forever. He was the Black Blade. The merman of whispers and shadows. I shouldn't have been surprised that the merman of shadows had slipped away into the night, leaving nothing but the trace of his darkness behind.

I ignored the rest of my duties that day. Even when Percival, servants, and guards came knocking, I called out from the confines of my room that I was feeling unwell. Of course, royal medics were rushed down, and they too went ignored.

Officially alone, I wallowed in words I'd wanted to forget. *You are more like the princess than you know.* Wear a face that wasn't yours long enough and you became the one you were impersonating.

But I didn't want to be like her. I realized, even as I told myself this, that Captain Saber had been right.

I'd possibly torn apart a friendship in Odele's cousins. I'd been rude to the captain. And worst of all, I'd done nothing to help the mer of Thalassar escape the shackles of Selection. And how could I help them? I was in over my head. Why had I even thought I'd be able to do this? I was no closer to discovering secrets or saving anyone than I had been when I first started this whole charade. I was no closer to getting answers and no closer to the queen or her council.

Odele had worked to get everyone in her court to hate and mistrust her. The only problem was that I was now on the receiving end of it. No one would ever take me seriously because of her, and everything I'd wanted to accomplish would be for naught.

With that knowledge, I went to sleep and didn't wake up till morning.

It was a knocking at the door that woke me. I tumbled out of bed, still half asleep and unaware of the hour. It was harder to tell in salt waters because of the depth and lack of sun or moonlight.

Rubbing my eyes, I reached for the handle and yanked it open. I was halfway through a yawn when he said, "Princess, I hope I didn't wake you."

My face heated into tones I couldn't imagine. Hair floated towards my yawning mouth which I almost inadvertently swallowed. I spat the strands out and sputtered, "Prince Kai!"

He floated demurely before me. No longer did his eyes gleam with the promise of danger and adventure. His brown eyes were set intently on me, roaming from my mouth all the way down my body.

It was then that I recalled what I wore.

A thin nightgown that left nothing to the imagination. The material was see-through, and my breasts pressed against it.

With a groan, I covered myself, crossing my arms over my chest. The prince's eyes followed the movement down there. He raised an eyebrow ever so slightly before his eyes found mine again.

His posture made it seem like he was unaffected, but the blush that suddenly sprouted on the height of his cheekbones told me otherwise.

"Prince Kai." My voice betrayed the nervousness I was suddenly feeling. "Is there something you required?"

He was trying really hard not to look down the length of my body. I could tell. "Princess…" His voice came out in a breathy rasp. "Today our schedules coincide, and I thought we could ride around Eramaea. I'm still relatively new to your city and I thought a… tour…" His eyes wandered down, then back up. Like his gaze was being pulled over every inch of me by its own volition. His face flushed even more.

"Sounds great!" I took a stroke back, grabbing the door and easing it closed. "Let me just get dressed, yeah?"

His eyes were once again glued to my body. He tore his gaze away long enough to nod. With that acquiescence, I slammed the door closed and let out a soft screech of mortification.

Oh. My. Gods.

The prince had nearly seen me naked. I may as well have been with this nightgown. I yanked it over my shoulders and tossed it into a bundle on the floor. I'd thoroughly embarrassed myself in front of the Dragon Prince. *Again.*

And he wanted me to take him out on a tour of Eramaea, I thought bewilderedly, as I pulled out a dress from the closet. It was bright yellow. I didn't even know anything about the city. It was as foreign to me as his own kingdom was. In all my life I'd never been out of Lagoona until the day Captain Saber had recruited me.

I yanked the dress over my head and smoothed it down my tail. I didn't notice much about it except it was a tuft of material with long sheer sleeves. Running my fingers through my hair, I pulled it behind my neck in a chignon.

I took a look at myself in the mirror. I supposed I looked decent, though not entirely royal. It was… simple. No jewelry adorned my neck or ears, my wrists were bare, and I'd never felt less like a royal than I did at that moment.

It's not like it mattered one way or another. I wasn't making a difference pretending to be her, nor would I make a difference pretending to be myself.

After everything appeared to be tucked into place, I took a deep, calming breath and went to the door.

Prince Kai wasn't waiting for me. One of his advisors was there, as well as a group of my own guards and his.

"We're to escort you to the stables." Kai's advisor bowed to me. It was still bewildering that mer bowed, when everyone here was likely higher ranked than I was.

They led me down to the stables where Prince Kai was smoothing down the mane of a hippocampus tethered to a shell carriage.

He was staggeringly beautiful and a little out of place next to the fuchsia hippocampus. Red robes flowed from his body, embroidered with a gold and black dragon as well as a pattern of flowers. A black sash was tied tightly around his waist. There was a theme to his clothing that breathed elegance and power.

"Ready, Princess?"

He was looking at me with intent. Gone was the blush from his cheeks. In his eyes, there was a glow, so brief it seemed I'd imagined it. He gave me a smile that was both warm and cold yet innately his own.

"Of course." A smile is what I gave, hoping he couldn't see the nervous quiver in my lower lip.

His gaze went there for the briefest of seconds. Thankfully, he didn't comment on it. Instead, he took my hand, bent over it, and pressed a kiss to my knuckles. Immediately, a feeling I'd grown accustomed to surfaced. Of nerves and a fluttering in my stomach and my heart.

"After you." He helped me onto the carriage, an enormous shell that closed off at the top in a curve. I would have preferred an open carriage but didn't argue as I sat in the soft cushioning. Kai settled in beside me, and at the snap of a whip, the two hippocampi took off at a steady swim.

My eyes stayed on the flicking of their long, serpentine tails. The beasts still unnerved me.

Kai pulled my attention back to him easily enough. "Where would you like to go?"

His question made my fingers tighten in my lap. I knew nothing of Eramaea. Nothing except that brief tour I'd been given by the Black Blade. Was it wrong, somehow, to take Kai to a place that could easily be deemed mine and Elias'?

I didn't have a choice.

I stuck my head from the carriage space window and gave the brisk command to the driver. He snapped the reins as I pulled my head back in.

The rest of the way was spent in companionable silence. Words were on the tip of his tongue. I caught him looking at me with yearning, though it was obvious he was unsure on how to bring up a conversation.

Finally, he spoke, but his voice was solemn. "I heard you were inquiring about marriage contracts. More specifically, *our* marriage contract…"

Freezing, I tried to steady my sudden labored breathing. Gods. This was why I hadn't wanted his guards trailing after me. What had they told him?

Probably everything. I could only hope that he didn't want to go to war because of my desperate inquiries.

"Princess?"

I couldn't bring myself to look at him. My hands were clasped tightly in my lap, my back rigid straight. My heart jumped, and jumped.

"Do you wish to break our marriage contract?" he asked coolly, darkly, and in his voice I heard the traces of the dragon. Something dangerous that lived within him, that I'd caught glimpses of in passing.

Instead of answering, I looked out the window and saw we were in the same park I'd been at with Elias a few days ago.

"You can stop here, please!" I ordered the driver quickly. He pulled the beasts to a halt. I didn't want to wait for Kai to hand me down, but he beat me to it, opening the door and swimming down. Instead of offering me his hand, though, he reached up in the floating carriage and grabbed me around the waist. He lifted me down easily. I had to hold on to his shoulders for extra support, in case my fin gave out and I fell.

When we were both steady near the ground, I found I could scarcely move. We stayed like that, hands on waist and shoulders. I could feel the water leaving my lungs, along with any traces of courage I might've had left. He was looking at me with that gleam of danger in his eyes. Still he didn't let go, almost as if he was awaiting my answer and wouldn't release me until I gave it.

An answer I *couldn't* give him with honesty. I couldn't tell him why I was really interested in the marriage contract, not without divulging every little thing. Who I was, and why I was here.

I let out the slowest of breaths. "I don't wish to end our marriage contract."

That seemed to be all the answer he needed, because his fingers slid slowly across my waist, a branding all on its own, and he smiled. "Good." He bent down so that our faces were but mere centimeters apart. So close, our lips nearly touched. "Because I have no plans of ever giving you up."

If only he knew. He would have no choice but to give me up, in the end.

Before I could say anything I might soon regret, I turned away from him, palms missing the heat of his touch as soon as I let go. "You don't even know me…" I swam forward and Kai followed. Our guards fanned out all around us, keeping at bay the crowd that had suddenly formed to watch the both of us. Self conscious, I tried not to fiddle with my body or clothes. What a sight I must be next to the beautiful Prince Kai.

"You couldn't be more mistaken." His voice was at my ear, causing my fins to curl. I turned, throwing him a look over my shoulder. He ignored me and came over to my side. "What would you like to do today, Princess? I confess, I've not seen much of your city since I arrived."

Neither had I. I glanced around the park. While children still played with their parents and schools of fish passed overhead, there was still a crowd forming. This wouldn't be the most private of dates, but one look at Prince Kai told me that he was used to the attention. I'd just have to push through it myself.

A smile broke out on my face as I caught sight of a street vendor. I gripped the sleeve of his robes and pointed. "Want to try some real food?"

His response was to take my hand. It was so natural a movement, our fingers threading through the empty spaces. I tugged on his hand, heart thumping, as we went up to the vendor.

His stand was a shabby thing, but the food displayed there looked delectable. Crispy snakes and shrimp, with kelp and greens.

I inhaled deeply and smiled. "Can we have two please?"

The mer behind the stand sputtered, eyes widening. "Your Majesties!" He bowed so deeply, his forehead nearly touched the silt. "What an honor!"

My face flushed. This was all so new. Kai didn't miss a beat. He held up his fingers, the ones that weren't clasped in my own. "Two, please."

The merman fumbled to skewer the food onto the long bill of a swordfish to form a kabob. Nervously, with shaking fingers, he handed them to us.

"Have you ever tried one of these before?" I asked Kai, turning to him. I was aware that the vendor was taking in the scene with curious, elated eyes. My sole focus was on the Prince of Draconi, and his curious expression as he took the food in.

"I haven't," he admitted somberly. He brought the kabob up to his nose and gave a delicate sniff.

"Consider it your initiation into Thalassar," I joked, bopping the end of my kabob to his. Then, I took a ferocious bite, savoring the explosion of decadent tastes swirling on my tongue. I barely held back my moan. "This is so good!" It wasn't princess-like to talk with a full mouth, but the food was just too good.

Kai took a bite, albeit a much smaller one than mine. I watched, waiting for his reaction. His eyes widened. "It is very good." He took another bite with much more enthusiasm.

"The future queen and king like my food," the merman breathed with astonishment.

I flipped him a thumbs up but continued digging into my food, Kai doing the same. Though we were being watched and trailed by guards, this almost felt normal. Like we were just two regular mer having a good time in the light of the waters.

When we finished, we discarded the garbage into a fisherman's net hanging from a hook on the side of his table.

"That was fantastic," I complimented the vendor.

He looked like he would burst on the spot. How something so little as a compliment could make the mer look this way. Happiness lit up his every feature.

"You may seek payment with my advisors." Kai pointed over his shoulder, where I was sure his advisors were watching us with rapt attention and disapproving stares.

Kai tugged on my hand and pulled me away from the stand. We swam, mer following us. It wasn't proper for us to swim together like this.

Without a proper chaperone other than our guards, with our hands close together, and through the streets of Eramaea.

Neither of us seemed to care.

Because as the hours went on, and we continued to swim, try foods, and make idle conversation, it seemed like an empty void between us was filling with something I could not quite describe.

Kai

We were sitting on a bench in an Eramaean park, finally able to rest. We had spent what felt like hours traveling from stand to stand trying foods and speaking to mer. On more than one occasion, the poorer mer of Eramaea came up to Princess Odele. The guards had tried stopping them, but she'd intervened, allowing them to come forward. They held her hand, bowed over her, and thanked her.

"You've given us hope," they whispered.

"Thank you, for saving the Black Blade."

She accepted their gratitude with a smile on her lips. I'd grown angry at the mention of that criminal, but it soon dissipated. I saw what their thanks did to the princess. I saw her eyes light up, and I saw just what it all meant to her. And to them.

The Black Blade had been a hero to these mer, and because she saved him, she was now one too. And because I swam at her side, hand protectively at her back, they kissed the tops of my knuckles, as if I'd done anything to warrant it.

Word had gotten around that two of the most popular royals were swimming through Eramaea. The crowds had gotten bigger, and news conches followed us. It was easy to pretend they weren't there.

When we finished our rounds, going through nearly every vendor in the capital, Odele had pulled me to the park and sat me on a bench. I had never sat on a bench before or watched children play without restraint. I'd never seen a life lived so simply.

Back home in Draconi, the royals were confined to palaces. The walls of ours had been my home, and my prison, for as long as I could remember. We saw little beyond it, except for the battlefields we shed blood on and the grounds where we bred our beasts.

Needless to say, the simplicity of this was enjoyable. I was full, content, and one look at Odele told me that she was as well, if a little thoughtful.

Her gaze lingered on where the children played, and there was something akin to longing on her features.

I wondered what she thought of. Was she imagining her own childhood? Or, maybe I was foolish for hoping, was she imagining the children we would have together one day?

Before, I would have relished in that fantasy. But after discovering what she was doing in her spare time, asking questions about marriage contracts, about mine and hers, I was nervous. Before, there had been plenty of time to break off the engagement had she wanted to do it. Our kingdoms desperately needed the Draconi-Thalassar alliance. Now, our joining went beyond duty. For me, at least it did. I had agreed to marry her, to sire children, and to be gifted their secret magic against two-leggers plaguing our homes. Then I fell in love with her, and I couldn't help but wonder if she didn't feel the same.

"If you could do one thing in the world right now, what would you do?" I asked.

She broke slightly out of her reverie to blink at me. Silence, as she bit her bottom lip before trailing her tongue across it. I followed the gesture with hungry eyes, but forced my gaze back up to her own.

"I'd stop a war." There was raw honesty in her voice.

The war between Thalassar and Kappur obviously affected her a great deal. My father was a war general, and I wasn't too far behind his swim strokes going in that direction. He'd spoken of battles, and I'd lived through a few myself in my short twenty-five years of living. The mer in Draconi grew up faster than in Thalassar. By fourteen, the females were considered adults fit for marriage, while the males were prepped for war at thirteen.

I knew the hardships. I'd lived to gain my own scars and tales of battle. I'd ridden fearsome dragons into the oncoming onslaught. I'd skewered mermen with swords, had let my dragon devour them in gruesome bites. I'd fought by my sisters' and father's sides, had mourned the dead and rejoiced for the living.

War with mer was a simple thing. It was something I had been trained for since my birth.

What I was not prepared for was war with the two-leggers. Whispers in my kingdom said a war was coming, unless I could stop it with the help of Thalassar and the princess at my side. So I understood what she meant. I understood all too well.

"Once we are wed, the dragons of Draconi will swim here. Our alliance will be a fearsome thing to behold, and Kappur will cease to attack. The Selection will be no more, and the war will finally end." It wasn't just empty promises. It was truth and strategy.

She sighed. "I don't want to *wait* until marriage," she muttered. "I want the war to end *now*. I want the bloodshed to be over."

My fingers twitched before curling tightly into the palm of my hand. "Without the war, you and I would never have come to pass." I wondered if those words had sounded cruel, if she would turn and slap me for such insolence. To say I was glad her mer were dying if it meant we could be together. But the deepest desires in my heart were dark things. I was forged in ice and jewels, in blood and war. Chaos and darkness.

She smiled though, the gesture rather sad. "There is that, my prince."

I reached for her hand, grasping it in mine. "Princess, if it is a war you want to stop, then stop it."

Her eyebrows rose, and her voice trembled. "How?"

Gods. She didn't know what power she wielded. "My gem..." I trailed a nail down the side of her cheek, relished in the sight of her leaning into me, closing her eyes. "You are blind to what you are. You are formidable. You are caring. You are fearless." Each attribute was punctuated with me trailing over different spots on her skin. Cheek. Neck. Lips. My fingers stopped there, and I felt rather than heard the gasp push from her mouth. "If anyone can stop a war, it's you."

"No, Prince Kai. If only you knew what I truly was..."

I pressed a finger to her lips. They were smooth against my calloused fingertips. I longed to bend across the space that separated us and take a taste for myself. "I know who you are, my gem. You are not the same princess you were before. You are better. Kinder. And I love—"

She shot back, not allowing me to finish my sentence. She knew what I was going to say, and she rejected me before the words were even out of my mouth.

She shook her head back and forth. "You can't, Prince Kai. *Please.*"

I frowned, and something rose in me. A battle of ice and heat, gorging its way up my body. A dragon awakening to roar and claim what was mine. "Don't presume to know what I feel, Princess." My voice was dark, face glowering. "I know what I feel for you, and your denial will change nothing." My hand encircled her wrist, and I felt the pulse beating there. "You are mine, my gem. You are *benitoaito,* the dragon stone, one of the most precious and valuable gems in Draconi." Her pulse was frantic now, and there was this sudden maddening urge in me to lick that spot on her wrist. But I let her go and turned. Calm settled over me once more. "You do not have to love me back."

Please love me back.

She did not reply, so I got up from the bench. News reporters were watching our every move. I'd nearly forgotten they were there, and I wondered if they'd heard the display, if they'd seen me practically tear my heart out and set it gently in her lap only to have her knock it over with distaste.

My skin prickled with defensiveness, just like it did moments before a battle. Nostrils flaring, I turned and offered my hand to my betrothed.

"Shall we get back to the palace now?"

Her eyes were wide, and from the corner of one of them, a small bubble swarmed out, floating above her head. My gut clenched at the sight of her tears. She swiped at her eyes discreetly and got up, ignoring my hand completely.

"I am sorry, Your Majesty," she whispered sincerely. "But I cannot—"

The rest of her sentence never came out.

My senses heightened, and I stilled. My body became the calm before the storm. The silence before a hurricane swept the ocean off its fins. Maybe I never would have noticed if my back had been turned. But because I was staring at Princess Odele, I noticed. And my blood boiled, and the beast inside me unleashed.

I thundered forward, gripping Odele by the neckline of her dress. I was not gentle as I yanked her away, pushing her aside, then behind. My body was the shield that protected her from the arrow that would have struck her head.

It pierced through my chest. A moment's worth of pain was all I gave it. Just a moment before I was shouting for guards, for advisors to come and protect the mer I loved.

Her breath came out in ragged pants, palm touching my arm. I could hear her words, yet they sounded so far away. "Kai, oh gods, Kai!"

Ice blasted through my veins. The magic of decades, of ancestors and dragons pummeled through me. I felt myself changing, rearranging, becoming something new. Something I'd never wanted Thalassar to see.

And yet for her, I would bare myself naked a thousand times over. If only to protect.

Guards swarmed in, pulling Odele back. She screamed and thrashed, hands pulling the back of my clothes. Like she meant to grab me, and pull me back into the line of protection of the guards. But my fury was overwhelming now. And the beast in me was out.

I straightened and heard the gasps. I knew what the magic of my ancestors did to my appearance. I knew it somehow elongated me. The scales on my tail hardened and sparkled like impenetrable diamonds, and where my nails had been earlier, talons grew in its place, curved and black. I was still mer, yet not. I was something wholly different now, a mixture of merman and beast.

Many thought magic was dying out.

But I bore the oldest of it inside me.

The arrow was stuck just below my collarbone. It had ripped through my clothes, embedded itself into my flesh. Pain was a miniscule thing when my rage had the power to freeze the kingdom over.

With a hard yank, I ripped the arrow from my body and let it fall. My eyes scanned the crowd of shocked Thalassarins. Then I saw him. The sniper. He wore all black, a mask, and a speargun was held in his hands. The weapon intended for the princess. For my betrothed. My mate.

I roared, trembling the waters, manipulating the drift of the current. I snapped my tail and charged forward. The guards trailed after, but they weren't as fast as me. Between one blink and the next, I was before the murderous sea scum and had him by the throat.

I hauled him by the neck, throwing him in the center of the park. Just seeing me made him tremble in fear. Foolishly, he fumbled with the speargun. With a jerk of my wrist, I pulled it away from him and crushed it beneath black talons.

Discarded pieces rained down over his face. He whimpered.

"Who sent you?" I asked calmly. My voice was different. Deeper. Sinister. Yet still understandable, all the same. "Why were you trying to kill the princess?"

Kill. Kill. Kill.

I thirsted for his blood. Why waste time on explanations when I could gut him with the swipe of a finger?

"Tell me!"

He didn't speak. Or maybe he did and I just couldn't tell. The waters around me spun like a violent riptide ripping through the water. I swayed and fought to keep my balance. The sea scum opened his mouth and laughed.

I swiped a hand out. Better to get this over with now, end his life, and get back to my betrothed. Yet my talons didn't reach him.

It was then I realized the severity of the situation. As my head spun and my limbs grew lethargic.

Poison.

The arrow had been poisoned.

Sound drifted away, and my vision darkened around the edges. My body turned, and beyond the fray of bodies, I could make out the one mer I wanted to get to above all others.

"Princess…"

That was my last word before I succumbed to the darkness.

Maisie

Lost in the fray of chaos. Bodies surrounded me, closing me in, when all I wanted to do was get to Prince Kai. Guards shouted and guided me cautiously back towards the carriage. The mer of Eramaea were screeching, shouting. Some swam away while others couldn't help but to stop and stare.

How could they not when Prince Kai had somehow *transformed* before them all?

The Dragon Prince, a nickname rumored to have been given because in battle he was as vicious and as bloodthirsty as a dragon. When I looked into those eyes, there had been nothing but kindness. Now, it was different. Because his body elongated, tail widening, hardening and sparkling like a hoard of jewels in a chest. His eyes had a savage glow about them, and his nails curved and tipped into long black talons.

Formidable.

Dangerous.

Murderous.

No wonder his advisors stalked his every move. No wonder they kept so tight a leash on him. Unleashed, he would have destroyed the entire kingdom.

All to protect me.

He roared and trembled the waters, and I could not tear my gaze away, even as I was pushed back, I kept my eyes on him. On the arrow protruding from his collarbone, on the blood rising in smoky tendrils. He ripped the arrow out and crushed it in half.

And when he found the culprit, the one responsible for making yet another attempt on my life, I trembled with true fear. Not fear that he would get to me, that I was in danger, but fear for what the Dragon Prince would do to him in such a state.

But then the Dragon Prince's body trembled, and he turned. His eyes found mine amidst the chaos, lips parting, his mouth formed one word, that I couldn't hear but didn't need to.

"Princess…"

And then he fell to the silt.

No one had been expecting it, so they were transfixed for a moment. Even the criminal. His bottom was in the silt, breathing heavy. He smirked, and I watched as he put his hand to the inside of his black tunic and pulled out something, something that shone against the light. Steel.

"No!" The scream ripped through me in a voice I hardly recognized as my own. Prince Kai. Prince. My prince… I struggled, trying to push past the guards surrounding me. "Kai!"

The sniper swung the blade down towards Kai's heart. The knife never struck. Because the sniper suddenly found an arrow protruding from his throat.

The knife fell from his grasp, and his hands went up to his throat. Blood bloomed around his face, choked gurgling emanated from his lips.

A second later, he fell dead.

I didn't want to take my eyes off of Kai for even a moment, but I couldn't help but turn and see for myself who had saved Prince Kai's life.

Behind me, floating near the palace carriage, was a single soldier, holding a speargun in his hands. And I'd told him to stay away, but I was glad he hadn't listened.

Captain Saber.

A breath of relief left me. A sensation that lasted but a second, because when I turned to look at Kai, he still hadn't stirred. His advisors leaned over him worriedly. Silently, they picked him up. His body no longer glistened like jewels and he no longer wore the aspects of the beast on his body.

"Why isn't he moving?" My voice shook with fear. The advisors looked at me solemnly and hurried past me into the carriage. "Why isn't he moving?" Hysteria rose up in my throat. They said nothing. They just pushed their prince inside the carriage, and a moment later it took off.

Something inside me broke. I rushed to the spot he'd just vacated, falling into the silt. Grains of sand dug beneath my nails, and a sob lodged itself up in my throat.

"Why wasn't he moving?"

And then I was being pulled up by Captain Saber.

"He wasn't moving, Captain."

"Not here, Princess," he whispered. It was the first time I'd ever heard his voice sound like that. Worried. Gentle. Tears poured from my eyes, and he pulled me to his chest, keeping my face pressed into his uniform jacket. "Not here, Princess," he whispered against the top of my head. "Not here."

I took in a shuddering breath. I pushed away my emotions, inhaling Captain Saber's scent. It was calming, and the erratic beating of my heart began to still, slowly, until it was a normal pounding. Captain Saber's heart pounded against my own, and he held me until the emotion eased, and I slowly drifted away from him.

His eyes searched my own, gentle. He looked ever so gentle.

"Come." He rubbed his thumb across my cheek.

I nodded once, and let Captain Saber pull me into the safety of his arms and take me from this place, now tainted with death and murder, and back to the palace.

I COULD NOT LET her go. Not when she wanted to fall apart. I was the only thing keeping her together. If I could loan her my strength, I'd give her every last ounce of it, if only to see that look wiped from her face.

Prince Kai was rushed to the palace ahead of us and into his rooms, where royal medics were ushered in to tend to the wound he'd sustained protecting Maisie. An arrow tipped with poison, poison that had been aimed at the back of Maisie's head.

This was the third attempt on her life. The one behind it all was becoming bolder, or desperate. But why? Why would anyone want Maisie—or

Odele—dead? Her life had never been in peril before, not in any obvious way, at least.

And now Prince Kai's life was in jeopardy because of it.

I ordered guards about the palace, posting them at every entrance and every door. There would not be another attempt on her life. Not while I still drew breath.

I opened the doors to her room and guided her inside, closing it behind me. Guards awaited my orders on the other side of her chambers. Inside, with privacy, Maisie finally crumpled to the floor. Sobs racked her shoulders up and down. She didn't care that I was there, that I was watching every move she made. She didn't worry about repercussions, about my judgments, but cried freely in front of me.

"This is my fault!" She dug her nails into the quartz floors, causing them to crack and bleed. "Someone is trying to kill me, and because of me, Kai was hurt. He could d-die!"

I pushed myself away from the door and sank to the floor beside her. There was no hesitation in me as I pulled her into my arms. She went willingly, her body curling onto mine. I held her tightly, rubbing circles across her back.

"No, Maisie." I tightened my arms around her. "It wasn't your fault."

Comforting someone was unfamiliar, and yet somehow it came so naturally. So many times I'd wanted to gift this, a shoulder to cry on, a word to lift spirits. There'd been no opportunity. How could there be? Princess Odele pushed me away every time I tried. So I'd given up. I'd hardened my heart, my soul, until I knew nothing but strength and quiet and anger.

To see Maisie this way was… crippling. It changed me. It hurt.

Yes, I compared them, a habit that was hard to break. I knew what Maisie was, saw all of her faults. I *knew* her, and so I knew that she was not weak. Not like Odele was weak. Maisie would never give up. She was righteous and kind in a way that had eluded Odele for so long.

It was only in this moment that I realized that what Maisie lacked, she made up for in other things. Stronger things. Like her desire to tear through the barricade of guards to reach Prince Kai. Her unwavering loyalty. The tears she shed for something that wasn't her fault.

She wept in my arms and clung to me as if I was the only one able to give her comfort. So I held her just a bit tighter and murmured just a bit gentler until her sobbing ceased, and all she did was shudder against my body. It was then that her mind seemed to clear, and she realized just who was holding her.

She pulled away, prying her body away from mine until there was space between us. She swiped at her eyes, but no amount of scrubbing would hide the puffiness, the evidence of her turmoil. When she looked at me again, it was with a hardened expression.

"That wasn't very princess-like." She barked out a bitter laugh and got up from the floor, straightening her clothes. She assumed a straight-backed posture, tilted her head up. The perfect image of royalty. Just as I taught her. She looked down at me. "Thank you, Captain, but I am afraid you must leave."

I got up slowly. "Maisie…" It was hard to admit that I was worried about her. Worried she would break again, and that she wouldn't let me pick up the pieces.

"I'm sorry, Captain. I shouldn't have done that. Rest assured it won't happen again."

What if I wanted it to happen again? What if I wanted to hold her and offer a brief comfort from the reality and death that plagued her? I shouldn't want such liberties, not with her. But the moment I'd seen her cornered by death, something in me shifted.

And things I should have realized sooner were suddenly as clear as crystal in my mind.

"Maisie…"

Her eyes narrowed. "You are *dismissed*, Captain."

My throat tightened with unspoken words I desperately wanted to say. Somehow, none of them came out. I swallowed, nodded, and bowed to the mer who had become a royal right before my eyes. It's what I'd trained her for. To be cold. To be like Odele. Now that she was, something about it just didn't swim right.

"As you wish, Your Majesty."

Turning stiffly, I left the room. She didn't stop me. She didn't say a word or call after me as I closed the door. My hands tightened into fists. I longed to drive them through something. To pummel someone. My mind whirled.

All I could see was that arrow zooming towards Maisie. How I'd been too slow to get to her. If I hadn't angered her, I would have been at her side, but I'd stayed behind in the shadows so she wouldn't see me. So she would not be blinded by her anger again. In my mind, I saw the arc of the blade intended for Prince Kai's heart.

He'd protected her in a way I couldn't. I wanted to despise him for it. A prince was a better guard than me. I was breaking my promise to Maisie. The promise where I said I'd protect her like I couldn't protect Odele.

What was I good for if not for this?

Anger pushing my tail, I turned through the hallways and made my way towards Prince Kai's rooms. I knew this wasn't the time for this. He could be on the brink of death, and I still pushed on.

Outside of his doors were the guards I'd posted there. They saluted me, but I found myself ignoring them as I rapped once on the prince's chambers and opened the door.

It was a breach of etiquette, but this was an emergency.

It was dragon fury within the room.

A blur of bodies fighting, screams that were guttural, more beast than mer. Transfixed, I watched as Draconian advisors attempted to restrain their prince. He thrashed his tail, bucking and fighting against them and the medics. Blood flowed from his wound in thin tendrils. The poison was making him delirious.

I knew there had been something strange about him, this foreign prince. His demeanor was calm, almost too calm. Like he had a restraint on his inner madness. Here was the proof.

The prince stopped thrashing and there was an eerie silence. Slowly, creepily, Prince Kai turned his head to look at me. Madness rested in his eyes. A beast waiting to pounce. He saw me and smiled. The twist of his lips was rather alarming.

"Captain," he purred. "What brings you to my rooms?" The voice didn't seem like his own. It was the same voice he'd used at the park. Deep. Threatening. Like a whole new entity resided at the back of his throat.

"His Majesty is suffering from the effects of the poison," a medic chimed in breathlessly. "He might say… things… and he refuses his medicine."

The prince let out a low rumble that emanated from deep in his chest. He sat up in his ivory shell bed, pushing aside his guards with annoyance.

"What do you want, Captain?" He leaned forward, pressing his forearms against the bend in his tail. There was a dangerous gleam in his eye, a hungry look there.

I went deeper into the room. The scents of the place tingling my nostrils. It smelt like heat. Like medicine, and something else. "Why?" It was one question. One he understood. One I didn't need to elaborate on.

Maybe because we both knew the answer.

The prince raised an amused, delicate brow. "Why wouldn't I? She is my betrothed, after all."

No, she isn't. My fists tightened, and his eyes followed the movement before flicking back up to my face. A smile twisted his features.

I wanted to hate him. Perhaps a part of me already did because of who he was and who he had. The one mer in the world who could never be mine. And because he no longer had her, but the one he so obviously wanted wasn't even a royal at all, and he hadn't even noticed.

"Have you come to presume my feelings again, Captain Saber?" He leaned back in the cushioning of his bed, and winced. More blood flowed. He closed his eyes, silent for a long moment. When he finally did speak, his voice no longer held dragon fury. "I know why you are so angry with me, Captain."

My eyebrows rose. His voice was becoming a whisper; he appeared to be in a dream-like state.

He opened his eyes, and they were feverish. "I pondered on it for a while, when I realized *why*." He chuckled. "So obvious… the Captain of the Royal Guard is in love with the princess, too."

My blood ran cold as he laughed, and laughed, and laughed. Until his laughter became coughing, and his eyes rolled to the back of his head until nothing was visible but the whites. Prince Kai's entire body began to tremble, and his advisors and the medics scrambled to get to him, forcing a tonic down his throat.

I swam backwards, shocked at the sight before me, his words ringing in my mind. My back hit the door, and I fumbled with the knob. Prince Kai was gasping for water now, his whole body seizing.

You're in love with the princess, too.

My eyes squeezed closed. I did not love the princess. Because the princess was really Maisie. And Maisie was someone I could never love.

When I opened them, I gasped out. "No, I'm not."

But my words fell on deaf ears.

He wouldn't have listened anyway. He'd come to his own conclusions, conclusions that were ridiculous, and yet they pained me. I realized then and there the impossibilities. The actions had been louder than any words he ever could have spoken. That Prince Kai loved Maisie in a way he never could have loved Odele.

No one heard or saw me leave.

WITH A WHIRLWATER MIND, I could not help but pace the room. Back and forth I went until my tail cramped up from the stiffness of my body posture. To distract my mind, I'd opened the telly shell, only to be bombarded with news and images of events that already plagued my mind.

Me. Prince Kai. The sniper. Captain Saber. Death.

I had promptly slammed the shell closed again and resumed pacing.

Now, I sunk onto the edge of the bed. The plump anemones must have sensed my distress. They caressed me, fat stinging tentacles curling around my arms and tail. I relished in the feeling for but a moment before my mind grew restless and I all but shoved them away again.

My thoughts would not ease. How could they, with Prince Kai dying in his rooms because he had decided to save *me*? Right after I'd publicly rejected his affections, had more or less told him not to love me, that I did not love him.

How could we?

We didn't even *know* each other.

The Black Blade's words came back to me. *I've no doubt in my mind, little fish, that Prince Kai Li of Draconi knows exactly who you are.* Did he? I mean, could he possibly? I wondered if it mattered.

In the short time we knew each other, I'd seen something in the Black Blade, like he saw something in me. It had been enough of a feeling, in so short a time, for us to give ourselves to one another. Maybe it was the same with Prince Kai. Maybe he didn't need to know my true name to feel something. Maybe he saw deep into the depths of my heart and soul and that was enough.

It still felt like a special sort of treachery to not tell him the truth. If he knew, it would change everything. I was terrified of him knowing. That realization struck me hard because I did not want his feelings for me to change.

Because maybe, just maybe, I felt something for him as well.

All I knew was that I could not sit here idly while Prince Kai was surely in pain in his rooms. I'd already waited too long to see him, and I could not put it off forever. I had to see him. Now.

Decision made, I swam out into the halls where my guards—thankfully not Captain Saber—were waiting. When they saw me, they bowed.

"Escort me to Prince Kai's rooms." The worry in my gut made me snap the demand. No please. No thank you. I was royalty, and I meant business, leaving no room for anything other than their obedience. They nodded stiffly and escorted me.

I was surprised to find his rooms were not too far from mine, though the appropriate distance to avoid a scandal. But the thought of a scandal would not keep me out. To the abyss with Odele's reputation, it was a ruined thing anyway. I had to speak to the prince alone, and so I would.

The guards outside the room bowed to me. I waved them off.

"You will wait here as I go see my betrothed," I commanded.

They dared not mention the impropriety of the situation. They just bowed, and one of them rapped his knuckles on the door.

A few moments later, one of Kai's advisors opened it. His dark hair was piled tightly into a bun on top of his head. There were crinkles just on the outer edges of his slanted eyes. He looked at me with disdain.

"Yes?" he asked. No respective titles. No beating around the cattails. I wondered if he despised me or somehow blamed me for what had happened to the prince earlier today. If he did, I avoided telling him that no one hated me more than I did myself right now.

"I'm here to see Kai." It was an intimate thing, to say his name like that. It nearly made my tail curl.

The advisor sniffed once. "The *prince*," he emphasized, accent thick, "is resting. The medics have ordered it. No visitors."

My heart sank like an anchor to the pit of my stomach. I tilted my chin up just a bit higher. "I insist." Though the tone of my voice said, *I command.*

He started to ease the door closed. "And I insist you go back to your rooms, Princess, lest someone else gets hurt today."

"Wait, I—"

"Dragons' sake, Ichiro, who's at the door?" Kai's voice sounded out from beyond the room, impatient, annoyed.

"No one, Your Majesty." The advisor—Ichiro—started to close the door in my face.

In a split second, I made my decision. I'd not let advisors and royals shut me out from what I wanted to accomplish. Not anymore. I shoved myself into the space that was left and pushed. The advisor called out as I forced myself into the rooms.

The first thing I noticed was that the room was as spacious as my own and consisted mostly of the same layout. The second thing I noticed was the smell. It was… strange… different. *Spicy.*

On two-legger land, there was fire, and it burned. I knew from stories told by the traveling market in Lagoona that two-leggers believed things beneath the sea could not burn. That wasn't true. While things did not ignite here like they did there, the lava of volcanoes could still heat and incinerate things in the water.

The lands between mer and two-leggers were alike, and yet so vastly different. Two-legger clothes floated in the water, while ours, being made from matter in the sea, did not wholly do so.

So, Prince Kai's rooms smelled like *burning.* Scents wafted in tendrils through the water that were both strong and calming.

I also noticed that Prince Kai's rooms were dimmed to a red glow. Red jellies floated like lanterns on his ceiling. He was not in his bed, a shell with black anemones swaying here and there. I didn't see the Prince at all really until Ichiro swam forward, further into the room, on the other side of the bed and bowed to the floor.

"It is—"

I hurried beside him before he could lie to the prince's face. But the moment I saw Kai, my face heated, and a lump formed in my throat that was hard to push past.

Prince Kai sat on the floor. He still wore the red robes from earlier, and yet there was something different about him. Maybe it was the sickness, or maybe it was because the robes opened at the lapels, and the material hung from his shoulders, revealing the skin underneath, and the strip of a kelp bandage that covered his wound.

My breath caught in my lungs and gills. I didn't dare breathe as I watched him. He was distracted and hadn't yet seen me. His arms were up, holding his long hair in his hands, as if he'd been in the midst of tying it back. And in the corner of his mouth, he was biting down on the end of the sash that went around his waist. It was loose around him, and I wondered if he'd been about to change, to take it all *off*.

My tongue darted out to touch my lips.

"This is highly inappropriate!" Ichiro sputtered. "You must leave. Now."

Kai looked up then, and my palms shook. In his gaze there were traces of that separate entity. The one who had fought me in the training room and had nearly left me naked. The one who had protected me in the park. Dark eyes nearly glowed as they took me in. The look he gave me chilled me. Like he was prepared to devour me whole.

He dropped his hands, and his hair fell slowly around his shoulders. Using long, elegant fingers, he pulled the end of the sash from his mouth and fingered the edges thoughtfully.

"Princess…"

I gulped. Menace. Danger. A promise and a threat, in one single word.

"Forgive me, Your Majesty, I told the princess that you were resting—"

Kai shot Ichiro a murderous look that shut his advisor up completely.

"Leave us," Kai commanded hotly.

Ichiro's face went red, though perhaps that was a result of the colorful jellies dancing above our heads. "Majesty, I do not think that is appropriate—"

"I said *get out*! And take Lee with you. Close the door and *don't* come back in."

His advisor's jaw worked tightly before he finally bowed. He started speaking in Dracon, words clipped and fast. A moment later, Kai's second advisor came out from the bathing room. He took one look at me, sniffed, but they didn't dally as they left the rooms, closing the doors behind them.

And Kai and I were finally alone.

He was observing me like I was a curiosity. It was unnerving, and words somehow wouldn't come. I'd been so determined before, but now I felt shaken.

"Sit, Princess."

His voice was like magic curling around my limbs, making me obey. I sat across from him, tail curling beneath me. Very little space separated us, and I could feel his heat, burning as hotly as a lava seam.

"Why are you here?" he asked darkly.

I finally loosed the breath I'd been holding since I'd seen him. "I wanted to see how you were doing…" The words sounded lame. I regretted them immediately. What was I? Some guppy?

"Does it matter to you?" His words weren't unkind, and yet they wounded me just the same.

I gripped the hem of my dress in my fists. "Of course it matters to me. How could you think it wouldn't?" My eyes went to the visible parts of his skin, to the kelp bandaged against his wound. I couldn't stop myself from scooting forward until our tails were touching. My hands went up to hover over the wound. "You got hurt trying to save me. Why wouldn't it matter?"

Kai's fingers wrapped around my wrist, and he pulled my hand away from his wound, bringing it up to his mouth instead. The tips of my fingers hovered just over the edge of his lips.

"I cannot read you, Princess." His breath was hot as it fanned against my skin. Too hot. Was he feverish? He sounded fine, if a little dark and dangerous. "Before, I could. Easily. You were unbearable. I dreaded marrying you." He pulled at my wrist until the tips of my fingers pressed against the warmth of his mouth. "And now…" His tongue darted out to lick my skin. I shivered, and not entirely out of fear. "I like this version of you so much more." He moved to the next finger, licking it. And then to the next. "Is it hypocritical of me to despise that other part of you and yet want you to want every piece of me?"

I swallowed. "No…" My voice came out a breathy rasp. He finished licking every finger and moved to the palm of my hand. He pressed a soft kiss there.

"Yet, you do not love me."

His words were an accusation, laced with dark amusement. My hand tensed, and I nearly pulled away, but he held me in place, hand tightening around my wrist, the other digging into my hip.

"You cannot make someone love you. I know that." He pulled me close. Too close. My body curved into his treacherously until I was on his lap. Our chests were pressed against each other. I could feel his heartbeat, the rasp of his erratic breathing. The hand at my hip slid around to my lower back and up the length of my spine. His fingers traced at the back of my neck just before he dug them into the roots of my hair. His rough touch sent the tie holding the pieces back snapping, causing my hair to tumble around my shoulders. He tugged, and my neck arched, naked and vulnerable to his ministrations.

A kiss was pressed to the base of my throat. I was wound so tightly, I could hardly tremble. Yet my breath hitched. He kissed my pulse, tongue warm, licking my flesh.

"But if I cannot make you love me for me…" He pressed a kiss to the side of my mouth.

I could do nothing but wait for the fallout. Wait to see what he did. I should've pushed him away, yet I couldn't bring myself to do it. Not when my gut was curling. Not when, despite my better judgment, I wanted him to continue. To see how far this would go.

The hand holding my wrist forced my palm to his chest, to touch the burning panes of his body. He slid my hand down. I did not fight it. I let him guide me, pushing past the material of his robes, down the ridges of his abdomen, past the sash…

"...then I will make you love me for my body."

He wrapped my hand around the hard length of him.

I gasped at the scorching feeling of soft steel against my palm. My eyes flew open—when had they closed?—and I took him in. His eyes were fixated on me, dark, and glowing around the edges. It was all daring. All consuming. I'd wanted to be devoured by the Dragon Prince, and now I was getting my wish.

"Make your decision now, my gem." He slid my hand up and down that part of him that was wholly male. Smooth, hard, and hot. "You can leave if you do not want any part of me. But if you stay…" He leaned forward, our lips touching slightly. "I will make you *mine*."

Subconsciously, my tongue darted out to lick my lips, and he was so close that I licked his, too. His eyes flashed, like what I imagined the strike of a bolt of lightning would look like. Still, he did not move. Awaiting my response, lava and ice raging a war in his eyes. Dragon eyes, I realized with a start. They were wider, pupils slit, a blue glow of ice around the edges.

I should leave. Get up and swim out. Prince Kai was not mine. We weren't meant to be. A wilder part of me thrashed like a fish on a hook. *Stay*. It begged. It begged for a sensation other than loneliness, a sensation of importance. To be held by a prince. To take and not care of the consequences. Did it matter if I wasn't who he thought I was? He knew my soul.

That was good enough.

"Stay," I whispered with a savagery I'd never felt before. *No longer will I let anyone else dictate what I could or could not take…*

Kai smiled, just before he pulled me into a hungry kiss.

His tongue dove in, exploring, hungry and demanding. He devoured me with his mouth, and I let him take all of me. Our mouths melded, dancing in a way that was foreign and familiar at once. A clash of tongue and teeth, just like the day we'd danced with swords. Daring each other to be bolder, to attack without restraint.

His hand covering my own moved. Up and down the feverish length of his member. He groaned against my mouth, sound rumbling deep in his chest. His hips moved, and the strokes of his hand—*my* hand—went faster, faster. I squeezed, closing tightly around him because as much as he was commanding my movements, I wanted to feel him too. The heel of my palm grazed the rounded head of his member.

Kai tore his mouth away and *growled*. He yanked on my wrist and I fell back. The only thing that cushioned me from hitting the floor painfully was his arm snaked around my waist. I gasped as his body loomed over mine.

There was something all too predatory about him when he leaned down and took my mouth again. It was a branding, a possession. He tasted like ice and spice, and I couldn't get enough of it. His nails dug into my waist, and the sound of tearing assaulted my ears.

I tore away from his kiss to look down. Inky black talons curved against my skin just where his nails had been. He pressed the tip of one against the dress and slid it up. Sharp as knives, my dress ripped at the seams. All. The. Way. Up.

He pinched the yellow dress between two talons and peeled it off. It ripped some more until the newly tattered garment was pulled entirely from my body.

I hadn't expected him to move with such fervor. Hadn't expected the ardent desperation he touched me with. Like I'd vanish if he stopped. I hadn't expected my own reaction, equally feverish, gripping, pulling, tugging. My body curved into his, shyness dissipating. I didn't care about my injury, didn't care that he'd see my scars. His teeth grazed across my collarbone, and I shuddered, responding by sinking my own teeth into the side of his neck.

It was rough, and his body was hot, too hot it couldn't be normal.

I pushed down at his clothes, desperate to feel every inch of his skin against mine. His fingers ripped at his own clothes, at the sash. The material was pushed to the side, and he lowered himself onto me. His body a brand. A claiming.

Mine.

Mine.

Mine.

Too late, I realized he was whispering those words across the surface of my skin.

"Mine." He nipped my collarbone. "Mine." His tongue traced across the edge of my nipple. I cried out, digging my nails into his shoulders at the sensation that spiraled through me like a violent tide. *"Mine."* His mouth closed over my nipple and I bucked against his body, tail curling around his to keep us close.

The heat of his member slid across my stomach, down to my opening. I craved that friction I was now familiar with. Wanting him desperately, I angled my hips, tail tugging him closer until I could feel his tip shy at my entrance. I moved upwards, and he slid in. The length of him stretched me slowly, filling my body and making me cry out almost immediately. The feeling, everything, it was just too much.

He entered me to the hilt, sliding my body across the floor.

I felt too full that my next breath caught in my throat as I clenched around him, needing that movement of our bodies.

"Mine." He thrust against me and I cried out. His taloned hands grabbed my wrists, his grip firm yet gentle, as he rose them above my head and pinned me to the floor. "Mine." He thrust again and I gave into the pleasure, moaning and crying out in a voice that sounded far away and too foreign to be my own.

"Kai," I whispered, pulling at the hands he held locked in place. I wanted to touch him. But he was claiming me, body and soul. I was shackled to him in every single way now. This was a mistake, but gods, it was a beautiful one. I was selfish. I wanted to have all of him, even if he wasn't even mine.

"Mine."

My thoughts flew as he growled this out. Each thrust was accompanied by a contradiction of my thoughts and reality. Like he knew what was in my mind, and he could banish it completely with this rough movement of his body.

"You are *mine*, Princess. My gem. My love. My life." Each thrust was a promise. Promises I wanted him to keep. "You don't have to love me yet…" My body exploded into one enormous wave of sensation. It dragged me under, sinking me into an abyss where I found nothing but pleasure. Once

I came up from that wave, it was to realize he was still inside me, still moving, and still promising. "…but I know that someday you will."

He followed me into that chasm of pleasure and pain, darkness and light. Only, Kai did not follow me back up. His body slumped onto mine, breathing in little rapid pants. We stayed like that for a moment. His hands had eased their grip, falling to my sides.

"Kai?"

He didn't stir.

It was a struggle to slip from under him and sit up. I pressed a hand to his forehead. He was feverish in a way that had nothing to do with what had just happened between us and everything to do with sickness.

I panicked, lifting him up with difficulty and lying him on his back on the floor. His body floated up a few inches from the ground, but he remained steady.

His brows pulled together and he tossed feverishly. He'd fainted. Prince Kai had fainted.

What he needed was rest and medicine.

Body still tingling, I got up and looked around. My dress was in tatters. I couldn't leave his room wearing nothing at all, so I bounded over to his closet and peeked inside. There were many kimonos, and traditional dress clothes from Draconi. I pulled one out at random and slipped it on. It was a robe similar to the one he wore, and I didn't know the proper way to tie the sash around my waist so I went with a bow.

The clothes fit me largely, sliding down my body. I held them in place with tightened fingers and swam back out into the room. Prince Kai still turned a bit restlessly. I hated to leave him after what we'd just shared, but his advisors needed to give him medicine, assuming the medics had left some behind.

Slowly, I opened the door. In the hallway, only his advisors remained. My face heated with mortification as Ichiro and Lee floated like sentinels before the door. They took me in, my floating tendrils of hair, and the robes I now wore. I hadn't thought about the fallout of our actions, but surely the guards had swam to tell Captain Saber–or worse yet, the queen–what had happened between us.

Ichiro looked at me with narrowed eyes. "I sent your guards away," he said finally as if he'd read the panic in my eyes. "So they would not comment upon your indiscretions." There was judgment laced on his every feature.

The judgment annoyed me. "Your Emperor has concubines," I reminded him unkindly.

He sniffed once. "Yes. Do not think I worry for our prince's reputation. Our laws of marriage are much… freer… than those in Thalassar."

Lee looked as equally disdainful as his companion. "It is your reputation that risks being tarnished. We cannot have any mistakes or slights in the eyes of Queen Circe. Draconi needs an alliance."

My heart thundered. If Queen Circe discovered what had happened here, would she be capable of canceling the marriage contract with Draconi? Would it be justified, considering I wasn't really the princess? They didn't know that, and still, my blood ran cold.

"Hurry to your rooms and change," Ichiro ordered. "We will not speak of this again."

Cleansed and changed, I ventured back out to the hallways of the palace. Being cooped up in the princess' rooms didn't help my mental state at all. All I could think about was Prince Kai, his injury, and the Black Blade.

He had left me, claiming we'd see each other again. Had it been a betrayal to him, to be with Kai the way I'd been with him? No. The sentiment couldn't wedge itself in my chest. Somehow, I figured he'd be strangely proud of what I'd done. Happy I'd taken what I wanted, to the abyss with the consequences.

I was still restless, though. So I wandered the palace until I came to a stop in the hallway with the portraits of the royals. Odele's portrait hung there. As did her father's, and more importantly to Thalassar, the Malabella ancestry. Queen Circe, her gaze regal and cold. Queen Odette, Odele's mother, was painted there. She was a pretty mer, with the purple-blue hair and black eyes that was common in the Malabella lineage. Stories whispered of her kindness and the love between her and King Xristo.

Beside the portrait of Queen Odette, there was another one. Identical, save for a few changes in features. An upturned nose, darker eyes, higher cheekbones. My hands went to this portrait, fingers tracing along the contours of her face. I couldn't help but wonder if the artist had captured her likeness or if she'd been different in real life.

"Princess Odessa Malabella Sanitorum," a sleazy, oily voice interrupted my musings. My whole body tensed as Percival swam up beside me, staring at the portrait I had my hands on. I pulled them away, clasping them tightly at my stomach. "The elder sister to your mother, Queen Odette. Twins, in fact, though she was born mere minutes before."

Not tearing my gaze from the portrait, I snapped, "I know very well who she is, Percival."

I could feel his gaze swivel to me and then back. "Of course. Pity she died a few years before your birth. You never knew her."

How did she die? I didn't voice the question, but it was on the tip of my tongue, begging to be released.

"And then years later, your mother followed her to the grave." He spoke unkindly. So unkindly that, despite Queen Odette not being my mother, my hands still curled into angry fists on Odele's behalf. "And now, someone is making attempts on your life. Strange, don't you think?"

My throat tightened. I cocked my head to the side. "Strange?"

"Strange, how the Malabella lineage is slowly dwindling. First, your aunt Odessa, then your mother, and now…" He shrugged.

An uneasy feeling slipped through my stomach. "In case it's escaped your notice, I am not dead."

"No," he agreed. "Yet I cannot help but wonder if your lineage is somehow…" He gave a slight pause to look at me. I was too cowardly and could not meet his gaze. "…cursed."

Chilling words, and they sounded like a threat. A promise. Luckily, I didn't have to reply, because he bid me a good day and swam off, after asking me to be careful and to not leave the palace.

My skin and body felt dirty even minutes after he'd already left.

His words kept trilling through my mind.

Cursed. Cursed. Cursed.

I didn't believe in curses. Magic existed, but I knew there was a limit to certain things. The Malabella line wasn't cursed, but I didn't doubt they were being hunted. Why else had Odele gone away? How had her mother died? And her aunt? I couldn't quite remember the details.

A thought occurred to me. Perhaps the details of their deaths were important to my own investigation. And there was one place that could give me answers. One place where only royals were allowed. One place that Odele had, surprisingly, spent a great deal of time at.

The royal library.

"Princess!" The old, glowing librarian smiled warmly at me. His skin went from a soft blue to a bright yellow at the sight of me. He was sitting behind his desk, old bent fingers studying the ledgers. He put his quill down when I approached, flipped to a clean page, and let me sign my name in. When I finished, he said, "You came alone today. Is there something I can help you with?"

"I'd like to see the royal records, please."

He nodded. "Of course, of course. Follow me, Your Majesty."

I swam after him, to the room set apart from the rest of the library. *Royal Records. Royal Access Only.* He produced a key ring, fiddled with the dozens of keys there, and finally slipped one into the lock. He pushed the door open for me but didn't go in himself.

"Remember now, if you need anything, just call out to me."

I told him I would and went inside the room, closing the door behind me. It was a small space, with hundreds of conches and kelp parchments, like the outside. Little jellies glowed in a canopy above my head, buzzing in soft colors of yellow, orange, and white.

There was one table in the center of the room, a stone slab with rose quartz bleeding through the cracks.

Taking a breath, I made my way over to the shelves. They were dated back years before I was even born. Years in Thalassar, and in the entire ocean, were not measured like in two-legger lands. The twelve months existed, yes, and yet times changed with the phases of the moon, earth, sun, stars, and tides.

In Draconi, years were measured by seasons and named after their Dragon deities. In Thalassar, the years were measured by the reign of the Malabellas and the queens' respective consorts.

We were in the forty-fifth year of the Malabella Oriana reign, and yet when Odele married Kai once she turned eighteen, it would become the forty-sixth year of the Malabella Li reign. It was all to make royal records easier, I supposed. Nowadays, the mer tended to speak like two-leggers. No longer speaking of moon months, but of *years*.

Each shelf was labeled into sections. Royal Deaths. Royal Marriages. Marriage Contracts. Royal Births. Each marked with a different reign, number, and moon phase.

I scanned the shelf of Royal Births, picking up one labeled with Queen Odette's name on it. I pressed the conch to my ear.

Two-leggers were said to be fascinated with ocean shells, that they could hear the crashing of waves inside. That was only because air and water weren't compatible, and the vibrations of air on two-legger land could not relay messages or images in conches.

Conches weren't just for recording images, but for recording voices as well. Documentation in the oldest form of technology.

A low voice spoke into my ear as I pressed it there. "On this Starsday, on the sixth Waning Moon of the Malabella Oriana reign, Queen Odette Malabella Sanitorum has given birth to a healthy mermaid, with all the respective Malabella features. Purple hair and tail, black eyes, refined features. Healthy and baptized as Princess Odessa Malabella Oriana." I pulled the conch away, confused. The sixth moon? How was that possible if Princess Odele had been born around the thirteenth New Moon after the start of the Malabella Oriana reign? If this was true, that would mean that she had an older sister named after her aunt.

I put the conch back and went over to the Royal Death shelf, and scanned the names. My eyes stopped on a conch with the name: Princess Odessa Malabella Oriana. My heart sank as I picked it up. Odele's sister... The breath whooshed from my lungs. I placed the conch to my ear.

"At only three Waning Moons old, Princess Odessa Malabella Oriana, daughter to Queen Odette Malabella Sanitorum and King Xristo Oriana, has died of fever, on the ninth moon month of the Malabella Oriana reign."

I placed the conch back onto the shelf with shaking fingers, and scanned the rest of the shelf, eyes catching attention on another shell, this one dating a few years before the death of Odele's sister. Princess Odessa Malabella Sanitorum. Her aunt.

I picked it up and pressed it to my ear.

"On this day, Tidesday, Crescent Moon, of the forty-forth year of the Malabella Sanitorum reign, Princess Odessa Malabella Sanitorum, was found dead in her chambers. As the royal medical examiner to the Malabella family, I have studied the cadaver to determine what exactly could cause the death of a seemingly healthy mermaid.

"After examination, the results are conclusive. The princess shows signs of abnormal paleness with blue coloring along the gums and red eyes. The princess died of substance overdose. Likely sea wasp poison."

I pulled the conch away from my ear, unable to listen to more. The princess, Odele's aunt, had been poisoned. How? Why? My hands shook. Someone had tried giving *me* sea wasp poison in my wine. That could have very well been *me*. Pale, blue gums, red eyes. A cadaver in a morgue.

But how did the kingdom not know how their princess had died? I'd been a baby at the time, so I wouldn't have known, but surely if she was murdered, it'd still be talked about. The information was lost in time. Or maybe...

My gut clenched uncomfortably. The war with Kappur. Had it been because of this? Had Kappur started the war by poisoning a princess? It was unclear. There was still more to the conch, but I couldn't listen to it. Not yet. First, I had to know.

I set the conch down on the table and swam out into the library, finding the old, glowing merman behind his desk.

"Find everything you need?"

I shook my head. "I have a question for you..." My breathing was harsh. I fought to steady it. "Do you happen to know how Princess Odessa Malabella Sanitorum, my aunty, I mean, died?"

His old face set into grim lines. "A sad, sad day that was. I've worked here for so long. Why, when your mother and aunt were children, I was here." He stroked his chin, skin dimming to a dull glow. "Now that I think back, there wasn't much information regarding her death. Heart troubles, they said. You never would have known if you'd seen her and your mother swim about the palace. Wild little things..." He chuckled, then scratched his neck and looked at me curiously. "I'm confused, Your Majesty. You asked me this months ago. Don't you remember?"

My heart almost stopped right then. *You asked me this months ago...* I hadn't been here for that long. Which meant that the real Princess Odele *had* been. That she'd discovered the exact same thing I had. She'd asked him the same questions. I was on the right track to the truth. I knew it.

I thanked him and went back into the royal records room, picking up the conch again. It had paused where I'd stopped listening, and continued to play when I pressed it to my ear.

"Upon further studious examination of the princess' body, marks were found to be formed around the area of her stomach, appearing like stretched skin. Because of these indicators, I closely inspected her insides, and what I found was rather alarming. Please note, all of this information was taken to the queen and king on that forty-fourth year. There was a tracing of placenta stuck to her inner uterine walls." I pulled it away, staring at it with confusion. Placenta? Wasn't that…? I pressed it back. "After further searching, I've concluded that Princess Odessa had given birth, just before she died, and her body hadn't been properly examined or cleansed."

Slowly, I placed the conch back in its place and sank to the floor. My brain swam laps, trying to process the information. The queen's twin sister, Princess Odele's *aunt,* had had a child before she died. But, the mermaid had never married. She'd died before her wedding with King Xristo could take place. Her sister, the queen, had married him instead, and then Thalassar and Kappur were plunged to war.

I took a deep breath.

If Princess Odessa had birthed a child out of wedlock, then where was it? And why had they killed her? Who had been the father? I'd come to find answers, and all I got were more questions and confusions.

Somewhere out there, Odele had a cousin, assuming the child had even lived. If they killed Princess Odessa for her indiscretions, wouldn't it stand to reason that the baby had been killed as well? Or had the child lived, and had Odele discovered this truth and gone in search of her cousin?

I'd come here to pretend to be a princess. To stop a war. Now I found myself on a chase to find the real princess, and suddenly, another missing royal. A royal I knew nothing about. Had the baby been male? Female? Was it dead or alive? Who was the father? *Where* was Odele?

And more importantly, why was someone out to kill the Malabella family?

My life in the palace was just about to become a whole lot harder.

I dropped my head into my lap and murmured, "Well, silt."

CARESSES BETWEEN THE SAND

"ON THIS MOONSDAY, NEW Moon, nearing the sixth year of the Malabella Oriana reign, Queen Odette Malabella Sanitorum was found deceased in her royal chambers. Having been feeling unwell for nearly a month, she finally succumbed to the sickness that ailed her and passed."

The voice in this conch was so unlike the other one I'd grown accustomed to. *This* one lacked depth. It was curt, quick, and simple, different from the honest precision that had been delivering bad news and answers from conches for the past hour. It had been a baritone that inquired, studied, and gave the best possible answers to this whole confusing mess that was now my life. I suspected he'd been changed, replaced by a mer who was less sympathetic to death and who gave vague answers that left me with more questions than answers.

A life I never wanted, but still found myself sunken deep into it. Like falling into a darkened abyss with an anchor tied around my stomach that was hauling me down… down…

When I'd first come to Thalassar—it seemed so long ago now—I'd thought it would be a simple thing to achieve my goals. I soon realized that anything you really wanted to achieve was never easy. It was something you had to fight tooth and claw for.

If I thought I would be sitting in on meetings with the queen and royal officials, chiming in with opinions and thoughts on the war of Thalassar against Kappur, I was wrong.

See, I wasn't even the Princess of Thalassar. I was a waitress from Lagoona, parading around in *her* silks and jewels, sleeping in her chambers, living her life, kissing *her* prince.

I lost sleep many nights over the mystery of Princess Odele's disappearance. I'd found her hidden cove, a secret passageway behind a tapestry in her rooms. I'd watched hundreds of conch recordings she'd left behind, and yet none of them pertained clues to why she had left.

It wasn't until the threats against my life that I finally started to understand. Death followed me—*her*—and her whole lineage. I'd discovered evidence these past few days that could change my fate, the fate of the kingdom of Thalassar forever.

It had started with the marriage contract. A piece of kelp parchment hidden in a shell in the cove. A contract that promised Princess Odette of Thalassar to Prince Dorian of Kappur, and Princess Odessa of Thalassar to Prince Xristo of Brague.

These marriages never took place. Because Princess Odessa had died, and then Princess Odette had married Prince Xristo instead of Prince Dorian. And then Thalassar had been plunged into war with Kappur.

Why? The obvious answer was because of the broken marriage contract. But royal secrets had so many layers I couldn't even begin to fathom. Just when I thought I had the answers within my grasp, more secrets unraveled, leaving me with far too many questions and very few answers.

Like the fact that Princess Odessa had a child before she'd been killed by the same poison that had almost ended *my* life. Or that Queen Odette had a child before Odele.

Somewhere out there was a missing royal. A cousin to Princess Odele. A bastard child, yet with royal blood nonetheless. A cousin I *assumed* Princess Odele had gone in search of.

That would certainly explain her disappearance. All this time I'd thought she had abandoned her duties, selfishly leaving behind a kingdom that needed her, when the reality very well could be that she'd gone to find her family.

This didn't change the fact that she was an awful mer, and it didn't eradicate the cruel things she'd said and done. It hardly made up for anything, really, but it was an explanation. And that was a start.

It didn't explain the death attempts I was now experiencing either. Could it be related to this? It must have been, if the whole Malabella lineage was dwindling due to "ailments." The lines were all connected somehow, I just couldn't see how yet.

I stared down at the timeline I'd made. It started with the marriage contract and ended with Odele's disappearance. On my kelp parchment, I'd scribbled in the deaths of the royal family, the missing royal, and the war, adjusting things as I remembered or discovered them. I ferociously drew a circle around the words: 'missing royal?'

I had no way of knowing if the baby that Princess Odessa had given birth to before her death had been male or female, or if it was even still alive. I wanted to hope that it was, given Odele's absence. In order to find both missing royals, all I had to do was follow Princess Odele's fin strokes. If I found her, I'd find the missing royal.

And then what?

I dropped my head unceremoniously onto the table, winced at the pain, then sat back up, rubbing my forehead. Then what? What could *I* do? I couldn't even get anyone to listen to me about the war with Kappur. What did I expect to happen if I found Odele *and* her cousin? If he—or she—was brought to the palace, I doubt they'd be welcomed with open arms. Bastard children of royals were rarely cared for or even acknowledged.

But I'd already decided hours ago that I was no longer going to feel sorry for myself. I would no longer allow other people to tell me what I could and could not do. I decided to take control, and after all this information, I was determined now more than ever to unravel every single royal secret in Thalassar.

Someone was killing royals. I wasn't one, but I'd been pretending to be one long enough that I was starting to take it personally.

Someone had *poisoned* me. I'd gotten shot at in the gardens. Prince Kai had almost gotten killed by a poisoned arrow that had been meant for me.

I was done playing the victim. Done looking over my shoulder, done with guards trailing after me, done with waiting for someone to attack and end me. No longer. To end this, I had to solve the mysteries, all while trying to stop a war…

I suddenly missed Elias, cripplingly so. He'd been the only one in the palace I could trust. The only one who had been willing to *help* me. The only one who knew my secrets. It'd only been two days since he'd left, but I still felt his loss like I was missing a limb. He had said that he was going to meet up with his mysterious *contacts,* but I wasn't sure if I believed that. I should have trusted him, but I couldn't deny the ache of sadness he'd left behind in my chest.

I'd wallowed in self pity for hours after he'd left, wondering if he'd left because of me, because of what had happened between us. I'd given myself to him. He'd been *inside* me, and then he'd left. The thought of betrayal was soon shaken from my head. I knew Elias. He flowed with current and shadow, went where he wished and didn't owe anyone an explanation. Not even me, even if we had been intimate.

It appeared as though, for the time being, I was alone.

I got up, spending a few minutes organizing everything back into place with shaking fins and fingers. Finished, I folded the kelp page I'd been writing on and tucked it neatly into the bodice of the dress I wore. With everything neatly in place, I swam out of the royal records room and to the front desk.

There was a glowing merman there, his skin giving off a slight yellow hue. He smiled as I approached, pushing a quill, ink, and ledger towards me. "Find everything you needed, Princess?"

I was too distracted to gift him with a smile. I pulled the ledger towards me, dipped the quill into the vial of squid ink, and signed Odele's name and time on the 'sign out' side of the kelp page.

"Unfortunately, no," I answered slowly, looking up to find his eyes staring at my hands. I tightened my fingers self-consciously.

His eyes rose, eyebrows creasing. "Really? Well, maybe I can help you with something."

I tapped the quill against the edge of his desk before sticking it back into the vial. "I was listening to a few royal death conch recordings that were made during the Malabella Sanitorum reign. I was wondering if the merman who recorded them was still around..."

He stroked his rounded chin with wrinkled fingers. "Hmm. Well, I am not sure *who* recorded the conches, as no one but royalty is allowed in that room. I'm merely a keeper of the keys, you see. Yet if it's royal deaths you wish to inquire about, I would suggest the royal morgue."

The royal morgue. I wondered why in gods' names Thalassar just threw the word royal in front of everything. As if that made it any more special than it really was. Royal library. Royal morgue. Royal lavatory. As if they weren't just rooms for reading, dying, or...

"Of course, thank you." I pushed the ledger back to him and swam from the library and into the hallways. Everything in the palace had gone dark, though that was no surprise. The capital of Thalassar, Eramaea, was located in saltier waters. My freshwater home, Lagoona, was located in the northern parts of Thalassar and surrounded by two-legger territory. Here, sunlight did not completely reach down below. We relied on phytoplankton, lava globes, and jellies for illumination. The soft glow of floating jellies guided me through the halls now.

I had no guards following me. They should have been, considering the fact that hours before I'd been nearly killed. Somehow, Prince Kai's advisors had convinced them to let me be alone for a while. That was more due to the fact that I had risked Odele's reputation by visiting him in his chambers.

He'd just been shot protecting me and I'd wanted to see him. High with fever, running on the adrenaline of battle and poison, the dragon entity that lived inside him had controlled his actions. The whole interaction had been unlike the prince I'd come to know and *like.* He'd been a new being entirely. Someone I'd only caught glimpses of in passing. Daring. Dangerous. Sensual. That fervent sensuality had been a contagious sensation. For weeks I'd tried to ignore that I felt something for him. Something that was similar to what I felt for the Black Blade, yet a feeling belonging innately to the Dragon Prince.

They were both completely different mer. Elias was as mischievous and secretive as the shadows of the night. His actions were unpredictable, exciting. Beyond that, we understood one another. We knew our struggles. We wanted what was best for the mer of Thalassar.

Prince Kai was a mystery. Unlike other royals, he was kind and quiet, and I liked both sides of him. The gentle prince and the vicious dragon.

What I felt for them was so intense, it was overwhelming.

I wondered if it was too late to pay a visit to the morgue. A stifled yawn answered that question for me. I was exhausted, body weary. It had been a day of surprises, revelations. I should sleep and then visit the morgue in the morning.

I swam in silence, until the silence broke in shards of whispering. The smallest breath of a rushing current pushed past me, chilling my bare arms. I turned sharply, looking for an open window but saw none. The whispering continued. One voice, deep and eerie, repeated one word over and over again.

"Princess..."

I felt the word like the tips of claws sliding down my spine. I shivered, bumps rising over my arms. I stared into the darkness of the hallway behind me, but the jellies didn't illuminate anyone there. Maybe I'd imagined it.

I started to turn, but the whisper stopped me mid-action.

"Princess..."

My heart pounded. I'd never actually roamed the palace at night. I didn't believe in ghosts and the like, but right then, I was frightened enough to be convinced that apparitions were real.

But then something unfurled from the darkness. *Elias?* His name stuck in my throat, not daring to push past my lips as the figure seemed to materialize. A merman in sinister shadows, covered entirely in black. I took a frightful stroke back. And when the figure moved, I caught a glint of something shining silver. Steel. A blade.

I turned and swam.

Kicking my tail, I put in as much speed as my limping form would allow. I wasn't fast, and the sudden strain caused me to swim jerkily. I rounded a corner and slammed into a wall. A portrait of a royal shook from its hinges and came crashing to the floor. I winced, heart pounding, breath coming out in heavy pants. I swam as if gators were behind me ready to tear through my flesh. My mistake was chancing a glance backwards.

The knife-wielder stalked behind me, steel glinting beneath the glow of jellies. It followed, hot on my fins. I kicked my tail. In my fear, I had no sense of direction; I barely knew where I was going. But I pushed forward with all of my might.

An involuntary sob burst past my lungs. My fins could barely keep me upright anymore. I rammed into another wall, knocking over a vase. Still I did not stop. I could feel the shadowed merman closing in on me, reaching out to take me.

I rounded the corner and rammed into yet another wall, but this wall gave out a soft noise of surprise from my collision.

Heavy hands clamped down on my shoulders. A scream almost tore through me, but I refused to give the stalker the satisfaction. I kicked my tail and jerked away, thrashing about.

His voice tore through my panic. "Princess? What's wrong?"

I stopped struggling and looked up into the eyes of Captain Tiberius Saber.

Relief was instant. I forgot all about my anger with him and all that he'd done, the hurtful way he'd treated me. It didn't matter. Nothing did except the safety of his arms. I threw myself into them, willing the sobs to go away before they could embarrass me in front of the ever-demure and strict captain. Never before had I been so happy to bury myself into a military jacket. The gasps and thundering of my heart, I couldn't control.

"What's wrong?"

I pulled away from him, turning around, but nothing emerged from the shadows. As if it had been entirely my imagination. But I knew I hadn't imagined it. Shadow and steel had been as real as Captain Saber was before me now.

"Princess?"

His fingers pushed into the roots of my hair, near the back of my neck, pulling my gaze back to him. There was genuine worry there that I didn't have time to ponder at the moment. He was looking at me like he really cared. And I wanted to believe that he did.

"What's wrong? Talk to me."

Nothing came from the shadows. My mind whirled. Had Captain Saber's presence scared it off? Had it even been there to begin with? What should I even tell the captain? He would believe me, but the worry on his features would be accompanied by a lecture and his everlasting disappointment. Then more guards.

I let out a shaky breath. "Nothing. I just—" It was hard to speak past the lump in my throat. "It was nothing. I panicked because I got lost." I hoped he couldn't smell the lies on my breath.

He did. His eyes flashed with hurt before he shuttered his gaze, every feature hardening.

"Of course," he said coolly. "Let me escort you to your rooms, then."

Despite myself, I felt suddenly safer because of the offer. I had this maddening urge to loop my arm through his for extra protection, but held myself back. He, of all people, would hate that the most. Captain Saber appeared to be one of those mer who despised contact with others. He was too cold for that.

Of course, hours ago he'd held me close as I wept for Prince Kai's safety. I thought it was more because he thought I looked like the princess he was in love with, rather than to comfort *me*.

I pulled away, putting distance between us.

He accompanied me down hallways, and I scarcely paid attention to the path or how far I'd veered away in my panic. My thoughts were plagued with that shadow, the steel of the knife. If the captain hadn't shown up, I likely would have been captured. Killed. Just another royal dead.

Fear had made me lose myself. I'd forgotten everything I'd vowed and had given in to helplessness. I was going to have to start carrying my blade around with me for protection. It wasn't conventional for a princess to do such a thing, but I needed to feel safe. I needed to feel like I wasn't going to be killed at every turn because of what I knew or because someone wanted the lineage dead.

After tonight, I'd arm myself.

Never again would I be helpless.

Never again would I let a murderer in the shadows try and get the best of me.

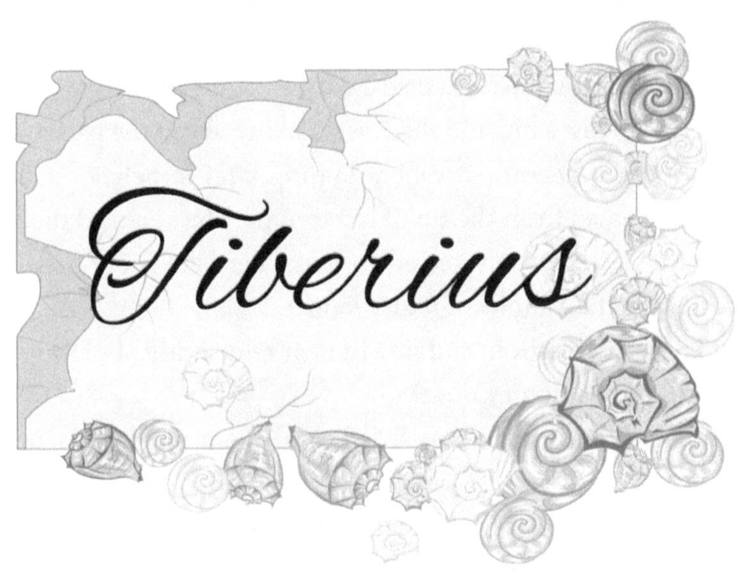

Tiberius

I COULD SEE THE pulse beating on her throat like the thrashing of a fish caught within a net. The rapid thumping of it made me want to interrogate her, but I didn't want Maisie to know that I was staring at her, that I was concerned. Last time I had, she'd promptly pushed me away. Though what else had I expected? I'd treated her so badly that she didn't care for my touch.

It was easier this way. Easier to balance ourselves on the edge of the line that separated us in the sand. Friends? Enemies? We were neither, yet we were both. It was just blurry right now. Everything was a mess; it was chaos.

I'd promised to protect her like I'd not protected Odele and I was failing. No wonder she couldn't stand my touch. Maybe next time I would be the one to swim in front of the arrow for her. Would she weep for me as she wept for Kai?

"Where are your guards?" I asked hoarsely. My eyes narrowed. I'd left her alone for a bit. Just a bit, and she was sneaking about the palace at night without anyone to accompany her. Typical Maisie behavior. Lectures begged to be released from the tip of my tongue, but I choked them down my throat. My lectures only served to make her hate me more. I wasn't sure I could bear the weight of it any longer.

She tensed at my question, and slowly, near reluctantly, she shrugged her delicate shoulders. "I don't know."

My hands tightened into fists. "I will find them and reprimand them immediately."

Her hand went to me then, gripping the hem of my sleeve tightly. The action shocked me into complete stillness. She looked at me, obsidian eyes wide and pleading. "Please don't," she begged. "It's not their fault. I sent them away… I had to be alone."

My throat tightened as I took her in, face betraying none of the turmoil I was feeling inside. In the soft, buzzing glow of the hallways, shadows and light flickered across the elegant curve of her face. She looked… different. She no longer seemed that awkward mer I'd picked up in Lagoona all those weeks ago. There was confidence around her, a surety that hadn't been there before.

She filled out the dresses now. Her body and posture were elegant, royal. Her cheekbones were high, chin pointed, neck arched and long. She looked like a real Malabella now. The realization of that was staggering.

"They had a job to do, and they failed." I hated to sound like such a cad when she was looking at me like that.

She tugged at my sleeve once before letting go, releasing the spell of immobility her touch had seemed to cast over me. We swam again.

"I'd just hate to see them get in trouble because of *my* decision."

Gods. I closed my eyes for a second and opened them again. Why was she so kind? She cared about mer. All of those less fortunate. She had so little herself, and still she *cared*. She would have given the clothes off her back, knowing it would leave her naked. Royals were born with everything, and so they wanted and cared for nothing. Everything was easily replaceable. I knew this, because it was their way of life here.

Life for us guards and servants was different. If something didn't get done properly, there were consequences.

If she'd been attacked without the protection of palace guards…

"You're to be protected, Mai—Your Majesty." I couldn't forget myself, make a mistake. Just because no one seemed to be around, it didn't mean they weren't. Even barnacles spoke and spread news and rumors.

Maisie fiddled with her fingers. "I know."

"I'd hate to see anything happen to you."

She stumbled at those words, then righted herself, casting me a long sideways look. "Captain…" A warning. One I didn't quite comprehend.

We stopped in front of her chambers. I turned to her, so many words I wanted to say, though nothing seemed appropriate. "I want you to be safe."

She reached for the handle of her door, looking at me a little sadly. "Is it really *me* who you want safe, Captain?" She twisted the handle and pushed the door open.

"Of course."

Her lips pulled into a tight, thin line. I already knew what she was thinking before she even said it. Still, when she spoke, my heart nearly ceased beating. "Do not confuse us, Captain Saber." She didn't need to specify who 'us' was. Odele, and her. "I know who it is you really want." There was a pause. "Goodnight." Going into the room, she closed the door softly behind her. The soft clicking of the lock settling into place resonated louder in me than slamming the door ever could.

I did not wait by her door but retraced our strokes, back down to the hallway I'd found her in. Taking the turn, I stopped. She'd swam about the palace as if someone had been after her, but there were no signs of anything. Not an overturned picture or vase, and no one was about either. It wasn't surprising, as the castle's inhabitants were all resting.

Swimming down the length of the hallway, I stopped short when I felt the slightest of breezes. I turned and noticed that a window had been left open. The current from the outside was getting in.

I stalked over and pulled the window shut. When I took a stroke backwards, my peripheral caught sight of an object glowing on the ground. Unmistakably steel. I bent low and picked up the knife by the hilt, bringing it to my face for closer examination.

It was a common enough weapon. Every mer in the streets likely had one, but what was it doing here in the palace? Palatial weaponry was more refined, showy and adorned with jewels for flourish rather than made for slicing. I doubted a servant had dropped it.

I leaned forward and sniffed the blade, edging back with a start. A bitter scent emanated from it. One that was all too familiar to me.

Sea wasp poison.

Someone had been in the palace. Someone had been carrying this around.

I recalled Maisie's expression when she'd rounded that corner. The obvious relief on her face. The pounding of her heart against my chest. And her fear.

Had someone chased her around the palace with this? My hand tightened around the hilt until my knuckles went white. Had she thought me unable to protect her? Was that why she hadn't told me about this?

No more, I vowed.

There would be no more secrets between us.

And the only way to keep her safe was to get her to trust me. Completely.

I DROPPED ONTO BED and was lulled to sleep by the soft kissing of anemones. Dreams and nightmares clashed together in my mind. One moment, I dreamt of Prince Kai and the Black Blade. Side by side, they looked formidable, and my heart accelerated as they both reached for me. I couldn't tell whose lips were on my skin or whose fingers wrapped around my body. Their images soon faded into tenebrous shadows with steel eyes. I swam and swam, but it didn't matter how hard I pumped my tail because the darkness swallowed me whole.

I thrashed all night, and when I awoke the next morning, my entire body was weary. Secrets did this to a mer. They made the mind weaken, filled it with erratic thoughts and nightmares. Once I rubbed the sleepiness from my eyes, I got up and got ready for the day.

I undressed, making sure to slip my timeline beneath a dolphin figurine on a coral shelf, and bathed and bounded into the closet, contemplating dress. I would be going to the morgue after I was finished with whatever it is I was to be doing today. I was sure there was a whole long list of things Princess Odele was meant to get through today. Like another endless lesson with Percival in history, riding, and other things I did not care for at the moment.

The backs of my hands had hardened from Percival's whacking. I didn't want to repeat those punishments. Besides, I'd almost been murdered yesterday and Prince Kai was on his sick bed. Surely they could give me the day off?

Thinking of Prince Kai, I made a mental note to go and visit him later in the day. Not after my visit at the morgue. How morbid, to bring the stench of death and decay into his rooms while he was unwell.

Granted, I wasn't entirely sure his advisors—Ichiro and Lee—would even let me go in to see him. They'd disapproved last time I was in his room alone. I suppose they had good reason, as I hadn't left entirely virtuous. Not that my virtue had even still been intact when I had gone in the first place.

Elias Blackfin, Thalassar's most notorious criminal and my *friend,* had been the one I'd given myself to first. I tried to summon embarrassment because of my wanton actions, but couldn't quite muster the sentiment. I did feel guilty, though. By doing this, was I somehow tricking them? Had I used them to satisfy my own selfish needs?

The Black Blade wouldn't care, I told myself. He'd encouraged my affections towards Prince Kai often enough. He told me to not be afraid to take what I wanted. I supposed it was his twisted sense of humor, or honor. He was *free,* and he wanted me to be free as well.

But Prince Kai didn't know who I was. He assumed I was Princess Odele because I'd led him to believe so. He thought he'd lain with a princess, but instead it had been with a poor waitress. I tried to tell myself it didn't matter. He'd confessed his love to *me,* not the princess. He had said that he hated who I was before, hated who the princess was. Did it matter that I wasn't royalty? Did it matter that he didn't know my real name?

It did. Kai needed an alliance with a princess to help his kingdom. I had nothing to offer.

I shook those depressing thoughts off as I pulled a dress from the closet and a chemise. I slipped the undergarment on and then the dress. It was a fanciful thing in swaths of light pink, periwinkle, and sky blue with long sleeves and a high neckline. I went to the mirror and started parting tendrils of hair to braid it down my back.

When I'd first come to Thalassar and had been transported into this room, I hadn't been given servants or lady's maids. Perhaps because they would have known I was an imposter immediately simply by looking at my scarred tail and mauled fins. I was glad I didn't have them, but couldn't help but feel as though one of them could have done something to my hair to make me look more princess-like. I was stuck with this. Endless chignons and braids. My fingers worked quickly before the mirror, and when I finished, I tied the end with a strip of pink cloth that looked bright against my dark purple-blue hair.

Once finished, I went for my timeline, tucking it into the bodice of my dress again, then made way for the door. I'd send for a light pastry before I got to work. If there was one thing I still was after living lavishly, it was hungry. Even if the food here wasn't entirely too desirable.

I opened the door and jumped with surprise.

Captain Saber floated on the other side, fist raised as if he'd been about to knock. Behind him, more palace guards floated.

"Captain..." I pressed a hand to my chest, as if I meant to calm my sudden erratic heartbeat. The sight of him provoked too many nerves. "You gave me a fright."

He lowered his hand and gave me a bow. "Forgive me, Princess, but I've come to escort you to the royal state rooms."

My eyebrows rose at that. I'd never been to the royal state rooms, but they sounded important. "Why?"

His penetrating blue eyes found mine. "The queen wishes to see you."

Queen Circe Malabella was a regal beauty. She was all sharp, refined features with clear skin and golden hair coiled tightly atop her head. The only evidence that she even belonged on the Malabella family coral branch was the coloring of her long tail, though it was more blue than purple.

Every time I saw the queen, I was struck with the slightest pang of fear. Today was no different, especially when she wore robes of state, royal blue with glittering diamonds and silver on her shoulders. A crown adorned her head, towering over her. Its enormous height didn't make her look smaller. It made her look powerful. And she knew it. Knew she was beautiful, with the long arch of her throat and piercing eyes.

To her left sat her advisor, Percival, who hid the glare aimed in my direction beneath the sagging wrinkles of his eyes. And to her right, King Xristo. He wore similar robes, and a smaller crown over his dark hair.

In Thalassar, the queens ruled supreme and kings, though they had power, seemed a bit more for show. In comparison to his wife, King Xristo's appearance was dimmed, but he was no less beautiful. And his eyes lit up when they saw me.

Around the table there were more royals from different kingdoms. More advisors and representatives. Some I'd met at the anniversary dinner and others who had obviously just arrived, as I hadn't seen them before.

Fear gnawed at my gut, making me feel suddenly inadequate among such important mer. Even Ichiro, Prince Kai's advisor, was there. This was obviously very important, and the presence of the future leader of Thalassar had been required, or else the queen would have been content to keep me oblivious to this meeting.

I pushed my fear aside and channeled my inner Odele. Not the selfish version of her, the one who didn't care for others, but the one who was regal, beautiful, and commanding. Wearing her personality came easier to me now. I tilted my chin up, assuming the waters of importance.

Captain Saber had placed a tiara, a dainty thing that glittered and dangled with diamonds, over my brow before entering. The change in me must have been a miraculous likeness because I noted how King Xristo's eyes widened, and the slight twitching of annoyance on the side of the queen's cheek.

I spoke to no one, even as the mermen got up from their seats and bowed. I merely nodded in acknowledgment and glided towards the empty seat beside the king.

Captain Saber pulled out my chair for me and I took a seat. He didn't leave but took a few strokes back as he surveyed the room, eyes and senses alert.

"Now we may begin," the queen said. Her voice was like the crack of a whip. It was law. She looked around the room with a hard gleam in her eye. "As you were all informed, there was an incident yesterday afternoon. Due to the recent events, I understand some of you must be feeling particularly… *unsafe*… but I called this meeting to assure you that you are."

It was quiet for what felt like an eternity before someone dared speak first. He was a merman with brown skin and eyes as white as snow, ringed with silver. He was rather thickly corded all over, massive, even bigger than

Captain Saber. He looked like he could take down a hippocampus with his bare hands. His voice had an icy chill and was laced thickly with a harsh accent as he spoke in Thalassarin. "If that is true, then where is the Draconian Prince?"

I looked at Ichiro, but his expression betrayed nothing. He was all solemn lines. I looked over to the queen. A muscle at her jaw was working furiously.

"Forgive me, but who are *you* to speak here?"

A blond merman sat beside him, his eyes fierce and blue. I didn't recognize him from Prince Kai and Odele's engagement party, but his frosty features and brown skin gave his heritage away. Captain Saber and I had gone over the long line of foreign royalty and allies for days. He was the Prince of Iol, the northern, icy sea kingdom. His accent was equally thick and rolling. "He is *my* advisor and guard, and he will speak as freely as I or you. *Majesty*." He threw that last word out so last moment, it could have been construed as disrespectful.

Sure enough, the queen looked like she was leashing her fury. We were in her kingdom, and she was the supreme ruler, but everyone at this table was royalty. She could not risk angering any of them.

"We have all seen the news recordings," the white-eyed merman continued coldly. "The prince was shot down protecting your step-daughter. Before that, she was nearly shot down in the royal gardens. Before *that,* she was poisoned in front of all of you at a royal dinner."

My face heated at the disdain in his voice. I couldn't help but feel guilty. Like it was all my fault. The hands clasped in my lap tightened.

"I am aware of the incidents—"

"Are you?" he interrupted arrogantly. "Because no suspect has been detained yet."

The queen scraped her nails across the quartz surface of the table. It was Percival who answered, directing himself to the Iolish Prince. "Your Majesty, this is obviously the work of King Dorian and his Kappurin assassins. They obviously want to break the engagement between Thalassar and Draconi before it begins, so they can win the war."

The Prince of Iol—whose name eluded me at the moment—narrowed his eyes. "Dangerous accusations, Percival. I suggest you tread carefully. Iol and Kappur are on good terms, and you'll recall that we in the ice waters do not take sides in this war."

Percival's saggy, wrinkly face fumed.

Iol had always been a neutral, secretive kingdom. There was very little the rest of the sea kingdoms knew about the ice kingdom of the north. The royals rarely left their home waters, there were no conch recordings, no paintings, and scarce information about them. All negotiations were made through their Prime Minister or Mister Shallows, Iol's foreign diplomat.

The war with Kappur had been a slow going thing, dragging on throughout the years. The death toll was incredible, but neither side had allies, as none of the other kingdoms had wanted to get involved in a war that wasn't their business and knew nothing about.

"Regardless of who is behind it, I want to assure you that you are in no real danger here." The queen spoke with a surety that could have convinced them, if they'd not seen the threat for themselves.

The white eyed merman raised his eyebrows. "If you really thought that, then why have you doubled guards around the palace?"

I could understand their hesitation to remain here. No one wanted to go away in business with another kingdom only to turn up dead because some trigger-happy moron was out for royal blood. But I also understood why the queen needed them here. A show of strength and support, to celebrate my—Odele's—wedding to Kai. It would be an insult to the kingdom if they left. And Thalassar needed allies.

Good thing they were after Odele's royal blood and didn't want the other royals. They would be safe as long as they didn't interfere in the murder attempts. And perhaps Kappur had nothing to do with the attempts at all.

The timeline tucked into my bodice suddenly burned, begging me to find the missing pieces of this puzzle.

I couldn't hold back my words any longer. "Your Majesty." I directed this to the Prince of Iol. He stared at me with surprised eyes. I fought not to blush. Odele had obviously never spoken at one of these and he'd likely heard about how careless she was. "Please, do not leave Thalassar out of fear."

My words had obviously offended both him and his guard. "The Iolish are *not* afraid of death, Princess. We survive in harsher waters and conditions that I doubt you and your ilk could even begin to fathom."

I smiled a little at that. "I do not doubt it. I merely want to reassure you that if it's death you're worried about, worry not. They're after me and no one else."

"And what of Prince Kai?" the Iolish diplomat, Mister Shallows, chimed in. "His absence at this table says otherwise."

I tried not to glare at the smugness in his voice. The tadpole had given Kai such a hard time at the anniversary dinner that it was no surprise he'd choose to attack him now when he wasn't here to defend himself. He didn't even hold back his vicious words in the presence of his own prince. All it served was to remind me of the strain between Iol and Draconi. The two kingdoms hated each other, and I couldn't remember why.

"My dear betrothed was being heroic. He pushed me aside and took the arrow that was meant for me. You don't have to worry." I smiled at him. "Not everyone is capable of such displays of heroism. You should be perfectly safe."

The Prince of Iol's guard didn't bother holding back an amused snort. It was an inappropriate sound for anyone in royal company, but it also made me inexplicably content. The fact that he hadn't defended Mister Shallows meant there was some strain there as well.

"The problem here isn't that it happened," King Xristo spoke for the first time. "The problem is that it happened publicly. The mer of Thalassar demand blood. They are unhappy that someone tried to murder their princess."

A princess that they wouldn't have cared for if not for me. It was my turn to feel smugness.

"Understandable." The Iolish Prince nodded.

"As you can comprehend, we mustn't let matters spin out of control," the queen told them. "The mer of Thalassar should see us all in unity. They must see that we are alright and safe. Anything else and they will panic."

"How *is* Prince Kai? Is he really alright?" Iol's guard directed the question to Ichiro. Surprisingly, there seemed to be no hatred in the question. Just scholarly curiosity.

Kai's advisor looked at me with an expression I couldn't quite decipher, though I supposed it was similar to every other look and glare he gifted me with.

"The prince is recovering speedily."

As if we'd summoned him, the state room doors opened and the Draconian Prince swam through.

I shot up from my seat. Entirely inappropriate, but the surprise kept me upright.

He trudged in slowly. He looked surprisingly elegant and healthy in his traditional black and red robes. His hair was swept into a tight bun above his head. There were no traces of fever on his features and no sign of that other entity, either. The one who was daring, dangerous, and straightforward.

A chair was immediately pulled over for him. His eyes found mine, and his smile was breathtaking. "Please, my gem, sit."

Face flushing, I slowly sank into my chair and he sat in his own. He turned his dazzlingly soft smile to the others around him.

"Forgive my tardiness," he apologized. "I was indisposed." A light laugh trickled out of his mouth, others soon echoed the sound.

"Well then, this confirms your advisor's words." The queen's voice burned like lava. "Now that our circle is complete, to pacify the unease in the kingdom, I'd like to propose a royal ball."

A ball. I'd just been attacked, Prince Kai hurt, and she was suggesting a *ball*.

Josiah had spoken of this many times at Tides' Tavern. With a pocket full of conspiracies, this one had been one of the last I'd heard before coming here. To distract the mer from wars and unpleasant things, royals often threw lavish parties and balls, or planned weddings; a curtain, so the mer could forget their troubles and what ailed them. It was a distraction for the mer. Because they couldn't focus on their problems when parties were announced.

I never thought I'd be involved in one.

"A ball?" The Prince of Iol sounded as disbelieving as I felt. "Is that wise?"

The queen flicked her manicured fingers. "It is customary to have a royal engagement ball after a royal engagement dinner. I think it is very wise."

"I agree," said Prince Kai.

Surprised, I turned to find him smiling widely at me. Too widely. His eyes were flashing, knowing. I flushed, willing it to go away. Even from the opposite side of the table, I could feel heat emanating from him, and I knew where his thoughts were. On his body over mine, his hips snapping against my own. On his lips tasting every inch of my skin. I could almost feel the phantom touch of his fingers gripping my wrists down against the floor. It was a memory I knew would be with me forever.

"I will be honest, Queen Circe; I think we should proceed with the wedding as well."

My heart thundered too fast and too loud. I was sure they could all hear it.

Queen Circe seemed taken aback. King Xristo's face betrayed nothing but slight amusement.

"That's so sudden…"

"I think we have delayed long enough. Odele's sickness set our plans back a few months. Now that she is well, I see no reason to wait."

I saw reason. I saw plenty of reasons. The first being that *I wasn't Odele.*

I looked to the queen, wondering if my panic showed in my face. She wasn't even looking at me. Her hardened features were trained solely on Prince Kai. Contemplative.

"Of course, Prince Kai. We could formally announce the wedding date at the ball."

What?! I tried not to shriek. We couldn't have a wedding date! Captain Saber hadn't even found the real Princess Odele yet. And I certainly couldn't get married to him! I wasn't royalty. What was the queen thinking? Perhaps she was just agreeing to buy us time…

Kai's answering smile was the widest I'd seen yet. Ambitious. Anxious.

The Prince of Iol cleared his throat. "This is all very romantic," he said, a hint of sarcasm in his voice, "but if it's true and an assassin is after the princess, who's to say they won't try to murder her halfway through the engagement toast?"

"Our Captain of the Royal Guard will ensure that everyone is well protected for the event."

Iol's guard snorted, which told everyone what exactly he thought of Captain Saber and his security measures.

I didn't dare turn to look at the captain's expression, fearing it'd be murderous.

"So it's settled, then," the queen concluded. "There will be a ball in a week's time."

In a week? Surely that wasn't enough time to plan an entire ball? I dared not say anything. Fear would have cracked my voice. I hadn't expected any of this, and it interfered with my plans of unraveling secrets. Balls meant dresses, food, and dancing. It meant lessons upon lessons, leaving little room to breathe.

My gut twisted.

I'd survived a gator attack, near murder, and a poisoning. Yet a ball? That seemed like the most dangerous task of all.

THE MEETING ENDED AND every royal and advisor present got up slowly, lingering. I could feel eyes draw to me, curious and eager to see fault in me. Maybe they were hoping I would fall over and die. Yet I'd never reveal to them just how much pain I was in, just how much the wound beneath my collarbone agonized me. It wasn't so much the wound itself, but the traces of poison still flushing through my system. My body tried expelling it, and I'd thrashed all night with fever.

Nightmares plagued me vividly. In them I'd been devoured whole by the dragon entity within me, whipped into a bloody mess of flesh by my father, and cursed to the abyss by the Great Dragon. Nothing had been clear. Reality and dream melded together until I could hardly tell either of them apart.

Except her.

Always her.

I'd memorized her touch and taste, keeping it all close to me like a fevered dream that became memory. It had been real. All of it. Her hands over my body, teeth at my neck. I still had the marks, just where my neck met my shoulder, as proof of what had happened between us.

In Draconi, it mattered little if the mer were married before sharing intimacies. My father, the emperor, had one wife and many, many concubines. Marriage did not matter. What mattered was the feeling. The only reason we bothered with a slow courtship was because my kingdom was desperate and Thalassar's propriety dictated it.

After what happened between us the night before, well, it was one of the main reasons I suggested a speedy marriage. Last night could have very well resulted in heirs, and I'd protect her reputation. I'd not let her be shunned by her kingdom and the royals here.

I had to speak with her and explain myself. I'd noted the suddenly pale pallor at my suggestion. It wasn't something she'd been expecting, and I thought I'd ease her mind.

Brushing aside Ichiro, who had swam to my side to glare and possibly lecture me in our mother tongue, I maneuvered past bodies and to the far side of the room.

Odele was there, but she wasn't alone.

Captain Saber, ever faithful, was rigidly posed behind her. Too close, for my liking. But even more unnerving was the fact that a blond merman held her hand in his. His lips hovered over her knuckles, and I was forced to watch as he pressed them to her skin. Not once, but twice. He kissed his way up to the back of her hand, to her wrist.

Ice and lava warred within me, but I kept my outer composure cool, even if all I wanted to do was rip his arm from his shoulder for touching my bride. My mate.

He pulled away, but did not let go of her hand. I was within hearing distance, so I could make out his every filthy word.

"You've enchanted me, Princess." His voice was rather wistful, a lilting elated tone to it.

"Thank you, Prince."

"Please, call me Ytgar."

Ytgar? My eyebrows rose as I stared between the blond, dark merman, and the dark skinned, white-haired one. The frost of their features, as well as the garments they wore—long blue and white furs that covered them from shoulders down to their tail fins—told me they were Iolish.

Odele smiled, her high cheekbones blushing hotly. "Of course I shall." She turned to the white-haired merman with eerie eyes, obviously waiting for an introduction.

"This is Valmundur." *Ytgar* gave a brusque roll of his R. Their language was a harsh one, so every word seemed made to sound like an insult when they spoke in Thalassarin. "Val for short." He winked, and Princess Odele giggled.

Containing my rage, I started forward, settling beside her. "My gem," I greeted, ignoring everyone else. I could not forget that our kingdoms were at odds, and the insults their diplomat threw my way every chance he got. "Are you well?"

"I am, Prince Kai." She tried to pull her hand away, but the blond held strong. My eyes narrowed on his thumb, tracing circles around the back of her hand. When I looked into the ice blue of his eyes, he was smirking. This merman was too daring for his own good, his actions meant to irritate me.

"It was a pleasure, beauty mine, and I look forward to seeing you at the ball. I trust…" He brought her hand daringly up to his lips. "…you'll save a dance for me?"

She was breathless when she replied, “Yes, Prince—”

“Ah, ah. Ytgar, remember?”

“Yes, Ytgar. Of course.”

He smiled triumphantly and pressed a kiss to her knuckles, and though he didn’t look at me, I knew it was directed towards me. He finally let go and bowed arrogantly to me.

“Prince Kai.” After that farewell, he turned and left the room, his *guard* and his diplomat dutifully following behind.

The princess turned her flushing face to me, and the smile on her lips was not on account of anything I had done.

“He’s very charming,” she whispered, a little wistfully, herself.

“Hmm.” And insolent. I kept my snide commentary to myself and offered Odele my hand. “May I speak with you, Princess?”

Her face flushed an even brighter color, making me wonder what she was thinking about. If her thoughts wandered back to where mine had been since last night, to the press of our bodies and the heat of our joining skin. Slowly, she gave me her hand, and I took it in my fingers, thumb sliding across her knuckles. As if that could banish the imprint of Ytgar’s lips from her skin.

I pulled her to my side, and together, with Captain Saber following behind, I led her out into the hallways. There was nothing proper about the way I held her hand, the way I threaded my fingers between the spaces of hers. I didn’t care. We were past the bounds of propriety already. It wasn’t as though I wanted everyone to know what we’d done. I wanted everyone to know what I felt.

“How are you feeling? Truly?” There was worry in her voice.

“Better.” There was no need to worry her with details of my pain.

“I didn’t get the chance to thank you yesterday… for what you did for me. I’m sorry you got hurt on my behalf.”

I shook my head. “Don’t fret, princess. I’d throw myself in front of a thousand poisoned arrows if it meant to keep you safe.”

Her high cheekbones flushed, the thick lashes lowering against them as she cast her gaze downwards. "I'd prefer it if you didn't do that. I'd like to keep my betrothed intact."

"It would take a lot more than one arrow to kill me. Don't worry."

"Good."

My fingers tightened on her hand as I tugged her closer. Her arm brushed against mine. Odele was much smaller than me. My tail was long, wide, and while she was a bit on the taller side, to me she appeared petite.

I had to bend down to whisper, my lips brushing against the warmth of the lobe of her ear. "We need to talk about last night."

She jerked away from me, fingers pulling away from mine for a second before she latched on again. Panicked, she threw a glance over her shoulder at Captain Saber. The guard was following at a steady distance, but he was still close enough to hear and be heard. My eyes narrowed.

"No," she answered quietly, shaking her head so vigorously, the tiara poised there almost fell off.

We stopped swimming, turning to face each other. Pulling my fingers from her grasp, I readjusted the crown on her head, fingers lowering and lingering a bit too long on her skin. She fought the shiver that coursed through her, but I still felt her tremble. I trailed my fingers down to her cheeks, cupping them.

Her eyes closed, as if she meant to block out the sensation my touch provoked. As if it pained her.

"Princess, I love you." The confession was pulled from my lips as if by magic. We'd been down this current before, and I'd been rejected. Last night hadn't been a rejection. It had been our beginning. Something was just holding her back. "And I want to marry you. Now. Tomorrow. *Soon.* I want to be with you." A small bubble rose from the corner of her eye. I wiped my thumb across the curve of her cheek. "Odele—"

She pulled away from me violently, eyes snapping open. "Don't…" she pleaded, keeping her palms up, open, warding me off. Pain tore through me at the sight. Was I truly such a monster incapable of being loved? Was I not good enough? What had last night been?

I reached out for her and she took a stroke back. Away from me. "I thought—"

"Please *don't*," she interrupted.

I wanted to say more. I was desperate to say more. To the abyss with Captain Saber, who was watching, listening. I wanted to pull her into my arms, hold her and demand answers. Before I could do any of this, Odele spun away from me and darted down the hall.

Captain Saber let out a whisper of a curse and shot after her.

And all I could do was watch her go.

His confession had been too much. It had reminded me of my treachery. I didn't regret what had happened between us, and I wanted to speak with him. A part of me had even wanted to tell him the truth. But this wasn't the time for that. Not in the hallways of the palace. Not where anyone could overhear. Not with—

"Princess!" Captain Saber's hand clamped on my forearm, forcing me to stop. "Are you alright?"

Even if I wasn't, I had to pretend to be. I'd embarrassed myself enough in front of the captain. A lecture couldn't be too far behind.

"I'm fine." I straightened my spine, steeled my gaze. He would see no weakness in me or my posture. I was the perfection he'd molded me into.

A frown pulled his features. He didn't believe me, but he didn't have to. All that mattered was that I was immaculate in everything. Like Princess Odele had been.

The captain still didn't release me. His hand tightened, though not enough to hurt. He cast a look around, assessing the halls. Servants swam about, dusting off portraits and vases with sea sponges.

He turned back to me. "Princess." His voice was a low, forbidden plea. "Come with me." He tugged lightly.

I stiffened. Honestly, I didn't want to go anywhere with Captain Saber. I didn't want to endure another lecture. I didn't want him to see just how much his words had affected me since he brought me here. Whenever I saw him, all I could see were my imperfections. All I could feel was the prominence of my limp, hear the imperfect accent curling off my tongue. Around him, I felt like I was *less.*

"I don't think so."

Besides, I had things to do. The timeline tucked in my bodice burned as a reminder. I had to get to the morgue, speak to the merman there, the one in charge of the royal conches. There were so many secrets to discover, and with the announcement of the oncoming ball, I feared I'd be swamped in studies and other things the entire week.

"Please…"

His soft tone broke my resolve. It could have been construed as manipulative, the tone he was using to get what he wanted, and I should have denied him, but gods, there was sincerity etched on his every feature. An emotion I had yet to decipher, one I'd never seen him wear before.

I sighed. "Fine," I conceded.

He nodded gravely and led me away.

I wasn't sure where we were going. Not until we exited the palace through the back and made our way to the royal gardens.

Colors in every shade brightened the waters. Bushes of coral, swaying plants of seaweed, water lilies and sea fans were ornamented just so, giving the place a beauty that rivaled Lagoona's.

Back home, the waters were filled with cattails, grass, and lily pads that floated up like clouds. When they parted, sunshine pierced past the waters and our world brightened in an array of colors.

That was home. It was familiarity. It was my comfort.

I couldn't deny there was beauty here, and it wasn't artificial.

The captain guided me past the maze of underwater shrubbery, deeper into the forestation, until we were far enough from the castle, hidden behind them. There was privacy here, and it would obviously give him a good opportunity to lash out at me. It was a nice change of pace from the princess' chambers. At least here I'd have something pretty to look at while he yelled.

There wasn't anywhere to sit, so we both floated there, facing each other awkwardly before the captain turned away from me.

I had to admit, he was beautiful. Not in the way Kai was beautiful. Captain Saber was all hard, jagged lines, strong jaw and muscle. There was no softness in him. Even his eyes were hard and cold. His entire posture was rigid, back steeled straight, and there was nothing out of place with him. His military jacket was impeccable, the star fish that marked his rank moved slowly against the lapels. Even his hair, blond and cropped short, was in perfect place.

He was a merman who thrived in perfection and would accept nothing less.

He looked so out of place here in the gardens that I couldn't help but stare as he took the petal of a water lily between his fingers and rubbed it slowly.

"I'm not good with words," he began slowly, softly. "I never have been." He released the leaf and turned to me, forcing his hands behind his back. His jaw worked, a muscle near his eye ticked. Something in him was warring, that much was obvious. "I know that since we met in Lagoona, I haven't been..." He cut off, turned. I watched the workings of his strong throat as he swallowed. "I know I have been hard on you."

I blinked, sure I'd heard wrong. This sounded an awful lot like an apology, and Captain Saber didn't seem the type to apologize. Maybe the real changeling was him.

"Maisie..." He started forward, and I couldn't move. Even as he placed his hands on my shoulders, I was too shocked to do much but stare. "All this time, I've lived with this secret, and I've safeguarded it so deeply, it was... eating me inside." He was having so much trouble getting the words out. I didn't dare interrupt. "And then you came and tore it out of me. I hated you for that."

My hands tightened in front of me. He pulled away, keeping his body in constant, changing motion.

"I... loved... her." Those seemed to be the hardest words of them all. "For so long and she never noticed. But you did. It made me wonder if perhaps she did know, the whole time, and never acknowledged it." He huffed a bitter laugh, turned to trace his fingers across a new plant. "I knew we could never be, and I was content enough to see her happy. Even when she treated me like I was scummy staff, I told myself it didn't matter."

I could hear the heartbreak and resignation in his words. It *had* mattered. To him, it had. I was seeing him in a new light, and my heart beat harder, and I hated Odele so much more.

"I gave everything to her and was content with nothing in return." He turned back to me, his eyes fierce. "Then she disappeared, and I found you." He came forward. I let him take my chin in his fingers and tilt my face up, examining it. "You look so much like her that I wanted to *make* you into her." He released me, but I still felt his touch like a brand. "So I pushed you, like I never pushed her, hoping that you could replace her somehow." He looked regretful now, and a little embarrassed. "Everything you did was *wrong.* Every time I saw you, I thought, Odele would *never* do that. And now—" He let out a sound of frustration. "I tore you apart, Maisie. And I'm—I want to thank you."

I blinked. "Thank me?"

He laughed, an empty, bitter sound. "You opened my eyes, Maisie. Thanks to you I realized what she was—is. A part of me even wishes that she'll never come back."

A soft gasp came out of me involuntarily. "You don't mean that, Captain." He loved her still. He was just angry. Confused.

He shook his head. "You're right," he said softly. "I don't mean it."

I took a stroke forward, reached out to touch him, palm splaying over his shoulder. "You're allowed to be angry," I reassured.

He opened his mouth, closed it again and nodded gravely. He'd spoken so much, way more than I'd ever heard him speak. He'd confided in me his feelings, something that was monumental. And he looked like he wanted to say more, so much more but still held himself back.

"I am sorry, Maisie." His thumb came up to the curve of my cheek, just where Prince Kai had stroked so lovingly. Captain Saber did it just as gently. "I am sorry I never told you before, but I think you do fit in here, with the royals. You are not like them, but you care more than they do. I may not agree with you on certain subjects, but you are doing a good job."

My heart clenched at his words before starting to beat against the cages of my ribs. Never, in all my time faking to be the Princess of Thalassar, did I *ever* expect to hear Captain Saber's praise. Never before had I believed I could earn it. That he would see me as anything other than what I was. Or that he'd ever think ill of Odele.

Yet here was the proof. That all my hard work had paid off. That all of that training, all of the tears, and jabs had led up to this moment.

Suddenly, everything changed, shifted.

His words filled me and I didn't feel less like I had only moments ago. Captain Saber had given me a gift; since the very first moment it had all been a gift. I now knew things I hadn't before. I knew how to portray myself as a royal. I knew secrets and was looking for answers. I'd made friends with the Black Blade and the Dragon Prince.

Thanks to him, I had hope that I could make a change. Like no one else ever had before.

"Thank you, Captain." Warmth spread throughout the veins in my body and I shifted closer to him. I wrapped my arms around him and dared to tug him close. A hug that lasted the briefest of seconds before I was pulling away. "Thank you."

For the gift of royal secrets, and the education I now had to unravel them all.

I'd bared myself before Maisie, expecting… Well, I wasn't sure what it was I'd expected. Certainly not this. Not the feel of her arms wrapped around my body for a moment. Not the blinding light of her smile, and not the shine in her obsidian eyes.

I was so used to rejection, to Odele pushing me away, laughing at my gestures and caring, that I had not been prepared for this. I was unused to it, so when her arms wrapped around me, I uselessly floated there and did not hold her back.

I should have, but it ended all too quickly.

She pulled away. "Thank you."

I nodded, clasping my hands behind my back. We stared at each other for a moment, and it should have been uncomfortable, but it wasn't. My heart was thundering, as it had been since I'd brought her out here. Baring my feelings had been more nerve wracking than going to war.

I'd never had to explain myself to anyone before. I spoke and mer obeyed. With Maisie, it was different. I challenged her as much as she challenged me. This experience had made me stronger. It was another stroke towards earning the trust I so desperately wanted, and needed, to protect her.

There was still so much I wanted to say. So much I wanted to confess. Like how my feelings were ever-changing these last few weeks, and how my heart was slowly pushing Odele away. Like how it physically hurt to watch her and Prince Kai, in a way that was inexplicable madness.

One stroke at a time.

"We should get back," I commented.

She nodded and turned. Dutifully, I followed as she led us out of the gardens and into the palace. I'd expected her to swim down the hallways that led to her rooms, but she made a series of turns that were off track. My eyebrows pulled together.

"Princess." My respectful tone fell back into place. I had to keep to decorum for appearance's sake. "Where are we going?"

She smiled over her shoulder. "To the morgue."

I stopped, blinking at her swimming back. I willed my limbs to move as I followed beside her. "Why?" The tones of lectures were in my voice, I knew. I couldn't help it. The morgue was not a place for a princess.

"I'm curious, and I know you aren't going to leave me alone—not after yesterday."

My eyes narrowed. Maisie saw right through me. It was unnerving. I didn't like it.

"Princess," I warned.

"Yes, Captain?"

I sighed. I wanted to argue, lecture, haul her back to her room. But surely the morgue wouldn't bring any harm? I would just follow her closely and keep an eye out on my surroundings, hoping there was nothing eerie hiding in the shadows.

"Why in gods' names do you want to go there?" It was an odd request. In this, she reminded me of Odele. Odd, that she was also traipsing about the palace in the most random places.

"I just realized you never gave me a proper tour of the palace, and I'd like one."

My face must have shown my confusion, unfortunately she didn't see it. "And you thought you'd start your tour with a visit to the morgue?"

She laughed, the sound a little nervous. "Where's your sense of adventure, Captain?"

I stopped mid-stroke, looking at the back of her head. Why had her words sounded like something Odele had once said to me just before she went missing?

Dread curled through my body, but I kept up with her, determined, now more than ever, to keep her safe.

Maisie

THE CAPTAIN DIRECTED ME to the morgue and didn't once protest. I could tell he was itching to know the truth about why I really wanted to go down there, and he couldn't seem to fathom any plausible excuse himself.

It was so strange to travel around the palace with him like this. Without him lecturing and judging or trying to control my every move. His earlier words had meant so much, but I still didn't let my royal facade drop. I swam with dignity and poise. It was obvious he was trying very hard not to fall into his old ways. The grumpiness. His strictness was still there in his posture, in the set of his jaw. Another thing I noticed was the way his eyes kept darting around, as if he expected a sniper to come out from every corner and barrel me down.

I couldn't fathom why he had told me those things earlier, why he had laid his feelings bare for me and hadn't once commented on what Prince Kai had said, or what had transpired between the two of us. It was just as well. I didn't need him asking questions.

He'd been nice, and he seemed bent on change—I could see it in his eyes—but I still wouldn't trust him with this truth. He'd apologized, though that didn't mean he was loyal to me. Not like Elias was loyal to me. Not like he was loyal to the Malabella bloodline.

We made it to the morgue; a very, very large room at the bottom of the palace as if it had been hollowed out in the earth and constructed with white stone. There was a large black door, wide and tall enough for a small whale to fit through.

"Wait here," I ordered the captain. I never would have ordered him about, not before. But the mask of a royal was still on. I was politer than Odele about it, though.

He tensed and, despite his earlier words, I could feel the lecture he was about to spew, but all he said was, "No."

"I need to go in alone, Captain."

"Whatever for?" His arms crossed over his chest.

I didn't have an excuse. Not now. The 'tour of the royal palace' could go only so far. I crossed my arms over my own chest, giving him a matching look of disapproval. Silence stretched out between us, and neither of us spoke, neither of us blinked.

But one of us had to give up soon.

The captain was the first to give in.

His arms uncrossed, falling to his sides. "Why?"

"I can't answer that, Captain. Can you trust me?"

There was a pause as he thought this over. He didn't want me to go in alone, and I wasn't sure if he trusted me either. Eventually, he sighed.

"Fine. But keep a distance from the mortician or anyone else. If you ever feel threatened, scream and I will barge in there to protect you."

"Okay."

He grabbed my wrist, the palm encircling my skin burning. "I mean it." More a demand than a plea, and there was soft desperation in his eyes. His jaw was working, and I could tell he was struggling. Struggling not to take control and order me around.

He was *trying.* So I would try, too.

I let out a soft breath. "I promise."

After a moment, he nodded and released me. I turned to the doorway, fighting my instinct to knock. Princesses did not knock. And they didn't open their own doors either. The captain fell into his role and opened it for me, though I noted how his eyes were glittering with amusement as my façade snapped into place. I swam inside, and he closed the door behind me.

The room was so white, it was blinding. My eyes squinted to make out shape and form. Stone slabs erected from the floor, held up with little pillars. Each slab was roughly as long as Captain Saber and as wide as the merman Val. On the walls, there was the outlining of what looked like two-legger drawers, except these were made of coral and stone.

There was a merman inside, wearing long white robes and gloves. He was bent over a stone slab, and the dead merman weighed on it.

He looked up at my entrance, dark eyes widening with surprise. "Your Majesty." He was holding a sharp, knife-like instrument in his hand. A mask and glasses covered his face, muffling his voice behind the cloth.

Dropping the instrument and pulling off his mask to reveal the face underneath—a prickly-looking thing with barbed whiskers and sharp teeth—he started forward.

"That's quite enough," I commanded before he got any closer.

He froze, then swept into a proper bow.

"Princess, I'm afraid you've caught me off guard. I was in the middle of an autopsy..."

I recognized his voice from the most recent conch I'd listened to. The one reporting the death of Queen Odette. He was a different merman from the one who had reported the deaths of Odessa and Odele's sister. His conches weren't as detailed as the other merman's had been. They'd revealed nothing.

Gaze wandering to the slab and the body there, my heart gave a lurch when I recognized who it belonged to.

It was the sniper who had nearly murdered Prince Kai.

Now a pale, dead shell, he was bare everywhere. A cruel incision had been made in his chest, the flaps of his skin pulled apart to reveal the hollowness behind ivory bone. A gaping hole ripped at his throat. Right where the arrow had struck. Right where Captain Saber had ended his life.

Revulsion should have churned my stomach. Instead, curiosity prompted me to say, "He's not a royal."

The mortician blushed. "I know, Your Majesty, but I was merely studying him from a scientific point of view. I'm sure you understand."

I leveled a cool gaze with his. "I don't."

This mer was a murderer. He'd attempted to end royal life—well, *my* life—and had harmed the Draconian Prince. For all I cared, he could have been tossed into an abysmal ditch somewhere.

The mortician sputtered. "W-well, you should know, Majesty, that there are always new things to be learned. W-with death, I mean. It's interesting to detail them."

"He was shot through the throat. What else is there to detail?"

His fingers twisted his white robes. "There's so much the post-mortem body can tell us—"

"Oh, really?" I interrupted, gliding forward, yet keeping distance between us. I swam around him, over beside the dead body of the merman who'd tried to kill me. There was no remorse, but a vicious satisfaction. "And what did my mother's body tell you?" I cocked my head slightly to the side, assuming the waters of innocence, though the inquiry was anything but. It was an accusation, brittle and brutal.

His twisted features paled. "W-what do you mean?"

My hands flicked up, and he watched the movement with curiosity and nervousness. I let my fingers hover over the dead merman.

"You're so interested in documenting this merman's death—studying him—but the conch recording of my mother's death was… Well, it was short. A disappointment, rather." I dropped my hands back to my sides and gave him a shrug. "One would think you didn't know how to do your job…"

This offended him. His face lit up with the beginnings of rage that he tried masking quickly. I was royalty, after all. He could not show his anger towards me unless he wanted to find himself kicked out of the palace and without a job.

"I have executed my duty according to Malabella Oriana standards *perfectly* well."

"Perfection is a relative term. Yet you are wrong. There were no details in my mother's death conch. The mortician before you… now *he* was perfect at his job…"

"Well, the mortician before me is dead for defying the royal family he served." There were no more niceties to his voice. I smiled at that. I hated the whole façade, playing nice. I'd rather see his true colors. "So his perfection only got him buried in the silt."

So it was true, what I'd suspected before. The merman who had recorded the conches before this one had been killed all for reporting the truth. But who would order his death?

There were only two people in the realm powerful enough to hide this sort of thing.

The queen and king.

"How did my mother die?" I asked.

"Princess, I already told you the first time…" The first time. This meant Odele had been here before. I was on the right current to the truth. "…that I'm not authorized to disclose that information to you. Besides, everything you need to know is on her death conch."

A death conch he recorded at the behest of the queen and king. A death conch that was vague, at best. A death conch filled with lies.

I swaggered around the dead body, breaking my promise to Captain Saber and moving close to him until we were face to face.

"Just answer me one last question."

"Yes, Majesty?"

"Was it sea wasp poison that killed my mother?"

His silence was answer enough.

There were two reasons that royalty would cover up a murder of their queen.

One, they'd done the murdering.

Two, they'd wanted to avoid a scandal.

I was betting on the former, but couldn't entirely discard the latter. But I couldn't help the thoughts that plagued me as I left the morgue behind with Captain Saber. Who could've done it, hidden this truth for years? Who could have murdered them? Why? Who had the most to gain with all of these deaths?

Had Princess Odessa married Xristo like the contract ordered, she would have inherited the Malabella throne. With her death, it had landed in the lap of the late Queen Odette. Odele was her heir, and her marriage to Kai would gain her ascension to the crown. Yet she was missing. Off finding a royal, Odessa's first born, when there was no way in the abyss that a bastard could ever inherit the throne.

The answers were pretty clear to me.

"What are you thinking?" Captain Saber's baritone interrupted my thoughts.

I shrugged. Maybe if I told the captain, I'd very well gain another ally. He was loyal to Odele, and if he knew why she'd left, perhaps he could bring himself to forgive her for leaving in the first place. Maybe he would understand. The captain had connections, his insight could help push this investigation along quickly.

And the sooner it ended…

…the sooner I'd leave.

"Nothing," I answered casually.

I could feel the narrowing of his eyes on me, ignoring it as I rounded the hallway.

"Hmm." He lapsed into silence, not pushing or forcing it. I supposed that was what I liked the most about the captain. He didn't force anything, yet his silence was somehow forceful, discerning, a slow thing that tried to pry the truth from me with the mere essence of it.

"I think I'll retire to my rooms now." I had things to do, still. Change. Speak with Prince Kai. Continue my investigation. "Thanks for stalking—I mean, accompanying—me." Jokingly, I nudged him with my elbow.

The side of the captain's lip twitched. The closest thing to a smile I'd get from him.

"Sorry to bring you the bad news, but you can't retire just yet."

My skin prickled. "And why not?"

In a surprising moment, he nudged his elbow into my side as well. It was so brief, the touch so light, I thought I'd imagined it. "You heard what they said in the meeting. There's to be a ball."

"So?"

"So, I'm familiar enough with the routine that I know I am to escort you to your rooms for a dress fitting, and then you will be required to look over the menu with the queen, as well as look over the guest list."

I almost tripped on my fins and blanched. Luckily, the only sound to come out of me was a soft one of disbelief. "I'm not even the real—" I cut off abruptly, looking around. Other than the occasional servant, the halls were relatively empty. "Why would I have to go through that?"

He didn't comment or chastise my error. "It is customary."

Right. And I was sure that if a royal mer were to swim around wearing two-legger clothes, it'd be deemed customary eventually.

"Don't fret," the captain reassured. "I will be there to guard you."

"I'm not worried about death threats, Captain. In fact, I'd much rather face them than a seamstress."

"Oh, be sure that the seamstress is a vicious mer. I've seen many mer felled by her cunning. Which is why my presence shall be your shield against her."

I groaned. "You're lousy at making someone feel better. You know that, right?"

"I've been told…"

Instead of escorting me to my chambers, where I'd been desperate to relax before I continued my investigation, he escorted me there for dress fittings. The seamstress barged in moments after we arrived. Her prompt timing made me wonder if we'd been watched and someone had informed her the second we were back. She was a rotund, proficient mer, who quickly rang for afternoon tea and got to work on me.

After making me discard my clothing, I was forced to float there in nothing but my shift, a sheer material that pressed against every pane of my body. The captain had promptly turned around when I'd started to undress. When the knock at the door came for tea, he propped open the door a moment, grabbed the tray, and brought it in, all while blindly averting his eyes to my form.

The seamstress took a small cake molded like a starfish and began munching on it. I floated with my arms out. The position was starting to cramp my fin.

"Can we get this over with?" I grumbled.

The mer shot me a withering look that was even more frightening than the queen's glare. "Suffering gods, we've only just begun, Odele, and you're already whining."

I blinked at the informality in her tone. No one had ever spoken to me that way. After the initial shock, it was refreshing and made me smile.

"Now," she said between bites, dusting crumbs from her ample chest. "What color gown are you thinking?"

"Uh… pink?" It was a color that Odele had in her closet in abundance.

The seamstress dusted the final remnants of her snack off and circled me like a shark going in for its prey. She snorted. "No. What do you want to do, blend in with the walls? It's your engagement ball. You must outshine even the queen herself."

Bold words that, if heard, would be taken like a knife to the gut by Queen Circe. As if the seamstress had knocked the crown from the queen's head herself and left her in disgrace.

Good thing there were no servants present who could take this conversation back to her. Well, save for Captain Saber, who didn't look inclined at all to go about and gossip.

"I'm thinking…" The rotund mer put her hand in her chin as she surveyed me. One would think she'd never surveyed Odele before. If we looked alike, as everyone thought, it should have been no problem to pick out a color fabric and be done with it. "Blue. Ice blue. What do you think, Captain?"

Captain Saber's back was too us, his hands clasped together. I could not see his face, but there was the slightest hint of amusement in his voice when he answered. "It does not matter what the princess wears; she will be stunning."

I couldn't help but blink, not sure if what he was saying had been sarcasm or truth. Of course, it may not have been me he was speaking of, but the real mer I represented. And I didn't know why the smallest part of me had flared with hope that I'd been the one he was talking about.

"Fish-fosh, Captain," she grunted, finally moving forward with her long strip of kelp tape to take the measurements of my shoulders. Efficient fingers spread the strip from one end to the other. "The only reason I keep you in here is because you know how to flatter a lady."

"I can hardly contain myself when I am surrounded by such exuberant charm and beauty."

I blinked. Who *was* this merman and what had he done to Captain Saber? The captain was acting charming, and he never acted charming. He was strict, and quiet, and rigid. He didn't make jokes or charm old mermaids with compliments.

"Oh, stop it," she flirted back at him with equal charm as she moved to the front of me, measuring the length of each arm. She looked at the numbers, a crease forming between her brows. "You've grown a few inches, Princess," she commented offhandedly.

My body stiffened involuntarily. It needn't have, because she resumed her task with quick fingers and flickering movements. There'd been no seed of suspicion in her voice at all. That didn't calm the thumping of my heart. Not until I saw Captain Saber turn slightly from the doorway and give me an encouraging nod.

That small act of faith warmed me, as well as calmed me. I nodded back and he smiled, a slight twitch of his lips. The action surprised me so much, that too late, I realized what the seamstress was up to as she slowly started hiking the shift over my tail.

I jerked back. "W-what are you doing?" I clutched at the clothes.

She rolled her eyes. "Really, Odele, now is not the time to get squeamish. I have to measure your tail and your waist."

If she did that, my secret would be exposed. She would catch glimpse of my torn fin and know.

"No."

She scoffed. "Don't be silly." The mer made a dive for the hem of the shift, which I dodged by swimming a bit to the side, panicking.

"You already know my measurements," I said tersely. "Go by those."

Her eyes rolled again. "You've grown, so your old measurements will do no good. You got sick and lost too much weight." Her tongue clucked with disapproval. "All skin and bones now…"

"I think it's been a long day for Princess Odele," the captain cut in. He was turned fully now, facing us, but averting his eyes appropriately from my figure. They were set entirely on her. "You're smart enough to calculate the size of her hips based on the size of her arms, I'm sure." He winked and she beamed.

"Well, yes, I can, but—"

"See? No problem. Have a cake and I shall escort you out, Madame."

Blushing, the seamstress packed up her belongings, swindled a plate of cakes and let Captain Saber swim her from the room, flattering her the whole way.

With the door securely closed and locked behind her, he turned back to me, eyes set on mine, not daring to travel further down.

My body was on display, yet the only thing embarrassing about it was the fin flapping viciously at my side. The seamstress hadn't looked at me closely; how could she, when he'd been charming her ears off? But the dress was see-through, and the fins were surely on display.

Don't look. Don't look. Don't look.

His eyes didn't once stray from my face. Belatedly, I reacted, wondering if it was gratitude he sought.

"Thank you," I whispered.

He nodded and started forward. I watched his slow movements as he came to the edge of Odele's bed, looking down at it like some foreign, forbidden thing. Indecision warred his features before he finally decided to take a seat. He patted the side next to him. An invitation. A breach of propriety that no doubt cost him.

I gladly sat next to him. A modicum of space loomed between us that had much more to do with the unspoken words than the distance.

I knew he was itching to ask.

Don't ask.

Just ask and get it out of the way.

Don't.

Do.

"When I finished my training," he started slowly, surprising me, "I was sent to the front lines in the war." His words ensnared me, a horrific melody that sang of loss and sadness. "I'm sure you've heard stories about the first few years of the war with Kappur. My father was a fin soldier at the palace, so he told me the stories. There wasn't outright fighting, not at first. War can begin in the most subtlest of ways… A cease in trade. Pulling ambassadors from kingdoms. Insulting each other publicly…" He let out a bitter laugh. "It lasted for so long. My father said he thought it would never move past what it was. But then it did…

"I was positioned at the front; it was the third battle, and one of the most brutal." His fingers went to the immaculate jacket he wore, touching the edges of the starfish adorning the lapels. "I won the rank of captain for my valiancy in the war. Because I saved lives, because I plotted the victorious battle when our captain died on the battlefield." Slowly, he began undoing the pearl buttons of his jacket. One by one, they slipped from their loops and opened to reveal the white, spotless tunic underneath. He pulled the jacket from his arms, and then the buttons on his tunic followed.

The panes of his chest looked golden-kissed, like skin favored by the rays of sun, captured by his body. I stared, heart thumping, water stilling in my gills.

"A Kappurin soldier put up a fight. I'd watched him tear through my friends." He spoke the words with cold detachment, like he was pulling himself from the memories that haunted his soul. "When he got to me, I put up a fight, and I earned *this*." He pulled down the material of his tunic and I saw it. The jagged scar on his hip, made by the blade of Kappurin soldier. It was a glimpse, a brief flash before he covered himself again, quickly buttoning everything up and shrugging his jacket back on. "We all have scars, Maisie." He turned to me. "I know you don't agree with my decisions, my opinions on this war. You don't have to. But I just want you to know…" His hand reached out to grasp mine, in a gesture that was all comforting. "Our scars are not a weakness, and they are not ugly. I—I'm sorry if I made you feel that way."

The fin on the left side of my tail flared with heat, a burning that spread throughout the entirety of my body, settling just in the center of my chest. Sensations inside me bloomed to impossible depths of darkness, making me lose sight of myself in the shadows.

Pain and embarrassment were nothing anymore. My greatest shame was torn away with the passing of the current of his words. He'd shared a piece of himself. Another one in a single day. It only seemed fitting that I gave him a piece of myself. A piece I'd shared with no one but the Black Blade.

My story was easier to tell when I thought the words would weigh in the back of my throat like an anchor falling to sand. They rolled off, quickly, easily. The same detached voice that the captain used, I mustered in my own recounts of the tale. Of the story that, in the span of a few exchanged words between him and I, lessened the shame I'd carried with me the entirety of my life.

By the time I finished, it had dissipated.

The captain did not release his hold on my hand.

"What was his name?" he inquired coolly, in the same tones of murder that Elias had used when I'd told him.

"It doesn't matter."

"Maisie." His voice was halting. A command straight from a captain, a superior. And surprisingly, a friend. "Tell me."

My lips formed the name I'd fought hard not to say since the accident had happened. Since the merboy I'd had a crush on tricked me, lured me into gator grounds and abandoned me to a fate of pain and blood.

"Gilbert Eaton."

His grip eased, and he rubbed his thumb across the skin of my hand. I watched the movement with nothing short of fascination. This was the closest the two of us had ever been. The closest we'd likely ever be. I relished in the moment, knowing it would not last.

"Promise me something, Maisie."

Promises were sacred things, things that shouldn't be thrown around like grains of sand. They were to be dispersed in small amounts, and to few who deserved them.

Yet I nodded. "Sure."

"Please do not leave the palace without an escort, and do not wander around the halls either. Promise me. Let me protect you."

It was a promise I could keep only in halves. So, for the part I could keep, I nodded.

"I have things I must see to. Guards will be posted at your doors, and I will be back later."

I loathed to see him go. Something about our shared moments had eased an ache inside me, an ache I hadn't even known was there. Captain Saber was as grounding as an anchor, yet in no way did he make me feel chained. Not after today. Perhaps not ever again.

He got up, hand pulling from mine, and he gave me a bow. As if I was truly royalty. Then he left.

And all I could do was ponder at this new side of the captain, and hope it wasn't as fickle or as dangerous as the sea.

Tiberius

The name echoed inside my mind, but it gave me focus.

With the same cold efficiency I always possessed, I ordered about my soldiers, posting my most trusted at her doors, knowing they would not abandon their post and they would inform me of every coming and going.

I had other things to do.

It was a quick swim down to the stables, to saddle my hippocampus and to ride away from the palace. I'd be only a moment, just a few hours, maybe even less. Geronimo, my faithful hippocampus, thundered through the waters of Eramaea, swift fins gliding behind us in powerful strokes.

The mer bowed as we passed, as if we were of the same royal stuff the queen and king were made of.

We weren't.

I wasn't.

I was a merman from Eramaea. The oldest of five, with a soldier for a father and a humble stay-at-home mother. We came from an average background, not poor or rich. We'd made enough just to get by.

I'd followed in my father's fin strokes. Painted images of the heroism of war were embedded deeply into my history, my soul, and beneath the outer layers, there was fear and death. Stories my father told me melded together. The lines in the sand separating heroism and death weren't drawn. It was a conjoining of the two. It was trauma and loss, blood and pain, victory and friendship.

I never thought anyone could understand the depth of my scars. Maisie did. Her scars were like mine. We weren't similar, and we hadn't been through the same hardships, but they were hardships just the same. Scars had a funny way of bringing mer together, and mine had given me a piece of Maisie, a piece I'd never known I'd wanted.

I steered Geronimo through the streets until I found the building I was looking for. I passed pillars of quartz and marbles, erected proudly, shaded with ceilings engraved with symbols of the kingdom. The ornate double doors were wide open, and mermen and mermaids swam in and out of the building, some dressed casually in tunics, others decked out in military jackets.

I jerked Geronimo to a halt and hopped from his back, tugging tightly at his reins. A young soldier, obviously around fifteen, came to me to take care of my mount. I handed him over with a word of warning before I swam inside.

The place, as always, was immaculate. Pictures aligned against the walls of generals, captains, and royalty in high ranks. Medals and maps, statues from shipwrecks and from six of the seven sea kingdoms—obviously, not Kappur's. There were even things from beyond, from far out west of the globe. To the continent beyond the waters of Draconi where savages dwelled and roamed, uncharted waters filled with mer and creatures of all types and races unknown.

Desks were arranged across the floors. Behind them sat mer in military jackets, writing on kelp parchments and speaking their recordings into conches.

I swam up to one of the desks and to one of the secretaries sitting behind there. Every secretary, groomsmer, and janitor in this place was a select. Not all of them were sent directly to war. That was one of the parts of Selection that Maisie didn't know about. There were two rounds of it. They were chosen for training, and then after training, they were once again selected for a different job here in the capital or on the front lines of war. Some were chosen as spies, others as guards, or even—to my own horror—*secretaries*. Nothing was wrong with them, of course. But I couldn't imagine living my life behind a desk. I'd hate the feeling of being caged.

"Good afternoon," I greeted.

The secretary looked up, gaze going for the lapels at my jacket there, taking in the stars of my rank. Immediately, she shot up and saluted. "Morning, Captain."

"At ease."

She slowly lowered herself back into the chair. "Is there something I can help you with, Captain?"

Two words fell effortlessly from my tongue, with enough command for her to know what I wanted her to do. Who I wanted her to find.

"Gilbert Eaton."

WHEN CAPTAIN SABER LEFT, I allowed myself to stare at the spot he'd vacated a mere two minutes before I got up and dressed. We'd had an entire conversation while I wore nothing but the thin shift, and his eyes had not strayed once. My face heated a bit, thinking about it now. But even more baffling was the piece of him he'd dared to share with me.

He was right. We didn't agree on things, and I understood why. He'd grown up in a family of soldiers, with a mer who'd decided that there was glory in fighting, and had followed in those fin strokes. He'd seen war and still bore the scars of it.

I didn't agree with war or violence, but I understood. Understood that he fought to protect the home he loved, and the mer in it. Our goals were the same, even if we had different ways of going about it.

I grabbed the timeline I'd hidden and made my way into the cove. It was echoing emptiness, though I'd expected nothing less. Something about the darkness of this place helped me think. Maybe it was the secrets it held, or something else entirely. In here, I was closer to the princess than I felt out there in a palace of fine jewels and servants. Here, there was raw honesty. There were words and images hidden behind recordings, layers I hadn't yet peeled back fully.

It was a frustrating process. I picked up a conch and placed it on the recording, then sat down as the bubbles emerged and her image became a clear, silvery sheen before me.

And so, for the next few hours, I sat and watched Princess Odele's life unfold.

Tadpole, tadpole, tadpole, tadpole!

Princess Odele was the biggest tadpole I'd ever known, and we hadn't even met.

Why had I thought that she was capable of intelligence, of placing secrets here in her cove? Of giving me even the slightest of hints as to where she had gone, or what she had learned?

Frustration swelled inside me. I didn't have *time* for these games of hers. I didn't have time to comb through every single shell, some lasting hours of nothing but the latest court gossip. Raging, I grabbed the conch shell, prying it from the recording, and turned to chuck it across the cavern. It hit the wall and shattered, broken bits of shell raining down through the water.

"Stupid princess," I yelled unkindly, grabbing another shell and throwing it with all the strength my arm could muster. It shattered.

And again, I picked another conch up, a series of the ones I'd watched, the ones I'd tortured myself with hours and hours down in the loneliness of this place. I threw, and they shattered.

Again, and again, and again.

I tossed the proof of her life into scattered pieces around me, letting shards swirl down and slide across my exposed skin. I didn't care. I thought I was close to the truth, that I was following the right tracks. But there was nothing in here.

Nothing.

My fingers scraped across the ground as I bent to pick another one to toss, to let my anger breathe the scents of violence and destruction. When I brought the shell up, I noticed that this one was different from all the rest. The others had numbers etched on the sides in small indentations. What caught my attention about this one was the emboldened black.

My thumb rubbed across the sigil there, not numbers, but twin black blades criss-crossing. A symbol I'd come to recognize like a second beating of a heart.

The symbol of the Black Blade.

What was it doing here on a conch belonging to the princess? Hidden beneath a pile of her lavish life?

I darted over to the recorder and placed it in the center then swam back as it started.

"I discovered something today." I'd grown so accustomed to seeing Odele in nearly all sorts of states. So I knew that this one, the one on *this* recording was genuine. The worry, the breathlessness. The wide, fearful eyes. "Something that could get me killed." Her eyes darted a little distractedly to her surroundings. Was someone in the room with her? Was she worried someone would swim in on her recording? I could make out the background of her bedroom behind her. "I can't say what I found, because if this recording falls into the wrong hands…" She broke off, swallowed. "But there's still more to be discovered. Things I can't find on my own. But I know someone who can help." I slowly sank into the couch, grasping onto every word. "A servant told me about him. She said if anyone had the answers, it would be him. So tonight, I'm going to find him. Tonight, I'm going to pay a visit to the Black Blade."

Rushing white noise thundered in my ears as the recording died, bubbles popping, and the spinning of the recorder settling into a stillness that I felt through the entirety of my body.

The Black Blade. The Black Blade. The Black Blade.

Princess Odele had gone in search of Elias Blackfin. Had she found him? No, she couldn't possibly have found the Black Blade. He would have mentioned that fact to me. Right? If the princess had gone to look for him, if she'd met with him, Elias would have said something to me. He wouldn't have lied or kept such an integral truth from me…

I had to find him.

He'd told me not to look for him, that one day we would see each other again. But when? Time was thinning. There was going to be an engagement ball, and the queen had said that they would announce an earlier date for the wedding with Prince Kai. I had to figure this stuff out. I had to find her before it was announced. Before the wedding actually came.

Things needed to fall back into place.

I strapped on the blade of Elias' making and donned on a dark cloak before I ventured out into the night. The stone doorway scraped closed behind me as I was swallowed by the shadows of Eramaean streets. Night befell quickly in the salt waters of the city, and phytoplankton glowed and floated around me like tiny sparks of stars.

Caution would be my only friend as I swam through the city. The shadows cloaked me. Under the cover of darkness, I dodged guards and street merchants, couples strolling and carriages being pulled by hippocampi. I was unfamiliar with the streets and took a couple of wrong turns until I finally recognized the direction I was headed. This was the poorer parts of Eramaea, the place with escaped selects and shabby houses.

Guards were here when they hadn't been there last time, patrolling the area. I had to backtrack and find a way around the small area that was separated from the rest of the city. It looked like a small village, ominous in the dark of the night waters.

I swam past the backs of houses, knocking on doors. The first to answer was an old mermaid, confused as to why someone was knocking at the back door to her home at such an hour. I made sure to keep my face hidden in the shadows of my hood as I asked, "Do you know where I can find Elias? Elias Blackfin?"

I could practically hear the tension coiling tightly through her body. I knew what she'd say before the words were even out of her mouth.

"I don't know who you mean." And slammed the door in my face.

And so my night went.

House after house, the same question, the same answer and detached rejection. Eventually, I stopped waiting to hear them tell me they didn't know who he was. The look in their eyes was answer enough, and I swam away before even giving them the chance to reply.

I reached the last house on the edge of the community. When the owner had promptly slammed the door against my face, I sighed and turned slowly. I had no choice but to make my way back to the palace. Back to the cavern of so many questions and too little answers. Back to the façade that was now my life. Back to it all.

I started forward, distracted when I probably shouldn't have been. Maybe if I'd been paying attention, I would have noticed the shadowy figures before they were upon me.

Three of them spanned out to give me less room to swim by, or at least enough space between us so that they could grab me if I swam near. Their faces were unfamiliar, though I didn't care to know them. I just wanted to swim past. My hand went to the hilt at my waist, but I didn't unsheathe the blade. Not quite yet. Not until I'd assessed the threat.

"Evening," one of the mer called out.

Features were blind to me in the dark, but I could make out the gleam of bright eyes, tough barbs spiking out against thin upper lip, and rows of sharp teeth.

I did not reply.

"We hear you're looking for Elias Blackfin," another one added, body shifting closer.

They weren't as elegant as the shadows that moved and swarmed, yet there was a prowess in these three that was dangerous.

This time, I found my voice, glad when it did not quiver. "I am."

I could make out the gleam of sharp teeth as one of them sneered. "We can take you to him."

Liars.

"Can you?" I asked, voice steady, as I cocked my head to the side. The grip on the hilt only became tighter. If I unsheathed it now, they would undoubtedly attack. I had to play this safe, and pray that my ten minute lesson on defense with Prince Kai would be enough to get me through this.

My future looked bleak.

"'Course we can, little one. He's a friend of ours. We'd be happy to take ya'."

"That'd be so kind of you." I angled my body, moving casually away from them, towards where there was the most space between them and the exit. If I made a speedy retreat and kept further to the side, maybe they wouldn't be able to grab me.

I took small, even strokes to the left. Their eyes were keen, and their bodies shifted that way too. It looked like I'd have no choice.

I pulled out the black blade and brandished it in front of me unwaveringly.

"The problem is..." I slowly swam to the right. "... I don't believe you."

I made a dash to the side and swam straight, as fast as my torn fin could carry me. I was a breath away from them, and their fingers grazed against me, tugging at my clothes. I turned, viciously bringing the blade down. It struck, and a painful scream filled my ear, quickly cut off by panting, angry breathing.

"You bi—"

I swung the blade before my assailant could get the rest of the word out.

They were on me at once, the three of them dodging my vicious, unrelenting swinging. I was pulled against a body, and before I could scream or cry out, a hand clamped over my mouth. Panic burst in my chest, and I bucked against them. Pain exploded in my wrist, causing the blade to fall from my trembling fingers.

"We got a feisty one," one of the mermen commented, his fingers going to my throat.

I thrashed, feeling the hood slip from my head.

There was a moment of silence as they took me in. And then, "You're the Princess of Thalassar."

I closed my eyes, praying to the gods that that knowledge would be enough for them to let me go.

"I ain't never met royalty before." There was a yank on my cloak, the material tore. "How much you think she's worth?"

No!

I thrashed and bucked, but the grip around me, behind me, was vice. As vicious and painful as the gator who had shredded my limb all those years ago.

My mind went back to that date, pulling the memories to the front until that moment and this one overlapped in vicious panic. My heart thundered, and all I could think of was that I was going to die here, that they would kill me, all because of who I was.

No.

I was not a victim. I wouldn't be prisoner to the same terrors.

"If a gator gets you again, don't fight it, because you won't win. It'll be hard, but you gotta relax your body. Let it think it has you and that you won't fight back. When you do that, it will slacken its hold. Once it does, catch it by surprise and swim for your life."

Josiah's words, straight after those days I'd been lying near comatose in his home, echoed in my mind. A bit of advice, in case I ever found myself in the same predicament.

I'd vowed I never would.

My body went limp, even as my limbs threatened to shake.

"No more fight, eh?" More tugging at my clothes.

I closed my eyes, unwilling to watch what atrocities they wanted to commit. All I could do was focus. When my captor felt I would no longer fight back—for no doubt, he must have thought he had an advantage over me—I'd be the most formidable thing he'd ever seen.

And I'd make him regret ever crossing me.

As soon as his hold loosened, I threw my head back, hearing the satisfying crunch of his nose against the back of my head. My tail shot forward, thumping against the mer in front of me. The surprise of my sudden violent gestures had them doubling over, gasping. That left the third one. I side stroked them, just as the third merman's hands came for me. They clamped on my wrist, and I opened my mouth to scream.

To hell with them, their safety. To hell with the fact that I was a princess—or supposed to be—and was out of the palace at this hour. The guards would come swimming the minute I let out a shriek, and when they did…

My plan was cut off by the sudden banging open of a door, and a brittle voice in the night.

"Get yer hands off her right now."

A brute command that was obeyed immediately. The merman took a few strokes away from me, looking behind me at the merman who had interrupted their nefarious plan.

"If you know what's good for ya, get! There are soldiers swarmin' everywhere lookin' for a reason to shoot. You know better."

They sputtered, and after sharing a glance between the three, they darted away.

Finally gone, I allowed a shuddering breath to escape my lips. Once it did, I turned slowly and faced the merman who had saved me from those criminals.

He was old and bent, and that was all I saw beneath the light illuminative glow of the jelly globe held in his hand.

His eyes squinted, then widened as they took in my hair, my face. "You're the Princess of Thalassar," he gasped.

Before he could say anything else, I spun and swam away from him. Away from this cursed part of the city, and back to the comforts of just another prison. The palace I now called home.

I yanked the tattered remnants of my cloak from my shoulders, tossing it to the ground with a furious yell. My hands shook, not from fear, but from a kaleidoscope of emotions coalescing inside me. Anger. Indignation. And courage. So much courage.

I stripped down to nothing but my shift. The sword was shoved into a corner of the room, placed carefully there even when all I'd wanted to do was toss it and rage, wishing it was Elias instead. If only so I could hold the blade to his throat and demand the answers I so desperately wanted.

A soft knock at the door tore me from the viciousness of my thoughts.

Calming my breathing first, I took a few slow strokes towards the door, opening it to reveal none other than Prince Kai on the other side.

Beautiful, in flowing robes obviously meant for sleep, his brown eyes took me in, roaming over every inch of my body, until they finally came to settle on my suddenly flaming face. Behind him, my guards—Captain Saber's mermen—were eyeing him warily.

"Princess." His voice was smooth in the dark. "May I speak with you?"

The guards behind him shuffled uncomfortably, like they should say something but didn't dare bring themselves to do so. We were royalty, and they had no right to say anything to us, yet the situation made them uncomfortable. This was improper. Not just because of the hour, but because of our state of dress. Nightclothes. This was an intimacy reserved for after marriage.

I supposed we'd already breached the wall of propriety. What was one more mistake among many?

"Of course," I answered, surprised to find my voice husky.

He gave a pointed look beyond my shoulder, to the room behind me. Right. I pushed the door open, knowing that the light blue light inside illuminated me in a soft limelight, and no doubt every curve pressed against the shift.

The guards turned their heads to the side.

Prince Kai pushed his way inside, closing the door behind him to give us privacy.

"Come in." I made sure he followed me deeper into the room before I sat down on the bed. He sank into the spot next to me. Beneath us, the anemones caressed our scales, tugging our tails closer together. "Is there something you need, Prince?"

"Back to formalities, then?" His eyes shone in the darkness, flashing blue for a split second.

My gulp was audible, as I became aware of how close he was to me. Of the heat of his body radiating onto mine. There was no fever in his eyes.

No sign of dragon blood coursing through him, riding his actions like they had that night.

Maybe having him that way would have been easier. If it was the dragon controlling what he did, it would have been easier to fall into his arms. I could give in to my own weakness for a moment and forget about this talk he wanted to have. His boldness in that state was contagious. He filled me with courage and desire in equal measure. He could make me give in, but I knew I'd regret it afterwards. I'd regret it because then he would look at me like he was looking at me now.

Having him like this, without the dragon at the forefront of his mind, was different. The raw honesty in his eyes, the expectation, the *love.* It all reminded me of why we could not be, and that I was nothing more than a liar. I was deceiving him. I was pretending to be something I was not and if he ever discovered the truth, he would hate me.

I couldn't bear his hatred.

"Is there something you need, Kai?"

His eyes seemed to sparkle while his mouth twisted up into a smile. "I wanted to see you, to apologize."

I blinked. "Apologize?"

"I came off as too strong earlier, in the hallway, and I placed our secret—what happened between us—in jeopardy. And my confession…"

His confession. It had been everything I'd ever desired to hear, but not from him. We were leagues apart, and he didn't even know it. He didn't know that he'd lain with a waitress, not a princess.

"We don't have to talk about that." I bit my bottom lip nervously.

"We do," he argued passionately. "Princess, do you regret what happened between us?"

I tried summoning that emotion. Regret. The only regret I had was lying to him about who I was. As for what we'd shared? I would never regret that. For as long as I lived, I would cherish it. Slowly, I shook my head. "There are many things in my life I regret, yet what happened between us is not one of them."

He took my hand, squeezing it to his warmth. "I know," he began almost reluctantly, "that arranged marriages rarely bring love…"

"Can we not talk about love?" My voice was tight in my throat.

His expression fell. "So it is true. You do not love me."

Not a question, but I felt myself answering just the same. "Why is it so important?" A foolish counter, even to my own ears. Who didn't want to be loved? It was just one of those things that a mer craved with every fiber in their body. To make them feel a little less alone.

"Because I would prefer to have the mer I marry to love me as much as I love her."

My heart pounded, twisted in my chest. Love. I could not deny that what was between us was strong, a sentiment even I could not describe. Was this love? This heart pounding, hand shaking warmth? Was it the desire to touch him, to run my fingers through the length of his hair? To share whispers in the current and caresses in the sand?

I love you.

The words were caught in my throat.

Could it be true love if I was lying to him about who I was? The feeling, would it vanish from him entirely if he knew?

I squeezed his hand, and he squeezed back. The simplicity and the steadiness in the gesture gave me strength. "There are… things… I cannot tell you yet, Kai," I confessed. "Royal secrets that you cannot yet know."

His gaze was piercing, vicious, in a way that almost made me falter. Like his silence intended to probe for secrets, rip them out of me with just a look.

"Can you trust me?" More a plea than a question.

Still, the look faded from his eyes into one of warmth, and he nodded. "I trust you."

The ease with which he placed his trust in my hands… I could only hope I didn't shatter it before his eyes.

"There are things I want to tell you, but it's not the right time to do it. I will. Eventually, I think I will." I could make no promises, fearing that if

I did, and broke them, he would never forgive me for it. I'd never forgive myself. "But trust that there are things that I can't talk about right now."

Slowly, his hand went up to cup my face, thumb trailing light circles across the curve of my cheek. The quiet in his features assessed my own. I wondered what he saw in me.

He smiled. "I trust you, my gem. With my heart and with my soul." And then he kissed me.

A soft brush of his lips against mine. A heat ignited within me at the touch, causing my body to curve into his. When had we gotten so close? He tugged me closer, an arm snaking around my waist to pull me atop him. Our bodies moved, angled so that there was no inch of space between us.

My mouth slanted over his in this position. His mouth opened for me, for my explorations. I took the lead this time. This time there was no dragon, no fever, no sickness or threat of death. It was just us, raw and aching.

The breath of his fingers trailed over my body, pushing down the straps of my shift from my shoulders. My own hands went to his robes, pushing aside the lapels so it slipped from his body. My nails curved against his skin, traveling from the panes of his chest to his shoulders, curving to his back.

He was smooth everywhere, soft as royals were. But when my fingers met his shoulder blades, I noticed the skin there was raised in a pattern that was familiar to me.

Tearing my mouth from his, my gaze found Kai's. He did not look at me with shame as my fingers dared to explore more, sliding down bumps and ridges that should not be there, where smoothness should be.

Ever-growing horror filled me, and angry protectiveness must have shown in my eyes. Prince Kai cupped my cheeks and pressed the tip of his nose against my own.

"What happened?" My voice was a hoarse whisper.

His answering smile was heartbreaking. "My father."

The Emperor of Draconi had done this? Had given him this latticework of scars along his back? His own father had inflicted this pain?

"Don't fret, my gem." He pushed aside a stray strand of hair I hadn't known was there. "It doesn't hurt. My father said it would make me stronger." His hands slid down my face, to the front of me so he could reach for my hands and finger the backs of my knuckles. There were no scars there, but he touched them tenderly as if there were, as if only he could see them. "Do you think less of me now?" Somehow, when he said that part, he couldn't meet my gaze.

My fin throbbed in response. Scars spiderwebbed at the roots of them, trailing against hardened scales. Captain Saber and I weren't the only ones with scars, however hidden they may be. We all bore pain. Some pain was invisible and others lived on our skin. Hidden, but there. A constant reminder what it meant to survive.

I kissed him, slowly and thoroughly. When I pulled away, my head was spinning. "We all carry scars," I echoed the captain's earlier words. "They do not make us weak."

And because he'd shared this bit of himself with me, it was high time I gave him something, some bit of my own truth. I got up from his lap, taking a stroke back. It was dark, but not dark enough that my form couldn't be seen. That *this* couldn't be seen.

I let the dress fall from my skin, flicking it off of my tail. There I floated. Naked. Exposed. My fins flapping at my sides, and that was what he took in first. Not my breasts, not lower, to the evidence of my arousal, my want, but to my fins.

To my scars.

His eyes widened. Not something he'd been expecting from me. The *princess.*

He was silent, spoke nothing. He just took in the fin, one and then the other. The holes on one side, the shredded tips. Finally, he looked up at me, and his eyes were beginning to glow with the hint of power and danger.

"They do not make us weak, my gem." He opened his arms, an invitation. One I took, slowly gliding into his arms. He wrapped them around me, encircling my waist. "You are no less beautiful because of them." He didn't ask me how I got them. If he had, I probably would have broken, told him the truth. He just pressed his hot lips against my neck, and then his tongue.

Open mouthed kisses went along my skin. Down a pathway he invented. The base of my throat, my collarbone, the swells of my breasts…

When his tongue touched my nipple, I nearly came undone. Crying out, I arched into him as his mouth encircled it. Long fingers pressed against my body. Arms, waist, stomach. I leaned into him, my own hands trembling, but eventually pushing away his robe to bare him.

My breath came out in ragged pants. I wanted more. More of him. More of this.

But Prince Kai pulled himself away somehow, and our foreheads touched. He sighed. "This isn't what I came here for."

My eyebrows rose. "No?"

He smiled and ran his fingers down my arm. "As lovely as this is, no. I—" He cleared his throat. "I do not want to risk your reputation any more than I have already. I want to do this right."

My throat constricted. "But—"

"We have time, my gem. We have our whole lives."

If there was one thing we didn't have, it was time. Not when someone was actively trying to murder me. Not while I was actively looking for the real princess. Not when they would never let a poor waitress from Lagoona truly marry the Prince of Draconi.

No, Prince Kai, I refrained from saying, *if there is one thing we do not have, it is time.*

I COULD READ THE sadness in her eyes the moment my lips formed those words. If only she knew that this abstinence was as much a punishment for me as it was for her. But I would wait. For her, I'd wait. Marriage came first, the rest later.

She had not said so but I knew from the look in her eyes, from the fervent way in which she touched my body, that perhaps she loved me too. Words weren't a necessity, not when her actions were so much louder. Not when her expression said so much more.

I pressed a kiss to the skin by her collarbone, having the satisfaction of feeling her shiver, her body lean into mine a fraction.

"I love you," I whispered against her flesh.

Her body melted against me. I smiled.

Yes, words weren't necessary at all when her body screamed the truth that words couldn't.

"Goodnight, Prince Kai."

Her eyes twinkled with the lights of mischief, a double meaning seemed to lace her words. Goodnight, indeed. I smirked, bringing up a tendril of hair between my thumb and forefinger. Twirling and twirling, I did not break her gaze.

Heat flared between us, like a living thing that pulsed and pulled, drawing us together in the light of the blaze. My resolve melted like the molten core of lava. Honorable, that's what I was trying to be. But what did it even matter? We were engaged, and though I had been dead set on following her kingdom's traditions and her rules on propriety to the letter, I could not bring myself to want that, with as much as my kindling need for her was.

We'd already broken the rules, anyway.

My fingers dropped her strands of hair and pressed to her bare shoulder, sliding down… down…

I leaned down to her height, smirking against her cheek. "Tonight, leave your door unlocked." When I pulled away, her face had heated, and she was staring at me with something akin to desire in her eyes.

A feral smile pulled at my lips. The hint and promise of the dragon, and all the passion and the depths he—we—would take her to.

"Goodnight, Dragon Prince." Her answering smile was confirmation enough.

As long as no one saw me slip in and out, I would come to her.

Tonight, I would hold my mate in my arms, and maybe, just maybe, she'd finally find the courage to say the words I longed to hear.

Elias

THEY WERE IN A tavern drinking. The bastards were oblivious to my presence as they tossed back tankard and tankard of frothy sea ale. I watched them cackling from the shadows and I heard their whispered words as they leaned towards each other and spoke. Of the Princess of Thalassar. What a shame the old merman chased them off before they'd gotten a taste.

Foolish mer.

Didn't they know that she belonged to me? I may have left her without a word, and maybe I hadn't seen her since she'd shared a part of herself with me that she hadn't shared with others. But that didn't mean she'd stopped being mine.

And no one touched the Black Blade's property.

So I waited patiently until they stumbled out of the tavern on drunken fins. Waiting served my purpose. It made my anger rise. It was beneath the surface of my skin. So when I moved, I became night. I became shadow.

I became death.

They didn't know what hit them. They didn't know whose fists connected to their jaws and bodies. All they knew was pain until they slumped against a crumbling wall, gasping for breath, adjusting their drunken vision as they searched for me in the darkness.

"Who's there?"

I swam out from the shadows then. I let them get a good look at me in the dim illumination of the alley. I let them see the rings on my fingers and the blade in my grasp. Then, they trembled in fear.

"Black Blade," one of them gasped. "We've done *nothing*—"

"Silence your lies before I cut your throat." I was going to cut his pathetic throat anyway, but I needn't hear his excuses before he died. "You touched my property today." The blade in my hand lifted, the sharp point aiming at their bodies, one after the other.

"What—?"

The fool didn't get the rest of his question out because a single swipe of my blade across his throat had blood pooling from his body. He choked, gasped, and died.

It sobered the other two up quickly.

"As I was saying before I was rudely interrupted, you touched what belongs to me, and I cannot let you live."

"Please, Black Blade, we meant no harm!"

My brows rose, visceral amusement and anger together. "No? You did not mean to harm the Princess of Thalassar tonight?" At the surprised widening of their eyes, I smirked. "I know all about that. I know everything that happens in Eramaea because this is *my* kingdom. I am the king, the soldiers, the servants… And I am the princess' blade."

My weapon met their bodies.

They didn't even get a chance to scream.

Their bodies would stay here in a heap for the soldiers to find. No one would care about three drunken thugs murdered in the middle of the night. Just like they wouldn't care that I had offed them. My hands were stained with their lives, but I didn't care what it meant for my soul.

I didn't care about anything.

Just Maisie.

And the fact that she'd disobeyed me. She'd went out looking for me and these fools had attacked her. My knuckles ached, but I ignored the pain. My wrath was still building in my chest and it wouldn't ease. Not until I saw her.

Not until I asked her what she'd been thinking.

I slept peacefully.

Prince Kai had left hours before, after we both hurriedly fixed our clothing, I saw him out the door, gifting him and the narrow-eyed guards beyond the door a smile, and then retreated back inside—leaving the door unlocked, as per his request—where I fell to the cushioning with a sigh. Moments later, I was asleep.

No nightmares plagued me. How could they with this contented feeling coursing through my body? I still felt the imprint of his hands, his lips against my skin.

When I did wake up in the middle of the night, it was to the press of a sharp blade against my throat.

I gasped, skin at my throat pressing tighter against the razor edge as I swallowed. I tried refraining from doing so. Just like I tried refraining from looking around, from searching the shadows for the mer who wanted to end my life on this bed.

"I told you…" a recognizable voice whispered dangerously in my ear. "… not to come looking for me."

A moment later, the blade was pulled away, and I shot up in bed to face Elias Blackfin.

Clad in dark colors, he blended in with the shadows so well he may as well have been one himself. The only thing shining was the glint in his eyes, and the edge of his obsidian blade.

"Elias." His name came out like a breath of relief. His body floated just above the bed. When I said his name, he sank onto the cushions beside me.

The smile, his expression, everything about him was familiar. So familiar, something in me ached at the sight of him.

"Do you always find it so hard to follow directions, little fish?" His voice curled around me like a phantom menace.

Those words, the carelessness… Anger shot through me like a hot rod being shoved into my chest.

"You left," I accused quietly, yet viciously. "You left without saying anything."

His eyebrows rose, and the twisted smile on his lips was not one of happiness. "And you care?" His finger went to my lips. "Based on the swelling here, I'd assumed we owed each other nothing."

I shoved his hand away, face heating at his words. He knew. Knew I'd been with Prince Kai. I did not ask myself how he could have possibly known, because he was the Black Blade. He knew everything. Whatever. I'd not feel embarrassed about something I'd wanted, about taking it and damning the consequences.

"I think you, of all mer, would be proud of me for it. It was your idea after all. To seduce the Dragon Prince."

"Oh, I am, little fish. I knew you had seduction in you this whole time."

I took him in, the tightness in his brow, the thinning of his lips into a line. "Yet you're angry," I observed, "when you just said we owe each other nothing."

He made a sound of exasperation. "No. I'm *angry,* little fish, not because you took the Dragon Prince to bed, not because I am jealous, but because you ventured out to look for me and nearly got yourself killed, and gods knows what else."

My heart thumped. He'd heard. Of course he'd heard. He traded in secrets, specialized in lies, and blended with the shadows. It'd be odd if he hadn't heard what had happened to me.

Defiance slipped through me. "And you care?"

His gaze narrowed, pupils thin slits of accusation. "Of course I care."

"Why?" I challenged. "If we owe each other nothing—"

He interrupted by stealing a kiss. Not a soft one. It was rough, thorough. A punishment and a curse, but something else equally sweet and bitter. He pulled away before I could react, respond, and glared at me.

"You know very well what we owe each other and what you are to me, little fish. You know how I feel, and you know that I care about you enough to be angry that you disobeyed and were attacked."

Disobeyed. "I am not your property, Elias. And you are not my keeper. Do not act like it."

He growled. "This is serious. Do you know what those mer would have done to you? The atrocities—" He cut off, ran a hand through his hair in frustration. He brought them down, tightened them into fists. It was then I noticed they were cut and bruised, swollen. As if he'd fought. The fact that he was here in my room meant he'd been the one to swim away with his life. When he looked back at me, I could see a burning need, and an anger in the depth of his eyes. "I told you I'd come back to you, little fish. And you didn't believe me. You didn't trust me."

I glared. "How can I trust you when you lie to me, Elias?"

He blinked, the only tell that he was surprised.

I crossed my arms against my chest when he remained silent. "Tell me the truth. Did the Princess of Thalassar come looking for you?"

I held my breath as I awaited his response. *Please don't be true,* my eyes screamed. But his own hardened, unforgiving. As if he owed no one, not even me, an explanation for his lies.

"She did," he confessed. "Odele found me months ago, and she asked me for a favor."

I'D KNOWN THIS DAY would come. When Maisie would discover the truth. How could she not, when she'd been actively looking for answers? I'd have been a fool, if I assumed that Odele would not leave clues in her wake. Clues for someone else to find.

The mer who found them just happened to be the one I'd fallen in love with.

The confession that exited my lips was spoken strictly, yet my insides were a rushing current. The blood in my veins warmed, and this sensation

I was feeling, the innate pounding of my heart against my chest, was nervousness.

It was the betrayal on her face, an expression that nearly crippled me. I sat firm, eyes boring into hers, daring, challenging. I was the Black Blade. Keeping secrets, trading them, it was what I did. And this secret I'd held onto, what had transpired between Odele and I, had been safeguarded. She would not make me feel guilty for doing what I've always done.

"Why?" The word tore from her throat.

Nothing else needed to be said when that one word conveyed it so perfectly.

Why didn't you tell me?

"We owe each other nothing." Such a lie. Maisie was everything. *Everything.* I'd save thousands of mer from Selection if it meant she would smile. I would kill every blackheart in the city if it meant she would be safe. The truth was, she owed me nothing, but deep inside, I felt like I owed her the world.

Her answering slap was well placed, and well deserved. I felt the deep sting on my cheek.

"Tadpole," she cursed. "I should've known. Should've remembered what you were—" She cut off and turned away, not before I saw the glistening of a tear and a bubble rise a moment later.

I truly was a tadpole.

I could not let this go on. Could not let her believe the worst of me, even if I wanted to believe the worst of myself.

"You know what I do, the things I have to do to survive."

She looked at me, giving me a grave nod.

But she didn't know the extent of it.

"I do bad things, little fish. I steal and harm and kill. I trade secrets and collect them. I am the most wanted criminal in Thalassar, and despite that I still spy for the royals who reside here."

I worked with the very mer who wanted me dead. No, not the queen and king directly; I doubted they even knew that their lords and ladies employed me. Favored me. All because I could accomplish what others could not. I could find secrets others could not. I could kill when others could not.

"And I will keep lying, and murdering, and spying. That will not change."

Her eyes flared with something. Acceptance? Good.

"Odele was not the first royal I've dealt with."

Maisie broke her silence. "Why did she go looking for you?"

I recalled the moment months ago when Odele had come to me. She'd stood out greatly in a tavern full of blackguards and criminals, with her richly embroidered cloak and hood that did nothing to hide who she was.

"Are you the Black Blade?" she'd asked, though it seemed more a formality than anything else. One pointed look at my obsidian sword had been answer enough. I was the only mer brave enough to openly carry such a blade in the waters of Thalassar. Soldiers actively looked for me, for anyone carrying evidence of my whereabouts. "I need you."

"When the princess came to me," I began, "she was shaken." I'd only ever seen recordings of her, seen her in passing, but her distress had been obvious. "She kept looking over her shoulder, as if she thought someone had followed her, was watching. I wanted to believe she was being a silly little royal. But we had a private meeting, and she told me that someone was trying to kill her."

Maisie let out a small gasp. She'd known this already, yet that was genuine shock on her features. "Did she say who?"

I shook my head. I'd asked, of course, but she had blatantly ignored me. "No. She didn't tell me much. She dumped a bag of gold on my lap and demanded I discover secrets for her."

I remember looking from the gold to her black eyes, more brown than anything, with the slightest flecks of gold. Maisie's were darker, I realized that now. I'd pushed the bag of gold from my lap and watched it plop to the floor, the coins jangling inside and then settling.

"I don't want your money," I'd purred, pressing my fist into my chin as my eyes roamed over her. She'd misread my stare and had tensed.

"Then what payment do you require?" Her hand had gone into the pocket of her cloak, gripping a dagger, no doubt. As if she could best me. The little fool.

"I have no interest in your body, Princess," I'd assured her. "My interests lie… in a more lucrative direction."

"She asked me to find out all I could about the deaths of her mother and aunt. She gave me a list of names, asked me to investigate them."

"Do you remember the names?" Maisie seemed to lean closer to me.

"Yes. Little good it did me. Every single mer on the list was dead. Save one. She paid me for the information in royal secrets, but by the time I'd learned everything she wanted, she was just gone." I shrugged. At the time, I'd thought her frivolous and annoying. "But then you showed up, and you handed me the answers I'd never gotten. You followed the same path Odele had, and I started to piece things together."

Maisie chewed furiously on her bottom lip. I could see the workings of her mind, see her trying to piece everything together herself. "Do you know why she wanted you to investigate those mer, specifically?"

I shrugged. "Now that I know more, I suspect she thought they had something to do with the royal deaths."

She grumbled, shaking her head back and forth, causing the tresses of her long hair to float and curl against her cheeks. "If only I knew more about it…"

She sighed and told me everything she'd found since I'd been gone. Just like that, I'd been forgiven. Maisie had such a kind heart that I smiled, even as she weaved a tale of tragedy. About every royal who had mysteriously died, the pregnancy of Princess Odessa, and the possibility of Odele's missing cousin.

"I think that knowledge threatened her life. I think someone was trying to kill her—just like they're trying to kill me—because of what she discovered. I think she went to find her cousin, wherever this mer may be."

I took her in. The darkness could not hide her coloring. The purple-blue of her hair, the dark eyes and refined features. The desperation for the truth in her eyes.

"When you told me what you'd discovered, the contract, all of it, I left," I explained. "Not because I wanted to be away from you, but because I wanted to check again." I paused. Something in me yearned to grab her, so I gripped her hand in mine. "I have contacts in the city, so I went to them. I went to ask for help. Maybe there was something I'd overlooked, but I asked them to investigate those names again. To find out everything they could about those mer." I smoothed my thumb over her skin, my eyes begging her to understand.

I didn't leave you, they said. A silent conversation, a silent plea passed from me to her.

Her nod was her only response.

Leagues of silence pressed up into the spaces between us, broken by her sharp-tongued inquiry. "So you knew. From that first moment you knew I wasn't the princess."

Though their resemblance was quite staggering, and had taken me aback for a moment, I'd known since I saw her attacking those mer in the alley for me. Perhaps I hadn't known Odele personally, but I knew she would never throw herself into the path of danger for others. Maisie was different. She cared so deeply, too deeply.

"Your eyes are darker." And so full of life. I did not spend my time imagining life on shores or what occurred beyond the waters. Yet her eyes reminded me of the dark, starry nights of two-legger skies. They held desires and wishes, an endless expanse of dreams.

"Why couldn't you tell me?"

It wasn't an accusation. Sorrow kindled her words.

I was truly a tadpole.

"I—" I almost choked. Swallowed. I finally admitted, looking her straight in the eye and not daring to turn away. It would be a coward's move. "I don't know. I've... never had to explain myself to anyone before. And I... I wanted to bring answers back to you."

Answers I could lay across her fins, like a bouquet of lilies to buy her affection. For her to trust me, wholly, completely.

I was not a swaggering prince of the dragon waters. I commanded no armies. I did not guard her night and day or morph into a whole new entity. I was no self-conscious fool. I knew that, when faced with these adversaries for her affections, *we* were an unparalleled match. I knew her, like she knew me. I was secrets and shadows, and she was truth and light. Wholly different, yet the same goals pushed us to strive for a better world.

"I was waiting for the right time."

Can you forgive me?

A breathy sigh escaped her. "Yes."

Smiling, I pulled her close to me. I'd missed this the past few days I'd been gone. Missed her warmth, the flush of her skin against mine. My lips found their way home, at the space where her neck met her shoulder, just below the thin line of gills. I pressed them there, whispered against her skin. "I am glad."

A tremor traveled up her body. "Elias," she whispered.

I groaned, my body tightening at just the sound of her lovely voice. "Maisie?"

I heard the gulp, and seconds later she was pulling away. "We have to talk."

That didn't sound good. I schooled my features into careless frivolity, raising an eyebrow, twisting the side of my mouth into an arrogant smirk. "Yeah?"

"I—" She cut off to bite her bottom lip, and then blurted, "I've been intimate with Prince Kai."

She blinked, and I waited the span of a heartbeat, two.

"I know."

How could I not have known? Her swollen lips when I'd arrived had been a dead giveaway. That, and I'd been behind the tapestry when he'd left her room. It took me what felt like hours to finally deign to come in, make my grand entrance.

By pressing a blade to her throat.

I really was a tadpole.

"Don't you care?" she asked tentatively. "I mean… we owe each other nothing, but…"

She was looking to me for permission, I realized. For acceptance.

"You want to label this." I gestured between us. "You want to know what we are."

A stiff nod.

Slowly, I spread my palms wide in front of her, displaying every single ring that adorned my fingers. They'd been lost to the guards when I'd been captured, but a few favors called in had brought them back home. To me.

I pried off the one adorning my pinky. A heavy stone, black in appearance. I'd stared at it often enough to know that it was actually a dark purple. Or maybe the two colors danced together inside—something I'd contemplated before.

It was my most prized ring.

I grabbed her wrist, pulling it to me and dropping the ring into the palm of her hand. Her fingers trembled, but I closed them over the stone. "In two-legger lands, rings are exchanged between lovers and betrothed." Her eyes widened at my emboldened words. "It was a gift, given to me by an immigrant mer from the west, from the Uncharted Waters. A mer who saved my life when the time came for me to escape Selection." I paused, made sure the weight of my words reached her. "I want you to have it."

I could still remember that day. The day I'd been selected, and a young merman with vicious yellow eyes had saved me, buying me just enough time to slip past the guards. What had become of him and his sister, I didn't know. Though not a day went by when I didn't think of him, and feel overwhelmed with gratitude. He'd made me who I was. His words had created the Black Blade.

To a free world.

Her palm opened as she looked down at it. Indecision flickered in the dark of her gaze. "Elias," she breathed. "I can't."

She was so easy to read, my little fish. I smirked. "You love him don't you? The prince?"

Denial pulsed around her, but I pierced her with a look. The same look I used on those I wanted to pry secrets from. It worked just the same, though unnecessary. "I do," she confessed, looking ashamed.

"Do you love me?"

Obvious.

The answer was so obvious.

Still, I wanted her to say it.

"I do. I love you, too."

I smiled and closed her fingers around the ring once more. "You can love us both, little fish, and I will still not want you any less than I do now, any less than I would in two days, years, centuries. You are mine, and I will never give you up."

In my life of lies and secrets, this was one thing I would voice proudly. I did not care if she loved me *and* the prince. I did not feel insecure and did not think any less of her for it. I'd steal her the stars if I very well could.

Maisie made her decision. Not with words, but by slowly opening the palm of her hand, gazing down at the ring balanced there. She picked it up, looked at it, and I watched with a thumping heart as she placed it onto her ring finger.

A perfect fit.

She turned her hand about, this way and that, in different poses and positions as she took in that piece of me I'd gifted. She lowered her hand.

I love you, her gaze whispered.

Smiling, I replied, "I do, too." And then my hand circled around the nape of her neck, to pull her in for a kiss.

It didn't speak of softness, but of urgency and quickness. Silent conversation flowed with every touch. Like a spoken word, her hands sliding up my chest, stopping at my neck. For every touch was a question, and my every kiss a reply.

I slid closer to her, bringing her up with me so we weren't lying on the bed, but facing each other, bodies and curved edges of tails touching. My hands framed her face, and her own dug into my shoulders, grasping tightly at me, begging me to stay.

Don't go. Don't go.

Don't.

I pulled away, her nose touching mine, our lips a hairsbreadth apart. "I won't," I promised. "I won't."

I leaned in to kiss her again, to devour her, make her wholly mine. And she let me. Maisie opened up to me, mouth and soul. My hands roamed over the fine angles and curves of her body. I memorized the shape of her all over again. As if I could ever forget.

She was the one thing that had filled my mind for hours in the darkness since I'd left. So little time knowing each other, and such a strong feeling pressurizing my chest. I'd been a husk before. As hollow and empty as the inside of a shell. The only thing that kept me going was helping others.

Now I had Maisie.

And I never planned on letting her go.

ELIAS RAN LONG, DARK fingers over shelves, stopping to linger on glass figurines. His finger trailed over the dorsal fin of a dolphin. Though his movements were precise, calculated, his eyes looked far away and wistful.

I sat up in the ivory shell bed, pulling the blanket tight around my chest.

"What are you thinking?" I whispered.

I may as well have been speaking to silent darkness. Elias did not reply right away. He gave no indication that he'd even heard me at all. I debated repeating the question, but he finally turned to me, the smile curving on his lips genuine.

"About you," he admitted, causing a flush to rise to my cheeks. He couldn't see it in the shadowy room, but I'd no doubt he knew it was there, staining my cheeks. He prowled forward. His chest was bare, as was the rest of him, really. No evidence of that which made him male opening at his tail, but his prowess was there, and obvious.

He stopped just at the edge of the bed. That smile on his face was a dangerous thing, and still it curled my insides, made me weak.

"About how happy I am right now. About how much I love you."

There. An admission. One that wasn't silent, passed between the secrets of touching.

And it being said aloud, the confirmation of it rippled through me, and made me question it. "Why?" My voice cracked.

"Because you are brave, and smart. You are the light to my shadows, the truth to my lies. Because even though you knew it could cost you your life, you came here and pretended to be a princess you hated, and risked everything for a better Thalassar, risked everything to save me from the gallows. You may not be a true royal, Maisie, but you are a damn fine one, just the same."

Tears slipped in air bubbles from my eyes unbidden. I didn't bother to swipe them away as I got up, letting the blanket slip down the front of my body. Until we were face to face, body to body. Skin touching skin.

"I love you," he whispered again, this time to my lips. "Despite the circumstances, I am glad you came here, glad you are not the real princess. Glad I even got this opportunity to be with you."

I didn't have the words. Didn't know if they were even needed. Perhaps they were, but they eluded me. Left me altogether.

Especially when the sound of the door clicking closed made us jump apart. I barely had time to scramble for the blanket to cover myself again, barely had the time to do much of anything. Elias pushed me behind him, shielding my body with his own. My heart thumped loudly against the back of his bare chest, begging to be unleashed from the confines of my ribcage.

The silence that ensued was a roar, deafening. I could only hide behind Elias and wonder who was there, and what would become of us.

The image of a swinging ax and heads rolling through the water gave me enough bravery to peek over his shoulder…

And look directly into the eyes of Prince Kai.

Shock rippled through my body.

A roaring filled my ears, the guttural sounds of that dragon beast being unleashed. The tether holding it back snapped, filling me to the core. My body began to change, slowly. And I relinquished that control in my shock.

"You." The word came out a guttural growl. More beast than mer.

Curved black talons poked into the palm of my hand, making me realize I was clenching them too hard, and I did not care.

Betrayal. Anger. Hurt. It all coalesced inside me, like a riptide wave. Like a tsunami crashing to a shore. Chaos could only follow.

It all made sense now. With the eyes of a dragon, I observed what I'd been too stupid to realize sooner. A newfound clarity was there.

I'd wanted to come to her room, to see her without the suffocating pressure of guards on the other side of the door, of them straining to hear every word we said. I'd been under the impression that she wanted it too. That she wanted *me*.

But here she was. My princess. My gem. In the arms of another.

A criminal.

No wonder she had risked everything to protect him. Not because it was the right thing to do, not because she despised the barbarity of the execution, but because she was in love with him.

Mine.

The beast in me growled the word, over and over again.

Mine. My mate. My gem. *Mine.*

I pointed my talons in the direction of Elias Blackfin. The Black Blade.

"You." The word tore from me again, unbidden, yet filled with growling menace.

My eyes flicked to Odele. She hid behind him, the brightness of her eyes peeking over his shoulder to take me in. Yes, that was true fear there. Her fingers curled on the Black Blade's shoulder, as if she meant to seek comfort.

Mine!

A growl ripped from my throat. A mighty roar of anger. An anger that I could not pass off as just the beast's, but my own as well.

"Let her go."

The Black Blade held out a hand. His voice didn't shake, but he also didn't display that same arrogance he had in that arena, when we'd faced off much like this. Except, that time, Odele had been between us. His shield. A shield I'd wanted to protect with my last dying breath.

"Calm down," the Black Blade ordered firmly, quietly. "Calm down and we can talk about this."

No talking, the dragon inside roared. *Kill. Kill. He touched our mate. Ours. Mine. Mine.*

I prowled forth. Her voice stopped me before I made a whole fin stroke forward. "Kai, please, let me explain." She swam around him, clutching a blanket to her very naked chest. Her black eyes were wide with fear, worry. Yet she still swam up to me, with my beast-like features. The Black Blade made a move to pull her back.

I growled at the gesture.

Mine.

"It's alright," she whispered, swimming up to me until our bodies were mere inches apart.

"Little fish…" the Black Blade warned.

My eyes shot over to him, narrowing.

Kill.

"Did he hurt you?" I asked. Because I had to know. Had to cross out every viable possibility. Anything but to accept what could be the truth. That my mate did not love me, because she loved someone else. Was that why she'd never been able to say the words, why she constantly pushed me away?

"He didn't."

Pain ripped through my chest. Then it was true. She did love him. Like she could never love me.

I swallowed past the pain tightening my throat.

"So you wanted this." It was more an accusation than a question, quietly placed.

Her eyes fluttered closed, as if she were in pain. But what pain she felt right now could never compare to what burned deep inside me.

When she opened them again, there were tears in the corners of her eyes. Little bubbles rising up, and glistening in the dull glow of her room.

"Yes. I—I love him."

She said those words with such ease. Words she never could have said to me. I staggered back. A blow to the chest, that's what this was. It was pain incarnate. It was death itself.

But the dragon inside gave me strength, hardening me in ice.

I straightened, turned an unfeeling gaze to the Black Blade. I'd kill him. Everything inside me screamed to do so. The only thing holding me back was that, if I did, Odele would never forgive me. And I wouldn't forgive myself.

My steely gaze went to her. "It doesn't matter," I said viciously. "Because you are still my betrothed. You've given yourself to me. We will be married soon." I hated to sound like this. Like my father. Possessive. Jealous. I hated to be a demanding conquerer. But the words spilled from my mouth like sand falling from a jar. The truth was, I didn't care if she loved someone else. It did not take my feelings away from her. I loved her. And someday, I could only hope that she would love me, too.

"Kai…" My name was a breath pushing past her lips. "*We* won't be married."

"We *will.*"

She sighed, a long suffering sound. Her eyes closed once more. This time, when she spoke, she didn't open them and brave me as she suddenly confessed, "We will not marry, because I am not the real Princess Odele."

Behind her, the Black Blade tensed.

I could only stare at her, and only her. I took her in. Every inch. Her hair flowed in disarray around her face. Her posture was… slouched… And her eyes, glaring dark daggers. As if daring me.

Shock pushed the dragon back once more.

I felt my body shrink, the talons go back to fingernails, and the rage dissipate into tepid curiosity.

"What?"

"I'm not the real Princess of Thalassar." She threw a hand up, exasperation seeming to wear her down. As if this was some secret she'd kept for so long and was glad to be rid of it. "I'm not Odele. I was brought here by Captain Saber to pretend to be her because she is missing."

I blinked, unable to believe such a thing. How could she not be Odele? This was ridiculous. The very notion that I'd been duped…

"She swam away, so the queen and king made up the whole charade that she was sick while the captain went out to look for her. He found me instead. Odele's look alike. My name is Maisie Fauna. I'm a waitress from Lagoona. Don't you understand?"

I didn't. I couldn't possibly comprehend the level of treachery that was going on here.

"We won't marry, because I'm not her. Once she gets back, they'll either kill me or send me back home. We won't ever see each other again. And we can't do anything about it. You need a princess to help your kingdom, not a waitress. I am sorry I deceived you. I'm sorry I lied, but I had to. I thought I could mend things between you and Odele so that when she got back, the two of you could be happy. I never thought I'd—" She broke off with a gasping breath. "Don't you see? Even if we love each other, we could never be, Kai."

Silence followed, as my mind struggled to swim and keep up with all this information. Odele. She wasn't Odele. This mer before me was not the princess. Her name was Maisie, and she'd lied to me this entire time.

It made sense.

I thought back on it now.

The sudden sickness of the princess. How no one would ever let me see her, and whenever I inquired, they would say, "She's in recovery." How she had looked so different once I saw her again, how her whole attitude had changed. That was because it hadn't been Odele at all, but Maisie.

Maisie had been the one to enchant me. Maisie had been the one I'd fallen in love with. Maisie was my mate.

It had been Maisie all along.

"You knew," the Black Blade finally spoke, and I looked up at him slowly. His gaze was calculating, assessing. Like a thief looking for jewels to plunder, looking for the easiest entry into the coffers. "All this time, you had to have known that there was something different about her, regardless of the striking resemblance."

I had known. From that first moment I saw her—*Maisie*—I'd known she was different. And my heart had called to her like it'd never called to Odele.

"I lied," Odele—*Maisie*—whispered, shame filling her voice. "I tricked you. I pretended to be someone I wasn't and you gave yourself to me, and I'm sorry I didn't tell you the truth. I'm sorry you gave yourself to a liar…"

My growl shut her up. I couldn't help it. It came out of me, a savage sound that brought about the quiet. I needed silence. Needed to think. And I could not stand to hear her speak one more moment. To keep apologizing. As if giving myself to her had been a chore of some sort.

She'd betrayed me in the worst possible way. She'd lied. She'd let me fall in love with her, knowing she wasn't who she pretended to be. Easily, so easily she could have pushed me away, pretended to be like Odele and hated me. Yet she brought down my barriers, melted the ice encased around my heart and made me care for her. Love her.

She could have kept going with this charade, but she was telling me the truth now. My eyes narrowed on her.

"Why?" I asked. "Why tell me now?"

Maisie bit her bottom lip. Despite everything, burning hunger roared to life within me. "Because you deserve to know the truth."

Not good enough. That answer was not good enough.

My eyes flared to life, talons curved on my fingertips.

It was the Black Blade who interrupted impatiently, "It's because she loves you, lizard boy. Get it through your thick skull. And you, little fish, need to learn to be honest in regards to what you feel."

Even in the dark, I could make out the flush of her cheeks. She threw him a quick, accusatory glare over her shoulder.

Love.

Could it be true?

I searched her face. Searched for a lie. By now I supposed I realized, I was no good at looking for a liar. At least, not when it came to her. Which made me realize that maybe she'd been telling the truth. I was good at sniffing out liars and traitors. Which meant that Maisie had never lied. She'd lied about her name. But who she was deep down shone through. It was something that couldn't be tarnished or hidden. It was that part of her that I fell in love with. That part I'd been attracted to from the beginning.

"Is it true?"

"Does it matter? We can never be."

"Is it true?"

She flinched, then glared. "Yes."

She loved me, and she also loved Elias.

I knew, from years of watching my father and his concubines, that it was possible to divide a heart. To love multiple mer, to give yourself wholly to them, knowing they were not the only one in their heart. My truth was that Maisie was the only one in mine, and she always would be.

Even if we truly weren't meant to be.

It was a long time before anyone dared to speak again. I could not stay here forever, and the knowledge was weighing on me. I took a deep breath, straightened, and put on the face of the prince.

"I will keep your secret," I said, though it was not what she'd asked of me. Still, she nodded with gratitude. "We will keep pretending. We will go on as we have been until the real princess is found." Another nod. I swallowed past the tightness in my throat. I didn't want to contemplate what would happen if she wasn't found. Or if she was. I didn't want to think about Odele at all. "But you are right. We cannot be."

My kingdom needed a princess. We needed Thalassar. Draconi was suffering. Two-leggers were polluting the waters, pulling creatures from their homes, fishing them to the brink of endangerment and extinction. It was a war with creatures who didn't know of our existence, who were likely soon to find out. I needed this alliance. I needed the magic of

Thalassar, to push the two-leggers away from our borders. To save my mer.

I would not get the answers I sought with Maisie, a waitress from Lagoona with the heart of a royal.

My gem. My love.

My mate.

For my mer, I would make the ultimate sacrifice. I would have to give her up.

The dragon in me whined at the thought, pleading not to do this, to not swim away from her.

It took everything within me to turn, even if my every instinct fought and thrashed against my soul to turn back. Face her. Kiss her. Claim her.

I could not.

"Thank you for your truth."

I swam to the door, placing my hand on the knob. I willed myself to turn it. To leave. My body didn't comply.

"Coward."

I froze, but didn't turn around. Even as the Black Blade hissed the cruel word at my back.

"You are a coward, Kai Li. You want her, but you're too afraid to take what you want. Too afraid to damn the consequences to the abyss and back."

My hand tightened around the knob. "I have a duty to my mer." The words came out tight, clipped.

Behind me, the Black Blade snorted. "If you can swim out of here and go on pretending, if you can turn your back on Maisie and when the time comes, for it *will* come, marry Odele, then you never deserved Maisie in the first place."

Those words sank into me. I counted the heartbeats. I was sure they did too. They wanted me to turn around. Were willing me to do so.

Duty. Honor.

The terrible scars on my back throbbed, begged me to whirl around and take her in my arms.

I could not.

"Goodnight, Maisie Fauna."

I opened the door, and swam out. His voice trailed after me, even as I closed it.

"Coward."

Loving my kingdom did not make me a coward. Wanting to protect the mer was not a weakness. Maisie knew this. I saw the way she spoke of ending Selection. The hardships of war in her eyes. She would not think me weak, would not hate me for the decision.

I leaned my back against her door, dropping my head against it and closing my eyes.

Mine, the voice whispered in my mind.

The dragon in me bristled, spread its wings and sharpened its claws. Dragons hid jewels, protected them with their lives. They pillaged and devoured cities whole for something as simple as a pebble.

And I was the Dragon Prince Kai Li of Draconi. I had the blood of dragons coursing through my veins. I'd been forged in ice and jewels, in death and shadows, in darkness and chaos.

Like my ancestors, beast and mer, I would pillage and destroy, if only to possess the one jewel that mattered above all others. To bring the mer I loved just a little closer. To claim my mate.

Body and soul.

No.

A coward I was not.

I whirled, yanking the door open and swam into her room. Maisie floated there, frozen in the position I'd left her in, hand clutching the sheet at her chest. She took one look at me, her eyes wide with surprise.

"Kai… what—"

She didn't get the rest of the question out.

Because I took her face in my palms and claimed my mate in a scorching kiss.

HE'D LEFT. SWAM OUT and left me. It had been more of a civil reaction than I'd expected, and still it scorched something deep inside me to see him turn around and not come back.

"He doesn't deserve you," Elias whispered darkly.

I wanted to believe that those words were true, but the reality of it was the opposite. I did not deserve him. Prince Kai was too good, too kind. Even now, as something in me tore painfully, I could not fault him for his decision to leave.

I'd lied to him, and while he may have wanted me, he *needed* Odele, the real Odele. Not some pretender who could bring him nothing, who did not have the backing of a kingdom ready to go to war for him. I possessed no magic that would help his kingdom. And he loved Draconi and his mer enough to sacrifice anything for them, even his own happiness. He loved Draconi more than me.

A tear rose from my eye.

"Maisie?" Elias seemed to swim closer. I felt his heat at my backside.

"He needs a royal," I answered numbly, staring at the place he'd vacated. I felt suddenly hollow inside with his absence. "He's just doing what's best for his mer." And I could not fault him for that. Not when I'd come here to do exactly the same thing. To build a better kingdom. To help those who could not help themselves.

It did not make it hurt any less.

The door to the room opened, and Prince Kai swam through once again. My eyes widened at the sight, and my heart flared, though I did not dare hope. He closed it, and took me in from across the span of the space that separated us. His eyes glowed around the edges, the sliver of the dragon beneath.

"Kai… what—" I didn't get the rest of the question out.

Because Kai swam forward, took my face in his palms, and kissed me.

It was a claiming. A brand meant to possess and demand every piece of me. He tilted my head back, tongue pushing past my lips to tangle against mine. I accepted his ardent kisses, moaning when the sharpened points of his teeth grazed over my lips, when he bit possessively and sent desire spiraling through every nerve in my body. It was the perfect mixture of pleasure and pain.

He pushed me back, as if he meant to throw me onto the bed, but I rammed into the solidity of Elias' chest instead. His warm hands went to my arms, holding me steady as Kai kissed and kissed, as if it would be the last chance he got to do so. It didn't feel like a goodbye so much as a desperate attempt to consume me. Caged between the two, I could only give in to the sensations of being protected, enveloped in warmth and passion, in two mer that were wholly different, but whose feelings matched my own.

Kai finally pulled away, leaving behind the warm bruising of his lips against mine.

"I am no coward," he declared feverishly against my skin, eyes glowing.

No, you're not. The words somehow stuck in my throat. Behind me, Elias chuckled. The sound made me acutely aware of our position. Our closeness. I felt every inch of their bodies on mine, all three of our breaths mingled, heart beats synchronizing like we were interconnected with every steady pound. Every pane of Kai's chest was tight against my own, every solid ridge and muscle of Elias against my back. His hands slid up and down my arms, and Kai's thumbs trailed circles around my cheeks.

There was nothing more intimate than this, than having them on either side of me, stroking my skin, filling me with delicious sensations of want. The underlying need and desires pulsating from the both of them. The promise behind every stroke of their fingers. As if they both meant to have me.

What I suddenly wanted, I probably shouldn't.

"We…" I swallowed past the pain of my desire. "We can't… Can we?"

Kai looked at me before his gaze flicked up to stare at Elias, who towered over me from behind. I could not see his face, but I could see Kai's well enough and knew a silent conversation passed between them. One I couldn't decipher.

Then Kai said, "I do not know whether to kill you or keep you." He said the words as if Elias was some jewel he found on the ground. A dragon contemplating treasure. A shark contemplating the severity of the threat before it. Like he still couldn't quite get over the fact that Elias had threatened my life and wanted to punish him for the offense.

Enemies or allies?

The lines in the sand were still unclear.

Elias chuckled. I felt the rumblings vibrate along my back. "I'd be disappointed if you didn't at least try to hurt me *a little.*"

Kai's eyes flared.

My heart stuttered at the innuendo in his words. They sounded like a promise of a good time to come. "Are… are you two *flirting*?"

Elias's hand flicked aside my hair to bare my neck, where he traced his thumb across the nook where my neck met my shoulder. "Perhaps."

I shivered, but willed disbelief into my voice. "Just a few minutes ago I had to talk him down from killing you, and now you're flirting?" There was something here I obviously wasn't comprehending.

I knew Elias liked mermen and mermaids both. He'd said as much and I long suspected he'd harbored a secret crush on the Draconian prince. But did Kai lean towards that direction as well?

Kai pulled away briefly, bringing his hand up between us. I watched as polished nails suddenly lengthened into sharp talons. I remembered the feel of those tips scraping down my flesh and shivered.

The prince must have sensed where my thoughts were, for he smiled, a feral twist of his lips and brought one taloned finger up to my face. It scraped over my flesh, starting at my forehead and down… Down my nose, past my lips and chin, and lower still. Desire followed his slow movements. The scraping of his talons did not hurt so much as provoked a different sort of sensation. Anticipation. He drew it slowly out of me. My breath hitched as his nail made it to the top of the sheet that I still held tightly to me. He stopped there for a brief second as his eyes searched my own.

If it was permission he wanted, he had it.

He smiled and yanked.

The sheet tore down the middle, slipping from my fingers, the scraps piling onto the floor.

I shivered, bare before the Dragon Prince.

"I thought he was harming you," Kai confessed, his voice a near guttural rasp. I wondered how tight of a leash he was keeping on the dragon, if he only let it slip in rage and passion. Not that I was complaining. Not when his nails were raking across my flesh, scraping a pattern across my collarbone and throat.

"I'd never hurt her." Elias squeezed my arm. I could not see his face, but had no doubt he was glaring.

Black-blue eyes flared as they took Elias in. Gauging. Searching. For what, I wasn't sure. The truth? He must've found it, because he gave the smallest dip of his head.

"My dragon says we should keep you," he commented darkly, running those delicious talons of his down the length of my chest, stopping at the swells of my breasts. I barely heard what they were talking about, trying to grasp some sense of the conversation but couldn't because of what Kai was doing. Because of the patterns he traced against my breasts like he was mapping out veins and scales and memorizing every inch of me.

"How does that work?" Elias asked, rubbing his hands across the back of my neck, traveling at a leisurely pace down my spine. "Is it just a voice whispering in your head?"

Kai paused, cocking his head a bit to the side. "It is hard to explain." His talon circled my nipple, and I gasped, arching into him. I wanted more than that. My body ached, desperate to have his touch, his mouth. I wanted everything, and yet he kept speaking as if he wasn't driving me mad with soft caresses. "It's like having a separate being inside of me, but it is also me."

"And you can become this being?" Elias' breath was now at my ear, his teeth scraping against the lobe.

"Yes. In every way." Kai's talons scraped against the underside of my breasts. I felt too empty, and every part of me was on edge like I would burst.

"Your darker self," I gasped out, causing both mer to pause.

Then Prince Kai smiled in that feral, dragon grin. "Exactly like that, my gem."

It was a darker self that was contagious, making me drunk with want. Elias was just as affected as I, trailing his hands over my hips, pulling me closer to his chest.

"We… we can't…" I repeated.

They froze, and I almost regretted the words.

"It will be difficult," Elias commented, and I could hear the smile in his words. "You have, after all, only one entryway." His hand snaked around to my stomach, fingers hovering over my slit. The warmth of his close contact had an embarrassing sound keeling from my throat.

My cheeks heated.

"It does make for difficulty with sharing," Kai added, his eyes twinkling with mischief in the dark.

"Sharing?" I asked incredulously. Was that even possible? Would they even want to? Why?

"If it pleases you…" Kai's lips curled deliciously and his talons slid down the curve of my stomach, stopping just near Elias' hand.

I gulped.

"Is that… I mean… You two…" I had no words to express what I was feeling. How could I? This was uncharted territory. I didn't know how to proceed. "How does it work? I mean… You don't like each other… Do you?"

They'd almost charged at each other for gods' sakes. How could there be any attraction? I knew Elias found mermen beautiful; he'd said as much to me. But Kai?

Kai searched Elias' face. "I did not," he admitted. "But I cannot deny that you intrigue me. You are the Black Blade, the most notorious merman in all of Thalassarin history. If you have earned Maisie's love, then it must be for a reason."

I could feel Elias smiling behind me.

"Don't let it get to your head," I muttered under my breath.

Elias ignored me, and I had the satisfaction of watching his hand reach out from over my shoulder to grasp Prince Kai's loose tendrils of hair.

"Ever the dragon, aren't you? You'd add mer to your collection like rubies and gold."

"I have no interest in rubies or gold," Kai purred. "For what is it but a pile of stones? Contact, relationships, are far more precious."

Silence stretched out for a few heartbeats.

"We could take turns," Elias suggested.

"That would be the civil thing to do," Kai agreed with a smile.

"Is that what you want, little fish?" His voice was a dark promise in my ear, his hand a hovering desire that went unfulfilled. I clenched on empty water, aching everywhere when he used that voice. I ached everywhere just watching them carry on this absurd conversation.

"The three of us?" I pondered breathlessly.

"If that is what you prefer." Kai smiled.

"And… will you two…?"

They shared one glance. Only one.

"We could… if it pleases you."

"Would it please *you*?" I countered.

The prince only shook his head back and forth with amusement, a chuckle pushing past his lips.

"Perhaps… we could see…"

"See what?"

They did not reply. Instead, a silent agreement, they pressed me tighter between them. I tilted my head up to watch as they edged closer, *closer,* faces inches apart. My throat suddenly went inexplicably dry as their mouths melded together.

Holy. Mother. Of. Gods.

Kissing. Kai and Elias were kissing.

Their heads were right above me, angled so I got a perfect view of the way their mouths worked together. There was nothing tentative about it. It was violent. It was an ire, like watching battles waged between two conquerors. Their mouths opened together, breathing each other in. Teeth scraped against lips, and a beastly growl emanated from someone's chest, though I couldn't say from whose.

They took each other in as if they were punishing each other, pushing and pulling, with me in the center, melting between the two in a way that only fueled my desire.

Elias released my arm to grasp for Prince Kai's. He pulled him closer until not an ounce of space lay between the three of us. I could feel their own hardness against my body. A strange emptiness and longing were prominent against my skin. I ached for that friction and gave it to myself, grinding against Kai while Elias pushed me against the prince's chest. But it wasn't enough. It could never be enough.

Too soon, they pulled away from each other, lips hovering inches apart. Gauging each other, deciding…

"You'll do," Kai said dangerously. "You'll do nicely."

Elias' answering smirk melted my insides entirely. No longer was there a threat or a rivalry between them. Nothing but the dark promise of danger and passion.

Elias blinked and shifted his gaze down to me. "What do you say, little fish?"

The lump of desire in my throat rose painfully to the surface that it was hard to swallow past. But my voice was surprisingly steady and bold when I replied, "I feel thoroughly ignored."

"Well, we can't have that, can we?" Kai slid a black talon between my breasts, down to my navel and lower still, shy at my entrance.

A gasp pulled shakily from my throat.

I angled my hips, jerking forward a fraction, my body begging—demanding—his touch. But it seemed the closer I pushed, the further away he went, teasing me with the presence of his fingers, though not satisfying that need deep inside me.

Behind me, Elias pressed kisses against my neck, scraping teeth and tongue across the most sensitive areas of my flesh.

"Please," I begged quietly. My body jerked in demand.

"Of course, my gem."

Kai's talons curved softly into my hips, the touch scorching, demanding. He took control, whipping me around in the water so that I was facing Elias now.

"Elias…" Kai's voice was a quiet command. It was kingly, and Elias obeyed the command in that one word. He shoved his fingers into the roots of my hair, angling back my head roughly. His lips inched down, grazing mine. Kai's lips went to the lobe of my ear and whispered, "Claim her."

Elias' mouth devoured mine.

His tongue swept past the barrier of my lips, demanding, taking, *claiming.* He kissed me thoroughly, roughly, and I grasped for his shoulders to keep me floating upright instead of spiraling to the floor like my body demanded.

Kai's hands covered mine over Elias's shoulders, sharp talons digging into the Black Blade's skin. His every move was a command, his voice and every word a threat that we would both gladly obey.

"Take her," he urged darkly. "Now."

One hand grasping my hip, Elias angled his naked body and pushed deep inside me, filling me to the hilt. I gasped against his mouth.

"Yesss." The word came out like a hiss of satisfaction from Kai's lips. He pressed tightly against my backside, letting me feel the extent of his desire. I groaned, pulling and tugging at Elias closer. More, I wanted more. Even as he moved in and out of me, I was selfish, my body demanding everything.

But then Kai's talons curved down my spine, and I arched behind him. Lips soon replaced hands. Soft and warm, they trailed the pattern his talons had followed. Tongue tracing movements and patterns along my skin. I shivered between their bodies, hips thrusting against Elias' as he pumped his length in and out of me. My inner walls squeezed him, pulling him tighter. Our tails entwined, my nails digging into Elias' hips. Our bodies slapped against one another, the force of his thrusts pushing me against

Kai's chest. He ground tightly against me, wrenching cries from my lips. My body and pleasure soared higher, the sensations coalescing through me, just spiraling until he pressed tightly against that one sweet spot that sent me over the edge.

When I floated back down to reality, I was shaking all over, aware that Elias was still pumping into me, his movements languid, almost lazy. Like he had all the time in the world with me.

"It's my turn now, my gem." Kai was at my ear again, but his hand went to Elias' cheek, fingers tracing circles against the curve of it. Elias pulled away, eyes fluttering as he surveyed the prince. Silence. It was a blanket weighed heavily over us. Words were not needed. Not when we had this.

Kai leaned over my shoulder and took Elias's mouth. His own claiming, his own form of branding. His talon curved into his cheek, splitting the skin. Elias gasped as thin red tendrils floated up above him. That one simple move awoke something in Elias. He thrust harder in me, and I could make out the beginning of Kai's triumphant smile just before he devoured those lips with his own. The harder he pressed and pulled against the Black Blade the harder Elias' thrusts became.

My body trembled, and I cried out as the sensation became overwhelming. It was too much, too much…

I threw my head back to cry out to the ceiling. I fell apart against them, tears stinging the backs of my eyelids. They rose from my eyes and swarmed above us, catching the light of the jellies that illuminated the space. Elias slowly pulled away from me, gazing down at my eyes with such an open tenderness.

"Did I hurt you?" he asked quietly.

Behind me, Kai's hands stroked softly, as if he meant to ease any aches and pains.

I sighed contentedly. "No."

"Would you like to move to the bed?" Kai asked.

My fins were shaking and my tail was curled beneath me, ready to give in. The only thing holding me upright were their bodies.

"That would be nice."

They smiled knowingly at each other before Kai scooped me up in the strength of his arms. Elias led him over to the bed, where he laid me gently on the soft cushioning. Kai and Elias laid on either side of me.

"I think we got too carried away," Elias mused, his fingertips stroking my bare skin.

"Apologies..." Kai pressed a kiss to my shoulder.

I waved them off. Or tried to with a shaking hand. "I'm fine," I whispered.

"Do you want to stop?" Hands began stroking down my stomach. Elias'. I had the texture of them memorized. I groaned, my body alighting all over again.

"Is that a no?" Kai mused.

My reply was to moan.

How was this possible? How could my body react like this to them?

My eyes fluttered open, though I hadn't even realized they'd been closed and I looked back and forth between them. "Will you two kiss again?" The words came silkily out of me. It had been an enjoyable sight, to watch two beautiful mermen equally formidable and dangerous come together in a passionate embrace. I wanted to see it again, this claiming between the three of us.

Kai and Elias obliged. I liked how they felt, leaning over my chest to kiss. I watched them, their tenderness as they sipped from one another slowly. It was erotic to watch the way their tongues danced together, to hear their breathless murmurs against their lips.

"Don't hold back," I whispered, digging my hands into the roots of their hair, as if that could make them press closer together.

One of them groaned before they kissed more fervently. They didn't break apart, and when they did, it was to lean up and kiss me. Gods forbid I felt ignored. One after the other, we claimed each other until the heat between us became an explosion of something grander.

Kai hovered over me, tearing at his robe with impatience. He leaned down and kissed me heavily, thoroughly. I arched against him, and his taloned hands gripped my waist, bringing me up, aligning his warm length against my entrance to thrust into me. I cried out, tail wrapping around his.

He began to move, and we floated together.

"Elias," Kai spoke gutturally as he moved inside me.

My eyes flew open. "Do you feel ignored?" I was surprised the words could even come out of my mouth at all. My head spun, my body quivered. I was balancing on that edge, ready to plunge into the abyss all over again.

"Come here," Kai ordered.

Elias obeyed, sliding his body closer.

"Grab him, my gem. Take him down to the abyss with us."

My throat and body tightened, but his firm command was followed by a thrust that had me obeying. I reached blindly for Elias, grabbing his smooth length in my hand. Heat scorched my palm. He was hard as steel in my hand but as smooth as silk.

"I—I—" I swallowed.

Kai pressed a kiss to my brow. "I will teach you how, my gem." And then his hand closed over mine. Elias sucked in a sharp breath as we began to move. Up and down our hands slid, squeezing Elias' length from the hilt upwards and back down again. When we reached the base, Kai's hand squeezed roughly over mine, pulling a groan from Elias' lips.

Kai controlled the pace, the movements of our hands mimicking Kai's hips as he slammed in and out of me. Pleasure mingled until it was impossible to tell our feelings apart. Until it was impossible to discern where pleasure ended or began. All we had was this moment. This moment as I spiraled first, Kai hitting that spot inside of me that made me scream without reservation. Elias soon followed and Kai, he had been waiting for the rest of us first before he finally took the plunge into darkness.

We fell side by side by side, sounds of content echoing across the chamber rooms.

We belonged together now.

We shared the same secrets.

And that was a bond that could never be broken.

The next morning I awoke to an empty bed. Hardly surprising, considering our situation. I had no doubt that Elias had slipped through the tapestry and out the cove, while Kai would have had to exit quietly through the front door to my rooms while the guards switched their watch.

We'd spent most of the night in each other's arms. It was a strange thing, unburdening the truth. I felt lighter, now that we all knew each other, and the depths of each other's secrets. Spending all of last night talking—when we weren't doing other things—speaking truths of the palace and our lives.

It was comforting to know that my feelings weren't misguided and that I was not thought less of because of the callings of my heart. It was empowering to have Elias and Kai and for them to know the truth and not care.

"You are the mate of the Dragon Prince," Kai had whispered against my skin last night. "Dragons hoard treasure. It's only fitting that you do so as well."

I suspected he was hoarding us as well. The three of us, we were formidable together.

And for once, here in this palace, surrounded by all this finery, I finally felt content.

I got up and started getting ready for the day.

After I'd cleaned away all evidence of last night's rendezvous from the room, got cleaned, and dressed—stashing Elias' ring into a place it wouldn't be found—, my whirlwater of a day began.

Captain Saber hadn't been lying when he said that royal balls were hard work. And I was required at every single part of the planning. He'd gotten there this morning with the seamstress in tow. The plump mermaid had dropped her bag on the floor, rang for tea, and efficiently began pulling out swaths of fabric, unfolding it until it became a dress, swaying in the water.

"This is all I have so far, but I wanted you to try it on before I got any further with the details."

It was a dress of ice blue that she slipped over my raised arms and began tugging and pulling at the waist. The dress was heavy, and already I didn't like it. It wasn't the craftsmanship, because that was beautiful. It was just... too much. It was like something Odele would wear.

I didn't let my discomfort show on my face. I did not want to offend her when she'd obviously worked so hard on it. So I suffered through the fitting, trying not to fidget with impatience. The only thing that got me through it were the looks Captain Saber kept throwing my way.

As if to say, *It's alright. I am here.*

And that was enough to get me through the two hours of fitting, tucking, and fixing.

"I'll have it done in two days," the seamstress said as she packed up her bag for the day. "The dress will be delivered straight to your rooms."

I nodded, and Captain Saber escorted her out. As he did, I slipped on another dress, but before I could even think about plopping onto the bed for a much needed rest—that my sore body was demanding—the captain was in my rooms again. Immaculate, and hands behind his back.

His gaze roamed over me, and my face flushed. It was almost as if he could see through me. As if he were peeling back my every layer to reveal the nakedness underneath.

"You look happy," he commented curiously, head cocking to the side.

I gulped, but did not reply.

I don't think it was needed anyway, because the captain just smirked a bit. "I hope you keep that attitude on for the rest of the day, because we have more work to do."

And so my day began in earnest.

MAISIE BRAVELY TOOK THE tasks head on without a word of complaint. I trailed after her, leading her from one location to the next without a breath in between.

Still, she kept her head high as she was bombarded by servants and royals alike. She even faced the queen with dignity as they kept up with appearances and went over the guest list and decorations. I was sure Queen Circe was surprised at her efficiency.

As if Maisie had been born for this.

She very well could have been a royal in a past life.

When the last of the decorations had been chosen, the last dance rehearsed, and the last of the food tasted, I finally was able to lead Maisie away. Not towards her rooms, but down further in the palace.

"Captain, where are we going?" she asked suspiciously.

I didn't know why my body had led her down here, all I knew was that there was a giant part of me that didn't want this day to end. I didn't want to lead her to her rooms, where she would lock herself in and not emerge unless she was needed.

I wouldn't admit it, but I'd had fun at her side, watching her. Seeing what she'd blossomed into was staggering. There were moments throughout the day when her gaze would find mine across whatever space separated us. As if she were searching for recognition, or searching for a friendly face in the crowd to get her through something so difficult.

I'd blink at her as if to say, *I am here, Maisie.*

Her answering smile each time only made me want to prolong our tasks.

And so here we were in the stables.

Maisie froze at the entrance. Wide, frightened eyes taking in the beasts tethered behind their stalls.

"Why are we here? Riding wasn't on the schedule, was it?" There was a note of fear in her voice, making me recall the first time she'd laid eyes on Geronimo. There had been fear trembling through her body, and at the time, I'd been nothing but harsh. Annoyed. Frustrated. Because I'd sought out to find one mermaid and found Maisie instead.

Now I didn't feel an ounce of annoyance at all.

I stopped in front of Geronimo's stall. A groomsmer swam towards me, eyes offering help. I waved him off with my hand.

"Would you like to ride?" I asked.

Her face flushed brightly and my eyebrows pulled together with confusion when she started sputtering incoherently. Finally, she stopped, took a deep breath, and replied, "I don't think so… I mean…" Her eyes went nervously to Geronimo, his height, the vicious strength in his serpentine tail.

"It's alright," I assured her. "It will be alright." I turned to my hippocampus and he stuck his beastly head from the stall, whinnying softly as I stroked my hand down his nose.

There was comfort in animals. To them, status didn't matter. Rich, poor, captain, servant, queen… What mattered was affection. Geronimo was a faithful companion and could sense my moods. Sometimes he knew me better than I did.

He bumped his nose against mine and I smiled, rubbing my palm down his neck. "Ssh, ssh," I reassured him, even if he needed no reassurance. He bumped me again. "I missed you, too, Ger."

I felt Maisie's tentative presence at my side. "You're good with him," she whispered, voice trembling slightly.

I smiled at her. "You'd be surprised by all the things I'm good at."

Her face flushed brightly, and in turn, mine did too. Where had those words come from? I nearly sputtered with sudden nerves, but straightened my resolve. I was Captain of the Royal Guard, not a blushing mermaid in her teens and wouldn't be reduced to one. No one had ever made me feel this way before. No one had ever twisted nerves in my stomach the way Maisie suddenly did.

Since that first moment, her presence had been overpowering, had filled me with something I hadn't recognized, had pushed away with every fiber. Now, everything was different. A trust was starting to build. A trust I needed to ensure her safety. A trust I was suddenly beyond desperate to attain. And perhaps it had nothing to do with her protection at all.

Perhaps, I just wanted a friend.

"Do you want to touch him?" I asked, equally tentative, my voice a breathy rasp.

Her body tensed. "Oh, I don't—"

"Do you trust me?"

She blinked. "What?"

I held my hand out to her. "Do you trust me?"

She stared at my hand for the obvious offering that it was. My breath caught tightly in the back of my throat as I waited, heartbeats counting the seconds.

Ba-dump.

Ba-dump.

Ba-dump.

As if this moment would determine everything.

Slowly, she placed her hand on mine.

The breath I'd held pushed past my lips softly. I tugged at her hand and she swam in front of me, Geronimo looming over her smaller stature. A gasp escaped her throat, but I held her hand firmly.

"It's okay," I reassured, both mer and hippocampus. My hand encircled her wrist and slowly, I brought her hand up and placed it over Geronimo's nose.

My hippocampus sniffed once, twice, and nuzzled her hand, as if sensing her nerves. That gentle action from him was just enough to have her tightly coiled body relaxing in front of me, nearly curving into me.

"See?" It was difficult to even speak, and I couldn't quite determine why. "He's harmless."

A shuddering laugh escaped her. "Right. It's not like his hooves could trample me through the silt or nothin'."

She'd dropped her practiced Eramaean accent, and I could tell she regretted it immediately. Her following gasp had been as great an indicator as any. But I did not reprimand her. It had been so long since I'd last heard her speak that way, I'd nearly forgotten what her real accent sounded like.

"Sorry," she apologized, smoothing her palm up and down Geronimo's nose. "I guess I'm a little nervous…"

"Don't be. It's fine." I swallowed, willing myself to be brave and to ask, "Is it… is it hard? The accent…" I hadn't asked before. I'd only pushed and pushed until her speech had been close to perfection. I never bothered to question if it was a burden for her or not. Why would I, when I'd swam around like an entitled tadpole? We all had burdens to bear, and I hadn't cared if Maisie had just a bit more than most.

She shrugged, her shoulders pressing into my chest. I hadn't realized how close we were. "I'm used to it," she said distractedly. "Sometimes, I forget I had an accent to begin with."

"I suppose to you it wouldn't have been an accent at all…"

She laughed softly. "I guess not."

Another breath of silence stretched. I cleared my throat. "Would you ride with me through the gardens, princess?" A formal offer. Nothing more than a guard offering to escort his princess.

Maisie turned so she was looking over her shoulder. Her dark purple lashes were curved and coquettish as she blinked up at me. When she smiled, I was almost blinded by the radiance of it, and almost hated myself for the offer. For the real reason behind it.

"Sure."

I gave her a nod, and then began prepping Geronimo. I combed him down before putting his saddle over his back and then leading him out of the stall. Maisie gave him a wide birth until I beckoned her over. She came over tentatively, limbs shaking. I made sure to give her hips a reassuring squeeze as I lifted her up and set her down on the saddle, and didn't dally as I jumped up behind her.

My arms caged her in. I felt the press of her deep in my core. The curve of her back against my chest, the soft tendrils of her floating hair caressing my cheeks…

I nudged my tail into Geronimo's side and he started forward at a slow pace, swimming out of the stables and around the palace until we made it to the gardens. The mer didn't tend to ride their hippocampi through here, fearing the plants would be trampled to the silt, but I'd seen Maisie's face that day in the gardens with Prince Kai. She liked it here, more than anywhere else in the palace.

I wanted her to look at something nice, something beautiful, when I broke the news.

My heart thundered against my chest as my mind fought to form the words I wanted to tell her. I was no good with words. I was no good with anything. I had no idea how she'd even react. Perhaps she would be horrified, and perhaps not.

"When mer are selected," I blurted, causing her to tense. "They go through a stage of training. They're brought here to the capital and taught the art of war."

"Captain, why are you telling me this?"

I pushed on. "By the end of their vigorous training, the mer go through a second round of Selection. They are chosen based on skill, and placed in different areas. The front lines, desk jobs, guards, spies…" There was a whole list of things the mer could be doing after Selection.

"Captain…"

That was a tone of warning in her voice.

Still, I pushed on. "They aren't all sent to war. Not without training. Even then… it's rarely the selects who get chosen. Unless they show apt talent for fighting, that's where they'll go." I was nervous, and my stomach was roiling, hands tightening on Geronimo's reins a little too tightly. "Sometimes they're stationed somewhere in the kingdom, other times they're stationed in Kappur."

"Captain…"

"So not every Select goes to war, but they do take part in it. In some way. Not many of the mer know that, and Thalassar does not go around advertising it. Even the selects are prohibited from speaking of it. If the mer knew that there were two parts to Selection, they would fail during training if only to be placed in a lesser ranked position. So the queen instills fear so that they obey, though by the end of it, it's all rather lenient."

"Why are you telling me this?!" Maisie shouted. I could feel the ragged inhalations of her breathing against my chest.

"I—" I did not want her to see us as complete barbarians. "I—"

"You're telling me," she interrupted slowly, "that there's a possibility that all my friends are alive? That… that they may not have been fighting in the war in the first place?"

"I—"

"Why?" Her voice broke. "Why are you telling me this *now*? Why couldn't you tell me this on the way *here*?"

Mistake. Mistake. I'd made a stupid mistake. I'd been so preoccupied, plagued with thoughts of Odele that I hadn't thought to mention it. Just another stupid mistake from me. Something else Maisie could hate me for. Perhaps it had been a bad idea to tell her. Perhaps I should have just kept this information to myself. She probably hated me more than she ever did, and any hope I had of gaining her trust was now lost.

"I tried…" I whispered weakly, hands tightening so hard, I thought my fingers would snap. "I tried to tell you we weren't…" Barbarians. I broke off. Could I even claim that?

"The queen still sentences those who flee to die."

"I know." Thalassar was not perfect. Far from it. But the queen was trying as best as she could to get this war with Kappur over and done with.

"Why?" Her voice was venomous. "Why are you telling me this now?"

This would be the hardest part.

I took in a breath.

"I went to inquire about Gilbert Eaton."

Her body tensed before she whipped around. Her glare was like a dagger that pierced straight into my heart. Disbelief widened her obsidian eyes. Shock. Anger. Hurt. An array of emotions kept her frozen.

"As Captain of the Royal Guard to the Malabella family, it is quite easy to get what I want. Within moments, I had everything about his life in my hands. I didn't know why, but I wanted to know what became of that sea scum. He was stationed at the palace. Did you know that?"

She didn't. I hadn't known that, either. There were so many guards stationed there, and I was supposed to know every single one of them. Things had changed when I'd gone in search of Odele.

"So I paid him a visit."

The sea scum had been strutting around as if he'd owned the palace. He exuded arrogance and importance, and all I'd wanted to do when I saw him was slam my fist into his face. To make him feel the pain he'd put Maisie through. To change his life as irrevocably as he'd changed hers. But even a beating would never compare to what she had endured.

"Wha—I—"

"I demoted him."

She froze, mouth dropping open in surprise. "You what?"

I steeled my spine. "You cannot make me regret what I did. I'd have killed him myself if I could've, but even as the thought crossed my mind, death seemed too good a punishment for what he did to you. So I stripped him of his rank where he floated." And watched his life crumble to pieces before my eyes. Saw the light leave him. Saw the arrogance stripped away along with the decorations adorning his jacket, marking his rank. "And I would do it again in a heartbeat."

"Why?"

I tugged on the reins, pulling Geronimo to an abrupt halt. "Gods, Maisie," I said with frustration, forgetting myself entirely. "He hurt you. Isn't that a good enough reason to send him on janitorial duty for the rest of his miserable life? Death was too good for him, so I sent him, far, far away from you where he'll be shoveling silt until he dies. Do you want an apology? Because you won't be getting one from me."

Tears suddenly burst from the corners of her eyes, little air bubbles rising in a swarm above her head. She batted them away like she would pesky packs of shrimp swimming by.

She swiped at her eyes with the back of her hand.

Gods. I'd made her weep. My fingers tightened on the reins. She undoubtedly despised me now, and I could hardly blame her. I'd lied from the first day and now I'd taken a vengeance that should have been hers into my own hands. I'd fallen in too deep with Maisie, far deeper than I ever had with Odele.

Was I destined to ruin every good thing that was placed in my path?

"Gods, Ma—" I cut off, cleared my throat. "I did it for you. Maybe I had no right, but I couldn't bear the thought of him swimming around the palace, that blasted smile on his face, as if he hadn't completely ruined your life so long ago. As if—"

"It's fine," she interrupted.

I stopped my nervous ramblings to take her in. The tears were gone. All of them. Any traces of sadness she'd let show were now replaced with strong determination.

"I—it is?"

She let out a breath. "Just tell me this, Captain Saber, was he utterly and thoroughly crushed?" There was something there in her voice. Hope. Joy.

A smile touched my lips. "Well and truly destroyed, Your Majesty."

Her smile brightened. "Good." And then she turned away from me, but I could still feel the curve of her lips burning like a tangible thing. As brightly and as hotly as the radiance of the sun.

CAPTAIN SABER SURPRISED ME. Completely. As if something in him had changed overnight. He'd gone from the stiff, irritating guard and became something else entirely. He had loosened that tight hold on the imaginary reins he'd wrapped around me. Now, there was something there and I couldn't quite make out what it was.

I liked it. Liked this change in him. He seemed more relaxed, as if there was a weight lifted from his shoulders. It was the first time I'd actually seen him on the brink of smiling throughout the day.

It was a rather pretty smile.

Until I ruined it by asking, "Why did you fall in love with Odele?"

The smile touching his lips vanished in an instant, forming a thin line of displeasure. His body had tensed, and his stance resumed that of a royal guard rather than a simple merman escorting a mermaid through the gardens.

He held Geronimo's reins, but we'd stopped riding him after a while, even though the hippocampus could have swam for hours. I swam at Captain Saber's side, surrounded by hedges of coral in an array of sizes.

He looked past me, at the waters above and beyond, as if searching for a threat or an eavesdropper, I wasn't sure.

It was a long time later before he deigned to answer. "I don't know," he confessed. "It's not like we had any sort of relationship that ever went beyond guard or princess, but…" He paused, and I wondered if he was thinking back on the specific moment he realized he'd fallen in love with her. I didn't understand the hot twist of my gut that followed. "You have to understand," he went on. "I was with her, night and day, and though she was always surrounded by such wealth, I could not help but think she looked rather… lonely…"

Princess Odele, lonely? My mind wrapped around it. Perhaps it had been true. When I'd first arrived, I could feel it. Feel the vast space of the bedroom, the weight of jewels and crowns, with no one to share it with. No one until Elias and Kai. It *had* been such a lonely existence. But Odele had been born here. How was it she had no friends? No one to confide in beyond empty shells of recording conches?

"I guess I thought her loneliness matched mine. I never wanted to be her guard, you see. The honor of being the youngest Captain in Thalassarin history—at only twenty-three years old—and I was stuck playing babysitter. I wanted to be out there on the front lines, doing something." *Avenging my friends*. Those words went unsaid, but I heard them just the same. "I left everything to be a guard to an ungrateful princess. That's what it felt like. But eventually, I saw past her mask, saw how desperate she was to be free." He stopped speaking to pat Geronimo on the side of his neck in silent reassurance. For himself, or the hippocampus, it wasn't clear.

"She reminded you of you," I whispered, understanding dawning.

He bit his bottom lip, but nodded. "I guess that's true. Lately, though, I've realized…" His voice trailed off. His eyes got a far-away look in them, and I had a feeling Captain Saber wasn't physically here with me.

"Realized what?" I asked, bringing him back.

He shook his head, as if clearing the memories there. "Nothing. Never mind."

He lapsed into silence the rest of our swim, but I couldn't help but be plagued by thoughts and questions and the maddening desire to know what it was he was about to say.

"What do you miss the most about Lagoona?" Captain Saber asked.

It had become a game of ours. He would ask a question, I'd answer honestly, and then ask him one of my own. We'd been going at it for hours now, as we leisurely paced the gardens. As if we had nowhere else to be. I realized that maybe he was doing it on purpose, giving me a break from the pressures of palace life and the ball that loomed over me.

So we swam, and we sat, and we rode Geronimo, and we swam some more. Silence hardly pressed between us, yet when it did, it was companionable. And for once, I did not feel the anxious need to be perfect for Captain Saber.

I felt like I was in the presence of a friend.

"The *foooood*," I hummed, leaning back on the coral bench in the royal gardens. My stomach nearly growled in response. "Tides' Tavern made the *best* frog liver stew in all of Thalassar."

Captain Saber chuckled.

It was still surprising to hear such sounds come out of his mouth when I'd hardly been able to get him to smile before. Things were different now. We were both different. He did not have to pressure me into perfection because I'd already attained it. I was Odele, yet not. A waitress turned royal. I knew, without him having to say it anymore, that I was doing a good job.

"How many siblings do you have?"

"Four brothers and sisters," he answered. "Syberia, Liria, Thomas, and Rhia."

I blinked. "Syberia Saber?"

The captain stretched his tail out in front of him. Though his entire demeanor seemed careless, his eyes never ceased to remain alert. They darted to all places, gauging any possible threat, and his hand hovered close to the hilt of the sword at his waist.. "Much to my sister's delight..."

I always wondered what it would be like to have a sister or a brother. A family. Someone to care for you and take care of you.

My silence must have weighed heavily on Captain Saber, and my expression must have given away my thoughts. He cast me a long, sideways look.

"Do you remember anything about your parents?"

I swallowed the sudden rising lump in my throat. My grandmother hadn't told me much about my parents. She'd been my father's mother. Perhaps the memory of them had just been too painful a thing to recall.

"Not really." I tapped my fingers against my tail. "My father died before I was born, and my mother soon followed him to the grave. My grandma was my only family. Raised me since I was a baby." I shrugged, as if this meant nothing, yet my heart thundered inside. There was always a gaping hole, a longing inside me when I saw families, when I saw children. It reminded me of everything I never had and always wanted. Things that seemed so far out of my grasp.

"If it's any consolation..." he drawled slowly. "...I've learned that family isn't just blood relatives, but friends you find along the way." His own voice had taken on a sad tone to it.

I looked at him, and he stared back at me. Our eyes held. Blue on black for a long moment and communication, reassurance, passed between us. My hands trembled at the intensity heating in his depths. I had to tighten them into fists, to avoid him noticing the way they shook.

"We should probably get back," I breathed heavily.

Captain Saber nodded slowly. Finally, he got up, gaze breaking away from mine, posture straightening into cold frigidness. I took a moment to calm my nerves before I got up after him.

He placed me on top of Geronimo's saddle, climbing on behind me. With a flick of the reins, the hippocampus darted back to the palace.

And the whole way there, I could do nothing but concentrate on the sensation on my hips, right where Captain Saber had touched me.

For the life of me, I couldn't quite figure out how, or why, his touch had burned like a brand.

THE DAY OF THE engagement ball was nearly upon me, upon us. And my nerves were frazzled. I'd spent the entire week ushered from one room in the palace to another, helping the queen put together the last bits of decorations and details for the party. Or rather, watch her scream at the servants until they finished. Even though I'd done an exceptional job at every task the queen had thrown my way—and I swore, I saw surprise on her beautiful features—I was still nervous.

The dress arrived the day before. Swaths of blue silk and gossamer, diamond studded top, and long, sheer sleeves. It was beautiful. Made of crystals and jewels, it shimmered in the light of glowing jellies.

It looked so expensive I was almost too afraid to touch it.

A knock on the chamber doors distracted me from the pretty gown. I went and opened it to find Prince Kai on the other side of the door, holding a folded piece of black fabric in his hands.

"My gem," he greeted, warmth showering his every feature.

The warmth he greeted me with had me answering with my own, even if my face heated.

I hadn't seen him since the other night. Not since he, Elias, and I…

"Prince Kai, what brings you here?" I asked politely, perhaps overly so, but there were guards posted behind him, watching his back with their hands tightened on their spears, being over protective.

"I come bearing gifts." He gestured at the cloth in his hands. His dark eyes twinkled with mischief and danger as they roamed over my body.

My throat tightened as I pushed the door open. "Come in."

He swam past me and I kicked the door closed behind him, setting the lock in place.

Kai swam slowly but with a purpose in each stroke. He made his way over to the bed, where he gently placed the folded cloth, right next to the gown. When he straightened, he was eyeing it carefully.

"Is that your gown for the ball?" he asked.

I swam to his side. "It is. Pretty, isn't it? Almost too pretty to wear."

He hummed in response and turned to me, heat filling his eyes. They glowed briefly, the only sign he gave of the dragon beneath. And then he kissed me.

As if we had been apart for centuries, rather than days.

His arms snaked around my waist, pulling me up to his chest. I threw my own around his neck, kissing him back with equal parts desperation and happiness.

He pulled away long enough to murmur against my lips, "I missed you, Maisie."

The sound of my name—my real name—coming from him had me trembling all over.

"I missed you, too." And Elias. That remained unsaid, but the words pulsed between us both.

Slowly, I slid down the length of Kai's body, his hands holding my hips to steady me in the water. "I brought you a gift," he whispered shyly.

My eyes went to the cloth he'd laid on the bed.

"Open it."

Pulling away from him, I swam over to the edge of the bed, pushing away the fat, swaying anemones. I unfolded the piece of black wrapping, setting it aside to reveal the contents underneath.

When I picked the garment up, a black dress slowly unfolded, the edges floating up. My fingers held it lightly, recognizing the precious material that it was. A dress, made up of fine Draconian silk. White thread embroidered along the high neckline, and when I turned it over carefully, the pattern trailed to the back. A dragon of white, baring teeth and claws.

"You have a dress already, but I thought you could wear this instead." He sounded suddenly nervous. I stared at the dragon embroidered at the back of the dress. It was a vicious thing, with knowing eyes, waiting to attack. "Perhaps it goes against Thalassarin etiquette, but…"

"I love it," I whispered, turning to him. Emotion made my voice crack. "It's beautiful." I held it to my chest, inhaling the scent of it, the scent of him that lingered on it.

Relief and affection shone in his dark eyes. "I am glad."

We stayed like that for a moment before Kai finally cleared his throat.

"I would offer to stay, but if I don't get back to my rooms soon, Ichiro and Lee will come find me." A half-hearted laugh that I echoed.

They tried to keep a tight leash on him and lectured him if he did not follow the rules of Thalassar's etiquette. No doubt they told Kai's father everything that happened within the palace. What had happened between us. I wondered briefly what the emperor thought of that, and what he would say when he realized I wasn't who I said I was.

"I understand." I carefully placed the dress back on the bed and started to escort Kai from the rooms. We made it to the door, where Kai stopped me from opening it by pulling me into his arms and kissing me thoroughly.

"Until tomorrow, my gem." A promise. One that curled darkly down my body, leaving me wanting more.

"Until tomorrow."

And then Prince Kai left the room.

It was the day of the ball, and I barely got a moment to breathe. I was hauled from the comforts of my bed early morning by a knock on the door. A hearty breakfast had been ushered in, which I ate quickly, and then I was escorted by a group of Captain Saber's most trusted guards to speak with the queen and king in private about my role at this ball.

That meeting had been filled with threats, mostly spat from the queen's lips, about how she wanted nothing more than the most perfect behavior. That I was to act like Princess Odele at all moments. "And for the love of gods," she'd pleaded, "do not start talking politics with the guests."

It hadn't even crossed my mind to do so. In fact, it had been a long while since I'd last thought about Selection. Perhaps it was a selfish thing, but ever since Captain Saber had told me the truth about it, it did not weigh upon me so heavily. How could it when there was a possibility that the mer were alive? Everyone I had known might be out there somewhere. Stationed at different places around this kingdom or another. Unable to breathe a word to their families, to anyone about what had really happened to them.

The war was still there, a looming, terrible thing. Thalassar was far from perfect. My goal was still the same: to end the war and better the kingdom. And yet, it was Odele and the missing royal whom I had to find first.

So I nodded my acquiescence to the queen, ever the picture of a demure servant before I set about my day.

I hadn't seen Prince Kai or Captain Saber at all. The former presumably getting ready for the ball, the latter preparing security measures throughout the palace.

I sat in my room afterwards, soaking in the sand-filled tub, hoping that no one would make an attempt on my life that night. I hated that life-threatening attempts had become my norm now. Couldn't I have one relaxing day?

I must've fallen asleep in the tub, because when I awoke, the sands were cold and it was late into the evening. I got up, wrapping a silk robe around myself, and made my way into my room. My gaze stopped short on the bed where two dresses sat side by side.

One that was appropriate for Thalassarin royalty, and another that was obviously meant for a Draconian princess. I looked over both of them carefully.

Prince Kai had really wanted me to wear that to the ball tonight. But the queen had made me swear to be the perfect royal. To be Odele.

My hands hovered over the black dress, a thing made of less jewels and layers than the other. It was simpler in make, yet somehow was much more beautiful.

I sighed and picked up the blue dress.

I dropped the silk robe from my shoulders and slipped on the beautiful blue dress, pulling it over my tail first. My fin got caught on the layers, and hours in the cold sand suddenly made it cramp up. I cried out as I went tumbling through the water, throwing out my hand to right myself on a coral shelf. My fingers bumped into the leather bindings of a frayed, two-legger book, sending it sliding across the shelf and ramming onto an old, chipped conch.

The conch toppled to the floor.

With a very un-princess-like curse, I righted myself, yanking the dress up and shoving my arms through the sleeves. Heavy, tedious thing. I grumbled as I bent down to pick up the shell that had fallen. When I straightened again, I ran my fingers over it.

It was an old conch shell, thin and cracked in certain parts. Algae covered it in a second layer, and I scraped it away with my fingernail.

Princess Odele had a collection of things throughout the room. Glass and diamond figurines arranged neatly side by side on shelves. But this shelf had been reserved for things that were not so nice looking. Things I couldn't imagine a princess would even want. Two-legger objects, the teeth of alligators and sharks, pebbles and sea glass, and this shell.

My heart suddenly thundered.

Many, many nights ago, I'd dreamt of this. I'd dreamt of a mer holding this shell just like I was right now. I wondered if that dream had meant something, if it'd even been a dream at all.

I whirled from the shelf, conch in hand, and hurried my way over to the secret passageway. I swam through without the guidance of light. Not that I needed it anymore. I knew this tunnel as much as I knew myself now. I swam straight until I reached the dead end, then bent low, feeling for the hole in the wall. When I found it, I swam-crawled through it, careful to keep the conch ahead of me and unscathed.

There was a ripping as I slipped through the tunnel and came out the other side. I ignored it and swam down in the cavern, all the way to the conch recorder.

Please be something important, I begged as I placed it face down on the recorder. The machine started up, twirling and twirling. Bubbles rose from it, a familiar silvery sheen around the edges. Slowly, I sank into the couch as it started.

All was quiet at first. Nothing but a white-silver bubble stared back at me. A few minutes passed, and I nearly got up and ridiculed myself for my silly notions, when a voice on the recording suddenly spoke.

"On this Sunsday, we gather together in the Tides, as Stars, Moon and Skies do witness, the joining of these two mer in holy matrimony."

My breath suddenly held as the image in the bubble changed, and two mer appeared there. A mermaid and merman, dressed impeccably in royal gown and jacket. Facing each other, they were both incredibly beautiful. And I knew them right away.

"I, Princess Odessa Malabella Sanitorum, first born daughter of the mer kingdom of Thalassar, hereby take and accept this mer as my husband, and promise to love and to cherish him for the rest of my life. So the Seas, Tides, Stars, Moon, and Sun be my witnesses."

A long strip of cloth wrapped around their joined hands.

The long dead Princess of Thalassar.

Odele's aunt.

"And I, Prince Dorian Knoll Gennivus, first born son of the mer kingdom of Kappur, hereby take this mer as my wife, and promise to love and to cherish her for the rest of my life. So the Seas, Tides, Stars, Moon, and Sun be my witnesses."

A second piece of cloth wound around their hands, joining the two mer who had been promised to others in holy matrimony.

The King of Kappur.

Thalassar's enemy.

My heart nearly burst from my chest as I watched the two mer kiss. Kiss as if they were in love and knew nothing and no one else but each other.

"And I promise to help give Kappur and Thalassar many, many heirs," King—at the time of the recording, *Prince*—Dorian joked.

Princess Odessa laughed, a joyous, heartfelt sound. "Don't say that while we're being recorded!"

His laughter rose up to mingle with hers, and then he picked her up and twirled her round and round.

And then the recording died in tiny silver and gold bubbles.

I sat in dumbfounded numbness for what felt like hours, until I finally found the will to get up, and play the recording once more. As if something in it would change. As if I'd seen wrong. As if it would make it untrue.

But it wasn't.

Princess Odessa and King—Prince—Dorian had wed. Even when Odessa had been engaged to Xristo and Dorian had been engaged to Odette, they'd wed.

Suddenly, all the pieces fell into place. One after another, they tumbled through my mind, stacking high until it all, finally, made every bit of sense.

A broken contract. A dead princess. A missing royal. A war with Kappur.

Oh, gods.

The missing royal was heir to the Kappurin throne.

That was why Kappur had waged war on Thalassar. That's why King Dorian had let this go on for so long. There had been whispers that the war had started between Thalassar and Kappur because of a love gone wrong. They'd been discarded as ridiculous.

And yet it was the ridiculous explanation that made the most sense.

They'd wed, and she'd been murdered, her child gone—taken?—and in his grief, or in search of his heir, King Dorian had waged war against his dead wife's kingdom.

No one had known why the war had started, because this had been kept secret. Because the royals of Thalassar didn't want the kingdom to know that their princess, that their *heir,* had eloped and broken contract. That she'd defied them, their rules, and chose to follow her heart instead.

For there was no question about it, I thought, as I watched the recording, as I watched King Dorian take Princess Odessa into his arms and kiss her. There had been the greatest of love between them.

"Gods…" Everything was so much clearer now.

Odele had known. She had somehow found this conch recording, had left it in plain sight. There was no doubt now in my mind that she'd left to find the missing royal. Had she just wanted to know her cousin, wherever he—or she—may be, or had she thought that bringing this information to light would stop the war that plagued her kingdom?

Technically, if Odessa and Dorian had wed and had had a child after, it would mean that their child was not only the heir of Kappur, but of Thalassar as well. Odessa had been the elder sister, and had she not died, she would have ruled.

But even if they'd wed, would Thalassar consider the legitimacy of the union? They'd broken contract, after all. And who had wed them? There hadn't been a face behind that first voice. I had to find out. If the mer who had wed them was still out there… maybe he knew something. Royal children were baptized once they received their name, blessed by a royal priest.

I got up, a new urgency in my strokes. I had to tell Elias and Kai this new discovery. Elias could help. Princess Odele had hired him to look for mer. Maybe one of them on that list had been the priest. I pried the conch carefully from the recorder and then turned to swim up the cove. I crawled through the tunnel, down the passageway, and pushed aside tapestry and emerged into the room.

I held the secret of all royal secrets within my hand. The one thing that could determine the future of Thalassar and Kappur forever. Carefully, I placed it back in its rightful place. Hidden in plain sight.

I took a moment to admire Odele's cleverness. Everything I'd wanted to know hadn't been in that cove, but here in this room. I'd been none the wiser.

"Clever, clever princess," I muttered with a smile, then turned from the shelf. The sight of myself in the mirror made me cringe.

The dress, the beautiful, beautiful dress had been thoroughly ruined with mud and silt.

If the seamstress saw this, she would tear my hair out, royal or not.

I quickly undressed and washed up again, shaking dirty silt from my hair. I had no choice now but to slip on the dress Prince Kai had gotten me. I'd wanted to preserve it, to keep it for myself. Wearing a dress he'd gotten for me was like shouting out for all of Thalassar to see that I belonged to him. Me. Maisie Fauna, not the princess. And it only hurt, because when

I eventually left and he wedded Odele, I'd have nothing left but this dress to remember him by.

Shaking off those negative thoughts, I pulled a jeweled comb through my hair, pulling it back into the most elegant bun I could muster. When I finally turned to look at myself in the mirror, a small gasp escaped me.

I looked…

I didn't dare think the word.

The dress fit me like a second skin. There were no flowing layers to it, but it was loose enough in the tail to allow for free movement. A slit rode up the right side of me, showing off the elegance of my bright, aquamarine fins on my good side. The top was tight against my chest, but not constricting, and the neckline was a high thing, pressing up against the base of my throat, where little white buttons trailed down the front.

I would have looked like a Draconian, if my features had been darker, my eyes more curved. And yet there was no greater acceptance than this, than wearing the clothes of his kingdom with pride.

I did a vain twirl, admiring the dress in the back, the white dragon embroidered there.

A knock sounded at the door, and then Captain Saber's voice drifted over from the other side. "Princess, it is time to leave. You're late for the ball."

How long had I been down there? I tried not to dwell on that as I went over and opened the door.

"The queen is—" Captain Saber's voice nearly choked off as he saw me and what I wore. His golden skin seemed to heat, cheeks reddening as his eyes breathed me in. As if he'd never quite seen me before. I suddenly felt very nervous, and I couldn't explain why. Especially when I took him in. He wasn't wearing his usual military jacket, but a different one. A decorative one in blues and golds, an ornate sword sheathed at his hip. "Princess…"

"Yes, Captain?" My voice came out rather husky. With a start, I realized it was the same voice I used on Elias and Kai when I was being kissed.

I cleared my throat.

It seemed to break him out of his staring spell. "The queen and king are waiting for you, and Prince Kai has already arrived and is waiting for the first dance." His voice came out strong, stiff, yet his eyes warmed on mine.

"Of course, Captain. Please, lead the way."

MY BLOOD BOILED TO impossible temperatures at the sight of Maisie in Draconian wear.

It wasn't anger that spurred the heat in my voice, but something else entirely. Something I wasn't sure I could admit to myself.

Like the feelings I once had for Odele, I would push this away too, whatever it was, even if a more primitive part of me was screaming to give in to it. To give in to *something* for once. To be selfish. To take, regardless of the consequences.

I hadn't been able to feel for Odele freely because of our differences in station. But with Maisie… Well, there wasn't much of a difference at all. A princess and I could never be, but *Maisie*? We were a possibility.

Except for the way she looked at Prince Kai, and the way he looked at her.

Impossibilities lied between us. A frustrating sensation, one that made me think that perhaps I was just destined to be alone. I wondered if Maisie was destined with the same fate as I. To love those who we could never truly have.

My hands clenched at my sides as I forced myself to look around for threats. To focus on the one job I'd been tasked with. To protect Maisie with my life.

Her life had been threatened publicly many times. I would not let it happen again.

"You look handsome tonight, Captain." Her voice weakened me. I almost tripped stupidly over my own tail and righted myself into a strict posture, hoping the other guards hadn't seen me fumble.

"Thank you, Princess. As do you." Stupid. Why was I so stupid? "Look beautiful, I mean. Not handsome, I mean." Stupid, stupid, stupid. What was wrong with me? This had never happened before and I felt entirely out of my element.

I didn't like it.

"Thank you, Captain. That's very kind of you."

I strengthened my resolve, pushed nerves aside. Diving into these depths would do no one any good. Not me, and certainly not her. So I gave everything an enormous shove and focused on the one task I needed to excel at.

Protecting her.

I gave a silent wave of my hands to the guards as we approached the wide, double doors to the ballroom. They fanned out ahead of us to scour the halls and the room beyond. The queen and king were already waiting on the high balcony that led down quartz stairs. Waiting for Maisie.

"Just like you practiced," I reassured her when I saw her body tense. And much like the first time she'd attended a royal party, my hand inadvertently reached out to the back of her dress and gave it a slight tug of reassurance.

She visibly relaxed, held her head high, and swam forward.

And all I had to do was follow.

THE BALLROOM HUSHED THE minute I swam on that balcony. I held my breath and kept my head high. I did not look down, didn't see anyone. I could barely feel anything past my nerves. How could I, when there were recorders everywhere, each one pointed straight at me? Waiting for me to mess up. Waiting for me to be attacked. Waiting for… something.

I turned to the queen and king, both of them stunning in dress and robes of dark blue. I wondered if there had been a theme to the dress code and I'd ruined their plans by donning Draconian attire.

Slowly, I bowed to them.

"Mother, father," I commented demurely. When I looked up, the king was smiling at me, his eyes warm with affection. The queen's gaze was serious, yet she bowed her head just the same.

"You're late," she whispered from the side of her mouth, even as she smiled at the recorders pointed our way.

"Forgive me," was all I said.

"Nothing to be done about it now." She clapped her hands, and everyone in the ballroom turned to look at her. "Thank you all for attending this ball to celebrate my beloved step-daughter's engagement to Prince Kai Li of Draconi." Slow, polite clapping was the reply. When it died down, she continued, "In honor of the union of our two kingdoms, the princess and the prince will now join together in their first dance."

Music began rippling through the water, the slow melody of a waltz. I gulped. That was my cue. I'd swim down those stairs to the center of the ballroom, where Kai would meet me, and the royals of Thalassar would crowd around and scrutinize us.

I prayed to the gods my fin wouldn't cramp up.

I straightened and then slowly made my descent to the floors below. Mer, faces known and unknown, crowded around and watched me. I met no gazes, but could feel the shock travel through them as they beheld what I wore and whispered about it behind open fans.

It was a break of etiquette, or perhaps just strange, to see who they thought to be Odele wearing the colors and silk of a foreign kingdom, without jewels decorating her neck or any sign of superfluity.

Finally, I made it to the center of the room, where Prince Kai was waiting for me.

The sight of him melted my dignified façade. Because when I saw him, all I could do was freeze and breathe him in.

Every. Single. Inch.

He didn't wear ceremonial robes today.

In fact, his outfit matched mine perfectly, save for the color. Draconian wear in white, black buttons followed the material up to his neck. The material covered him like a second skin, tight to show off the wide set of his shoulders and the strength of his arms. White to my black. And where white thread embroidered against my chest and shoulders, disappearing at my back, black thread adorned his.

He didn't need to turn around to show me what I already knew would be there.

A black dragon to match my own.

His long hair was tied back with white ribbon, away from his face, gifting all of Thalassar with the beauty in his refined features. His eyes seemed to spark, and the side of his mouth lifted up into a smile as he took me in. And then he bowed low to the waist with an absolute flourish.

"Princess…" His whisper carried out through the water like a caress everyone could feel. I swore the waters trembled along with them.

I willed my body to move and made my way towards him. Face to face we floated, music echoing around us. We stared, and stared.

"You wore it," he finally whispered. Affection glowed in his eyes.

"You didn't tell me it was part of a matching set."

I was aware of all eyes on us, of the recorders aimed our way. I wasn't sure I could bring myself to care when Kai was looking at me like that.

He smirked and reached for my hand, bringing it up to his lips. His mouth hovered over my fingers. "Now the whole world knows, my gem."

I swallowed past the lump in my throat and somehow managed to ask, "Knows what?"

"That we belong together." He kissed my knuckles and then swept me into his arms.

Beautiful.

There was no other way to describe the mer in my arms right now. She made my heart thunder with desire, made me want like I'd never wanted anything before. I didn't care if she was royalty or not. She had the heart of one.

And I had a plan.

I twirled her along the dance floor, holding her steady with one hand on her waist, the other clasped lightly in her own.

It was obvious she was no expert in the ballroom, and the scar on her fin made dancing difficult, but I would hold her, guide her, and catch her if she tumbled.

"Smile, my gem," I leaned forward to whisper along her cheek. The simplicity of the action caused onlookers to murmur behind their fans. Like public displays of affection were so scandalous. I could've sneered down at them all, but my only focus was her. The way heat rose to her cheeks at the feel of my lips against the softness of her skin.

"Everyone is staring," she muttered, her lips barely moving.

"That's only because you're the most beautiful mer in the room." I twirled, gently tugging her along with me. I could feel her body trembling with nerves. "Relax," I urged. "Enjoy the ball."

"Would you believe me if I told you I've never attended one of these before?" Her eyes darted around the ballroom, nervously taking in everyone encircling us.

"Do not look at them, my gem. Look at me. Only at me." My words had some hypnotizing affect on her, because her gaze snapped up to my eyes and held. She sucked in a sharp breath a moment before her body relaxed. I couldn't help but smile widely at her, to bathe myself in her expression. Her lips were full, beckoning me forward. Maisie was tantalizing and she didn't even know it.

"You're way too good at distractions," she whispered, blushing furiously.

I twirled her again, pulling her closer. My nails dug into her lower back, our bodies pressing intimately together. She made a soft sound of contentment that I felt deep in my bones. I could not help but lean over her, teasing her with my proximity.

"Perhaps I am…" My eyes locked on her lips. Inviting.

I couldn't hold back any longer.

I didn't care that there were hundreds of Thalassarins present, or that the queen and king were watching. Perhaps it was the moment. Perhaps it was seeing her in Draconian dress, a stake of my claim on my mate.

The dragon inside roared, one ferocious cry, before urging me forward.

I bent down and kissed her.

She tasted like freedom and adventure. Like secrets and light. I wanted to drown in every inch of her. To the abyss with everyone else, to the abyss with Thalassar and their propriety. She was mine. Ours, if I included Elias, which she obviously did. And after the other night, I did, too. We belonged to each other.

And nothing, no rules, status, or kingdom would ever tear us apart.

"I hate to interrupt…" a deep, accented voice commented, making me break away slowly from Maisie's mouth. Her flush rose to impossible heights as we froze our dancing and turned to face *Prince* Ytgar of Iol.

The blond mer, I dreadfully admitted, looked impeccable in his own foreign dress. A jacket of white and ice blue, the collar and lapels lined with white fur. The material flowed around his waist and down the length of his tail, keeping scales and fins hidden. A golden belt was secured at his waist, from which hung an ornate sword that appeared crafted of ice. His family crest stamped at the hilt, the image of a powerful orca.

"May I have this dance, Princess?" His ice blue eyes were focused solely on Maisie. He never even spared me a glance. As if I wasn't there at all. As if I was a hindrance or garbage floating in his way.

I fought to keep my temper level, even as the dragon in me growled possessively.

Iol and Draconi did not share love. Trading gone wrong in the past, I assumed. Who knew? Grudges were tricky little things and could last lifetimes without either party really knowing why. Iol was a closed off kingdom, their Prime Minister a worthless, thieving cad. What the kingdom had in strength, they lacked in everything else. Riches. Tact. Friendliness.

Yet Prince Ytgar assumed the waters of a charmer. His short, ice-blond hair was fanning over his head messily, yet it did not take away his appeal. If anything it made him look more beautiful.

I despised myself for thinking it.

"Um…" Maisie looked a bit indecisive, her hand squeezing gently over mine. She did not wish to leave me. That was enough reassurance for me to let her go.

"Of course." I smiled coldly at the prince.

But he and his ilk were the masters of ice and frost. I'd never been, but the northern waters were rumored to be made entirely of ice and snow. Unforgiving and cruel.

"Dance with your guests, my gem. I must speak with the queen for a moment." Before she could protest, I bent and placed another kiss on her lips. This one a brand. A possession. A claiming.

Strange that I'd felt the need to do so. When it had been Maisie, Elias, and I, there had been a claiming between the three of us. A way for each of us to place our mark, to get to know one another in every aspect.

With Ytgar, it was different. I did not feel the sensation I did with Elias. Of wanting to punish and be punished. To kiss and taste. To *share.*

There was something feral in the eyes of the Iolish Prince, hidden behind exuberant charm.

When I pulled away and slashed a grin in his direction, all Ytgar did was raise a bemused brow and tilt his lips slightly.

With that, I turned and swam away from them.

The crowds gathered, parted to let me by. I swam at a slow pace all the way up those steps and to the balcony, where the queen and king were watching everything as if it were a spectacle rather than their daughter's engagement party.

"Quite the display," the queen said icily as I slid in next to her. Her chin dipped, indicating the ballroom below where Maisie now danced with the Iolish.

"I'd like to speak with you about the wedding," I said. I would not have her dallying about when she knew what I really wanted. It was part of my plan. My plan to have Maisie as my bride and save Draconi in the process.

The queen flicked her fingers across the balcony railing, nails scraping along it quietly. The only sign of her annoyance, I supposed. "What about it?" she inquired leisurely.

"I wish for the date to be moved up. Within the next week."

King Xristo threw me a look of disbelief, his blue eyes widening. Queen Circe just tossed her head back and laughed.

"Look at you," she mused cruelly. "Making demands as if your voice had any holding here." She'd dropped the pretense of amity with those words and the look on her face. Why wouldn't she, with all the recorders pointed in Maisie's direction? "Your request is denied. We have a contract; you'll do well to stick to it."

I'd expected this. Had expected ardent denial. Maisie was not Odele, and that's why she was saying no. But I needed her to say yes. I needed to marry Maisie now, within the week, before the real Odele could be found. By the time we signed the marriage papers I'd have Thalassar's secrets against the two-leggers and my mate.

"Funny you should mention the contract, Your Majesty, because I looked it over just last night." The queen tensed. "Of course, with you going on in years, I assumed that was the reason as to your forgetfulness, but I won't hold it against you."

Her fingers tightened on the rail. "How dare—"

"The contract states that once the princess turns eighteen, we are to wed. Her birthday is in but a week and a half. We can wed on the day of. I do not see why you're objecting so heartily on the matter. Unless… there's a reason for it?"

Silence echoed, but I remained calm.

"Of course not," she snapped. "But Odele is not yet ready to take the throne."

King Xristo glared at his wife, but said nothing. A sad, pathetic merman who had lost his voice when he'd married this shark. Perhaps she wasn't objecting to the marriage itself, or of Maisie at all, but the fact that once we did wed, she would be forced to give up her position of power.

"Regardless, there is a contract we must keep. We wouldn't want to break that, now would we?" There was an underlying threat in my words, one she read all too well. They couldn't afford a war with Kappur *and* Draconi.

Her teeth grinded together almost painfully as she mulled this over. Finally, she replied, "Of course, Your Majesty."

I pushed away the smile of triumph that threatened to emerge, and instead, held out my hand to her. "It would be rude not to ask you for a dance, Queen Circe. Would you do me the honors?"

"Of course…" she ground out tightly, and still, she took me hand.

And I led the queen to the dance floor.

Prince Ytgar's palm was warm as it encircled my own and he pulled me close. As close as Kai had dared to hold me. I may not have been a royal, but I knew that the very little distance between us was improper. I could feel his every inch. And the ice in the Iolish Prince's eyes made me nervous, despite his beauty and charm.

"You look very beautiful tonight, Princess," he commented as he twirled me. My gaze tried to focus on his eyes, but they were as piercing as sticks of jagged ice. "Then again, there is never a day when you don't look beautiful." He smiled fully, revealing his bright teeth. There was a way in which he spoke that made me want to believe every word. Like his voice forced everyone around him to accept what he was saying as truth.

"Thank you. You look handsome yourself, Your Majesty."

"Call me Ytgar. Please."

I smiled at him. "Of course."

We danced in torturous silence for a few moments before I couldn't stand it any longer.

"How are you liking Thalassar thus far, Prince Ytgar? I confess, I wasn't aware you'd even arrived."

"Val and I arrived while you had the misfortune of lying in bed with poison coursing through your system." He twirled and then dipped me. My head spun and my fin nearly cramped with the exertion.

"Then I'm afraid you arrived at a terrible time, indeed."

The hand pressed against my lower back dipped a fraction. "I'd say I arrived at the most opportune moment. We never get out, see. I was hoping to fortify alliances and plan trade routes with Thalassar. I was expecting it to be dull." His eyes shone with mischief. "It's all actually rather exciting. Death attempts, jealous princes…"

My blood flared. "I'm glad my near death experiences have served to amuse you, Your Majesty." I suddenly stiffened in his arms and reached behind me to grip his ever sliding hand to yank it up and settle it on my back. Where it should be.

"Don't take offense, Princess. Think of it as a compliment. I was told you were spoiled beyond reason, yet you do not strike me as so. I dare say, I wish I'd gotten here sooner to procure a marriage alliance with Thalassar myself…"

"May I cut in?"

I was saved the embarrassment of replying by the sudden appearance of King Xristo. Ytgar froze, pulling away from me to bow deeply to Odele's father. Then he turned and brought my hand up to his lips for a kiss.

It was all so polite, and even if his words had been offensive, how was it possible that he still exuded charm as he swaggered away, casting me a flirtatious wink?

Those thoughts were blown away when the king took me in his arms and the tempo of the song changed.

I suddenly felt much more nervous than I had before. I was dancing with the King of Thalassar. He knew who I really was, and though he had not mistreated me since I'd been here, I did not want to give him a reason to do so.

I straightened my posture and twirled through the dance strokes, just like Captain Saber had taught me during this last week of activity. My fin cramped and I ignored it.

"How are you feeling?" the king asked. I didn't want to imagine it, but there was genuine, soft concern in his voice and expression as he took me in.

My heart seemed to flare to life with longing. I'd vowed I wouldn't feel this way, that I wouldn't let his words get to my head, but I couldn't help it. I was an orphan. I'd never known my family, never had a father. And a king was looking at me with fatherly love. Even if it was only because I resembled his missing daughter, I was desperate for whatever scraps of familial love I could get.

"I'm fine," I replied.

The dance required we separate a fraction, dancing between other couples before joining together again. When we did, there was a frown on his face.

"You're sure? We haven't had time to properly speak to one another, least of all in private."

The king's eyes were looking at me like sad, blue orbs. Like a lava globe with dimming light. As if he had no hope in them at all.

"I suppose Queen Circe doesn't want us speaking too closely." It was an off-handed comment, one I probably shouldn't have even said. But I couldn't help myself. Could the king possibly be an ally? Had he known that his intended had wedded another and been murdered for it?

"She is intimidated by you." He twirled me, the motion whirling the shock of the words out of my mind, only to come back when I caught sight of Kai and the queen dancing a few strokes away from us, though not close enough to hear. "You look so much like her."

My body tensed. "Like Odele."

His blue eyes widened, and when he shook his head vigorously back and forth, his braided beard shook with him. "No, no. I mean, yes, you look like my daughter, but you also resemble her mother a great deal."

Queen Odette. I'd studied her portrait for such a long time, her features were branded in my brain. Odele did look quite a lot like her mother, and if I looked like Odele, then it only swam to reason…

"She, too, was very kind," the king went on sadly, lovingly. His eyes got a far away look in them and I knew he was remembering her. His wife. "She loved her subjects and fought for her ideals, for what she thought was right." His gaze finally flicked down to me. "You are a lot like her in that regard."

"Odele…"

He got that sad look about him again, and he sighed. "You must understand. Odele lost her mother when she was very young and was raised by her mother's cousin. I gave her all I possibly could to make the pain of her loss ease. She still hurts and expresses it the only way she knows how."

I had nothing to say to that. How could I? The king loved his daughter. He wasn't blind to the terrible way she treated others, but he allowed it. He made excuses for her behavior and spoiled her beyond imagining. He thought he was doing her a favor, and who was I to tell him he'd done more harm than good?

"You must've loved her mother very much," I finally commented.

His eyes seemed to spark. "I did." Raw honesty.

"I've heard stories from the older mer in Lagoona that your wedding was a grand affair…"

He chuckled. "Quite. We were so young at the time, and we were both nervous for what awaited. A whole kingdom, the pressure to make heirs. I nearly vomited on the priest."

Thalassar was not a religious kingdom. We worshiped no specific gods, but paid tribute to them anyway. The rules of old were already embedded so deeply into our society that it hardly mattered where it all came from. Yet there were still priests. They baptized young mer, wed couples, and resided over death beds.

"Do priests marry all royalty?" I asked, palms suddenly growing warm. I kept thinking about that conch, the strips of cloth joining Dorian and Odessa's hands, the voice of the possible priest, and the happiness in their eyes.

"But of course. It wouldn't be legitimate otherwise."

I knew it.

I loosed a breath. "Is there a priest charged with marrying the entire Malabella lineage?"

"The priest who married Circe, Odette, and I was also the priest who married Odette's parents, and their parents before that."

"Will he be the one to marry Kai and—"

The king stalled answering by twirling me slowly. When I went back into his arms, he nodded. "He is the only royal priest in Thalassar. After… after Odele's marriage to Kai, I'm sure the priest will announce his successor." He must have been aware what I was about to ask because he answered me before I even got the chance. "I'm not sure how the priests do it. There's a secret ceremony in their temple. I assume the successor makes vows and receives honors. If they do not go through this ceremony, they are not considered a true royal priest."

Had Thalassar's royal priest been the one to marry Princess Odessa and Prince Dorian so long ago? No. If this priest had resided over the entire Malabella lineage, he'd be an old mer, bent on tradition, following the rule of the queen and king. If there had been a contract, the priest wouldn't have dared interfered, and he wouldn't have kept the elopement a secret.

It must have been someone else. A Kappurin priest, perhaps?

Thankfully, the song came to an end, and King Xristo bowed over my hand, making me flush. "I shall now take my leave," he said politely. I inclined my head, and he left.

Couples parted and then regrouped as a new song began to play. I wove my way through the bodies. I didn't think I could stand another dance. Not when my fin was cramping up painfully. It had been easy enough to ignore when I'd been in conversation with the king, but in its stillness, it flared.

I needed a breath of fresh water, away from the confines of this ballroom and its mer.

But then Prince Kai was before me again, eyes roaming over me and stopping on the left side of my tail. As if he could see through the material and the pain there. His eyes again found mine.

"Are you alright?" he asked quietly.

If I lied, he wouldn't believe me. Yet I didn't want him to see me as weak, as someone who could barely handle the span of two dances before she was panting and begging for rest.

"I'll deal with it," I replied.

Kai opened his mouth, obviously to argue, I could see it in his eyes, when we were suddenly interrupted by the presence of his advisor, Ichiro. The mer glared between the two of us. From the tension in his body, it was obvious he was in disapproval of our public display of affection earlier. At first I'd thought he disliked me because of my obviously wanton ways. He confessed it was because Draconi needed Thalassar, and they couldn't afford a single misstroke.

If only he truly knew all the misstrokes we'd had up until now, the poor mer would keel over in an early grave.

"Yes?" Kai demanded with impatience.

Ichiro replied in their mother tongue, a language I didn't understand. His words were hard and clipped, and he handed Kai a folded slip of kelp parchment before he turned and swam away.

"A servant handed him this missive and said we were wanted on the balcony."

"We?"

I swam to his side and watched as he carefully opened the slip of parchment. The letter for us both. There was no address, no name. But no name was needed when I beheld the bold strokes there. The image of twin black swords crossing.

The symbol of the Black Blade.

Kai crumpled the parchment, shoved it into the pocket of his outfit, and gestured with the slightest jerk of his chin that I follow.

Wide double doors were thrown open to reveal a veranda. The white marble balcony was twined with flowers of all kinds and the dark waters of night beyond.

Swimming to the balcony, I inhaled deeply. The waters outside were warm, but not suffocating. A steady current drifted past and schools of fish swam all around at leisurely and fun paces. It was true freedom.

I sighed, placing the palms of my hands onto the balcony rail and staring down at the drop below. The sea was a vast place. A whole world lived beneath these depths, just like a whole world lived on the surface, and surely a whole world lived in the skies.

Elias' face suddenly appeared, seemingly out of nowhere, in my line of vision. I startled, jumping and ramming into Kai's chest.

"Gods!" I pressed a hand to my chest, as if that could steady the rapid beating of my heart.

"Not the gods." Elias smirked. "It's just me."

I could feel Kai rolling his eyes behind me.

Elias' hands gripped the balcony, and he dangled from it leisurely, black tail gently swaying back and forth beneath him like a shadow. Such a careless demeanor, coming from an outlaw to the crown.

"What are you doing here?" I hissed. "If someone sees you—"

"No one will see me. I bribed the guards on watch with secrets so they'd leave their post for an hour. We are perfectly safe."

I still looked cautiously over my shoulder, to the doorway and the party beyond. The music was an upbeat tune now, and everyone was so busy with the revelry, that no one was even looking out here. Not even for the prince and princess.

It still didn't stop the anxiety from thumping in my chest.

"What's wrong?" I demanded.

Elias' eyes were alight with mischief. Something that shouldn't surprise me, but did. He took his safety way too lightly. Thought himself invincible. How irritating.

"Why does something have to be wrong? I just wanted to see you. The both of you." His eyes flicked up to Kai and remained, the dark depths heating. Kai tensed behind me, chest pressing closer to my back as he closed me tighter against the rail.

"We missed you, too," the prince purred seductively.

My face heated and I slapped a hand against Kai's chest. "Now's not the time for that!"

Elias pulled himself up onto the balcony, perching himself on the edge. Once again, I found myself sandwiched between the two mer. There was desire in infinite amounts pulsing between the three of us. But more than that, I felt panic.

"There's always time for a quick moment of passion…"

Kai snorted in response "Perhaps for you," he said mockingly. "But I never do anything *quick*."

I shivered.

How was it that his words could sound like both a promise and a threat and send delicious shivers of sensation through the entirety of my body?

Elias took this as a challenge as he leaned forward, so close his lips grazed against my cheek. "But it'd have to be quick. We have, after all, only one hour. If it's beyond your abilities, maybe you could just watch."

The suggestion heated me all over.

Oh, yes. Yes, please.

I gave my head a sharp shake. "No. We don't have time for that." I pressed my palms to Elias' chest and gave him a hard shove. He pulled away, eyebrows raised as he took me in. "I'm actually glad you're here," I rushed. "Not because of that, but because I have something to tell you both."

Black eyes went alight with the prospect of more secrets to be learned. Kai's hand slipped up my arm, a comforting and warm touch.

"What is it, my gem?"

I took a breath and began recounting it. All of it. Everything I'd learned from the conch, from the king, and my thoughts on the whole thing. When I finished, I swore no one was breathing.

"A missing royal, heir to the Thalassarin and Kappurin throne…" Elias mused, his eyes bright in the darkness.

"Perhaps. If the marriage was legitimized by a priest."

"That should be easy enough to find out." Elias cracked his fingers, danger thrumming off him in waves.

"It'd have to be a Kappurin priest," I pointed out. "I haven't met Thalassar's, but I'm assuming he's a stuffy, barnacled old mer with no sense of adventure."

This brought out a chuckle from both of them. And then Elias stroked his chin and said, "I have contacts throughout the city. I can ask around about Kappur's priests and customs…"

I breathed a sigh of relief I hadn't realized I'd been holding. Leave it up to Elias to work out a mystery and want to get to the bottom of things with quick efficiency.

"Meet us tonight in my room," I told him. "And we can plan our next strokes there."

He smiled, and his long fingers went to his cheek, to the thin cut there that hadn't yet healed. A mark of possession, and insinuation, as his finger slid over it.

"Is that all we'll be doing, little fish?" His voice became a deep rasp.

I swallowed past the sudden lump in my throat. "You're insatiable."

He leaned forward to take the lobe of my ear into his mouth and sucked. I shivered, vibrating onto Kai's body. Kai, whose hands snaked around the flat of my stomach and traveled higher to stroke my breasts.

"This is a bad idea," I whispered, even as I leaned into them.

"Relax," Elias murmured.

"Enjoy the ball," Kai added, as his fingers tweaked my nipples through the material, causing me to moan.

"Anyone could swim out and catch us." My protests fell on deaf ears as Elias kissed his way down my neck.

"Fifty minutes," he whispered hotly against my skin.

"We can't possibly…"

His lips on my mouth cut off any more protest I could have. His tongue explored the depths of my mouth, taking and demanding, pulling sounds from deep in my throat that made my exposed skin flush. And Kai… Oh, gods… His fingers were flicking the buttons of my dress, parting the material, he slipped his hand inside. His palm came into contact with my breast, holding me tightly.

I arched, moaning into his grasp. Demanding. My body demanded more. I wanted to be devoured by them, and all logical thoughts sank somewhere in my mind. Instead, passion buoyed. I could no longer think. All I could do was feel.

And this felt so good.

Elias tore his mouth from mine. "I'll be quick, little fish." His hand grasped the lower part of my dress and he hiked it up.

"But not *too* quick," Kai added, his lips at my ear.

Oh, gods.

I dropped my forehead to Elias' chest as his fingers made quick work of pulling my dress up to expose my waist and my slit. It pulsed for him, crying for his length to move inside me. Kai pressed a kiss to the back of my exposed neck.

"You're ready for me—for us—aren't you?" Elias pressed his fingers right at my entrance. I cried out, hips thrusting into his hand. "Gods, you're beautiful."

I buried my expression and cries of pleasure into his shirt front.

"C-can't—" I breathed, not able to form coherent words or thought.

"What was that?" His fingers stroked inside me.

I groaned, digging my nails into his black tunic.

"Elias…" I gasped.

But my words were drowned out by another voice. A voice belonging to neither mer that held me so tenderly. It was a voice of rage, and murder, and one that I recognized so well.

Elias pulled away from me with a start, letting the dress fall back into place. Kai's hands left my body as he whipped around, assuming a protective stance. As if he could cover me, and the sudden embarrassment that flushed through my body.

As if he could shield me from the eyes, and wrath, of Captain Tiberius Saber.

SURELY MY EYES WEREN'T seeing correctly.

Surely it was just the darkness of the waters and the swift bubbly current passing through casting an illusion before me.

Surely that wasn't Maisie in the arms of both Prince Kai and the Black Blade.

A strangled noise ripped from my throat. Surprise, and something else I could not quite describe. Shock froze me a few strokes away from the entrance of the balcony.

I'd seen Maisie swim out here with Prince Kai. I'd have followed them immediately, but the lack of guards had been disconcerting. And when I found them lagging about in the ballroom, I gave them a stern talking to, before hurrying out here.

To find *this*.

Something I never imagined I'd find.

The three of them...

I swallowed the lump in my throat. My heart palpitated like the rapids of a current, like the viciousness of a wave crashing to shore, over and over again.

Prince Kai shielded Maisie with his body, and in turn, shielded a wanted criminal as well. A criminal Maisie had risked everything to save. I had wondered feverishly what she had done that day to escape unscathed. Now I knew.

It had all been a show. Just a show. They were involved in the most vile of ways. And not just them, but Prince Kai as well. I shouldn't have been surprised. His father was a greedy thing who hoarded concubines like jewels, why wouldn't his son be as well?

My hand reacted on instinct, going for the sword I kept sheathed at my waist. I pulled it out and aimed it at Elias Blackfin.

"I will *kill* you," I threatened, just before I charged.

The wise decision would have been to call my guards out here. To have them arrest him. But my mind wasn't thinking clearly. All I knew was anger. That, and it would make a spectacle. It would exhibit Maisie in an unflattering light.

And why was I still protecting her?

"Swim away, Elias!" she cried out, pushing on his shoulders. He cast her a look, one I couldn't decipher, but she could read all too well. Like their own personal language composed entirely of stares. "I'll be fine. Just go!" She pushed again and he dove off the balcony. I made my way there, chest pressed up against the rail and looked down.

Elias disappeared into the shadows.

Cursing and pounding my fist into the rail, I whipped around. Maisie had taken a stroke back. There was fear in her eyes, as she took in the point of my sword. Yet still, her chin tilted up in a small act of defiance. Prince Kai was at her side, holding her arm, eyes narrowing on me.

I pointed my sword at him. A giant gesture of disrespect, one that could have caused a war. One that could have landed my head within the mouth of a dragon.

"What in gods' names is going on here?" My voice was a menacing rumble.

Kai's chin lifted, brown eyes beginning to take on an icy glow. His fingers lengthened into black talons. Talons that could surely rip my throat out with a mere swipe. "You saw what you saw, what need do you have to ask?"

What I saw… What I saw, I didn't want to believe. What I heard I wish could be unheard. The sounds of Maisie being pleasured… the sight of their hands on her.

What had the little fool been thinking? She obviously hadn't been thinking at all. She never did.

"Kai… can you give me a moment to speak with the Captain alone, please?"

Kai's eyes never once drifted from mine, even as he replied with a voice as hard as ice, "I don't think that's such a good idea, Maisie."

My whole body rippled into stillness.

Maisie.

He'd called her Maisie.

Because Prince Kai knew the truth. Knew that she wasn't really Princess Odele. And if he knew, did the Black Blade know as well?

"I'll be fine. He isn't going to hurt me."

The prince finally tore his gaze from mine to look at her with firm tenderness. Slowly, his talons sank back and his eyes lost their feral glow. He sighed and shook his head back and forth.

"I can deny you nothing, my gem." And to my never-ending shock, he bent and pressed a quick kiss to her lips before piercing me with a threatening glare. "If you harm her in any way, I'll drag your body through the streets of Draconi and feed you to my dragon."

I believed every word.

That being said, he turned and swam away, leaving Maisie and I alone.

She stared at my sword for some time in silence.

"Shouldn't you put that away?" she inquired softly. Even if her voice spoke of defiance, I could hear the slight tremble of nerves in it.

I glared but shoved the sword angrily back into its sheath.

So much swam through my mind. So much. I didn't know where to begin or what to say.

"I can explain," she began.

"Yes. Yes, you will explain to me just what in the abyss is going on, *Princess.*" I put as much emphasis and anger into the word as I possibly could. She barely even flinched.

"Perhaps, we could speak over there?" She inclined her head towards the more shadowy areas of the balcony, a place out of eyesight and earshot of the guests in the ballroom beyond. I resisted the urge to comment about how she should've taken such measures with Kai and the Black Blade rather than with me.

Still, I obliged, letting her lead the way towards the shadowy part of the veranda. If only to give me something to do. I needed to move, needed to pace. As if physical movement could help get my scrambled thoughts in order.

What I really wanted to do was shake Maisie senseless. Perhaps punch my fist through a wall. No, those wouldn't do. My body was wound so tightly, I needed *something*. Something I couldn't yet fathom.

"So explain." I crossed my arms over my chest, uncrossed them. I was raging inside. "Why does Kai know your real name and why—?" I cut off, unable to finish the question. *Why were you with Kai* and *the Black Blade? Why were you with them* both?

She took a deep breath, her lips parting. My eyes flashed to the movement before flickering back up to the obsidian orbs that were her eyes. She placed her hand lightly on the railing, like she meant to steady herself for the lies—or truth?—she was about to spew.

Her eyes pierced mine, down to the very depths of my soul I was sure she could see. And curse me, something inside stirred, despite it all.

"I told Kai the truth," she confessed. "All of it. I couldn't bear to lie to him anymore."

Shock rippled through me for the third time that night. I was tired of the sentiment already, but I couldn't even chase it away. "Why?" The word ripped out of me like a cry of pain. She swore, she'd *sworn* she'd keep this secret. The most precious secret in the kingdom and she'd told the prince meant to wed Odele. She'd told… "Did you tell the Black Blade?"

She tensed, and that was answer enough.

"You did," I accused. I couldn't believe it. Thalassar's biggest secret, and she'd entrusted it in the hands of a common criminal.

"To be fair, the Black Blade guessed my identity. He knew right away I wasn't the princess."

"Right. How could that sea scum possibly have known you weren't the princess?" She opened her mouth to reply, but I cut her off, holding my hand up. "I don't want to hear it."

Her eyes narrowed. "Of course you don't. You don't want to hear anything that would remotely speak ill of your precious Princess Odele. Which, by the way, is how he knew I wasn't her. Because she knew him. I bet she didn't tell you *that,* did she?" When I didn't speak, when all I could do was curl my hands into fists, Maisie laughed, a sound that was entirely without humor. "Of course she didn't. For all the love you profess to have for her, you didn't know a thing about her. I bet for my few months of being here, I know her a lot more than you ever did."

"Stop," I demanded with quiet rage. Not because I couldn't bear to hear it. No, I knew what she was saying was the raw, honest truth. I could hear it in her voice. And I didn't need her to tell me what I'd started to realize on my own these past few weeks.

I knew who Odele was. Every ugly, honest aspect of her.

"I will not." She swam a stroke too close to me, rammed a finger in my chest. There was a ferocity in her gaze that had been building up for so long, leading to this exact moment when we would both undeniably explode. "You've tried to keep me quiet for far too long, *Captain.*" She spat out the word as vehemently as I'd called her 'princess'. "You'd close your ears to the truth that's staring you in the face because you can't bear to face it. Well, let me be honest with you now."

She jabbed her finger into my chest. Like she meant to inflict pain. It hurt less than the pain I'd felt upon seeing her giving herself to Kai and Elias. So I welcomed every jab. I welcomed every sensation it spurred deep inside me. Like the swell of a rising volcano, I wasn't so far behind in the explosion.

"Your princess wasn't who you thought she was. Her, and this bloody kingdom, and the lineage you love so much have secrets that could fill up the great abyss." Jab. "And I've had to put up with pretending to be as selfish as she is, all while dealing with the queen…" Jab. "…Percival…" Jab. "…and *you.* And I will not be bullied by you, and I will not apologize for what you witnessed here. I will not apologize for falling in *love*…" Jab. "...with two amazing mermen. Not when they've been here for me in this shell of a palace, doing much more for me than you *ever*—"

I exploded.

Anger rose hotly and burst me into action. I moved, grabbing her by the upper arms and ramming her unceremoniously into the edge of the balcony railing. The rest of her words were cut off by a gasp as the water was knocked from her lungs. I should have been more gentle with her, but if she thought me such a brute, then a brute was what I would give her.

"I've done nothing for you?" I demanded darkly.

In the spanning breaths of my rage, I'd somehow come close to her. So close that I could feel the rapid rise and fall of her chest pressing up against my own. So close that I could count every individual eyelash framing that obsidian glow. That I could make out the exact shape of her plump bottom lip, and the small indent in the center of it that begged for attention.

"Nothing but demand everything of me, while expecting the absolute worst." Her breathing was a rasp, her words hoarse. Like it was a struggle to bite them out.

The venom was there, in her tone, in her eyes. But there was something else there as well. Something that curled slowly, dangerously down my spine.

All my life I'd controlled my every action, moved so precisely. I had my every move on a tight leash, too afraid to let go. I was dangling on that precipice now, by a mere strand. All that was left now was to fall.

"Oh, Maisie." I dropped my voice to a low whisper. "If I'd demanded everything, you would have *given* it to me. As freely and as fervently as you do to them." There was a pause, as the heat of my vicious words sank in. Even in the dark, I could make out the rising flush on her cheeks, the hitch in her breath.

"I despise you," she whispered ardently. "And I curse you to the deepest depths of the abyss."

My nails curled on her skin, tightly but not enough to hurt, just enough to make her body shudder. "Curse me all you'd like, Maisie. It doesn't matter. It won't change the looming truth of your future. That in the end, you can't be with either of the mermen you love. If you had as much courage as you pretend to have, you'd admit that's the reason you hate Odele so much. Because she has the life you want, engaged to the merman you love. She has the life you wish you'd had."

Her eyes narrowed, and I knew I'd struck a nerve of truth. Perhaps her biggest secret, one she hated herself for. The fact that she was more noble than any royal, and had been born a peasant.

"Admit it." I pressed her tighter against the rail so her body bent just a fraction. I loomed over her, putting weight onto her body. She squirmed, but it only served for me to press tighter, to hold her still. "You love the royal life. I can see it in your eyes, no matter how hard you fight or hide it."

"I don't have to admit silt to you. Now let me go." She struggled, thrashing her tail about. To keep her still, I wrapped my tail around hers and squeezed. She gasped, arching into me.

A cruel smile touched my lips. "It's true, and you know it."

"So what?" she spat. "You want me to admit it? Fine. I like feeling important. I like feeling like I have the opportunity to change the kingdom for the better, which is more than what your precious princess was doing. Does it make you feel good, Captain? Cornering me like this? You're so used to everyone obeying everything you say that you can hardly stand the sight of me because I don't."

My hand slid up her arm to her chest. Her body stilled at my slow ministrations, but she didn't fight back. Not even as my fingers slid past the open buttons of her bodice, across the sharp ridges of her collarbone, and higher to cup her chin. She swallowed.

"I like to be obeyed, Maisie." I tilted her chin up so she had no choice but to glare angrily into my eyes. My thumb stroked across her bottom lip, pausing at the indent in the middle. I felt rather than heard her next shuddering breath.

"I'm not a soldier, Captain. And I will not obey you."

I squeezed her chin and finally felt that tether on my control snap. "I will *make* you obey, Maisie. I will make you *beg*."

And then my lips went crashing down on hers.

Her mouth stayed clamped tight, and she moaned against me, digging her fingers into my side.

"Open your mouth," I commanded against her lips. I wanted her. All of her. Like I'd never wanted anyone in my entire life. And it took seeing her in another pair of arms for me to realize just how hot my blood coursed for her. Just how deep the yearning ran. "Do it."

Her eyes fluttered. She did not want to yield to me. She'd rather put up a fight than give me what I wanted.

One hand cupped her chin, the other traveled down her bodice and gripped her breast tightly. She let out a gasp and her mouth opened and I dove in, tongue digging into depths I'd been too controlled before to explore.

Why had I waited until now?

Maisie tasted like heaven. Surely the gods were real.

I bent her over the railing and explored the inside of her mouth. I took, demanded her pleasure. She warred with herself, fingers digging tightly into my skin, and when my hand slipped into the crevice of her dress to finger a bare nipple, she gave in. Maisie kissed me back, a feverish war clashed between our mouths. I punished with tongue and teeth, biting and nibbling. She retaliated with as much anger and venom as me.

Her nails raked through my scalp as she tugged my strands of hair, pulling and clinging to me.

Nothing had ever felt better.

"Yes," I tore from her mouth to say. She felt so good against me, body curving perfectly into mine. As if this were meant to be. As if it had always been meant to be, and I'd just been too blind to see it.

"We shouldn't be doing this, Captain." Her breaths were ragged things, panting against my cheek.

Why? I wanted to demand. *Because I'm not Kai, because I'm not Elias?*

I said none of this. I merely ripped apart the lapels of the dress, sending buttons flying through the water. Her gasp filled me to the core.

"We will." I bared her breasts to the chilly currents of the night. They were ripe for the tasting, lush peaks that beckoned my mouth to them. I bent to have a taste. Her fingers dug into my hair, and I couldn't feel if she was pushing me down, begging without words, or clawing at me. It felt good either way. Even better when my tongue flicked out across her pebbled nipple.

A sound caught in her throat that she dare not unleash, but her body said it all. The way she jerked closer to me was all the reaction I needed to confirm.

She wanted this as much as I did. She was desperate for my touch and would never admit it.

But I'd make her scream and beg with my mouth and tongue if that's what it took.

I would dominate her every inch until she forgot their names entirely and could only utter mine.

"Get away." Her nails clawed into my shoulders.

I stopped, lips hovering over her pert nipple. I looked up at her. "Do you truly want that? Do you truly want me to get away? Look me in the eyes and say it."

She looked down, eyes meeting mine, eyelashes fluttered. Her breath hitched, and the pulse at her throat beat in a rapid rhythm. She swallowed before she answered. "Yes. I want that."

I started to pull away from her, my heart beating up to my throat as I stared into her half-hooded eyes. As I pulled away, she followed, gripping tightly to my shoulders like she loathed to let me go.

I couldn't help but smile. "You're lying."

The softest of sighs left her lips, the sound morphing into a growl. "So what if I am?" The words almost sounded like an accusation. Like she wanted me just as much as I wanted her, and blamed me for it.

I blamed her too.

She was maddening and yet I still sought her out with an ache in the very depths of my soul.

"Look me in the eyes," I repeated. "Tell me you want me to go away."

She growled, the sound of frustration her surrender. "Damn you," she hissed. "I don't want you to."

I took her in my mouth again. She didn't push me away, but she dug her nails into my skin, her punishment for my arrogance, for my earlier words, but she had no idea how much her aggressive touch spurred me on. It made me want to touch her harder, make her *scream* and writhe beneath me.

My tongue trailed down her stomach and lower to where her body betrayed her. To the evidence of her arousal. I bent low, and at the first lick of my tongue at her entrance, her hips bucked into my mouth. She was hot with sensual desire, and I was smug to know that I was the one who put her there.

Whether she hated me or loved me, it didn't matter.

All that mattered was this. This primal urge between us, the need pulsating, begging for release.

I slid my tongue inside, and she responded, not by screaming, but by digging her nails deeper into me.

"I'll make you come so hard, you'll scream," I promised darkly. And I *would* hear it.

My words made her shiver, the dark sensual promise behind it that she so obviously wanted. And then I licked her again, tongue delving in and out, up and down, her hips jerking against my face set the rhythm. And when I found the nub at the apex of her sex, my teeth grazed over it, and a sound of raw pleasure emanated from deep in her throat.

I looked up to find her biting down on her lip so hard, blood floated from the corner of her mouth.

"Just scream, Maisie." I gripped her hips, pushing her back against the railing. "Tell me you want more." *Tell me you love it. Love me. Even if it's a lie, I will take it.*

"Never," she gasped, but the way she clawed at me betrayed the lie for what it was.

"But you will."

I went back to my ministrations, tongue licking up her nub. She gasped and trembled but did not scream. Her hands held me tightly, as if she would fall if she didn't. I held her hip with one hand, and the other I slowly slid into her, feeling all her warmth and desire enclose around me.

"Gods, you're so tight." I slid a second finger inside, stretching her. "Aah," I sighed, pressing a kiss to her stomach and then to the nub of her desire. "You feel so good." My fingers began to move within her, stretching her, driving her to the pleasure she would deny.

"Captain…"

"Don't." I pressed a warning kiss to her nub, and flicked out my tongue to taste. Her body shuddered into me. "Say my name, Maisie," I ordered, pressing a third finger in.

"N—no."

I slid in and out, causing her to gasp. "Say it." Gods, I wanted to hear her say it. I wanted to hear her scream it with reckless abandon.

"C—Cap—aah—"

I sucked on her nub, scraped my teeth against it, all the while my fingers dove in and out. She rode my hand, bucked against my mouth. I was doing this. I was giving her primal pleasure, feeling her against my mouth, listening to her helpless pants. I demanded more with every thrust of my fingers, every taste and tease of my lips and teeth.

"Tiberius," she moaned finally. "I—I—"

Triumph swelled within me. "Are you close, love? Do you want me to end this torment?"

She was gasping, even as my fingers moved, and she bit her lip, feral sounds clawed from her throat. It was begging just the same. My thumb pressed against her desire and she cried out, loudly and with abandon. Close, she was so close to falling into that abyss, but I wanted to be inside her when it happened. To feel her shudder and fall and know that I was the one who took her there.

"Saber…" she groaned, nails digging into me.

"Beg me, Maisie. Tell me you want me." I was desperate now, desperate for her. I wanted her, wanted to feel her. My fingers were still inside her, my thumb caressing her gently, pulling gasping noises from her throat.

"I—I—"

Just say it, I willed. *Say it and end the torment for us both.*

Her fingers wove through my hair, and she pulled my head back so I was looking up at her and the feral glance in her eyes.

"I want you," she nearly spat with hatred, and a hint of something else, too. "Inside me. Now. *Please.*"

That was enough for me.

I slid up her body, tugging aside the buttons on my uniform, pushing aside the long tunic underneath until I was bare and aching for her body. I pulled her close, letting her feel the strength of my own desire against her stomach.

"This is what you do to me," I whispered gutturally.

I jerked my hips against her stomach, and she gasped. The sound was a beacon, begging me to come home. I groaned as I gripped the side of her hip and her lower back, angling her up, so my tip pressed against her entrance.

"You make me forget my self-control. You make me angry." I slid inside her and hissed out my pleasure while she sighed it. *Yes.* The gods must be real. And this felt like paradise. "You make me want you." I thrust in to the hilt, hitting her just right. Her whole body trembled as she took me in. Her tail wrapped around my own in her desperation, as she went into the abyss where I wanted to do nothing but follow.

I thrust, slow and hard, pressing her tighter against the railing.

"This is what you do to me." I thrust. She gasped, clinging onto me, digging her nails in as if she meant to punish. So I punished her back, taking her mouth in a kiss that left us both blind. I set the pace, slow and hard, and she clung to me, moaning and gasping as if she couldn't get enough. As if she wanted more, wanted me to drop her into the depths all over again.

Maisie pulled away from my kiss to bite at the lobe of my ear.

That single action sent me spiraling. I pumped faster into her, stomach coiling tightly just before I spun down into that chasm of pleasure.

I leaned against her, aware of my heavy weight, as I tried to catch my breath. Our chest pressed, back and forth, as we both struggled to regain our control. My heartbeat refused to comply. It banged and banged against my chest like a war drum.

"Gods," I whispered against her temple. My hand holding myself up on the railing curled into a fist. "Gods," I repeated.

"We probably shouldn't have done that," Maisie rasped. There was no more hatred in her voice, at least. Just quiet resignation. Like she regretted what had just transpired between us. I felt it like a blow to my chest.

"Probably not," I agreed, pulling away to look into her eyes. I tried not to let her see the hurt in my eyes, masking it with cool indifference. "But we both wanted it." I pulled her dress back together, but with the missing buttons, all it did was flap open again. Shrugging out of my military jacket, I wrapped it around her shoulders. And then, because I could, I bent down and kissed her one last time. "And that is something I'll never regret."

Mother of gods.

That was the only thought that slashed through my mind as I swam.

Mother of gods.

Captain Saber… he… well, he'd been quite thorough with my body. It was something I never imagined could have happened between us. The bout of passion that overtook us had been unexpected, had been filled with more anger than anything. It had been his way of punishing. Of taking control.

My thoughts had completely scattered the moment I first felt the heated rasp of his tongue against my skin. All I could do was feel and want more. The boundaries of our friendship had undoubtedly changed the moment he had pressed his lips to mine.

Had we even been friends to begin with?

Now we were something more. An indescribable relationship lay between us. It wasn't like what I had with Kai or Elias. What had happened between us had been angry, a punishment, a reprimand. It was uncharted territory, and I didn't know how to proceed.

What did this make us?

I scanned his face, the frigid indifference masking his beautiful features. He began straightening my clothes with quick efficiency and didn't speak to me at all. Not after that dark confession.

That is something I'll never regret.

Had he read regret on my features? Is that what I was feeling? No. *No.* It wasn't as if I felt regret at what had just transpired between us. But the whole time we'd been together, the whole time he'd been inside me, a part of me couldn't help but feel like I was Odele. At least, in his eyes I was. It was the only reason he touched me with such fevered passion. Even as I thought it, and pain had sliced through my chest because of it, I knew it didn't matter. I would take those scraps of passion and love he bestowed, even if they weren't really meant for me at all.

Because I wanted him. Whatever he could give me.

It had taken that blinding moment of rage for me to realize that what he had said was true. I did despise Odele, not only because of her inability to help others, but because she had Kai, and she had the captain's love and appreciation. And that was all I had ever wanted.

Even if I hadn't realized it before now.

Our relationship had been slowly building, like lava climbing, *rising*, up the length of the cavern in a volcano. It had been filled with anger and judgments, all to come up to this one explosive moment of melting heat.

I only hoped it wouldn't leave chaos in its wake.

"You can't go back in there." The captain finished looping the last button of his jacket that I wore. Then, he straightened his palms against his immaculate tunic, as if to smooth out wrinkles that weren't there. It flowed over his tail before settling. "They'll wonder."

Of course they would. They'd wonder why I'd gone out on that balcony with Prince Kai only to return with a tattered dress and Captain Saber's jacket. I may not have been the real princess, but I still had an image to maintain. If I didn't want to find my neck exposed to the blade of an ax, I would follow the rules of Queen Circe.

"We will go to your room, and you will explain everything." An order, not a request. One he uttered brusquely. He didn't even look me in the eyes. As if I shamed him.

That hurt worst of all.

"Come." He tugged at my arm, and I followed silently. I probably should have spoken, should have raged. But I'd said all I'd needed to say moments ago.

Besides, I was confused.

My mind pounded and my heart swirled in a tidal wave of sensation. I couldn't seem to sort through the emotions that plagued me. I wanted him, but did I love him? Hate him? And for the love of gods, what did he feel for me?

He led me over the balcony. If the Queen saw me, she'd surely die of apoplexy. Decent mer didn't swim out of windows or over balconies. But I wasn't decent right now, and neither was Captain Saber. So he led me through secret parts of the palace where we wouldn't be seen, until we made it to my room. We entered alone, and for some reason, my heartbeat froze in my chest.

The sight of the plush bed, anemones swaying around it, looked inviting. But not for sleeping.

My face flushed.

"Now..." The captain swam around to face me, muscular arms crossing against his chest. I recalled the feeling of them around me as he pumped in and out of me. His grip had been strong, demanding. My eyes trailed over the curve of his muscle, the veins straining against his skin. My tongue ran across my bottom lip, and I struggled to focus. When I looked up, the captain was staring at my mouth. "Tell me everything."

I had no choice but to speak the truth. It wasn't as if a lie could come easily to me, anyway. He'd seen me with Kai and Elias. He'd heard Kai call out my name.

"I'll tell you everything, but you have to promise me you'll keep it a secret. From everyone, including the king and queen."

He uncrossed his arms and pierced me with a cold stare. "When I brought you here, I made you promise not to reveal your identity to anyone, and that meant nothing to you. So, *no,* Maisie, I don't have to promise you a thing."

But you will. Those words went unspoken on my lips. He would promise, once he realized the severity of everything I'd found. Once he realized I was looking for Odele, that I was close to finding her, he wouldn't breathe a word. For me, there'd be no promises, but for her there would be.

I ignored the painful lurch of my heart.

"Promise me." I took a stroke forward. "Promise me you won't say a word."

His jaw worked furiously as he struggled to contain something inside him. Another explosion of fury? I almost shuddered at the thought.

"I owe you nothing, Maisie," he finally ground out tightly. *"Nothing."*

I had to calm the beating of my heart, for I feared if it raced any faster, it just might shatter against my ribcage. "So what just happened outside was *nothing*?" I demanded.

His eyes narrowed into thin slits, eyebrows pulling together. But he didn't respond. I wanted him to. I wanted to spew his anger like honesty, and then maybe it'd all come to light.

"It didn't seem like nothing," I went on bravely, taking another stroke forward. This was dangerous territory. He could explode all over again. Maybe that's what I wanted. Maybe I wanted to argue with the push and pull of our bodies instead of a clashing of words. “In fact, it felt like *something.*”

It had felt like something to me. Or maybe it was all in my mind, a fantasy I’d fashioned in those few moments of vulnerability to make myself believe that we meant something to each other. It couldn’t all have been a lie, could it? The thumping of his heart against mine hadn’t been a lie. Did he see me for me? Or had he only seen Odele? When he’d been inside me, had he been wishing it was her?

“It *was* something, Maisie.” My heart thumped a few painful beats at those words. “But if you think what happened between us changes the fact that you’ve been lying to me…” He shook his head back and forth. “Tell me the truth now. *Please.*”

My next breath came out, a shuddering broken thing.

So I told him.

I told him everything and held nothing back. I told him how I’d found the secret passageway when I’d been feverish with poison. The cove. The recordings, her confessions, how I’d come to know the Black Blade. I spoke to him with an even voice about following her fin strokes to what she’d discovered about the mysterious deaths in her family, how someone had been trying to kill her, the missing royal, and finally, the conch I’d found that could help prove the legitimacy of Odele’s cousin.

I left out no detail and kept my voice steady throughout it all. Captain Saber didn’t interrupt me once.

And when I finished, all he could do was stare at me, as if his mind was still processing all the reveals, all the royal secrets he obviously had no idea even existed.

His whole body was rigid, his jaw working furiously. Finally he commanded, in a voice that was soft, yet firm. “I want to see the cove.”

The captain said nothing as I led him through the passageway, through the tunnel and into the cove. He just kept his eyes wide and alert, taking everything in. The only sign of his surprise was the slight twitching of his fingers.

I led him down to the cavern's floor, where the glow of the lava globe illuminated the hundreds of conches littered on the ground. His gaze swept over them. I could read the question in his eyes, so I answered before he got the chance to ask.

"These are all her recordings." Silence responded, so I went on. "I've watched a lot of them since I discovered the place. She made so many recordings of her life here…"

The captain swam slowly over to where the recorder was, empty of a conch. It was impossible to read him, his emotions. He kept everything bottled so tightly, I couldn't discern what he was thinking. He floated, frozen as he took in the machine.

I picked up a conch from the floor and went over next to him, placing it on the machine. "We can watch one if you want, so you can see—"

He placed a hand on my wrist, squeezing slightly. "Don't," he warned tightly.

I looked up at him, a question in my eyes, but he wasn't even looking at me. He was staring at the conch I'd placed on the disc. Like it was a menace, like he expected it to attack.

Finally, the captain turned away, eyes boring into mine like the twin, heated licks of two-legger fire. "I've seen enough."

"I need to go make an excuse for you at the ball. I'll tell them you were feeling ill."

Captain Saber floated by the door to my room, hands clasped behind his back. He was back to his strict formality, pretending as though nothing had happened between us. There was no evidence of that heated passion in his body. I almost wondered if he'd been so quick to push it away, but then his eyes found mine and hinted at the dark, promising whisper of desire.

"Come tomorrow morning," I told him, cheeks flaming, wondering if he'd think my words had a double meaning. "So you can help us plan our next stroke."

He tensed at the word 'us'. I understood it would be hard for him, hard for him to trust the criminal he'd hunted down, hard for him to trust either Kai or Elias. But if he wanted to find Odele, he would do this. He didn't even need to promise to keep it a secret. I'd seen the look on his face down in that cove. In the place where I'd felt closest to Odele, where he had felt closest to her, too, no doubt. Promises were unnecessary when his love was obviously stronger.

I still didn't let the pain of it cripple me.

"Tomorrow, then." He gave a stiff bow. He'd forgotten himself. And when he straightened, his eyes strayed to my lips. I held my breath, daring to hope he'd close the space between us to kiss me.

He didn't.

"Lock your door behind me," he commanded before he whirled, opened the door, and left.

The quiet clicking of the door made my whole body shudder. As I reached over to set the lock into place, I *thunked* my forehead against it. It was only a few minutes later that I finally gave into my emotions and let the tears come.

"LITTLE fish..." I SHOOK her lightly awake, even though I loathed to do so. She looked so peaceful, hand pressed against her face, eyelashes pressed against the high curve of her cheek. She had let her hair loose, and it floated in coquettish tendrils around her face.

She was so beautiful it hurt.

My fingers fluttered against her skin softly. I'd be content in my life to simply watch her. She was the perfect puzzle piece that fit in that missing spot of my heart.

Her eyelids fluttered as she slowly opened her eyes. When she saw me next to her, she let out a slow breath. "Elias…" She started to sit up, but I stopped her by pressing my hand to her arm.

"Rest," I whispered.

She laid back against the cushioning with a sigh. "Did you discover anything?" Her voice was a dreamy whisper, balancing on the precipice between the realms of sleep and reality.

"We can talk about it tomorrow, little fish." I trailed my fingers against her arm. She'd fallen asleep with her dress on. Too exhausted to change it, most likely. As she moved on the bed, I noticed the flaps of her dress part. All the buttons appeared to have been torn off. My eyebrow rose at the sight.

I never imagined Captain Saber had it in him. Then again, he'd needed that shove to finally give in to his feelings and urges. The moment I'd seen him draw his sword and Maisie had urged me to swim away, I'd only done so because of her. Because of the worry in her voice. If not for her, I would have faced off with the captain in a battle that wouldn't have ended until one of us was dead. But the evidence of what Tiberius and Maisie had shared changed everything. She had feelings for him, too. Which meant that he was off limits.

I didn't comment on it, I just pulled Maisie closer to my body, tucking her head on the crook of my arm. She snuggled in close, and I held her. Whatever bad news and plotting could wait until morning.

For now, I'd enjoy her like this. Vulnerable and safe in my arms.

Right where she belonged.

I AWOKE WRAPPED IN Elias' arms, a vague memory of our short conversation from last night surfacing in my mind. Our tails were entwined tightly, bodies pressed close together. I'd fallen asleep with tears rising from my eyes, so waking up to him holding me was bliss. Pure and simple.

I got up, stretching my aching limbs. Elias reached for my waist, but I pushed his arms aside. He groaned. "Come back to bed, little fish."

"I would, but I can't. I have princess duty, remember?" Especially after I'd escaped the ball last night in secret. I needed to suck up to the queen and king and make up some excuse. My fingers smoothed down the lapel of the dress and the missing buttons there. "And Captain Saber is coming this morning…"

Elias pulled a pillow beneath his cheek to hold instead, letting out a soft snort. "Coming…"

My face flushed. "Don't be infantile." I slid off the bed, swatting away anemones as I swam over to the closet. "Why do you mermen like ruining perfectly good dresses?" I complained as I began pulling out a simple day dress. I slipped the Draconian wear from my body, letting it sink to the floor. Pity. It was so beautiful. I hoped the buttons were an easy fix. I pulled the new dress on.

"It's all about power, little fish," Elias replied.

I swam out of the closet, running fingers through my hair. "Power?"

He nodded against the pillow, eyes still closed. "It feels good to rip things. Makes us feel powerful while we leave you vulnerable. A type of foreplay, if you will." His eyes finally opened and roamed over me. "I'm sure it satisfied Captain Saber to try and get you to submit."

"I—I don't want to talk about that."

He sat up stretching his tail out before him. He still wore the same clothes from last night, a black tunic and jacket. His obsidian blade had been placed against a nearby dresser, close enough for him to reach, should the occasion arise.

"Suddenly shy? Alright. I'll let it go."

My eyes narrowed. I didn't believe him. Elias didn't just let things go, and he looked suspicious anyway. He started getting up, straightening out his clothes and securing his blade at his waist. I watched him go about, his movements confident, fingers quick.

Just then, a knock sounded at the door.

"Hide," I hissed. I turned, unsure if he'd done so or not and went to crack the door open a fraction. Captain Saber and Prince Kai floated on the other side. A sudden knot formed in my stomach as I let the two of them in, closing the door once they were safe in the room.

Kai greeted me with a gentle kiss. His hands cupped my face as he bent down, lips lingering softly. "All is well, my gem?" he asked against my mouth.

"Yes." My reply was breathless.

He smiled and pulled away. I turned to greet Captain Saber, only to find him frozen in place, hand lingering at the hilt of his sword as he took in the Black Blade from across the room.

Elias was perched by the window leisurely, his sword out. He used the obsidian blade to trim the nail on his thumb, but his eyes were focused on the captain. A challenge glowed in them, and nothing but mischief twisted the side of his lip up into a mocking half smile.

"Mornin', Captain Saber." He gestured at his forehead with the hilt of his black diamond studded blade. "How's the head?"

Captain Saber let out a low growl at the reminder of what had happened weeks ago. When Elias had used me as a shield to escape from a beheading. Captain Saber had caught him and stabbed him, just before Elias had bashed his head with two-legger kitchenware.

There was tension and unfinished business between the two. It was obvious they despised one another, the feeling palpable in the water, causing goosebumps to rise on my arms.

"Behave," I commanded, putting as much of my teachings into my voice as possible. I sounded like a royal.

Elias' eyes flickered to me. "As you wish, little fish." And then he shoved the blade back into his sheath. Only then did the captain put away his own sword, though he still stared at Elias cautiously.

I sighed.

"Everyone should sit down. This might take a while." Even if the captain didn't take my suggestion right away, Kai went with me to sit at the edge of the bed. "So, I told Captain Saber everything."

"Hence why he's here…" Elias muttered.

The captain's gaze hardened like jagged pieces of ice. If looks could kill…

"Please don't argue." I rubbed my temple, feeling a headache starting to form. Kai pressed his hand against my back, and began rubbing in circles. The action soothed me, giving me confidence. "We're all in this together."

Elias' eyes narrowed. "Are we, though?" He pointed a finger at the captain. "Can we really trust him?"

"Last night—"

"I don't care what happened last night or what you told him," Elias interrupted, his voice every bit the criminal Thalassar believed him to be. "We trust one another because we had to build it. We are loyal to one another because we love one another. You…" He made a jab with his finger in the captain's direction. "…are loyal to the Malabellas. The very family we do not trust."

Suspicion hung in the water. Even Kai regarded Tiberius thoughtfully. I released a slow breath, knowing that it did not matter what I said here. Captain Saber would have to prove himself, show where his loyalties lay, all on his own.

He must have realized it too, because his body was tense, his voice tight when he said, "The fact that you are still breathing should be enough proof of my loyalty."

Elias made a face. "Not good enough. You need to state your loyalty. Who are you loyal to?"

Captain Saber's hand curled into an angry fist. Elias' dark eyes lit up at the sight.

"Are you loyal to the Malabella family, or are you loyal to Maisie?" he repeated darkly.

I held my breath. Of course he was loyal to the Malabellas. Anyone with a set of eyes could see that truth. He loved Odele. He would be loyal to her. Likely, the only reason he even agreed to be here was because he wanted to finally find her and bring her back home.

I cast a glance down, unable to read that truth in his eyes.

"I am loyal to Maisie," he surprised me by saying.

"Then prove it."

My eyes went up to Elias at the sound of that curling mischief in his voice, at the danger. Yes, he was planning something, though I couldn't be sure what.

"How, exactly, am I supposed to do that?"

"Let's call it an initiation into our little group, shall we? We are all Maisie's lovers, right?"

Both Captain Saber and I tensed at the words. What was he playing at? My eyes narrowed on him. He ignored me.

"We've all had her, tasted her, individually…"

Oh gods. My face heated and I turned sharply to take in the captain's reaction. He didn't move, but his nostrils were flaring. I wondered how much it took him to hold back from drawing his sword and skewering it through Elias' chest. If the Black Blade wasn't careful with his words, it would come to that.

"And Kai and I have had her together. It was rather lovely…"

"Elias," I hissed. This was vile and embarrassing. The captain didn't need to hear this, didn't need to despise me any more than he already did.

Again, I went ignored.

"To be a part of us means to share her. To *be* with her. Together."

My heart stuttered. Oh, no. Oh, gods, no.

My face must have been fifty different shades of crimson.

"That's how you can prove your loyalty to Maisie, and to us. Make her come. Right here. Right now. It shouldn't be hard to do, should it?"

"Elias!"

How could he be so… so… crude? I'd not deny that the idea of them, of the three of them sharing me, sent a tiny thrill down my spine. The idea was intriguing. Wanted, even. But Captain Saber wouldn't see it as thrilling.

The captain snorted. "You expect me to play along in these vile games of yours to prove that I want to find Princess Odele as much as you do?"

To find Princess Odele as much as you do…

Of course this was all about Odele. His loyalty, after all, was to her.

"Humor me." Elias spread his arms out at his sides.

The captain's eyes narrowed. "No. I won't fall prey to your petty games."

"I wouldn't say they're petty," Kai chimed in with slight amusement. "Pleasurable, yes. But petty?"

"Regardless of what it is, I will take no part in it."

"So we can move on, then." I tried not to let the hurt show in my voice, but the feeling was there, lodged tightly in my chest and throat. Not because he refused. I understood why, I really did, but because of everything else underlying that refusal. Because of what it meant. For us. Just because we'd shared one night together meant nothing. It didn't mean he'd suddenly become as free as Kai and Elias and kiss me with abandon. Especially not now that he knew the truth. Now that he knew Odele had left because her life had been threatened, because she went to find her cousin.

"No. Now Tiberius here can get out of your room and let us do the plotting. Without him." Elias' voice was venomous and filled with every inch of shadow and darkness befitting the Black Blade.

"This concerns me, too," the captain ground out. His fingers flexed near the hilt of his sword. Like he wanted to end this incessant talking and just run Elias through and get on with his day.

"It doesn't. And we can't trust you."

"You can't trust me because I won't take her in front of you? That's preposterous."

Elias smirked. "We can't trust you because you will only take her in the shadowy corners of a balcony. You think that's love? You think it will be *enough*? This is a *test,* Captain. Prove to us that you can give her the love she deserves. Right here. Right now. Prove it." He paused, cocking his head to the side and throwing me a sharp smile. "If that would please you, of course."

"Oh, so now you'll take my opinion into consideration?" I crossed my arms over my chest.

"I know your every desire, little fish," Elias purred. "Captain Saber might be new to them. He doesn't know how much you like being touched, watched, and adored. You could tell him, though. You could get him to agree."

I uncrossed my arms, feeling a sliver of awkwardness beneath my skin. I tried not to look uncertain and shy as I contemplated my answer. Did I want this to happen? I was sure if I said no, he would drop it. Leave the choice up to me, though it was Captain Saber's as well. I didn't want to force him, and I needed to make that clear.

"I do like being watched," I whispered. "But I won't force you to do anything you don't want to do. If you don't want to, we'll drop it. Right, Elias?" I threw the question and a glare in his direction.

He held up his hands in surrender. "Whatever you say, little fish. Now, Captain Saber, what'll it be?"

Silence stretched out. My heartbeats measured the seconds. A minute passed. Sixty torturous heartbeats later, and Captain Saber finally turned to me, the unmistakable flare in his eyes heated me down to my very core.

Slowly, with prowess and purpose, he went over to me, stopping only inches away. Our tails touched, and I felt that small contact down every nerve ending in my body. Like a small buzz of electrifying jellies, my body was suddenly alight at his nearness.

His eyes pierced me so intensely, I felt he was pulling out the deepest recesses of my soul. One look and he could wrench everything out of me. That's what Captain Saber looked like. Like pure, intoxicating power.

My breathing grew shallow and labored. They could all hear the hitching in my chest, read the anticipation in the trembling of my body. Captain Saber fed on it, nostrils flaring as if he were some primal beast scenting in my fear, my desire.

Everyone was quiet.

I held my breath as he reached his hand out and cupped my chin, squeezing and tilting my face up to his. His grip was brusque, but not painful. His thumb swiped past the edges of my lips, and I was suddenly emboldened by the gesture. I couldn't help myself. I sucked his thumb into my mouth. Desire flared in the twin icy chips of his eyes, and a shudder racked through his body. He leaned down so our faces were an inch apart. An inch that felt like leagues.

"Maisie..." he whispered, a dark promise of what was to come. He leaned forward, closer still, and pressed his lips to the corners of mine. His mouth skimmed the edges of my jaw, traveling over my skin only to come back up. He tilted my chin, pulled his thumb from my mouth, and then kissed me ferociously.

I was angled in such a way that I took all of him, that he dove deep into my mouth. Like last night, there was no exploring. It was just a taking and punishing. And a part of me trembled with the hope that this was a claiming as well.

His tongue clashed against mine, fighting for dominance, something I was glad to yield, if for but a moment. He was making me feel things, delicious things. I couldn't hold back any longer. My hands flew up to grip his shoulders, to dig my nails into his jacket as if to say, *Don't stop. Please, don't stop.*

And he didn't.

The hand cupping my chin went down, both hands, sliding down my sides, thumbs stopping to rest on the underside of my breasts.

My noises of desperate desire were swallowed with his tongue and teeth. Every movement I made against him that felt *good*, any sign of pleasure that I gave, he duplicated.

Thumbs caressed my nipples through the material of the dress. I arched into the touch, just as he pulled away. His movements were quick, efficient. When I wanted them to take the time to explore one part of me, his hands were already moving to touch another. Everywhere his fingers traveled, a sizzling was left behind until my whole body ached with impatience.

I wanted him. I wanted him now.

His lips tore from mine almost violently. I couldn't help but feel like he was reading my thoughts, or maybe our bodies were so in tune with one another, maybe his need ached as hotly and desperately as mine.

His teeth scraped along my chin, down to my throat, grazing across my collarbone.

And then his hands were at the hem of my dress, hiking it up so it floated around my waist. I wanted to look, but couldn't bring myself to. My eyes squeezed closed at the first touch of his fingers in my entrance. My hips nearly came off the bed, but he held me steady with his other hand, palming my waist, nails digging in to taste.

His fingers slipped inside me, and I couldn't help the sound of desperation that scorched from my throat. There was something triumphant in the next few strokes of his fingers, the way they curled in and out of me, drawing me up… up… My head spun as if it lacked water. As if I was floating near the surface of two-legger territory and was gulping down air.

I gasped, clinging to him. I could do little else. My body was useless. I couldn't move. I could only feel.

When that final sensation rose to a crescendo and exploded, I cried out my gasping pleasure with a vicious tremble. When it ebbed, I leaned against him, holding him, wanting something more that I couldn't quite say.

Finally, he pulled away from me with a pained look on his face that he quickly masked into indifference. But it was too late. I'd seen it, and hurt spiraled through me.

Captain Saber took a few strokes back. His entire body was stiff, as he slowly turned back to Elias. Play time was over, his body said.

Elias chuckled, and I turned to glare at the Black Blade. "I'd hit you, if I didn't think you'd enjoy it."

Elias laughed harder, and when the sound died down, his black eyes met Captain Saber's bright aquamarine ones. Mischief met anger. "Welcome to the club, Captain."

They gave me a minute to compose myself. A minute in which I had to go into the bathing room and breathe. In. Out. In. Out. The fins on the side of my tail flared, both angrily and with embarrassment. I tried not to let my hurt show out there. Even though I'd been more than willing, I knew the only reason Elias had forced Captain Saber's hand was to spite him. Because he'd stabbed him.

Sure, both Captain Saber and I had a choice in the matter, and I was sure we'd equally enjoyed it, but the feeling of hurt still slid through me.

The only one showing any bit of decency was Kai, who had decided to keep mostly quiet during the whole exchange.

I'd not deny that I wanted every bit of what the captain had given me. I'd wanted it like I was starving. For him, for all he had to offer. And I would have rejoiced, would have possibly declared my love for him right there, if I hadn't known his heart belonged to another.

I supposed it didn't matter. We were all gathered in my room for one thing only. For the truth, so we could begin planning.

I set myself to rights and swam out. Elias still sat on his spot by the window, looking casually mischievous. Captain Saber was regarding him suspiciously from across the room, and Kai's eyes danced with amusement between the two.

At least they hadn't killed each other.

"So," I began, going to sit beside Kai on the bed. He seemed the safest of them all, and I put just enough distance between myself and the other two, that if they tried to lunge for each other, they'd meet me in the middle instead. "Elias was supposed to inquire about Kappurin priests. How did that go?"

"Like trying to find an obsidian stone in the abyss, as you can imagine, little fish." His attention went to me. Though his eyes still shone, his mouth was pulled tightly in a grave line. "There are so many Kappurin priests, it's impossible to know which one performed Odessa and Dorian's marriage ceremony. I don't even think it had to have been the royal priest from the king's castle. It could have been any bloke in a temple."

I figured as much, but straightened my spine. I'd not give up. "Then what we need to do is retrace Odele's strokes. Try and find out where she last was."

"You don't think we've done that already?" Captain Saber snapped, with only a small note of impatience in his voice. "We've searched everywhere for Odele and found nothing."

I tightened my hands into fists.

"That's because royal guards aren't very good at searching," Elias chimed in with dry humor. "But I am the Black Blade. What you are afraid to find, I will."

The captain's eyes narrowed. "With illegalities."

Elias winked. "I am a criminal, after all."

Before they could argue, I cut in, directing myself towards Elias. "While you're searching, look at orphanages. Try and see if someone ever abandoned a newborn around the time of Princess Odessa's death."

Elias nodded and got up. "If the baby was given up, I find it very unlikely they would have kept it in Thalassar, but I'll inquire, anyway." He swam over to me and bent so we were face to face. "I'll come when I have information. In the meantime, I know I'm leaving you in capable hands." Before I could comment upon his sarcasm, he pressed a fierce, thorough kiss to my lips before he got up and left through the tapestry.

Once he was gone, I sighed, rubbing my temple.

"Are you okay, my gem?" Kai's hands were suddenly at my neck, soothing and massaging the tension there.

I decided to settle with honesty. "I just keep thinking about everything we've discovered. I can't stop wondering who would do all these terrible things, why they let it get so far."

"Perhaps someone who had a lot to gain." Kai's hands paused at his own words, and then, between the three of us, we shared looks that went back and forth, back and forth.

"Who has the most to gain with all these deaths and disappearances?" I voiced aloud.

Obvious. The answer so obvious.

Yet Kai still said it. "Queen Circe. With all these deaths, with Odele gone, she has claim to the throne. And she doesn't seem too inclined on giving it up."

My breath hitched and my heart pounded. I had always suspected, if not outright, that something was wrong with the queen. It was in her power-hungry gaze. It was in the deaths of all these royals, and the disappearances of others.

With everyone else gone, the throne was hers for the win.

My eyes sought the captain's for his opinion on the matter. He did serve the family, after all.

His eyes were cold and calculated. "Heavy accusations," he murmured. "Yet at this point, nothing would surprise me."

I loosed a breath. What did we do from here? What did we do with this information? I supposed I had no real answers for this. There was hardly a thing we could do except twiddle our thumbs as we waited for Elias and the information he could provide.

But time seemed to suddenly press down on me, making me feel like I had only a certain number of days, hours, or minutes left before something bad happened.

The sudden flash of the steel of a blade invaded my mind, causing me to shiver.

And here I thought being a royal was going to be easy.

Prince Kai left, but I asked the captain to stay a moment longer. I wanted to speak with him. I needed to. After what had happened in this room, the waters needed to be cleared. At least, that's what I told myself. The truth could have been a far more simpler notion. I wanted him to linger here, purely out of selfish reasons. Because I relished in the feel of my pounding, nervous heartbeat.

And I wanted to know that he truly had no regrets.

"Thank you," I told him. We were both floating by the door, a safe distance away from each other. Close enough to reach out, but far enough to back away if we so wished. "For being here, for helping us."

He snorted, though it wasn't an unkind sound. It seemed a sound aimed more at his own expense. "The Black Blade is doing most of the work. I'm just going to float about being useless with nothing to do."

I huffed a small laugh. "Still, thank you. I know it can't be easy, working with someone you hate."

He didn't deny it. He just shrugged, the gesture seeming nonchalant, but his eyes seared through me. "If working with him is what it takes, then I'll put aside my own feelings."

A lump rose in my throat. He was so difficult to read. With Elias, we could communicate without words, using eyes and facial expression in lieu of speaking. Kai was always so honest and forthcoming, so *sweet.* The captain was a different story. I couldn't quite place where he sat on the line of our spectrum. What he thought.

If there was one thing I was positive about, it was that he was doing this, not only because it was his duty, but for Odele as well.

"I hope you know how grateful I am." Almost absently, stupidly, I added, "And I'm sure Odele will be grateful as well. Once we find her."

Captain Saber blinked. "Odele?"

I nodded, trying to appear calm even if on the inside I was a mess of nerves. Why was I still talking? I was just trying to get information out of him. Trying to get him to confess. Trying to get him to say those words, so I could hear them for myself. Then maybe my heart would stop beating wildly, and I could move on with my life, to the way things were before. When I was sure Captain Saber despised me instead of wanted me. That way I could ignore my own feelings, push them back as if they'd never been there in the first place.

"Yeah. I know you're helping because you want to find Odele as soon as possible." *To get rid of me.* Those words went unsaid but lingered in the space between us.

"Gods," Captain Saber muttered, turning his face away. His expression was all hard lines and disapproval. The sight of it had me straightening my posture and chastising myself internally, though for what, I wasn't sure. He turned back to me, his eyes twin orbs of burning lava. And the way he stared at me, I felt like I was being scorched to the core. "Is that why—" He broke off. "I don't *care* about Odele. I care about—" He broke off again and ran his hands through his short, blond hair.

You care about what, Captain?

I didn't speak, and neither did he for a long moment. Even if I wanted him to finish that sentence, to say the words I hoped they'd be, he didn't.

He let out a resigned sigh. Defeated. Like a mer who had lost a war.

"If you need anything, Maisie, I will help. No matter what it is."

His hand went to rest on my shoulder, but the action brought no comfort. It felt like a detached sort of movement, and it made me wonder if Captain Saber was truly there with me in the room at all, or if he'd gone far away inside himself and his memories.

"Good day, Princess." He pulled back and gave a strict yet proper bow before he opened the door and left.

I stared at the spot he'd vacated for a long while after he'd left, unable to move, unable to blink. All the while, doubts coursed through my head like the whiplash of a strong moving current. What had he been about to say? I dared not hope.

I feared that if I did, I'd find myself plunged into the bottom of an abyss alone, with my heart breaking into millions of little pieces, with Captain Saber's face in my mind, hearing the echoes of laughter in the darkness. Nothing but jokes at my expense, for being stupid enough to fall in love with a merman who could never love me back.

THE WORDS I so desperately wanted to say were at the tip of my tongue, begging for release, begging to take that dive into the unknown. Uttering them could either make me surface to brilliant, impossible heights, or make me sink.

They were better left unsaid.

I was neither the Black Blade nor the Dragon Prince. I possessed no eloquence at the face of my torrent of emotions. So I opted for silence instead.

Even when I'd wanted to confess the truth, when the words had almost spilled from my mouth, a desperate confession I'd realized the night before.

I don't care about Odele. I care about you.

The truth was, I'd stopped caring about Odele a long time ago. Slowly, she'd been ejected from my mind, and Maisie had filled her place. Not a replacement, no. It was in these past few weeks that I started to realize for myself that the truth of the matter was. I had never really loved Odele in the first place. I'd fashioned an illusion of her in my mind. I'd seen a lonely, broken royal beneath the pristine surface and had led myself to believe that she was as lost as I was.

I believed that she pushed those she cared about away, because it was easier to be cruel rather than to face her own emotions and be abandoned. And while that was true about Odele, that did not make it *love.*

Love was not cruel.

It was Maisie who opened my eyes to that last night. Love was devotion. It was caring. It was the conversation passed between silent stares, lips lingering on a forehead, and eyes shining with affection.

It was honesty.

It was proving a point.

Like Elias had so cruelly proved his point in that room moments ago. Maisie may not have seen the intention behind his actions, but I was not a complete fool. He'd done it, not only to spite me, but so I could come to the realization on my own.

I loved Maisie.

But she didn't love me back.

I despise you, she'd said last night. She'd never know how deeply her words had sliced into me. I would never tell her. If she wanted me for nothing more than my body, then I'd give it to her. It was more than I'd ever gotten from anyone before. More than I could hope to have.

Someday, I'd find it in myself to brave the words looming over me.

Someday, I'd find the courage to tell Maisie the truth about what I felt for her.

But it would not be today.

Maisie

Queen Circe called me into a private meeting late in the afternoon.

I'd spent most of the day in my room. Captain Saber had made the excuse that I hadn't been feeling well since the ball last night, explaining my absence then and all day today.

I should have gone to the queen sooner, to apologize for my lack of etiquette, but my own investigation—not to mention, fear—held me back.

I tried to be brave, donning the perfect afternoon dress in the demure color of white, and clasping my hands so she wouldn't see them tremble. I was swimming—surrounded by guards—to meet the queen who had the power to destroy me where I floated. At the snap of her fingers, an ax could come swinging down on my head.

I'd been too bold before, I realized. I'd challenged her at every turn in my feeble attempt to get her to see reason on the topic of the Selection. I'd done nothing but anger her since I'd been here. At first, I hadn't cared. But after all the information I'd discovered, after realizing that she was a possible suspect on so many murders and disappearances, I had to play it safe.

I had to yield.

The guards escorted me to the queen's sitting room. They merely opened the doors, let me swim in, and then closed them behind me.

The sitting room was blinding in its dainty superfluity. Pinks, golds, and purples adorned it ostentatiously, blindingly. Curtains were tied back from the opened windows, the outer edges of which were furry with colorful tube worms in bloom. A diamond chandelier hung from the ceiling, hundreds of glistening orbs dangling from it, soft blue lava glowing on the inside of each one. Tables and couches obviously sea-make, with plush purple cushioning, coral legs and anemones around the edges adorned the spacious room. It was blinding, but pretty.

Queen Circe sat at a high back chair of brilliant magenta and gold. Looking regal, as she always did, in brilliant colors of blue and yellow. Today, surprisingly, no crown adorned her head, and her hair was unbound, the golden tresses looking like beaming rays of sunlight illuminating the perfection of her face. Though she was in informal wear and in an informal setting, she looked no less powerful or deadly.

And we were alone.

I went forward with trembling fingers and dipped into a polite curtsy before her.

"You sent for me, Your Majesty?"

"Yes, have a seat, my dear." She spoke the words with sweetness, but with the slightest edge of poison beneath. Sea wasp poison.

I took the seat she'd indicated with her fingers, the high backed chair across from her own of much smaller make. Not even the chairs dared be taller than her own.

Her eyes flicked over my figure, stopping at the left side of my tail, as if she could see through the white, beaded dress I wore and to the mauled fin beneath. Everything in her gaze screamed at me, saying, *Imposter Princess.* I fought not to fidget.

"Captain Saber said you were feeling unwell." Her tone held a bit of inquiry.

I dipped my head in a nod. "I was. My stomach was feeling a bit uneasy last night and this morning, but it is starting to pass."

Her long fingers reached up to scrape along her chin. Every movement was precise, the slow coiling of a sea snake readying to spring. "It's disappointing, indeed, that you could not brave your discomfort enough to see the party through." I ground my teeth together. "All royals are taught to hide their deepest discomforts, their weaknesses. You could have been seconds away from death and still would have been expected to dance with your guests." She dropped her hand, letting it hang leisurely over the arm of the chair. A queen on her throne. "Yet, you were not raised a princess, and do not possess the knowledge to know your obligations."

I let out a slow breath. "Forgive me, Your Majesty, if I committed a slight."

Her eyes regarded me curiously, the blue in them lighting up. "I see you are finally learning to keep your mouth shut. Good."

I wanted to snap at her, but I bit the inside of my cheek to avoid doing so. I chanted things inside my head, truths to help me get through this smart, and unscathed.

Odette.

Odessa.

Odele.

The missing royal.

Sea wasp poison.

The queen either didn't notice my rising anger, or chose to ignore it entirely. "I know you think me to be cruel and heartless. No need to deny it, I can see it in your eyes." I hadn't even thought of objecting, or contradicting her. She went on, "So many mer find this hard to believe, but I care for this kingdom. The Malabella line has been full of such sickly mermaids... None of them survived long on the throne."

My blood ran cold at the words. My fingers trembled, and I clamped them in my lap to keep myself steady.

Odette.

Odessa.

Odele—

"But I have." Her voice held the unmistakable rise of vicious passion in it. And it made me afraid. "I have survived because I have followed the rules of our ancestors, because I do not question the hierarchy. My cousins, Odessa and Odette, gods rest their souls, were too kind. They cared more about the love of the mer rather than their fear."

As she spoke, her voice rose, and my own fear with it. I feared interrupting her. I feared breathing.

Odette.

Odessa.

Odele.

"And Odele—" She cut off with a scoff, only to continue in a more vicious manner. "Spoiled little mer. Her father gave her the world, and she threw it back in his face by fleeing." She shook her head back and forth. "My lineage is tainted. Cursed, some say. But we have not thrived or survived because of this weakness. Do you know *what* weakness does?" She looked at me intensely. I could only shake my head. "It *poisons* the rest of the family coral branch."

I almost gasped at the word 'poison'.

Odette.

Odessa.

Odele.

Sea wasp poison.

Poison.

The missing royal.

"The only way to rid ourselves of the poisoned branches is to eradicate them entirely." Her fingers curled along the arm of the chair as she took me in. "That is the way to deal with weakness, Maisie."

I nodded, as if I understood completely. Inside, I was reeling. Struggling to keep water into my lungs.

"You understand, don't you?"

Since she looked like she genuinely wanted an answer, I swallowed past the lump in my throat. "I understand, Your Majesty."

She leaned back into the cushions and smiled. "Good. Do not be a weakness." And then she flicked her fingers in a sure sign of a dismissal. I was all too eager to leave this room and conversation. A conversation that hadn't been one at all but something else.

A warning.

A threat.

"Thank you for your wise words, Your Majesty." I curtsied and slowly backed out of the room. I wasn't stupid enough to turn, lest I find myself with a poisoned dagger through my back.

The queen's eyes never strayed from my face, the side of her mouth twisting into a cruel smile that disappeared once the doors behind me opened. I backstroked past them, and they closed once again.

Once she disappeared from my sights completely, I turned and bolted.

Oh my gods. The queen had practically confessed to killing her family because they were weak, because they didn't follow the hierarchy. I knew she was vicious, knew she was power-hungry, but to have everything confirmed, and from the prime suspect herself?

I pushed my tail harder, faster. I swam as if I could swim away from her entirely, put as much distance between us as possible. The closer she was, the more the palace confines closed in, threatening suffocation. Threatening *poison.*

I swam until my fin gave a screaming protest of pain. I cried out and tripped, colliding into a wall and a portrait there. I looked up, coming face to face with the image of Princess Odessa. Her pretty, dark gaze bore into me. Seeming to say, *Justice. Justice. Sea wasp poison. Justice.*

I turned, gasping, and slid down the wall, crumpling to the floor. I tucked my tail under me, suddenly not caring if this wasn't princess-like. I was too overwhelmed. The truth lurked over me, mocking. I knew what I was saying, but I was somehow helpless. The queen had killed her cousins. What made me think I could stop her? What made me think I could do anything about it?

I wasn't sure how long I sat there, hyperventilating into my palms. All I knew was a small voice pulled me out of my panic.

"Your Majesty, are you alright?"

I looked up slowly to find a servant hovering above me, looking down at me with concern. How long had I been sitting in the hallway, overrun with all the thoughts of what the queen could do to me?

"I'm fine…" A blatant lie, as my voice broke.

The servant, to her credit, didn't blanch. She looked at me curiously, then down the hall. When she looked back at me, her eyes were rather wide, and she dropped her voice to a whisper. "I've been lookin' for you, Majesty."

I blinked, my brain trying to grasp her words, understand them. "Why?"

She looked around again. Was she waiting for someone to come? Making sure no one did? "I was told to give this to you, miss." From her pocket, she produced a small conch shell and handed it to me.

I looked it over, then back up to her. "Who gave this to you?" I asked, eyebrows pulling together. And why would they be sending this to me? I hadn't gotten a single conch since I'd been here posing as the princess.

"No one, Majesty. It was left in the kitchens with a note addressed to you. I'm lucky I got to it before Clarissa. Right nosey, that one."

That was so very odd. It instantly made me distrustful. "Did you listen to it?" I demanded.

Her face paled, and her eyes went wide. "Of course not, Majesty. I'd never do such a thing, especially not to you. Especially not after what you did to defend me with your cousins."

I took her in, realizing who she was. I hadn't recognized her. She'd been the maid who had been serving Jessinda, Silviya, Scarlet and I months ago. They'd vilely insulted her, and I'd put an end to Odele's cousins' bigotry. How had I not recognized her? Had I been so absorbed in myself that I'd seen right through her sweet face? Was I more of a royal than I knew?

"I'm sorry. I didn't recognize you."

She smiled a little sadly. "That's okay, Majesty. I wouldn't expect you to, but I appreciate it all the same."

That just made me feel worse.

"It's not an excuse. Forgive me?"

Her cheekbones reddened and she nodded. Then, she curtsied. "I'll leave you now. If you don't need anything else from me, that is." She gave a pointed look to my crumpled form.

I sat up straighter, mustering up the most fierce royal voice I could muster. "That will be all."

She curtsied once more and turned down the hall, leaving me in my solitude.

As soon as she'd gone, I stared at the conch in my hands then slowly, I lifted it to my ear and listened.

The voice inside that spoke was a deep rasp that sent chills curling down my spine. Bumps rose up on my arms, and my gut clenched. Something about this voice seemed familiar…

"I know you're lookin' for answers about Princess Odessa's missin' bastard. I have them. Meet me at Siren's Song tonight. Come alone or you'll get nothin' from me. Smash this conch when you're done."

That was the entirety of the message. I waited a few heartbeats, keeping the thing pressed to my ear until it began again. I listened to it twice until I had the whole thing memorized.

And then I smashed it against the ground.

Broken bits littered the quartz floors. I stared at them for a moment. Once a conch was broken, the message inside disappeared, and no matter how long you took to place the pieces back together, the words or images would be gone forever.

No one would know about this but me.

Taking a breath, I got up and swam back to my room.

It was risky to leave a message of that nature lying around, but whoever had done it had known I'd receive it. He had to have known.

Who was he, and what did it mean? How did this merman know the answers and how did he know that I was searching for them?

Going alone would be dangerous. I should tell Captain Saber. The smart thing would have been to preserve that conch and let him listen to it. Maybe have him trail after me.

But the instructions had been specific.

Come alone.

If he knew what it was I searched for, then he surely knew who Captain Saber was.

I couldn't risk not getting the answers we'd all been searching for. Answers that could end this once and for all.

So I would go alone to Siren's Song. I would don a disguise and slip through the cove unseen, undetected, with the weapon of the Black Blade strapped to my waist.

I was no longer a victim. The glow of steel flashed in my mind, and all sense of helplessness dissipated.

Because I was Maisie Fauna, waitress at Tides' Tavern. I'd survived gators, Selection, poisoning, assassination attempts, and life at the palace. I could do anything. I'd no longer be a victim.

Because I was not afraid.

I slipped on a dress and cloak of black, tying my hair into a knot behind my head. The hood shadowed my features, and the blade at my side was well hidden.

I was ready when night descended over the waters of Eramaea. Determination powered my every stroke; not even my fin ached. I felt powerful. Invincible.

Inside the cove, I filled a pouch with coins and jewels from the two-legger chest. Never once had these riches tempted me. Never once had I thought to use them for any selfish purpose. As if that feeling had been pushed beyond me by some invisible force, waiting for this exact moment.

I wasn't stupid enough to assume this information would be for free.

I filled enough so it wouldn't clink as I swam, to avoid any attempted muggings. Though if anyone even tried, they'd find themselves with my blade in their gut before they got the chance. I was focused enough that I believed it could come to that.

With everything ready, I made my way to the alleyway and onto the streets of Eramaea.

I swam with shadow and current, keeping to myself. I spoke to no one. Instead, I listened. Listened like I imagined Elias would do. That was how I navigated my way. I followed the sounds of vile depravity until I made it to a shabby little tavern.

I looked at the place with distaste. A sign made of shipwrecked wood with the vulgar image of a mermaid hung from a chain at the top of it. It was covered with furry algae around the edges, a sign that looked as if it had seen better days.

The whole place looked like it was made from an overturned sunken pirate ship. From the round, opened windows, sound and music spilled. The sounds of drunken voices drifted.

The Siren's Song.

Tides' Tavern definitely put this place to shame. A thousand times over.

Steeling myself, I ventured inside.

Bright lights illuminated the disgusting little tavern. It was as horrid inside as it was outside. Covered in barnacles, crabs and lizards scuttled along the rotting wood and along hastily put together tables and chairs. Mermaids in skimpy, see-through outfits, swam about serving frothy ale and wine out of two-legger bottles. Mermen—obviously of ill repute—sat around in drunken laughter, pulling the serving mer into their laps.

There was a makeshift stage in the corner of the tavern where a band played. Using instruments made of shell and bone pipes, they fiddled an upbeat tune. A mermaid wearing close to nothing on her body and too much on her face was belting out a song.

Hm. Siren's Song, indeed.

I turned throughout the tavern, searching for the figure who could have possibly called me here. Could it be the merman drinking alone at the rotting wood of the bar? Or maybe it was the middle-aged merman stroking his fingers along the arm of a server. Could it be the lone, dainty figure in the corner of the tavern, face obscured by cloak and shadows?

I took a seat at an empty table and waited.

A serving mer came over, eyeing me curiously. To avoid suspicion, I ordered a tankard of moonshine.

She brought it over quickly and I flipped her a gold coin.

When she left, I lifted the glass up to my mouth and took a generous swallow… and nearly gagged the stuff out.

This was what they called moonshine in Eramaea? It was despicable. Disgusting. It tasted like one tiny part moonshine and the rest tasted like slime. They'd diluted it.

I pushed the glass across the table, just as a merman took a seat across from me.

My whole body tensed as I took him in.

I couldn't quite discern the mer's age, but there was a peppering of gray throughout the roots of his sideburns. He was a bit on the rotund side, though there was no mistaking his build of a laborer. His arms were large. The shadow of a beard covered his jaw. His eyes were small, but shot through with red. Either he was drunk or hadn't slept for weeks.

My hand fluttered to the hilt of my blade. Even skimming it, I felt Elias' presence, and it gave me valor.

He was dressed entirely in black. Not ominous here in a tavern full of unsavory characters. He grabbed my discarded tankard and brought it to his lips, taking a very large swallow. When he put it down, he smacked his lips.

"You come alone?" he asked.

So this was him, then.

I nodded.

He looked around as if he didn't quite believe me. When he was satisfied, he picked up the tankard again and downed the whole contents in one go. Then, he wiped the froth from his upper lip with the back of his hand.

"Well, follow me."

He got up, gesturing with his fingers that I follow.

I furrowed my brows, staring at him distrustfully. But he cast me an impatient look that had me mustering up my courage and getting up to follow him.

We went out of the tavern. He led me off to the side of it, and gestured that I swim in first, to the end of the dark alleyway there.

I realized my mistake as soon as I made it to the end.

I was trapped, and he blocked the exit.

I whirled, fingers resting near the hilt of my blade.

But the merman was just regarding me. Eyes roaming over my every inch. Not lustfully, but with something else I couldn't quite place.

I was the one to break the silence. "Who are you?"

His eyes seemed to spark. He pressed a hand to his chest. "A mere mercenary."

I tensed further. "Why did you send me that conch? How do you know I'm looking for answers?"

He sighed. "It's a long story…"

My patience already wore thin. I wanted answers, and I wanted them now. I reached inside my cloak for the pouch of coins and tossed them to the ground at his fins.

"There's your money. Now spill."

He bent and picked it up, opening it to look through the gold and gems. Satisfied, he pulled the string closed and pocketed it.

Then he looked at me, and there was a sudden viciousness in his eyes.

"I was hired during the Malabella Sanitorum reign to do a job."

My breath and next words caught in my throat. By who? The current queen?

"Thought it'd be easy. Do the job, collect my money, and move on." He shook his head back and forth. "Never thought what I did years ago would catch up to bite me in the tail now."

My eyes narrowed. "What are you talking about?"

"Princess Odessa's bastard babe."

The babe wasn't a bastard. She'd married Dorian and had a baby before she was killed. He didn't know that, of course.

"Do you know something about the baby?"

He nodded. "Oh, ay. Wee little thing she was."

She.

Princess Odessa's baby had been female. Which meant that Thalassar could be rightfully hers.

"What happened to her?"

He ran a hand through his hair. "Wasn't supposed to be a hard job. But I'm not an uncharted savage. I got morals just like anyone else."

None of his babble made any sense. "*What* are you talking about?"

"They wanted me to kill Princess Odessa, they did. Had to off the nurses, too. Pulled the squalling babe right out of her arms and poured the poison down her throat myself."

Holy gods.

It had been him. He had killed Princess Odessa on someone's orders. Whose? Gods… and I was alone in an alley with him.

My hand gripped the hilt of the blade, but I didn't pull it out. Not yet. No sudden moves.

"And then they told me to off Queen Odette, too. She fetched me a hefty sum, she did. Pity, she was so kind, even in those last moments."

Holy gods. He was insane. He was crazy. But he had all the information. I needed him to keep talking. And then make it out of this alleyway alive.

"She went diggin' for stuff she shouldn't have. It got her killed. And then that prissy little Princess Odele went diggin' and they told me to off her, too."

My palms heated. "I *am* Odele."

His haze sharpened. "No you ain't. But you ruined everythin' by coming here. You shoulda' stayed where you was at."

Silt. He knew I wasn't the princess. How? My grip tightened. I unsheathed the blade a fraction.

"You coulda' stayed where you was and no one would've been the wiser."

My heart beat rapidly in my chest. "What do you mean?"

"Wanted me to kill the babe, too, they did. I ain't no babe killer."

Gods. Whoever it was who had hired him… this mysterious 'they' had ordered him to kill a child? The queen…

"So I took her. Gave her to an older mer with no children or family. Told her it was my sister's. She left and I ain't heard a thing since."

Would my tail cramp up if he attacked me and I defended myself? Where could I stab him so he'd go down, giving me just enough time to swim away?

"But then Princess Odele got away from me. They was furious. And then you came. You fooled me at first. Thought you was her. I tried finishin' the job." My breath hitched. "But they realized who you was. And now they want *me* dead. Because I didn't finish the job. Now I gotta remedy it. It'll all be better then. Don't worry… *Princess…*" He reached into his tunic and pulled out the glinting steel of a dagger.

The shine of it made me catch my breath.

Princess… The glint of a blade. The mounting fear.

He'd been the one to chase me in the palace that night.

He'd tried to kill me.

My voice shook. "If I'm not Odele, then why do you want to kill me?" *Keep talking,* I begged. *Please keep talking.*

He barked out a bitter laugh. "Because you ruined everythin'. You weren't supposed to come back." He took a stroke forward.

I brandished the blade then.

I will not be afraid. I will not be afraid. I am not a victim.

"You've ruined my life, Odalaea."

"My name is Maisie."

"Your mum put up a fight for you. And you've proved difficult to kill as well. But I won't fail this time."

"Wh—"

"I shoulda' killed you when you was a babe, Princess."

And then he lunged for me.

I dodged, breaking out of my surprise. His dagger sliced at my cloak, snagging. I swung my own blade with such a force that would have made Kai proud.

But this merman was skilled and I was not. He was a mercenary. But I still swung.

He overpowered me. Somehow, he overpowered me. The blade was knocked from my hands. It fell to the silt. And then he pushed me and my fin gave out. I fell to the ground, gasping.

The merman loomed over me, raising his dagger high over his head.

"I shoulda' done this when you was a babe," he cursed, and a single tear rose from his eye. "I shoulda' put that poison in yer mouth, too, but the princess begged me not to." He sniffled. "But you aren't a babe any longer, and I gotta kill you now."

Before he could bring the dagger swinging over me, a gasp ripped through his throat as blood bloomed through the water at his chest.

I could only stare numbly at the tip of the sword sticking from his chest. It dug through and he let out a sound that I knew would haunt me forever.

And then he died.

The sword was ripped from his body, as if it had been keeping him afloat, and he crumpled to the silt.

I watched his body fall first. And then I looked up.

A cloaked figure floated there, shaking the plumes of blood from a steel sword. The weapon was sheathed, and delicate fingers pushed the hood of the cloak away to reveal the face beneath.

I recognized the features as much as I recognized my own. I'd studied them for weeks. I'd been told the resemblance was uncanny and hadn't wanted to believe it until now.

It was like looking into a slightly distorted mirror. Her body was a bit wider than mine, curves fuller, cheeks rounder. But our hair and tails were the same, eyes nearly so. She was as stunning in beauty as the recordings made her out to be, as everyone said she was.

Then Odele Malabella Oriana, Princess of Thalassar, smiled at me, and she spoke, "Hello, cousin."

DEATH
BEYOND THE
WAVES

"Hello, cousin."

Shock unhinged my jaw, making me numb to my surroundings. In this breathtaking moment, I knew nothing but the sight before me, or rather, the mermaid before me.

I had the sinuous curves of her features memorized for months now, all from the portraits in the castle and the recordings sequestered deep inside that secret cove. But the silver-gold sheen of a moving image hardly compared to the princess of flesh and blood floating before me.

I'd only ever seen her in the richest gowns Thalassar had to offer, ostentatious jewelry dangling from her ears, neck, wrists, and hair. It had become a uniform of sorts, one I associated with the mer whose place I'd taken, who I had been pretending to be for months now.

Having her in front of me right now was different. She was different.

Instead of gowns in pink and flashy colors, Odele Malabella, Crown Princess of the mer kingdom of Thalassar, wore the black tunic of a laborer and a dark hooded cloak to match. A simple leather belt hung from her hip, where a steel sword was sheathed.

A sword she'd used only a moment ago to run through the merman attacking me.

Her hair, similar in color and length to my own, was tied away from her round face, a face not unlike mine. Whatever image of her I had in my mind the whole time I'd been in Eramaea, this certainly was not it. I wasn't sure what I'd expected. Certainly not this mercenary-looking mer before me. Though pretty, she no longer looked the part of a royal. It was still there, in the elegant cock of her hip and the arrogance flaring in eyes that were more brown than black.

I was so distracted staring at her, almost certain she'd be a phantasmal illusion my distressed mind had conjured up, that I didn't really register her words.

I shut my open mouth and swallowed past the tight lump in my throat. I looked down at the merman slumped in the silt, his body already starting to rise and twirl through the water. Plumes of blood still flowed in little smokey tendrils. His mouth hung open, and I could almost hear the sound of his last dying cry, echoing in the ripples of water around us.

"You killed him," I whispered. Inexplicably, anger swelled to the roots of my chest. She'd killed him. Odele had *killed* this merman. My gaze shot up to hers, and I couldn't hide the glaring rage.

Her own delicate, perfectly arched eyebrows rose, eyes shining with amusement as she pressed her fist into the curve of her hip and looked down at me, like she looked down on so many other mer that were lesser than her. "I just saved your life. I think gratitude is in order."

Because I couldn't stand to have her looking at me like I was less—though I probably was—I scrambled from my sitting position to float up and face her. I was taller by a mere few inches but she still had this look on her face, like she could belittle me, chew me up and spit me out for fun. She probably could, but I wouldn't give her the satisfaction.

"I needed information from him," I accused. "And you killed him before he could give it to me."

She scoffed, a sound that was both elegant and condescending at once. "He was too far gone into his craze at the end of that pretty little speech to reveal anything." Her eyes softened as she took me in. "Besides, he gave us the most important part of the story, cousin."

Cousin.

That word rippled shock through my entire body. I'd been too numb to hear it that first time, to process what she'd said and what the words implied. The heavy weight of them threatened to sink me into the darkness of an abyss I wouldn't be able to get out of.

"I am not your cousin." My hand tightened around the studded hilt of my black blade. It was a small comfort, to sense Elias here in the dark alley with me when the reality was that I was alone. Alone with a princess, a body, and heavy words that made no sense.

"Didn't you hear what he said?" Odele began softly, yet fiercely. "Aunty Odessa had a female babe. One he took and gave to an old mer. That baby was you."

The lump in my throat suddenly took the shape of steel, making it hard to swallow and speak. I had to breathe a couple of times before I could reply to her and even when I did, my voice cracked. "It's not true. That would make me—"

"A princess," she interrupted. "The rightful heir to the throne of Thalassar and Kappur. My cousin. Princess Odalaea Malabella Knoll."

Odalaea.

The merman had called me that when he'd taken a swing at me. It was all so confusing. I could hardly wrap my head around it. Me? A princess? It was preposterous. Ridiculous. Impossible.

"I am Maisie Fauna, a waitress from Lagoona," I told her firmly. Saying the words aloud helped settle them over me. They pushed past the tightness, the overwhelming sensation inside me. These words were real. These words were the truth of my life. Not hers.

Odele's lip twitched. "That may be who you thought you were, but it isn't who you are. You are a princess. My cousin."

I shook my head back and forth. It *wasn't* true. I couldn't quite possibly be royalty. Me. With my torn fin, my accent, and… well, everything else that was wrong with me. I was nobody, nothing special. Whatever she said to try and convince me otherwise didn't matter. In my heart, I knew the truth. My truth.

Instead of saying this, and possibly continuing an argument that could last hours, I looked past her shoulder. "We really shouldn't stay here," I whispered.

Odele looked inclined to argue more, but agreed with a shake of her head. Then, she crouched so she was leveled with his still-floating form and unceremoniously started digging through the lapels of the dead merman's jacket.

"What are you doing?" I hissed.

She pulled out the pouch of gold coins and rubies I'd given to him, jangling them in the palm of her hand. "I see you found my lovely treasure cove." She placed them inside the pocket of her own cloak and then went back to digging from his.

"Can't you let the dead rest in peace?" I was sure there was a special place in the abyss reserved for this kind of offense. Stealing from a dead mer was low.

Odele snorted, obviously not sharing in the sentiment. "These coins are mine, first of all. He would have taken them and left you dead in the street. I'm surprised you have compassion for him at all." When she finished emptying his pockets, she got back up. "I plan on leaving this… *mercenary*…" Her voice rang with unbridled hatred. "…here to be found in the morning. I want it to look like a robbery." She was still staring down at his form. Her hands were tightening into fists, looking as though she would erupt.

"Leave him here?" For a brief moment, I wondered if he had family. If he had anyone out there that was looking for him, would miss him.

"First kills are hard," Odele whispered, eyes not straying from that limp, floating body. "But I will shed no tears and feel no guilt for this scum." She looked up at me again, and despite what she'd said a single bubble, so tiny I almost didn't notice it, rose from the corner of her eye. "He killed my mother. *Our* mothers."

I didn't want to argue with her. Not when I knew she was right about him being a murderer. He had killed both Princess Odessa and Queen Odette.

"He deserved worse. Now come on. We've got to go before soldiers come poking around."

Odele whirled away from me and didn't wait as she swam to the mouth of the alley. I scrambled to follow, annoyed at her attitude. It was the very demeanor I'd hated while I watched those recordings of her. Like every mer was obligated to bow at her fins.

"Stick to the shadows," she ordered.

I wanted to snipe back, but held my tongue and did as told. We both drew our hoods over our faces before venturing out in the water.

Odele, I realized quickly, had expert knowledge of the streets of Eramaea. She knew where the shadows rested, areas that were sparsely populated, and seemed to know just how to avoid any soldier in sight. It was a skill that rivaled the Black Blade's, and I was sure it would have made Elias strangely proud to see Odele so at ease in the shadows, like a thief of the night.

We made it to the alley by the palace. When Odele pressed her hand to the wall to open that passageway, there was no fumbling, no feeling around crusted barnacles and algae. She knew exactly where it was.

The archway opened and Odele swam in quickly, flicking her tail in precise, elegant movements. There was no limp on her. No sign of imperfection like there was in me.

My heart gave a painful lurch at that as I followed, stone closing behind me.

Odele never stopped to pause once. She just reached into her cloak and tossed out the bag of gold coins with perfect aim and kept swimming up to that tunnel. I followed.

We made it all the way to my—*her*—room, and I breathed a sigh of relief when I realized no one was there to greet me.

"Ah, it feels good to be home," Odele huffed as she untied the strings at the neck of her cloak and let it slide from her body.

All I could do was watch her, take in her every movement. She was graceful, *beautiful.* The curves of her body were generous, the purple of her hair and tail literally shone. Even in rags she was regal and powerful. I couldn't help but compare myself to her, the way I'd been compared to her since I'd gotten here. Yes, we looked so alike it almost hurt, except she was more poised than I could ever hope to be.

It was a moment before I realized I was staring, and another moment for me to realize she was staring right back.

I startled, but she didn't rustle an inch. Her eyebrows were raised in amusement that slowly cooled into a softer, warmer expression.

"I never knew my aunt," she began. I tensed. "But I remember my mother speaking of her sometimes." She was speaking to me in hushed tones, sharing a small piece of herself she'd perhaps never shared with anyone before. And I knew this secret wasn't something to be taken lightly. It would now be a link between us, this piece of her past, and of her. "I always stare at the portraits of them, the ones in the halls." A little laugh trickled from her throat. "I mostly liked to marvel at how alike they seemed, and sometimes, in those moments, I'd find myself wishing for a sister." She gave a brief pause, and her stare seemed to bore into me. "But now I have a cousin, and that's practically the same thing."

Her following smile was so blinding, so *painful,* that I had to look away. Staring down at my fins seemed easiest. Kept me focused. "I told you," I ground out tightly, if a little sadly. "I'm not your cousin."

"You'd really float there, see the resemblance between us, and still deny it? Why, Odalaea?"

I ignored her question. "I told you to stop calling me that. My name is Maisie."

The annoyance was clear in her voice. "Odalaea is your birthright. The Thalassarin and Kappurin thrones are your inheritance. That name you're trying to carry is a lie, and I will not call you by it."

My rage flared then, and I took a stroke towards her. I wanted to grab her by the shoulders and shake sense into her, to scream. Instead, I calmly asked her, "Why are you so certain I am…" *A princess.* "...your cousin?"

"How are you so certain you're not?" she countered. "That mercenary admitted as much. He took you when you were a baby and gave you away."

My breathing grew shallower the more this conversation carried on. "He was just crazy."

Odele rolled her pretty eyes. "You were so keen to believe him when he said he'd murdered royals and when you wanted to know who hired him to do it. Why is this so hard to believe?"

I lost my temper, anxiety pulsating through me, like a wave crashing, exploding into a violent pull of ferocity. "Because that would mean my entire life has been a lie!" I shouted, causing Odele to still. "It would mean that the mer I called 'grandmother' my entire life was nothing to me but someone who took me off of someone else's hands. It would mean accepting all of this!" I gestured at the ceiling, at the richness of her room. "Accepting a royal life that I don't want. It would mean that I really have a father—a father who has waged war against the kingdom I love—and a mother who—" I choked off, unable to say the words but needing to get them out. I had to. "Who was *murdered.*"

Oh, gods.

The truth was out. The truth on why I couldn't accept this as reality, why I would deny it until my last breath. I'd never wanted a crown. I'd just wanted change. I'd wanted a war to end, a princess to be found, a murderer and culprit stopped.

I hadn't asked for *this.* I hadn't asked for the weight of a whole kingdom, for this sick, twisted family who lied and murdered one another.

"I don't want it," I told her viciously, my chest rising and falling with my anger. "I don't want it to be real, because it would mean my life is a lie. That I don't even know who I am."

There was silence for a long stretch of time after that, filled only with the rasping labor of my breathing.

"Whether you want it to be real or not, Odalaea, it *is.* It *is* real. You are my cousin. You are a princess. And you are heir to the throne."

It's not real. It can't be.

To avoid further argument, I plopped myself down on the edge of the bed, letting the anemones reach for me. I sighed into that small comfort. "Now what? Where do we go from here?"

Obviously taking the hint, Odele let the subject drop. For now. I didn't doubt she would keep bringing it up whenever she saw fit. It was a conversation I didn't want to have. Not now, not ever. I didn't even think I wanted to contemplate the weight of everything in my own solitude.

"Well, I don't know about you, but that tavern made me feel dirty." She shuddered. "It was likely crawling with unsavory diseases. I'm going to go bathe."

I could use a nice long bath myself. "Yeah," I agreed. "And when we're done and changed, we need to talk. Like about where you've been all this time." And why she seemed so at ease with thinking I was her cousin. She was taking it in stride and didn't seem the least bit bothered by the situation; by me or killing that mer in the alley.

"Sure thing." She waved my words off, and I wondered if she'd even heard them at all before she bounded into the bathing room, closing the door behind her.

With her gone, I was able to sort through a fraction of my muddled thoughts. The words echoed in my mind, a mockery if anything.

Princess Odalaea Malabella Knoll.

I repeated them over and over, trying to feel a stirring inside, a sense of rightness. Something that said, *Yes. This is you. Take it.* But no feeling came, because that name wasn't mine.

It belonged to another, to the baby who had been clutched in her mother's arms, and then ripped from them. And it had stopped belonging to her the moment her mother's murderer gave her away to a strange mer on the street.

My grandmother…

She'd been the mer to take me in. And she'd cared for me, loved me like I was her own, because I *was* hers. I doubted she'd even *known.* I recalled so vividly then. All the times when I was younger, when I'd tried finding pieces of myself in her. We'd looked nothing alike, and I had not questioned it. Why would I when she loved me so fiercely, when she had told me that I looked like my fabled parents…?

It had all been a lie. A lie I couldn't bear to accept. A lie I'd hold on to like it was the truth, because I couldn't stand to have my world suddenly sinking into the unknown. All my life, I'd known what I was, who I was, and now I couldn't even claim that.

Sighing, I got up and swam past the bathing room door. I needed to go into the closet and find something to wear. Granted, every scrap of clothing in this room was Odele's, and I wondered if she'd be infuriated at me for wearing what belonged to her. But I stopped in my tracks right before I passed the bathing room door, I heard muffled sounds coming from inside.

Loathing doing it, but not being able to resist, I pressed my ear up against the door and listened.

Listened to the sounds of Odele sobbing.

First kills are hard, she'd said with certainty.

I couldn't help but wonder if she'd said it more for my benefit, or for hers?

I didn't comment on Odele's puffy, swollen eyes when she exited the bathing room. She feigned confidence as she sauntered over to pull out an outfit. I quietly went in to bathe myself, nervous that if I turned my back for even a moment, Odele would disappear.

So I hurried through the process, dunking my head into sand, and scrubbing it and my skin raw. I quickly donned a robe and swam out into the room, nearly out of breath.

But Odele was there, lounging across the plush cushions of her ivory scallop bed. One hand was propping her head up, and she admired me with amusement.

"Still here, O."

I tried to compose myself, assuming a cool demeanor as I went to grab the nightdress I'd laid out. My hands paused, hovering over the material.

"I hope you don't mind me wearing your stuff…"

She just shrugged. "You've been using them for months now. Doesn't matter."

Not what I was expecting. What had I been expecting? Not this… friendliness… if that's what this could be called.

I changed, pulling on the nightdress and hovered just at the edge of the bed. I felt suddenly out of place and chastised myself. This room had never been mine to begin with, and I'd gotten too comfortable. Now, Odele was back and there was no place for me here.

Not that there ever had been.

But I hadn't really planned this far ahead. I didn't know what to do, where to go from here. Would I be kicked out of the palace? Or would the queen have my head for my disobedience? The future was a dark, blurry thing, and I didn't know what mysteries waited for me inside it.

I started to turn from the bed I'd grown used to for these past few months. I could always fashion a hammock out of a sheet. It's not like I wasn't used to sleeping in discomforts. That had been my life. The only life I knew and accepted it.

"There's plenty of room on the bed for the both of us," Odele quietly offered, as if she sensed where my thoughts were taking me.

I stopped, turned to look at her. "I don't want to impose."

She scoffed, waving my words away with her delicate fingers. "Nonsense, we're family." She patted the empty space next to her in invitation.

My teeth ground together in annoyance, but I loosed a breath before slowly trudging over and sliding into the spot next to her. I kept distance between us, afraid to get too close. She had no such qualms about me, and obviously no concept of personal space, because she scooted closer until our arms touched. The contact jolted me, but I fought to keep very still.

"You need to relax," she commented. "I'm not going to hurt you."

"I know."

She didn't seem the murderous type. Not like her stepmother, anyway. The mer in the alleyway didn't really count. After that initial shock, after hearing her sob in the bathing room, I'd understood. It had been about revenge, and it had been about justice. The moment her sword had pierced the mercenary's heart, the lines between the two terms had blurred. It had been about saving her mother's honor. It had been about saving me, even if I couldn't accept the possible connection lying between the two of us.

She had saved me regardless of what I thought.

"Where have you been all this time?" I asked.

Odele's fingers started plucking at the cushions beneath us, the only sign she was even remotely nervous, even when her voice was calm and confident. "It's a long story…"

"We have all night."

She sighed. "I guess the whole thing started *months* ago. I—" She paused, and I didn't turn to look at her, but I imagined she was chewing her lip, debating how much truth to tell and how many lies. "I really enjoy reading, and I enjoy listening to conches. *Don't* tell anyone I told you that." Her nails dug into my arm in threat. "I will deny it with my last breath."

"Alright."

She loosened her hold and continued, "I spend a lot of time in the royal library. I've read through almost every parchment and listened to nearly every conch there. The selections here aren't quite as extensive as they are in other kingdoms…" Her tone grew wistful. "I hear the great library in Brague has millions of conches and the libraries of Draconi record messages in dragon eggs…"

She was getting off track, and the grand library that wasn't extensive to her had been quite impressive to me. That comment only served to remind me how different we truly were, how much more knowledgeable she was regarding the world.

"So I started poking around in the Royal Records room. Out of boredom, you see. No one usually goes in there except the queen and my father, or their closest advisors. The conches were really quite boring. Just a bunch of stuff on our long dead ancestors…" She paused, and her fingers slid down my arm. I wondered if it was a nervous gesture, or if she was seeking comfort in me. "I came across the conch on my sister—I hadn't even known I'd had a sister—and the conches on Aunty Odessa and my mom." She sucked in a breath, shuddering and painful. I couldn't help but take her hand then, to loan her my strength. The way I wished so many times before that someone would've loaned me their strength so I didn't have to battle harsh truths alone.

"You can imagine what a shock it was to me… to hear that my aunt had been poisoned after giving birth. And who would have known? The queen didn't like me meddling in that room, said I'd break important records with my foolery…" She scoffed. "Anyway, everything after that kind of just… fell into my lap. I started digging. I discovered that this room…" She gestured with her free hand. "…had belonged to Aunty Odessa. I found sketches of blueprints of the palace, old and new, and realized some sections had been cut off. I found the secret cove only days later."

So the cove had not only been Odele's, but Odessa's as well.

"It's a good place to hide things you don't want others to see…"

I imagined her hundreds of conches littering the floors.

"The more I dug, the more I found out and started to put things together myself. I found a discarded marriage contract, then a conch with your parents getting married, and it opened my eyes to everything. I had a cousin out there somewhere. Not just distant cousins, like Jessinda is, but an *actual* cousin. My mother's twin's child." Her hand squeezed mine, as if that simple motion could implant the words into me and make me believe them.

"I knew I had to find him… or her. To discover all I could. That's when the attempts on my life started. Someone knew what I was looking for and was trying to keep me quiet. At first, my goal had been only to find my cousin—to find you—but with the assassination attempts, I looked deeper.

"I knew there'd always been something suspicious about my mother's death. She'd been healthy, so how was it she died of a supposed attack or sickness? Odessa had been killed with poison, so I took a trip to the morgue. The merman there was obviously following someone's orders. The more I dug, the more vicious the attempts got.

"It was all kept quiet, of course, and I had to pretend like nothing was happening. Like I hadn't *accidentally* been thrown off my hippocampus. Like I hadn't noticed the shadows following me with the glint of steel shining beneath the glow of lava globes. Like someone wasn't trying to murder me for what I knew." A shuddering breath racked through her body. "No one would have believed me. So I kept it to myself."

My heart constricted at her words, so sure they weren't true. "Captain Saber—"

Odele scoffed. "Tiberius would have smothered me, had he known, and that would have been worse."

Tiberius. Even I rarely called him that, despite what we had shared, what intimacies lay between us. And here Odele was, using his first name as if it meant nothing. Like it was so easy. The jealousy that seared inside me came unbidden, and I tried to expel it before she could glimpse it.

"So I came up with a plan. I started sneaking out of the palace dressed as a commoner. I learned what I could on the streets of Eramaea and from what few members of the staff I could trust. I learned about the Black Blade. I gathered what information I'd collected, names of nurses and doctors who had worked for our grandparents, the names of those who had died the same day as aunty Odessa, and I took them to him."

Just the mention of Elias warmed my heart. He'd been telling me the truth. Not that I'd ever doubted him.

"I knew some of them had already died, but I wanted to make sure, to see if any of them were still alive. Anyone who could tell me what had happened to you. Where you were. By then, I'd already decided to flee. I couldn't risk the attacks getting more aggressive. Not before I found you. So I escaped through the cove and went to search for the names on the list.

"Most of them were old and had died. There was only one name on that entire list that had survived. And the old mermaid was in a nursing home here in Thalassar. The doctors let me see her—they didn't recognize me, of course—but told me to be gentle, because she was out of her mind."

I vaguely remembered Elias saying that everyone on the list Odele had given him was dead, save for one. This old mer. Had *he* spoken to her, or had he deemed it hopeless?

"But she was as sane as you or me. She saw me and recognized me right away. I asked her if she had been there that day my aunt had given birth. She said yes, she'd been head nurse at the time.

"'She'd been locked in the hospital for months, away from the public eye,' she told me. 'It was improper for someone of her station to have a baby out of wedlock, but I knew she had to be married.'"

"Why did she think that?" I asked, speaking for the first time.

"I asked the same thing. She said she wore a ring on her finger like two-leggers do when they get married. And during the first few days of her lock up, a merman kept trying to get in to see her, but was never allowed."

King Dorian. Had he gone to find her? Begged to see his pregnant wife before he'd been brutally chased from the hospital, the kingdom?

"The nurse said that the day you were born, a merman barged into the hospital, claiming he had royal business to see to. She wasn't there at the time; she'd gone to get medicine or something. When she came back, the nurses were dead, and she thought Aunty Odessa was too. She said she went to check her pulse and it was weak. She thought she could save her, but all Odessa could manage to say was 'Odalaea' over and over again before she died."

I hadn't realized the tears were pouring from my eyes until it was too late. Until a sob lodged tightly in my chest and rose, coming out of me in a strangled sound. I muffled it, yanking my hand away from Odele's to bite down on my skin. Maybe the pain of a physical injury would make me forget this story and all it implied. Make me forget the sadness of my origins.

"Why are you telling me this?" My voice came out as a whisper as I tried holding back the sobs that trembled my body.

"You wanted the truth. This is it. The nurse said she swam to look for you, but it had been too late. And after everything was cleaned up, those who knew of Odessa's stay at the hospital had started disappearing. She knew she would have been killed eventually, so she hid in that nursing home, all those years, keeping this secret with her."

What must have it been like for this old mer? To hold one of the greatest secrets in Thalassar, hiding because of what she knew, unable to tell anyone what had happened that day, that somewhere out there, a criminal had stolen a baby. A princess. *Me.*

"You want to know what else she said?" Odele asked, breaking a silence that had seemed to stretch out for leagues. I didn't answer before she continued, "She said she knew, in her heart, that someone was caring for the baby. That she had always hoped the baby would be found and that she would retake the throne that was rightfully hers, putting an end to the corruption of the crown." Odele reached over and squeezed my wrist. "She's right, you know. You're a royal, and you're ready."

She let the weight of all she'd said settle on to me. I wanted to reply, to say something, ask more questions, but I couldn't bring myself to say a thing. Having royal blood didn't make me one. Odele was wrong. So, so wrong.

It was hours before I finally replied, my voice the mere caress of a whisper, "I'm not ready. I'll never be."

But Odele didn't hear me.

She was already fast asleep.

The thunderous pounding on the door jolted me from a dreamless sleep. It took a moment for the grogginess to clear, for me to get my bearings and remember everything that happened to me the previous night.

Odele was sprawled beside me, occupying most of the space on the bed, keeping me confined to the very edge, where the only things preventing me from toppling to the floor were the soft, balancing brushes of the anemones.

The thundering continued, followed by the voice of Captain Saber. "Princess! Is everything alright?"

I groaned and rubbed my eyes before I was fully awake.

Silt. Captain Saber was at the door. I couldn't very well open it, could I? Not with Odele here. I didn't like the idea of keeping secrets from him, but this wasn't just my own. It was Odele's too, and we had to decide what to do together, whether or not we could keep her presence a secret.

I glanced down at Odele. She slept with her mouth wide open and hugging at the pillows. It was odd to see her so mussed and vulnerable, but also refreshing to see her look so… normal.

"Odele," I shook her shoulder. "Wake up."

She groaned and batted my hand away, turning away from me.

Annoyance flared through me, and the pounding at the door just became more insistent. I reached out and shook her shoulder again. "Odele," I said a little louder. "Wake up."

She pushed me away. "What do you want?" she complained, her voice muffled as she buried her face into her pillow. "It's early. Go sink in the abyss somewhere."

So we were back to hostility? Gone was last night's sliver of kindness she'd displayed, and once again she was an arrogant princess. Fine. I shouldn't have expected otherwise.

"Wake up." I shook her, hard. She didn't even stir. I groaned to myself and contemplated my next move. She was a princess, the future ruler of Thalassar, and it was hardly wise for me to do what I was about to do, but I couldn't help it. I was annoyed, and she needed to wake up. Now.

I pinched her.

She yowled and jumped up, rubbing the tender spot at her side as she turned to glare at me. "What the—Odalaea, you may have been raised in the freshwaters where you had to be up early to milk your catfish, but royals are allowed to *sleep in.*"

I ignored every offensive word she said and pointed at the door to her room. "Captain Saber is at the door." The knocking continued.

"So?" She dropped herself back onto the bed, hiked a blanket over her shoulders and turned away. "Who cares? It's his job to float at the door."

I sighed with deep annoyance. "Then do you want to answer it?" I almost loathed the idea. If Captain Saber knew she was here, everything that had happened between us would fall apart. He'd escort me home and would be free to live life as though he'd never met me in the first place. The idea sent my heart thundering in my chest.

"Gods, no," Odele replied. "Let him knock."

The knocking continued.

I looked from the door to Odele, and she must have felt my gaze heavily on her, because she finally turned and arched a brow. We stared, like we were silently communicating, and I won. She groaned and sat up.

"Fine," she grumbled. "Open the door. But please, for the love of gods, keep it short. I want to rest." She got up and swayed—like a drunken mer—over to the bathing room. "And don't tell him about me," she called over her shoulder.

I waited until she was in the bathing room, the door closing behind her, before I scrambled to answer the door. Captain Saber floated impatiently on the other side.

"Princess," he greeted, offering up a bow.

Before, I'd thought nothing of the title I was thrust into. It was just pretend, after all. It didn't mean anything. But now, as he said it, there was a weight on the word that hadn't been there before. Something about it was mocking me, a shadow looming over my consciousness. One I didn't want to acknowledge as truth.

Something I only hoped not to spill in his presence, even if everything inside me begged to confide in someone.

Tiberius

"May I come in?" I asked, fighting back the twitch of amusement that threatened to pull at my mouth.

Maisie was floating there, her hair in loose and wild tendrils. She was staring at me with wide eyes, and I could just make out the tightness in her jaw, as if there was something she wanted to say, but was physically holding herself back from saying it. I wondered about it before she took a stroke to the side to allow me entry.

I went gratefully inside and my eyes scanned the room for danger, an instinct that was hard to fight. I did a sweep along the floor, coming to a stop at the discarded pile of dark clothing in the middle of the room. They looked like commoner's clothes and a cloak. Another sweep showed me Maisie's black blade leaning against a wall.

My eyes narrowed.

"What's going on?" Maisie asked casually after she closed the door. She swam around to face me, the smile pulling at her lips obviously forced.

I'd come in here this morning because all I could think of last night was her. Everything I'd wanted to say and confess to her had me tossing and turning. I'd braved it enough that I decided on telling her my feelings. Even if she didn't reciprocate them, I'd tell her.

But the words I'd spent hours practicing last night disappeared as a fierce wave of protectiveness nearly drowned me, and the strict words came out of me instead.

"Did you go out last night?" I asked.

Her eyebrows rose and she followed to where my fingers were gesturing at the clothes tossed onto the floor. I tried to gauge her reaction, as her every emotion was so open. Easy to read. Panic, and the sudden fumbling of her mouth, could only mean that she was about to lie to me.

"I—I mean—no—"

"You're lying." It was a brusque accusation that had her freezing. I was aware of what that tone did to her. I knew it made her strive for perfection, to be more like the princess I used to compare her with. I tried to soften my voice. "Why did you go out?"

Maisie bit her bottom lip but didn't speak. Frustration swelled through me at that.

"You still don't trust me," I whispered. Her eyes were guarded, but the flash in them spoke more than words ever could. *No.* And that hurt. "Why?" I asked. My voice was cold steel, so as to not betray the real emotions I felt beneath.

"I—"

I didn't let her finish before I was taking a stroke towards her, startling a gasp from her mouth. I didn't mean to frighten her. It was the last thing I wanted. I willed my shoulders to loosen, and when my hands reached out to cup her shoulders, I did so lightly.

"I would do anything for you, Maisie," I promised. "I said I'd protect you with my life and I will. But how can I keep that promise if you don't trust me? If you don't tell me things?" I was sure she could hear the insecurities dripping from me, and I wondered if she was disgusted. For a brief moment, I didn't care.

Her gaze averted away from me before traveling back slowly. Something in her black eyes glossed over. "I do trust you," she whispered.

I wasn't sure if it was a lie.

"I just want you safe, Maisie." And because I couldn't help myself, I had to lean forward. Even if she pushed me away, at least her feelings would be clear enough to keep me away the next time. But I took the risk, and pressed my lips to hers. It was slow and soft to give her a chance to decide if she wanted me or not.

Before on the balcony and here in this room in front of Elias and Kai hadn't counted. The first time had been angry and vicious desire, the second time had been for an audience.

I wanted this time to be more real. I wanted her to feel how much I cared, without anger or anyone else in between us.

So I kissed her, and when she opened her mouth to accept me, my heart thundered and I pulled her close so she could feel it. Our tongues met in the middle. We gave and took in equal measure, a soft exploring of lips that didn't quell the desire building in my stomach.

I pulled her closer, needing to feel every inch of her. My hand slid up to cup her cheek, and she gripped the lapels of my jacket tightly. She tugged, as if the space between us was just too wide. Like she planned to breathe me into her very soul. If she did, I wouldn't have minded.

I wanted her.

Maisie Fauna of Lagoona, waitress at Tides' Tavern, who had yelled at me for knocking her over, who had slapped my hand and swam away, who had led me onto gator grounds and had swung a kitchen knife at me in self-defense. Who had gone from waitress to princess, saved criminals and challenged royals all because she thought it was right.

She was the one I wanted.

I conveyed this as best as I could. Not with the words I had practiced, but with my body, with the movement of my hands and with the touch of my lips. I could only hope she understood. And the way she responded meant she wanted me just as much as I wanted her.

Maisie pulled away and struggled to catch her breath. Her chest rose and fell against mine in rapid little movements. I searched her eyes for regret and there was none. Her hands slid up to my shoulders, and she gave a soft little sigh that made me want to take her mouth in mine all over again.

"I do trust you," she repeated firmly.

I nodded. "Then please, don't leave the palace without me. I—" I took a breath. "I don't know what I'd do if something happened to you. Something I could have prevented—"

"It's okay." Her hand came up to pat lightly at my cheek. "I promise, it won't happen again."

I didn't ask again why she'd left the palace, as I doubted she'd tell me anyway. Maybe she'd gone to see Elias. If that were the case, next time I saw the Black Blade, I'd have to have a few words with him regarding Maisie's safety.

"Well, thanks." I cleared my throat, suddenly feeling very awkward. I wanted to kiss her again, but duty was calling. I took a stroke away. "You should get ready for the day," I suggested. "There's much to do."

Maisie smiled at me, and I didn't wait for her dismissal or give her a goodbye as I whirled away and left the room. Once I was out, I could finally breathe and see clearer. I hadn't told her what it was I'd wanted to say, but my actions seemed effective just the same.

"Well, he seems as stiff as ever."

I hadn't noticed the moment Odele had swam out of the bathing room and plopped herself down on the bed. She laid against it casually and was giving me a knowing, sarcastic look that I fought to ignore.

"Even when he's trying to be romantic, he sounds so… *rigid.*" She laughed mockingly, and my annoyance with her flared.

"You know he cares for you, right?" I snapped.

Odele's eyebrows rose. Her lips twitched. "It seems like he cares for *you.*"

I growled, forgetting she was a princess. I glared at her, mer to mer. "He was in love with you, Odele." I don't know why I threw it out like an accusation. Perhaps I wanted some trace of emotion from her, to be reminded that she wasn't just a crown and the jewelry she wore. To get a glimpse of the vulnerability underneath, at the mermaid who cried while locked in a bathing room after confronting the mer who had killed her mother. I wanted to see that mer. Not this doll, not this *princess.* I wanted to see a trace of the mer that Tiberius had fallen in love with. The lonely, vulnerable mermaid he'd wanted me to believe she was.

"I know that," she replied, clearly annoyed.

I tried to control my angry breathing. It was hard, so hard to not want to reach across the space that separated us and throttle her. I settled for a question instead, one I had to know. Even if the answer could threaten to destroy me entirely.

"Did you ever love him back?"

Odele paused as she stared at me, reading me. I didn't squirm. I just lifted my head in a confidence and defiance I didn't truly feel. Inside, I felt weak.

Finally, after what felt like an eternity, she replied. "No. I never loved Captain Saber."

Something in me eased but a fraction. "Why not?" I knew it was a silly question as soon as I asked it. She could ask me why I loved Elias, Kai, and even Captain Saber, and I'd be able to answer thoroughly, but I doubted she'd understand just how deep the depths my feelings for them ran. The heart wanted what it wanted, and mine tore me into three different directions, not forcing me to choose, but wanting them all at once.

Odele shrugged and leaned forward, hugging her tail, expression suddenly serious. "I don't know," she admitted. "I guess… I mean… I watched you both just now." My cheeks heated at the admission, but she didn't say it to shame me. "You do something to him, something I was never able to do." She shook her head back and forth. "I'm not explaining this right… You challenge him, cousin, and he challenges you, but me and the captain? We never had that. He never questioned me or defended himself when I was rude to him. That's how I know it wasn't love. That maybe, he never really loved me in the first place."

We were both quiet after that, both lost in our thoughts, seeming to contemplate the words she'd just said. I wondered if it could be true, if Captain Saber had never really loved her. Maybe she'd known and that's why she never reciprocated those feelings. Because they weren't meant to be.

But if Odele and Captain Saber weren't meant to be, then who was he supposed to be with? Was it selfish of me to want him, Elias, and Kai? Probably. I wanted them all regardless.

"So now what?" I asked after a while.

Odele looked up at me with curiosity. "What do you mean?"

I shrugged. "You heard him. There are things you have to do today. What should we do? Should we tell everyone you're back or…" I let the sentence trail off; let her fill in the blanks, even if I loathed what she might say.

Odele's eyes widened before she made a face of disgust. "Oh, gods, no." She stuck out her tongue. "Do you know what would happen if we told anyone I was back, cousin?" I'd had an idea before, but hearing her say it aloud, solidifying it, made my whole body tremble. "My stepmother, the evil barracuda, would have us both killed."

"You think?"

"I may be rich and vain, but I am not daft. You think I haven't figured out why my stepmother didn't want me in the royal records room? Who is the one who has benefitted from all these deaths, and who is trying to keep me from uncovering the truth?" She shook her head furiously. "It's her. I know it. And if she knew I was back, the attacks on *both* of our lives could get more aggressive."

The mercenary had said that someone—the queen, most likely—had discovered the truth of who I was, and wanted him dead for not being able to finish the job. It would explain her not-so-veiled threats towards me. Because she knew who I was and the threat I posed to her throne. The threat both Odele and I posed to her. She'd do anything to keep the throne, and she was capable of anything, like killing her cousins and trying to kill her cousins' daughters.

"We have to keep this a secret," Odele urged. "For both of our sakes."

I agreed with a nod of my head but looked at her with narrowed eyes. "So where will you be? Come to think of it, where have you *been*?" I doubted she'd been staying at shady night inns.

"I told you, I got the blueprints to the palace. That means I know routes and secret passageways no one else does. I know how to stay hidden."

I blanched at that. She was telling me that she'd been hiding in the palace this whole time, right under everyone's noses? I had the sudden vague flash of memory, of her in this room one night, lingering by the shelf of coral that held her little trinkets.

I grinded my teeth together to hold back my frustration. It hadn't been a dream at all. It had been real.

She'd played us all for fools.

I crossed my arms over my chest with annoyance. "What if I refuse to do your duties?" I snapped. All she'd done this whole time was sit back and watch as I suffered through her royal life. Through Percival's beatings, the poisonings, and the queen's threats. And she'd done nothing to help, nothing to stop it. And now she would sit back and let me continue through this, while she was tucked safely away, hidden from the mer who wanted us both dead.

Odele's eyes twinkled. "You could, but you won't refuse. You forget, dearest cousin, I've been investigating for months and have been observing for just as long." She leaned back on her palms, kicking her tail out carelessly. "For as much as you claim to despise royal life, I can tell that you actually love it."

My whole body jolted, as if I'd been stung by a jellyfish. I uncrossed my arms, clasping my hands in front of me. "You're wrong," I replied weakly.

She snorted, telling me how much she disbelieved me with a simple sound. "You don't have to hide it from me. I recognize that look in your eye. You enjoy the privileged, lavish life. You enjoy having my prince—and apparently a guard—to yourself. It's okay to admit it, you know."

Captain Saber had said much the same thing. Words I didn't want to believe. I didn't enjoy getting almost murdered at every turn and I didn't enjoy not having any power to protect anybody. How was any of this enjoyable?

"My life is in danger." My voice cracked. "I'm out here taking arrows that are meant for you." And she didn't seem like she cared one bit.

"My life is in danger, too," Odele argued. "And those arrows weren't just meant for me. But as long as you keep pretending to be me, she won't harm you fully."

"What, because she hasn't harmed me at all thus far?" I scoffed.

Odele shook her head. "The attacks have ceased, at least for now. Why do you think that is?" When I shrugged, Odele went on. "Because the public loves you now, Odalaea. She wants to keep you in line for now. And she also wants to find me. The minute she has us both together, she won't hesitate to take us out. That's why my appearance has to be kept a secret, if only to buy us a little more time."

"Little more time for *what*?" I nearly shouted, waving my hands in the water with exasperation.

"To take down my stepmother, and to place you on your throne."

Those words, once more, dawned on me. She would not let this go. She wouldn't let me rest until I accepted what she said as truth. Until I sat on that throne, whether I deserved it or not.

"Why do you want me on that throne so badly, Odele?" I asked, not caring if I was speaking to her with familiarity. We were past propriety now, each of us knowing hidden aspects of the other to give us that right of speech. "I've seen your conches down in that cove. I've seen you prepare yourself to be Queen of Thalassar."

My question made Odele's careless movements suddenly freeze. Her jaw clamped closed, and the expression in her eyes shuddered into one that was almost unreadable. Then she loosed a small breath and tried to assume that same blithe spirit as before, flicking floating tendrils of hair over her shoulder. Her movements just came out terse.

"The throne belongs to you, Odalaea…"

"No, it doesn't," I snapped sharply. She glared at me, and I did not back down from her stare. "Even *if* Dorian and Odessa's marriage was legitimate, there was a contract promising her to another. They both broke that contract, and Thalassar wouldn't recognize them, or their child, as heir to the throne. You know this. So *why* are you pushing it?"

There had to be a reason she was doing this. I wanted to believe what she'd said last night. That she had gone through such lengths to find the missing royal—to find me—because of her sense of honor, her sense of family. But I knew her. I'd seen her personality shine through in the silver-gold glow of secret conches. I'd seen cruelty in her, and shallowness as well.

Odele must have known that. For all the secrets she kept, for all she claimed to know me, I knew her too. And like Captain Saber, I wanted to see the good in her. The vulnerability. I wanted to see the mer who cried behind closed doors. A mer who didn't hide what she was feeling.

But Princess Odele let out a sound of eternal exasperation, her voice suddenly a tone more serious when she replied, "I told you last night, cousin. You and me, we're the closest things left of our mothers. I searched for you because I wanted family, a friend. Do you think Jessinda is that for me? She's not. She gossips and talks behind my back. At least you're brave enough to say what you think to my face. That's what I want. I want what my mother had. A sister." She paused, like she was letting those words sink in for a moment. "But I can tell that you don't feel the same."

She got up then, ever the image of grace and refinement. She smoothed out the nightgown she wore, pushed back her tendrils of hair until they stayed. Every movement was precise, holding an edge of finality, and I couldn't help but feel like every swipe of hand, and finger, was equivalent to the swing of a blade, readying to come over my head.

"If you don't want my royal duties, that's fine. I know they're not ideal. They may not be what you imagined when you came to Eramaea, so I won't burden you with them any further." Her narrowed eyes focused on me intently. "Just do me a favor when you leave; do it secretly and get as far away from Thalassar as possible. Even if you don't care about me, I care about you. I want you safe."

A lump had caught tightly into my throat. I couldn't swallow past it; I couldn't do anything but stare at her, breathe her in. Compare us once more.

Over the years, there were things I'd learned while living a lonely life in Lagoona. When my grandmother had died, I felt more alone than I ever could have imagined feeling. All my family was dead; what did it matter if I died, too? But then Josiah had pulled me up from my sinkage. He'd been the only father figure I'd ever had in my life. And it was thanks to him that I realized family wasn't just about blood.

And here was Odele, a Princess of Thalassar, claiming a blood right that neither of us had known existed until recently. Claiming me as hers, wanting me as I was, limp and all.

I saw it then. Saw that her desperation for a family to call her own was an equal match to my own desires. Not a family who was dead, or the murderers, but actual blood. That loved with honesty, with their all. She was offering it up to me, and I was pushing her away.

"I—" The word came out a rasp. I cleared my throat, and tried again. "It's hard for me… to accept all of this as reality," I explained. Her eyes were on me cautiously. "It's obviously easier for you, but I'll need time, okay?" She opened her mouth to speak, no doubt to tell me we didn't have time, but I spoke over her. "I cannot accept the throne or the crown and riches that comes with the Malabella lineage. But I can try to accept you. As family."

One moment she was stern and the next, alighted with happiness. Odele squealed loudly and rushed to me. Her arms enveloped me in a crushing hug of strength that was surprising. It took a moment to push past the incoherent screeching to realize that she was speaking words in her excitement. I floated numbly in her arms, unsure of what to do at first, before I slowly wrapped my arms around her and gave her an equally strong squeeze.

We stayed like that for a moment, wrapped in each other's arms. In that moment, everything fell apart, fell away. I could forget who I thought her to be, and what she was inside. None of it seemed to matter then, because all I cared about was this.

Being in the arms of family.

"I can't breathe," I gasped.

Odele ignored me and yanked the strings tighter. "Suck it in," she ordered unkindly, yanking once more.

My hands were on the curved ivory edge of her bed for support while Odele was behind me, pushing and yanking as she tried to fit me into, what she called, a corset. It was more like a torture device that threatened to squeeze my bones until they snapped.

"Why do I have to wear this?" I asked breathlessly.

Odele finally stopped pulling and began tying. When she finished, she spun me around unceremoniously. She was making noises that ranged between approval and disapproval, but didn't answer right away. She grabbed for a dress, a solemn looking thing in black, and pulled that over me as well.

As if I was a child that needed help dressing.

"You've been half-tailing the way you dress for months now. It's embarrassing, and you're making me look bad." She started fixing the dress at the hem and then straightened to fix the low neckline.

My face heated at her honesty. I knew I wasn't princess-like; the fashion critics on the telly had made that abundantly clear after my first anniversary dinner. I just hadn't expected her to say it with such disgust. It made me want to bury my head in the sand.

"It's not my fault you don't have maids," I grumbled.

Odele clucked her tongue. "I don't have maids because I don't want them snooping around my stuff. Also, no one does a better job at dressing me than me. Now, let's brush your hair." She pulled me away from the bed and sat me in front of her little vanity table. It was of Thalassarin make. A blue clamshell opened, the edges rimmed with jellies glowing a natural light and held a mirror in the middle.

I avoided staring at myself while she got to work, instead focusing my gaze on the pins and brushes she picked up and set back down in a pattern.

She worked in silence for a while before I couldn't take it anymore.

"If you were hiding in the palace the whole time, why didn't you ever make yourself known before now?"

Her fingers paused on my scalp before she resumed working, pulling apart strands to comb them out. "I wasn't sure if I could trust you yet. If you would tell the queen about me or not."

Perhaps I would have, those first few weeks. I was miserable enough to want to end the whole charade, to go back home to Lagoona and never have to set fin in Eramaea again.

"What made you decide to trust me?"

"I saw the broadcast on the telly where you saved the Black Blade." I felt the hair begin to tighten, and stole a small glance in the mirror to see her braiding it. "I thought anyone who publicly defies the queen and the law like that is deserving of my trust." She bent over me and picked up a string of pearls that were a mixture of white and pink, and one by one, she began integrating them into the braids.

"But you still didn't show yourself right away."

"No," she agreed. "I couldn't find the right time to do it, and I was nervous you'd dislike me."

My eyes widened as I took in her reflection. Her? A princess of the realm nervous I'd dislike her? I couldn't fathom it.

"There." She placed the last pearl into place and took a stroke back. "Stop ogling at me and look at yourself." She gestured at the mirror.

I tore my gaze away from her to finally stare at myself.

I froze.

"Pretty, right? We look nearly identical, but this way it's more believable." Odele's face appeared next to mine, but all I saw was my own.

She'd taken the stubborn strands and pulled them back, creating braids at my sides in a way that kept the strands floating in what looked like magical curls behind me. Pearls shone, pink-white against the dark strands of my hair, forming a discreet yet beautiful crown around my head.

"You have elegant cheekbones and a slender neck that should be showed off. Your eyelashes are dark enough to not need cosmetics, and your eyes are super intense. I wish mine were that dark." Odele sighed wistfully into my ear. And each word she spoke, I saw. I saw what she meant, what I'd never seen in myself before.

I *was* beautiful.

"Thank you," I whispered, emotion tight in my throat. I never thought I could be beautiful. Even as I spent months in her fins, wearing her dresses, I'd never felt the sensation I was feeling just then.

She waved me off. "You're beautiful, cousin. I mean, duh, you're a Malabella. Our mothers were gorgeous."

They were. I'd stared so often at their portraits in the hall that I knew it for a fact. Even if I hadn't been able to see a royal in myself then, I did now.

"I look like her," I said, so quietly that it wasn't meant to be heard.

Odele heard it anyway, her smile radiant. "Of course you do. Although your nose is a bit straighter, and your cheeks aren't as round. I suppose you get it from King Dorian."

"Do you know what he's like?" I asked. "King Dorian, I mean." I couldn't refer to him as my father, like I couldn't refer to Princess Odessa as my mother. Not yet.

Odele nodded. "He's very beautiful, so I hear."

I hadn't ever actually seen any recent recordings of the King of Kappur, but I didn't doubt her words. Most royals were quite beautiful, and even if he'd waged war with Thalassar for years, I didn't doubt the truth of his appearance. I'd seen him promise himself to Odessa. He'd been young then, probably younger than me at the time. He'd been handsome in his youth. But I couldn't help but wonder if, like King Xristo, the light had extinguished from his eyes, if he was nothing but a simple, hollow shell of a merman.

"Anyway, I'm done now. You can get up and go about your duties."

I got up slowly, getting a good look at myself and the dress she forced me in. I couldn't take my eyes off my reflection.

The dress was scandalous. Perhaps the most revealing thing I'd ever worn. The neckline was plunged relatively low, and the corset pushed my breasts up, holding them firm. The décolletage was low, the edges trimmed with a thin pattern of sea lace. Despite the revealing neckline, the dress had long, sheer sleeves, a cinched waist, and a long, light train that flowed down to my fins.

I tugged at the neckline, trying to pull it above the swells of my breasts, but it didn't budge.

"Just leave it," Odele ordered with irritation. "You'll rip it if you keep doing that. Here…" She was in front of me suddenly, swatting aside my hands and—to my numbing shock—grabbing my breasts. She stuck her fingers in the neckline and adjusted, then pushed my breasts up so far, it seemed like they'd spill out.

"Why?" I beseeched, crossing my arms over my chest. "Why is this dress necessary? And why black?"

Odele rolled her eyes. "It's not black, it's violet."

I looked down at it again with raised eyebrows. At first glance, it looked black. But I obviously hadn't been paying much attention to it. When I moved, the dress seemed to shimmer, and it *was* violet. A violet so dark it looked black, two colors clashing together in every strand as I moved, battling for dominance.

It would look absolutely perfect with…

I whirled away from Odele and rushed to the spot where I'd hidden Elias's ring, my ring, now. It matched perfectly with the dress, too.

Odele eyed it and smiled. "I was just about to suggest jewelry. Give it here." She held out her palm, and when I hesitated, she pulled the ring from my fingers. She looked at it curiously for a moment, obviously noting that this piece wasn't hers, but after a moment, she merely shrugged. I watched as she rummaged around in one of her drawers and produced a dark, delicate chain from which she slipped the ring onto. "So riptide," she smiled as she went behind me to clasp the chain around my neck. The heavy weight of the ring settled in the curve between my breasts. Just the sight of it there felt intimate. Odele circled back to face me, eyes bright. "The tides will love it, cousin."

I looked down self-consciously. "The cleavage is a bit much."

"Nonsense. You look like a confection."

An eyebrow rose. "I look like a pastry?"

Odele pointed. "Exactly. A delectable, sweet, and delicious *snack*."

I'm sure what she said was meant to be a compliment, but all it did was make me flush and look down, where the first thing I saw was the rise and fall of the swells of my pink skin, and the color was only darkening. I bit back the groan that tumbled up my chest. Yes, I did look good, but I was also embarrassed by it.

Odele must have sensed the turn my thoughts were taking, because she swam into my personal space, so close our noses touched. She brought her hands up and clapped them on either side of my cheeks. "Own it," she commanded. "You're a Malabella, a princess, and you're beautiful. I know for a fact you'll have Tiberius ensnared in seduction the moment he sets eyes on you. Be confident."

Her words sunk into me, into the hollow pits of my mind and heart right next to my insecurities. A million protests sprang to my lips. *I am not beautiful. I have a limp. I am a waitress. I'm not royalty.*

None of them came out.

I saw myself as she did, pressing those words so tightly into my chest until I believed them. I *was* beautiful, limp or no. And I was descended from two beautiful mer. I carried their blood in my veins, the blood of greatness, of two mer who loved each other.

And for once in my life, I felt that swell of power rise in me, shifting me entirely.

Odele smiled. "Good." And she took a stroke away.

I felt the change in my posture, the straight back, and the tilted chin. It wasn't just because I'd perfected that pose in order to be her. It was a pose of confidence and regal command.

Mine alone.

"Go forth and prove to them how much of a royal you truly are."

I swam out into the hallway, closing the door behind me, while Odele's words echoed in my mind.

Prove to them how much of a royal you truly are.

I wasn't a royal, but I sure felt like one, for the first time since I'd come here. It was all thanks to Odele. Funny that, how the royal I thought I'd come to despise had become an ally of sorts, a tentative member of my family. I still couldn't read her as well as I hoped. She was still somewhat of a mystery, though not quite as selfish as I imagined her to be.

Oh, her vanity was there and strong, like the crashing pull of a vicious wave. Yet I couldn't help but wonder—hope—that there was more beneath the surface of her. The way Captain Saber had hoped as well.

"Princess…"

So engrossed in my thoughts, I hadn't noticed the guards surrounding me, Captain Saber leading them in the middle. Every single one of them took me in with wide, surprised eyes.

I did not feel an inch of shyness as I lifted my chin and smiled at them each in turn. Some of them flushed and looked away. Others had their eyes focused on the revealing décolletage and couldn't seem to look up. Captain Saber took one look at me, and his expression shuttered into one of scrutiny. Just as quickly as he took me in, he fixated his gaze on his mermen and snapped at them.

"Eyes ahead, soldiers. You have a job to do." His tone held a hint of irritation, which I couldn't help but find amusing.

The soldiers all assumed their positions surrounding me, like mer-shields on my every side. The captain took his place stiffly to my left, and we began to swim.

As the hallways widened, so did the mermen's stances. They put space between us, giving me an illusion of privacy, though they were undoubtedly close enough to hear anything I had to say.

Captain Saber was the only one to stay by my side, and he didn't say a word.

"What's on the schedule today, Captain?" I broke the silence between us.

"The queen requests a meeting with all of the royals currently present." His blistering reply thawed at the confidence I'd so surely built. There was no trace of the caring warmth he'd displayed that morning in my—Odele's—room. He was back to his rigid old self. Someone who couldn't be bothered with me at all.

Just as I started to retreat into my silence, I felt a warmth slide across my knuckles and the tips of my fingers. I looked down slowly, finding Captain Saber's own fingers ever close to mine. He flexed them, and the tips grazed across my skin.

It was a simple touch, but one that seemed to melt me from the inside out.

My own fingers reached for him, not to hold or to grasp, but to convey a silent message between our hands. A message I couldn't really decipher at all, and I doubted he could either. But we were there, and we were touching.

And that was enough.

I COULDN'T GO ANOTHER moment without touching her. Not a second passed when I didn't want to feel the warmth of her skin pressed against my own. The selfish, reckless part of me surfaced and demanded. It wanted me to disperse the guards, pull her into an abandoned room or other, and claim her for my own.

Today, Maisie was not that simple, conservative mer. Today, she was a seductress. She was alluring. Whatever spell she'd weaved through the threads of the clothes on her body was working. They held not only me but every single guard under its enchantment.

Jealousy seared through me every time I caught them staring down her front. But I could say nothing, do nothing but shoot them commanding glares, reminding them of their duty and task at hand.

Protect her. Like I should be protecting her.

But her body was distracting, inviting.

She always had been.

It wasn't just that the dress did wonders for her figure and pushed her breasts up to almost impossible heights. It was her posture, her expression. It was no longer practiced perfection. It was no longer a mask.

It was her. Wholly, entirely, and seductively *her*. There was a confidence in the set of her shoulders, the tilt of her chin, the steady stride. It was new. Like somehow, within the span of a few hours, Maisie had found herself. Her beauty.

My fingers grazed along the skin at her knuckles once more and she responded in kind. To touch her was a privilege, one I shouldn't possibly take but still selfishly wanted.

So we touched. Light caresses back and forth, back and forth. A dance. A rhythm. A challenge. Like this stolen, secret intimacy was a game we'd both just invented with rules that were unclear, and the goal too far away to reach.

Yet we both wanted to make it to that end.

Victorious.

A ROYAL MEETING IT WAS.

Everyone was in attendance. The queen and king sat at their respective places, a chair empty next to King Xristo for me to take. Mister Shallows was there, glaring at Ichiro and Lee—Kai's advisors—and Prince Kai himself. Prince Ytgar of Iol and his second-hand, Valmundur, sat side by side away from the rest of the royals and far away from Mister Shallows. Advisors and diplomats from foreign kingdoms all sat around the table, eagerly awaiting my arrival, so this meeting could get on and over with.

I'd not donned a crown for this meeting, but it was unnecessary. The way Odele had done my hair, the pearls woven in each strand, pushed close enough together to form the illusion of one on my head.

The queen glared at me as I swam in.

The mermen all got up and bowed.

I smiled at them. "Please, do not trouble yourselves." When they sat back down, I swam around, escorted by Captain Saber to take my seat next to King Xristo.

The king gave me a soft smile that didn't quite reach his eyes. For a moment, my heart hurt for him. What must he be feeling? I wondered if the loss of his wife and daughter were what had snuffed the light from his eyes. Did King Dorian look like that as well? The thought physically hurt, building an ache in my chest until I had to look away.

My eyes met Prince Kai's from across the space that separated us, and my skin flushed brightly, hotly. His dark eyes glowed as he took me in, pupils becoming thin slits. The hand he had rested on the table curved, nails lengthening into black talons.

Ice and heat warred on his features, and I felt every myriad of emotion, of sensation he conveyed.

"Thank you all for coming on such short notice, and please forgive any inconvenience it may have caused."

I tore my gaze away from Kai with difficulty and turned to look at the queen. From the look on her face, I knew this wouldn't be a pleasurable meeting. Her bright eyes were mutinous, her jaw working furiously, like she had to physically fight back the urge to spit and scream. Her long nails tapped impatiently against the table, and everyone eyed them cautiously.

"What is this about, Your Majesty?" Ytgar asked, his voice charismatic, despite the tension roiling through the room.

The queen's nail scraped along the table, creating a screeching noise as she forced a smile onto her mouth. "I gathered you all here to announce that in two weeks' time, we will be witnessing—at Prince Kai's incessant behest—the union of Draconi and Thalassar."

My throat tightened painfully.

What?

"Once my daughter comes of age, which is within two weeks, she will marry Prince Kai Li and ascend the Thalassarin throne."

My tongue felt as heavy as an anchor, and I couldn't swallow past it. I could only stare numbly at the queen, a torrent of emotions going through me until I didn't know what exactly I should be feeling.

"Well…" Mister Shallows broke through the array of my emotions with his greasy, disapproving voice. "I believe congratulations are in order?" Though he said it as if he meant anything but.

Ytgar made up for his foreign diplomat's lack of enthusiasm, clapping his hands together excitedly. "Congratulations to you both. What a joyous event! A wedding! But, two weeks is rather short notice…"

The queen shrugged one delicate shoulder and gave a venomous smile. "Worry not. Prince Kai and I had a lengthy discussion before this meeting, and invitations have already been sent out with the swiftest of our messengers, as well as being broadcasted on every telly in the kingdom."

Gods. My hands went to tighten in my lap. This couldn't be happening. My mind was reeling. Odele was back, so that meant she and Kai… But they didn't know she was back. I was the only one who knew. Did that mean I would have to go in her place? Would Odele allow it? Why was the queen even allowing it? She was adamant that the throne was hers. She'd killed her cousins to possess it; surely she wouldn't relinquish it that easily. What was she planning? And why had Kai planned this without telling me?

I avoided his gaze, even as he spoke. "The Emperor knows the contents of our marriage contract," Kai explained. "Even with such short notice, I do not doubt he has sent warriors and family to Thalassar. They should likely be here before the wedding."

Wedding. Wedding. Weddingweddingweddin—

"I am sure you are most anxious to wed," Ytgar commented. It took a moment for me to realize he was directing the words towards me and was expecting a response. His blond eyebrows rose, and the bright blue of his eyes were shining with equal parts mischief and curiosity.

I swallowed past the lump of panic. "Of course," I replied tightly. "Most anxious." I was sure everyone in the room could see past my lie.

Ytgar just looked amused and turned to whisper something in Val's ear. The dark-skinned, silver haired and eyed mer nodded in response, a smile twitching at the side of his lip.

"Do not fret about the short notice. Even if your guests cannot make it to the actual wedding, there will be days of celebration afterwards. I can assure you. Now, if you all do not mind, I would like a word with my daughter alone."

The mer all began to murmur as they got up from their seats. I could only stare at the hands clasped in my lap as I listened to the sounds of them vacating the room, leaving me alone with the queen.

I feared looking up at her, feared breaking some sort of spell and finding her holding a dagger in her hand aimed for my throat. Would she kill me? Would she do it before the wedding? It was all a possibility, one I'd be powerless to avoid.

"I am sure you think yourself quite the lucky mer," the queen commented cruelly.

I finally looked up at her, but she wasn't staring at me. The queen was looking down at her crown. A massive looking thing made of silver and diamonds. When had she taken it off? I hadn't realized… She was looking at it like it was a real living, breathing thing. Like she couldn't bear to let it go.

"You came from nothing, and now you are here. A pretend princess, ready to wed the Dragon Prince…" She sighed and turned to me. There was a burning fever in her eyes. Madness. It looked like an eruption waiting to happen. "I hope you do not think you will truly wed the prince."

Because I wasn't sure, I said nothing.

The queen let out a tinkle of a laugh. "You will sign the paper with Odele's name, yes. You will join Kai in union. But the moment my daughter is found, your places will be switched. You will go back to your filthy little pond with nothing but your silence, as if you'd never been here in the first place. Do you understand?"

If she had any intention of letting me out of this palace alive, Odele's words echoed in my mind. She wanted the both of us dead, and I didn't doubt she would try and accomplish it. I just couldn't be sure when.

"I understand," I breathed.

Her eyes bore into mine, and I wondered if she was searching for a lie in me, for something to exploit. Then, she turned back to the crown placed perfectly on the table before her. She fingered the jagged edges at the top.

"My cousin wore this crown," she said gently, running her finger across the tip and holding it there. "There are many crowns in the vaults, too many to be worn in a lifetime. But my cousin Odette wore this one during her coronation, when she ascended the throne." Her voice held a whisper of remembrance, and the madness in her eyes slowly faded, like she was vanishing into an ancient memory. "We used to have so much fun together, the five of us."

I blinked and dared interrupt. "The five of you?"

"Odette and Odessa, of course. They were inseparable, even as they grew older. But we were children then. And Xristo and Dorian…"

I tried not to suck in a breath, tried not to let any surprise or emotions show on my face. She'd known them when she was young. Xristo. Dorian.

"I always felt like an outsider looking in at them, the odd one out. No one ever looked at me. They were too busy looking at my cousins. Dorian was such a pretty mer. We'd been friends once…"

Before you murdered his wife and ordered me stolen from her arms.

My jaw locked to avoid saying anything I'd soon regret.

"I know everyone thinks me cruel." She sighed and picked up the crown. "But I am queen, and what I do, I do for my subjects." She placed it on her head, and it was a perfect fit. "I often tried to mend the rift between Thalassar and Kappur. I tried to appease King Dorian time and time again, but he would not even see me. As if the friendship we'd shared so long ago no longer meant a thing to him. Fickle little mer, with moods that change like the waters and a thunderstorm." Her hands came to rest on the table. "He's been dragging this dreadful war on and on and on. I need not tell you it is taking a toll on Thalassar. You've seen the broadcasts for yourself. The mer are angry."

They were. I was. This war was pointless and wrong, even if I was slowly beginning to understand the reason behind Dorian waging it. He'd lost everything. He was a broken mer trying to find what was his. Yet to kill hundreds, thousands... It was inexcusable. Like killing your cousins for a throne was inexcusable.

"This alliance with Draconi is what we need to put a stop to it all. So you will do your duty perfectly, as if you were really and truly my daughter. You will marry Kai, we will stop this war, and when my daughter is found, you will go home and breathe not a word of this to anyone. We cannot afford any failures. Do you understand?"

I swallowed. "I do, Majesty. I understand perfectly."

She nodded. "Good. Now leave and send Captain Saber in. I would like a word with the guard."

"LEAVE ME BE," I hissed to Ichiro and Lee in our mother tongue. They both opened their mouths to reply, but my glare cut them off. They presented me with twin, stiff bows before they turned and left. They were becoming insufferable, the both of them. With news of the wedding and my intentions, they'd become even more annoying than usual. All they wanted was to ready me, feed me lessons of marriage traditions I already knew.

And I, well, I wanted to see Maisie.

She'd barely met my gaze the entirety of that meeting, and there had been a sudden, obvious nervousness about her that I didn't know how to interpret. Was she happy, angry? I couldn't tell.

So I'd wait for her with my own thrill of nerves trickling down my spine. She was still inside, speaking to the queen. I fought not to tighten my nails into my palms. What could the queen be doing to her, saying to her? I hadn't wanted to leave her alone with that shark, given all that we knew. But one moment, my eyes were on Maisie, and the next my advisors were hauling me from the room, chattering away in my ears about all the preparations left to make.

The Promising. The Gift Exchange. The Claiming. Dragon Riding. Dragon Choosing.

A myriad of things I had no desire to think of at the moment, when all that possessed my body was *her* and the thought of finally wedding her, of having her as my bride. The Dragon Princess.

That thought made me smile through my nerves.

Maisie showed all the signs of being a true Dragon Princess with all the qualities of a great ruler.

If only she could see it.

"You're going to marry her…"

I glanced up at Captain Saber with surprise, not having realized he was there. In fact, we were mostly alone now, with a mere handful of guards. The captain and I were closer to the doors, further away from straining ears. Though his words were a tight whisper, I still swept a cautious glance around before replying.

"That was always the plan."

His back and blue tail were so straight; it was a wonder he didn't sink straight to the floor with the rigid posture he was holding. His hands were at his sides, but I was well versed in the stance, hand hovering near the hilt of his sheathed sword, eyes darting from every angle in search of danger.

"The plan was to marry—" He paused, not saying it out loud, but I knew perfectly well what—rather, who—he meant.

Odele.

"Yes, but she is not here." And while she was nowhere to be found, and the public *thought* Maisie was Odele, it was her I would marry. It was her I would fight for. It was her who I would take back to Draconi if the secret were discovered. Because it was her name I'd ask her to sign on the binding marriage contract.

"What if she comes back?" the captain asked skeptically.

My eyebrows rose as I took him in, not quite knowing what to think. He was a difficult merman to read, the captain. Yet his frustration, and his love, shone as brightly as Draconian waterworks. But whether that love was for Maisie or Odele, I didn't know. Maybe it was for both. And even though Maisie loved us all equally, and could have us all, I knew that someday Captain Saber would have to choose between the two.

"Then I would still choose *her*, because she is the one I love. The one I want." My lips pulled back into a mocking smile. "Can I say the same for you?"

A jolt seemed to shoot through the captain's body before he tensed again. Instead of looking around for danger, he finally deigned to face me. His lip nearly pulled up to his teeth. A sneer. "What are you talking about?"

"You care about her, even if you won't admit it. But do you love her, or is it *the other one* you prefer?" I did not like referring to them like this. Yet I couldn't very well throw both of their names around without a care. So I would speak of them like this, in terms we both understood.

The captain bristled. Surely if he had spikes running down his body, they'd have perked by now. The glare he shot me was nothing short of mutinous, but didn't affect me in the least.

"How dare you?" he ground out.

I smiled, shrugged. "I'm asking you a simple question. Your unwillingness to answer leads me to believe that maybe you do prefer the other one."

Captain Saber took one stroke until our bodies touched, and though we were the same height, he straightened in an ineffectual attempt to loom over me. There was lava blazing in his eyes, molten blue exploding. Fury. I welcomed it.

"I care about *Maisie*," he punctuated on a hissed whisper. "I will not lie and say that I don't care about Odele, because I always have. But if you think you can turn my doubts of your plan into something it's not…" He broke off, casting a furtive glance around before turning back to me. "I will not play these games with you, Dragon Prince. I played them already at the behest of that criminal, and I won't do it again. I don't have to prove to you that my feelings for her are genuine, that I would protect her. Die for her."

A smile pulled at my lips, wide and content. I was not the sort to play the same games as Elias. The sheer ferocity in his words was proof enough for me that he cared, and that he loved. I needed nothing else. I lifted a hand and set about patting his shoulder like he was nothing more than a child. A gesture that made him bristle.

"Good mer," I complimented. "Good mer."

I was spared his tedious reply when the door opened and Maisie emerged, her facial features pulled tight. She stopped when she saw us by the door, and her eyes narrowed in on our close proximity. I took a deliberate stroke away from the captain and smiled at her.

She didn't meet my gaze.

"Captain, the queen wishes to speak with you."

Captain Saber's eyes traveled down the length of her in question. He gifted her with a bow, murmuring, "Your Majesty," before pushing slowly past her and through the door. I noticed as he passed, his fingers grazed over Maisie's knuckles, like an act of quiet reassurance, but just when her fingers extended to reach for his, he was already gone with the door closing behind him.

Maisie floated in front of the closed door awkwardly, eyes staring past my shoulder.

"My gem?"

She finally looked at me then, but there was no softness in her gaze. Her eyebrows pulled tightly together to form a frown, her lips thinned into a tight line. And she did something I didn't expect of her.

She ignored me.

My eyes widened as she swam straight past me, like I was nothing more than a disturbing piece of furniture placed in an unconventional spot.

I whirled, watching her retreating back, posture tight and angry. The guards did not hesitate to follow her, forming a wall of protection around her figure. My body moved, weaving my way between the guards until I swam at her side.

She didn't even acknowledge me.

"My gem, what is it?" I asked. Still, she did not reply. Panic and irritation surged through me. I gripped her upper arm, pulling her to a stop. "Princess, *talk to me.*"

She glared vehemently at me and yanked her arm away from me. The simplicity of the action hurt.

"Leave me alone, *Prince.*" She sneered the word like it was an insult. I fought not to stagger back from the hatred she packed into the word.

"What's wrong?" I demanded. "I cannot make it better unless you tell me what's wrong."

I was aware that the guards had given us distance to argue, but not enough so as to not be able to jump in between us, should they need to.

"What's wrong?" she hissed. "What's wrong is that you went to the queen and demanded a speedy wedding without talking to me first. That's what's wrong!" She turned and began swimming vehemently away from me. I followed.

"How can you be mad about that?" I asked. "The date of our marriage is set in the contract…"

She whirled angrily and shouted, "No, it's not!" Her exposed chest rose and fell angrily, the light pink of her skin flushing a bright red. Her black eyes were as wide as jewels, glossed over as if they'd been polished one too many times.

She didn't need to say the words aloud for them to hang thick in the waters between us.

The date of yours and Odele's wedding is in the contract. Not mine.

"But..." I was at a loss for words. What could I say? I knew what I wanted to say to reassure her, but I couldn't utter any of it with the guards present.

"Don't bother." She sniffed, and for a moment, I wondered if she was going to cry. "There's no point in arguing about it. What's done is done." She started away again, and I stopped her by grabbing her wrist. This time, when she tried to pull away, I didn't let her.

Mine, the dragon in me growled. *Mine!*

I let a sliver of my other self slip through. She didn't cringe at the sight of the dragon in my eyes, but tilted her chin higher in defiance.

A worthy opponent.

"I thought you'd be *happy*."

Her eyes blinked rapidly. Then, she let out a bark of bitter laughter. "And why would you think that?" When I didn't reply, she tugged her arm lightly. "Did you think I'd bow at your fins and be grateful? Because you're the Dragon Prince and because I'm..." She cut off, bit her lip, but pushed through. "...Me?"

The dragon inside roared in anger. How dare she? How dare she think so low of me? Had I not proved to her time and time again that I loved her? That despite what my kingdom needed, I had chosen her? She was my mate.

Mine. Mine. Mine.

When would she realize this?

"Of course not." My voice had become a guttural growl. "I love you. Does that mean anything?"

Her posture slackened, and she looked suddenly very, very sad. A single bubble tripped from the edge of her eye. "Of course it means something," she whispered, voice cracking. "It means I would have thought you'd have the decency to at least ask me first, to include me in your plan. But *you* are so used to getting everything you want. Of everything being planned for you. The marriage date was set in *your* contract. But it was never set in *mine*."

I still didn't understand. I thought… I thought she'd want this, as much as I wanted this.

"*So* sorry to interrupt…" I turned sharply to the voice that had sounded anything but sorry. Charismatic ice blue eyes met my dark ones, and a wide mouth was quirked up into a smile.

"Prince Ytgar, Val." Maisie's face flushed. Because she was embarrassed Ytgar and Val had caught us arguing, or because he inspired that color on her cheeks with his flirtatious face? "Hello."

I growled. "Leave."

His icy-blond brow rose as he took me in. "I think I won't. In fact, I may just stay. The princess looks rather winded…" he trailed off. The implication in his words said I'd hurt her, that I would do it if he didn't stay.

"This is a private conversation…"

The blond—I refused to call him a prince—flicked long fingers in my direction, a sign of dismissal. "Not so private if you're shouting at each other in the halls for all to hear. And I don't think the princess wants to continue this conversation any more than I do." He gave a pointed look down at the hand I still had clasped around her wrist. "Princess, would you like Val and I to escort you to your rooms?"

She gifted him with an unwavering smile. "I am feeling a bit… winded… and would like to lie down."

The blond looked at me triumphantly. "The princess has spoken. If you'd kindly release her."

Mine.

Possessiveness burned through my insides in a way I'd never felt before. But a casual glance over my opponents showed me the tension in their bodies. The way the blond's hands were casually at his back, though no doubt reaching for a hidden dagger somewhere. The darker skinned, silver-eyed one was more obvious in his hostility. His hand wrapped tightly around the hilt of his ice-like sword.

"This conversation isn't over, my gem," I promised darkly, letting my words settle over her like a blanket. They were the whispering promise of something else as well. Of stolen kisses and bodies joining, of claiming.

Her cheeks flushed as my dark meaning registered.

Only then did I release her wrist.

She flexed her fingers, as if my touch had burned. And I could only watch with ire as she turned and smiled at the Iolish merman, settled her arm into the crook of his own, and fell into easy chatter as the three of them turned away from me and left.

"You wished to speak with me, Your Majesty?"

"I did." Queen Circe's gaze was trained on her long, painted nails, each one tapping a dangerous rhythm against the quartz tabletop. *Click. Click. Click.* The movements of her long fingers were both distracting and a threat. The tips of her fingers were a dark red. Like blood on the tip of a steel blade.

A part of me was too frightened to move.

Queen Circe was regent, at least until Odele ascended the throne. But now I was not blind to the truth of the curse in the Malabella lineage.

Not a curse at all, but her.

She'd killed every threat before her, and she'd surely kill Odele, were the princess before her now.

"The doppelganger is to pose as a bride in but a short two weeks," she commented all too casually.

Had she thought I'd forgotten? No one who was present in the room would be likely to forget.

"How goes the search for my stepdaughter?" The clicking of her nails ceased, and her preternatural stillness seemed much more dangerous somehow.

"I regret to inform you that the search for her has proved fruitless. She is nowhere to be found in the kingdom of Thalassar." The way the queen's features slashed with unconcealed rage made me glad for it, too. Hopefully she was far away from here, so far away that the murderous grip of the queen would not reach her.

Queen Circe straightened in her chair, as if it were the royal throne itself. *Click. Click. Click.* "Tell me, Captain Saber, is your family well?"

A shiver of unease slid down my spine. I let my cool composure and obedience fall into place, the mask I wore to serve the royals. I would not let her scent my fear. "I believe they are, Your Majesty." It was dangerous to answer any other way.

"It'd be a terrible shame if, in a few weeks' time, they find themselves unwell."

"Majesty?" I had to feign ignorance, even though the threat didn't go unnoticed. Oh, it was very well implied in her tone, in the nefarious clicking of her fingernails against the table. Like they were the blades she intended to slit through my family's chests herself.

Click.

Click.

Click.

"You have one week, Captain," she ordered with finality. "One week to find my stepdaughter. If, by the end of the week, she is still gone, then consider it your resignation. Are we clear?"

I swallowed the lump of fear that tightened my throat. "Very clear, Majesty."

Her lips curled into a smile. "Good. Now leave."

As I turned to leave, my thoughts whirled like the stirrings of an oncoming hurricane. Without saying it directly, she had threatened my family. She had threatened *me.* Perhaps she thought me a stupid guard and captain, and maybe I was. But I was not a stupid merman, to think they were idle threats.

For Queen Circe had never specified as to whether it would be the resignation of my job…

…or of my life.

I TRIED NOT TO think about Kai, his expression, or the dark and dangerous promise of his parting words. It wasn't hard to forget him the moment Ytgar held my hand firmly into the crook of his arm, chattering away in my ear.

Though I followed the conversation, it was hard to grasp the actual point of it. Then again, maybe there was no point to it at all. Maybe he was just talking to take my mind off of the Dragon Prince and our argument.

I hated that it was starting to work.

Soon, there was nothing on my mind but the comfort of Ytgar's warm touch, his lighthearted words, and the protective presence of Val at our backs.

I turned over my shoulder to look at the silver-eyed merman and was taken by surprise at the gleam in his eyes. I hadn't really gotten a good look at him before. How could I when Ytgar stole all the attention for himself? But there was something formidable about the dark-skinned mer. He was commanding in his own right and wore a much more serious expression than I'd ever seen on Captain Saber. His silvery-white hair was tied away from his face. He wore a tunic in dull tones of gray, partially exposed beneath the long, thick cloak of velvet he wore. The garment was so long, and lined with the thick fur of some northern creature, it covered his tail entirely. In fact, I realized with a start, both Iolish mermen wore clothing so long neither of their tails were visible. Surely they felt the suffocating heat?

"Why don't you swim next to us, Val?" I offered with a smile. His protective presence had been welcoming at first, but now, after getting a good look at him, I felt suddenly nervous, and I couldn't quite place why.

His grave expression never changed, but his lips did twitch slightly into what I believed was a smile. "How am I to guard your backs if I swim next to you, Princess?"

My cheeks flushed, burning warmer when Ytgar laughed. "Always so grave, Val."

I quickly turned away from Val to focus on the hallway before us. I chuckled a little bit with Ytgar. "I'm sorry. I should have known better. My guard is the same way; never wants to relax around me."

Ytgar's warm hand covered my own. "Oh, Val isn't a guard."

I blinked. "But…" *But you introduced him as your guard and advisor.*

"You're aware that Iol breeds whales?" I barely got my nod out before he kept going. "Valmundur here is a whale trainer and my closest friend since infancy. I'm hopelessly lost without him, I'm afraid. So I lie and say he's a guard, or else they'd never let him into those fun meetings of yours."

He waited a breath, and I wondered if he was expecting a reprimand for such an action. Really, if he thought so little of me, I don't know why he'd bothered to share that secret in the first place.

"I hope you do not think less of us for it; for his position, or for the deceit."

I wondered if Odele would have minded the position. If she would have been upset that a whale trainer had been allowed into royal meetings, had given his opinion so freely?

Well, I wasn't Odele, despite my origins or whatever relations lay between us. I was a waitress from Lagoona, with a position perhaps lower than even Val's, and here I was, being escorted by the arm of the Prince of Iol.

I smiled up at him with reassurance, and I swore his breath caught. "Of course not. What should it matter where someone is from or what position they hold? It's the heart that counts, I should think."

Both mermen went very still, and despite earlier protests, I felt Val's presence on the other side of me. I felt suddenly very small, caged between the two mermen.

"Ah, you are so very lovely, Princess. And not at all what we expected."

"And what did you expect?" I asked, merely for my own amusement. I was already sure of the answer.

"Fun," he replied, and I took immediate offense. Was I not fun, then? "Also rude and sarcastic. I admit, I imagined all the lovely arguments we would have, and here I am. Disappointed."

"Ha, well, I'm sorry I am not much more fun than this. It's been a trying morning."

He patted my hand just as my room came into view. We started towards it, and he released me. Just as I turned to thank both him and Val for escorting me, he gave me a breathtaking smile. "Perhaps we will not quip with words, but there are other ways to have a good time," he offered. I stilled as his fingers went to my cheek and trailed low to my chin. His eyes were fixated on the ring heavy between my exposed cleavage. I flushed all over at the insinuation.

"How *dare* you?" I demanded.

He blinked, as if a spell had been cast over him to make him say those words. Or maybe he was just surprised by the anger in my voice.

"Um..."

I straightened into a posture that was formidable in my own way. That was commanding. Queenly. "I am engaged to be married—within two weeks—to the Dragon Prince, Kai Li of Draconi. I am sure your brain is not so small that you cannot recall the meeting where it was announced?" I had the satisfaction of watching Ytgar's mouth drop open.

"But... I..."

I held up a hand, and he shut his mouth. "Regardless of what you saw or overheard in that hallway, he is my *betrothed.* And if he knew you were propositioning his soon-to-be wife, he would cut you into pieces and feed you to his pet dragon." At the mention of violence, both mermen tensed. I merely smiled and added, almost as an afterthought, "And he'd do it with his bare hands, too."

Ytgar's mouth opened and closed in silent stammers. "I—I meant no offense..."

My eyes rolled. "Of course you didn't, Prince Ytgar. But please, next time, find your cheap entertainment elsewhere, because you won't find it with me." I looked over his shoulder at Val, who looked to be either suppressing a cry of rage or a laugh. I smiled at him. "Have a good day, Valmundur."

And then I turned and opened the door to my room and swam inside, but not before I heard the harsh bark of laughter, no doubt coming from Val's throat. Their voices muffled when I closed it, and I leaned the back of my head against it to take deep breaths.

Really. The nerve.

When I opened my eyes, it was to find Odele on the bed, lounging luxuriously and feeding herself little fruits.

"Who's at the door?" she asked, her mouth full.

"Prince Ytgar and his whale trainer friend, Val," I answered almost absentmindedly as my gaze swept across the sights before me. Platters and platters of breakfast food lay all around the room. Frothy tea, pastries, cakes filled with fruit, bowls of fruit and greens, salads, honey dripping onto the floor…

Even as my stomach gave a rumble at the delicacies, I glared at her. "Where did all of this come from?" I asked tightly.

She swallowed and reached for a pastry, a delicious looking thing that bled red berries. She licked them from her fingers before taking a large bite, and spoke around her chewing. "I rang for a maid."

My temper flared, but I tried to reel it in. "And what, please tell me, did you do that for?"

She shrugged, took another bite. "I was hungry."

I couldn't hold my anger in then. "Because you were hungry?" I laughed harshly, though she'd find no joy in the sound. "I'm hungry, *too,* Odele."

Odele held out her half-eaten confection in offering. "Want some?"

I shrieked and darted over to a platter of food, and in an angry, impulsive move, I flipped the contents of the tray violently, watching as it crashed to the floor.

"What's got your fins flaring, cousin?" She only sounded amused by my outburst.

I was not.

"I can't believe you," I accused. "I am out there suffering through *your* chores while you're in here eating the day away."

"Well, I have to keep my arrival here a—"

"A secret, yes, I know," I spat. "And how do you pretend to do that if the whole palace knows you're here? You think the maid who brought this up won't talk? What will mer say when they realize that one princess was in the meeting with the queen while the other was ordering *room service*?"

Odele swallowed the last bite of her food and shrugged. "I didn't think about that."

"No, you didn't, did you? You don't seem to do much thinking."

Her eyes narrowed and she sat up straighter on the bed, eyebrows pulling together. "Don't talk to me like that," she hissed.

I couldn't help myself. I was angry. I was a volcano on the verge of eruption, and all I wanted to do was damage everything around me. I wanted her to burn. "Don't talk to you like what? With the truth? Because that's what this is! You're a spoiled brat, Odele. You think of nothing and no one but yourself."

"How *dare* you—"

"No. How dare *you*? Do you even realize what you're doing? Everything we set into motion this morning could be *ruined* all because you felt the need to play princess again. I can't believe I fell for your load of silt. You probably don't care about my life at all. You'll gladly sit back while we take the risks in your stead!"

"We?"

"Yes, *we*. Captain Saber, Prince Kai, Elias, and I are all sacrificing things for *you,* for *your* kingdom and *your* mer, while you've done nothing but hide away this entire time!"

A slash of hurt crossed her features, so brief, it was like I'd imagined it being there at all. Anger and entitlement were pressed down on her. "I have *too* been doing stuff."

"What stuff?" I crossed my arms.

She bit her bottom lip in thought. "I left to find *you*."

I scoffed. "But you didn't find me, did you? Captain Saber did."

Princess Odele waved the words away, assuming an air of impertinence. "He had a stroke of luck. And anyway, we shouldn't really be doing anything at all. We're princesses. If you'd accept your heritage and title, you could just take the throne back, we'd out the queen, and then all would be well."

Because it was so easy to take down a monarchy, right? If it were, she could have done it herself by now. But like every other royal I'd ever known, she wanted things handed to her. She wanted everything to solve itself without really lifting a fin to help. Oh, sure, it was easy for her to do a little digging, escape to inquire about me, but actually making the trek to find me? She'd stayed hidden within the secret passageways of the palace, for gods' sakes!

"You have done nothing since this whole thing started. You've been waiting behind the comfort of these quartz and stone walls for all your problems to solve themselves." My hand went to my chest, to grab the ring hanging there. I touched the smooth edges and was reminded of Elias, my heart suddenly hurting. A tear slipped unbidden from my eye. "You are a Princess of Thalassar, and you've done nothing for this kingdom. Gods, Elias has done and is doing more than you ever have." I dropped the ring, the heavy weight of it resting over my thumping heart. I turned away, unable to look at her any longer. "Gods, and he left to search *orphanages* for information you had all along. Information you never bothered to share. You… *time waster!*" I couldn't help but throw that last bit out like a bitter accusation. I should have regretted it. I should have taken care with how I spoke to the future ruler of Thalassar, but my anger had taken over. It was an uncontrollable current inside of me releasing in a rush. Once it started, it could not stop.

There was a deafening silence, and I dared to look up to see what my explosion had caused.

I refused to look away from the hurt on her face. I relished in it, in that brief moment of anger and cruelty. What pity should I feel for her? For this mer who had abandoned her kingdom, who had lied to me, and was risking our plan to fulfill her own capricious needs?

"You think so little of me, cousin." Her voice was hollowed out. No trace of the entitled princess, no trace of any emotion. I'd taken it from her. "And you really made me believe that you were interested in being a family…" She sighed and slowly got up from the bed. Without another word, she turned, swimming towards the tapestry. I watched numbly in the aftermath of my angry words as she pressed her hand to the stone and slipped through the passageway.

She didn't once look back.

TRY AS HARD AS I might, I could not get the look of Odalaea's face out of my mind. The look of disappointment, anger, and finally, her simmering hatred. Each emotion packed tightly into one facial expression, able to convey every single one with her narrowed eyes fixated on me.

And every single emotion was precisely why I had not wanted to come forth.

I'd expected it, of course. I'd expected such a reaction. After observing her from behind stone and quartz walls, and in telly recordings, I knew her. Knew that the moment she met me, she would despise me, if not for bringing her the truth, then because we were nothing alike.

I liked to believe we were two halves of a whole, the different sides of a coin. My side was polished, shining, *perfect.* Hers was varnished, rusted. But we occupied the same space. She was mine, and I was hers. Her blood was my blood. And even if she was everything I despised, poor, righteous, and somewhat pitiful, I loved her despite it all.

And despaired because she didn't feel the same for me.

My cousin thought me worthless. She would not be the first to think it. Most everyone in the palace believed that of me. That I was daft, shallow, selfish. I'd not deny I was different. But for the first time in the entirety of my life, I wanted to prove those judgments wrong.

So I would take risks, and she would see that I did care. I cared more than she could ever know. I cared about her, and I cared about *me*, I cared about our family, and that the world should know the truth.

I slipped into the spacious cove and immediately felt at home. Well, as at home I could feel in a dirty, barnacle-infested cavern. I'd loathed to admit it, but this place was a second sort of sanctuary for me, the first being the royal library, with all its kelp parchments and conches.

Swimming down to the floor, I rummaged inside the chest of gold and pulled out a spare cloak I kept at the bottom, along with a bag of coins, a belt, sword and sheath. Over the past months, I'd practiced in the music of silence, and in the art of weaponry. I was a quick study, a virtue of mine no one knew I had, and many overlooked. I was good at memorization, at studying things around me.

It's what made slipping in and out of the palace without being seen so easy.

I pulled the hood of the cloak onto my head and slipped out of the cove and onto the streets of Eramaea.

The secrets of Eramaean streets were no easy thing. At least, it hadn't been at first. As I couldn't afford any errors, I spent days, weeks, observing until my eyes hurt. Until I found the perfect angles of shadows and darkness, of whispers and secrets, and followed it.

Maisie told me that her precious Elias, who I knew as the Black Blade, was scourging orphanages in search of any trace of me, any trace of her.

Since I'd gone through the exact same route and had turned up entirely empty, I knew where he would be. After all, my vast city had only two orphanages, and he'd likely already searched them. And if I knew the Black Blade, which I did in rumored whisperings, I knew he had connections. Likely, he'd try using them, calling in favors to discover all he could about every single orphanage in Thalassar.

He was nothing if not thorough, from what I'd gathered.

I also gathered, from the way that my cousin spoke of him, that she was in love. It'd been so obvious, from the way her fingers fluttered to grasp at the ring between her breasts. A ring made up of the same stuff as the Black Blade's legendary weapon, the color of obsidian, sharper than steel. Very few blades of that make existed.

Apparently, a ring did too.

I was huddled into a corner in a tavern of ill repute. Not the Siren's Song, but one as equally disgusting, if not more. The ambiance was deader than a funeral. I'd seen more light in the soulless eyes of my stepmother than at this place.

And the stench was disgusting, too.

It smelled rotten, mossy. Like something dead was decaying in the crumbling wooden and coral walls. I bit back the bile rising in my throat. Ugh, why had I sought out to do this in the first place? Hunting down a criminal to my crown to bring him back to my cousin. And all for what?

To prove I wasn't as worthless as she thought me to be? Well, if this was what it would take for her to trust me, I should have just stayed at home. The stench of ferment and depravity was hardly worth it.

Who knew what kind of diseases lurked through these waters, what kind of ailments these disgusting mer brought with them.

I didn't want to wait too long to catch anything.

Thankfully, I didn't have to. The criminal I had my sights set on this whole time got up from a far away table. He was dressed all in black and traveled with no cloak, so his exposed face was easily recognizable. His black hair swept over dark skin, black eyes shining as fierce and threateningly as the blade hanging from his hip. I was too far away for my staring to be noticed, but as I narrowed my eyes, I could make out a thin, pink scar along his cheek.

He swam with purpose in his stroke, a king of criminals, confident in his rule.

The Black Blade.

I got up and followed him out on quiet fins.

The trick to stalking was staying at a far enough distance that you wouldn't be recognized, but close enough to follow. I prided myself in my self-taught abilities of stealth. My eyes never once strayed from him as he swam through the near desolate waters of this part of Eramea, the home of criminals and their place of business.

His back was to me, and his confident swagger unmistakable. So I knew the moment he suddenly disappeared right before my eyes.

My body came to a stop as I looked around but found no sight of him. It was as if he'd somehow become the shadows and slipped away from me. But that wasn't possible.

I swam faster, closing in on the space I'd last glimpsed him at. The moment I stepped fin in the spot, I felt a grip on my arm. I was suddenly hauled away from the street and pulled into shadows and darkness.

I did not scream.

It would go ignored here.

I started to struggle and was whipped around, my back colliding into a wall. I gasped for breath, but didn't let the pain stop me from whipping out my sword, brandishing it in front of me, the tip pointing at the feral white grin of the Black Blade.

"Hello, *Princess,*" he purred.

I thrust the sword forward in warning, but he slid back, pushing the side of my blade away with his hand. He was too confident for his own good, with all the arrogance of a shark, and all the brains of a blob of dirt.

"Want to tell me why you're following me, Odele?"

The inability to use my proper title infuriated me. How dare he, the sea scum? I was his superior. He should be *groveling* at my fins instead of smiling like a sneaky little catfish.

"You don't seem surprised to see me," I commented, fighting back breathlessness. This scum didn't intimidate me. He hadn't the first time I met him, either.

"You've been stalking me since I was in the tavern, so no, I am not surprised."

I bit the inside of my cheek.

He was observant, taking every inch of me in. A chuckle escaped his mouth. "I'm sorry, did you think you had me fooled?"

Because I had, I didn't reply to the question. I lifted my sword and pressed the tip into his chest. He barely wavered.

"Enough talking. You're coming with me to the palace, criminal. *Now.*" My commands were usually followed by immediate obedience, but only mocking laughter followed this one.

"Oh, I think not, Princess. You see, you have no power here." He took a stroke back, away from the sharp point of my sword and slid his own out of its sheath. I listened to it slide, watched it glisten beneath phytoplankton glow.

His blade was the same as my cousin's, except the hilt of his was studded with rare, black diamonds instead of sapphires, the blade longer, heavier.

"But I suppose if you wish for me to accompany you, you'll have to beat me in a duel first."

My heart thundered. A duel I could do. After all, I was the Royal Princess of Thalassar. I'd been trained in fighting and strategy since my birth. There was no way this criminal could beat me at my own game.

"Fine," I conceded with a smile. "Loser owes the other an immediate favor."

"Deal," he smiled.

And then he struck.

His move was fierce and strong, the blade arcing down from above, threatening to slice me in half. I blocked it, steel scraping obsidian and causing sparks to rain over us like dozens of tiny fallen stars. The Black Blade was strong. I'd give him credit for that. But he was also an amateur fighter. There was no refinement in him like there was in me. No perfect gliding movements or hand-held positions. He hadn't been trained for this since birth like me.

I pushed against him and twirled under the swing of his blade. Turning, I struck, and he struck back. Our blades met, clash for clash in an implacable sparring dance, where the strokes were mismatched and savage. We swung, ducked, pushed, and pulled.

I'd hardly call the Black Blade a formidable opponent. He was nothing but a street urchin, sea scum, criminal to my crown and my family.

And I could easily disarm him.

Growing tired of the games, I made my final move, smashing the hilt of my sword onto his face. He didn't cry out, but he did wince, taken aback for a moment. That moment was all I needed. I slapped the side of my blade onto his wrist and his hold on his weapon slipped. It clamored to the silt in a cloudy puff and I hit my tail against his, sweeping it out from under him. He fell to the ground beside his blade.

Triumph swelled within me. It had taken hardly a few breaths to knock him down, only a few to prove that I was better than this filthy criminal.

I pointed my sword at him, a smile pulling my mouth. "You lost, scum. Now you have to come with me to the palace."

His chest rose and fell steadily, and he was using his elbows to prop himself up in the sand. His black eyes regarded me with a look I couldn't quite decipher, but had no desire to do so. All I wanted was for him to uphold his end of the agreement and come with me to the blasted palace, so I could present him to Odalaea and show her that I was as valuable as this scum, the prince, her, and the captain.

That I mattered.

Because I *did* matter.

"There's just one problem, Odele," the Black Blade said coolly. "I don't play by palace rules."

In a move so fast, I could hardly see it, he kicked his tail up, hitting the hand holding the hilt of the sword so hard, it smacked onto my precious face. I cried out, and a moment later, my own tail slipped from under me, the sword was torn from my hand, and a heavy body hovered over mine in the silt.

The Black Blade smiled down at me.

"I win."

Princess Odele squirmed beneath me, and the thrill of winning shot through the core of my bones. A thrill that was only heightened by the look of pure hatred in the depths of her brown-gold eyes.

"Let go of me, scum. I am the *princess*," she commanded, her voice the perfect tone of entitlement and indignity. She pushed her body up against mine, her pathetic attempt to throw me off.

I smiled down at her, hands gripping her wrists above her head. "Careful with how you move, *Princess*. Do not forget that I am a male made of flesh and blood, and my moods are as sporadic as the ocean we inhabit."

She tensed at the lie, which was precisely what I'd wanted her to do.

I took her in in this moment of stillness, noting the differences and similarities between her and my little fish. Not that I needed to memorize them. With just a glance, I could tell who was who. And the moment I'd caught the glimpse of her in the tavern, I knew I was about to be greeted by the true Princess of Thalassar.

Her eyes were the burning tones of copper, dark and light, dancing together. While Maisie's were twin orbs of obsidian and violet, as dark and vast and secretive as an abyss. They tempted me.

Odele's did not.

"I will order you only once more to get off of me," she hissed between gritted teeth.

I raised an amused brow. I could make out the spot on her forehead where the hilt of her blade had rammed into her skin. It was red, though it would not leave a bruise. "I find it amusing that you think you can order me about. Like you said, I am a criminal, I am scum, so what should your orders be to me but empty words falling through the water? You are not, after all, *my* princess."

My princess was at the palace, pretending to be Odele. *Suffering* because of her. *Looking* for her.

And here she was.

"Your princess is in the palace right now," Odele breathed. "And she wishes to see you."

I smirked. "Does she now?"

"Yes, now get off of me so I can take you to her!"

My heart thumped in my chest, so rapidly I was sure she could feel it against her own. That pounding was likely the only hint that I felt anything at all. My face remained impassive, one eyebrow arched, the rest of my features calm.

"How do I know you speak the truth?" She could be pulling me into a trap for all I knew. While I trusted Maisie to follow her to whatever ends, I did not trust Odele, nor would I ever.

"You don't," she hissed, baring her teeth in such an un-princess-like manner that I smiled. It seemed even she could be ruffled. "But my cousin needs you right now, and you'll go to her."

Cousin.

A jolt swept through my body. Maisie, she was still talking about Maisie, but she said the word 'cousin' so surely, with so much confidence, that I smelled the truth on her breath, in her expression.

Slowly, I eased away from her, keeping my eyes trained warily on her as she rubbed her wrists, as if my touch had pained her. She was looking at me with narrowed eyes, perhaps wishing me dead on the spot. Even if she was a royal, there were just some things even they weren't capable of.

"You are a brute," she snapped unkindly. "I'd have your head for this." She gestured at her wrists, jerking them in my direction.

I waved off her foolishness and got up, picking up my blade and sheathing it. She stared up at me from the silt with expectant eyes.

I sneered. "If you're expecting me to help you up, you'll be waiting for an eternity."

I could make out the flush of her face and anger pulled tightly at her features. Obviously embarrassed, she got up, muttering nonsense that sounded like curses and dusted off the back of her dress.

"You're despicable."

I smiled and gave her a mocking bow. "I never claimed otherwise."

She scoffed and retrieved her own sword. "So?" she demanded impatiently. "Shall we go? I don't have time to hang around in a disgusting alley all day. My cousin needs us."

And I needed her like a dull ache in my chest that wouldn't cease. Since the moment I'd left her side, I missed her terribly. Like a part of me was missing. But I'd gone away for her, to find out the truth. And now I was being called back to her side. Perhaps I was a fool, at her beck and call, doing her bidding, doing everything she asked of me. But where my pride was concerned, it didn't matter.

For Maisie, I would shatter the world and rebuild it anew if she so wished.

So I smiled at Princess Odele and waved a hand with a flourish. "Lead the way."

I LAY AGAINST THE cushions of the bed—Odele's bed—feeling miserable and entirely too alone. First, I'd practically exiled Prince Kai for having the audacity to plan a wedding without consulting me, and then I'd yelled at the princess in her own room. Captain Saber hadn't come looking for me and was perhaps still with the queen. Elias was gone, searching for Odele when she'd been at the palace the whole time.

My life was falling to tatters.

And I only had myself to blame.

If I'd just gotten here and done what I was told, if I'd just shut up, kept my head down and pretended to be Odele in every way, then my world wouldn't have been in upheaval.

Perhaps the truth would have found its way to me eventually. Eventually, I would have discovered who I truly was, that I came from two royal families and two powerful kingdoms. But would have I accepted it? *Did* I accept it?

I wanted nothing more than a mother, a father. Two things that seemed entirely too impossible had become even more so in an instant. Having royal parents seemed an even more unattainable thing than wanting parents who were just un-dead.

If King Dorian *knew* who he'd waged war for, would he regret it? Would he take one look at me and decide I was better off a figment of his imagination? Would he look at my fin with disgust and mourn the daughter he wished I was? Would he rage upon looking at me and see that I was the reason his wife had been killed?

I could not accept it.

Some secrets were better off buried.

My throat tightened painfully. I tried to swallow past it, but my body was unresponsive. I wanted to cry. I wanted to scream.

I wanted this to be over.

"Cousin…"

I jolted up in bed and turned to the tapestry. I had been so lost in my thoughts that I hadn't noticed the sound of stone scraping away. Odele was holding the tapestry aside and looking at me with uncertainty. Around her shoulders there was a dark cloak of poor make and a sword at her hip.

"You went out," I whispered, in a voice that was surprisingly steady. Odele looked uncomfortable for a moment. I noticed her forehead was red, as if she'd been smacked across her skin. "Are you okay?"

She waved off my concern with a flick of her fingers. "I know you think I can't do anything right," she said. Guilt shamed me. Even if what I said had been true, it hadn't been the way to say it. It had been cruel, rude. "But

I hope this makes up for it." She moved aside to reveal a merman behind her. A merman I knew and recognized as if he were the very beating of my heart.

"Elias…"

The tears swelled from my eyes then and I cried, stifling my sobs by slapping my hands against my mouth. In all the world, if there was one mer who understood me, it was Elias. If there was someone out there who would understand, it was he.

Seeing him before me could almost make me forget how angry I was with him for showcasing me in front of Captain Saber like a slab of meat for a hungry shark.

Almost.

"You tadpole!" I shouted, grabbing a pillow and hurtling it at him.

He dodged, and the smirk he gave was familiar, almost comforting. "Hey, little fish. Nice outfit."

My face flushed profusely. I'd almost forgotten what I was wearing. Now that he'd seen me in it, he wouldn't let me hear the end of it, I was sure.

Odele looked between the two of us. "I'm confused. Are you two lovers or not?"

"You embarrassed me in front of Captain Saber and then just left!" I accused, ignoring the princess.

Elias rolled his eyes. "I left because you asked me to."

"But you didn't even apologize for acting like a total barnacle!"

Odele sighed, a lengthy and annoyed sound. "*Ooookay…*" She swam deeper into the room. "You two obviously need to have a very private and personal talk. I'm just gonna…" She slipped into her swim-in closet and closed the doors behind her.

Elias didn't spare her a glance as he swam into the room to sit across from me on the bed. "Little fish…" His hand reached out to cradle my face.

I pushed him away angrily. "Don't touch me."

He masked the flash of hurt by arching a dark brow. “What’s got your fins flaring?” he asked with little mirth.

My fingers went almost involuntarily to the ring settled warmly between my breasts. His eyes flickered to the ornament then back to my face, assessing, calculating, and gauging my secrets with the depths of his eyes.

“Don’t do that,” I whispered, closing my eyes as if in pain.

“Don’t do what?”

“That,” I accused, opening them again to glare at him. “Look at me like you can pull out all of my secrets with your inquiring gaze.”

His lip quirked into a mischievous smile. “Can’t I?”

The door to the closet opened, and Odele swam out, interrupting my reply. We both looked her over. She’d changed into a simple day dress in a very light blue. Her hair was swept over one shoulder, the tendrils magically curling down to her chest.

She looked fabulous. And she’d managed it in less than a minute, too.

“Since I can hear everything from there, I’m going to take a turn about the palace while you two work things out.”

My heart thundered. “But—”

“I know, I know. I’ll be careful. As long as you stay in here there shouldn’t be a problem. No one will suspect a thing.”

I was sure I looked doubtful, but she waved me off with her fingers. “Please, go back to your stimulating conversation.” With that, she went to the door, opened it, and swam out, leaving Elias and I truly alone.

I sighed, a long suffering sound. She was too much.

I looked back at Elias. He was staring at me with dark, expectant eyes.

“I’m mad at you,” I told him, though there was no anger in my words, just a bone-deep tiredness.

“So I’ve gathered. What I don’t understand is why.”

“Don’t you?” I asked. “You’re great at swindling secrets, after all.”

Elias scooted closer to me and took my hand. This time, I didn’t pull away from the warmth of his touch. I let our fingers entwine, and his own fit through the spaces like it was meant to be his home.

"Talk to me, little fish."

I sighed. Of course, he had his perfect ways of stealing my secrets. With a look, with a touch, with nothing more than the softness in his voice…

"You used me to satisfy your own amusement. Me and Captain Saber." My fingers tightened on his, as if I could transfer the pain I'd felt in that moment to him. "You ridiculed me. Despite knowing how I feel about the captain, you put me through that. You must have known how it hurt me."

Of course, the captain and I made our decision. We'd chosen to do it in front of the others. Maybe I was just grasping at whatever excuse I could find to be angry with Elias, to be angry at anyone else because of this mess that was now my life.

Elias, for the first time since I'd known him, looked honestly bewildered. "Little fish, I didn't…" He broke off, ran a hand through his dark tendrils of hair. "You have to know that wasn't my intention, to humiliate you."

"But you did."

He winced, as if my words were slaps to the face.

The action had me softening. I was unjustly taking my ire out on him. At the end of the day, I had free will, and I chose to do what I did.

"I'm sorry," I whispered. "You don't deserve that. We did what we wanted to do, even if you were poking the shark."

Elias observed me, his dark eyes seeing all too much. "I didn't do what I did because of you, little fish. I did it for Captain Saber. You have to know that."

My eyebrows pulled together. "I don't understand."

He let loose a small breath. "I didn't do it to ridicule either of you. I did it because I *know* the captain has feelings for you and I wanted him to open his eyes. I wanted him to realize *what* he felt for you."

"That doesn't make any sense." I frowned.

"Doesn't it?" He smiled. "Mermen, especially one like him, like the competition, the *challenge.* I wanted to prove to him that he could let go of the feelings he so tightly leashes. He just needed that push."

I shook my head, disbelieving. It was more likely he'd done it to thwart the captain. That he'd done it to infuriate and mock him by waving me in front of his face; me, the mermaid who looked like the lost love of his life.

Elias put his fingers beneath my chin and lifted my face up to meet his gaze. "Why do you doubt his feelings for you?"

I shrugged. *Because of his actions. Because he seems to despise me and push me. Because it'd be easier to accept his hatred.*

Of course, Elias read every thought on my face and he shook his head, cupping my cheek in his palm. "He doesn't love *her*, little fish. I wonder if anyone ever could love her, if I'm honest. She hides what she is so tightly, and even if she didn't, she could never compare to you. So if he chooses her over you, more the fool he is."

I let out a breath through my nose and found myself smiling, a slight turn of my lips. "I'm still upset with you, you know."

"I'd be disappointed if you weren't." He pulled away and leaned back on his hands, smirking with that mischievous grin of his. "So tell me, how does it feel to be actual royalty?"

My whole body jolted with hyperawareness. "How—"

"Odele told me everything. Though I can say I'm not surprised."

My eyes narrowed, distrust shamefully filling me. "Was this another secret you knew and kept from me?" I demanded.

Elias flicked his fingers across the bed casually. "A secret? No. But I did have a feeling…"

"A feeling?" I echoed.

"Tell me you didn't have it as well, little fish? There is no possible way that you two could look so alike and not be related. And when you told me about the missing royal… well… it just solidified my belief."

"Why didn't you say anything?"

His eyes narrowed at my accusing tone, but he merely shrugged. "Would you have even believed my suspicions? Do you even believe the truth? Don't answer, I can tell that you don't."

A part of me despised that I was so readable, but another part was relieved. I didn't have to voice what he already knew.

"Why do you doubt so much?" Elias inquired. He held his hand up, and began ticking off on his fingers. "You doubt Captain Saber's love for you. You doubt my honesty. You doubt you are of a royal bloodline." He dropped his hand, raised an eyebrow. "Why?"

The hardest part of all this was explaining myself. I'd told Odele why, but I hadn't given her the truth, at least, not entirely. I braced myself to tell Elias the truth now.

"All my life, I thought I was one thing," I explained quietly. "Everything I thought I was has suddenly changed. Yesterday I was an orphan with no family, today I have a cousin and a father. If I accept this role, if I accept my lineage, it means accepting this…" I gestured to the room around us. "Accepting that my mother is dead." My throat tightened, and I couldn't seem to get through the rest of the truth.

"So?" Elias asked quietly, fiercely, though not unkindly. "You thought both of your parents were dead before. Now you discovered only one of them is. What's the *real* reason behind it, little fish?"

My fingers went to the ring for strength. "I keep thinking that maybe he won't want me. That maybe he'll take one look at me and I won't be enough. I won't be what he expected. This truth has changed me, Elias. Everything about me is different now."

He shook his head. "That's bullshark, Maisie." I blinked at the ferocity in his voice. He leaned forward, so close that our noses touched. "If he didn't want you, he wouldn't have tried tearing this kingdom apart to find you. He will want you, all of you. I'm sure of it. As for the other bit?" He closed his eyes briefly, the shadows of his lashes swimming against the top curve of his cheek. "This information doesn't change you. Not at all." He pressed a hand to my chest, right over the rapid thumping of my heart. "This is still the same. Perhaps the only thing that's changed is your knowledge of who you truly are. But deep down, you are still that mer from Lagoona.

You are still the mer who wants a better Thalassar. Except now, you finally have the power to change things, if only you dared."

"So you're telling me to accept it," I breathed. "To be a princess."

He shook his head, dark eyes piercing mine. "Accept it. Don't accept it. That's up to you. But don't let anyone force you into any roles, little fish. You are *you.* You are Maisie *and* Odalaea. You were born a royal, but raised in Lagoona. You are a waitress *and* a princess. And no one can take that away from you except you."

Was it possible to not just be one thing? Was it possible to be a myriad of emotions and things? Wasn't Elias here proof enough of that? A criminal who saved mer, secretive yet honest. Dangerous but safe.

Was I proof enough of this?

Could I accept the role as Princess of Thalassar, of Kappur, and still be me?

"You'll never know unless you try," Elias answered my unasked question.

And maybe he was right.

Odele

It was a strange sensation, to swim so openly through the palace after so long. In the months I'd been gone, I'd gotten used to hiding and sneaking through shadows and secret passageways. Of hiding and observing. I couldn't quite say I missed sneaking around like a common thief. I wasn't meant for that life, for a life of hiding.

I was meant to be seen and heard. To be worshiped and lavished. Not scuttling around like a crab, or hiding in the silt like a rockfish.

I glanced down the hallways, hoping to spot a servant I could command, just for the pure joy of it. Perhaps I'd make one of them clean the ceiling with a sponge, even if it currently appeared spotless.

Smiling to myself at the idea, I swam forward, searching for a servant that could be mine to command. Really, where were they? There should have at least been two posted in every hall and bend of the palace. *Commoners*, I thought with disgust, rounding the corner of the hall. *They could be so stupid sometimes.*

A warm body rammed into mine so suddenly, I took a staggering stroke back. I looked up with a glare, "How *dare* you—" I cut off when I beheld the merman before me. Dark robes flowed around his body, covering the black, orange and white koi fish pattern of his tail. His black hair was tied back with a red ribbon, exposing the sharp angles of his cheekbones and pointed chin. Warm brown eyes settled over me with familiarity.

My betrothed was attractive, if one found disgusting dragon half-breeds to be that—which, I could assure anyone who asked, I did *not*. His soft good looks had absolutely no effect on me, and were entirely too unimpressive.

"My gem." His eyes warmed to entirely impossible temperatures. His gaze roamed over me, a slice of blue cutting through the brown as he took me in, in a way that made me feel too exposed, too naked.

"You—"

He cut me off, gripping my arm tightly and pulling me towards a wall that he pressed me up against. His body slid over mine, and I felt his every pane and joint poking into my delicate skin. Gross.

"Don't say anything," he whispered. He bent down close. Too close. I tensed. "Please just listen. I do not understand why you are so upset about the marriage. You know I love you and want to be with you. I assumed you felt the same way. If you do not, then tell me now. I do not want to keep believing that we have a future together if we don't. You have to know that I came back to you despite being duty bound to another, because I want *you*. All of you."

My head whirled at the tenacious confessions. He hardly breathed as he spoke, and his eyes were wide and frantic with worry. Long fingers skimmed down my arms and made goosebumps rise over my flesh.

Not the good kind, either.

I couldn't speak for a long while, I was so stunned.

My silence seemed to fill him with hope. "So you'll marry me?"

I blinked rapidly. "I—"

"Say yes," he nearly begged. Pathetic Draconian lizard boy. What fool had to beg for love? "Please say yes. I will give you love, and..." He broke off, hand reaching up to stroke the side of my breast. I jerked away from the touch, back hitting the wall. "I can give you pleasure, too." And then his eyes flashed a violent shade of blue, right before he bent down and kissed me.

I gasped in surprise and he shoved his tongue in my mouth.

It would likely take me weeks to get the taste of reptile out.

Closing my hand into a fist, I brought it up and punched him on the side of his face.

Startled by the force of the blow, he jerked back, cupping his cheek in his palm. He took me in, the blue fading back to brown.

I spit and gagged. My throat, my tongue, oh gods, it *burned.* "That was the most disgusting thing I've ever had to endure." I swiped the back of my hand against my mouth. "Oh gods, I think I'm going to be sick." I gagged and cut him a vicious glare. "How dare you touch a Princess of Thalassar, you disgusting half-breed lizard?"

He blinked in surprise. "Wha—*Odele*?"

Oh, silt.

I wasn't supposed to tell anyone. Oh, well. I was sure Odalaea would forgive me.

"Duh," I snapped imperiously. "Who else would I be? Years of breeding with beasts has obviously made you as brutish and as dumb as one. Oh, ugh." I gagged and whirled away from him.

Silt, silt, silt.

If he'd kissed me, if he was spewing nonsense about weddings and love, it could only mean that he was involved with my cousin.

And he'd just kissed me.

It felt like a betrayal to the blood of my blood. Yet I couldn't think about that right now. All that whirled through my mind was the fact that he'd kissed me, and it was disgusting, and I felt like I was going to toss up my breakfast.

"Oh, gods," I muttered, slapping a hand to my mouth.

"Odele?" Prince Kai still sounded incredulous behind me.

But I didn't have time to float around and wait for his miniscule brain to catch up to the facts.

I was about to be sick.

So I swam, hard and fast, all the way back to my room.

STUNNED, I COULD DO nothing but float there and stare at the spot she'd vacated.

Odele.

Odele Malabella, Princess of Thalassar, was *here.*

The dragon inside berated me, but no more chastising than the way I berated myself. How had I not realized she wasn't my mate? How had I not recognized that the body I caressed, that the lips I'd tasted, had not been Maisie's?

Questions floated through my mind. Too many to shift through. When had Odele arrived? And if she was here, then where was Maisie? Panic seized me in an iron fist, and every worst possible scenario swam through my mind. Had I pushed her away with my insistence? Or had Odele showed up of her own volition after all this time?

Oh, Dragon Gods, had Maisie *left*?

No, my gem, my *mate* couldn't be gone.

She *couldn't be.*

I darted after Odele, as if the Great Dragon himself were snapping at my fins and prayed I wasn't too late. And if I was...

The dragon inside me roared with fury. If she'd left me, I wouldn't stop until I found her. I would tear apart Thalassar to get her back in my grasp. She may have been upset with me, but she was *mine.* My love. My life. She was the very water I needed to breathe and survive.

I would haul her back screaming and crying if I had to, but we *would* work it out. We would fix our problems. And we *would* be together.

If it was the last thing I did.

Odele burst through the room, startling both Elias and I. We looked sharply at her and I got up, worry weighing in my stomach as I saw her heaving and gagging over her palm.

"What's the matter?" I asked quickly. "Were you poisoned?" Gods, no. Not poison again. If she'd been poisoned, I had no idea how I'd handle that. I wasn't a doctor. I wouldn't be able to heal her.

"No—" She heaved, gagged. "Not… poison…"

I went over to her, placing my hand on the small of her back. Where she'd seemed like such an extravagant impossibility before, it was strange how touching her now was as easy and as comfortable as breathing. "Deep breaths," I suggested calmly. "Breathe through the nose."

Of course, she didn't take my advice. She gagged, shook me off, and turned to glare at me. "How many are you involved with?" she accused.

"What are you talking about?"

She started forward, her body moving jerkily as if she really had been poisoned. She went over to the foodstuffs and trays she'd left that morning. She picked up the pitcher of frothy tea, and poured it into her mouth. I watched with astonishment as she gargled her mouth and spat it back into the pitcher.

"Gods, that was disgusting…" She shivered. "Just thinking about it makes me—" Odele broke off, gagging. "Oh gods, I need to brush my teeth." She started to turn around.

"What is going on?" I asked.

A suffering sigh escaped her. "We're busted, cousin. Your Lizard Prince discovered me and—" She gagged. "Oh, gods, I can't even say it out loud, it's so vile." She disappeared into the bathing room. The next few moments were filled with the sounds of Odele vigorously brushing her teeth.

I shared an exasperated look with Elias, both of us clearly unsure as to what exactly was happening. She emerged a moment later, swiping at her mouth. If she scrubbed it hard enough, there was a possibility it would fall off.

I opened my mouth to comment on her odd behavior when the door to the room suddenly burst open and Kai swam through, closing it behind him.

There was a look of absolute panic on his face, a panic that surely I was now mirroring. The prince froze, looking back and forth between Odele and I with obvious astonishment, while all I wanted to do was screech at Odele for foolishly leaving the door unlocked.

"Maisie…" he breathed, looking towards me.

Odele scoffed. "Oh, *now* you can tell us apart, Lizard Prince? You should have used your beastly instincts to figure that out earlier before you kissed me!" She slapped a hand over her mouth, whether it was because she wanted to take the words back, or because she wanted to gag I wasn't sure.

Not when shock rippled through me entirely.

"You—you *kissed* her?" My heart thumped and cracked against my ribs. My chest lurched painfully, and my stomach roiled. Kai and Odele had kissed. I suddenly felt like I was far away, and everything that had suddenly been so close and in my grasp was unattainable once more.

"I thought she was you!" Kai explained, eyes pleading mine.

"You can't tell them apart?" asked Elias. I could hear the smile in his voice, and it wasn't helping the situation. It felt like a blow to the stomach.

"I'm sorry, my gem!" Kai swam over and took my stiff fingers in his hands. "It was a momentary lapse in judgment. I was desperate to speak with you, and she was there and I thought…"

"Do you like her? Did you enjoy the kiss?" Elias asked mischievously.

Kai glared at the Black Blade, a threat swiping over his features. Elias laughed in reply.

"My gem…" Kai's fingers swept over my cheeks.

"Helloooo, is anyone listening to me?" Odele's voice broke through my haze of pain. We all turned to look at her, to find her *glaring*, and rather formidably. "I don't know what kind of sick, weird and twisted relationships you have, cousin, but please note that the kiss? It was the most disgusting thing I've had to go through in my life. It was worse than sleeping on mossy floors." She shuddered.

Kai's eyes narrowed on her, clearly offended. A moment later, they widened, and he turned to look at me inquiringly. "Cousin?" he echoed.

We all went suddenly still. I felt like ice had suddenly dribbled down the length of my back in slow, torturous movements. Kai obviously tried to process this information. *I* was trying to process it.

This secret knowledge was difficult to fathom myself, and now Kai knew. Could I bear to recount the events? No, I didn't think I could get through the story. My heart felt like it would suddenly burst into thousands of irreplaceable pieces despite Elias' earlier words of encouragement.

Silence stretched to impossible lengths as Kai stared between the three of us, obviously waiting for an explanation, for the truth. I couldn't look him in the eye, even as I felt his gaze fall heavily on me. I was too afraid I'd find an accusation in his eyes and I couldn't deal with that, atop everything else.

Thankfully, Odele spared me the hardship of explaining. She let out a dreadfully weary sigh. "Okay, look," she began. "Aunty Odessa had a baby with King Dorian of Kappur who was stolen from them, and that baby is her." I looked up to find Odele gesturing vigorously in my general direction. "So meet Odalaea Malabella Knoll, Princess of Thalassar, rightful heir to the throne of this kingdom and Kappur. If you have any questions, keep them to yourself, because she doesn't want to answer them, and frankly neither do I."

"Oh, gods." I dropped my face into my palms and tried taking deep, calming breaths. Her explanation had been short, terse if anything. Of course Kai would have questions. He'd be crazy not to have them. After a moment, I finally felt brave enough to look up at the prince.

He looked to be grappling with the information Odele had just given him.

"Don't hurt yourself trying to process it," she commented unkindly.

Kai ignored her and looked up at me. Our gazes held, my own was fearful, waiting for judgment, accusation, for *something.*

"You are the daughter of King Dorian and Princess Odessa?" he asked quietly.

I swallowed the lump in my throat. Daughter was a title I could not yet accept wholly as a part of myself. And yet when Kai asked, I found myself nodding, forcing down a swallow. "Yes," I replied, equally quiet.

"How long have you known?" His eyes flickered away from me and onto Elias for a brief second.

Odele let out an exasperated sound. "She's known for less than twenty-four hours, and the Black Blade has known for an hour. Are you done? Because I'm bored. This *whoooole* conversation is boring."

I opened my mouth to comment on what she thought would make the day more interesting? Explosives?

I never got the chance, though.

Because a few quick knocks sounded on the door, and we all turned to glance at it with horror as it opened, and a moment later, Captain Saber swam through.

"I sent the guards away," he commented, almost distractedly, and froze.

My heart would surely cease beating now, I thought. There was no way I could continue living. Not when Captain Saber's gaze settled slowly, ever so slowly, like the workings of a recording, over each one of us. Me. Elias. Kai.

And finally, Odele.

His mouth dropped open, rendering him speechless momentarily, before a strangled word tore from his throat like a gasp of pain.

"Odele."

Tiberius

Surely this was the working of my own overactive imagination. Surely this was some sort of spectral shadow, some sort of recording.

Surely this wasn't *real.*

"Odele." The word tore from my throat without meaning to. She was here. The Princess of Thalassar was here, alive, in this room.

I had long given up the idea that I'd ever see her again. I never imagined our reunion. All I could imagine was the hope and relief I would feel once she was back home in this palace. How we would go back to our normal, regular routine. How my feelings would finally settle into the stillness that her absence had obliterated.

Looking at her now, I felt none of what I thought I'd feel coarse through me.

I felt only a sense of dread and confusion, as it tore out of me like the last striking of a blade set to kill. Like the soundlessness of a bomb exploding on a battlefield before chaos erupted into a cacophony of confusion, blood, and death.

A small part of me wanted to reach out and touch her, grasp her at the shoulder to make sure this was all real, that my mind wasn't playing some cruel, ironic trick on me. I didn't dare take a stroke forward.

I feared I'd throttle her if I did.

"You're alive…" My eyes couldn't seem to tear away from her figure. I should look away. My eyes should find Maisie's, I should be giving her a smile of reassurance. One that said, *All is well. I am here.* But Odele was hypnotizing, keeping me focused.

"Of course I'm alive, Tiberius, don't be ridiculous." Nothing about her had changed. Not her voice, not the impetuous way in which she answered, she was the same.

I cringed. How had I never realized before the venom in her words, the terrible, terrible way she looked at me?

"Where have you been?" I threw the words out like the accusation that they were. "Everyone has been worried about you. I—" I broke off, all too aware of everyone staring at me. Of the Black Blade's amusing glances drilling between my shoulder blades. I could practically hear his own accusations and mocking laughter in my mind even though the room was silent.

I reeled in my emotions, tightening everything on a steel hook and pulled them, tucking them tightly into my heart. My shock could wait a moment, and my anger could wait even longer.

Right now, I wanted answers.

"Why are you *back*?" I demanded tightly.

Odele's eyebrows rose in amusement. "Well," she pointed out sarcastically, "this *is* my house. And honestly, that isn't the warm welcoming I was expecting from you." She smiled, the type of smile that used to make my heart thump wildly and my palms itch with a burning need to touch her.

I tightened my hands into fists and whirled away from her to look at Maisie.

And for the briefest of moments, I caught a glimpse of *something* in her eyes. Of that confidence she'd displayed being suddenly demolished into broken little pieces, like a conch shell crumbling to dust. As she caught me looking at her, I could see the struggle it took to rebuild that structure, around her soul and around her heart.

And I couldn't help but feel like I was on the outside looking in, and that with the return of the Princess of Thalassar, Maisie would undoubtedly lock me out.

For good.

I COULDN'T HELP BUT feel like I was on the outside looking in, watching desperately from a barred window in a high tower as the captain was reunited with his first love. As he looked at her with shock and admiration, his hands curled into fists at his sides, almost as if he were holding back from reaching out to her. From touching her, to assure himself that this was real.

It shouldn't have been such a grand shock. After all, we all assumed the princess would come back eventually. I was just fulfilling her role for the briefest of moments. But I'd gotten so caught up in it, that I'd fallen for the façade. I'd fallen for those in her life that were never really meant to be in mine.

Watching Captain Saber take Odele in was a sharp reminder that we never truly belonged together in the first place.

I'd merely been her replacement.

"Explain," the captain demanded coolly. I could make out the strain in his voice, the difficulty he was having at keeping everything rigidly contained. Maybe all he wanted to do was break down and grasp for her. Hold her. Love her fully, fervently, like he never could with me.

My heart broke, and I took comfort in the fact that Odele did not love him back, but my guilt at the emotion was immediate. His suffering shouldn't be comforting. I'd known this whole time who he really cared about, and it shouldn't bother me now, whether Odele returned his feelings or not.

"Ugh, do I have to explain *everything*?" Odele complained. "Fine, but only one more time, so listen up. Maisie is my long lost cousin. Her real name is Odalaea Malabella Knoll, and she's the heir to the Thalassarin and Kappurin thrones. Got it?"

After hearing the story so many times, my heart should have been numb to the repetitive news. It wasn't.

Captain Saber's eyes widened to impossible fractions. He looked even more surprised at that news than he did at Odele's presence, honestly.

Why wouldn't he be surprised?

I was a mess.

"If Maisie is heir to the throne… then that means…"

"Thalassar is hers. She can stop the war and marry Kai and do whatever else she wants," Odele interrupted the captain's musings.

My whole body tensed at her words. "Thalassar isn't mine," I choked out. "Because I don't *want it.*" How many times did I have to tell her? I wasn't a royal. I didn't want her life.

Elias' warm hand touched my lower back, steadying my emotions and me. I drew on his strength.

Odele looked at me with exasperation. "Odalaea," she began arrogantly. "We have the proof. Your claim to the throne is irrefutable. It's yours, you just have to take it back."

I snorted humorlessly. "And how do you propose we do that?"

There was silence afterwards. I looked from face to face. Odele, who I could tell was mulling it over in her mind, trying to come up with a plan. Captain Saber, his gaze never once straying from her. Elias, who was staring at me with lazy concern in his dark gaze, and Kai, who was chewing ferociously at his bottom lip.

"That's what I thought," I said with finality. "There is no way to fix this, except for you to take the throne you're meant to take, Odele." I pressed my hands into my tail as I leaned forward, conveying with my eyes the decision I'd finally taken. I would not take the throne. She would. It was hers. She was the princess the kingdom knew. I was just a baby stolen from my mother's arms.

"But it's rightfully *yours,* cousin. I won't steal it from you."

"It's not stealing if it was never really mine in the first place," I pointed out. "Keep it. Because even if I wanted the throne, there's no way I could keep it. No way I'd be accepted."

"Actually…" I turned abruptly at Kai's slow interruption. His brown eyes were shining through with a blue that I recognized as the mischief of his dragon entity. "Perhaps there *is* a way."

Odele's eyes shone at the prospect of a plan. Lazily, she dropped herself onto the bed, looking quite graceful as she did it. She sat up straight, and placed her hands in her lap as she smiled at the prince. "Do tell," she ordered casually, as casually as if she were ringing for tea.

"The wedding…"

I sucked in a breath. No. Not this again.

"The wedding…" Odele pursed her lips. "What about the wedding?"

"You'll be eighteen in two weeks," Kai commented.

"Aww, you remembered my birthday."

Kai ignored her and continued, “We are to be married the day of. The queen wanted to postpone it because we fell behind schedule when you ‘fell ill’.” He used water quotes mockingly. “I convinced her not to.” He smiled almost triumphantly.

Odele snorted at the expression. “Don’t look too smug, Lizard Prince. If she acquiesced, it’s likely because she has a plan.”

Kai’s smile didn’t die. He just looked at her with eyes that seemed to burn for a challenge. “Which is why we will have to counter with a plan of our own. Maisie is the first-born heir; let her marry me in your stead. Let her sign her given name upon the marriage documents. Let her be crowned, and once it’s done, we expose Circe for the usurper she is.”

Odele opened her mouth, closed it again, searching for a flaw in his plan. “What if she tries to kill Maisie before the coronation?”

Captain Saber tensed. “I will not let that happen,” he hissed venomously.

I startled at the tone.

Odele looked at him curiously. “Well, it’s quite a possibility that she’ll do it. Perhaps that’s why she accepted your proposal, because she doesn’t plan on keeping Maisie alive.”

“Then we protect her,” Kai suggested. “I set my guards on her.”

“I will protect her,” Captain Saber added.

“Very well, then we can play the proof at the wedding, the recording showing Aunty Odessa and King Dorian getting married. We’ll tell all the guests the truth.” She clapped excitedly.

“My father has likely already sent my mer here to celebrate. We will have dragons and Draconians here to help secure her safety when the truth unfolds.”

“The queen will get thrown into the dungeons for the murders, Kai and Maisie will be married, you’ll stop a war and rule Thalassar *and* Kappur. It’s perfect.” Odele was smiling widely at the plan and then turned to look at me. In fact, they were all staring at me, as if waiting for some sort of reply.

My mind was whirling with their words, trying to take it all in, process the plans they were making.

"But Kai is *your* betrothed, Odele," I argued weakly.

Odele waved my words off with the fanning of her hand. "I don't want him. Besides, you two obviously have a thing for each other. I'm happy to take a stroke aside for your happiness, cousin."

My eyes narrowed suspiciously. "Why?"

She looked shocked I'd even asked. "Well, these beautiful possibilities, this palace, everything was stolen from you. I'm just trying to give it back."

My temper rose, flared like the blinding light of sun rays. I pushed myself up from the bed, glaring at her, glaring at all of them. "I don't *want* it, Odele. How many times are you going to push this on me?"

Odele's perfect demeanor crumbled into annoyance. "As many times as necessary. Until you accept who you are and what belongs to you."

My nails curled painfully into my palms until I felt a cold sting. "You are taking *my* life in your own hands. *All of you.* Floating around deciding what my future should be, what I should do, and who I should marry." I saw Kai flinch at those words. "You all *get* to decide these things because you're so used to everyone bowing to your every whim and wish without asking if it's what they truly want. That alone is why I cannot accept this role of a royal. Because that is not me, so no," I snarled. "I don't want it, Odele. I don't want your throne, or your crown, or you betrothed." My heart shattered as I admitted those words, but I pushed through, glad when my vision blurred with tears so I might not see the expression on their faces. "I don't want *any* of this."

Before I could give them the opportunity to speak, I bolted, swiping at my eyes as I swam past them and out of the bedroom, into the halls.

Taking nothing but my broken heart and loneliness with me.

I GOT UP FROM my place, staring at the spot Maisie had vacated, feeling the echoes of her hollowness flow through me as well.

None of them understood. How could these royals and rich mer ever understand the burdens she carried, the burdens *we* carried? It was such an easy thing for them to snap their fingers and expect obedience. Expect their every wish to be granted, to take control of another's life.

"Stop pushing it," I said darkly, dangerously. The threat unveiled from my eyes and settled over them. They'd hurt her, and Maisie was a part of me, so intricately woven into the very fibers of my soul that what she felt, I did too.

"I am going after her," Kai declared, ignoring me. He got up and swam after Maisie, letting the door click into place behind him.

I turned my glare to Odele. More the fool she was for not trembling, but taking in the full force of it. "If she doesn't want it, don't force it on her."

Odele frowned and pursed her lips. "It doesn't matter what she wants, *criminal.* She is a princess. This is her life now."

"Her life is whatever she wants it to be, and the more you insist, the more she will push you away. Give her time."

"We don't have time," Odele snapped impatiently. "This needs to be done *now.*"

My eyes narrowed upon her, much like they did when gauging secrets and sniffing out lies. I could practically hear her every anxious thought that she so desperately wanted to keep hidden. But I tucked those secrets away without ever asking her for them, without even elaborating on them. They'd all come to the light soon enough.

I looked over to Captain Saber to find him watching Odele. He'd watched her throughout the majority of the exchange, his eyes wide with disbelief. For a moment, my gaze was so penetrating, the force of it seemed to curl around him tightly. He turned from Odele to glare at me.

I smirked. "Remember who you belong to, Captain," I reminded him, just before I turned away and slipped through the tapestry.

Because she swam blindly, knocking herself into walls and onto vases, she left a trail in her wake, one that was all too easy to follow.

I found her, finally, still and unmoving in the hall of portraits, staring almost angrily at one in particular. The one of Princess Odessa Malabella Sanitorum, her mother.

I stopped beside her silently, watching her expression, staring from the portrait to her face.

She looked breathtakingly similar to Odele, and that hadn't meant a thing to me before. After all, the ocean was a vast, vast place. Surely every mer had someone out there who looked like them. But this made sense. It explained so much.

She had the elegant arch in her neck, the same one as Princess Odessa, and her coloring was that of the Malabella lineage, purple-blue hair and tail, pink tones of skin. Her eyes seemed wholly her own. Or maybe those were her father's or some Kappurin ancestor's. Features pulled from both royal lines to make up the mer that I loved.

I pressed my hand lightly to her arm. "Would it truly be so bad to be a royal?"

Laughter trickled softly from her throat, and I could tell sheaa didn't mean it with humor but with bitterness. She turned to me and tears flowed freely from her eyes, rising like shining little clouds above her head. She looked so lost. And it broke my heart.

"Yes," she whispered. "Yes, it would be."

"Why?" I demanded. "Why is the idea so repulsive to you?"

"Because!" she shouted. "Because *this* is what it means to be royalty." She started forward and jerked the sleeves of my kimono up my arms, yanking my palms face down. Her fingers slid over my forearms, and the ridges of thin scars there. The scars my own father had given me. "It means cruelty and death. It's a whip coming down on hands for answering a question wrong. It's war. It's the lives of mer in inexperienced hands." She pushed me away, almost as if with disgust. "I don't want that, Kai."

I let the sleeves slide back to my wrists. "It's not just cruelty, my gem. It's so much more." I took a stroke forward, grabbing her wrist to pull her to me until our bodies touched. Until I felt every curve and angle breathing against me, until I felt the thumping of her heart like the second rhythm of my own. With one hand, I held her and with the other, I pressed it against her chest. "This is what being a royal means." I pressed my hand tighter against her chest, right against her thumping heart. "It's for the love of the mer, and the love they have for you. It is heart and determination. It is sensitivity and caring. It is *you*."

She stilled, black eyes trained on mine. She wanted to believe me, wanted to grasp onto those words like a lifeline. And I could see the precise moment when it all sank. She yanked away from me, shaking her head back and forth. "It's not," she whispered.

Those two words shattered my heart entirely. "It's not?" I repeated quietly. "Then is our shared love not enough to convince you? Is my love for you so awful that it prevents you from wanting to marry me?"

"You know that's not it." Her words came out weak and unconvincing.

"Then what is it?" I demanded, causing her to flinch. "What is it about?"

She paused, and I had cause to wonder if it was about anything at all. If she truly had qualms about the whole thing, or why she even had to stop and think on it. At this moment, I didn't understand anything. I didn't understand *her.*

"It just would have been nice to have been *asked*," she admitted quietly. Before I could comment on it, she was shaking her head back and forth and glaring at me once more. "The problem is, you're a royal."

"So are you!"

"No. I mean, you're a royal at heart. You didn't bother asking me, you just *expected* me to marry you, without talking to me first, because you're used to everyone obeying. I don't want that from you or from this life."

I ran a hand through my hair, stopping when I realized it was tied up. I dropped it again. "If that's not who you want to be, then don't be that mer. I'll admit, to be a royal sometimes means giving up a part of yourself for the mer, doing what you don't want to do for their safety and protection. Isn't that what you're doing already? You care about the mer, and they care about you. No one is saying you have to be like Odele or like me. Just be you. Caring, kind, and beautiful."

A sob burst past her lips, and her shoulders began racking up and down. "What if he doesn't *want* me?" She gestured at herself, in her imperfect entirety, taking extra effort to gesture at the left side of her tail, where I knew her torn fin was.

"He will want you," I said fiercely. It was all I could think to say, words I prayed to the Great Dragon would be proven true, because if they turned out not to be, I'd kill the King of Kappur for hurting my mate.

"How do you know?" she demanded angrily.

I pulled her into my arms and held her there, pressing her face into my chest. I let her sobs rack through me, felt her heartbreak like it was my own. Inside, my dragon roared at her pain. I pressed a comforting kiss against the top of her head. "He's tried to tear apart all of Thalassar to find you, my gem. He will want you. *He will.*"

She pulled away slightly to look up at me. She sniffled. "Kai," she whispered. Her words were an invitation to take the pain away with a ferocity that almost crippled me.

I bent down, more than willing to gift her with this, perhaps the only thing I could, when around the corner, a body appeared, stilled, and stared.

Maisie gave a small jolt of fear and turned to look at the merman there.

Staring.

I wondered how long the Iolish mer had been there. What he'd heard. One look into those knowing, eerie silver eyes told me all I needed to know.

He'd heard every bit of our conversation.

"Val," Maisie murmured nervously.

He looked between us, gaze gauging, assessing like a predator would its prey. There was no mistaking the threat there. A threat that passed over neither of our heads when the side of his lip twitched into the semblance of a smirk.

"Good evening," he murmured, his voice like black ice, before he swiftly swept past us.

Maisie's face was white with horror. "He heard us."

He had. It had been obvious in his expression, the expression similar to a two-legger gloating upon catching game. And we were the fish on his hook.

"What are we going to do?" Maisie looked to me for guidance to fix this. I'd nearly ruined everything else for her, including our relationship. I'd almost pushed my mate away because of my arrogance. The least I could do was fix this.

Determined, I bent and took her lips in a ferocious kiss that left her breathless. All too soon, I was forced to pull away, even as she reached for more.

"Go to your room, my gem," I ordered gently, yet firmly. "I will sort this out."

I half expected an argument, but she sighed and nodded. Before she left, she pressed her hand warmly against my arm, like an offering of peace between us, as if our relationship hadn't just shifted into something more. Boundaries had been tested, threatened the balance of the love we shared. I could only hope that our honesty strengthened it, helped us love deeper, wholly.

She turned from me, and I watched her go briefly before I whirled and swam to catch up with the Iolish.

He swam at a sedated pace, with all the stance of a mer who had nothing to worry about. He tensed when I swam up to him, and I noticed his hand skim over the pommel of his sword.

I decided to do aside with niceties. "You heard," I accused without preamble.

He didn't break his stance. Didn't slow, or hasten. I took in his cool demeanor. The merman looked every bit a warrior. He was fairly tall, taller than even me, with a wide expanse of muscle. He looked like a block of ice, and his silver eyes were eerie, with something absolutely vicious in those depths.

"Perhaps," he answered coolly. "It did not make sense at first, but I understand it now. Why she is so different from what we heard of her." There was a smile in his voice, even if his lips were forming a thin, serious line.

A hot wave of rage swept through me, causing me to give free reign to the dragon inside. It reared up, spreading its massive wings. I could feel the change take over me in an instant. Nails lengthened to talons, scales hardening, pupils splitting, eyes changing. Everything about me was suddenly menacing.

But the Iolish did not quiver, foolish mer.

"You will tell no one," I growled, my voice low and guttural. I'd do whatever it took to protect my mate and her secrets. Even if I had to leave this one bloody in the waters. "You will speak to no one about what you heard or saw."

The Iolish stopped and turned abruptly to me, silver eyes blazing like starlight. "I do not respond to threats. So you will do well to hold your tongue."

I smiled, a formidable twist of my lips that was mocking, and knowing. "Perhaps not, but if you share her secrets then I will be forced to share yours."

He did tense then, fingers tightening around the hilt of his sword of steel and ice. His eyes narrowed, as if to say, *I don't know what you mean.*

I smiled cruelly. "You Iolish may frown upon mingling with the rest of the kingdoms, and you may close yourselves off, but you are not as secretive as you think." Daringly, I lifted a talon up and traced it down the length of his smooth cheek. He kept still, as still as a block of ice. "You thought I wouldn't know? We are neighbors, after all."

He did knock my hand away then, without fear, yet with impatience. He had assumed a battle-ready stance, but I had no desire to fight him. All I wanted was assurance, assurance that he would not tell our secrets. In exchange, I would not tell his.

"I assume you are keeping your secrets for a reason, just like we are keeping ours."

The Iolish growled. "What do you want?" he demanded.

"Your silence is all I seek."

"Then you have it."

He held his arm out to me. A Iolish tradition, to seal deals with a hard shake. I clasped my arm in his, gripping his forearm while he gripped mine. We shook tightly, brusquely, and then pulled away.

"So it is done," he murmured.

I smiled. "So it is."

"WHY ARE YOU HERE?" I could not contain the words any longer. It had been merely a few seconds after the Black Blade had disappeared through the tapestry before they had slipped out. They'd been on the tip of my tongue the entire time I'd watched the exchange.

I felt the vast space of the room pressing in on us, all too aware that Princess Odele and I were alone. I should have gone after Maisie, but Kai had done that. I should have spoken to Elias, but he had left. And now I was face to face with the mer I'd been searching for, and the anger slowly bubbling inside me was rising.

She looked at me with arrogance in her dark eyes. Unchanged. She was still a beauty, and she still acted as though the world was hers, and all who inhabited it should bow before her. Maisie had been right about that. About who she was.

"I already told you why," Odele replied with exasperation. "I'm here to give my cousin her rightful place." She smiled, and I could see it for what it really was. Venomous. She got up and fluttered about the room, hands passing over pastries on trays, picking them up and setting them back down again. I could only observe, and recognize her movements for the nervous gestures they were.

"It seems rather convenient that you came back just a few weeks before your birthday."

She sighed and dropped a pastry. It thumped to the floor and bounced slowly. She turned to me, her every movement sinuous and inviting. Her eyebrow arched, her head cocked to the side as she studied me, observing and taking in pieces of me, much like the Black Blade collected secrets.

Except her glances affected me no longer.

Slowly, she sauntered over, swaying her hips in seductive movements that went ignored. When we were face to face, close enough to touch, she lifted a hand and ran a sharp nail down the side of my cheek. "You don't seem so happy to see me, Captain," she purred. "I thought you'd miss me most of all." Her fingers stroked across my skin. "*Didn't* you miss me?" She was slowly rising up so that our faces were level, so that our eyes met, and I could stare into those copper depths.

Copper depths that had me wishing for the polished glow of obsidian instead.

"Why are you here, Odele?" I repeated tightly.

"I told you—"

"I don't believe you."

Why would I, when all she knew how to do was lie? When that was all she'd ever done to everyone? What made this time any different? A liar then, a liar now.

"Oh, silly captain." She rose higher, leaned in, until our lips were but a breath away. "Wouldn't you rather kiss me instead of talk?"

I growled and pushed her away, slamming her body into the wall. She gasped out with shock at the action. I should have been shocked myself, but the feeling didn't register. In my anger, I was blind. I pressed my forearm against her throat, keeping her pinned and at my mercy.

"You're a liar, Odele," I accused vehemently. "They don't know you well enough to see it, but I do. You're lying about why you came back here, and I want to know why."

She squirmed against me, her nails clawing at my arm, pulling at the sleeve of my jacket. "What do you think you're doing, Tiberius?" she demanded angrily.

I pressed tighter against her throat and then eased my grip, leaving her gasping and clawing at me. "Why are you here?"

"I told you! I want my cousin to have what was stolen from her!"

"You expect me to believe you'd be that selfless?" I pressed tighter, closing her waterway. It was like a demon had taken over me, and I wasn't even a Draconian to claim that it was a separate being deep inside me. This anger, this rage directed at her was wholly my own, brought on by the fear of a threat against the mer I loved. "I know you, Odele. You haven't done a selfless act a day in your life. Tell me the truth." I eased my grip, but she didn't reply. She glared, her eyes tiny arrows that bounded off my body. I didn't care what or who she was. "Did you come back to harm Maisie? Are you merely befriending her as a trap, and when her back is turned will you help the queen stick a knife in it?"

It was the only explanation I could muster as to why she'd returned, to get rid of Maisie, the true heir to the throne, and then to get rid of the queen as well.

So that she could rule, without the weight of usurpers looming over her.

I'd not let that happen.

"I'm sworn to protect you," I whispered darkly. "It was a vow I did not take lightly. But I swear to the gods, Odele, if you are here to harm Maisie, I'll kill you myself."

"Gods, lay off, will you?" She clawed at me. "I'm not going to kill my cousin, what's wrong with you?"

"Then tell me the truth!"

"Alright!" she shouted. "Alright, I'll tell you the truth, just get off of me." I hesitated a moment before I pushed off of her. She glared and rubbed her neck with long, delicate fingers. "Ugh, you'll leave a bruise."

I frowned. "Talk."

She blew out a breath. "Fine. I didn't come back purely because I want Odalaea to take the throne, though that is a big part of it."

Snorting, I crossed my arms against my chest. "Why should I believe that you're willing to give up the throne?"

She kept rubbing at her throat. "You obviously don't know me all that well, *Captain*." She shook her head back and forth. "I don't want the throne, that much is true. When I learned I had a legitimate cousin out there with an irrefutable claim to the throne, I had to find her. Because I don't want it."

I blinked, not quite believing that last bit. "You'd give up this lavish life?"

"Gods, no. But I would give up the throne. I'd give up ruling, because it's a hassle. I don't want to take care of mer I don't care about. How boring. And I don't want to marry that lizard prince, either. I'll leave the boring stuff to Odalaea. She can have the kingdom she wants to save, the prince she loves, and I can have my freedom and just live here richly and happily."

Gods.

This, I could believe. Even when she presumed to be selfless, it was all only in her best interests. She hadn't done any of this because she actually cared about Maisie, because she cared that she had the life she'd missed out on. She'd only done it because she didn't want the responsibilities that being a royal implied.

How had I ever imagined her to be vulnerable and sweet beneath this façade, if it was even a façade at all? Disgust with myself tremored through me. I'd been fooled by her pretty face too many times, by the imaginings of my own treacherous mind, hoping it'd find something that hadn't been there at all.

So much time wasted on this mer who cared, as always, about nothing and no one but herself. And I doubted she ever would.

"Do you believe me now, Captain?"

I did, but I didn't say it.

"You're willing to harm Maisie to get what you want, aren't you?" Despite them being cousins. Despite the way Maisie so obviously already cared for her.

"I'll do whatever it takes, Captain."

I reached for the front of her dress and tugged, pulling her close, so close that she could see the threat in my eyes. So she could see that I meant it. "Harm Maisie," I whispered, "and I'll kill you."

Odele smiled and reached up to pat the side of my cheek mockingly. "Oh, Captain. I'd always wondered what it would take to get you to go against me. Now I know."

I was going to reply, something vicious and cruel, when the door to the room opened. The small gasp that reached my ears was enough to tell me that Maisie had once again found her way back.

THEY WERE PRESSED SO closely together, it was almost as if they belonged there. Her hand cupped his cheek, and she was smiling up at him in a way that pressurized my chest and made me feel like I was being pulled into darkness by an anchor.

Upon seeing me, Odele pulled away from Captain Saber, and cast me a guilty glance. Her face reddened and I could only imagine what had been going on before I'd interrupted. She'd told me she didn't have feelings for him, but maybe that had been a lie.

She pulled away from him, darting around his body. Odele came up to me and took my hands in hers. It felt like a burn.

"I'll let you two talk, okay? Clear the waters." Before I could reply, she was gone.

With inert slowness, the captain finally turned to me. "Maisie," he breathed.

I closed my eyes against his voice, because it pained me. It pained me to hear such gentleness in his voice, knowing it was feigned. Wondering, perhaps, if he was using it on me because I looked like her.

"You must be glad she's back," I blurted, opening my eyes to take him in. He had paused mid-stroke, as if he'd meant to come towards me, but stopped as soon as I'd said those treacherous words. My heart was beating rapidly against my chest, like the fluttering of a swarm of shrimp, tickling my insides. I willed myself to calm down. "You spent all this time looking for her, it must be a relief to see she's alive and well."

"Maisie…"

"It's kind of funny, isn't it? She was right under our noses this entire time. You searched all of Thalassar for her and couldn't find her, only because she hadn't left at all." I chuckled, though I was sure he could hear there wasn't any amusement, any gaiety in the action. My hands fluttered around nervously. "I understand if you don't believe the news she brought with her. I can hardly believe it myself. I mean, me? A princess? It seems like some kind of a cruel joke."

"Maisie…"

"I lived in poverty my whole life. I can't imagine my childhood any different than what it was. I mean, imagine me in a palace…"

"Maisie…" The captain swam forward until we were close. So close, I could feel the warmth of his body searing onto my skin, singeing me yet making me tremble.

And even if he wasn't mine, even if he had never been mine, I still longed for his touch like a two-legger beyond the deathly crush of waves craved air and sunlight. My body was hyper aware of him. I was aware of the steady breath in his chest, the way it rose and fell gently. Of the determined set of his shoulders and tilt of his chin, and the way lashes as bright as sunlight framed blue eyes, like rays against a cloudless blue sky.

His fingers skimmed across the skirts of my outfit, and I shivered, feeling his touch as if he'd laid his hand upon my bare skin.

"You shouldn't touch me," I breathed, the words coming out a heavy rasp. My tongue felt anchored, and it was very hard to swallow. "I-it's not wise. Odele could come back at any moment, and she'd be furious if she saw me with you… like this…"

Captain Saber froze and he looked down at me with hard eyes. His jaw worked almost angrily. "Is that what you think was happening?" he finally asked tightly.

It was a struggle, but I managed a weak nod. "I know what she means to you…"

"Nothing," he growled. "Odele means *nothing* to me."

His words were what I'd always longed to hear from him, and yet, I couldn't believe the truth behind them. "That's not true," I argued. "You—you love her. You never stopped."

"I never stopped, because I never truly loved her in the first place. Gods, Maisie—" He broke off to grip my skirts and pull me forward, his movements rough but not at all painful. My body collided against his, and a moment later, his hands were on my waist, palms scorching through the material. "I *don't* love her. I am in love with *you.*"

I stammered through the myriad of emotions that suddenly assaulted me, not quite grasping a single one of them, until I finally could. Disbelief. I grappled for it and tugged it to me impossibly close. I placed my hands on his arms, both to steady myself from the shock and to ready myself to push him away.

"No, you don't," I whispered.

His expression hardened, as if those hadn't quite been the words he'd expected to come out of my mouth. "You presume to know how I feel."

"I don't presume. I *know*. You don't love me. You can't. What's more, you *think* you love me because I look like Odele." Even pressed close together, I could feel the sudden chasm of space stretching before us, so vast and empty. If we plunged into it, I feared we'd never come back up again. "This…" I gestured at us both with a jerk of my chin. "…it was always about Odele. You loved her for so long, that when she disappeared and I took her place, you didn't know what to feel, or who to feel it for. I've always been second to her in your heart, an adversary for your affections. But she's back, and I won't get in the way of it."

I started to push him away, but his hands held me tightly, pulling me back into place as if he meant to fit me against him.

"This whole time we've been together, you thought it was because I was using you to replace her?" His voice sounded so betrayed, the guilt pierced through me like the tip of a spear. "On the balcony… and even after…" His fingers tightened into my waist. "I am many things, Maisie, but I am not such a cad to stoop so low."

"You said yourself, Captain, that you thought to make me into her."

"That was before! Before I truly knew you. Before I started *loving* you. If there is one thing your arrival taught me, it was what it truly means to care. To feel this, what I stupidly thought I felt before. To realize finally the line between a fantasy I created and the reality of this. I love *you*, Maisie, because you are smart and kind, because you listen. Because you are mischievous and exasperating, and because you make me smile. But most of all, I love you because you are wholly, entirely, and irrevocably *yourself*. You are not a consolation prize. You are not a replacement. Her arrival did nothing but solidify my feelings towards you. *What* do I have to do to prove to you that I am yours? Wholly, entirely, and irrevocably, I am *yours*."

I took in a shuddering, unstable breath. My throat tightened, yet I still managed to choke out, "Captain…"

"Believe me," he begged, pleaded. His eyes shone with the glossiness of unshed tears. And then, Captain Saber did what I never pictured him doing. His body slid down mine. He dropped at his tail. And he bowed before me. "Please," he whispered, burying his face into my stomach. "Believe me."

I was too stunned to reply. Captain Saber, the mer who was used to giving orders, to listening to nothing and no one but the crown, who had promised to make me *beg,* was bowing at my tail. Like I was royalty.

Like I was his everything.

Something inside me shattered in a maelstrom of emotion.

His grip at my waist was tight, and I could see the now rapid rise and fall of his shoulders as he breathed unsteadily. His forehead was buried in my stomach, almost as if he were too afraid to look up and see a rejection he no doubt thought was coming.

I dug my fingers into his short hair, nails scraping his scalp. He trembled, his body vibrating my own.

I sighed. "I believe you," I decided.

Slowly, he looked up, blinking at me with disbelief.

"I believe you."

He dropped his forehead to my stomach and murmured, "Thank the gods." His hands snaked to the back of my dress, digging into the skirts before running up my spine. He looked up at me again, and this time, his expression was so easy to read, so filled with desire that my breath caught in the back of my throat.

My fingers loosened in his hair, sliding down to his face to cup his cheeks. I made sure he could read my own expression just as clearly. The desire mirrored there, the desire that had suddenly raked through me without restraint.

"Say it again," I whispered a hoarse demand.

"I love you."

I crashed my lips down onto his. The force of it was as strong and bright as a bolt of lightning. Sensations splintered through me, tearing me apart in fragments. I gasped against his mouth as his hands tore at the back of my dress, demanding, pleading.

I pulled him closer, our bodies melding together, and finally it felt like they belonged, like we belonged. It was warmth, it was the clash of a storm.

His arms snaked around my waist, and in one strong, deft move, he was lifting me up through the water, and twirling around, all while keeping his lips locked tightly against mine. He only broke away for a moment, and that was to place me softly against the cushions of the bed.

His body loomed over mine, though not in an intimidating stance. He looked desperate, elated. When the soft tendrils of anemones climbed up the side of the bed to caress his scales, he pushed them away with impatience before bending down and kissing me once more.

Hotly. Thoroughly.

I felt this second kiss straight down to my core. I felt it to the very tips of my fins, and I couldn't help but to curl them under him and relish in the sensation of his own tail curling around mine, keeping me pinned to the bed.

Then he was pulling away from me. My lips gave a cry of protest that quickly turned to a moan as his mouth traveled down the length of my neck, to the pulse at my throat, to my collarbone, stopping just above the valley of my breasts.

"I love you," he murmured against my skin.

I shuddered in his arms.

He must have liked my response, because I felt his lips pull into a smile against my skin. "I love you," he whispered again. The words became a reassurance as much as the molten heat of lava that had me trembling for more with each passing breath.

"I love you."

His fingers hooked to the insides of my bodice.

"I love you."

He pressed fervent kisses down the valley of my décolletage as he yanked the dress down.

"I love you."

He admired the corset pushing my breasts up to his view for merely a moment. Hooking his fingers into the material, he gave a sharp tug, pulling a breast free to his ministrations, to his tongue. The first rasp of teeth had me crying out, pressed the back of my hand against my mouth and biting down on the skin to avoid making too much noise.

The sensation was over all too quickly. The captain—Tiberius, he was Tiberius now—pulled me up so we were sitting, facing each other. He didn't give me much of a moment to take him in before he turned me around, so that my back was to him. Still, I nearly jumped out of my skin when his fingers touched my shoulders. Smooth movements slipped the sleeves of the gown down. He bent forward and pressed a kiss where his fingers had been.

The next thing I knew, he was making quick work of divesting me of the dress, slipping the top down to my waist; I had to work to slip it from my tail. Then his fingers were at my back, unlacing the corset. Instant relief found me, helping me breathe again. His fingers were quick with the lacings, yet it still felt like there were leagues left of the ribbon to unhinge.

I cursed Odele and her frivolity.

After odious waiting, the corset and shift were finally free, and I tugged it off hurriedly, discarding it off to the side and turning to face him, fingers already pushing aside his lapels. He chuckled slightly, but helped me remove his jacket. When we reached the immaculate tunic underneath, I tugged it upwards, yanking it off his body.

Until there was nothing between us at all.

His eyes flared to life at the sight of me, and my cheeks flushed at the sudden exposure, at the way his gaze raked over me. I wanted to cross my arms over my chest. I hadn't ever really felt this exposed before. The lights in the room were bright, and every bit of me was on display. From the flush over my pink skin, to the pathetic flapping of my torn fin.

"I love you." Tiberius tore my insecurities away with those three words.

Yes, it wouldn't do good to let my insecurities best me now. After all, I wasn't the only one with a scar. We reached for each other at the same moment. My fingers went to his hips, touching the rigid scar raised over immaculate, unblemished skin. His own hands grabbed me by the shoulders, his tight grip easing to slide down the contours of my body.

He left no part of me untouched. Fingers slid up and down my spine, across my shoulder blades and back to my collarbone, down my breasts where he paused to torture my nipples to peaks. I arched into his ministrations, gasping at the sensations he pulled from me, slowly and thoroughly. Like he meant to savor every single inch of me. No matter how imperfect or impossible.

And I meant to give back to him in equal measure.

I wrapped my arms around his shoulders, pulling myself closer to the warmth of his body, sliding myself down until I felt the rigid hardness against my core. It slid against me, slick and hard, pressing against that spot of sensitivity that had me tearing my mouth from his and gasping, groaning. Wanting more.

"Please," I whispered against the crook of his neck. I was drunk on my own desire in a way that felt impossible.

Tiberius' fingers slid up the arch of my neck, where he took my chin. Gripping it lightly, he tipped my face up so that I was staring into the radiance of his eyes. "We've only just started." He looked amused but no less affected than I was.

"I know," I groaned. "But… I need…" I couldn't quite say what I needed. Not when he knew. Not without my face brightening to an array of colors.

"Then let me look at you." His grip on my chin tightened, thumb pressing circles around my cheek. A move that was comforting, and arousing at once. "I want to watch you while I enter you. I want to see you come."

His words sent a thrill fragmenting through me, a thrill that was followed by the vicious gasp that tore from my throat as he thrust into me in one. Delicious. Move.

He began to thrust. Not the hurried, angry thrusts like our time on the balcony. This was different. It was slow and torturous. It was a promise, a question, and an answer. He slid out, the tip of him teasing my entrance before going back in, taking me to the hilt. I felt him deep inside me, pulsating and large.

My eyelids fluttered closed.

Just like that, the sensations stopped.

"Don't," he ordered. My eyes opened. There was chastisement in his gaze, and my cheeks flushed in question. "Don't close your eyes," he said. "I want to see you, and I want you to see me." He moved against me slowly, his length pulling a cry from me. "That's it," he praised. "I want to see every glorious inch of you. I want to hear your cries and smile knowing I elicited them."

Oh. My.

My face flushed, but I found myself biting my lip with nerves.

This was most definitely different from before. It was more passionate. It wasn't just some tryst in the shadowed corners of the balcony. Now that I thought about it, at the time, he hadn't looked at me, not like this. And he hadn't savored me, either.

And I wanted to savor this.

Him.

I bent down and kissed his lips. When I pulled away, he was smiling.

And then he thrust.

A slow movement of his hips against mine, he held me, his hands sliding over my body, leaving no inch unexplored. I touched him back with equal fervor until my hands finally settled on his shoulders, nails digging into his skin.

All the while we stared. I couldn't break away. His gaze was captivating, hypnotizing. He kept me locked there, watching the flare of blue as he moved against me. I bit my lip in an ineffectual attempt to keep from crying out, but it did not work.

Eventually, the gasps and moans poured from me. I threw my head back as I felt the pressure build deep inside me. My eyes closed involuntarily and…

He stopped his movements.

The sensation faded.

"Open your eyes, Maisie," he whispered. "I want to see you."

So I did. Even as he rode me through that vicious rogue wave with his slow, sensuous movements, and I screamed as tremors racked through my body, even as he followed the wave after me, pumping in and shuddering against me, we did not look away.

Odele

When had palace life become so boring?

To be honest, it had always been boring. Such a vast place and I was hardly ever allowed out of it. I'd never visited anywhere beyond the confines of my own kingdom. Being closed in had led me to the royal library in the first place, a place that, against my better nature, had become my sought after sanctuary.

But even now, I couldn't seem to bring myself to venture there. I'd read and listened to everything, so it didn't sound appealing.

I sighed, a long suffering sound that was unbidden and unattractive. I was just so *bored*. This was why I didn't want the responsibility of being queen. To be shut in the kingdom of Thalassar forever?

I think not.

There were places I wanted to see before I withered away and died an old mer. Sights I'd only heard about but could never dream of.

The kraken sculpture and libraries in the kingdom of Brague.

The lush forestation of Kappur.

The vicious Great Dragon of Draconi—even if I did despise the Lizard Prince, I could still have a fondness for the sights of his kingdom.

The vast abyss of Ventlair.

The orca breeding grounds in Iol.

Even to the dangerous waters of the Uncharted, where vicious, ugly and savage mer dwelled. Where mer were rumored to have ventured and never come back alive.

As "future queen" I was to be locked in a prison of propriety in Thalassarin standards, to never see what I wanted, when I wanted, how I wanted.

I'd die before I let that happen. I'd die before I became queen. Odalaea would be put on that throne, if it were the last thing I did. Then, I'd finally be free to do as I wished, plunge into the royal coffers, take money and travel. Take money and live richly, anywhere but in this suffocating palace, with its terrible decor and even worse memories…

"Princess!"

Speaking of…

I tried not to cringe as I turned and found Percival, my stepmother's sluggy-looking advisor, swim hurriedly towards me. It was too late now to pretend as if I hadn't seen him, though I suppose I could have. I despised the mer, and it was all too obvious he despised me as well, if the way he was glaring at me with disapproval was of any indication.

"Princess, a word." He stopped before me, appearing slightly out of breath, though composing in his posture.

He disgusted me down to my very core.

"Say your word and be done with it then, as I have a great many things to see to," I snapped impatiently.

Percival looked at me, appearing to be taken aback momentarily at my words. "I—"

"Really. You have the usage of merely one word and you decide to say 'I'? How incredibly wasteful." I looked him over. "And yet so incredibly you."

He emitted a shocked gasp. "Princess!" Oh, how he sounded perfectly scandalized.

How perfect. Now I could leave.

I started to swim away, and the sleazy mer did something I'd make sure he'd regret later.

He grabbed my arm.

"We must prepare you for the wedding ceremony. You must be schooled on etiquette and customs of both Thalassar and Draconi!"

I yanked my arm away, keeping the perfect demeanor of composure. He would see nothing but the perfect picture of an immaculate princess. Beneath my façade, I was seething, feeling his touch on my arm long after his fingers had vacated the spot, like a burn, a brand.

I'd never show him how much he unnerved me. How much I truly despise him. Percival would never see to what extent my hate went. It was, after all, his fault the backs of my hands were as hard as a workmer's. How I hardly had any feeling in them anymore because of his constant punishments.

Punishments that he'd been delivering since I was a child.

"No," I said coolly, confidently. "We will not."

His fists tightened, likely on the invisible strap of leather.

I could almost feel the pain on my hands. Even if my feeling was gone, I *remembered* the pain of it. That was terrible enough.

"We *must*," he urged. "There is a schedule we must keep."

I looked around for some sort of escape ploy I could use to get away from him. Leaving my room had been a bad idea, but I'd had no other choice. I hadn't wanted to be in the middle of whatever sick love games my cousin had going on with Tiberius.

As if being with the Lizard Prince wasn't bad enough, she went after a commoner, and a stiff one at that. I mean, the Black Blade was even worse than commoner filth, but at least he was a king in his own right, even if it was of ill repute. At least he had *money.*

But there was no one around to save me from this situation, nothing but a flock of servants averting their cowardly gazes as they swept their sponges across vases and picture frames. And then my gaze landed on a merman swimming leisurely about the halls and winking at the mermaids as he passed.

This merman was obviously of rich make. He was wearing what looked like thick draperies of velvet—*rich,* of course—lined with thick fur that hung down to hide any evidence of his tail. By the gods, wasn't he scorching in that get up? Never mind that, I told myself, as I took him in further. He wore a belt and scabbard, from which hung a sword that appeared to have been carved from ice, the pommel bearing the symbol of an orca. Hm, Iolish then. My eyes raked over his face for my final assessment of his usefulness. He was blond, rather, his hair was white-yellow, and wisps of long curls that swept over light brown skin and pale lashes. Lashes that framed eyes as blue as jagged chips of ice.

He would do fine.

The moment he came towards us, he stopped to gift me with a bow that would have been proper had I not sensed the mocking in the way he purred, "Princess."

"I have plans of my own, you see," I hurriedly told Percival. "See, I promised our Iolish visitor I'd gift him with a proper tour of the palace." I made an absentminded yet elegant gesture in the Iolish's general direction. "So you see, I have my own schedule. Such a shame I'll have to miss such a stimulating lesson on smelly reptilian mating dances."

Percival opened his mouth to argue, but before he could say a thing, I grabbed the Iolish stranger by the arm and tugged him away, past Percival and rounding the corner until the merman was out of sight. Even then, I did not stop. Taking various twists and turns about the palace, until I finally deemed it safe, with enough distance between me and the advisor.

I took a breath, releasing the Iolish's arm. Immediately, he leaned against the nearest wall, propping a shoulder up against it to stare down at me with mocking eyes.

I straightened and glared at him. "Pray tell, what are you still doing here?" I demanded, shooing him away with a wave of fingers. "You've served your usefulness. Leave."

An irritatingly perfect eyebrow rose, and his full lips quirked into a half smile. "I don't think I will."

He stared at me challengingly. All it did was make me scoff and tear my gaze away. "Whatever. Loiter around if you must, but I'm leaving."

"What about the tour you promised me?" he demanded good-naturedly. I despised the good-natured. They always seemed to be hiding something.

My eyes narrowed on him. "As I'm sure even your tiny Iolish brain can comprehend, that was a lie."

He blinked at my words, and then threw his head back with a bark of laughter. I chastised myself for being momentarily distracted by the arch of his throat, and the way he laughed in a way that seemed so sincere, and according to my treacherous thoughts, *pretty*. Ugh. I had to leave. Now.

I started to turn away from him, but for the second time within a few minutes, the Iolish grabbed my arm, right over the spot where Percival had touched me. And as if by magic, the warmth of his touch banished the other entirely, leaving no memory of that disgusting creature's handprint at all.

"Wait," he pleaded. "Stay, please."

I yanked my arm away, startled by the command, and unnerved when I felt the need to do what he asked. I glared. "You're no one to be giving me orders, Iolish."

His smile didn't even falter. He took my insults in stride, as if the words just bounded off of his body like a lumpy sea sponge. "I'm 'Iolish' now?

Please, you can still call me 'Ytgar.' Especially since I wanted to apologize to you for my earlier behavior."

I blinked. Ytgar. Gods. I knew who he was. Recognition of the name hit me like the collision of a hippocampus. Prince Ytgar Neves Isolde of Iol. And he was apologizing for his earlier behavior. I blinked again. What behavior?

He probably meant something offensive he'd said to my cousin.

I recalled then when she she'd come bursting into the room, face flushed.

"Who were you talking to?" I'd asked.

"Just Prince Ytgar of Iol and his whale trainer friend…"

I looked him up and down.

Some prince.

Okay, I'd not lie, he was attractive. But he smiled too much, as if he knew some massive joke no one else did and had no plans to share it. It was unnerving.

"I should have never insinuated we should… begin an affair… and on the eve of your wedding to Prince Kai."

My gods. He did *not.*

I startled, staring at him, searching for some sort of lie. There didn't appear to be any. Gods, he'd propositioned my cousin, the kelp.

I laughed, cold and cruelly, straight to his face.

"You and I?" I gestured back and forth between us. "You insult me by even imagining it, Princeling. As if I would ever stoop so low." I snorted. Really. The nerve.

He looked briefly offended. "Well, why would *this…*" He gestured between us. "…be so disgusting?"

I made a point to look at him, from head down to his hidden tail fin with disgust. "Need I give you a list of all your flaws? You live with yourself on a daily basis. Surely you know what you lack by now."

The hurt left his face quickly, replaced with swagger and arrogance. By gods, his moods seemed as interchangeable as two-legger weather.

"I'll have you know, I am considered a *catch* by the mer at home."

"Oh?" My own eyebrows rose in response. "By who? The blind and the deaf? Or perhaps the homeless."

Ytgar laughed again, and again my threat had no effect. It was growing quite irksome that nothing I said was absorbed. "By many, *many* mermaids back in Iol. I am quite popular."

I snorted. "I can't see why." And this bragging about the many, *many* mer who wanted him did nothing to impress me.

"No?" He took a stroke forward that I was sure he meant with swaggering arrogance and threat. I straightened my back just a bit more as he came impossibly close until I felt his arms brush against mine. Arrogant stick. As if he were entitled to share the same space as me. Yet for some maddening reason, I could not bring myself to move. And when he bent down so our faces were but an inch apart, my breath held. "Possibly," he whispered, "because I am an *excellent* kisser."

My heart thumped so loudly, I feared he'd hear it. Blast my body, being treacherous and infuriating. I swallowed, and glad my voice came out steady. "I doubt that."

His eyes glowed with the promise of a challenge. "You be the judge of that."And then Prince Ytgar Neves Isolde of Iol kissed me.

My hands gripped his shoulders, my mind screaming at me to push him away and punch him straight in the jaw. Even as my body melded closer to his, even as I opened my mouth to let him slip his tongue inside to tangle with mine, my fingers curled into his fur-lined coat to hold him tighter.

Treacherous, foolish body.

But, oh, his touch felt so good.

It was like I was drowning on air, and he was the only thing that could supply me with the water I needed to survive. A strange notion, to think of a kiss that way. To feel it so refreshing and down to the marrow in my bones, the blood in my system, the beating of my heart.

And like everything in my life, it lasted too short a time.

We pulled away slowly, and even if I was aware of the flush brightening my cheeks. Slowly, he pulled back from me, a gleam of triumph in his eyes.

Well, we couldn't have that, could we?

I willed the blush away and snorted.

"Apparently, our definitions of the word 'excellent' are quite different, indeed." That being said, I whirled and swam away.

"WHAT DO YOU THINK I should do?"

Tiberius stilled his fingers at the question for but a moment before resuming tracing lazy circles around my skin. He was silent for a while, so long, in fact that I thought I'd receive no answer. But when he spoke his voice was calm and reassuring. "What do you want to do?"

I groaned, burying my head into the crook where his arm met his shoulder. "I don't know," I confessed. "That's why I asked you." I sighed and turned, only regretting the loss of his touch as I did so, to look up at the canopy of buzzing jellies above us. "It would be infinitely easier if someone just told me what to do."

"You know you wouldn't like that." I could hear the smirk in his voice.

"You're right, I wouldn't. But, really, what should I do? Should I go along with this maddening plan to marry Kai and take back the kingdom?"

Tiberius sighed and pulled me close. He'd been doing a lot of that the past few minutes. Whenever we suddenly found distance between us, he'd pull me closer, as if he couldn't quite stand the concept of space. It was a warming feeling, to be in the circle of protection his arms provided.

"I won't pretend to understand every aspect of politics and hierarchy, but I do think you have a good chance of winning back your throne. If you are able to gather up enough evidence."

I turned up to him, eyebrows furrowing. "Is my existence not evidence enough?"

"Unfortunately, no. That conch is good evidence, as well as all the conches in the Royal Records room. The old mer who witnessed the event, maybe even King Dorian himself. Even the mortician…"

I slumped back down on his arm. "So I'll have to make a whole case for myself so that the royals can evaluate my claim?"

"Perhaps…" His voice trailed off in a way that was slightly suspicious. I wanted to ask what was on his mind when he answered before I even could. "You know, you could always go to Kappur instead. King Dorian… He's been searching for you for years. He will welcome you back with open arms and place you on the throne without a trial, if you don't want to go through everything else…"

I thought of the possibility he was placing before me. If I rose a claim and ascended the throne, it'd mean I'd reside over two kingdoms: Thalassar and Kappur—three, if I agreed to marry Kai and Draconi. Who wanted that much on their hands? That many kingdoms, triple the lives. Such a simple thing it would be to abandon Thalassar and go to Kappur, where I was wanted, where I wouldn't have to fight. Where I'd likely be accepted unconditionally.

Could I do that? Could I abandon the only home I've ever known to live at the root of all my problems? Kappur had waged war. Perhaps I understood the why, but would I really be comfortable living there, father or no?

"It's the safest thing to do," Tiberius went on. "To give up Thalassar and the scheming and the death threats for a home, a family." He pulled me closer still, as if we weren't close enough. "I just want you safe, Maisie. If anything were to happen to you, I—" He broke off, emotion filling his voice that tightened my stomach into knots. "If something happened to you, I would die."

The words seemed to gut me, waking me up to reality. This wasn't just some game Odele was playing. This was dangerous. Our mothers had already died for it, and we were being hunted just as viciously. If I risked this, I not only put myself in danger, but those around me. What was to stop the queen from finding out what I cared about the most, who I cared about the most and taking it from me?

I gripped Tiberius just a little tighter and pressed a kiss to the edge of his exposed collarbone. "I'll figure it out." I tried to sound reassuring, but all I felt inside was fear. "Eventually, I'll figure it out."

Tiberius pressed a kiss to the top of my head. "I know you will," he whispered. "And I don't want to rush you but I fear we don't have much time left."

We didn't have time.

I didn't have time.

The next few days were a whirlwater of activity. With Odele tucked safely away in the room, I was forced to go through the tedious routine that she should have been doing. Hauled from one end of the palace to the next, I was forced through hours of dress fittings with the seamstress, where we poured over her sketches of the wedding gown. It was a monstrosity in white with glittering diamonds and sapphires, to bring out the color of my skin and hair.

If I wasn't with her, I was being ushered into the royal coffers, where I was forced to undergo crown fittings, to see which fit me, and which one I'd wear for the wedding, and then the coronation. These things weren't just the dainty little tiaras the queen and Tiberius had fitted on me for last minute events. These were the real deal. Thick and heavy, I could hardly bear the weight of them.

There were lessons with Percival, which I dreaded the most. Not only because of the way he whacked my hands on occasion—despite Prince Kai's dire warning—but because he made me feel very much the fool. A servant playing princess, who knew nothing about royal etiquette or how to address the Emperor of Draconi or the Draconian Princesses. By the time lessons with him were done, the backs of my knuckles were always scratched and bleeding.

Preparing to ascend the throne was a lot more complicated than I ever could have imagined. There was so much it entailed… I thought it was 'receive the crown and be done', but apparently not. There was a whole series of swim strokes and words, preceded by the coronation and many days of celebration. I'd thank the queen for her assistance to Thalassar, promise to follow in our ancestors' swim strokes, and rule Thalassar with dignity.

Or something to that effect.

I kept getting it wrong.

"I vow, as the Tides, the Sea, the Stars, Moon, and Ocean as my witnesses—"

"No, no, no! Stop!" Percival shrieked at me with fury. "Foolish child, this is the sixth time you have messed up."

Fifth, but who was counting?

My face flushed brightly at his scrutiny. I shouldn't have cared what he thought, what any of them thought. But I had an audience, and I was sure they all thought the same thing. I was doomed to fail.

I was in the presence of Queen Circe and King Xristo, as they looked in on our rehearsal. Prince Kai was at my side, his advisors watching from a few strokes away with obvious disapproval. Servants had stopped to stare, and to make matters worse, Prince Ytgar and Val were also in attendance. Granted, they were at the very back of the room, but their presence was dominating, overpowering and intimidating.

"One more time," Percival ordered. "From the top. *'So the Seas, Tides, Stars, Moon, and Sun be my witnesses,'* is the line." He clapped his hands together, and Kai and I, once more, swam down the steps and took our places.

The nerves in my stomach were making me forgetful. I could hardly retain the information Percival was throwing at me for more than a few minutes at all. I'd thoroughly ruined practice, and wanted to do nothing more than cry.

Through the pain of my own helpless thoughts, I felt a firm squeeze on my hand. When I looked down, Kai's fingers were intertwined through my own. I tried to fight away the tears that glossed over my eyes as I looked up at him, and his soft smile.

"It's alright, my gem," he reassured.

Something about his patience made me feel worse, especially since I still wasn't sure if I could go through with his and Odele's plan. After they discussed it a few days ago, we'd all gone our separate ways and hadn't discussed it again. I didn't want to, even if I was aware that we were swimming out of time. The wedding was practically around the corner, and I had to decide what I wanted to do, and more importantly, who I wanted to be.

Slowly, I pulled my hand from his and turned back to face the front, not before seeing the brief look of hurt slash across his features. It wrenched my heart. I hadn't meant to hurt his feelings. The stress of everything was weighing heavily on me, and Kai had so many expectations. He was happy to be here doing this, to make wedding plans, picturing a future we would have.

I wanted to picture it, too.

But with the threat of death over us all, I couldn't bring myself to come to a decision.

The music started, breaking me out of my depressing thoughts. Trying to muster whatever was left over of my dignity, I started forward, in slow, easy strokes. I counted the seconds, and when I made it to the front, where two chairs had been arranged side by side—where Queen Circe and King Xristo would sit—I bowed deeply and stayed. I'd done this enough times already to expect the cramping in my fin. It'd been hurting for a while now. What I hadn't expected was the zing of pain to cripple me the moment I bent low.

I cried out softly, fanning it rapidly to no avail. It cramped up painfully, and I toppled to the side, hitting the ground with a painful thud.

How embarrassing.

There was a shift through the water, the sound of whispering and choked back laughter coming from Ytgar at the far end of the room. That was even worse. I started to get up, but then Prince Kai loomed over me and bent to help me up.

"Are you all right, my gem?" he asked with concern.

I grit my teeth. "Fine." Not entirely a lie as the pain was already ebbing. I just didn't think I'd be able to get up and continue right away.

"You stupid mer!" Percival came over to spit at me. "Can't you do anything right?"

"Obviously not," I muttered sarcastically, leaning onto Kai and hiding my face in the silk material of his salmon pink robes. Really, he looked lovely in them. I focused on that instead of on Percival's insults.

"Get up," he commanded impatiently. "Get up and do it *again*, and do it *right*. I'll not having you embarrassing this kingdom with your stupidity—"

Kai nearly dropped me in his swiftness to get up and grip Percival by the collar. I startled and looked up, watching as he shook the older mer so hard it looked like his head would rattle right off his neck.

"You will speak to the princess with respect, you blubbering slug."

Percival muttered noncommittal noises. The sight of him being jarred around brought me slight relief, a relief that shattered when the queen's voice rang out angrily. "Enough!"

Everyone froze and turned to look at her.

She had risen from her throne and was glaring in our direction with a vengeance that could have killed me had she possessed magic.

"Get out. All of you. Leave."

She was instantly obeyed by everyone, save myself, Kai, and Percival. Though, Kai did release her advisor and take a stroke back to try and pick me up.

"Leave her," the queen ordered before he could even take my hand.

Kai glared at her with disbelief. "But—"

"I said leave her. And you..." She turned angrily to Percival. "Get out of my sight as well."

"M-Majesty..."

"Now."

He bowed deeply before scuttling away. Kai left much more slowly, casting me discreet, reassuring glances. Once he was gone, and we were alone, the queen looked down at me and snorted.

"I confess, I never thought I'd see this task beyond you. You always like to pretend to be so intelligent." She kicked her tail lightly, the movement sending my skirts floating up to reveal my scarred fin. Panicked, I pulled them back down to cover me. "I do hope you won't make such grievous mistakes the day of, dearest daughter. It would be such a shame if the coronation were at all ruined by you falling to your death, thanks to this." She gestured at my fin again.

The threat didn't go unnoticed.

I had to pretend I *didn't* notice. "Forgive me for my slight, my queen." I hated this. I hated the pretending, acting as though everything was alright. As if the queen didn't make me sick to my stomach every time I saw her. *Murderer*, my mind screamed. She'd had my mother killed. And for that, every fiber in me despised her.

The queen smiled radiantly, and it transformed her whole face. "It's not your fault you weren't raised to know these things."

No. It's yours.

I bit my lip to avoid replying.

"You and your ilk cannot be expected to be refined in the finer arts like we are here at the palace, and you likely never will. Mer who hovel at the bottom hardly ever float to the top, if you understand my meaning."

I did, and it was demeaning. To think, this mer was ruling Thalassar. It was no wonder those of us at the bottom couldn't go places besides war. Because of mer like her at the top pushing us back down.

Then, the queen held her hand out to me. "Let me help you."

I stared at it with wide eyes for a moment before I quickly took it, and she hauled me up easily. Once off the floor, she snatched her hand back as if my touched burned, and I dusted off the back of my dress and fixed my skirts.

"Do not forget your place, little mer."

How could I forget my place when she never ceased to remind me? I knew very well what I was without having her there to whisper my worthlessness in my ears. I knew I was from Lagoona, a small pond that wasn't lavish in riches or the like, but it was *beautiful.* It was a place full of life and quirky mer. It was a place of sunlight and wind, even beneath the depths.

It's not your fault you weren't raised to know these things…

The queen's words had me wondering, moments after she dismissed me from her presence and I treaded slowly back to my room, what my life would have been like if my mother had never died. If I'd grown up in a palace, here or in Kappur, what would I be like? My fin cramped in response to the question. I'd be whole and plump, without a deformity, with a mother and father who loved me, and perhaps a few siblings.

But if I'd been raised in a palace instead, I'd not be who I was. Caring and compassionate. Perhaps I'd be like Odele, or maybe even like Queen Circe.

I would have certainly never met the Black Blade, or Josiah, or my grandmother. I wouldn't have fallen in love with Tiberius or Kai or Elias…

I wouldn't have been me.

But I would have been able to make a change… The moment the thought fluttered through my mind, another voice inside overpowered it by a thousand.

"Be the change you wish to see."

Josiah had said those words to me at Tides' Tavern. He'd been so thoroughly convinced at the time, even when I hadn't been, that I of all mer could make a change. That I could make my mark in the sea. At the time, I'd been so eager to believe him, so eager to believe that his words were the truth. Arriving at the palace had only broken me down. It had chipped me apart, little by little, until I'd become this. A mer who doubted her worth because of an injury and because, in my nerves, I failed at reciting a few lines.

But I wasn't that. I wasn't Odele. I wasn't just a poor mer with little education and a penchant for trouble. I was strong, I'd survived. I was caring, and kind, and the mer of Thalassar loved me. I had a father out there tearing kingdoms apart to find me.

I was a princess.

Odalaea Malabella Knoll.

Heir to the thrones of Thalassar and Kappur.

And I would not be afraid to take back what was mine.

That night, we all got together, because I'd finally made a decision. I finally knew what I wanted.

The queen wasn't going to sit back and watch as her throne was taken from her. Her increasing verbal threats the past few weeks had made it all but clear. She knew who I was, and thought I didn't belong. I didn't doubt that, come the day of, she would try to assassinate us both. She'd stop at nothing to keep her throne and the crown.

"I am going to take my throne back," I announced without preamble.

I was met with shocked stares.

Elias dropped his tail from the chair he had it perched up on and fumbled with his blade.

Kai, perched at the end of the bed, smiled almost shyly.

Tiberius looked at me gravely, his posture tensing.

Odele was the one to break the silence by bursting into a thunderous applause and twirling in circles. "I knew you'd see reason!"

It was Tiberius who asked, in a voice tight with an unknown emotion, "What made you change your mind?"

I sighed, placing my hands behind my back. "The queen did." They looked at me with even more confusion, so I explained, "She murdered my mother and my aunt. She tried to murder me. She's a tyrant who doesn't care about the suffering of others or the poverty in Thalassar. But I do. And I want to change it. I want to be queen." *I want to be the change I wish to see.*

"And an amazing queen you will be," Odele complimented with giddy excitement, swimming up to me to take my hands. Her smile was a radiant thing on her beautiful face. When she smiled genuinely, she looked almost younger. "You'll be perfect."

Emotion swelled tightly in my throat, but instead of giving in to it, I nodded my gratitude. "Thalassar deserves better. It deserves a ruler who cares about them. Not someone who doesn't want to see them advance. Not someone who will kill anyone who gets in the way of a happier future."

Odele nodded, almost knowingly. "And if there is one mer in the world who can give that to them, it's you." She gave my hands a tight squeeze. "I just know it." She pulled away, still smiling at me.

"Are you sure about this?" Tiberius asked with uncertainty. He looked like he was ready to strangle something or someone. I wasn't sure who.

I tilted my chin up. "Yes."

"Right, then." Elias sheathed his blade and hopped up from his chair, his mischievous smirk in place. "What do you want us to do?"

"Well…" My gaze passed over all of them, and my heart swelled to impossible sizes. I loved them. Every single one of them had a special place in my heart. I felt differently for each, and loved them all for different reasons. I no longer felt selfish for it, but empowered, and humbled that in my life, I'd gotten these mer who I cared about above all others, and they for me. This time, a small tear slipped out. "I want you all safe," I confessed. "Because I think the queen is going to try something nefarious at the wedding, and I'm afraid she's going to use you all to get to me. So if you all want to leave, and save yourselves, I will understand."

I waited the span of a few breaths that were slow and torturous.

Tiberius got up from his place and swam over to me, his height and breadth slightly imposing. He stopped before me, and bent to take my mouth in a scorching kiss. He pulled away, leaving me dizzy. "We will never leave you, Maisie. *Never.*"

Relief made me sag against him as the others murmured their agreements.

"So what do you need? What's the plan?" Elias asked with enthusiasm.

So I told them. Bits and pieces of what they'd already plotted, adding my own details to it. The mortician would be taken up to testify, as well as the old nurse. The conches would need to be protected until the day of the wedding, when we could out Queen Circe before her whole kingdom and the visiting allies.

We spent the next few hours together perfecting the plot, deciding who was going to do what, when, and how. Finally, when every detail was memorized, I bid everyone goodbye and watched them go, my heart suddenly weighing heavily in my chest.

Kai and Tiberius were the first to leave. Kai stopped and gave me a hug and a kiss, murmuring a fast and passionate 'I love you' in my ear. I nodded in response. When Tiberius came before me, his whole body vibrated with tension.

"I don't want to see you get hurt," he whispered gravely. "I don't think any of this is a good idea."

The sweet merman. I placed my hands against his chest and leaned up for a kiss. When I pulled away, I gave him the most genuine smile I could muster, and hoped it was convincing. "I'll be fine. Don't worry." Even if I didn't quite believe the words myself.

He looked inclined to argue, but I shooed him out and he reluctantly left. Once he was gone, I locked the door and turned to Elias as he made a move to slip behind the tapestry.

"Wait!"

He froze, eyebrow raised.

"Can you do me a favor?"

"You know you don't have to ask, little fish."

I smiled, knowing that would be his reply. "I need you to send out two messages for me with someone fast, someone you trust."

Obviously intrigued, he leaned against a wall. "Oh?"

"And afterwards, I need to meet with you somewhere. But it has to be a secret."

"You're doing the right thing, cousin." Odele gave me a small pat on the shoulders.

The action didn't reassure me.

I looked around the room, taking every detail in as if it were very well my last. I'd grown fond of the place, the place where I'd discovered royal secrets, where I'd battled death, where I fell in love and gave myself to them entirely. Where I learned the truth of who I am, and where I'd found a family.

Odele plopped herself onto the bed with a deep sigh of contentment. "After this is over, I want to travel. To Ventlair, or the great library of Brague. Or Iol, perhaps…" Her tone had gotten slightly wistful around the edges.

I couldn't bring myself to comment on it.

"Odele," I whispered, finally having memorized every crook of the room and saving it in a far corner of my mind. "Do you trust me?"

Odele looked at me sharply with her eyebrows raised. "Of course I do. You know that."

"Can I trust you with my secrets?"

She sat up straight, tucking a stray bit of hair behind her ear. "You kept mine, so of course I'll keep yours. "What's this about?"

I took a deep breath, and blurted. "I can't marry Kai."

She looked at me as if I'd grown an extra head. "What do you mean you can't?" she demanded, almost angrily.

I shook my head back and forth. "*I* can't. It has to be *you.*"

Her eyes narrowed. "Explain yourself."

So I did.

I AWOKE THE NEXT day to an empty space on the bed beside me, feeling sick to my stomach. I pressed my palm into the space, assuring myself it was true. The cushions were cold. Vast. Empty.

I sighed and got up, aware that the room felt suddenly much more empty without Odalaea to fill the spaces. Even if she'd only filled it with judgmental glares and disapproval, I still missed it.

A part of me suddenly hated her for this. For what she was forcing me to go through, but I pushed those emotions aside and got up to get ready for the day ahead of me.

It felt strange, to prepare to do something other than sneak around the palace. But do it I must.

After I got dressed for the day, I braced myself and swam out into the hall to meet with my gaggle of guards. Tiberius wasn't among them. Good. This would be difficult enough without him there. I straightened, tilting my chin up in a gesture of defiance I'd long since dominated.

"Take me to the queen," I commanded.

So they did.

My stepmother was every bit as regal as I remembered, even so early in the morning. Even I, with all the hatred I possessed solely for her, was impressed with how put together she seemed. She sat tall upon her coral and gold throne, stroking the arm of it almost menacingly. Her hair was coiled tightly upon her head, pulling her face into an equally tight expression. Her dress was simple, in colors of bright yellow and orange, the colors making her blinding. As if she wanted to deter the mer from looking her in the eye.

So I met her gaze straight on, the gaze of my mother's murderer. I was hardly able to spare a second glance to my father, seated quietly beside her. It hurt too much, the sight of him with her, a broken merman in the place of what he used to be. No, instead I looked to the mer responsible for his hardships, for mine. The one who had driven away everything I loved, any happiness I might have had.

"Mother," I greeted. "Good morning."

She glared at me without reservation. "What do you want, little mer?" she demanded. "I grow bored with your presence already."

Ah, I smiled. So she couldn't tell Odalaea and I apart.

I spread my hands wide, made my smile even wider. "Is that a proper greeting for your beloved stepdaughter? And here I thought I'd be welcomed back with hugs and tears after my long absence."

There was satisfaction in seeing her face suddenly pale, her lips forming into a thin line. Her eyes widened as she took me in, her gaze roaming down to my tail, where her eyes narrowed. As if she could see through my skirts to ascertain whether or not my fins were whole.

Whether I was who I said I was.

To ease her doubts, I hiked my skirts up scandalously to expose my fins, the wholeness of them. A moment later, I dropped them, and a gasp tore from my father's throat.

"Odele?"

I finally turned to look at my father, loathing to take my eyes off of the queen for even a moment. "Hello, daddy."

The king got up from his throne, his eyes wide with disbelief, as if he dared not hope I was real lest he find himself heartbroken all over again. The one thing I regretted about this whole thing was hurting him, for I loved him dearly.

He swam with uneven strokes towards me, his movements jerky and inelegant as he descended his dais and came before me, so close that we could touch. "Is it really you?" he pleaded.

"In the flesh, daddy."

With a cry, my father pulled me into a tight hug, an action that made me blink with surprise. I couldn't quite remember the last time he'd hugged me. I'd been a child, for sure. After the death of my mother, we'd grown apart, drifted in different directions of pain and coping until we hardly knew each other at all.

The queen's voice tore us apart. "Captain Saber!" she shrieked. I looked up at her, watching as she seemed to fall apart before my eyes like the crumbling dust of old stone. She frantically turned to a guard. "Bring Captain Saber here at once!"

The guard bowed and quickly swam away. When he did, the queen glared at me.

"Where have you been, you foolish child?"

My father put a protective hand over mine. "Perhaps we should wait—"

"No!" she shrieked at him. "Mind yourself, King, for you are not ruler here. I will know what your spoiled daughter has been doing, where she has been, and I will know it now."

My whole body tensed. I didn't like the way she was speaking to my father, the way she'd always spoken to him, as if he were somehow less than her.

"I will tell you everything, of course." I smiled venomously, as venomously as she taught me to be.

Just then, the doors opened, and I didn't need to look to know that it was Tiberius. He'd followed me so long, I recognized the loom of him like a shadow.

He stopped by my side, bowed to the queen, then to my father and I, keeping his face impassive. "You called for me, Majesty?"

The queen pointed an accusing finger in my direction. "Why did you not inform me that my stepdaughter had returned?" she accused.

Tiberius turned to look at me, and his eyes widened, his mouth dropped open when his eyes searched mine, obviously recognizing me for who I truly was. He hadn't known it would take this turn. None of us had. And I'd be the one to bear the bad news.

"He did not know." I smiled. "No one did. I only arrived last night."

The queen's nails dug into the arm of her throne. I saw bits of it crumble down to the floor. Her anger only fueled my own desire for vengeance. She turned to Tiberius and commanded him from between gritted teeth, "Go fetch me the other one."

Tiberius stilled, and with good reason. It's what we'd thought she'd try to do all along. Get us together… and kill us both.

"If by 'the other one' you mean that filthy Lagoona commoner you tried to replace me with, then she's not here."

"What do you mean she's not here?" the queen shouted.

An eyebrow rose high on my forehead as I let amusement flitter through the words of my reply. "Precisely that. She is gone. Left, in the middle of the night."

The queen rose then, straightening in her formidability to loom over us, her and the ostentatious crown of my mother, and my mother's mother before her. But I was not frightened, if that had been what she'd set out to make me feel.

"How did she leave the palace with no one taking notice? And who helped her leave?"

I shrugged a shoulder. "I let her go." When the queen's glare seemed to become a prominence on her features, I added with glee, "I hardly saw the need to keep her here since her purpose has been fulfilled."

"Where is she?"

"Gods if I know. I gave her a handful of coins and she left. My guess? Probably Brague. Or Ventlair. If we're lucky, Kappur."

"You insolent little—"

"Do not speak to my daughter that way," my father interrupted, a slow sign of rising rage over his features. It startled me, to hear him defend me so openly, so freely.

The queen sat back down on her throne. Her anger heating the waters, palpitating around us, making goosebumps rise over my skin. I fought back a shiver of weakness, trying not to let her affect me.

After a few tortured moments of silence, she finally spoke, her words coming out in a whoosh of breath. "Very well, then. It is done, and now we can proceed as originally planned." She looked me straight in the eyes. "You will marry Prince Kai. I trust you are here to stay and do your duties this time around?"

Like I had a choice?

"Of course."

"Good," she sneered. "Now get out and go do them."

"What's going on?" Tiberius hissed, so obviously fighting the urge to tug at my arm like an Uncharted savage.

"Not here," I replied. There were eyes everywhere, and it was hard to discern who we could even trust. Anyone of his trusted guards tailing after us could be in cohorts with my stepmother. I'd not risk our mission. *My* mission. "Find Kai," I ordered quietly, too worried to bother with any unsavory nicknames. This was too important.

And I needed to speak urgently with them both.

And prayed they could handle the truth of our betrayal.

They assembled in my room for a chat before the seamstress was to arrive for the final gown fitting. Dread coiled in my belly as I took a seat demurely before Tiberius and Kai. Both looked confused, and both looked eagerly around the room for Odalaea.

"You won't find her," I told them. "She's gone."

A breath of silence followed, one I could only interpret as disbelief. Nothing was doused in clarity yet, but soon they'd see. A part of me hated Odalaea for this. Usually, I didn't care who I hurt, because after all, nobody truly mattered to me. And while I didn't care for Tiberius or Kai, the news would be a blow to them, one I knew they'd not swim away from intact.

But they had to.

For the good of Thalassar, they had to.

"What do you mean she's gone?" Tiberius demanded impetuously. "Stop kidding around. This isn't funny, Odele."

"I'm not joking. Odalaea left. She's gone." And every moment of her absence killed me inside.

"Well, where did she go?" Kai asked, his voice a quiet calm that rose the flesh on my arms uncomfortably. There was a hidden danger in those depths, like the calm before the storm. Like the calm before a volcano erupted.

"I do not know. She did not tell me. She just left with Elias." I could still remember her parting words like a blow to the face. *'I can't marry Kai. It has to be you.'* I took a deep breath, and my throat tightened. I was not one to convey my emotions so openly, so I tried to push the sensations aside. Tried to tilt my head just a bit higher. "She said she doesn't want to be queen. That she's not suited for the role."

Kai's brown eyes flashed blue, giving me the desire to flinch. "You lie," he hissed.

My chin tilted even higher as my eyes narrowed. "She's the liar. She told us all what we wanted to hear last night and escaped with Elias. Neither of them looked back." My heart thundered, and my stomach lurched.

Captain Saber took me in, from head to tail fin. He'd find no lie, because there was none. Slowly, he let out a breath through his nose. "You're telling the truth," he whispered darkly.

"How is that possible?" Kai jerked back. He looked like he'd been punched in the gut, and was reeling from the pain. I'd felt the same way when she told me she was leaving.

"Did you even try to stop her?" Tiberius accused.

I glared at him. "Of course I did. She didn't listen. I don't want to be queen, either. I don't want to marry Kai, but we have no choice now. If we both disappear, the queen stays on the throne forever, and we can't let that happen."

Tiberius growled, a low rumble. "You expect me to believe you care?"

Tears welled in my eyes, but I pushed them away, piercing him with a glare. "I don't. But I promised her…"

'Promise me you'll do it. For our mothers, you must promise.'

So I had.

"It doesn't matter. She's gone now, and you are stuck with me. The plan is still on, but we will have to make do without Odalaea. Just because she isn't here doesn't mean her existence should be hidden any longer. My stepmother must be removed from the throne, and we will do it. Do you understand?"

In their shock, they couldn't do much but numbly nod.

Good.

I'd thought it'd be much harder to get them to agree.

"You both have jobs to do. Do them." As the words escaped my mouth, I realized just how much I sounded like my stepmother and felt the curdling pain deep inside me. If that wasn't proof enough that I didn't belong anywhere near the throne, then I didn't know what was.

But I promised Odalaea, on the graves of our mothers, that I would do this.

And it was a promise I dared not break.

Tiberius

THE PAIN OF IT all was almost crippling. But even if it hurt, even if I felt something inside me crumble, I kept my head high, determination the only thing willing me to continue. I didn't want to believe that Maisie had gone, that she'd just leave without a word. But she wasn't in the room and she wasn't in the cove.

My mind kept flashing back to the day before, searching for any signs I might have missed, anything that would have told me to expect this, but for the life of me, I couldn't seem to find that hint of her plot of betrayal.

Was everyone I loved destined to leave me? Every time I tried to open up, would they swim away? First Odele had left, and even if I hadn't truly loved her at all, the pain of her departure was very much real. And now Maisie was gone, and everything was worse.

Maisie was eternal.

Or so I'd thought.

The truth was, I didn't know what to think anymore, didn't know what I should feel besides catastrophic heartbreak that threatened to end me entirely. It was all I could to keep from falling apart, focusing on my duties. On getting rid of the queen I served and replacing her with the mer I thought I once loved.

Maybe if enough time went by, Maisie would return. Or maybe, she'd never been destined for this life at all. Maybe the pain of her leaving would ebb into a pang instead of this vicious throb.

And maybe, if I made enough excuses for her departure, eventually I'd believe one of them to be true, instead of thinking that maybe, Maisie never really loved me at all.

The dragon inside roared in fury and betrayal. It spit ice and lava. It raked its claws down my consciousness, demanding I relinquish control, so that it may tear all of Thalassar apart if only to get my mate back.

For that reason alone, I kept him tightly tethered.

There had to be some explanation for her departure, even if I didn't want to accept it to be true. Had I pushed her away with my insistence that we wed? Despite what she'd said last night, inside, had she been afraid? And could I really blame her?

We were so different. She came from a line of powerful royals and love, and I came from a line of hybrids. And like a beast, I'd been relentless in my conquest of her. Like a dragon, capturing a fish to play with it, tossing it from one clawed hand to the next, only to find it dead in its paws.

I should have been more careful with her. I should have listened and not forced my status and my love on her so viciously.

But, like Odele said, I was a beast.

A beast desperate for love.

Instead of getting the happy ending I longed for, I destroyed the future I'd dreamed of.

THE DAYS CLOSED IN on me, suffocating and demanding. Though I was frightened of what lay ahead, I dared show it to no one. I was back to the way things had been before. I had no allies, and I had no friends. Tiberius and Kai barely spoke to me unless it was necessary for the plan. They looked utterly destroyed, the both of them just trying to get through this wedding and usurping as quickly as possible. Perhaps we should have gotten together, the three of us, to share in our pain and abandonment.

But I was alone, and preferred it that way.

I'd not deny that Odalaea had left an ache in my chest. For a moment, I'd been so blinded with the prospect of family, of a true friend, that I'd forgotten to encase my heart in ice and steel to avoid this hurt. I thought, with her, it wouldn't have been necessary.

How wrong I was.

So, I threw myself into my duties with ease. Truly, I'd been trained for this my entire life, and if the mer in the palace suddenly found it odd that I was way better at this than my cousin who had pretended to be me, well, it wasn't that much of a surprise.

I'd ordered the seamstress to make me a new wedding gown. No different than the one she'd already tailored. Odalaea was taller than me, and slimmer, so her measurements would not fit. Altering the one she'd already made had felt like a betrayal of my own, somehow. Like I'd be wearing her skin, and that was just too morbid to contemplate, so a new dress had been made. My crowns had been picked out for the ceremony, practice had gone without a hitch, and soon, the palace was hosting new visitors.

We swam to the balcony the day the Draconians arrived. We watched as they paraded through the streets, making a show of arriving at the palace for our wedding. I tried to look unimpressed, but I could not deny that seeing dragons in the flesh was as frightening as it was breathtaking.

The beasts were massive creatures, bigger than any hippocampus I'd ever seen, as big as large orcas, *bigger*. I knew from my studies that dragons could stretch to the size of humpback whales, but the ones the Draconians had brought seemed tamer than the ones I'd heard about in conches.

Their skin looked leathery and sheer on the wide expanse of their claw tipped wings—wings that, according to conches, helped for easy gliding through the water. Their hides and scales looked as hard as diamonds and sparkled in different colors of blue, red, white, black, and even purple. Spikes ran down their spines like the jutting points of thick, threatening blades, and the many rows of sharp teeth were overwhelming in their gleam.

Leading the procession was a dragon the color of blue ice. It was a massive thing, with slim muscle and an elegance in the long arch of its neck, and the steadiness in its black eyes. It had four legs, with sharp, curved talons that it used to push through the Thalassarin waters. A long serpentine tail, barbed at the end, swished behind it. The wingspan on the creature was impressive and dangerous looking, elegant and vicious in equal measure.

I didn't even need to look into the longing elation in the eyes of Prince Kai for too long before I realized that this was the mount he boasted of.

Suddenly, I could very well picture him atop it. They both had a stillness about them that was matching, almost eerie.

There were more dragons of course, but none of them stood out as much as this one. Neither, really, did the warriors atop their own mounts. Draconian males and females shared in Kai's features of dark eyes and varying shades of skin tones ranging from white to a light brown. Some wore kimonos, others wore steel armor shaped like the overlapping scales of a dragon.

"I never thought a Draconian display could ever impress me," I murmured conspiratorially to Kai.

He cast me a sideways incredulous look when I spoke. Either because of the words, or because they were perhaps the first words I'd spoken in what felt like days. His lip merely twitched in response as he swept past me to go down and greet his mer as they swam up to the palace.

He greeted them in his own language, and I feigned indifference, even as I grasped the words. I'd always been desperate for a piece of the outside waters, and the fact that a bit of Draconian culture was here in Thalassar now, well, I was desperate to grab on to whatever knowledge I could.

"Impressive," a voice at my ear suddenly whispered.

I sighed with exaggerated exhaustion as I turned to look up at Prince Ytgar. His eyes weren't on me, but on the parade of Draconians dismounting and greeting their prince and his advisors with respect. One mermaid, with features similar to his, the angle of her sharp cheekbones, and color of her koi fish tail told me they were siblings, especially when she rushed to him and he wrapped his arms around her.

I cripplingly missed Odalaea.

"Of course, the orcas of Iol are much more impressive."

"Are they?" I asked with bored disinterest. My eyes were still on Kai, who was twirling the mer through the water and laughing merrily, despite being surrounded by dozens of royalty who would judge him for a display. It was the happiest I'd seen him in days.

"Of course," Ytgar replied. "Val can attest to that. Can't you, Val?"

"Yes."

I turned, my eyes narrowing on the merman I hadn't noticed before. And *how* had I not noticed him? The mer was massive, built as solidly as a block of ice. He put Tiberius to shame with all that muscle. His skin was brown, his straight hair silver and tied back. Eyes as silver as the glittering of diamonds or snow, found me and an involuntary shiver sluiced down my spine.

The merman—Val—bowed to me. "Princess," he acknowledged.

"What are you doing here?" I demanded with irritation. More because of my body's treacherous reaction to Val—who I now remembered to be a whale trainer—rather than their presence.

"We came to greet the Draconians. Perhaps rile them up with our sharp wit and humor."

"Riiiight." I rolled my eyes and turned back to watch Kai. He'd finally released the mermaid, and she was speaking to him rapidly, with quick gestures of her fingers and wrists through the water.

"You don't have to do it, you know," Ytgar whispered.

"Do what?" My eyebrow rose.

Ytgar smiled knowingly, though what this tiny-brained Iolish could know was a mystery to me. He leaned down, so close, *too* close it could have been construed as offensive to our visitors. His lips brushed the lobe of my ear, and I fought not to shiver. "You don't have to marry him," he whispered.

Behind him, Val warned darkly, "Ytgar…"

Val's warning went ignored. "You know you don't want to."

I turned my head, ever so slightly, that his lips grazed along the edge of my cheek, and when I looked into the ice blue of his eyes, I found them looking down at the space that separated our lips.

"What would you have me do instead?" I teased.

He almost seemed too distracted to answer that question. His tongue darted out to lick his lips, and for a moment, I almost felt the brush of the tip of his tongue against my bottom lip.

"Marry *me*."

My whole body went rigid at that. Those words, I hadn't been expecting them. I'd expected teasing, a joke, and banter. Not that.

"Ytgar," Val admonished darkly. "Leave her be."

And then Ytgar's lips twisted into a slow, mocking smile that made a flush shine across my cheeks. Oh. Oh gods, how embarrassing. He *had* been joking, and I'd taken his words seriously.

To save my dignity, I tossed my hair back, and looked him straight in the eye, my lip curling to the side in a mocking smile of my own, lest he see too deep. "How *cute*," I complimented sweetly. "To think I'd ever sully myself with the likes of you orcas."

Ytgar blinked. "Orcas?"

My lips pursed. "Isn't that what your ilk breed with up north? I've heard the stories, don't think I haven't." I turned away from him. "Dragons are much more suited to me than orcas. I mean, look." I gestured at Kai's dragon, who he was now greeting by running a hand down his snout. "Powerful, majestic. And orcas?" I turned to look at him with mocking, raised eyebrows. "Cold, smelly creatures."

"Smelly?" Ytgar echoed.

"Disgusting, really. As if you've been shoveling their waste all day. I'd sooner let a dragon eat me than lie with a mer who shovels orca feces."

I didn't contemplate the brief slash of hurt to cross his features, because I didn't care, and because I had to go greet the Draconians.

Even if the words he'd muttered had excited me, despite them being a joke, I couldn't think them over and wish, because I'd made my cousin a promise.

A promise I intended to keep.

The day of the wedding came.

The day I'd fulfill my promise and get Thalassar back.

I bathed quickly, and soon, servants were bustling into my rooms, bringing in the newest dress for the wedding. They set it on the bed beside the old dress, by Odalaea's. Fear suddenly gripped my gut as I looked at both garments. With difficulty, I pushed the sensation away and let myself be tended to by the servants.

They slipped the dress onto me, fixing the fluff of the skirts before sitting me before my vanity and brushing out my hair. Before they could begin parting the strands in an intricate braid, I stopped them.

"Leave it down," I ordered. They looked at me incredulously "No fancy braids. Today, I want simplicity." It almost hurt to utter those words. Since when did I not like ostentatious hairstyles? Today was different. And it didn't matter what they thought, anyway.

Once they finished dressing me, I shooed them out, my eyes straying to the dress and then to my shelf, where the conch, old and chipped, sat. I'd have to leave it here, but Tiberius would take it into the throne room after the wedding to expose my stepmother.

A sudden twist of nervousness spiraled through me. This had been all I'd hoped to accomplish when I'd discovered the truth so many months ago. Perhaps not in the way I'd envisioned it, but vengeance was so close, too close within my grasp that I feared, for the first time, that I'd ruin the plan entirely.

No.
I couldn't think that way.
I had to get through this.
I had to be strong.
Or else the whole plan could fall to pieces.

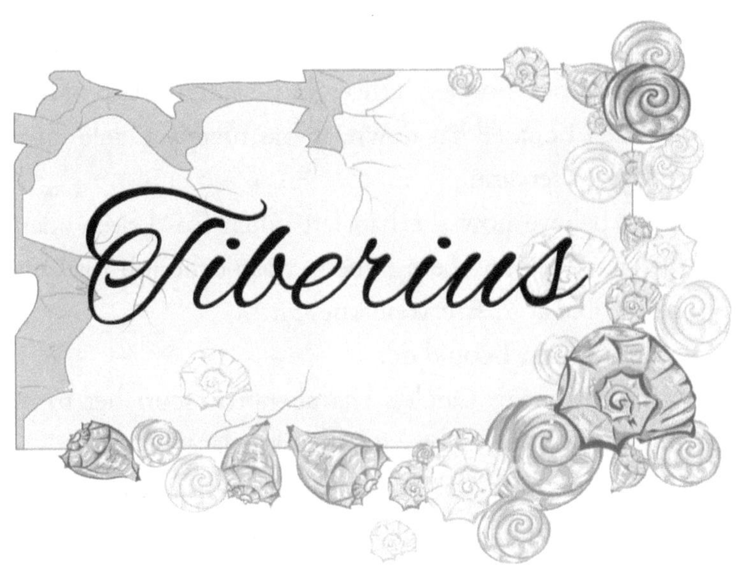

Tiberius

I'd never known nerves quite like I did on the day of the wedding. Probably because I was fervently working with Odele in a plot to usurp the throne and take down the queen I'd spent most of my life serving.

The reality of our actions hit me full force as I realized the implications of what this meant. If things went well, then Odele would take her throne unscathed. If things went terrible, we could find ourselves thrown to the dungeons or beheaded. Even worse, my family could suffer for my actions.

In my worry for Maisie, I'd agreed to help, to protect the love of my life no matter the consequences. But she'd left us. I didn't fully understand why, but maybe it was because of this, because she hadn't wanted us to get hurt. But we were continuing with the plan, and surely, we'd get hurt anyway.

Truth be told, I wasn't entirely sure what I was supposed to be feeling beneath the tight coiling of my stomach. The past few days had been nothing but a haze of emotion and confusion. I felt Maisie's loss like the loss of a limb. For a brief moment, I thought I'd catch a flash of her around a corner, but when I chased her down, it was merely Odele, sneering or yelling at some poor servant.

I still couldn't believe how she had left when she'd been adamant on taking the throne. We knew being queen wasn't the job for Odele. The mer would be terrible at it. Everyone knew it.

But there was nothing I could do.

So the day of, I went to Odele's chambers to escort her to the royal throne room, where the ceremony would take place.

The guards were on high alert today, just as I'd ordered them to be. We couldn't afford any attempts on the Princess' life, especially not today.

When Odele emerged from her room, she was dressed in a gown swathed in white, pinks, and blues. Her hair was in smooth, floating tendrils surrounding her face.

I couldn't help but feel like Maisie would have looked prettier by far. Yes, they looked alike, but Maisie had a different aura. It was in her smile and posture. She wasn't solemn or irritable. She was kind. She would have been smiling, instead of glaring.

"What are you staring at?" Odele demanded, breaking me out of my thoughts.

I ignored her snap and bowed deeply. "Are you ready, Your Majesty?"

She snorted and shrugged. "I suppose. It's not like I have a choice, do I?"

My lip twitched with an annoyance that I had to force back. "Then let us leave."

We swam through the halls, my eyes alert for any and all possible threats. Everything was quiet; it was eerie how quiet it was. I paused, cocking my head to the side, listening. Surely there had to be some noise, servants bustling around in the fray of the day. Not this… absolute silence.

I lifted my fist, and everyone stopped moving. Odele rammed into the back of a guard who swam before her, causing her to let out a sound of surprise and exasperation. "Oof." She righted herself, straightening out the tendrils of her hair. "Move aside, you big oaf." She pushed him, and in his surprise, he staggered and she swam around him.

"Princess," I warned, starting forward…

But then all hell broke loose.

Something exploded, though I couldn't be sure what. All I knew was that one moment, I was staring at Odele, and the next a bright light was blinding me. It encompassed the entire hallway like magic. Debris flew, vases cracked and exploded. Coral pelted us across our bodies, and in the fray, I kept screaming Odele's name but heard no reply.

My eyes burned in pain, and it felt like forever before I could finally open them. When I did, some of the guards were on the floor, groaning and rubbing at their eyelids. Others were up, blinking as rapidly as I was. A quick headcount told me everyone was well and accounted for.

Everyone except Odele.

"Princess!" I bellowed.

Her answering groan had me moving fast to find her.

The explosion had blasted her further down the hallway, where she'd hit a wall and was crumpled to the floor.

"Are you alright?" I asked her, reaching down to help her up.

"Do I look alright?" she snapped impatiently, swatting away my hand and getting up herself. She smoothed down her skirts, and fixed her hair. "What was that?"

"A light bomb, most likely. It doesn't do extensive damage, but it's a nuisance." I snapped my fingers and the guards immediately surrounded Odele, forming a protective circle around her. "Eyes alert!" I commanded.

"That bomb could have been a prank by the servants, or it could have been nefarious. Keep your eyes peeled."

"A prank?" Odele echoed incredulously. "What absolute bullshark. Find who did this!" she snapped at a nearby guard. "See to it they are punished for this! I could have broken my neck, and even worse, they could have ruined my dress!"

I pushed away the eye roll that threatened and placed my hand against her lower back. We started forward again, and I'd placed myself closer to Odele, to protect her and prevent her from bolting. She tensed at my nearness.

"Personal space," she grumbled unkindly and went ignored.

I didn't care what she complained about, not when her safety was at risk. The daft mermaid didn't even seem to be worried that the whole hall had exploded and blasted her back. She treated it more like a nuisance or an inconvenience at best. I'd never understand her and her way of thinking.

Even if she had no regard for her own safety, that didn't mean that I would take it lightly.

I had a duty to protect her, and I didn't mean to fail.

I KNEW THE MOMENT Odele swam into the royal throne room because the music started, marking the beginning of the ceremony. The guests in attendance floated up to demonstrate their respect for the princess and future leader of Thalassar.

I floated near the dais and thrones of Queen Circe and King Xristo, turning when she arrived. A space had been cleared for Odele to swim through, an aisle decorated in anemones and sea flowers, lava globes in varying colors of blue, pink, and purple.

The room was full of guards and guests. Captain Saber had strategically placed them near every window and exit, as well as near every important mer who had come from other kingdoms for the nuptials. Reporters had been allowed inside where they would broadcast the wedding through every one of the seven kingdoms. My marriage to Odele.

Dread curled in my stomach that I tried very hard to mask.

At the end of the aisle, Odele stopped and bent low, allowing Percival to place a crown on her head, the last crown that marked her as princess of the realm before she ascended the throne.

I barely took her in. I didn't want to even look at her. The dragon inside roared. This wasn't my mate, she wasn't Maisie, and I felt nothing for her. But Maisie was gone. She'd left me alone, abandoned Captain Saber and I to carry on without her. The dragon in me thrashed at this, fighting me every stroke of the way, so hard that I almost let slip my hold on it more than once. It didn't want Odele. It wanted Maisie. *I* wanted Maisie. But she was gone, and this was the sacrifice I'd been expected to make this whole time.

I'd just never expected it to hurt so much.

Percival swam down the aisle first, the slug wearing the mixed colors of Thalassar and Draconi to symbolize the union of the two nations. He took his spot on the dais before me and next to the Thalassarin priest, an old merman in older looking robes.

My eyes scanned the crowd assembled. As the wedding had been a hasty thing, there weren't thousands of guests in attendance, yet there were still quite a few important ones. Three of my sisters had traveled here to witness my wedding. They'd witness instead the end of the happiness I'd found with my mate. If I'd known it was to be such a fleeting thing, I would have never allowed myself to feel.

The thought felt treacherous as soon as it entered my mind, so I shoved it away and focused. Odele was swimming up the aisle now, her gait perfectly practiced, her expression somber, and her eyes downcast. When she finally made her way up to me, I took her hand in my own stiff one, and bowed lightly over it before guiding her to the table perched in between us, Percival and the priest. Atop it sat a marriage contract, with lines to sign our names, ink and quill, as well as my gift to her.

I released her hand and reached for the gift. The Exchange was a tradition dear to Draconi and happened when couples were married. The males gifted the females with a gift, and because I was a royal, mine was rare, beautiful. I only regretted it would be for Odele instead of the mer I'd truly meant it for.

The egg was big, the shell as thick as diamonds and the color of a moonstone. Ridges of scales bumped around it, digging into my palms from the nervous force in which I held it. I turned, and presented Odele with the dragon egg.

"In Draconi, a gift exchange is tradition," I explained, loud enough for her and the guests assembled to hear. "Among the royals, it is customary…" I placed the dragon egg in her outstretched palms. "When a dragon dies in battle and leaves behind an egg, it is up to us to care for it and nurture it until it hatches and can be released to its own kind. Let this be a symbol of our union, Draconi's acceptance of Thalassar, and of you, Princess."

I stared at the egg, at the way her fingers curled beneath its heavy weight. "Thank you," she whispered softly and turned to set it gently back on the table.

And then the ceremony began.

Music played, our vows were said; she with excellent precision and a soft, confident voice, and me rather stiffly. Strips of cloth in our kingdoms' colors were wrapped around our joined hands, blessed by the priest and declared legitimate. Once it was done, I bent over the page and signed my name quickly, not allowing my hand to tremble. I handed the quill to her, watched as she dipped it in the vial of ink and bent to sign her name. The large flourish of the O… and I had to look away. I couldn't bear to see my fate sealed so harshly.

When she finished, the priest blessed us one last time, and the table was moved a few strokes aside.

Now came time for Odele to ascend the throne. She would swim before her stepmother, recite her vows to Thalassar, and then the crown would be placed upon her head, and she'd take her place at the throne.

And our plan would begin.

But before Odele could swim up to continue in the rest of the ceremony, the doors to the royal throne room burst open. The sound was distracting and unplanned. We turned sharply to the noise, to see who would dare interrupt a sacred ceremony. A hush fell across the guests, followed by fevered whisperings.

And with good reason.

Because I recognized the merman floating there at the door. Not only because I'd seen him in conches and painted portraits, but because of those eyes. Rounded orbs as rare and as black as obsidian. Eyes that matched his daughter's like twin jewels.

King Dorian Knoll Genivus of Kappur.

Shock and outrage rang out through the assembled crowds, others merely whispered disbelief. I was frozen in shock myself as I took in the King of Kappur, as I took in Maisie's *father*. He was easily recognizable, though he wore no finery save for the golden crown perched on his brow. He wore a black riding habit, dark tunic and leather jacket, the hemmed ends floating down to his tail, the color of green and copper. His dark eyes contrasted the paleness of his skin and the light hue of his hair. A beard ran along his jaw. Not elaborate and decorated in jewels like King Xristo's, but a mere shadow forming in haste.

He swam into the royal throne room, flanked by guards both Kappurin and Thalassarin, and found himself an empty seat. His posture was stony, and he stared straight ahead without even twitching a brow.

The queen slowly got up from her throne, her face marked red with obvious fury. Even King Xristo looked taken aback by the arrival of their oldest enemy.

"How *dare* you show your face in my kingdom," the queen hissed.

Odele, who had been all too quiet up until now, turned and smiled at her stepmother. "Do not be angry or alarmed. King Dorian is my guest. I invited him." Shocked whispers broke through the guests; it even rippled through me. Odele turned to those present and smiled widely. "As Prince Kai exchanges the gift of acceptance to Thalassar, I thought I should do the same. As a new reign begins, I bring with it an offering of peace between nations." She gestured at King Dorian, who was stoic as he stared at her. "A new alliance with Kappur and Thalassar. And…" She clapped her hands, and Captain Saber swam forth, placing a table and a device to play recordings on top of it. When it was settled, he pulled out a conch, chipped and withered with age. My heart began thumping in my chest. "I offer you truth."

At her words, the captain placed the conch face down on the device and it started. Guests sat forward in their seats, eager and aching with curiosity. I knew what would play before the words even began.

"I, Princess Odessa Malabella Sanitorum, of the mer kingdom of Thalassar, hereby take and accept this mer as my husband, and promise to love and to cherish him, for the rest of my life…"

And then came the answering reply, that shattered everyone into a silence that was eerie.

"And I, Prince Dorian Knoll Genivus, of the mer kingdom of Kappur, hereby take this mer as my wife, and promise to love and to cherish her…"

I watched King Dorian's reaction. Saw the stony facade slip for but a moment into grievous pain. He'd loved her. He had truly, unconditionally loved her.

"Don't say that while we're being recorded!" Laughter flittered from the recording, just before the bubble burst into tiny golden specks.

Everyone was too awestruck to speak.

Until the queen finally broke the silence, "Odele, what have you done?" It was a voice rife with accusation. She turned to the guests, saw them wide-eyed and whispering with each other. "Ignore my daughter, she is filled with nerves and childish fantasies. Captain Saber, please escort the King of Kappur out of our palace so we can continue this ceremony undisturbed."

"I can assure you, I am not a child filled with fantasies. And neither am I your daughter." Odele turned to the crowd then, and something in her voice changed, it grew, confident and sure. "It is high time I introduced myself. I am Odalaea Malabella Knoll, daughter of Princess Odessa Malabella and King Dorian Knoll and heir to the throne of Thalassar."

Chaos erupted.

Everyone began speaking at once, shouting, whispering, the words became a cacophony inside my head. But I paid it no mind. How could I? I was staring so intently at Odele, my eyes narrowing. She turned to me, and for a brief moment, I caught a glimmer of her eyes. Eyes I had refused to look into since the ceremony had started. Had I looked, had I willed myself to see, I would have realized the truth.

Odele wasn't Odele at all.

It was Maisie.

My heart did not stop thundering against my ribcage. Shouts of anger, confusion, and acceptance rang all around. As for me, I was staring at my father, at King Dorian, and he was staring at me. His expression had been stony, but at my announcement, his whole face changed, sharp features staring with painful longing up at me. But I didn't let myself fall into emotion as I took him in.

"Odele, stop this nonsense at once!" The queen came down from her throne, pushing aside a shocked Percival to come towards me. Kai was there before she could reach, pushing me behind him and assuming a protective stance.

"You will not touch her," he commanded, menacingly.

The queen glared at him and then me. "She is a liar! She is not daughter to Kappur!"

I tilted my chin up and faced the queen, and for once, I did not feel afraid. "I am."

"You are Odele, and you are causing a scene and embarrassing our kingdom for your own amusement."

"Actually, stepmother, if I wanted to cause a scene, I would have done so with much more flourish than this."

Everyone turned to the entrance to the royal throne room, and I smiled at my cousin. It was quite like her to announce herself in such a fashion, wearing a wedding dress identical to mine, her hair down and floating around her face, the Black Blade at her side, and a mortician panting at the end of her blade.

The queen let out a surprised gasp and stared back and forth between the two of us, as did the rest of the guests assembled.

"So you see." I turned back to the queen and smirked. "I *am* a daughter of Kappur and Thalassar." And because my heart was already pounding, and the whole affair was already drenched in scandal, I lifted up the skirts to my gown and flashed my torn fin to the queen. "I have been all along." I dropped the skirts again and turned to the crowd.

Odele pushed the mortician forward unkindly and he swam, cautious of the tip of the blade she had aimed at the back of his neck. Behind her, Elias strutted down the aisle, smiling with mischief, dressed head to tail fin in black, his blade at his hip, and a bag thrown over his shoulder.

"Little fish," he greeted with a smile.

Odele pushed the mortician to the ground at the dais, and turned to flash a smile at the mer. "I know this must all be confusing for you," she mused. "But it's all quite simple once it's explained. We are identical because our mothers were identical. I grew up in the palace, while my cousin's birthright was taken from her. After her mother was *murdered,* she was hidden away in Lagoona. And we are here to restore your rightful ruler to the throne."

Someone in the crowd got up and broke the silence. To my surprise, it was Jessinda, our cousin. "Murdered? Who murdered her?"

"An excellent question, dearest cousin," Odele answered. There was something absolutely gleeful in her tone, an anticipation at what was to come, at the vengeance she would finally claim. "The mer who murdered my Aunty Odessa was the same person who murdered the nurses that birthed Odalaea. The same mer who murdered *my* mother, your queen." She smiled widely and swiveled, pointing the tip of the sword in the direction of her stepmother. "Circe Malabella."

A gasp tore from her throat at the accusation. This time, she didn't let Kai stop her. She pushed him aside to confront Odele, anger marring her beautiful features like a scar. "How dare you accuse me?!"

"Don't deny the truth!" Odele yelled, thrusting the sword. No one moved to aid the queen from the potential danger. Everyone was just too dumbfounded to do much more than watch the truth unravel from its dangerous, entangled threads. "You had the most to gain with their deaths. You killed them, and you tried to kill us as well to keep the throne."

The queen's mouth dropped, and she pressed a hand to her throat. "I can assure you I have never harmed a mer in my life, especially not my family. And as for *you…*" She turned sharply to me, eyes roaming over me in an expression that, for once, I couldn't quite interpret. "I wasn't even aware Dorian and Odessa had married or that they'd had a *child.*"

"Liar!" Odele's breathing had gone heavy, and for the first time since I'd met her, I could see her composure falling apart entirely. "You knew, because you hired a mercenary to kill our mothers and us. You thought she had died as a babe, but when she turned up here to take my place after I went missing, you pieced it together."

She shook her head vibrantly. "I swear to my crown, I did not know."

My chest seemed to compress, tightening in on itself. Circe had threatened me; she had been so obvious since the beginning why she despised me, had made it clear she knew who I was. So then, why did I believe her now? She looked genuinely shocked at the accusations, but was it all an act? It had to be. She was the only one who benefited from all this death.

"Deny it all you want," Odele ground out. "But we shall have the truth soon enough." She swiveled the sword back to the mortician, jabbing the tip against the back of his neck and causing him to flinch and whimper. "This is the mortician who falsified my mother's death conch. The one before him was an honest mer, who unfortunately met with an untimely death." She turned a narrowed gaze to the queen before going back to the mer at her fins. "This one knows my mother died of poison. Who told you to keep quiet?"

The merman visibly shuddered. I almost felt sorry for him, felt sorry for the malice and murder in Odele's eyes. My heart ached for her, for what she must be feeling. I sought for justice, for all that I would have had. Odele fought for all that she had lost.

"Please, I was just doing what I was told!"

"Who told you? Who gave the order? Speak and you might live."

He took a deep shuddering breath, and he looked around, his head turning, not to look at Queen Circe, but to sweep past her and look at someone else.

"It was Per—"

He didn't get the rest out.

Because at that moment, an arrow whizzed through the water and pierced straight to his throat.

Blood rose up in the water as he gurgled and gasped. Odele took a surprise stroke back, dropping her sword to the ground with a clatter.

Several things happened at once. Mer jumped from their seats, some scrambled to get to the exits that the guards dutifully blocked. King Dorian got up and shouted my name, but for some reason, my eyes instead went to Ytgar and Val, who, like brave warriors, swam towards Odele, surrounding her with shields and swords. Queen Circe had gripped Kai, using his body for cover. In the fray, I couldn't find Tiberius or Elias.

But I felt the pull on my gown, the forceful tug that whipped me around to face the mer I instantly knew to be guilty. The one we hadn't truly expected at all, because we'd been too busy placing blame on the queen.

Percival.

The merman looked haggard and angry, and a moment too late, I realized there was a spear gun in his hands… and he was pointing the weapon at me.

I startled, trying to take a stroke back, but when his finger grazed the trigger, I froze in my fear. How had the merman gotten a spear gun? The ridiculous question drifted painfully through my mind.

Screams ensued at the sight of the royal advisor with a weapon he was so freely willing to use, followed by silence as Percival spoke. "Captain Saber, by order of the crown, I command you to arrest this would-be usurper and throw her in the dungeons!"

I felt rather than saw Odele's presence as she pushed past Ytgar and Val to come closer, and then I felt Tiberius's presence like a beacon of light and tranquility, like safety and a promise. I didn't dare take my eyes off the tip of the arrow pointed between my eyes, but I could feel him tall and proud.

"Arrest her!" Percival commanded again.

And Captain Saber replied, "I will not."

A shiver sliced through me. It was, perhaps, the first and only time he had ever disobeyed a direct command from his leaders. From those he had sworn to obey and protect.

Percival looked so taken aback, his grip on the spear almost faltered, before he held it tighter and waved it in threat. "Fine," he conceded. "Then I shall execute her now."

"Percival!" Queen Circe had come out from behind Kai to confront her advisor as if he'd sprouted a second head. "What in gods' names are you doing? Put the spear gun down at once! There will be *no* execution." Yes, that was genuine care and fear in her voice.

So it would seem that the queen hadn't been guilty after all.

It had been Percival all along.

"I fear I cannot obey your command, Your Majesty. This mer threatens the whole balance of Thalassar and our customs!" His hand was shaking, and I willed his finger not to tighten around the trigger accidentally.

"What are you talking about?" the queen demanded incredulously.

"This bastard cannot be allowed to usurp you and rule Thalassar."

I noticed then that King Dorian had pushed his way through the crowds, closer to me. "She is no bastard. She is my daughter and Princess of Kappur."

My eyes glazed over with tears at the words. I wanted to shout, *He accepts me, he really does!* but I avoided the urge, thanks to the arrow threatening my face.

"You will unhand my wife this instant," Kai demanded, swimming forward in my peripheral vision. Transformed into the other entity, he had never looked more beautiful to me. His hair was loose, his eyes with slit pupils and a glaze of blue. Black talons curved on his fingers menacingly.

"She is not your wife. This whole ceremony was a farce."

"Actually," I murmured to Percival, knowing I shouldn't provoke him, but not being able to help myself, "it isn't. I signed my name on the marriage documents. Odalaea Malabella Knoll. Our marriage is legitimate." I gifted Kai a smile and hoped he could forgive me.

Odele and I had to play the cruelest of tricks upon them. And my future was looking rather bleak, so I hoped he understood, that they all understood. I itched to let my gaze roam over them all. Kai, Elias, Tiberius, Odele, and my father.

"Like your mother before you, this marriage is despicable and goes against every Thalassarin tradition!" Percival spat. "I'll not have you tainting the Malabella lineage further."

King Dorian's eyes narrowed on Percival at the comment, but it was Odele who spoke, "You had our mothers murdered."

"They threatened the balance."

Queen Circe started forward, her eyes holding the fury of molten lava. "You murdered my cousins?"

How could we have been so wrong? So, so wrong? The queen was ruthless, she cared about the purity of the Malabella lineage, but it was Percival who was the extremist. It was Percival who had killed, ridding himself of those he thought too impure for the throne. And we hadn't seen it, hadn't contemplated that it was anyone but Circe.

And now my life was in his hands.

"And neither of you will rule now," he threatened quietly, just before his finger tightened against the trigger.

Odele screamed, and I was too frozen to do much but watch everything play out before me, too fast, too soon. The arrow whizzed towards me, and the impact of it piercing the flesh below my collarbone sent me hurtling to the floor. Pain spiraled through me, intensifying my whole body as I fell onto my bottom, on the ground. My teeth smacked together, and I gasped for breath as it painfully left my body.

A haze quickly fell over my body, but I fought for consciousness and watched. Watched as Percival notched another arrow and pointed the weapon at Odele. But he never got the chance to pull the trigger on her. Because in a move, brave and swift, Val pulled out the sword at his waist and threw it. His weapon of ice hurtled through the water, hitting the weapon from Percival's hands altogether.

The next moment happened so fast. Elias slammed the hilt of his black blade against the back of Percival's head, knocking him to the floor. Kai advanced, but it was Ytgar and Val who got there first, both of them wearing equal expressions of loathing.

"The line must be cleansed!" Percival shrieked. "And I shall cleanse it! It's too late! She will die! The poison is in her now!" He laughed, scrambling on the floor to reach for his discarded weapon. The last sound he made before Ytgar pulled out the royal sword of Iol and stabbed it through the merman's chest, killing him instantly.

I sighed, closing my eyes against the pain that suddenly assaulted me. Heat soared through my body in agonizing intervals. My limbs seemed to stop working, and I could no longer hold myself upright. I felt myself falling, falling into darkness, but Tiberius was there to catch me.

"Maisie!" he shrieked. Or at least, I think he did. Sound was escaping me entirely. I fought to keep my eyes open, but the agony. Was I screaming, or was that someone else? "Maisie, oh, gods, someone get a doctor!"

Numbly, I felt the pressure of hands against my body, though I couldn't discern whose they belonged to. It didn't matter. All that mattered was that I was being lulled into a painful sleep.

"Maisie, stay with me. Don't die on me."

"Get a doctor!"

"Cousin, oh, gods…"

"My gem…"

"Little fish, wake up."

"Daughter…"

I didn't hear the rest.

Because I succumbed to the darkness.

Maisie lay unmoving against the bed's cushions, veins stark against the paleness of her skin. It had been days since Percival had shot her with a poisoned arrow, and still she did not wake. She didn't even stir.

It was her stillness that worried me, her lack of reaction to pain, to the fever that had finally broken. The royal medics claimed it was the sickness of her body, as well as the sickness of her spirit that kept her unconscious.

For days, I had not dared move from my place at her bedside. None of us did. Kai sat at the fin of the bed, cradling his face into talon-curved fingers. Elias sat opposite of me, balancing his blade on his palm, as if he meant the movements as a distraction so he'd not have to focus on Maisie's immobility, but he looked no less haggard than the rest of us. His brown skin had taken an almost paleness to it, dark shadows rimming beneath his eyes. It hurt to look at them, hurt to look at anyone but Maisie, lest I find hopelessness in their eyes. Lest I find their thoughts written so plainly on their faces as they assumed the worst.

That Maisie would not wake up.

Unable to help myself, I reached for her hand, squeezing it gently in my own. Her skin was as cold as ice.

As cold as death.

I let her fingers slip from mine once again.

"Why isn't she waking?" I demanded angrily, to no one in particular. A surge of hopelessness overwhelmed me entirely. I was her guard. I'd been meant to protect her. The arrow should have been for me. But like everything else I set out to accomplish in my life, I had failed.

I did not deserve her. And now she was lying near death in this room, and if she didn't wake up at all, I'd never get to apologize for believing she had left me. I'd never get to hold her one last time, to kiss her, laugh with her. I'd never get to see her become the queen she was meant to be.

"She will wake up," Kai answered, equally quiet. I looked up at him to find him straightening, turning so his dragon blue eyes were fixated on Maisie's still form. "She is strong."

"She is," Elias agreed, twirling his blade through his fingers before sheathing it. He, too, turned to look at her with longing in the dark depths of his eyes. "She may be a little fish, but she is a fighter. Through and through."

Pain caught tightly in my throat. "You love her," I stated.

Elias' lip quirked into a smile, not arrogant or mischievous, but honest. "I do," he confirmed. "We all do."

I never imagined how such a love could feel. A love so strong and powerful, that the three of us, the four of us, could belong to one another so deeply. I could only hope that this would be enough to bring her back.

Slowly, I took her hand again and bowed over it. "Come back to us, Maisie. *Please*, come back to us."

There is so much I have to tell you, I added silently, hoping that my thoughts carried to her in her dreams. *There is so much I still want to confess. So much we still have left to share. Come back to me. To us.*

I love you.

And after what seemed like days, hours of waiting for something, for the tiniest of signs that she was returning to us, Maisie's breath hitched, and she turned, eyes closed in unconsciousness.

It was enough to make me hope.

I'D BEEN AT THE palace for days, ever since Maisie had been shot by the damned arrow, and no one had arrested me yet. Perhaps it was because the whole palace was in a state of sorrow and disbelief. They all mourned for Maisie, and the injury she had sustained, I doubted anyone had the energy to come after me. Not when I'd helped to put down that bastard. Not when it was so obvious how much Maisie meant to me.

I was not the praying sort of merman. I had not prayed a single day in my life. I relied merely on myself and my own devices. I had not sought the gods help since the day I'd been selected. I'd not sought them to save the merman who had given up his safety for my own, in exchange for a ring and a better life in the seas.

But now, seeing Maisie, a mer so full of life and love, lying still on a deathbed, I bowed my head and prayed for her.

If you take her away from me, I will hunt you and kill you myself, I promised the gods silently. Perhaps it wasn't wise to threaten all powerful beings, but it was a promise. One I meant to keep. If they took her away from me, I vowed to never stop hunting them until they restored the life back into her.

Maisie deserved more than this. She deserved the world, and if I had to destroy it to give it to her, I would.

Wake up, I whispered to her, mind to mind, as if it were some secret and shared power we had. She had been good at reading my thoughts, and I hers. Conversations flowed in the silences between us like bubbles on a current. Easily. Quickly.

And I prayed to the gods to send my words to her in sleep, so that she may wake up, and share silent conversations with me all over again.

For now and always.

THE DRAGON INSIDE flickered in and out of my own consciousness. I was growing too weary to keep the tether on it much longer, so I gave it free reign in those moments when feeling became too much. When my emotions curled deep inside me into a blinding pain that kept me on the precipice of control. So I relinquished it. I let the dragon take over, and it malformed my body into something vicious. But even as the roaring sounded, and the talons curved, and my scales hardened, the dragon did nothing but sit and watch Maisie in hopelessness.

There was only so much we could do, only so much we could take, before we broke entirely. And the both of us still held onto the hope that her eyes would open. That she would smile and kiss us. Our wife. Our mate.

I loved her so much it hurt, and if I lost her, then I would be lost too. It was a wound I'd not get back from. The Dragon Prince, the vicious soldier of Draconi who rode into battle on his great dragon, who did not bow down to enemies, who feared nothing, not blood nor death or war, would fall apart if Maisie died.

I couldn't bear the thought of losing her.

I kept my face buried into my palms as I prayed, over and over, to the Great Dragon, god of my mer, that if he brought Maisie back from the depths of paradise, that I'd give up Draconi, to Him and for Him.

All he had to do was bring my mate back.

"Do not swear what you cannot give up," a voice whispered into my mind, startling me into a straight position.

Great Dragon?

"She will wake," the mighty voice said. *"And you will give up nothing. It is a gift, freely given."*

And for the first time in days, I had hope.

Darkness swallowed me whole. I didn't know where I was, hardly remembering who I was. All I'd known at first was pain before it consumed me and kept me pinned down, numb. I gave into it without fighting. I let myself sink into the depths, I let that anchor pull me down… down… down…

And then I heard the voice.

Three voices, four, pushing down with me, wrapping around me in an attempt to bring me back up again.

Wake up.

Great Dragon, please save her.

Come back to me.

Cousin, please live.

Daughter…

It was that last voice that gave me pause, that awakened me in the darkness, made me grapple for a scrap of memory. When I remembered everything, when it all hit me painfully, it made me thrash against my invisible bindings.

They were waiting for me, praying over me. Who were they? That's right, my family. I'd never had a family before, but now I did, and they were calling out to me. They wanted me, accepted me, and I was failing them. I was giving in to the pain, falling deep into the depths of an abyss that would swallow me up and spit me from their memories.

I wouldn't give up.

I was not a victim.

I was not afraid.

Wake up.

Great Dragon, please save her.

Come back to me.

Cousin, please live.

Daughter…

I grabbed onto the voices like a lifeline, I let them wrap themselves around me, and I pulled with all of my might. There was no pain in my fins with the strain. There was nothing inside me but determination, and love, so much love. Whether it was mine for them, or theirs for me, I wasn't sure.

All I knew was that it saved me from the darkness.

And pulled me from that abyss.

"SHE'LL BE ALRIGHT," I assured the four mermen at her bedside. Even if I wasn't sure I believed in the words myself, I had to say them. I had to hold onto them, for I couldn't bear to believe the worst.

If Maisie died, I doubted I could ever go on. Perhaps my lineage truly was cursed, and everyone I ever let myself love was destined to die. But those thoughts were too morbid to contemplate. And I didn't want to say them aloud in front of Tiberius, Elias, Kai, and King Dorian. The four of them hovered over her bed, waiting for some sign of a flutter, whispering, praying in her ear.

The sight was enough to cripple me, as I remembered the time my mother had died. I'd been young, but I still remembered it vividly.

I pushed the painful memories away and straightened my shoulders, donning the façade that kept me sane and alive, donning the mask of a princess, pulling it close to me until it enveloped me like a second skin. I threw my shoulders back and ventured into the room.

"You all need to leave," I ordered.

Four hopeless gazes turned to me.

I rolled my eyes and let out sounds of exasperation. "She probably isn't waking because the stench of the four of you is keeping her knocked out. Seriously, when was the last time any of you took a bath? Get out, and get out now. Give her room to breathe for a moment before you come hovering again."

King Dorian straightened, piercing his gaze into mine. I met it unflinchingly. If he thought I was afraid of him, he had another thing coming. He was an attractive royal, with eyes that were like my cousin's, a slender neck and prominent cheekbones. All features she had inherited from him. Even the agony in his expression could not hide his beauty. And I liked beautiful things.

"She's going to wake up," I promised, dreading to do so but seeing no other option. "She just needs time and space. Bathe, fix yourselves, and then come to her later."

They still stared at me and didn't move.

I sighed. "Get. Out. Now." I used my most murderous voice, my princess voice, the one that bespoke of command and power.

The one that had them all obeying instantly.

I watched with satisfaction as they all began exiting the room, albeit slowly, but exiting just the same. Once they were all gone, I busied myself with opening the windows and straightening up the room. I called in servants to place flowers, lilies, all around the room for fresh scents and color. When she woke up, it would make her smile. I hoped.

When everything was ready, I sent my own silent prayer to whoever would listen to gift my cousin with life. As I did, her eyes fluttered, and her body moved.

Hope flared in my chest, it had seemed like days since she'd last moved about. The action, however small, gave me hope that the family I'd fought so hard for, would live after all.

"Princess Odele." The voice, a slow curl of promise, stopped me mid stroke. I turned, watching as Prince Ytgar swam hurriedly towards me, the blond of his curls bouncing slowly against his forehead.

His presence clenched something inside me, threatening to curl my tail fin and flare my other fins. His presence just reminded me of the way both he and Val had swam towards me all those days ago, to protect me from Percival's poisoned arrows. The way he and Val so bravely discarded him of his weapon. The way they'd had a hand in his downfall.

I should have been furious that they'd taken my vengeance from me. The kill should have been mine. The blade that skewered through his chest should have been mine, a bloody tribute to my mother and my aunt. But I'd killed the mercenary already, and it still haunted my nightmares. Even if I'd wanted to kill Percival, even after everything he'd done, it would have destroyed what little bit of heart I still had left.

So I was glad for him, and glad for Val, though I'd never show them just how badly they affected me at all.

I sneered at the prince. "What do you want, whale prince? I have things to do."

My snark only seemed to bring out a challenge and a smile from him. "Always so welcoming. I just wanted to make sure you were okay."

My heart clenched. No one had asked me, not when they were hovering so viciously over my cousin. Not that it mattered what I felt. I had not been shot. Still, his words warmed through my core, and I willed the sensation away, and the reply I truly wanted to give him.

"I'm not okay. My cousin isn't waking. My heart hurts. My mother is avenged, so why don't I feel at peace?"

"Fine. Now go away," I snapped impatiently and turned. He pulled me back around with a sharp tug against the skirts of my dress.

"You know, I've been thinking…"

"You don't say?" My eyebrows shot up sarcastically. "Please, don't harm yourself with such an arduous task."

He ignored me and went on, "I've been thinking about our every encounter, and I realized, I was finally able to separate you and your cousin in my mind."

I snorted. "So, you can miraculously tell us apart now?"

His answering smirk was gods' damned breathtaking. I ignored the sudden pounding of my heart. "I propositioned your cousin, but it was you I kissed."

"Well, if you call that a kiss…"

"I do. And I know you enjoyed it."

My hands curled into fists. By gods, I wanted to punch the smug expression off his face. "I didn't, actually."

"And I've been contemplating my marriage proposal quite a bit…"

I startled. "Proposal?"

"Since you are no longer promised to Prince Kai, I thought you would now be open for new suitors. Iol could use a princess."

My heart felt like it would explode inside my chest cavity. Nerves tingled through me, pleasantly and unpleasantly. And then the anger overtook. He'd already played with the question one time, why was he joking again? What would make him think that after one awful—joyous, wonderful, erotic—kiss that I'd ever meet him at the end of an altar?

Smug bastard.

I snorted. "Get this one thing straight, Iolish. I would rather take a poisoned arrow to the heart than to ever marry you or ally myself with your ilk. Do you understand? I would never, *ever*, marry you, even if you begged."

I whirled around and swam away as fast as I could, but my speed didn't keep his reply from drifting towards my ears or blind me to the smile I somehow knew was plastered onto his arrogant face.

"We'll see..."

Unlike the first time I'd been poisoned, I did not awake feeling quite so awful. My eyelids were a little heavy and my fin was throbbing, but I felt rested, relieved.

I opened my eyes and sat up, only to be bombarded with gasps and cries of happiness. Once my eyes adjusted, they found the faces of Kai, Elias, and Tiberius surrounding me, equal looks of worry and disbelief over their equally different features.

"Hi," I greeted, feeling my tongue heavy in my throat. I smacked my lips and swallowed, wincing at the pain in my throat.

"Lay back down," Tiberius commanded gently, yet firmly. His hand was suddenly at my back, guiding me against the pillows.

"How are you feeling?" Kai asked, reaching for my stiff fingers.

"Gods, little fish, you gave us a scare."

My head was whirling with the bombardment of questions and the worry in their gazes. I blinked, struggling to remember all that had happened before the darkness. When the memories returned, quite vividly, I groaned and lay back against the cushions.

"I'm quite tired of getting poisoned," I muttered unhappily.

They all seemed to breathe sighs of relief, and then I was being tugged gently into the circle of Tiberius' arms. His shoulders shook, almost as if he were crying. He pulled away, pressing a firm kiss to my forehead. "I thought I'd lost you."

The pain quivering his voice made my face flush with sudden shame. "I'm sorry," I whispered. "I know it was wrong, and I should've told you my plans, but I was afraid the queen would have killed you to get to me. I had to pretend I was gone from your lives. Odele and I arranged for a lava bomb to go off, and we switched places quickly before anyone realized. We had to keep it a secret in order to keep you all safe."

"Elias and Odele already explained it to us." Kai waved off my words with a sudden flick of his fingers. His expression was drawn tight, but his brown eyes spoke of warmth and relief. "And we understand."

My heart thundered a quick, hopeful rhythm. "You aren't mad?"

"We're furious," Tiberius said seriously. "But I'll forgive you if you promise to never almost get killed again."

He was perfectly serious. And he hadn't been talking about my sudden disappearance at all. When he said he thought he'd lost me, he'd meant my near death.

"You should be used to this by now," I murmured sarcastically.

None of them looked amused, and I quickly admonished myself for the humor at the most inopportune time. But I'd almost been murdered; surely I had a right to make jokes at my own expense.

"So, what happened?" I asked eventually. I'd been there, but those last few moments had been a blur of pain and poison on my mind. I knew Ytgar, Val, and Elias had worked together to kill Percival, the true villain of the story, but then darkness had consumed me.

"All of the seven kingdoms know of your existence. They know the truth. Everything that happened within the royal throne room was recorded and broadcasted far and wide. The matter was cleared up with the queen, the king, Odele, and your father. The truth is out, and the kingdom is eager to officially meet their newest princess," Elias explained, an elated grin pulling his lips.

Emotions tightened in my throat. The kingdom… They were excited at the idea of me? It was almost overwhelming, almost unbelievable.

"Your father remains a guest in the palace," Kai added, almost shyly. "He has been sitting with us waiting for you to awaken. Odele has been beside herself with worry as well."

Gods. It was truly unbelievable, that I finally had a family, and mer who would worry about me. I remembered the last two times I'd been lying in bed. The first at Tides' Tavern, with only Josiah and my shame to accompany me, the second had been here in this very bed, lonely and aching. And now, I had a family to call my own. Three mermen surrounding me, gifting me with stares of relief and love in equal measure.

The tears came then. They rose and rose and did not stop flowing.

I covered my face with my hands, sobbing into my palms. The emotions would not stop coming. Even here, lying in the bed where they were unsure which of my breaths would be my last, I finally felt whole, complete.

"Don't cry, little fish," Elias pleaded. "Gods, the tears do me in."

"Those are happy tears, I hope," this came from Tiberius.

"Cry, my gem," Kai whispered, contradicting Elias. "It's all over now. Nothing can ever harm you again. I swear it on my life."

And I believed his words like I'd never believed anything else.

"Great, now she's crying harder," Elias muttered like a curse. "See what you did, Prince?"

"Do not mock me."

"Will you two be quiet?"

I looked up then, brushing aside my tears and gifting them with a smile. "I love you," I told them. "I love you all *so* much."

And together, they pulled me close, arms wrapped around me tightly, as if by merely holding me close like this, they could push away everything on the outside. Every threat, and sadness, and wrap me in love.

Always their love.

Days passed and I'd been confined to the bed. Not that I'd truly needed such extensive rest anymore. I was feeling revitalized, and my body no longer hurt. But they were hovering over me and barely let me peek my head out of the room without trying to come to my aid.

It was suffocating, truly.

By the end of the week, I was bored with being treated like an invalid.

"Let me help you with that," Kai offered, reaching over and trying to pull from my hands the beautiful dragon's egg he'd gifted to me on our wedding. All I'd been doing was moving it from one spot to another, for lack of anything better to do.

I yanked the egg back to my chest. It felt like cold stone, heavy and extremely beautiful, but the movement rammed it against my collarbone, right where I'd been shot. I gasped for breath at the surprise pain that went through me, and took a vicious stroke back when Kai made a move to help me.

"Don't you dare," I warned. "Stop hoverin'. I'm not a helpless guppy. I can do stuff on my own, ya know." I'd dropped my Eramaean accent, no longer feeling the need to hide behind the perfection that Tiberius had instilled in me long ago. Everyone knew the truth and who I was, so what did it matter what I sounded like? I was a princess, after all.

"I just want to help," Kai assured.

"Well, don't. I'm not an invalid."

Kai pulled back, defeated. From somewhere else in the room, Elias laughed. I turned sharply, watching him emerge from the bathing room, his body entirely bare and dusting stray grains of pink sand from his long, black hair.

"Leave her alone, Kai. Our little fish is tough."

My tongue suddenly felt heavy as I took in Elias' lithe form. They'd all taken up residence in Odele's—now my—rooms, and had made themselves at home. Elias was not entirely shy, and this wasn't the first time he'd taunted me with his body, though unfortunately, between the three of us, nothing had gone beyond light kisses or cuddles.

I was hoping to remedy that.

If they ever stopped treating me like I was incapable.

My eyes followed the path where stubborn grains of sand still clung to the contours of his body and slid down his chest invitingly. It was a sight to see, the way the grains clung to him. It made me almost envious. I was crippled with the sudden urge to hold him, to kiss and taste, and my whole body flushed at the thought.

"My gem, are you alright?" Kai broke through my thoughts by taking a stroke forward and pressing the back of his hand to my forehead. "You're feverish…"

I jerked away and stared up at him, at the worry in his brown eyes looking down on me, at the panes and curves of his beautiful face. Even though he hovered, I wanted him with a need that was baffling. I wanted them both. Gods, I wanted all *three* of them.

I was breathless with my cravings and almost too embarrassed to give voice to my desires. I doubted Tiberius would want to share, anyway.

I looked over to where he sat at the desk, kelp parchments placed before him. He claimed to be studying the safest routes from Thalassar to Draconi, just in case. In case of what, I didn't ask.

Now, I focused on his form, hunched over the kelp parchments studiously, his eyes intense with concentration. I admired the breadth of his shoulders, the muscles teasing against the tightness of his tunic.

Gods, what was wrong with me? I was acting like a shark deprived of a meal.

My face heated to levels that were almost impossible.

"I don't think it's a fever." Elias had swaggered up beside Kai, and his gaze roamed hungrily over me, leaving no inch of my body unexplored with his dark eyes. Like always, he knew exactly what I was thinking, was so in tune with the rhythms of my breath and the beating of my heart, the shaking of my limbs that he sought to ease my aches. He reached out, sliding his fingers down the skin of my arm. I shivered so hard, I nearly dropped the dragon egg to the ground.

"Elias…" My voice was a breathless rasp that stoked the heat between us. Kai read it too, but he made no sudden moves to touch me. Instead, he reached forward and plucked the egg from my fingers and turned to deposit it safely away from us. When he came back, his eyes had lightened to that dangerous blue hue.

"If this was what you wanted…" Elias pulled me close by the skirts so that my body pressed tightly against his, so that I felt every pane and glorious inch of him. I felt the way he opened up to me instantaneously, the warm hardness of him pressing against my stomach. He bent down, brushing his lips across my temples, sliding them down, further and further to the corner of my mouth. "…then all you had to do was ask."

And then he kissed me.

My response was immediate. my body burned from the inside, desperate for contact, for *him.* I pressed myself against him, grasping his shoulders to tug him closer still. His mouth explored mine as if we didn't already know the architecture of one another. As if it were the first time and the last time.

And then I felt an extra set of hands, not Elias', who had wrapped his around my waist, but Kai's, whose long fingers danced up my neck to hold me in place against Elias.

His face came close to us, lips grazing across my cheeks, alternating between Elias and I, talons scraping deliciously along my skin.

"Kiss her neck," Kai ordered firmly in Elias' ear.

Elias obliged, breaking away from my mouth to trail his own down the arch of my neck. He pressed open-mouthed kisses against my skin, inciting cries from my lips. I trembled at the sensation, already open and desperate for them.

I gasped, nails digging into Elias' shoulders. "Please…" I begged, hips pressing into him, eager for the hardness against my stomach to be inside me.

"Soon, my gem," Kai promised, his lips pressing to my cheek, and lower to my lips. He kissed my mouth as Elias kissed my neck, and by the time Kai pulled away, I was dizzy and shaking with need.

"Please…"

Kai smiled, a dangerous, imposing thing. "Lift your skirts," he ordered.

My head spun, and I dropped my hands from Elias' body to obey, sliding them slowly up the length of my tails, past my flaring fins to expose my opened slit.

"Elias… kneel before her…"

Elias was all too eager to oblige, dropping at the tail before me. I felt the warmth of his ragged breath across my stomach, blowing into my opening and causing me to shiver. Gods, I wanted him. If I didn't have him *now*…

"Soon, my gem." Kai's talons raked across my arm before pulling away. I watched, eyes half-lidded, as he hiked up his own robes and bared himself. He was erect already, and with one hand, he gripped his incredible length, sliding his palm up and down his shaft. With the other, he held the back of my neck and pulled me close so that our lips touched. And then he gave his order, "Pleasure her."

Elias' mouth crashed into my slit at the same time Kai's mouth plundered into mine. His tongue pushed apart my lips, tracing the inside of my mouth, commanding, claiming. And Elias was doing the same. Somehow, they worked the same rhythm until I was mindless, breathless. My hips jerked into Elias' mouth, desperate for release. I climbed high on that edge, waiting to drop into the chasm...

He pulled his mouth away, and a moment later, Kai tore his away to suck in a shocked breath. We looked down, only to find Elias had left me teetering desperately on the edge to switch the pleasure onto Kai. His mouth wrapped around the head of his member and slid down the length of him slowly.

Kai groaned, though it sounded more like a growl. "I didn't order you to..." He broke off and sucked in a breath as Elias worked over him faster and faster before slowly pulling away to look up at Kai with a smug expression.

"I think it's time you felt the pain you inflict, Dragon Prince." And then his mouth was on Kai again, sucking him, sliding up and down his shaft.

Gods, but it was a sight to see. My own frustration at the lack of release forgotten, I watched in fascination, gaze darting between one mer and the other. As Elias sucked harder and faster, Kai dropped his head against my neck, clawing at me, his hips thrusting, and his mouth desperate on my skin.

"Maisie," he groaned. "Elias..."

I dug my fingers into the roots of his silken hair, tugging and pulling him up to face me. I wanted to see his expression. Wanted to see that exact moment when he came undone. I wanted to feel it in my own bones, share this moment with them both.

"I want to see you," I commanded, feeling powerful, in control. As in control as he was when the three of us were together.

"Great Dragon," he cursed, and then his hands were on me, fighting for the control he had so obviously lost. "If I go, you'll come with me." His hands pressed into my opening, diving in and out, stretching and stroking my desire all over again. I cried out, clinging to him, but my eyes never once strayed. I watched his expression, following him on the current paved in pleasure. The thrusts of our hips matched, and when his eyes lowered and he bit his bottom lip, I knew he was close to his release, so I followed, plunging myself to the drop at the same moment he did.

He cried out, his hips thrusting against Elias' mouth, his fingers curling tightly into me, talons scraping across the nub of my desire that sent me spiraling after him.

We both sagged on shaking limbs, and Elias pulled away, a satisfied smirk on his lips.

Kai glared at him half-heartedly.

From his position at the desk, Tiberius groaned. "You are distracting me," he admonished.

"You're welcome to join us, if you like," Elias smirked in the captain's direction.

I heard the clatter of a quill dropping onto the table and turned in his direction. From what little I saw of his profile, his cheeks were flushed, his eyes widened. The strain of his muscles against his tunic was great, and looked as if the material was about to tear. I almost wished it would. Was I greedy for wanting to look at his body again?

When Tiberius didn't answer right away, I felt the smallest flutter of disappointment that was quickly whisked away when Kai lifted me in his arms. I gasped, hands wrapping around his neck as he swam to the bed and laid me gently down on it. He straightened and turned to glare at Elias.

"Lay next to her," he ordered, back to his dangerous, commanding presence, as if the last few moments of him losing control had never happened.

Elias joined me, his movements confident and smug as he slid into the empty space next to me on his back. He used his hands as cushions behind his head, and raised his brows up at Kai, who loomed over the both of us.

"Do with me what you will," Elias said.

"Oh, I will," Kai promised darkly. "First, I'm going to make Maisie *suck* you." As if to highlight his point, his hand went down to grasp Elias's shaft at the hilt. He squeezed, startling a gasp from Elias, and then he slid his palm up and down. His eyes flicked to me. "Would you like that, Maisie?"

I licked my lips, his blue gaze following the movement. "I would…" I'd never done it before, but I would. Kai made me bold.

Kai nodded, as if my words had been exactly the answer he'd expected of me. "Then when she's brought you to the point of coming, I'll make her stop until you're aching."

"Do it," Elias dared, his dark eyes glittering at the prospect of a challenge.

My body heated at the conversation passing between us, the words as casual as if we were merely discussing the weather. What I really wanted was for the words to cease. For their hands to be on me again, for them to take me to the depths of pleasure all over again.

I squirmed uncomfortably and turned, my eyes catching Tiberius at the desk. He was looking at us, ever discreetly, an intense look in his blue eyes.

I smiled. "Join us," I offered.

Kai's gaze snapped over to him, and he let out a mischievous smile. One I tended to only associate with Elias. "Yes, Captain. Come and play. Can't you see how much Maisie desires you?" His claw swiped down the bodice of my dress, tearing it so the flaps fell open to expose my breasts. A talon scraped down the soft mounds and to a peaked nipple, pausing there. I arched against him, needing the feel of his fingers, his mouth, his *tongue.*

"Please," I begged, straining against him.

"Don't you want the captain to join us, Maisie?" Kai leaned down to ask, his mouth hovering over my nipple.

"Yes." The word came out as a hiss.

"If he joined us, what would you have him do to you?"

My face heated and my eyes flew open—when had I closed them?

"Maisie…" Kai's voice held a hint of warning. "What would you have him do to you?"

"I—" I turned to look at Tiberius. He had turned, so I could see every shadowed angle of his face and the glowing desire in his eyes. "I'd have him touch me…" I answered breathlessly.

Kai's tongue swirled around my nipple and I moaned. "Where would you have him touch you?"

I couldn't look away from Tiberius. I was emboldened by Kai's strokes, by his words, even if my face flamed at all the thoughts pushing through my mind, all the things I wanted Tiberius to do to me. I gave voice to my desires. "I want you to kiss my breasts." I spoke the words directly to Tiberius. "I want you to kiss me until I'm breathless. I want you to touch me… *there*…"

"Where?" Kai interrupted. He licked my nipple again, then let his tongue travel to the valley between my breasts. "Where, Maisie?"

"At the heart of my desire. At my opening. My *sex*. I want him to touch me, and kiss me there, and then I want his member inside me. I want—"

Tiberius shot up from the chair, his brusque movements causing it to scrape against the floor and fall backwards with a clang. His chest rose quickly with the harsh breaths he took. "I'll do it," he said gruffly. That was all he said before he stalked forward, nudging Kai aside to loom over me. And then his hands were on me, touching and teasing, inciting cries from my lips. He pushed the flaps of my dress impatiently aside, and I lifted, helping him to tear them from my arms.

"Love her slowly," Kai ordered softly.

Tiberius stilled and turned a glare on Kai. "You are not my ruler, Prince. And I don't need you to tell me how to love Maisie or where to touch her or how to make her come, I assure you."

Kai smirked, but Tiberius was already turning away, back to me. His eyes were hungry, desperate to have me. Calloused fingers skimmed over my stomach, dancing over my skin in tantalizing movements. His fingers bunched into the material of my dress and he yanked them down, slipping them from my tail and tossing them to the side.

I reached up with anxious fingers, tugging at the hem of his tunic. Impatiently, he obliged, yanking it from his body. I watched the flex of his muscles, sliding my fingers up the ridges of his abdomen, palm stopping just over the rapid beating of his heart.

I smiled. “Make love to me.”

“Always,” he growled, just before he bent down and took my lips in a searing kiss.

I abandoned myself to his body, reveling in the sensation of the scrape of his teeth, the caresses of his tongue. The way his hands slid over me, leaving no inch unexplored. Beside me, Kai murmured delicious things to Elias, things that only made me groan.

Elias turned, capturing the lobe of my ear between his teeth as Kai slid kisses down the length of his body and lower still, where he captured the length of him into his mouth. Elias bucked, and I felt the pleasure of it spiral through me painfully.

I lifted my own hips in a silent plea to Tiberius, but he was taking his time, tasting and sucking. His lips went down my stomach and lowered right at my entrance.

Just like I’d begged him to do.

He pleasured me with his mouth, tongue and fingers diving in and out of me until I writhed beneath him. My hands dug into his hair to pull him closer, to keep him right where he was, even as I desired his length inside me.

Pleasure spiraled through me in painful waves. I didn’t know what sensation to focus on anymore; his tongue, Elias’ lips against my neck, or the sounds of pleasure coming from Kai’s throat? It was all too much…

I fell into that abyss.

And I screamed.

My body shot up from the bed as I cried out the sound of my release. When I fell back to the cushions, Tiberius slid up my body, his hardness pressing to my entrance. Even though I'd just found my release, a thrill went through me at the feel of him there. I clutched at his shoulders weakly, a gasp tearing from my throat when he pushed himself inside me to the hilt.

And then he was moving, and my hands fell back, where Elias reached for me and held on, as we rode that vicious, deadly wave of pleasure.

Together.

"I've been meaning to ask you…" Tiberius began lazily, his fingers tracing along my skin. "Do you worry… I mean… about… children?"

My eyebrows rose at the question. "What do you mean?"

He seemed to share a look with Kai and Elias, both of whom had suddenly stiffened. Elias shifted uncomfortably. "I didn't think about it," he murmured.

Kai looked chagrined. "I did think of it… but didn't take a care. I'm sorry. I should have taken more precautions."

"What are you guys talkin' about?" I sat up, looking left and right between them.

Tiberius scratched behind his ear and made a face. "I mean about… babies. What if you get pregnant?" he blurted.

My eyes widened, and I broke out into a smile. "Does that have you worried?" I teased.

"Well…" He looked at Kai, and Elias shrugged. "We all love you," Tiberius said firmly. "And if you had a child, any of our children, I wouldn't mind. I'd still want you, and I'd still love the baby."

I looked around, watching both Elias and Kai nod their agreement. I smiled. "Good to know." I flopped back onto the bed.

There was quiet, and then Kai asked, "*Are* you worried?"

I couldn't hold back the laughter that bubbled out of me. They all shared a look of exasperation and confusion, which only made me laugh harder. "When a mer turns eighteen," I explained slowly, "once a year, for a week, she will be fertile. It's when the body is ready for babies, and the only time a mer can get pregnant." I couldn't fathom how they didn't know this. Kai and Tiberius had sisters. But if they were anything like the mermen of Lagoona, I was sure they avoided those topics they deemed 'uncomfortable.'

"And, are you?" Elias asked. "Fertile. Right now, I mean?"

I laughed again. "Trust me, when my time comes, you'll know."

They looked doubtful, but I didn't go into a lengthy explanation of the mermaid mechanisms and bodily functions. They were grown mer and really should have had basic knowledge of this. But a part of me was glad they'd brought it up, because now I knew what everyone thought about it.

I hadn't really thought of having children with them before, but now that they mentioned it… I could picture it vividly. Kai and Tiberius would be such good fathers. Parts of Elias were still a bit of a mystery to me, but he seemed willing to stay by me, and that was all I could ever really ask for.

If I had been unsure about them before, I was positive now. This was a new start of my life, and I wanted nothing more than to share every bit of it with them.

"YOUR FATHER HAS BEEN stalking the halls of the palace like a guppy without his mother."

I sighed, dropping my head into my hands briefly. I'd been dancing around the subject of my father for days. Even if he'd defended me, had publicly accepted me as a daughter of Kappur, I couldn't bring myself to face him. A part of me feared that it had all been some type of farce, something said in the heat of the moment; that once he mulled it over and actually figured out who I truly was, he'd regret it.

Accepting he was my father, accepting that I was a princess, was easier than mustering up the confidence that he'd truly and wholly want me in his family.

"You're still on that self-pity current?" Odele sounded annoyed. When I didn't reply, she reached over and pinched my arm.

"Ow! What was that for?" I rubbed the sore spot.

"Wake up, Odalaea. He tore apart Thalassar and kept a war going for *years* just so he could find you. Rejoice, cousin, because at least your father fights for you."

I turned sharply to her, my expression softening into one of understanding and sadness. What must she be feeling? What must it be *like*? She was right; my father had fought for me, in methods I didn't entirely agree with, but he'd fought for me just the same. King Xristo had watched for years as Queen Circe treated his daughter ill. He had left her alone, had let her form her own way without a hint of guidance.

"Don't look at me with pity in your eyes. I can't bear it."

"Sorry," I apologized. "But you're right, I need to face him sometime."

Odele nodded her agreement. "Yes, you do. Perhaps you should go do that now. He's in his rooms." A delicate eyebrow rose. "Although, you should probably change into something more appropriate first."

I gave a pointed look down at my outfit. It was a simple black tunic, one of Elias'. I no longer felt comfortable wearing Odele's dresses. I hadn't really been *made* for them, like they hadn't been made for me. And what was the point, when every dress was destroyed in the throes of passion anyway? It was a waste. So I wore a black tunic, belted at the waist, where my black blade hung off the side. It was a simple garment, long enough to cover a little ways past my torn fin.

I looked like a mer from Lagoona.

I got up and sighed. "No," I decided. "If he's goin' to meet me, he might as well meet the real me."

Odele eyed the outfit distastefully, wrinkling her nose at it. "Well, good luck. You'll need it. He might take one look at that atrocity and tell you never to set fin in his kingdom. Ever."

I rolled my eyes. "Thanks for that vote of confidence."

She shrugged. "I'm nothing if not honest, cousin. And I honestly think you look like something scraped from the bottom of a rock."

I pulled my hair back self-consciously before shaking off the sensation and my cousin's words. I was going to meet my father, and I would do so looking like what I grew up as: a mer from Lagoona. Not a princess. It wasn't to make him feel guilty about anything that had happened, about what I'd missed out on. It was so he could see my humble origins. So he could see me for who I truly was, for I hadn't been raised royalty. I was hopeless, and yet so thoroughly me. And I wanted him to accept me for me, and for nothing else.

"Here I go." I breathed deeply and turned to venture out and find the King of Kappur.

His rooms weren't so far away from mine, and Kappurin and Thalassarin soldiers alike were guarding them on the outside. The distrust between them was obvious, though their reactions respectful the moment they saw me was the same. Each soldier present bowed deeply to me and greeted me with equal firm calls of, "Princess!"

I waved them off uncomfortably. It was one thing to pretend to be Odele and accept their respect out of obligation. It was another thing entirely to receive it myself, when I'd done nothing to warrant it.

"I'm here to see the K—" I broke off, shook my head, and continued, "I'm here to see my father."

The Kappurin soldiers bowed in acquiescence and turned to the door, knocked a few times, and when a voice bade they enter, they opened it and took a stroke aside so I could swim through.

No one followed me as I swam into the king's rooms, but they did close the door behind me. Awkwardly, I swam inside. It was so obviously a guest room and therefore held no personal touches. Light filtered through the open windows, illuminating the lone figure floating in the center of the room.

My heart jumped to my throat as I breathed him in. He wore a simple tunic of black and red, belted at the waist. His sleeves were rolled up to reveal his forearms, hands resting casually at his sides.

The moment he saw me, he tensed.

All my life, I'd wondered why I looked so different from the mer of Lagoona. I'd always wondered, in some shallow corner of my mind, why the strange, jagged pieces of me never seemed to fit.

Now I knew.

The arch of a throat, the jut of cheekbones, the darkness of my eyes, and as I took in the King of Kappur, I searched for what I'd greatly longed for my entire life, a piece of me within another.

And in him I found it.

In the eyes of King Dorian, I found my home.

"Odalaea—"

"King Dori—"

We clamped our mouths closed when we spoke at the same time. His lids lowered, and he let out a soft chuckle, gesturing at me with his hand. "Please, continue," he said.

I took him in. His hair was a mixture of brown and blond, as if streaks of sunlight had been captured in the strands. There was the slight graying at his temples, but other than that, he looked rather young, and as handsome as he had been in his youth. It was true. He *was* beautiful. The lightness of his hair and skin contrasted his darker eyes. I'd never really contemplated the color of my eyes before now, had never truly noticed the beauty of them on myself the way I did with him.

"It's been a while," I said lamely. What a line. But I was so nervous, the words I truly wanted to say didn't come.

"Nineteen years," he agreed. "I confess, after fighting for so long, a time comes when hope begins to fade." My heart clenched at the words, but he turned to the desk and picked up a conch in the palm of his hand. "And then I received this." His fingers traced along the outer edges of it, thumb grazing over the symbol of two black blades crossing.

I knew it well.

I'd recorded it.

"King Dorian, you may not know me, but I know you. I know you've spent nineteen years searching for your lost daughter. Like you, I've been lost. Without a family, without a mother or a father, because what we so greatly desired was stolen from the both of us. Like you, I just want the truth. I just want to see the wrongs set to rights. And that is why I humbly send this recording to you, to invite you to discover the truth alongside me. For, if I am correct, then I believe it is I you have been searching for. I am your daughter, Princess Odalaea Malabella Knoll. And it would be my honor to finally meet you."

Odele had been by my side as I'd recorded that conch, holding my trembling hand in her own as I pushed through my fears and gave them voice. When I'd finished, I'd given that recording, as well as an invitation to Odele—well, *mine*—and Kai's wedding, to Elias. He'd given them to a trusted messenger to deliver them as quickly as possible.

"I let myself hope again," he went on. "It was hard to believe that after all these years, I'd finally found you. Or rather, it was you who found me." He set the conch back aside and took a cautious stroke forward, almost as if he were nervous at how I would take his nearness. "I was starting to think you were dead."

"Well, I'm alive," I answered, again, lamely. I swallowed the lump in my throat and dared a stroke forward. "And so are you. I thought I had no family left."

We stared at each other, understanding pulsating between the two of us.

"You look so much like her..." the king murmured wistfully. "And you're as brave as her, too."

"What was she like?" I asked, wanting to grasp onto whatever I could. Another piece of myself I could find in another.

His eyes shone. "She was a thorn in my fin. Frustrating, bold, and brave. She was loud and slightly annoying, but I confess, I am hopelessly in love with her."

Am. Not *was*. He still loved her. Even after all this time, he had not let that love go.

"I am glad," I whispered. "That you had each other."

Silence followed, a silence in which neither of us really knew what to say. It broke when he took another stroke forward, bringing us closer together again. "Odalaea—"

"Please," I interrupted. "Call me Maisie. I—I know 'Odalaea' is the name you chose for me, but it is not the name I grew up with, and I find I can't bear the weight of it yet."

He nodded in understanding. "Of course. Maisie—I just want you to tell me something…" He paused, took a breath. "Were you happy? In Lagoona? You weren't… mistreated?" His eyes drifted down to my fin. The torn one I had impulsively flashed at the queen.

"I was happy," I assured him. And then, because I didn't want to hold back, I told him everything. "My grandmother raised me in a little blue boat, in a cattail forest. I grew up chasin' piranhas from our pond, and I waitressed at a place called Tides' Tavern. I used to go to the traveling markets every Finsday to look at the pretty stuff they brought in from the capital. I watched my friends die for tryin' to flee Selection, and I watched others get hauled away by soldiers. I grew up hatin' the royals of Thalassar more than I could have ever hated the kingdom of Kappur. My grandmother died when I was a teen, so I spent half of my life carin' for myself. The only father figure I ever had was Josiah, the owner of Tides' Tavern, a kind merman who nursed me back to health after a gator attacked me and mauled my fin.

"Months ago, a merman named Captain Tiberius Saber found me and brought me to the palace, where I discovered the truth of my origins. And I was too afraid to accept the truth, but now I have. Even so, I'm *still* frightened that *I*—" I gestured at the entirety of my body. "—am not enough. I still wanted to meet you, to see if I could find a piece of myself in you, even if you want nothin' to do with me. At least I know who I am now, and where I come from."

I took a breath, not having realized that as I spoke, tears had flowed freely from my eyes. As I bared my heart before a merman I knew had the power to destroy it entirely with something as simple as a rejection. And yet the words couldn't have been stopped. I'd needed him to hear them. I'd needed him to know.

He closed the space between us until we were almost close enough to touch. "I was raised back and forth between the courts of Kappur and Thalassar. I grew up with Odessa, and though I knew we were destined to wed others, it was too late, for I'd loved her since we were children. So we wed in secret, and we were happy. And when she grew pregnant with you…" His hand reached out tentatively and clasped over my arm. "It was the happiest moment of our lives. We were going to raise you in Kappur and take you riding through the forestation. But then you were taken, and I've spent the last nineteen years of my life in despair. The only thing that kept me going for so long was the thought of seeing you for the first time.

"And now I am before you, finally, and you tell me you are afraid that I won't want you. You think you are *less,* and you're afraid to accept the truth of us. I was afraid, too. Afraid that once you met me, I'd not measure up to the father you wish you had. That you'd not want me at all."

I took a shuddering breath. "It seems," I began, "our fears were similar."

"And now that we are finally before one another, I realize my own ridiculousness." His other hand clasped on my arm. "You are my daughter. Whatever you call yourself, wherever you grew up, you are my *daughter.* And there will always be a place for you. In my heart, and in my kingdom, for it is yours. If you'll have us."

"You are my father," I answered. "Of course. *Of course.*" And then he was holding me, and we were crying, sobbing into each other's shoulders. Gripping each other, because it was the first time we were meeting, though it felt like our love had been woven together in unbreakable threads throughout the years. It pulsated around us, settling on our shoulders, threading together to pull us close until we forgot all our fears and worries and cared about nothing at all.

Nothing but each other.

And the love between us.

Our family.

The queen sent for us moments after. The idea of seeing her after Odele and I had so viciously and publicly accused her of murdering our mothers didn't settle comfortably in my stomach. I was filled with nerves and dread. What did she want to see us for? There was still the possibility that she could order me dead, heir or not.

Still, I threw my shoulders back with a confidence I didn't quite feel. The only way I seemed to get through the swim to the royal throne room was because my father was at my side. I was only able to let out a small breath when we made it into the throne room to find Odele there waiting for us, Queen Circe and King Xristo sitting on their thrones.

They waved us in, and we swam forward, not bothering with the formalities of bowing, and the queen wasted no time getting to the point.

"Your identity has been proved true, and now all of Thalassar knows about the missing princess, heir apparent to the throne."

In my peripheral vision, I saw Odele throw me a smug smile.

"And I know you must be quite eager for a throne and power…"

"Forgive me for interrupting," I chimed in coolly, "but I never wanted the throne or your power. I just wanted justice."

Queen Circe's nails grazed across the arm of the throne. "Justice you both meant to impart upon me. You both treated me like a kinslayer and accused me as such before the entirety of the kingdom."

"Come on, you have to admit you are sinister enough to be capable of nefarious things," Odele said.

The queen slashed her with a glare. "Be silent, Odele. You are not allowed to speak after everything you have done." She turned back to me. "There is the question of the ascension of the throne. It is our tradition to change rulers, and I have made my decision." Her fingers unfurled. "The laws of Thalassar are clear. A contract was made, and it was not upheld. Therefore, the kingdom does not recognize the marriage between Odessa Malabella and Dorian Knoll as legitimate. As such, you are considered a bastard Princess to Thalassar and cannot be allowed to rule."

My heart plummeted to my stomach like an anchor.

Odele gasped loudly. "That can't be true! She's daughter to the eldest princess! The throne should be *hers*!"

"It is not and will never be."

My father took a stroke forward and gave a tight, formal bow before he spoke. "It matters not what the ruling of Thalassar is. My daughter is legitimate in the eyes of Kappur. A bastard princess she may be here, but in the kingdom of Kappur, she is heir to the throne and future ruler of my kingdom."

Just like that, my heart soared back up in my chest and thumped. I realized I didn't need kingdoms. I just needed acceptance. I just needed change.

"Of course," the queen murmured. "Which brings up another matter. Though a bastard, she still has Malabella blood running through her veins. And as heir to Kappur, and family, I propose an immediate cease of war and peace between our two nations."

"Yes," I answered. "I accept."

My father cast me an amused smile. "Of course. We will open our borders to Thalassar once more and trade goods as we did in the past. Once again, our kingdoms will be allies."

The queen nodded. "And our own contract with Draconi was broken, due to the stunt the both of you pulled." She gave a pointed look at Odele.

"Please do not hold Draconi or Prince Kai responsible," I pleaded. "He had no idea he was being deceived."

"Hmm. Indeed. Because I am feeling generous, and because of our new alliance with Kappur and Kappur's marriage ties with Draconi, I would hate to start a new feud. Because you *are* family, I will gift Draconi with everything that had been agreed upon, as per contract, save for Odele's dowry."

"That's very generous of you," I commented nervously. Was there a catch? There had to be a catch somewhere. I wasn't sure I could quite trust the queen, even if she hadn't been behind the assassination of my mother, she still believed the line was tainted…

"I know. And because my generosity extends only so far, I will urge you to leave my kingdom and be on your way as soon as you're recuperated. I tire of dramatics."

"Of course, Your Majesty." My father bowed low, and I followed suit. When I straightened, she was staring angrily at Odele.

"I will now ask you to exit the throne room, as I have words I wish to exchange with my stepdaughter."

Nervously, I turned to give Odele a look of reassurance. She smiled at me, a twist of her lips that didn't quite meet her eyes. Before I could say anything, my father was guiding me from the room, leaving Odele behind to face the consequences of her actions.

Silently, I wished her luck.

"I DIDN'T KNOW YOU had it in you to be so generous," I joked, crossing my arms against my chest. As if that action could act as a barrier between myself and the fury in my stepmother's gaze.

"The situation might not be as amusing as you think." Her nails flicked across the arm of her throne, a gesture I was already well versed in and knew it meant annoyance.

"It's pretty amusing," I assured her. "At least, Thalassar seems to think so."

The queen rose from her throne to loom over me and shout, "How dare you float before me and joke about the mess you've made? Your foolery and selfishness has cost us our Draconian allies."

I waved off her dramatics. "I'd hardly say it cost us our allies. They are still allies." Prince Kai would hardly turn his backs on us when he was married to my cousin who loved this kingdom very much.

This whole turn of events hadn't been what I was expecting. I'd been hoping Odalaea would take the throne and I would be forgotten. My stepmother had ruined it, and now I was stuck with the Thalassarin crown that I did not want. The only joy to be had from this was the fact that I no longer had to marry the Lizard Prince.

"You foolish child!" the queen shouted, making me flinch. "The only reason I am to give up the magic that was promised in the contract was to avoid the wrath of the Draconian Emperor. We do not need another war, and least of all with the royal dragons. Do not fool yourself into believing we are *allies*."

"But, Kai—"

"Is now married and allied with *Kappur*, not Thalassar. We risked everything to secure this marriage alliance, and like the petulant child you are, you *ruined* it with your stupidity. You think other kingdoms will trust us after this? You think we won't suffer because of what you've done? We need you to marry, Odele, and need you to marry well to help secure a safe future for our kingdom. Only then can you take the throne."

My heart thumped in both anticipation and fear at her words. "The ascension—"

"There will be no ascension! Don't you understand? If I had my doubts before, your recent actions have done nothing but solidify my decision. You are not ready for the responsibility of the throne, and therefore, you will not have it."

Hurt spiraled through me. I didn't want the throne, I never had, but to hear her so blatantly state that I was worthless, that I'd not have it, *hurt* in a way that was indescribable. I'd done everything to prove I was incapable of handling the kingdom, that I was incapable of following in my mother's fin strokes, and yet to finally have it thrown in my face was like having her return from the grave and spit straight at my fins.

"You cannot ascend until you prove yourself worthy of your bloodline. To do this, you will do your duty. You must marry and secure us an alliance."

Dread thrummed through me. "Surely there's another way to secure an alliance?" I almost begged, hating myself for reducing myself to such a level. "Any other way besides marriage…"

"You daft child. Marriage is the *only* way to ensure loyalty from another kingdom, which we now desperately need, no thanks to you. And yet, there are no princes left, and no widowed kings in all of the seven kingdoms. You'd be forced to marry beneath you. A lord, or a duke, even."

I cringed. "I am a princess," I argued. "You cannot expect me to lie with a lowly lord."

"You'll have no other choice. There is no one left. And I'm sure everyone has seen your disastrous display at the wedding already…"

"So?"

Her eyes narrowed. "Are you really going to make me say it, Odele? The truth is out. Everyone *knows* you now, and *no one wants you.*"

Her words hurt as if she'd slapped me against the face with them.

No one wants you.

Could it be true? Did it even matter? They didn't want me, and I didn't want them, either.

"So I am to be punished," I spat vehemently. "For wanting my freedom. It isn't fair. Daddy—" I turned away from her to look at my father. I waited for him to get up, to defend me like King Dorian so bravely defended Odalaea.

But my father did not get up from his throne. He turned sad eyes to me and murmured, "Sorry, Odele. It is decided."

"No! I'll not marry a lord! You can't make me!"

"Well, lucky for *you,* you won't be marrying a lord—as if one of them would even want you, anyway. No. We have a much better prospect in mind, and thankfully, he's already graciously asked us for your hand. So we must plan the marriage at once."

I blinked, disbelieving her every word. "What?" I demanded. "Who?"

My stepmother glared at me, and somehow, a deep, dreadful part of me knew whose name she would say before she said it.

"Prince Ytgar Neves Isolde of Iol."

That Iolish bastard.

Maisie

We would be leaving in a few weeks. It was enough time to pack up our things, plan a future, and say our goodbyes. It was a rather bittersweet feeling. For once, in my life, I did not have to fear the loom of Selection, the prospect that perhaps I would get chosen for an unknown future. Everything was clear.

I was officially Princess of Kappur.

I was wed to Prince Kai of Draconi.

I had a family.

I had a home.

And finally, I could make a difference.

I supposed I already had. By merely existing, everything that had fallen into place these past few weeks had finally ended the war between Thalassar and Kappur. The two long-time enemies had become allies. The Selection was no more, for that morning, the queen had announced it far and wide. They'd signed a new peace treaty and had sent the selected soldiers home.

In but two weeks, I'd be on my way. I'd say goodbye to the palace, and travel north, to Kappur, and then Draconi.

A part of me was sad to leave the kingdom I dearly loved, but I realized, there was nothing left for me in Lagoona. Nothing but a little blue boat that was likely already infested with piranhas, and that was fine. This was a new part of my life. A new journey. I was a princess now and there were so many things I still had to learn. I wanted to be a gentle ruler. I wanted to take the current of peace instead of cruelty.

I'd not use a strap of leather against gentle hands as punishment. There would be no scarred backs and arms. There would be no Selection or beheadings.

I saw what was wrong with the monarchies, and I aimed to change them.

One little stroke at a time.

"You'll enjoy Kappur," my father said confidently.

We were swimming together, taking a pleasure stroll through the gardens with our Kappurin guards, Kai, Tiberius, and Elias—who had been fully pardoned for his crimes, now that the Selection had been abolished.

I hadn't yet told my father about my relationship with the three mermen, as I'd hate for him to have an apoplexy because of my wanton ways. Even so, I think he assumed we all loved each other. They'd hardly left my side at all, and though I'd dreaded leaving Thalassar, out of fear that it would break the four of us apart, I needn't have worried.

Tiberius had resigned from his post as Odele's guard and Thalassar's captain, applying to be mine instead. He was now officially a soldier of Kappur and would follow me wherever I went.

Kai was my husband—it was still strange to say it—so where he went, I went, and vice versa.

Elias had been trickier. He was silence and shadow and secrets. He flowed as swiftly and viciously as a current and did what he pleased. I had prepared myself for the worst, for our goodbye. A goodbye to the merman who had given me confidence, the merman who understood me above all others, the opposite side of my tarnished coin.

My friend.

Like everything the Black Blade did, he did in secret and with surprise. As I'd prepared my farewells to him, he had held me tightly in his arms and whispered, "Selection is gone. I have no one left to save. So I will come with you. Wherever you go, I'll go. You are my home now." I'd cried, and he'd pulled away to swipe the pad of his thumb against my cheek. "Besides," he smirked, "I know everything there is to know about Thalassar. It's time to learn a few things about Kappur and Draconi."

"We have all manner of exotic creatures. I could take you to see the sea snake breeding grounds that the crown protects from extinction…" my father stated.

"It sounds wonderful." I smiled widely at him, earning a smile back. It had been easy for the both of us, after that initial meeting, to get to know one another, to truly act as father and daughter. There were years, nineteen of them, that we would never get back. But we had time now and that was important. Neither of us meant to waste it.

"After we spend a short while in Kappur, we will go to Draconi," Kai chimed in. "You'll meet my father and my sisters, and we will continue the second part of our marriage ritual under Draconian customs."

Kai had spoken to me of those customs. He said I would help hatch the dragon egg he'd given me and release it onto their breeding grounds. I would choose a dragon for myself, one to train and ride. My mount for war, he'd said.

I was averse to the idea. I didn't want a war dragon, because I didn't want war. I'd had enough of it already.

"Will I be forced to sit for hours of outfit fittings?" I asked with horror.

"Only if you want to."

"Absolutely not." I'd had enough of that, too. I'd had enough of corsets to last me a lifetime.

We swam around the palace, me leading the way. I wanted to get a good look at Eramaea and the palace of gold and pink that had so taken my breath away the moment I'd set eyes on it. Soon, it would be behind me for good.

As we rounded the corner and made our way to the front of the palace, a deafening roar crashed over us like a rogue wave crashing to sand.

I jolted at the surprise, and suddenly found myself pushed back by Tiberius as he took the place in front of me. Beyond him, I could make out crowds of mer. Mer with news recorders, mer with enormous kelp signs with words I couldn't quite make out. They were all shrieking and being held back by lines of guards.

"Let me through." I pushed Tiberius aside and started forward before he could stop me. I made it near the fray of mer, and at the sight of me, they all cheered.

"Hail Princess Odalaea!" they called out.

"Savior of the Black Blade!"

My face heated. These crowds were assembled here to celebrate *me.*

"Ender of Selection!"

"Hope!"

My eyes glazed over with tears as they called out and rejoiced, as I read sign after sign that spoke of nothing but praise for me.

It was overwhelming.

And then, "Maisie! Maisie!"

A voice from the crowd screamed my name. I searched, whipping from side to side. Then I saw him. An older merman pushed to the front of the lines. His graying hair was slicked back, and he wore his best coat in dark green with frayed hems. I recognized him immediately. The kind face, the long lower body of a gator, stumpy legs moving to keep him upright.

Josiah.

A smile broke onto my face. "Let him through!" I ordered one of the guards holding them back. He did, and Josiah, my former boss, pushed his way towards me. We met in the middle, and I felt the comfort of his arms wrap around me and pull me close. "What are you doing here?" I asked him, the rest of the world seeming to fade around me.

"I saw you on the telly," he explained. "I saw you confront the queen, and when it came out that you were the Princess of Kappur, I—"

"Who is this?" my father's smooth voice interrupted.

Josiah tensed, clasping his hands in front of him as he took in the King of Kappur. I wondered what he was thinking, if he felt hatred for the king who had waged war on Thalassar for all these years.

But Josiah was ever respectful as he bowed gracefully to the king. "Your Majesty, an honor. My name is Josiah."

My father's eyes widened and he turned to me. "This is the mer you spoke of?" I nodded, and Josiah suddenly looked nervous. But he shouldn't be. My father turned back to him and clasped his hand in the older mer's, giving it a vigorous shake. "Then I will thank you personally for all the years you cared for my daughter like a father would. Whatever you require, anything at all, you need only ask. Kappur is in your debt."

Josiah sputtered, his ruddy cheeks going red. When my father released him, he looked embarrassed for a few more moments before straightening and turning to me. "I thank you both kindly, I just... See, the reason I came all the way here was to tell Maisie somethin' of importance." He clasped my shoulders in his hands and squeezed. "I'm proud of you, Mais'. For everythin' you've done." He looked over at my father. "You have yourself a real treasure here, and the only debt I wish to claim from you is that you treat her well."

And my father, King of Kappur, bowed low to Josiah. "Always," he replied.

Then, Josiah was hugging me again, for this could very well be the last time we ever saw each other. I tightened my arms around the mer who represented my past, my family, my life, and my new future. As he pulled away, his lips grazed my ear as he whispered. Then, he was gone, disappearing back into the crowd, not giving me time to memorize his features one last time.

It was only later that I would take the words he'd whispered and hold them close to me, and smile through my tears at the truth behind them.

A truth I finally believed.

"I told you you were meant for greater things than Tides' Tavern."

If you want to read more in this world from Odele's point of view, check out the spin-off series ROYAL LIES

Aleera Anaya Ceres is the USA Today Bestselling author of several series including the Origins of the Six series and the Daughter of Triton series. Like most introverts, Aleera prefers to curl up with a good book, listen to music, paint, read tarot cards, and snack on the tears and heartbreak of her readers. A proud Mexican-American from the state of Kansas, Aleera currently resides in Tlaxcala, Mexico with her husband and children.

You can find/contact her here:
aleeraanayaceres.com
aleeraceres@aacbooks.com

Adult Fantasy series

Fae Elementals

A Dance with Fire

A Sword of Ice

A Shield of Water

The Dark Waters series

Riptide

Why Choose Series

Royal Secrets

Secrets Among the Tides

Whispers Beneath the Deep

Caresses Between the Sand

Death Beyond the Waves

Royal Lies

Slave to Ice & Shadows

Princess in Frost Castles

Queen of Frozen War

Origins of the Six series

Academy of Six

Control of Five

Destruction of Two

Wrath of One

A Daughter of Triton series

Triton's Academy

Triton's Prophecy

Triton's Legacy

A Daughter of Triton Box Set

Why Choose Standalones

Queenie & the Krakens

Lourdes & the Mafia

Paranormal Romance Series

Deep Sea Chronicles

Fall in Deep

Siren Queen

The Blood Novels

Love Bites

Blood Drug

My Master

Last Hope

Young Adult standalone

The Last Mermaid

www.ingramcontent.com/pod-product-compliance
Lightning Source LLC
Chambersburg PA
CBHW020303030826
48979CB00027B/2016/J

* 9 7 9 8 9 8 6 9 5 4 6 2 2 *